W9-BDP-265
DISCARD

WINDS OF WRATH

THE DESTROYERMEN SERIES

Into the Storm

Crusade

Maelstrom

Distant Thunders

Rising Tides

Firestorm

Iron Gray Sea

Storm Surge

Deadly Shores

Straits of Hell

Blood in the Water

Devil's Due

River of Bones

Pass of Fire

Winds of Wrath

DESTROYERMEN

DESTROYERMEN

WINDS OF WRATH

TAYLOR ANDERSON

ACE
NEW YORK

ACE
Published by Berkley
An imprint of Penguin Random House LLC
penguinrandomhouse.com

Library of Congress Cataloging-in-Publication Data

Names: Anderson, Taylor, 1963– author.
Title: Winds of wrath / Taylor Anderson.
Description: First edition. | New York: Ace, 2020. | Series: Destroyermen
Identifiers: LCCN 2019051132 (print) | LCCN 2019051133 (ebook) |
ISBN 9780399587566 (hardcover) | ISBN 9780399587573 (ebook)
Subjects: GSAFD: Science fiction.
Classification: LCC PS3601.N5475 W55 2020 (print) |
LCC PS3601.N5475 (ebook) | DDC 813/.6—dc23
LC record available at https://lccn.loc.gov/2019051132
LC ebook record available at https://lccn.loc.gov/2019051133

Printed in the United States of America
1 3 5 7 9 10 8 6 4 2

Cover art by Liddell Jones
Cover design by Adam Auerbach

ACKNOWLEDGMENTS

Thanks again to my agent, Russell Galen, who was sure from the start that the Destroyermen series had long legs. Without him it might still be just rattling around in my head. I've always thanked my editor, Anne Sowards, but she deserves much more than the usual short sentiment. Her assistance, supportive suggestions, and calm, steadying influence can't be overstated. She's firmly and insightfully corrective when I goof, but defends my "vision" of things, including the somewhat unconventional style in which I chose to write the tale. I fear I may occasionally frustrate various copy editors with antiquated nautical/military/technical terms and old-fashioned turns of phrase and colloquialisms (or stuff I just make up), little of which is supported by current dictionaries. Don't get me wrong—all the copy editors at Ace are great, and I hope they'll accept my apologies and admiration, but I can't measure my appreciation for Anne. She always has my back, but also has this graceful . . . *way* about her that helps me keep things in perspective and makes me ask *myself* if the fate of the cosmos truly depends on me defending whatever artistic or hard-history hill I've planted a flag on. Thanks, Anne. You really are the best. Period.

On a sad note, I must acknowledge the passing of a fine fellow named Charles Simpson. Many longtime readers of the series knew him as a tireless, cheerful, and dedicated supporter of the D-Men, who started the "Destroyermen Fan Association" page and was an early, driving force in expanding the informative wiki. I talked to him fairly often in recent years and was privileged to get to know him as an excellent historian and an enjoyable conversationalist as well. Even though I never met him in person, I considered him a friend. Fair winds, Charles.

Dispositions
Prior to the
Lake Galk
Campaign
May 1, 1945
Grik
Africa
Halik
5th
Lake
Uskoll
Lake
Ukri
Esshk
Lake
Galk
Esshk
Locks
Esshk
Galk
R.
Ukri
R.
Lake
Nalak
Ign
III
VI
XII
V
IV
I
Sofesshk
Saansa
Field
Zambezi
R.
Arracca Field

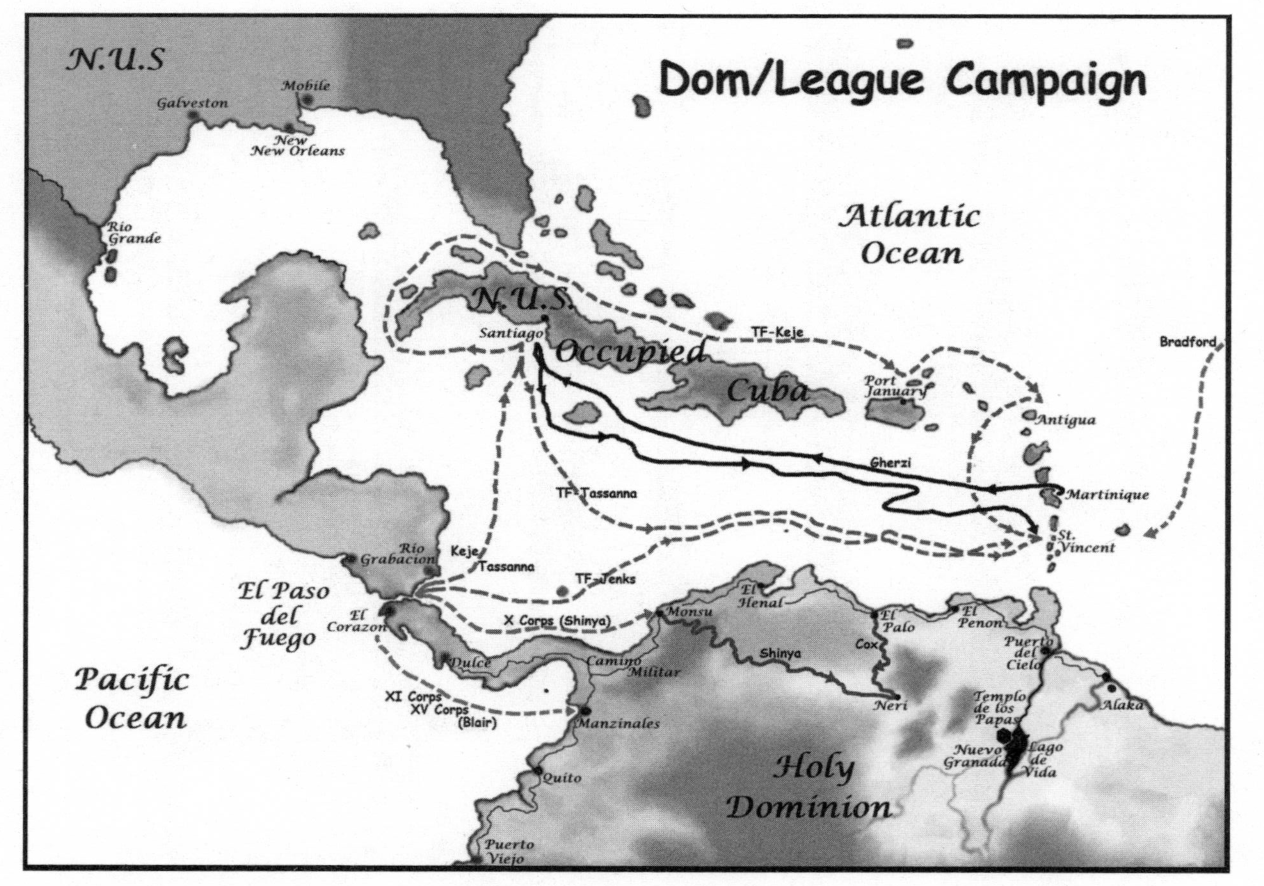
Dom/League Campaign
N.U.S
Mobile
Galveston
New New Orleans
Rio Grande
Atlantic Ocean
N.U.S. Occupied Cuba
Santiago
TF-Keje
Port January
Bradford
Antigua
Gherzi
Martinique
St. Vincent
TF-Tassanna
Rio Grabacion
Keje
Tassanna
TF-Jenks
El Paso del Fuego
El Corazon
X Corps (Shinya)
Monsu
El Henal
El Palo
El Penon
Cox
Shinya
Puerto del Cielo
Dulce
Camino Militar
Pacific Ocean
XI Corps
XV Corps (Blair)
Manzinales
Neri
Templo de los Papas
Alaka
Nuevo Granada
Lago de Vida
Quito
Holy Dominion
Puerto Viejo

Recognition Silhouettes of Allied Vessels

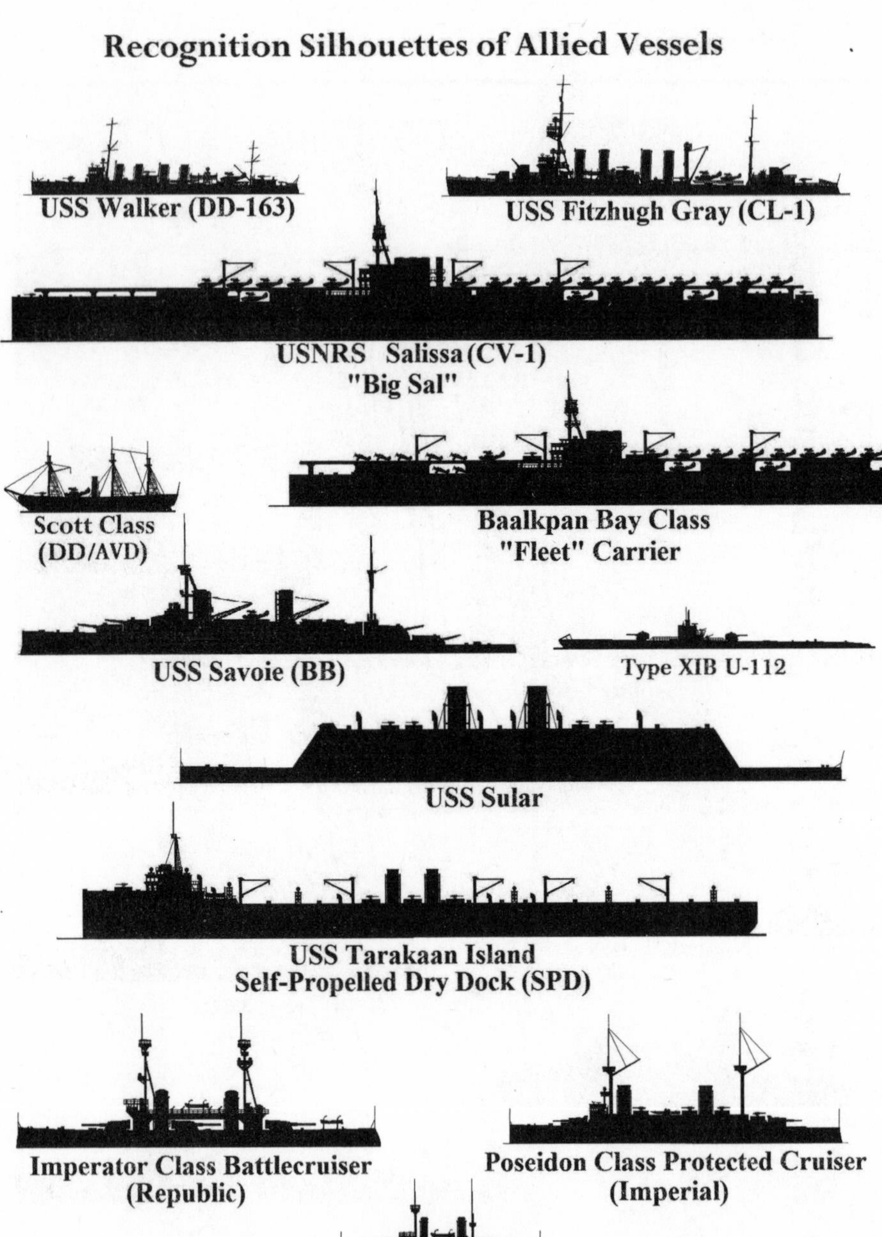

Recognition Silhouettes of Enemy Vessels

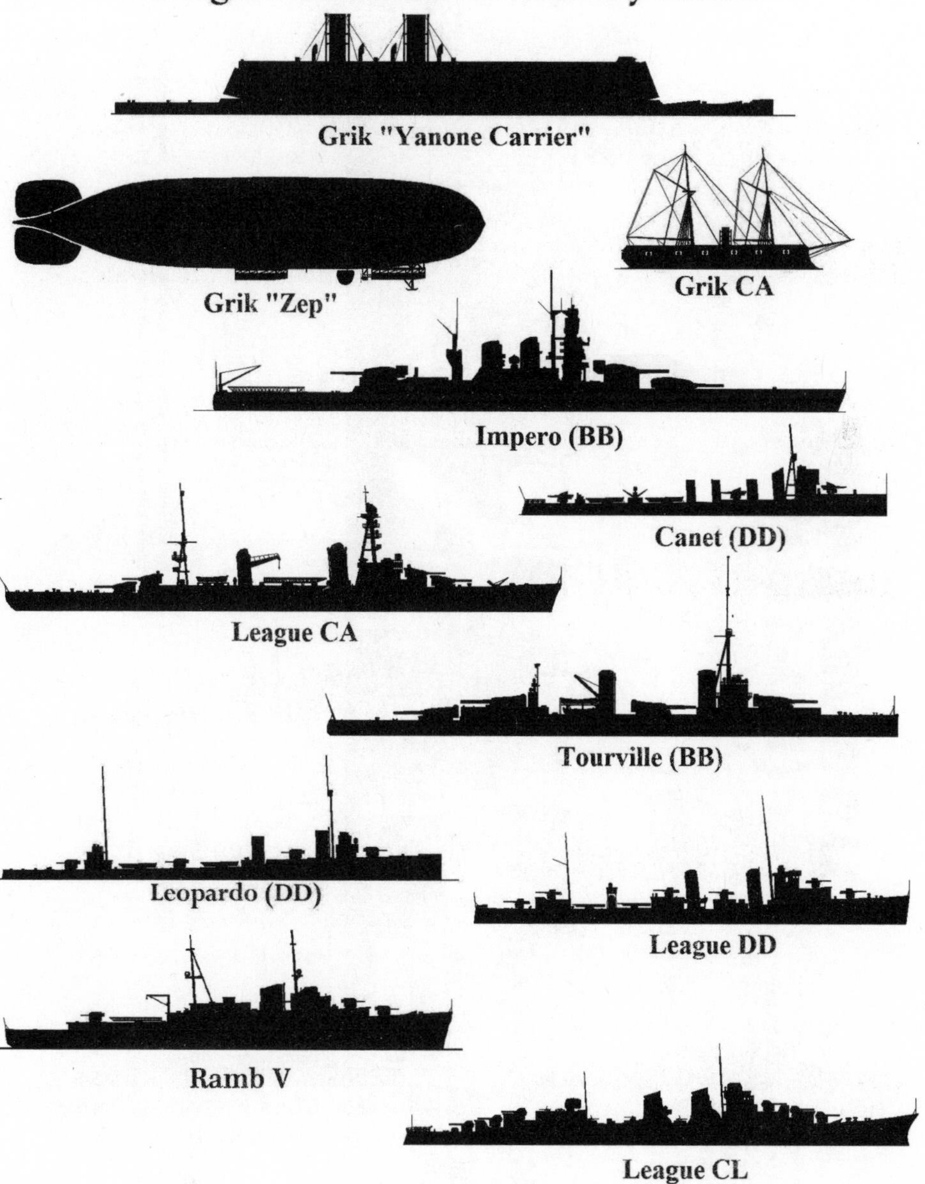

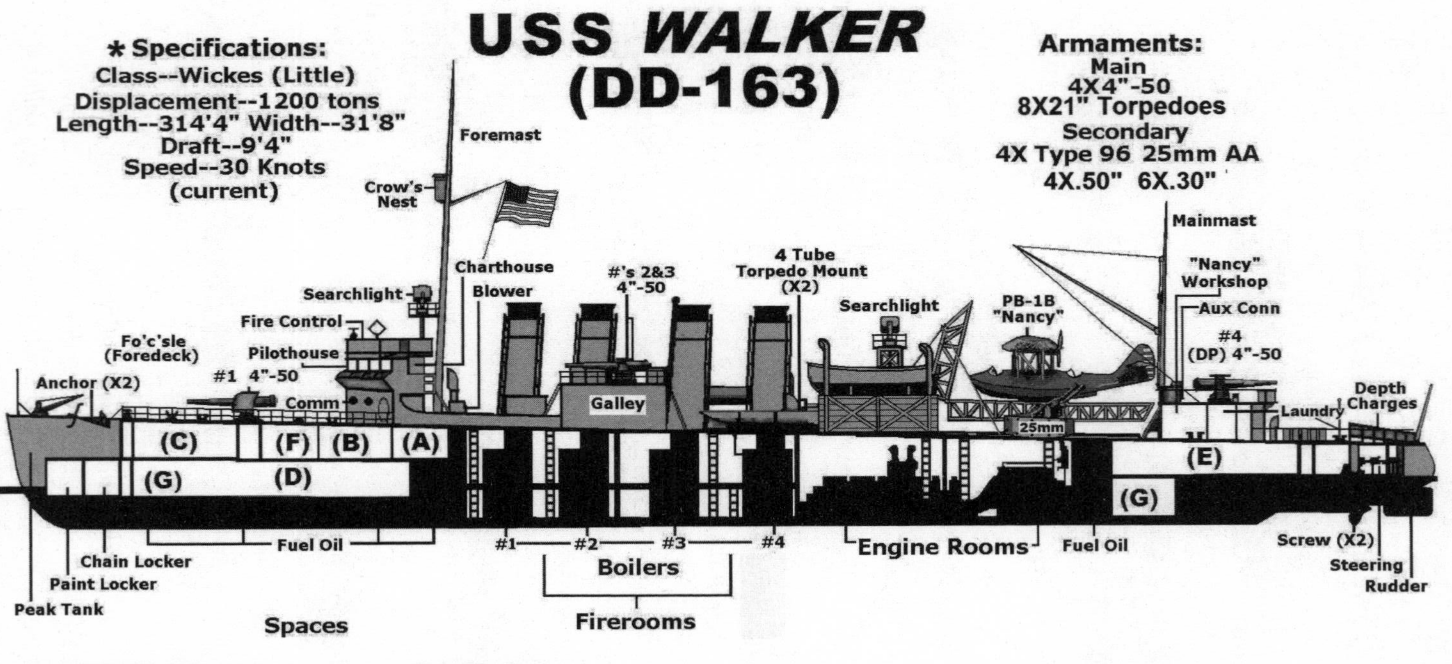
USS WALKER
(DD-163)
* Specifications:
Class--Wickes (Little)
Displacement--1200 tons
Length--314'4" Width--31'8"
Draft--9'4"
Speed--30 Knots
(current)
Armaments:
Main
4X4"-50
8X21" Torpedoes
Secondary
4X Type 96 25mm AA
4X.50" 6X.30"
Foremast
Crow's Nest
Charthouse
Blower
Searchlight
Fire Control
Pilothouse
Fo'c'sle (Foredeck)
Anchor (X2)
#1 4"-50
Comm
#'s 2&3 4"-50
Galley
4 Tube Torpedo Mount (X2)
Searchlight
PB-1B "Nancy"
25mm
Mainmast
"Nancy" Workshop
Aux Conn
#4 (DP) 4"-50
Laundry
Depth Charges
(C)
(F)
(B)
(A)
(G)
(D)
(E)
(G)
Fuel Oil
#1
#2
#3
#4
Boilers
Firerooms
Engine Rooms
Fuel Oil
Screw (X2)
Steering
Rudder
Chain Locker
Paint Locker
Peak Tank
Spaces
(A) Captain
(B) Officers
(C) Chiefs, Warrants, P.O.s
(D) Fore Crew
(E) Aft Crew
(F) Wardroom
(G) Storage/Magazine
* New Construction DDs such as USS James Ellis have similar specifications but are 5-7 knots faster and 150-200 tons heavier

OUR HISTORY HERE

By March 1, 1942, the war "back home" was a nightmare. Hitler was strangling Europe and the Japanese were rampant in the Pacific. Most immediate, from my perspective as a . . . mature Australian engineer stranded in Surabaya Java, the Japanese had seized Singapore and Malaysia, destroyed the American Pacific Fleet and neutralized their forces in the Philippines, conquered most of the Dutch East Indies, and were landing on Java. The one-sided Battle of the Java Sea had shredded ABDAFLOAT: a jumble of antiquated American, British, Dutch, and Australian warships united by the vicissitudes of war. Its destruction left the few surviving ships scrambling to slip past the tightening Japanese gauntlet. For most, it was too late.

With several other refugees, I managed to board an old American destroyer, USS Walker, *commanded by Lieutenant Commander Matthew Reddy. Whether fate, providence, or mere luck intervened,* Walker *and her sister* Mahan, *their gallant destroyermen cruelly depleted by combat, were not fated for the same destruction which claimed their consorts in escape. Instead, at the height of a desperate action against the mighty Japanese battlecruiser* Amagi, *commanded by the relentless Hisashi Kurokawa, they were . . . engulfed by an anomalous force, manifested as a bizarre, greenish squall—and their battered, leaking, war-torn hulks were somehow swept to another world entirely.*

I say "another world" because, though geographically similar, there are few additional resemblances. It's as if whatever cataclysmic event doomed the prehistoric life on "our" earth many millions of years ago never occurred, and those terrifying—fascinating—creatures endured, sometimes evolving down wildly different paths. We quickly discovered "people," however, calling themselves "Mi-Anakka," who are highly intelligent, social folk, with large eyes, fur, and expressive tails. In my ignorance and excitement, I promptly dubbed them "Lemurians" based on their strong (if more feline), resemblance to the giant lemurs of Madagascar. (Growing evidence may confirm they sprang from a parallel line, with only the most distant ancestor connecting them to lemurs, but "Lemurians" has stuck). We just as swiftly learned they were engaged in an existential struggle with a somewhat reptilian species commonly called "Grik." Also bipedal, Grik display bristly crests and tail plumage, dreadful teeth and claws, and are clearly descended from the dromaeosaurids in our fossil record.

Aiding the first group against the second—Captain Reddy had no choice—we made fast, true friends who needed our technical expertise as badly as we needed their support. Conversely, we now also had an implacable enemy bent on devouring all competing life. Many bloody battles ensued while we struggled to help our friends against their far more numerous foes, and it was for this reason I sometimes think—when disposed to contemplate "destiny"—that we survived all our previous ordeals and somehow came to this place. I don't know everything about anything, but I do know a little about a lot. The same was true of Captain Reddy and his US Asiatic Fleet sailors. We immediately commenced trying to even the odds, but militarizing the generally peaceful Lemurians was no simple task. Still, to paraphrase, the prospect of being eaten does focus one's efforts amazingly, and dire necessity is the mother of industrialization. To this day, I remain amazed by what we accomplished so quickly with so little, especially considering how rapidly and tragically our "brain trust" was consumed by battle.

In the meantime, we discovered other humans—friends and enemies—who joined our cause, required our aid, or posed new threats. Even worse than the Grik (from a moral perspective, in my opinion) was the vile "Dominion" in South and Central America. A perverse mix of Incan/Aztecan blood-ritual tyranny with a dash of seventeenth-century Catholicism flavoring technology brought by earlier travelers, the Dominion's aims were similar to those of the Grik: conquest, of course, but founded on the principle of "convert or die."

I now believe that, faced with only one of these enemies, we could've prevailed rather quickly, despite the odds. Burdened by both, we could never concentrate our forces and the war lingered on. To make matters worse, the Grik were aided by the madman Kurokawa, who, after losing his Amagi *at the Battle of Baalkpan, pursued a warped agenda all his own. And just as we came to the monumental conclusion that not all historical human time lines we encountered* exactly *mirrored ours, we began to feel the malevolent presence of yet another power centered in the Mediterranean. This "League of Tripoli" was composed of fascist French, Italian, Spanish, and German factions from a "different" 1939 than we remembered, and hadn't merely "crossed over" with a pair of battle-damaged destroyers, but possessed a powerful task force originally intended to wrest Egypt—and the Suez Canal—from Great Britain.*

We had few open conflicts with the League at first, though they seemed inexplicably intent on subversion. Eventually we discovered their ultimate aim was to aid Kurokawa, the Grik, even the Dominion, just enough to ensure our mutual *annihilation—removing multiple future threats to the hegemony they craved at once. But their schemes never reckoned on the valor of our allies or the resolve of Captain Matthew Reddy. Therefore, when the League Contre-Amiral Laborde, humiliated by a confrontation, not only sank what was, essentially, a hospital ship with his monstrous dreadnaught* Savoie, *but took some of our people hostage—including Captain Reddy's pregnant wife—and turned them AND* Savoie *over to Kurokawa, we were caught horribly off guard. Tensions with the League escalated dramatically, though not enough to risk open hostilities that neither we—nor they—were ready for. (We later learned such had already occurred in the Caribbean, between USS* Donaghey *and a League DD, and that Second Fleet and General Shinya's force had suffered a setback in the Americas at the hands of the Dominion.) But we* had *to deal definitively with Kurokawa at last, and at once. As powerful as he'd become, and with a battleship added to his fleet, we simply couldn't risk our invasion of Grik Africa with him at our backs.*

Captain Reddy conceived a brilliant plan to rescue our friends and destroy Kurokawa once and for all, and in a rare fit of cosmic justice, the operation actually proceeded better than planned, resulting in the removal of one long-standing threat, and the capture of Savoie *herself. The battle was painfully costly, however, and the forces involved were too exhausted and ill-placed to respond when the Grik went on the move. Our hopes now depended on the insanely, suicidally daring defiance of some very dear friends aboard the old* Santa Catalina. *Captain Russ Chappelle steamed the ancient armed merchantman up the Zambezi and fought the Grik Swarm to a standstill, ultimately blocking the river with her own half-sunken hulk. Even then her fight wasn't finished, and as reinforcements trickled in, the battle raged on. Finally blasted to utter ruin and with the Grik surging aboard, Commodore Tassanna brought her massive carrier* Arracca *to evacuate survivors, but* Arracca *was fatally wounded and forced to beach herself.*

Thus, most awkwardly, began the Allied invasion of Grik Africa. Captain Reddy and our Republic allies to the south (to whom, incidentally, I was at-

tached) brought everything at their disposal to support our people marooned behind Grik lines. Through daring, terrible suffering, and sheer force of will, "Tassanna's Toehold" held, and a bloody beachhead was finally secured in Grik Africa, from which we could strike deep against the ancient foe.

On the other side of the world, the vile Don Hernan and the equally unpleasant Victor Gravois finalized a treaty of alliance between the cruel Dominion and the fascist League, and General Shinya pushed north in a race with Don Hernan's General Mayta to secure the city of El Corazon and the fabled El Paso del Fuego. Mayta got there first and fortified El Corazon against Shinya's and High Admiral Jenks's inevitable assault.

And so the war began to build to an ever bloodier, more heartrending crescendo. Bekiaa-Sab-At and I, still with General Kim's Army of the Republic, battled northward to join Captain Reddy and General Alden, smashing their way up the bloody Zambezi to the very heart of Grik Africa. The decisive engagement was fought in the ancient city of Sofesshk, in the shadow of the Palace of Vanished Gods itself. The balance (against the Grik, at least) had tipped in our favor.

Or so we thought.

I was not at the Battle for El Corazon and El Paso del Fuego, of course, but the fighting in the city has been described in the most horrific terms. Ultimately, only valor and good fortune allowed General Shinya to evict General Mayta. But no Allied fleet remained to exploit this natural passage between the seas, or support the NUS invasion of the Dominion from the Caribbean. Worse, the fascist League understood the strategic threat posed by Allied control of the Pass, and in concert with the evil Don Hernan, Victor Gravois finally began to gather the powerful League fleet he'd always craved for his own murky purposes.

And then there was General Esshk, of course, who'd escaped defeat in Grik Africa to build a new army and new weapons—and prepare a final, obscene plot to ruin the world if he couldn't rule it. . . .

Excerpt from the foreword to Courtney Bradford's
The Worlds I've Wondered
University of New Glasgow Press, 1956

PROLOGUE

////// Old Sofesshk
Grik Africa
May 1, 1945

General of the Army and Marines Pete Alden hopped up on the freshly repaired dock on the Old Sofesshk waterfront and got his first good look at the ancient Grik capital. He was surprised. Every other Grik city he'd seen had been little more than a mazelike warren of jumbled adobe dwellings, reinforced with long grass and a few sticks here and there. They reminded him more of termite tunnels than anything a thinking being would build. But Old Sofesshk was different. For one thing, however long ago, it had clearly been *planned* and built with one eye for practicality and another to a recognizable—even to Pete—ascetic standard. Still more unusual, it was largely constructed of carefully shaped stones. Adobe had only been used to add or make repairs to far older structures. Much lay in rubbled ruin after the fighting, but a lot remained intact. And the predominating architecture reminded him vaguely of ruins they'd found in India, or even pictures he'd seen of ancient Greek cities—without all the columns and stuff, of course. He didn't know what to think of that.

He'd jumped from the bobbing foredeck of a battered MTB (motor torpedo boat) that had carried him east down the Zambezi River from Lake Nalak. His butt hurt after so long in the saddle of a me-naak, and it showed in his walk. Me-naaks were large, scary carnivores shaped a little like long-legged crocodiles. Mi-Anakka (Lemurians) from the Filpin Lands employed them very effectively as cavalry mounts, but not only were their saddles profoundly uncomfortable for large humans—such as Pete—the damn things gave him the willies. Particularly when the one he rode was hungry, and kept glancing back at him . . .

Several people were waiting on the dock in a light drizzle under an overcast sky, but before Pete acknowledged their salutes he turned to catch a couple of duffel bags and a pair of rifles tossed up by his new orderly, Kaik-Sar, a big, muscular Lemurian sergeant from the 1st Marines. He also threw a quick salute to the skipper of the MTB as it backed into the rain-swollen river and turned to pound back upstream. *The old "Seven Boat,"* Pete reflected. *I bet Nat Hardee misses her, but there was no sense sending her with him. He'll have a whole new squadron of better boats to pick from where he's going.* Shouldering his duffel and precious 1903 Springfield, Pete finally returned the waiting salutes of the three Lemurians—and two Grik—standing on the bright new timbers.

"Inquisitor Choon," he said, nodding at Kon-Choon, the "Director of Spies" for the Republic of Real People. As always, Choon was dressed in the stylish attire of a Repub civilian, complete with blue-and-white-striped kilt, coat, and vest. A dark blue cravat complimented the large, pale blue eyes protruding from the tan and off-white fur on his face. "And these are?" Pete asked, glancing at the other two 'Cats, also Repubs, wearing mustard-brown tunics, kilts, and campaign caps.

"Colonel Niaa-Taak—the Kaiser's niece," Choon said with added significance, "and Centurion Pyte." He swept his gaze to the left, at an ancient, almost toothless Grik. "You already know Geerki, formerly 'Hij,' now, um, 'Regent' of Grik City and Prime Interpreter to the Celestial Mother. His companion is Second Colonel Shelg of the First Brigade, Slasher Division."

Both Grik bowed.

"Stand up straight," Pete growled, grateful they hadn't hurled themselves to the dock, to squirm in front of him. That's how they'd shown obeisance to their own generals. "Nobody bows to me," he added sharply, then grinned. "How they hangin', Geerki? I hear you've been helpin' Choon rake up all the dope"—he regarded Shelg—"and working with our new . . . allies, to sort out who's for who, and recruit 'em to our side. Good work. Oh!"—he suddenly remembered—"and thanks for the lizardy interpreters you sent First Corps. Helped a lot."

"I all'ays told you I is a *good* critcher," Geerki replied piously.

"You bet," Pete agreed. Geerki had been a rare Grik indeed, their first "elevated" prisoner, and willing collaborator. Even now, though somewhat forcefully released, he considered himself General Muln-Rolak's property. Pete turned all his attention to Shelg. "And you're XO to First Colonel Jash?"

"I is—are . . ." Shelg shook his head, dissatisfied, but even Lawrence, who otherwise spoke perfect English and Lemurian, couldn't do words requiring lips. All the newly allied Grik officers had come a long way in a short time, if what Pete heard was true. They had good reason to. Careful communication with a minimum of errors was crucial to building trust among their former enemies, and thereby retaining a measure of independence. The old ways were gone forever, but after literally unremembered millennia of conflict, their largely Lemurian conquerors couldn't just flip a switch and love them overnight. So the new way could still go sour if they weren't careful, and they knew it.

"Take the general's bag," Choon instructed the Repub centurion, blinking self-chagrin that he hadn't thought to bring any enlisted men or 'Cats for the job. "My apologies for not greeting you more formally, General Alden. We weren't expecting you until morning." He glanced at Sergeant Kaik, as if also implying he'd assumed Pete would bring a larger entourage.

"I got it," Pete declined, bouncing the bag on his shoulder.

"He caan get *mine*," Sergeant Kaik murmured lowly.

Pete looked up at the fire-stained, shell-pocked Palace of Vanished Gods. "So that's the big Lizard Broad's digs," he said, then quickly added for the benefit of the Grik, "the palace of the 'Celestial Mother.' I caught a glimpse from a distance when we chased General Ign west, past here, on the other side of the river." He tilted his head south where New Sofesshk used to be. Nothing was left but charred debris, though a new airstrip was under construction on the northeast end, close to the water. Tens of thousands of local Grik, filtering back after the battles and commanded by their "Giver of Life" to obey the invaders, were levelling the ground of what would be Saansa Field with nothing but hand tools and rollers. No matter how hard they worked, it might be a while before the airfield was operational. The rainy season was here and new gullies opened in the completed part of the strip every few days. *Not much point callin' 'em "Old" an' "New" Sofesshk anymore,* Pete mused. *There ain't but one of 'em left. The "new" one's just . . . gone.*

Still staring at the dark, rounded, pyramidal palace, Pete shook his head. "Big," he conceded. "Almost as big as the one on Madagascar. *Still* looks like a giant cowflop, though." If he expected a rise out of Shelg, it didn't come. He'd probably heard the term often enough by now that he was used to it. Besides, Grik Africa had herbivores hundreds of times bigger than any cow, which left proportionate droppings. Shelg and those like him were obviously smart enough to survive the battles leading to the current state of affairs, and shrewd enough to make their place in them. Maybe the term struck them as appropriately descriptive too, if not very respectful.

"Shall we step inside and meet the others?" Choon suggested. The drizzle was coming down harder. "The pigment in my cravat will run and ruin my vest, I fear."

Shifting the rifle on his shoulder and nodding ahead at the bullet-spalled entry arch on the west side of the Palace, Pete grunted, "Lead the way."

Unconsciously, he and Sergeant Kaik kept a distance from Geerki and Colonel Shelg as they went. Pete trusted Geerki, but like many in his army—understandably—he would've scoured every Grik from the planet if he could. That was impossible, of course. There were just too many. It didn't mean he was happy with the peace Captain Reddy imposed on the Grik still loyal to the Celestial Mother, however. Ironically, Pete had once come to an "understanding" of non-aggression himself, with a remarkable Grik general named Halik, but that hadn't required Halik to accept—essentially—a defeated cooperative protectorate status. That never would've worked, and Pete figured he'd been lucky just to get Halik to march his army out of Indiaa.

Interestingly, though Halik kept his truce with the Allies (Pete believed, of all the Grik in the world—probably due to the influence of a Japanese officer named Niwa—Halik truly understood the concept of honor), he hadn't stopped fighting. He'd taken his increasingly competent and self-aware army into Persia, destroyed the Grik regent there, and set himself up in his place. Even more surprising, he'd done it with the occasional assistance of Allied cavalry, specifically Colonel Enaak's 5th Maa-ni-la and Colonel Dalibor Svec's "Czech Legion," originally sent to keep an eye on him. Reports indicated Halik was now marching south across Africa in response to a summons from the usurper General Esshk, still commanding vast hostile forces up around Lake Galk. But dispatches from Colonel Enaak and analysis by Henry Stokes, the Allied head of Strategic Intelligence, remained unclear whether Halik was coming to *join* Esshk or fight him. Chances were, Halik wasn't sure himself.

In any event, Pete was skeptical about the situation here. His army had been so focused on killing Grik, for so long, he didn't see how they were suddenly going to discriminate "friend" from foe. He suddenly frowned at his own inconsistency. The Allied Expeditionary Force on the Grik Front *already* discriminated the very Grik-like Khonashi of North Borno from the enemy. True, there were humans among them and they wore similar combat attire, carried the same weapons, and were increasingly fluent in English and Lemurian. Despite Pete's initial fears, there'd been amazingly few "friendly fire" casualties. So if the Celestial Mother actually accepted indefinite Allied supervision of her reign, and her Loyalist warriors were sincere about supporting her and crushing Esshk—and were made visibly distinctive from the enemy in some way—things *could* work out, Pete reluctantly conceded. Passing through the archway, heavily guarded by more Repub troops, he finally relinquished his duffel to his orderly. He wouldn't surrender his rifle to anyone. Ever.

He more than half expected to be escorted through a dank, creepy labyrinth leading to some gloomy, reeking chamber, high in the palace. *That's where Grik keep their CMs, right?* To his surprise, the first expansive ground-floor chamber seemed to be where everything happened now. The stone floor was damp, from people coming and going, but the space was well lit by dozens of oil lamps suspended from the walls. And the walls themselves, of this new "throne room," were festive with the hanging flags of every member of the Grand Alliance and each state of the new United Homes. Chairs, stools, and the saddlelike contraptions Grik preferred were arranged in a circle including—not surrounding—a modest throne designed to accommodate the oversized form of the Celestial Mother. Everyone stood as Pete and Choon approached, but for the moment, Pete only had eyes for the big Grik queen.

He'd never seen her predecessor, killed by Isak Reuben in the capture of "Grik City" on Madagascar, but he'd been prepared by descriptions. The new Celestial Mother of All the Gharrichk'k bordered on the obese and was easily twice as large as any Grik he'd ever seen. Her sharp teeth gleamed like fresh-cut ivory and her claws were polished ebony. Other than a gold-edged, dark red cloak and a few glittering jewels, she was covered only in a radiant, coppery, feathery fur. It was darker on her head and back, extending from snout to tail, and there was the beginning of what would always be a somewhat minimal crest and tail plumage (compared to adult males) but which promised equally brilliant colors. On the wall behind her, the same size as the rest, was a flag Pete had never seen. The field was the same bright copper as the Celestial Mother's plumage, but the center was dominated by what appeared to be a single word, painted in white, edged in black, printed in a flowing, Arabic style.

Realizing what caught his gaze, the Celestial Mother spoke. "Our new flag, First General Alden," she proclaimed. Pete understood "Grikish," he just couldn't speak it. Among the Grik gathered here, he'd been told the same would be the reverse. "The flag of the Gharrichk'k Empire." She glanced at a man with vaguely oriental features. "Though we won't *really* be an empire, of course, as we're emulating the system of our friends to the south and establishing"—she hesitated over the unfamiliar words—"a Monarchial Republic. I'm not yet certain how that works, but yours and Second General Kim's presence here implies that it does, so I'll endeavor to continue educating myself." She paused. "The color is of my bloodline, which should serve us well in recruitment. The word is simply 'Truth' in my tongue. Something I've rarely been exposed to," she added bitterly, "and will be my guiding principle. I'll never lie to you," she stated emphatically, her eyes sweeping the gathered soldiers and advisors, "and require the same courtesy from those represented here."

Pete was momentarily flustered by the nature and apparent sincerity of that greeting statement, clearly calculated to allay his concerns. Recovering himself, he finally managed the salute he'd been explicitly ordered by Captain Reddy to perform. The Celestial Mother was a head of state, after all.

No matter that everyone obviously knew who he was, Inquisitor Choon announced him. "I'm honored to present Pete Alden, General of the Armies and Marines and *First General* of the Grand Alliance in the West. He's come to report the outcome of his pursuit of General Ign, and assume command of all Allied Forces on this continent."

Pretty damn pretentious, Pete thought. *Before I came to this world, I was just a sergeant in USS* Houston's *Marine contingent, recovering from a leg wound ashore after a Jap bomb wrecked the ship's aft turret. Mrs. Alden's boy has come a long, weird way.* Sometimes he wasn't sure if limping aboard USS *Walker* to get out of Surabaya before the Japanese came had been a good idea, but the prospects for an injured man in Japanese hands hadn't been good. And he'd already missed his ship's final sortie—and her sinking in the Sunda Strait. *Probably came out on top,* he decided.

Assuming the position of parade rest, rifle still slung, he looked at all the faces in the circle. He only knew a few. Commander Mark Leedom was there, tall, lanky, brown hair almost blond, still looking younger than anyone had a right to after all he'd seen. Leedom had taken over Walt "Jumbo" Fisher's Pat-Squad 22 and its fourteen remaining four-engine, PB5-D "Clipper" flying boats. He'd also be COFO (Commander of Flight Operations) at Saansa Field when it was finished. Pete had lost Jumbo to the "bomber project" at Baalkpan, and probably, ultimately, to the Dom/League campaign. He felt a familiar tightening in his chest. He wasn't worried Leedom couldn't handle the job, he had plenty of experience, but he was concerned they'd sent *too many* of their experienced hands away, too soon. The Grik Front had received the cream of talent and war material from the United Homes for a long, long time, while the war against the Doms had been fought on the cheap. That was, of necessity, quickly changing. Captain Reddy knew it wasn't so, but after victory on the Zambezi led to the capture of Sofesshk and this . . . new arrangement with the Celestial Mother, Pete worried the brass in Baalkpan were starting to imagine the campaign in Grik Africa was little more than a mop-up operation.

Swell, he thought, *it's time General Shinya got a little real help. But now it's like they want me to* finish *this fight on the cheap, while Esshk and Ign are still out there. Maybe Halik too. If they combine against us, they'll run us all the way back to the sea.*

Standing by the Celestial Mother, Pete only barely recognized a Grik-like Khonashi named I'joorka under the hideous burn scars covering almost every exposed feature. Purple flesh was just beginning to resprout tufts of rust-colored feathery fur. Gingerly, I'joorka advanced, extending his hand. "It's good to see you, General," he said.

"You too. *Damn* good. You're what? 'Regent Champion' now?"

"In Ca'tain Reddy's stead," I'joorka agreed, "though su'ject to your orders, o' course." He lowered his voice. "She's trying to add 'consort' to the title, 'ut I don't think I is ready to such . . . exercise yet. Likely not a good idea any'ay."

Pete chuckled. "Oh, I don't know. From what I hear, poor Larry already declined the honor of becoming the 'father of his country.'" Lawrence was Chief Gunner's Mate Dennis Silva's particular Sa'aaran pal. Also "Grik-like," he'd been instrumental in arranging the Celestial Mother's surrender. Pete shrugged. "Somebody'll have to eventually. Why not you?"

I'joorka snorted.

"If you please," Inquisitor Choon interrupted impatiently, and proceeded to properly introduce General Kim and his staff, a Lemurian Shee-Ree major named Fuaal, two officers recently arrived as envoys from the Empire of the New Britain Isles, and yet more Repubs with similar credentials. Their names washed over Pete as he focused on General Kim. The man looked as stout and immovable as an oak and had a no-nonsense demeanor, making a favorable impression. Pete was impressed by almost everything he'd seen, in fact, but his frown had returned and it was growing. "Where's General Rolak and Courtney Bradford? Where's Bekiaa-Sab-At?"

Kim cleared his throat. "His Excellency Courtney Bradford retired south to Soala where he'll proceed by rail to consult with Kaiser Nig-Taak. From there he may return here, fly to Baalkpan, or accompany our fleet when it sails for the Caribbean to participate in our joint operations against the Dominion and the League. In deference to the system we've adopted to accommodate our new allies and avoid misunderstandings"—he glanced at the Celestial Mother—"I've assumed the post of 'Second General'—your second in command—by order of my Kaiser and agreement with your superiors. Also to avoid confusion, the three corps of my Army of the Republic have been consolidated into two, which will now be referred to as Fourth and Fifth Corps." Courtney Bradford's scratch "Provisional Corps" had been absorbed into the others as well. "They, and I, are at your disposal.

"As Second General, however, I thought it best to remain here until your arrival. *Third* General Rolak and Fourth General Faan have taken Third Corps up the Galk River toward Lake Galk. Legate Bekiaa and her Fifth Division are with them, marching along the shoreline and supported by the bulk of what remains of our naval elements. With First Fleet's departure, the most powerful of those are the Republic Navy monitors *Ancus* and *Servius*."

"What's Esshk got up there?" Pete asked Commander Leedom.

The young aviator assumed a pained expression. "Lots of Grik, we know that. Mostly up past the locks at the south end of the lake. Beyond?" He glanced at Kim. "We don't really know. The scuttlebutt is, Esshk and his Japs've been working on something scary that flies, maybe bigger rockets, but recon hasn't spotted anything other than some apparently unfinished ironclad battleships. Didn't see any guns in them either. Maybe they're using them to shuttle troops around? We'll sink 'em," he added confidently, "but whatever else they've got, if it's there, is hidden pretty well."

"Okay," Pete said. "What about Sixth and Twelfth Corps?"

"East of the Third, pacing its advance, but more closely following the Ukri River to its source," Kim responded.

"Why? That's all pretty pastoral country, right? There *were* Grik at Lake Ukri, but I thought they were already knocked out by our air, or came down here."

Kim hesitated. "True, but General Halik could approach from that direction as he nears. Not knowing his intentions, General Rolak and I agreed it would be best to interpose a significant force that's equally capable of moving to his relief, if required."

"Again, okay so far. I don't second-guess Rolak. *Nobody's* better than he is," he stressed. "But what about you? You have what, about seventy-five thousand troops?" He glanced at the preponderance of Repubs in the chamber. "I hope they're not all just hanging around here?"

Kim bristled. "Certainly not. While we do maintain a strong presence in the enemy capital"—he looked significantly at a group of Grik officers not yet named, who'd been joined by Colonel Shelg—"in addition to Fifth Division, already with General Rolak," he reminded, "another division of Fourth Corps is following him, and should join in a matter of days."

"Swell," Pete commended, "but this ain't the 'enemy' capital anymore, an' I've got a chore for your Fifth Corps. It'll head upriver to Lake Nalak, where I just came from, and jump off on the north shore." He sighed. "Maybe half of General Ign's Grik got away. Crossed the lake on *more* unfinished BBs. Jeez! It's a good thing we hit 'em when we did. I bet we've captured a dozen of those ships, some without armor, and most without guns. They're built around their power plants, though, so the majority can move. And like USS *Sular*, they make decent protected transports. Three we took are bringing First Corps here. They'll carry Fifth Corps back to chase General Ign. Before returning," he added cryptically.

Kim bristled again. "And what will First Corps do?"

Pete frowned. "Is *this* how it's gonna be? Bickering over who gets the shitty jobs and who gets the plums? That won't work," he stated flatly. "Trust me, First Corps won't sit on its ass for long, but the *first* thing it'll do is rest and refit." His expression clouded. "Goddammit, they've—*we've*—been after Ign ever since the battle that ran him off, while everyone *else* was taking a break." He shook his head. "And Ign's pretty good. Pulled us nearly two hundred miles away and ran us ragged before skipping across the lake. All our tanks broke down, not that they would've been much use. There's some pretty rough country out there and we had to leave 'em. Hopefully, most are already patched up and heading back here. We might need 'em again. Still, if Esshk had been in any shape to take advantage of Ign's diversion, he could've driven a wedge between us. Lucky he didn't. But First Corps is pretty hammered down."

Kim cleared his throat. "You're right, of course, and I apologize if I seemed insensitive and . . . provincial. You may be used to this level of cooperation with your other allies, but it's quite new to us." He took a breath. "So you want Fifth Corps to destroy Ign?"

Pete nodded gratefully, understandingly. "No apology necessary, General. And no, not specifically. I just need the Fifth to keep Ign pushed off, get between him and Esshk and stay there. Don't want them linking up."

"Why not just use cavalry then?" Kim inquired.

"It might take more than that. We slaughtered his rear guard," Pete said offhandedly, making light of one of the bitterest fights he'd ever seen, "but Ign's been raking in troops on the march." He noticed an arousal of interest among the Grik officers and the Celestial Mother. "More than us, despite what Geerki's translators could do." Pete finally addressed the Grik. "Sorry, Choon didn't introduce us. I met Colonel Shelg, but who are the rest of you?"

"I am First Ker-noll Jash," said one, in Grikish. He was surprisingly young, judging by his underdeveloped crest. "I was elevated to my current station by Second General Ign. I and these others command the Slasher Division."

"Promoted by Ign," Pete said dubiously, before recognition struck. "Hey, it was your Slashers that gave Chack's Brigade and Second Corps such a rough time."

Jash bowed his head slightly. "It was a great battle," he simply said.

Pete examined him speculatively. "Colonel Jash," he murmured, tasting the name. "What do you think of Ign now?" he asked bluntly.

Jash looked at the Celestial Mother for guidance but she merely gestured at the flag behind her and said, "No lies."

Jash took a long breath. "I admire him, but I also once admired the Usurper General—until I discovered how . . . faithless and false he is. Forgive me, these words are almost as new and difficult as the concepts behind them."

"No sweat," Pete said. "But what about Ign?" he pressed.

Jash looked at Shelg, then back at Pete. "He's tenacious, as you learned, and inspires considerable faithfulness—loyalty—among his troops. More than they feel toward Esshk, or if she'll forgive me"—he cut his eyes apologetically at the Celestial Mother—"to our Giver of Life. But Ign's own loyalty is . . . misguided. I think it remains with Esshk because he doesn't know where else to lay it."

"Are *you* loyal to him?"

"I was," Jash confessed, "and still regard him highly. How could I not? But my devotion is to the Giver of Life"—he looked directly at Pete—"and my allegiance, through her, belongs to those who conquered us and could've killed us all—and didn't. Considering what I've learned about what our race has done to . . ." He practically shivered. "All others, everywhere, for longer than anyone knows, your restraint and benevolence fill me with more faithfulness than I can express."

Pete grunted, reluctantly impressed. "So why are you here, just hanging out?" He looked at Kim. "Why aren't *they* with Rolak?"

Kim hesitated and his brows furrowed. "Honestly? Regardless how I personally feel about Colonel Jash, there naturally remains a question of trust. Even he recognizes that." His gaze shifted to their former enemy. "It will take time before our troops will be comfortable with Grik, no matter how devoted, guarding their flanks."

"Inquisitor Choon recommended they remain as a training cadre for recruits, and troops arriving from other regencies," the Celestial Mother supplied.

"Lots of that to do?"

"Less than we'd hoped," the Celestial Mother admitted. "Many regents have chosen not to participate in what they see as civil war. They wait to see who wins, and Esshk is their current favorite." Her crest rose. "I can't imagine how they perceive inaction as the safer path. I won't forgive it, when all is done, and Esshk won't wait. He'll destroy any in his reach, if he can, as an example."

"I doubt it, Your Majesty," General Kim disagreed. "He'll soon have more pressing concerns. He may outnumber us and have the high ground, but we have better weapons and control of the air. His few Japanese planes haven't been seen and he can't have many dirigibles left." He raised his eyebrows. Half a dozen Grik zeppelins had been captured intact during the recent campaign. "We may have more of them than he does."

"Regardless, you mustn't underestimate him—or the 'new weapons' he told me he was preparing. And as you say, even without further assistance, he retains a powerful force."

"Then we need to keep pestering the fence-sitters," Pete said. "Spread the word and remind 'em *we're* the ones who chased his shifty ass off, and the Celestial Mother and her *loyal* troops are on *our* side." He looked at I'joorka and waved at Jash. "Get these guys kitted out. With most of your Khonashi headed back to Baalkpan with Second Corps, there's plenty of replacement gear in storage at Arracca Field, or still in the pipeline."

I'joorka nodded. "What about weapons?"

"Surely we've got enough Allin-Silva breechloaders for General Mu-Tai's Austraalans in Twelfth Corps by now." Pete turned his gaze back to Jash and cocked his head to the side. "Issue their rifle-muskets to the Slashers. See they have plenty of instruction, but make it quick. How does that sound, 'First Colonel'? Ready to get off your ass and do some real soldiering, on the right side for a change?"

Jash perked up. "Quite ready."

The Celestial Mother leaned back in her saddle-throne in apparent satisfaction. Pete rubbed his chin, thinking. "Back to 'fence-sitters,' though, there's only one who really worries me: General Halik. I bet the rest of 'em know about him by now. They'd have to, with him fightin' *them* all the way down here!" Colonel Enaak had detailed how Halik's roughly hundred thousand troops had fought other Grik across Arabia and now northeast Africa. Unfortunately, that didn't mean much regarding his ultimate intentions, it simply meant he was crossing various regencies with more warriors than their regents were comfortable with. Combat in that situation was as much traditional as anything else. "I bet all the others are just as curious to see which way he'll jump as we are." His expression tightened with determination. "I believe it's time I visited him, in person, and pinned him down once and for all."

"Entirely too dangerous!" Kim protested.

"He's right," Choon agreed.

"How, General?" Mark Leedom asked, ignoring the others. "Our last report had him too far from water to fly you up in a Clipper, and it *is* too far and too dangerous to go overland."

"Easy. I'll take one of the Grik zeps." Pete grinned. "With a suitable escort, of course."

"One of *those* rattletraps?" Leedom objected indignantly. "Might as well just shoot yourself." Grik dirigibles, ships, guns—everything they made, in fact—had actually become surprisingly reliable, considering how relatively crude they were. This was simply because they'd made so many, the same way, for so long, with a fanatically specialized workforce focused only on their own small part of the whole. And "incentives" had been added to ensure quality components: build them to specs or be eaten. As for the zeppelins, however, even their most complicated parts—the five little engines that drove them—seemed able to chug along forever despite the crappy fuel they were fed. Leedom would never admit that, of course.

Pete laughed. "Silva flew one farther. *Twice.*"

"And crashed it both times," Leedom reminded. "Respectfully, sir, you're a little more important than he is."

Pete smiled ruefully and lowered his voice. "I'm not always sure about that."

Leedom was thinking. "What about this? How far is Halik from that other big lake, north of Ukri? What's it called?" He glanced at the Celestial Mother. They'd never flown that far, and without Grik maps, wouldn't even know the big, roughly rectangular lake was there. And when it was revealed, all they'd really cared about was that there were no locks and the river flowing down to Lake Ukri was unnavigable, descending hundreds of feet in elevation. There was even reputed to be something almost as impressive as Victoria Falls, which apparently didn't exist on this world.

"Lake Uskoll," Inquisitor Choon replied. "And I know where you're heading with this. According to Colonel Enaak's reports, Halik is within a hundred and fifty kilometers of its northeast shore. A meeting there would be out of his way if our assumption, that his army will cross the upper Ukri River before continuing south, is correct."

"Kind of 'out of the way' for us too," Pete stated wryly, "so maybe the best possible place."

"I wonder if he'd leave his army and let Enaak's cavalry escort him down?" Leedom pondered. "I could take you up in a Clipper and you could palaver there."

Pete scratched the dark beard along his jawline. "Maybe. Depends on how well they really get along, and how much Halik trusts Enaak—and Dalibor Svec, for that matter," he added darkly. "He'd have to know a meeting between us was intended to make him finally get off the pot and declare his intentions. Come to that," he added thoughtfully, "he'd also suspect Enaak, and *especially* Svec, might bump him off if he came and told us to our faces he was going with Esshk. Have to assure him of safe passage either way, and make him believe it. Just knowing what he'll do is worth armies. And whether he shows or not, he'll give us some idea which way he's leaning."

"In that case, issue the invitation—and any guarantees—in my name as well," the Celestial Mother said, looking defiantly at Pete, her tone brooking no argument. "I will go with you. I've always wanted to fly, since the first time I saw your wondrous machines," she confessed, "but mainly because if you can't persuade General Halik, perhaps I can."

Choon blinked unhappiness. "A great risk for all concerned. Even a simple engine malfunction might cost us the war. On the other hand," he continued, "if his own Giver of Life can't induce Halik to declare against Esshk at last, no one else possibly can." He blinked sternly at the Celestial Mother. "And you must allow him no flexibility." He flicked his ears at Jash.

"Just as others have done, he must declare his intentions, without reservation, to your face." He looked at Pete. "Certainty is indeed 'worth armies,' and with it, we can plan accordingly."

"And if he declares for Esshk?" I'joorka asked softly.

Pete shrugged. "Enaak and Svec take him back to his troops." His lips compressed in a thin line, fully conscious of the personal feelings the Khonashi might have about what he said next. "Then they spot for Pat-Squad 22 as the Clippers take as many incendiaries as they can carry, as often as it takes. Halik has no defense from the air, and we'll burn his whole damn army."

CHAPTER 1

////// *USS* Walker
Indian Ocean (Eastern Sea)
May 1, 1945

Damn, Skipper, it's *good* to be back at sea!" Commander Brad "Spanky" McFarlane proclaimed. Standing in his trademark pose—hands on hips, chest out, chin jutting—he always seemed bigger than he actually was. Short reddish hair ruffled in the wind on his uncovered head as he stared through the newly replaced glass windows in the pilothouse of USS *Walker* (DD-163), past the busy sailors around the number one gun on the fo'c'sle, and out at the white-capped, purple sea. The detail on the fo'c'sle was largely composed of furry, long-tailed Lemurian "'Cats," as was nearly all the old "four-stacker" destroyer's crew, these days. Similar details still worked all over the ship to patch her many, but thankfully—this time—relatively minor wounds. The ship *looked* like hell, battered and rust-streaked from battle and toil, but was steaming easy and the 'Cats at the big brass wheel and engine order telegraph (EOT) seemed relaxed and satisfied with how she handled.

Overseeing repairs to the forward 4″-50 gun, tracing balky wiring from the director, was an amusingly contrasting trio. The giant Chief Gunner's Mate Dennis Silva, the veritable Hercules of the Grand Alliance, seemed to be aping Spanky's pose as he loomed over the diminutive, furry fireplug that was Chief Bosun's Mate Jeek. And for no other reason than he apparently never left Silva's side, the Grik-like Sa'aaran named Lawrence was there, standing slightly back out of the way. Unlike the sailors in T-shirts and dungarees (or blue kilts on the 'Cats) Lawrence wore only a new tie-dyed combat smock, sunlight flashing on the dark plumage of his tail, crest, and orange and near black tiger-striped pelt on his arms and legs. Occasional humorous snippets of Silva's profane and bombastic declarations regarding how the work should proceed, and Jeek's adamant denunciations could be heard. All this was punctuated by the cawing shrieks of a small, fuzzy, tree-gliding reptile draped around the back of Silva's big neck like a sweat rag.

Captain Matthew Reddy, Commander in Chief of All Allied Forces (CINCAF) and "High Chief" of the "American Navy and Marine Clan" leaned slightly back in the chair bolted to the starboard side forward bulkhead of the pilothouse. The chair's shape and rigidity had always made it profoundly uncomfortable and only the soft, carefully embroidered cushion some anonymous Lemurian sailor secretly left on it one night made the long hours Matt often spent there physically bearable. And the responsibility the chair represented, not only to his ship but the entire Grand Alliance, could make it even harder to take. Matt was younger than Spanky, just thirty-five, but his brown hair was completely gray at his temples and the rest was starting to turn. His clean-shaven face remained boyish, but new lines were starting to undermine that impression as well. Turning away from the reassuringly normal entertainment below, he grinned at his friend and XO. "Considering you've said that *every day* since we left that nasty sewer river behind, I'm inclined to believe you're sincere," he noted wryly.

Spanky shrugged and made a noncommittal grunt. Matt chuckled and followed his gaze. A few heavy clouds were building in the humid afternoon sky and a squall caressed the sea with filmy gray fingers a dozen miles to port, but a cooling breeze generated by the ship's fuel-stingy twelve knots washed through the pilothouse and the eastern horizon they chased was clear. It was indeed a far cry from the filthy, muddy, blood-thickened waters of the Zambezi River. Most of First Fleet had been confined there for the last few months, after establishing a beachhead against the savage and seemingly numberless Grik. And these Grik were no longer the mindless mob of killing machines that relied as much on their teeth and claws as the other weapons they carried. They'd finally gotten wise and built real armies with thinking soldiers.

The battles that followed had been brutal and costly, and only a bloody, grueling campaign of misdirection and focused ferocity, capitalizing on dissension among the Grik themselves, allowed the Allies to shatter their way through to Old Sofesshk, capture the Grik "Celestial Mother," and command the cooperation of a percentage of her subjects. A larger percentage still opposed them, however, led by the cunning usurper Esshk, and the

Allied armies still had a momentous task before them. They were tired, worn down, depleted, and if Esshk's troops were on their heels at present, that could quickly change.

Matt frowned. Yet except for a little "brown water" work, the war in Grik Africa had changed to a land and air campaign. It would still gobble precious transports and supplies, and troops of course, but for the most part, the Navy had done as much as it could. Now it must race to confront an equally difficult, maybe hopeless situation, on the other side of the world. More than likely, they'd get there too late, with too little.

Matt looked back at Spanky. Despite all that, it was a beautiful day. *Walker* was plowing smoothly through the choppy swells and notwithstanding her many dents and patches, the rumble of her boilers and engines, vibrating through the chair into Matt's very bones, felt and sounded as healthy as he had any right to expect. And behind USS *Walker*, in a long straight line, steamed the pride of the American Navy Clan's surface fleet . . . such as it was.

Matt glanced over his shoulder, past his ship and the men and 'Cats going about their duties aboard her, and contemplated the massive form of First Fleet's most impressive element a quarter mile behind: the captured League battleship *Savoie*. She'd taken a serious beating herself when they took her from that madman Kurokawa—the League's former client in the Indian Ocean—but churning through the sea in her new "dazzle" paint scheme, she looked much better now. Some work remained, primarily to her sabotaged fire control system, but Steve "Sparks" Riggs cryptically promised they'd have it when they needed it. Like most of Matt's "old" destroyermen, Steve was still just a kid, barely twenty-two, but Matt didn't doubt the electronics wizard from Delaware, now Baalkpan's "minister of communications and electrical contrivances," would come through.

Savoie was French built, a Bretagne Class superdreadnaught from another, different "earth" where France, Spain, and Italy had all gone fascist in the wake of a broader war against Bolshevism as the Great War juddered to an end. Though crushed in Russia with the help of all the great powers, Bolshevism took firmer root in the rest of Europe and civil wars flared. That apparently triggered a quicker, more aggressive rise of fascism and despite their mutual animosities, the three chief partners in the "Confédération États Souverains" intervened in civil wars in Germany, Austria—and elsewhere, Matt supposed. Ultimately estranged from Great Britain, the United States, and Imperial Russia—virtually all its former allies—and requiring external threats and conquest to keep it together, the Confédération sent a powerful fleet to wrest Egypt and the Suez Canal from the British. That's when a similar . . . phenomenon . . . to that which brought *Walker* to this world apparently occurred. *And if Walbert Fiedler is to be believed,* Matt mused, and he didn't really doubt the German pilot who'd defected to the Allies, *the . . . event . . . brought over nearly the whole damn fleet and a fair portion of the city of Tripoli around the harbor where it had been at anchor.* Fiedler had described a cataclysm on shore, particularly where buildings—and a few ships—smashed down on *another* city already there.

Matt sometimes wondered how the Confédération fared on that other world after such a big chunk of its naval might simply disappeared. *I hope they got clobbered,* he thought. But its descendant here, ruled by a triumvirate of senior officers from its "big three" members, formed the League of Tripoli and commenced subjugating the Mediterranean's "indigenous" peoples, many of whom had arrived in a similar fashion through the ages. *And the League's starting to make itself a real pain in the ass for us,* Matt thought darkly.

Behind *Savoie* was *Walker*'s somewhat misshapen sister from another world, USS *Mahan* (DD-102). She'd been destroyed and resurrected—from less—even more often than Matt's own ship. She'd required two entirely new bows and been shortened the length of her forward fireroom. She'd lost a little speed, but no armament, and not much endurance.

Next came USS *James Ellis* (DD-21). She was another "sister," though maybe "daughter" was a better term. Copied from *Walker* and built on this world, she'd been the very first all-steel ship ever made in the Union capital of Baalkpan. Inevitably, she had a number of kinks. Her own first sister, USS *Geran-Eras* (DD-23), had been better, but she was sunk in the Battle of Mahe. Two more "Wickes/Walker-Class" DDs were supposedly complete, and at least two more were almost ready for sea. Others were being built in the Filpin Lands far to the East.

Bringing up the rear of the column was the light cruiser USS *Fitzhugh Gray* (CL-1). She was a beautiful thing, the most ambitious naval achievement of the Allies to date. Begun before they knew about the League, however, she'd been built to slaughter the big, tough, and frighteningly powerful Grik battleships and cruisers by running rings around them and outranging their big muzzle-loaders with modern 5.5″ rifles. But the Grik navy was finished and *Gray* didn't compare that well with what Matt knew of her League counterparts. And there was only one of her, so far. Another was finishing up in the Maa-ni-la shipyards using machinery shipped there from Baalkpan, but there was no way to know if she'd be complete in time. The Empire of the New Britain Isles, where the Hawaiian Islands ought to be, were drawing on their colonies on the West Coast of North America for materials to build steel-hulled "protected cruisers" of their own, but Matt had no idea about their particulars. And the Republic of Real People, their allies in southern Africa, was building "battlecruisers" as well. Matt had seen preliminary plans and was skeptical of their design.

But Gray *sure is pretty,* he thought wistfully. She was long and lean like the smaller destroyers, with a similar silhouette and the same four stacks. *She might even lick one of the lightest cruisers the League throws at us,* Matt cynically appraised, but then shook his head. *Not only is she a fine ship with a crew blooded in hard fighting, everyone aboard her believes the ghost of the man she's named after watches over her. She'll make a good account of herself.* Turning back in his chair, he stared out at the sea ahead.

They'd left La-laanti, where Diego Garcia ought to be, earlier that day after an overnight refueling stop and wouldn't see land again for two thousand miles. A convoy of oilers bound for where they came from and escorted by the last unaltered sail/steam DD, USS *Revenge*, would meet them around the halfway point. The task force would fill their bunkers again at the former League outpost of Christmas Island before steaming through the Soonda Strait to B'taava, Jaava. After taking on more fuel, they wouldn't stop until they crossed the Jaava Sea and opened Baalkpan Bay on the southeast coast of Borno.

It'll be the first time I've been home in the better part of a year, Matt realized, never associating the word "home" with the small ranch in Texas where he grew up anymore. *I wonder how it's changed?* He started calculating all the things they had to do once they got there, and grasped he wouldn't have much time to enjoy his "leave." Pushing that away, he decided, like his friend, to just enjoy the moment. "Not ragging you," he said at last, "I'm just as glad to be back out on the open sea."

"I think everyone agrees with that," added Sandra Reddy pleasantly, stepping up the ladder behind them. Matt froze after a quick glance in her direction because his wife had brought their infant son, Fitzhugh Adar Reddy, on the bridge, swaddled in a soft white blanket. *We've talked about this,* he inwardly groaned. He'd lost all preconceived notions against women aboard ship; a third of his crew was female now, both Lemurians and ex-pat Impie humans. Fully half the snipes in Lieutenant Tab-At's (Tabby had been the first female 'Cat to join) engineering spaces were female as well. And there'd been babies aboard before—briefly, either rescued from other ships, like *Neracca*, or twice when crew members gave birth. But it was still against regulations for "mates" to serve on the same ship, and infants were quickly transferred with their mothers.

But transfer to safer, more suitable transport hadn't been an option for Sandra and their son. Both the great carriers, *Salissa* (*Big Sal*), under Matt's best Lemurian friend, Admiral Keje-Fris-Ar, and *Madraas*, now under Keje's intended, Commodore Tassanna-Ay-Arracca, had offloaded most of their planes at Arracca Field and promptly left the theater right after the Battle of the Zambezi. Most of the other large ships in the fleet, like the floating dry dock *Tarakan Island* and the armored transport *Sular*, went with them, relying on the carrier's remaining planes for protection. Not only did they require refits and upgrades at Baalkpan, they carried most of the campaign's wounded, as well as Colonel Chack-Sab-At's extremely hard-used 1st Raider Brigade and the equally exhausted II Corps. II Corps' badly wounded commander (and Chack's mate) General Queen Safir-Maraan was in *Salissa*'s extensive infirmary with Chack by her side.

In any event, in the wake of the terrible battles and their child's birth at their height, Matt relented when Sandra insisted on joining him in *Walker*, as he'd earlier *promised* she could. But this wasn't part of the deal. Parading around the ship, *and on the bridge*, with infants hadn't been any part of the Navy he'd come from, or was trying to build on this world. More importantly, he had to set an example. If he let *his* wife cart babies up on the bridge—drawing along doting admirers, he noted, as Tabby, Surgeon Lieutenant Pam Cross, and Diania (Sandra's steward/bodyguard) tromped up the stairs behind her—how was he ever going to stop others from doing it? *And to top things off, Silva's here too!* he seethed, darting a glance at the fo'c'sle. *How did he get up here so fast, with Lawrence in tow?* And that ridiculous tree-gliding lizard named Petey was peering, big-eyed, from beside the big man's scarred, bearded face. Matt almost felt like it was mocking him too.

Sandra saw the thoughts behind his face as surely as if he'd spoken them and smiled sweetly. She looked so much better than after they'd rescued her from Kurokawa, and to see her eyes glitter with such genuine mirth . . . Matt's outrage deflated.

"You don't need to worry about having the carpenter build a playpen behind the chart table, Captain Reddy," Sandra said dryly, almost formally.

"And one visit by your son to enjoy such a wonderful day for a few moments with his father isn't going to set a corrosive example and crack the discipline of the American Navy Clan!"

"Damn straight," Silva agreed seriously, scratching the patch over his left eye. "Little scudder needs sunlight an' fresh air or he'll wither up. Why, look at all them wrinkles on him! Poor little Fitzy!" he cooed.

"All babies are wrinkled, jerk," Pam snapped at Silva. Everybody knew the petite, dark-haired nurse from Brooklyn loved him, but she rarely let it show. *Particularly* to Dennis Silva.

"Don't *ever* call him 'Fitzy,'" Spanky growled.

"Well, I reckon so at that," Silva conceded to Pam, ignoring the XO. "I ain't seen many o' the critters, mind, but it seems they were all a little creased. I guess they come that way, like folded balloons, an' grow so fast they gotta have room to shake out."

Pam rolled her eyes and Silva glanced at the gray-furred Tabby with his good eye and sniffed. "Still, no *proper* sailor can thrive in the dark, belowdecks. I noticed ol' Isak creepin' around on the aft deckhouse under the moon the other night, checkin' the voice tubes to the engineerin' spaces. He's lost all his tan an' I thought he was a spook."

Tabby laughed. "He might be. *Stinks* like he's dead, an' he never sleeps. Just haunts the firerooms night and day. Drives my snipes crazy."

Matt chuckled and took his son when Sandra thrust him forward. *What the hell? What're we fighting for, anyway?* He eased the blanket aside and saw a pair of dark green eyes regarding him intently from a round, pink face. "Isak's always been weird," he agreed, softening his voice unconsciously, "but he's the best there is. I told him he could be engineering officer aboard any ship in the fleet"—he glanced at Tabby—"including this one. It's time you moved up and out, Lieutenant." He looked back down at his child. "He refused. Said we'd have to pry him out of *Walker*'s firerooms like a hermit crab from its shell. Probably kill him, doing that."

"Same here, skipper," Tabby said matter-of-factly. "There ain't no 'up and out' for me. Not yet. I'm still not a good enough bridge officer for aany kind o' commaand," she added, but it was clear she'd stay with *Walker* until they dealt with the League, no matter what.

"I wonder how many others feel that way?" Pam speculated, responding to what Tabby meant, not what she said.

"Ha. I've been fielding requests from every ship back there," Spanky grouched, pointing aft with his thumb. "An' it ain't just the few guys left who came here with us, it's 'Cats too, them that started out in *Walker* or *Mahan*. Every one of 'em figures we're heading for the old girl's last fight. Ensigns, even a few *lieutenants*, have begged to come over as apprentice seamen if they have to! Shit!" He glanced quickly at Sandra. "S'cuse me."

"Stupid," Silva agreed levelly.

"The thing is, I kind of understand how they feel," Matt objected, "and I honestly wish we could oblige them, but we need them where they are."

"You don't really need *me*, Skipper," Silva said, surprising everyone. "Not aboard here. An' poor Larry's about to *die* with nothin' to do, to keep him from pinin' away over his lady love: the Sequestr'al Mammy."

"I *glad* to ha' nothing to do," Lawrence objected incredulously, his Grik-like face managing a hunted expression. "And I *not* going to die, *now. She'd* ha' killed I, sonhow. Squshed I . . . or torn I head." He shuddered at the memory of something he and Silva had seen.

"I reckon she might'a loved you to death at that," Silva allowed and shook his head. He looked back at his captain. "But you got Campeti for gunnery, an' he's trained up a whole new team."

"You're still their chief," Spanky pointed out. "Pack-Rat's gone off to *Mahan*."

Silva shrugged. "Anybody can do what I'm doin', an' Jeek's a good bosun too." He hesitated, exhibiting a degree of uncertainty, even vulnerability very unlike him. "*Walker*'s my home," he finally continued, "the only family I ever had is here"—he paused—"or was. But maybe me an' ol' Larry should'a stayed with Chackie an' his Raiders. Seems we do more good for ever-body when we're with them."

"No you don't!" Pam countered angrily. "You've done *more* than enough for everybody else already! It's time you quit goofin' off and stuck with your ship. You *said* you were 'back in the Navy for good,'" she almost pleaded.

Matt cleared his throat. Pam's personal considerations aside, Colonel Chack was physically and emotionally exhausted—who could blame him? His 1st Raider Brigade had been in the grinder for months and all its senior leadership, including his sister Risa, was gone. And now, after what happened to his beloved Safir-Maraan . . . Chack needed a break. They all did, but Chack was a special case. He'd gone from being a pacifist to one of the most lethal commanders in the Grand Alliance, fighting on every front. And so soon after Matt's own wife and unborn child had been threatened, he could particularly sympathize with Chack's mental state. There was no guarantee he was even fit to command his Raiders. And how would Silva function without Chack to guide and temper him? He wouldn't obey anyone else, and wasn't fit to lead the brigade himself. He was too impulsive to command that many troops, and he knew it.

Almost hesitantly, Sandra patted Silva's arm. Petey perked up, thinking she might be extending a biscuit. "Eat?" he inquired, rather softly for him, but then settled back on his perch when no food was forthcoming. "Colonel Chack's got some healing to do," Sandra said. "We'll see how he is when we get home. Safir-Maraan will recuperate at Baalkpan for quite a while. The hospitals are better there, and Chack'll be at her side. After that I suspect she'll resume her duties as queen of Aryaal and B'mbaado. We'll see what Chack's up for then. Few commanders in the Alliance can lead like he does, but we owe it to him to let *him* decide what's next." She squeezed Silva's tight bicep. "Same as you, Chief Silva. Captain Reddy and I already discussed it. But whether you're with Chack, or by your captain's side, nobody *fights* like you do," she stated simply. "And this ship"—she glanced at Matt—"and her crew, are going to be in the fight of their lives. One way or another, there'll be plenty for you to do."

Silva blinked, touched by the words of praise, then straightened and reassumed his normal demeanor. He thumped Petey on the head. "You hear that? I get to pick what I do next. What do you think?"

Petey seemed to contemplate that. "Eat," he decided.

Lawrence had been looking on, and now shuffled back toward the ladder in resignation. "I guess *I* don't get to choose," he murmured, the words whistling through sharp, Grik-like teeth.

Matt heard him, even over the roar of the blower. "Of course you do. Everybody has to fight this war, even those at home who make our weapons and keep us supplied. There aren't many of your people left, but most still work in dangerous occupations, making high explosive for our shells on Samar. Even so, you're the only one who's seen actual combat, lots of it, right along with Silva. You've earned the right to choose how you fight too. Same as him."

Lawrence looked at the big one-eyed man speculatively, eyes narrowing. Then he shook his head. "I guess I'll stay 'ith he. I don't know anything else. 'Ut I not get sad to stay in *'alker* a'hile," he added. "There's scary hoogers on shore!"

Nearly everyone laughed at that. Even Minnie the talker chimed in with her tiny, mousy voice. This whole world was frightening to everyone else, even without enemies to contend with, but Lawrence was originally from a small island in the Pacific and his race made a living from the terrible sea. He was used to it. He'd rarely encountered dangerous creatures on land before he met them.

Pam didn't laugh. She looked close to tears, in fact.

"This is all just a big damn game to you!" she snapped loudly, turning to look several of those on the bridge in the eye. "Just some damn *game*, a big adventure," she added, her voice dripping scorn.

Matt stood and walked to her, holding his child. The laughter and her raised voice had made the boy cry. Flustered, Pam took the baby when he handed it to her. "No, Lieutenant Cross, it's *not* a game, and never was. Not at all." He paused and glanced at Lawrence, then looked at his wife. "But sometimes you gotta laugh—or you'll go nuts."

CHAPTER 2

////// Near Puerto del Cielo
Holy Dominion
May 3, 1945

"I guess we're 'expend-aable,' now!" came Lieutenant (jg) Kari-Faask's tinny shout through the voice tube by Lieutenant Fred Reynolds's ear. It was midafternoon and they were flying their well-worn PB-1B "Nancy" floatplane five thousand feet above the Caribbean, just off the coast of the Holy Dominion. Fred heard his best friend fine, even over the roar of the wing-mounted engine above and between them. Holding the stick straight, he scrunched around in his wicker seat to look at her, sitting behind the tiny windscreen in the aft "observer/copilot" cockpit in the waist. Kari's goggles barely covered her large Lemurian eyes and the dark fur on her face was slicked back by the wind.

"Why do you say that?" Fred yelled back, disdaining the tube.

If Kari could've blinked cynicism around the confining goggles she would have. "Yesterdaay, they had us scout Maartinique Islaand, where Caap'n Gaarrett saank thaat League destroyer with *Donaghey* an' thaat Dom frigate she caaptured," she began. Their observation of the previously deserted island had been an eye-opener. Several modern ships, including a pair of oilers, a couple of tenders, and a large destroyer were anchored in the bay on the island's northeast coast. Not only had the sunken *Atúnez* been righted in the shallows, space for a significant presence—and what could only be an airstrip—was being hacked out of the snake-infested jungle ashore.

"Now we're goin' to scout thaat daamn 'Porto delsello,'" Kari continued. "They didn't waant us goin' *either* place before, scared they'd lose the only plane this side o' the Paass o' Fire." She nodded to the right where a virtually identical aircraft kept formation. Painted white below, just like theirs, the only apparent differences were the darker blue above, and instead of white stars and red dots in blue roundels on its wings and fuselage, it was marked by white squares surrounding what looked—to Kari—like a "raaggedy blaack lizardbird." It was the insignia of the naval air force of the Republic of Real People.

"Only we *ain't* the only plane no more," Kari concluded, "so it don't maatter whaat haappens to us."

Fred sighed. Part of what Kari said was true. There *were* more planes, now that a pair of beamy, wooden-hulled seaplane tender/oilers had finally crossed the Atlantic from the mixed-species Republic. The Republic was situated in a damp, chilly, southern Africa, populated by Lemurians, humans from different times in apparently divergent pasts, and some other folk called "Gentaa." Fred and Kari had fought their way here across the Pacific, however, and had almost no experience with "Repubs." Captain Garrett liked them and said they had the oldest (friendly) advanced civilization they'd met. Firm members of the Grand Alliance and now fully engaged in the war against the Grik in Africa, they'd also been preparing for a confrontation with the League of Tripoli, after a very unfriendly visit by them. Now that the League was allied with the Doms in South America—human enemies Fred bitterly considered the worst of the lot—the Republic was joining this fight too.

Despite their wooden construction, the new "Repub" tenders looked amazingly like any small freighter on the old world Fred remembered. That was understandable, he supposed, considering who influenced their design. More importantly, each carried half a dozen near exact copies of his Nancy, though the Repubs called them "*Seevogels*." If Fred understood the translation correctly, he thought it was a stupid, unimaginative name. *Not that "Nancy" is much better,* he admitted ironically. The Repubs also brought plenty of good gasoline their Allies' engines liked as much as theirs, and the ships, gas, and precious planes would've arrived much sooner—the tenders were surprisingly swift, capable of eighteen knots—if the heavy sail/steam frigates the New United States (Nussies) sent to escort them hadn't actually slowed them down.

Swept to this world in 1847, Nussies were descended from other Americans that had been bound for Vera Cruz to join Winfield Scott's campaign aimed at Mexico City. They'd retreated to occupy the south-central portion of North America (and now Cuba) after a bitter war with the Doms. That war never really ended, and though they weren't in the fight against the Grik, they were in it to their necks against the Doms—and now the League.

They'd just landed fifty thousand troops in the Dominion, in fact, aiming to capitalize on the Allies' conquest of the Pass of Fire to the west—a natural passage between the Atlantic and Pacific, about where Costa Rica ought to be—and drive south toward the Dom capital of New Granada City and El Templo de los Papas, the lair of the enemy's bloodthirsty "pope." Unfortunately, depredations by the heavy League destroyer *Leopardo*, now possibly at Puerto del Cielo, had made supplying the NUS Army extremely difficult.

Fred and Kari had watched from the air while *Leopardo* smashed a pair of Nussie transports. They hadn't seen her go on to destroy six of Admiral Duncan's most powerful warships guarding the NUS beachhead, but they'd witnessed the aftermath. And those ships hadn't been pushovers. In the century since the "1847 Americans" crossed over, they'd finally reattained and surpassed the technology they'd brought with them. And though still outdated wooden-hulled sailing steamers, their ships were more advanced than anything like them and mounted substantial broadsides of rifled muzzle-loaders up to 6" in diameter. Plenty big enough to smash *Leopardo*—if she hadn't used her speed to stay out of range and assassinate them from farther than they could even shoot.

At least the NUS Army was getting sufficient food from cooperative natives. No one outside the major cities loved the Dominion, and simply for having *seen* the "heretics" tread on holy soil, they were doomed to extermination by their own troops if the invaders were defeated. But battles loomed and the army must have military supplies. Nussie transports waited to bring them, but though the DD at Martinique seemed content to remain on guard, *Leopardo* had proven she'd attack. They had to confirm where she was.

Fred jerked his head at the plane nearby. "Somebody has to show these newies around or they'll just fly off in all directions until they run out of gas. *We're* the 'old salts' in this outfit," he told his friend somewhat wonderingly. He was barely nineteen. "Even most of our own people coming across are pretty green. New-fledged Impies who never *saw* a plane two years ago. And after the beating it took taking the Pass, they're all Second Fleet can spare. Our loss might be less tragic for the war effort now," he conceded, "but I don't think anybody'd just throw us away. Captain Garrett wouldn't," he defended loyally. Garrett had always been nice to him, even when he was *Walker*'s gunnery officer and Fred was just the youngest kid on the ship.

"Yaah, maybe," Kari allowed. "An' maybe it don't hurt thaat your *gurrl* is the daughter of the Nussie's Commodore Semmes."

Fred's face reddened and he shifted uncomfortably in his seat while making a show of looking around for threats. Grikbirds—aptly named flying monsters the size of a man that *looked* like Grik with wings—were dangerous to the slow-flying Nancys if their pilots weren't alert. They hadn't seen any "greater dragons," giant Grikbirds capable of carrying a man—and a bomb—on this side of the Pass, but there hadn't been any to the west either, before they suddenly made such a nuisance of themselves. They'd damaged all three of Second Fleet's carriers and one, *Raan-Goon*, was probably beyond repair.

"I, ah, don't really think Tabitha and I have much of a future," Fred admitted.

"You finaally figure out she's got nothin' in her head but air?"

Fred was tempted to lie. "No," he relented, "but I don't hang around Santiago much, see? And lots of high-up young Nussie officers do."

Kari said nothing for a little while, then finally retorted, "She faall for them over you, she's stupider thaan I thought."

Neither spoke as the hazy green, hilly coastline approached. Even hazier mountains reared to the south, almost indistinguishable from the sky. Fishing boats appeared more frequently below and for the first time Fred didn't avoid overflying them. None would have radios of course, but they'd report their sightings when they made port. It didn't matter. They'd probably been seen inspecting Martinique, and *Leopardo* had spotted them before so the enemy knew the Allies had planes in the Caribbean.

"That's gotta be Puerto del Cielo ahead," Fred said, pointing. The greenery had given way to a large white city quickly resolving against it. Fred squinted. The masts of quite a few ships rose above the sea, anchored offshore or snugged against the docks, but none had the shape of warships. As far as they knew, the Dom fleet had been annihilated in the west, and eastern elements sent to defend the Pass had also been destroyed. Obviously, the Doms now depended on the League to protect them at sea and these must be merchantmen.

"Wish we had bombs," Kari groused. Fred nodded. Captain Garrett hated the League above all their enemies, or at least he had. Their friends fighting in Africa probably hated the Grik the most. But Fred and Kari had actually been in the hands of the Doms before, personally enduring their depraved cruelty. Fred was tortured until he pretended to embrace the perverted blood rite faith of their foes. Kari, perceived as an animal at best, and possibly a demon, was seemingly tortured just for hoots and kept on display in a cage. Both escaped with the help of a Nussie "Ranger" calling himself Captain Anson, and a diverse group of rebels. Needless to say, neither was keen to fall into Dom hands again.

"Whaat's thaat to the east of the city?" Kari said, not really asking. Her eyesight was a lot better than Fred's and she had an Imperial telescope as well.

"Where?"

"Looks like two big forts to the east, on each side of the mouth o' thaat river. They're taall as the pyramids they tol' us to look for—which I see . . . maybe five? But the forts is faat an' round. See 'em?"

Fred thought he did. "So?"

"There's a couple steamers, no maasts, aanchored under their guns."

Fred believed he saw the ships as well, now, though it was difficult to tell. The shapes were light gray, not much different from the water. "Get on the horn. Tell our wingman to keep his eyes peeled," Fred warned. The Repub pilot was a 'Cat, and regardless how separated they'd become through the ages, most Lemurians—with a few exceptions—retained a strikingly common tongue. The accents varied wildly, almost unfathomably, but they could usually make themselves understood. To each other, at least. Fred could speak Kari's "'Cat" as well as she spoke English, but figured he was lucky to catch one word in three that an ordinary Repub said. Their senior officers were different, some even speaking English, but the other pilot was an "optio," whatever that was, and Fred barely understood a word he said.

"Wilco," Kari told him, then jabbered in her microphone. Fred sighed, wishing for the old days when they thought just talking in 'Cat made their comm secure. It never really had, of course. The League had abducted enough Lemurians to learn the language before the Allies even knew about them. They'd been reading their mail—and passing it to their enemies—almost from the start. Everything was coded now, and codes changed all the time. The naturally loquacious 'Cats still let real intel slip in the clear from time to time, but that was deliberate. Fred figured the snoops back in Baalkpan might use it to their advantage someday. In any event, there was no need for codes now. Alert lookouts on the ships should've seen them already.

Fred squinted again. Details of the city were sharpening and he saw it wasn't all white. The forts and walls around it were, but the roofs of the buildings, few over three stories, looked dark, reddish. Lots of the bloodred flags with jagged gold crosses whipped in the stiff coastal breeze, and Kari was right; there *were* five large stepped pyramids geometrically placed, with the biggest in the center. Fred looked back at the ships, just a couple miles distant now. There was the same dilapidated oiler he'd been told to expect—*Leopardo*'s personal fuel cow—but the other vessel looked different, bigger than *Leopardo*, with an indistinct outline.

"There she is!" Kari snapped.

"Where? That's not her, it's something else."

"Yaah!" Kari insisted. "Is something else *aalongside Leopaardo*!"

Fred blinked. Sure enough, the sleek, predatory shape of the Italian destroyer was snugged to a longer, fatter ship shaped like a small cruise liner. "Tell our friend to follow our lead. We found what we're looking for and it's time to go." Even as Kari passed the word and Fred turned sharply to the east, bright flashes lit both ships. Dark clouds of smoke burst right where they'd have been in another few seconds and Fred pushed the stick forward, accelerating into a dive to change his speed and altitude. More explosions cluttered the sky above and behind them. "Not bad shooting," he snorted, voice strained, as he turned north and steepened his dive. A final cluster of ragged black puffs pursued them. "And they said *Leopardo*'s guns weren't on dual-purpose mounts," Fred accused loudly. "Shouldn't have been able to shoot up so high."

"I guess they were wrong, or thaat other one did all the shootin'."

Fred nodded, but he was pretty sure both had fired. "Whatever. But what's that other ship? Where did it come from?" He shrugged. "Send the 'go' code to Commodore Semmes." That meant they'd spotted *Leopardo* and it was safe—for now—for transports to proceed to the Nussie beachhead at El Palo.

"Done," Kari confirmed a few minutes later. "Hey, maybe thaat other ship's the one *Matarife* met with at Ascension Islaand before Caap'n Garrett captured her. The 'Raam,' er somethin'."

"*Ramb Five*," Fred agreed. "Could be. The one with the League's area commander. That's what the prisoners off *Atúnez* said." He hesitated. "Which *could* mean the Leaguers are about to ramp things up."

"Them workin' at Maartinique, specially buildin' a airstrip, already proved thaat."

Fred pursed his lips but didn't reply. Now just a thousand feet above the sea, they flew north until Puerto del Cielo faded into the distant, greenish shoreline. Turning west, they crossed a prominent peninsula that would've been the Island of Trinidad, surrounding a little land-locked lake where Port of Spain should've been. It was risky flying over Dom territory, but there was no port, or even—supposedly—many Doms there. The Repub tenders were safely at anchor at Santiago and the two planes had been carried down by USS *Donaghey* and Captain Willis's NUSS *Congress*, currently just about in the center of the plane's operational radius. They'd head back for them after a quick look at El Penon. Local scouts said a Dom army was assembling there prior to pushing west along their military road, the "Camino Militar," toward NUS forces at El Palo. The final objective of their flight was to see if the Doms had moved.

"Draagons!" Kari suddenly snapped. "Three o'clock high!"

Fred looked up to the right—past the plane flying off their starboard wing—and sure enough, two of the giant Grikbirds were soaring along a mile away, paralleling their course, dark against the white clouds beyond. They'd been told Dom "dragons" were colorful creatures, even more than Grikbirds, but they couldn't see any detail. Their wingspan was as wide as a Nancy, however, and Kari confirmed Fred's first concern. "They got riders!"

That meant they could be controlled to an unknown extent. Just as important, riders could report what they saw and that gave the Doms a capacity for reconnaissance the Allies had never guessed they had. For an instant, Fred wondered what it would be like to fly like that, without a sound but the rushing wind. Then again, he suspected dragons were a lot like Maa-ni-la cavalry me-naaks, only with wings. Young "meanies" newly paired with riders often tried to eat them.

"They're faster than Grikbirds in level flight, but can't keep up with us," Fred reasoned confidently. "They'll see where we head, though. Might've been kiting around on the lookout just in case we showed. We were bound to sooner or later, and they probably hoped we'd show 'em the way back to our ships." He shook his head. "Well, we weren't heading to the barn yet, anyway. Keep your eyes on 'em, Kari, and make sure our Repub pal does too."

Over the next half hour, they crossed the peninsula and flashed over the water again. The enemy flyers diminished to specks, then finally disappeared. Fred turned southwest, followed by the Repub plane, and climbed to three thousand feet. The shadows of the clouds on the sea were beginning to lengthen when they made their approach to El Penon.

It was another coastal city with a respectable harbor, but not as large as Puerto del Cielo. It also lacked a broad river into the interior. But the architecture was identical, complete with a fort and wall around the older part of the city that boasted a single stepped pyramid at its heart. All Dom cities of any size on this side of the Pass of Fire featured a fort of some kind, probably a legacy of their hundred-year hostility with the NUS. They called Nussies "Los Diablos del Norte," and Fred figured that first, century-old conflict must've left quite an impression.

"Not maany ships down there," Kari observed. "No waarships at all. A couple traansports. The rest is just fishing boats. Where's this aarmy s'posed to be?"

"South side of the city on the flanks of the hills," Fred replied. The Allies had always been at a disadvantage from an intelligence perspective, particularly compared to the League and those it helped, who'd long monitored their communications, observed them from bases in the Indian Ocean, and even planted spies in the Republic. And the Doms weren't slouches when it came to that sort of thing. They'd infested the Empire of the New Britain Isles with spies, which then radiated into the United Homes from the Filpin Lands to the Malay Barrier. But the Allies had their own spies now: long-repressed subjects of the Dominion's bloody tyranny, prisoners, and even asylum-seekers from the League, disaffected with its fascism and brutal conquest of the Med, or perhaps just the neglect of certain factions within it. Even some Grik were on "their side" now. Sort of. Regardless, the Allies knew more about their enemies than they ever had, but for "right now" intelligence, they needed air recon.

Fred gazed down at the city and saw the same reddish roofs and profusion of fluttering Dom flags. *Mighty patriotic bunch,* he thought grimly. *Or spiritual. Not much difference here, I guess.* Hundreds of people, maybe thousands, were looking up from the streets below, garbed in a surprising riot of colors. *They can't* all *be crazy, can they?* He grimaced and looked ahead. *Can't count on that,* he reminded himself. *And the closer we get to their "El Templo," the more rabid they get. The city folk, at least,* he qualified. The vast majority of the people around El Palo were friendly enough, but they'd been serfs or even slaves. *The high-ups in the city skedaddled when the Nussies landed.*

A great camp sprawled on the open ground past the city walls ahead, invading a significant percentage of the nearby cropland. *What* used *to be a camp,* Fred corrected as they neared. There were still a lot of large tents and quite a few troops and wagons. Hundreds of giant, spiky, armadillo-like draft animals called "armabueys" were enclosed in vast, partitioned pens. Other pens held horses and Fred saw a column of lancers emerge from the forest to the east, trotting down the Camino Militar in a dense cloud of dust. But despite what was obviously a substantial supply depot an army on the move might leave in its wake, hundreds more tents had been recently stricken—he could see where they'd been—and their occupants were gone.

"The Doms've marched!" he shouted back at Kari, turning right to follow the dusty dirt highway. "Send it." He considered his fuel and added, "We'll try to see how far, but it might be hard to tell." The road entered a forest with trees tall and dense enough to hide an entire army. Their only hope was to catch signs of movement in sparser places.

They flew west for an hour, then two, the sun sinking lower in front of them. Try as she might, even Kari saw nothing beneath the dense canopy. Oddly, though they hadn't been precisely *here*, they'd experienced this forest and knew the ground was fairly clear around the great trunks, and visibility—though dim—was good. Little could grow in such deep shade and under the thick carpet of ferny pine needles, not even saplings of the great trees themselves. Probably, when one of the things finally toppled under the weight of its own sheer size or improbable age, saplings immediately shot up to replace it and only the fastest-growing survived. In any event, the entire Dom army out of El Penon could've been down there and they wouldn't see it.

"We gotta head to the ship!" Kari shouted. "We get low on fuel."

"We're closer to El Palo than El Penon now, anyway," Fred reluctantly agreed. "No way the Doms've got this far. Cap'n Anson's Rangers would've sniffed 'em out. Right?"

"Prob'ly," Kari hedged. "If they're lookin' this faar. But nobody knew the Doms'd maarched until we looked. Spies or scouts might, but they couldn't report to Gener-aal Cox faaster thaan we did. He might *just now* be gettin' the word."

The Repub plane to their right suddenly waggled its wings to get their attention and Fred heard Kari shout "Grikbirds, twelve high!" Barreling down from above the sun (Grikbirds always attacked from above), eight of the creatures plummeted toward them in a tight, streamlined stoop, every bit as fast as a Nancy. There was no way to avoid them with maneuvers and they'd strike before the observers could get a shot past the engines in front of them. "We'll meet 'em!" Fred hollered, advancing his throttle and pulling back on the stick. After a moment's hesitation, the *Seevogel* did the same.

Fred was unaware. Utterly focused on the sight in front of his windscreen and the rapidly growing targets, he opened fire with the single copy of a Browning .30-caliber machine gun mounted in the nose of his plane. The ship roared and shuddered as sparkling orange tracers arced toward—then across—one of the flying predators. It staggered and cartwheeled, shedding a trail of bloody, downy plumage. Its companions had to veer to avoid it. Green tracers from the Maxim in the *Seevogel* slashed through the cracking formation and another Grikbird tumbled away, then a third, as Fred's tracers struck again—but then they were upon them.

Teeth bared, toe talons extended, wingclaws deployed like great, wicked sickles, the first Grikbird barely missed Fred but slammed into the leading edge of the wing above. Liquid and furry feathers exploded all over him and he braced for the clattering impact with the engine and its spinning prop that would kill his plane behind enemy lines. But the expected jolt never came. The beast must've tumbled over the prop. Another Grikbird gave the plane a glancing blow below Fred's feet, raking a gaping hole in the tough rubberized fabric covering the hull. Fred instantly felt wind gust up between his legs. Kari's .45ACP "Blitzerbug" SMG rattled at one of their attackers and Fred pushed the stick forward before they stalled.

Whipping his head around, he saw two Grikbirds hit the Repub plane in pretty much the same place the first hit his; *they must be training them to go for the engines,* he realized, only this time the combined strike of *two* 175-pound animals shattered the wing and engine struts in a red cloud of prop-chopped feathers and the long, broad wing folded up around them. Fuel ignited and the *Seevogel* dropped into the trees amid a smear of flame that rose again in a rolling orange ball licking the top branches in a pall of black smoke.

Kari's Blitzer rattled again, probably at a Grikbird turning to chase them. *It'll never catch us,* Fred thought, but then he became aware of a nasty taste on his lips. There was blood from the Grikbird that hit them, but something else as well. . . .

"I got *gaas* all over me!" Kari practically shrieked. "We losin' gaas!"

Fred looked up at the leading edge of the wing and cringed at the damage. Shattered spars had been mashed into a jumble of jagged wooden splinters. Strips of ragged blue fabric fluttered violently. Worse, the plane's copper fuel tank was mounted in the wing, just in front of the engine, and had obviously been punctured.

"Don't . . . shoot anymore!" Fred shouted back, somewhat lamely, mind racing. There wasn't much chance Kari would light off the gasoline with her little Blitzer. Short as the weapon was, there was still hardly any muzzle flash. On the other hand, it was a miracle the engine's hot exhaust hadn't already set them on fire.

"You *think*?" Kari practically bellowed back. "The Grikbirds is gone," she added a little less hotly. "They give up after we paast, like usuaal. *They* don't know we fixin' to burn up an' craash anywaay."

"We're not gonna crash!" Fred shouted, glancing up and aft. A mist of fuel still blew, but maybe the Grikbird tore the tank up high. If he could keep them level, the leakage might slow. Not that it mattered. The gauge in the cockpit suddenly read "empty" and he had no idea if it was right. The wire from the sending unit could've been torn away. The backup gauge, basically a floating stick in the gas cap, had been broken off as well. But even if they still had gas and didn't lose much more, they'd never get back to *Donaghey.* Besides, a long flight over water, in a damaged aircraft with a possibly empty tank that might blow up any minute, wasn't something he craved. He wanted *down* and *out* of the damn thing. "We have to make for El Palo," he decided. "Can you send that?"

"I don't know. Aerial's gone. I'll try."

"They have wireless sets at the beachhead. We'll get word to *Donaghey.* Maybe we can fix the plane or Captain Garrett'll come get us. Worst case, we hitch a ride out on one of the transports."

"Okaay," Kari responded with what was suddenly a very small voice.

Fred gently descended just above the treetops and turned out over the coast so water would be near if they had to set down in a hurry. Nancys were dedicated seaplanes without any landing gear and even a smooth beach would probably crack them up. He glanced at the fluttering fabric past his feet and rudder pedals. *Not that we'll float for long.* But they were still losing fuel and he was terrified it would ignite. Kari was too, of course. She was soaked in it. And as much as they feared the Doms and the swarming predators in the sea, burning was an even less attractive fate. An eternal ten minutes later, they left the trees and crossed the lathering surf on the darkening beach. Dropping lower, Fred uncomfortably remembered the last time he put a Nancy in the surf when Doms were close. "Crank the wing floats down," he cried—just as the engine quit.

The sudden silence was shattering.

"Shit!" Fred shouted. "Hang on!" They were only about a hundred feet up and Fred barely had time to dip the nose and level off before they slapped down between the diminishing rollers. Fred slammed forward against the restraints he hadn't thought to tighten, smacking his head against the windscreen frame. Bright, swirling stars clouded his vision but he saw sandy water gush in around his feet. He didn't know it but the plane didn't dig in; it actually kind of bounced, dropping again on the crest of a wave and riding it toward shore. The port wing tilted and plowed into sand—Kari hadn't even started lowering the floats—and they twisted around, nose on the beach.

A grinding rumble caught up short brought Fred back to his senses and he saw Kari already beside him, waves washing past her waist, trying to get him out of the quickly filling plane. She'd slung her Blitzer and donned a pack containing basic survival gear and two canteens.

"Just a sec," he mumbled, unstrapping, and practically dove out beside her. Helping each other, they quickly thrashed through the shortening waves to shore. Flasher fish rarely hunted the surf, but the instinct to escape the water was strong nonetheless. Oddly, the plane followed them in, bouncing and pirouetting on jostling waves as if it had grown as attached to them as they to it.

"Where are we?" Kari gasped as they hit their knees in the sand.

"Who knows?" Fred replied, wiping watery blood from his eyes and slapping his right thigh where he usually strapped a small chart tablet. It was gone. "Just guessing, I'd say we're still eight or ten miles from El Palo, though. We better get under cover. The beach is deserted an' I didn't see any villages or anything, but we couldn't see the whole Dom army from the air. Doesn't mean they didn't see or hear us."

Kari stiffened beside him. It was midnight black under the trees of the forest, but her sharp eyes caught something. "Movement," she hissed, swiftly checking her Blitzer. Fred pulled the soaked 1911 .45 out of its holster, but then quickly fumbled in the pack between them. Retrieving a brass-framed copy of a Remington Mk III flare pistol, he mashed the button on the side and flipped the barrel up before inserting a 10-gauge flare. Glancing up, even he could now see the shadowy shapes of troops moving cautiously out on the beach about a hundred and fifty yards away. There seemed to be twenty or so, all carrying long muskets.

"Whaat're you gonna do with thaat?" Kari demanded, raising her Blitzer and nodding at the flare gun. Her voice was high, nervous.

"Burn the plane. They're not gettin' it—or us," he added grimly. "Cover me if you have to."

The stranded Nancy was only a few paces away now, rolling heavily against its port wingtip. The damage over Fred's cockpit was spreading and cracking, loud enough to hear over the surging sea, and the whole wing flexed, starting to break. He quickly covered the distance. Dom muskets were wildly inaccurate at this range but he still half expected shots. None came. Aiming the Mk III into the aft cockpit, most inundated with fuel, he murmured, "So long, plane," and pulled the trigger. The flare pistol bucked in his hand and a searing red ball blasted through Kari's wicker seat. He suddenly felt like an idiot, suspecting the thing had simply blown out the bottom of the plane, but then a rush of fire gushed out of the cockpit. Sloshing quickly backward, he saw the flames lick greedily forward, up the engine struts, and across the ravaged top of the wing. With an urgent *crump!* the fuel tank split and the whole plane was washed in fire. Some even poured into the sea, sweeping up near where Kari knelt.

The men on the beach were shouting now, jogging closer.

"It's been swell, paal," Kari hissed through gritted teeth, taking aim.

"Yeah," was all Fred could say. He raised his pistol.

"Hold your fire, for God's sake!" someone cried. The tone sounded . . . exasperated.

"Why?" Kari shouted back.

"Because we're on the same side, you fools!"

Kari abruptly stood, tail lashing angrily. "Says who? An' who's a fool? *I* think it's the fella runnin' straight at a auto-maatic weapon, caallin' people names."

Fred could now see that the men wore light blue uniforms with white trim and crossbelts. The man who'd spoken was an officer, in a dark blue frock coat. Uniforms of regular Nussie infantry. He began to relax. Doms dressed predominantly in yellow. Their regular infantry had white facings on their coats, but the vicious "Blood Drinkers" had red, and wore red trousers. "Don't shoot Kari, they're friends."

"They ain't *my* friends, runnin' up an' shoutin' at us like thaat," she grumped, looking at the officer. "Who the hell're you, an' how'd you know *we* was 'friends'?"

"Lieutenant O'Riel, Company A, Fourth NUS Infantry, at your service," the man replied curtly. Standing before them now, he didn't look any older than Fred. "And though the enemy can fly, it seems, he doesn't do so in machines." He nodded at the rapidly withering plane, its burning framework sagging and hissing in the sea. "Speaking of the enemy, they're quite close. The flames and smoke will draw them. We must be away from here."

Kari was looking at the burning Nancy now too. "Daamn it, that was *our* plane!" she said, dejection replacing her antagonistic tone.

"Yeah," Fred agreed solemnly. "And we've broken so many of 'em—not *always* our fault—I'm not sure they'll give us another."

Brusquely, the Nussie officer and his men ushered them off the beach and onto a barely visible trail paralleling it. No one spoke and all the men were clearly making an effort to move as quietly as they could.

"How close are they?" Fred finally ventured to whisper, catching the mood of his companions.

"I've no idea. Perhaps all around us," O'Riel confessed, less tersely than before. "We haven't seen any ourselves. We were forward pickets in an observation post overlooking the Camino Militar. Only Rangers and local scouts were beyond us, but it seems the enemy stole a march. They didn't come straight up the road as we'd so carefully planned for them to do," he added wryly.

Fred grimaced. NUS troops and sailors were professionals, well-trained and equipped to face the Doms, but aside from their navy, which performed very well against this enemy, their army hadn't engaged in a major land campaign in a generation. And it had been a century since it faced the Doms on their own soil. Fred doubted they were as ready for this as they thought they were.

O'Riel continued. "Our first hint something was amiss came when a pair of Rangers galloped through, informing us we'd been bypassed and must withdraw to El Palo." He paused. "There'd been nothing on the field telegraph and we discovered why. The line had been cut at another OP *behind* us, and those manning it annihilated without a shot. We weren't that far apart and should've heard any firing."

"Infiltrators sneaked up on 'em, or passed themselves off as friendly locals," Fred guessed.

"Precisely. In light of the apparent fact that *some* enemy elements, at least, are between us and El Palo, I thought it best to stay off the main road. Fortunate for you, or we wouldn't have seen your awkward landing."

"We reported that the Doms had marched," Fred told him, "but only a couple hours ago. We were trying to spot them from the air but couldn't do it along the road. That's why, I guess. Soon as they got under the trees, they left the road, or took another one."

"That's what I suspect as well," O'Riel confided. "Our local advisors describe a rather extensive network of well-worn paths connecting a number of villages. Our planners didn't consider them substantial or direct enough to move large forces. Perhaps the enemy isn't as concerned with 'directness' as we were, eh? Now there's no telling where they are unless the Rangers or dragoons can find them. I don't envy them that task in these woods at night."

"Well, we know where they're *headed*," Kari said, also whispering.

O'Riel glanced at her. Lemurians weren't unknown to the NUS, but remained something of a novelty. "Indeed, but General Cox had hoped to have at them on the march. Pure hubris, I suppose, to expect the enemy to accommodate us so. But worst of all, Cox may be slow off the mark but he's a fairly aggressive fellow, not much given to defensive tactics. If the enemy holds the initiative when they approach El Palo, from whatever direction they choose, we could find it difficult to deploy quickly enough to give them a proper welcome," O'Riel added worriedly. "It all depends on our scouts."

"Caap'n Anson'll sniff 'em out," Kari declared confidently.

O'Riel seemed surprised. "You know of him?"

"Not 'of.' We're old paals."

Fred couldn't see, it was quite dark now, but he suspected Lieutenant O'Riel's eyes had widened.

"That's as may be," the Nussie said at last, "but we've a long walk ahead. There may be hostiles—not to mention frightening beasts. I hope you two can manage in the infantry for a while."

"No sweat," Kari replied offhandedly. "We tromped haaff-waay across the whole daamn Dominion before you were even in this waar."

CHAPTER 3

////// Ramb V
Puerto del Cielo
Holy Dominion

"You're not going after them?" Contrammiraglio Oriani asked Capitaine De Fregate Victor Gravois, as he leaned back in a creaking wooden chair in the wardroom of his "flagship," *Ramb V*. Obese, pallid—except for a strikingly black mustache—and sweating profusely in the humid heat offshore of Puerto del Cielo, Oriani had been the resident supérieur at the League's outpost on Ascension Island. He was also the highest-ranking OVRA official outside the pretentiously named Palace of the Triumvirate in Tripoli. The "Palace," actually somewhat closer to where Tunis should be, was an ancient, drafty, somewhat gothic edifice, built by locals long ago. It was also the most impressive intact structure in the League's new empire. A few more imposing buildings, in what should've been Italy and Greece, had been demolished in the fighting there.

As always, Gravois was as impeccably turned-out as circumstances allowed, in a fresh uniform and brilliantly polished boots. Not a hair was out of place and his mustache was carefully trimmed. Yet despite his position in French Naval Intelligence, the Italian Oriani was his immediate superior. The OVRA (Organization for Vigilance and Repression of Anti-fascism) had increasingly accumulated responsibility over foreign (and domestic) intelligence for the entire League. To Gravois's dismay, Oriani and *Ramb V* had unexpectedly arrived the day before, and the man had assumed the grandiose title of "Gouverneur Militaire du Protectorat des Antilles."

It wouldn't do to have Don Hernan hear that title, Gravois mused, *but after all I've done to seal the alliance with the Dominion and subvert the forces opposing it, the position should've been mine. And it will be, if not something grander,* he resolved to himself. But he'd have to be careful. If the League had anything nearly as depraved as the Dominion's Blood Priests, it was the OVRA.

"It's obvious the scout was sent to determine *Leopardo*'s presence," Oriani continued, "so the NUS can supply their forces at El Palo. Such a shame the planes avoided your fire," he interjected. That was wildly unfair, particularly since Oriani's ship did most of the shooting, and even *Ramb V*'s rather puny antiaircraft capability was better than *Leopardo*'s. In fact, only a few of the newest League ships were properly equipped to defend against air attack. Politically . . . reformist . . . as its parent Confédération États Souverains might've been, its member fleets were largely ruled by traditional battle-line admirals before the "crossover," despite the potential modern aircraft had shown. Faced with pandering to or purging its highest-ranking naval officers, at the same time the Confédération's relations with many of the world's major naval powers were deteriorating, its chief partners, France, Italy, and Spain, had chosen the former. *That could've proven costly on our old world,* Gravois supposed, even if their old adversaries mirrored the prejudice to a large degree. *It might* here *as well,* he imagined darkly. He'd repeatedly warned his French superiors about the enemy's airpower, primitive as it was, and urged them to design countermeasures. He had no idea if they had. At the same time, however, he was *counting* on a number of those more traditional officers. They might prove useful to his ultimate scheme.

"But you could still intercept the transport ships with ease," Oriani urged.

Yes, quite simple, Gravois thought sarcastically. *I'll snap my fingers and have Capitano Ciano raise anchor and steam a tired ship and dispirited crew a thousand kilometers on a moment's notice. It may only be six hundred kilometers in a straight line, but there's the small matter of a conspicuous peninsula, countless islands, and dangerous shoals to consider.* The voyage would take thirty hours at top speed, and depending on where the transports lingered, they might come and go by then. *Leopardo* might chase them down, but what would be the point? Particularly since destroying the NUS forces in the Dominion didn't fit Gravois's plan just yet. His rationale, for that at least, he could share with Oriani. For that matter, there was no reason not to reveal his entire strategy—to a point.

"Perhaps, Contrammiraglio"—Gravois supposed that was still the safest way to address the man—"but is it truly in our—*your*—best interests? Don Hernan is dangerously intelligent, as I've told you, but foolishly refused *Leopardo*'s help defending the Pass of Fire, claiming his people must do it alone and *know* they had. He similarly rejected my offer to destroy the NUS invasion force before it came ashore—expressly so his troops could annihilate their hereditary enemy and *he* could take the credit." Gravois leaned forward. "I can't stress enough that 'allies' or not, even we are heretics in the eyes of those who adhere to the barbarous, dominant faith in this land, and therefore enemies of a sort ourselves. The Doms are amazingly obdurate when it comes to matters of their strange beliefs." He sat back. "Don Hernan has demonstrated flashes of pragmatism, even flexibility—*to me*—at times, but can't be *seen* to do so. Nor can he allow it to appear he relies too heavily upon us. That might undermine his near godlike authority, so he portrays us as 'tools' only he can wield."

Gravois touched his chin and his lower lip protruded. "He'll have to reinforce that notion as our presence in the region grows and he 'wields' us more openly. He *lost* the Pass of Fire to the enemy's 'Second Fleet,' though not without nearly destroying it, you'll be glad to hear. Only its admittedly slow and unsophisticated aircraft carriers posed the slightest threat to *us*, and all of them were damaged. It'll be some time before the enemy can take advantage of its victory—they have no modern warships in the Pacific at all. If we hurry our forces into the Caribbean, our position will be unassailable."

Oriani grunted. "Indeed, and work is already well along, establishing support facilities at Martinique, but the Triumvirate won't 'hurry' the task force it prepares 'unduly.'"

Gravois felt a stab of anger, but got the impression Oriani was as frustrated as he, and the last word he used was a quote. He sighed. "Very well, I'll speak plainly. The Pass *did* fall, the entire Dominion fleet is destroyed, and the gate is open to the west. The NUS has a foothold in the Holy Dominion, an Allied army will march east from the Pass to join them, and if we dawdle, Capitaine Reddy will bring every ship he can scrape together to secure the Pass and aid his allies *before* we grow too strong. A race has begun and we must win it."

"And if we lose?"

Gravois raised a crystal glass of Oriani's wine and studied the purple-red liquid. It was barbaric stuff, from one of the vineyards in the province of Egypt, but grapes wouldn't thrive on the newly conquered northern shores of this world's Mediterranean; it was too cool and damp. The climate wasn't at all what it should be. *Still,* he supposed wistfully, *it's better than that acid they're bottling in Algiers.*

"It'll likely make little difference in the end," he conceded. "I try not to underestimate Capitaine Reddy; the man exhibits flickers of tactical brilliance and has managed surprisingly well. But he seems overwhelmed by global strategy, and is ever *reacting* to events. Not his fault, I suppose. He and the alliance he built knew little of the world beyond their early operations for a great while, and nothing of us at all. He may now have a better idea of what we can bring to a direct confrontation, but can't possibly match it for many years. Don't misunderstand," he quickly added, raising a hand, "Reddy and the disparate allies he's amassed, particularly the, ah, 'Lemurians' who make up the bulk of his forces—much like the *hommes-singes* in the League—continually amaze me with their industry and creativity, but the conclusion of a confrontation *now* is forgone. That's precisely why we must *invite* it now," he added fervently.

"You've changed your position," Oriani accused.

"So it might seem, but I've never changed my *mind*. My 'official' position was dictated by orders, and the strategy I pursued to keep all our enemies at one another's throats facilitated the policy laid down by the Triumvirate." He straightened. "Despite various . . . criticisms from certain quarters, I believe that worked out quite well—until the *situation* changed entirely. The enemy has united more effectively than we ever imagined, and its focus has broadened. We *must* act while we retain overwhelming superiority."

A vicious-looking little lizardbird paused to flutter outside an open porthole, glaring in with large, yellow eyes. With a shriek, it darted away. Oriani snorted at the sight. "So what of Don Hernan? What do we do with him, here, now?"

Gravois appeared to consider that. "I *wish* we could simply eliminate him," he said with feeling, presuming that would appeal to Oriani as well, "but if we did, chaos would ensue. Perhaps they have an institutional mechanism to seamlessly replace him, but I think he's amassed more power than any Blood Cardinal ever wielded, purging others who might challenge him, so I suspect Dominion society might simply collapse. As would its war effort." He shook his head. "No, we must work with him, but it's essential you understand how absolutely he controls the minds and hearts of his faithful subjects." He shuddered. "If you'd only seen . . ."

He stopped a moment and had to remind himself the OVRA regularly committed acts almost as atrocious as those he'd watched on the beach, just not perhaps as wantonly and purposelessly. The thought chilled him and he shook his head and looked regretful. "If the enemy in the west hadn't come so soon and we'd had time to cultivate a temporary alliance with the NUS against Don Hernan, I might've counselled that we attempt it." He waved that away. "Just as well we didn't. The NUS is a fairly comfortable democratic republic. Enmity would've flared between us at once. The Dominion, on the other hand, presents an opportunity. You know I'm not squeamish, and our own conquest of the Mediterranean has required . . . regrettable extremes, but compared to the offhand, everyday flood of innocent blood in the Dominion, *most* of our methods can only be described as benevolent. And since the people of the Dominion are already accustomed to authoritarianism, they'll *see* us as benevolent when the time is right.

"For now, however, we must continue to appear to be Don Hernan's 'tools.' There's little else we *can* do until we're stronger here." He shrugged. "He can probably defeat the enemy armies on his soil alone. He has an entire continent with many more people than we have to draw upon, after all. But he couldn't oppose a dinghy at sea without our help and he knows it." He tilted his head at Oriani. "Yet regarding the transports that are, as you pointed out, no doubt already at sea, it doesn't hurt for Don Hernan to be reminded how *badly* he needs us from time to time, and allowing the enemy to supply their armies keeps him occupied. Keeps him beholden to us."

Oriani pursed his lips and sipped his own wine. "A risky scheme. It could strain the alliance if Don Hernan believed we weren't doing all we can to assist him"—Oriani's voice lowered—"and this alliance is *very* important to the Triumvirate." He drained his glass. "But it happens I agree with you, and approve."

Gravois was taken aback. Oriani had been his chief nemesis for so long, he didn't know how to react.

"Surprised? So am I." Oriani seemed to make a decision and his tone turned earnest. "As you said, the Dominion is vast, with many inhabitants. We have few, even counting the scant million or so we now rule around the Mediterranean. The *hommes-singes*, as you called them, are not even *people*, and those who are will never love us." His eyes gazed far away. "So cold and dreary there, it isn't *our* home at all. Not . . . here." His expression firmed. "And there's nowhere we can *go*. East would be no improvement, even if those few pesky British, Russians, and Turks hadn't closed the Dardanelles. Let them lurk in their little 'Lake' of Marmara—and welcome to their wasteland! The Bosporus is dry and they can't even access the Black Sea." He waved that away. "We can't go north. What for? The land's inhospitable even before one meets the marching ice. And beyond the narrow desert to the south are the Grik, of course." He drummed the table with his fingers. "Reports indicate our enemies have scored some major victories against them, but our sources there aren't what they were."

Gravois dipped his head, acknowledging the oblique compliment.

"Even if they're entirely defeated, however," Oriani continued, "there'll always be Grik." He shook his head. "Terrifying creatures. We actually owe a debt to our enemies for keeping those reptilian monsters focused away from us so long. But like the people of the Republic in southern Africa, no doubt, it troubles me to share a continent with Grik. It always will. No," he said, gesturing at the nearest porthole, indicating the city and land beyond, "*here* in the Caribbean and the lands around it, perhaps ultimately the Far East, are the only places a *real* civilization can flourish on this world."

Gravois was surprised to learn Oriani supported the growing "Equatorial Faction" (and its allies) in the League. Everyone knew the world they'd found themselves on was locked in an ice age of sorts. The lower sea levels and generally cooler temperatures away from the equator made that rather obvious. But many of the more scientifically inclined officers Gravois knew had long opined that the ice was *advancing*, the water receding, the ice age just beginning. It might take decades, even centuries, but sooner or later the Mediterranean would grow less suitable for the large, industrial society the League dreamed to build. Worse, some theorized that the Strait of Gibraltar might actually close. Where would the League be then? How could it ever dominate the world if it remained centered—trapped—in the confines of a giant freezing lake? What kind of world would that leave for their children?

Gravois seriously doubted things would ever get that bad. Alarmist movements always exaggerated things. But it *was* possible—and wasn't it really the *cause* that mattered, after all? At least to those whose support he needed. Doing nothing was unthinkable to many, and apparently Oriani as well. Gravois's eyes narrowed. *If he's sincere. If not, he'd be at the forefront of efforts to expose a coalition of factions bent on launching our global conquest sooner than our comfortable, complacent leaders in the fragile Triumvirate will countenance.* Gravois expelled a breath. *For whatever reason, Oriani seems content to endorse my policy of ensuring Don Hernan continues to believe he needs us more than we need him. And he does—for now. After the current threat is past, there'll be plenty of time to subvert the twisted faith of the Dominion, raise its people up—and join them here. Of course, that would all require more enlightened and aggressive leadership. . . .*

He gazed at Oriani. Despite their past differences and the reasonable concern he'd once felt that the man might simply have *him* eliminated—it had happened to other rivals in the various League members' intelligence services—Gravois caught himself wondering whether the man might prove an asset rather than an obstacle.

Oriani cleared his throat through a small belch, dabbing at his lips with a napkin. "Don Hernan is here, at Puerto del Cielo?"

"Indeed," Gravois agreed.

"And 'His Supreme Holiness,' the Dom 'Pope'?" Oriani's lips twisted. Unlike Gravois, or even most League officers, Oriani still made Catholic noises. "He's the only one Don Hernan answers to, correct?"

"There's a . . . pretense . . . that's the case," Gravois admitted.

"He's not here?"

"He never leaves their greatest temple in the capital city of Nuevo Granada, three hundred and twenty kilometers up the River of Heaven."

"So Don Hernan acts entirely on his own."

"Yes."

Oriani stood from the wooden chair and it rasped its relief. "In that case, why hasn't he come to greet me? *Ramb V*'s arrival can't have gone unnoticed."

"He, ah, doesn't consider himself bound by the same proprieties we observe," Gravois stated ironically. "Perhaps he's awaiting an auspicious day. Their calendar looms large in their social and religious life."

"Ridiculous!" Oriani spat, growing angry and beginning to pace. Finally he stopped and turned. "I *won't* be treated this way!" He measured Gravois with his eyes. "I understand you've never personally gone ashore, here or at New Granada."

"None of us have. It was made quite clear what would happen if we did, and I was explicitly ordered—by you—not to upset the natives in any way." *And I don't want to be tortured to death,* Gravois added to himself.

"Well, things are different now, and I'm no mere messenger—not that *you* are either, my dear Gravois," Oriani hastened to add. "But I'll command all the forces gathering in this theater, and if Don Hernan won't come to me, I'll go to him—and make absolutely *sure* he understands his very survival depends on us!"

Gravois's eyes went wide. He'd made the situation here as clear as he possibly could, reporting the barbaric practices of the Blood Priests, and specifically relating why none of them were ever *allowed* ashore, on pain of the most hideous death imaginable. Oriani must've seen for himself the rows of charred crosses and piles of blackened bones strung along the beach at the base of the fortress wall, a scant half kilometer away! The nightly executions of dissidents and accused heretics had tapered off, due to an "experiment" Gravois suggested to Don Hernan, but if any of *them* went ashore . . . They were *all* heretics in the eyes of these people. Gravois had just reminded Oriani of that. No "accusation" would be required to nail them up and burn them alive. "But surely—" he began.

Oriani waved off his objections. "I'm aware of the risk. But my orders—and inclinations—require me to meet Don Hernan at once. I'm willing to appear to be at his service, as you recommend, but I must be assured he grasps the reciprocal nature of our understanding."

"Sir," Gravois almost pleaded, "I'm not sure *you* understand—"

Oriani stopped him. "I'll take a suitable guard and interpreter. You say they speak some proper Spanish? I wish you could accompany me, since you've had dealings with the man before, but you must stay here." He paused and grimaced. "Just in case. You've been named as my deputy"—he'd been saving that little tidbit—"and will assume my duties if anything happens to me. I expect, in that case, you'll avenge me one day in some suitable fashion."

"I'll blast the forts to rubble and steam upriver and do the same to their great temple until they hand over their silly pope," Gravois declared.

Oriani seemed touched. "You'll do nothing of the sort. As I said, your strategy is sound, and is in the interests of the League. You'll continue to implement it and you'll find orders to that effect in my safe."

Gravois had never expected to have such mixed feelings about Oriani. "But why go at all?"

"Because I'm confident there's no risk, and our 'allies' can't be allowed to grow contemptuous of us, believing we fear them." He took a conciliatory tone. "In spite of the cloud you were under over that affair with *Savoie*, you've done fine work here, been the dutiful diplomat, and followed your instructions to the letter. And the initiative you've shown wasn't . . . over-the-top, shall we say, in regard to current circumstances." He lowered his voice. "And I believe you and I are of the same mind about the future of the League. We can't jeopardize what you've achieved by allowing the benign posture we've taken thus far to be interpreted as weakness.

"In any event, as you say, Don Hernan must be increasingly aware how much he needs us and it's time to assert ourselves. Bending their taboos a bit might be a subtle way of beginning the process." He chuckled at Gravois's dire expression. "Oh, don't worry. I'll loudly proclaim I'm responding to a summons as I go ashore. That should satisfy appearances."

"You may be right, sir," Gravois said, his tone one of respect. "I hope you are," he added, and found he actually meant it.

"They'll kill him, kill them all!" Capitano di Fregata Ciano growled harshly, standing by Victor Gravois on *Leopardo*'s bridgewing the very next morning. Brightly colored lizardbirds swooped and capered overhead, and snatched churned-up morsels from the wake of a gleaming white motor launch carrying Contrammiraglio Oriani ashore. Oriani was stuffed into his most stunning uniform and looked like a decorative ball on tall black boots. His Spanish chief of staff, a strange, thin little man named Roberto Francisco (Gravois remembered he'd been a fervent Carlist, of all things), was dressed the same, but with less ornamentation. They were accompanied by ten armed men in black tunics, khaki trousers, and black fezzes on their heads, each adorned with multicolored tassels. These were hard men, all volunteers, constituting Oriani's personal guard and half of *Ramb V*'s naval landing force. Two sailors manned the boat.

"I fear you're right," Gravois confessed, watching a rapidly escalating reaction near the dock the boat was steering for. People were running from everywhere, not just to look, but to confront. "I warned him repeatedly, but he doesn't understand these people." Gravois snorted. "*I* don't understand their self-destructive fanaticism, and never will. Not really." He considered. "At least not those in the cities, almost daily washed in sacrificial blood. I understand our enemies have had better luck with people in the countryside." He shook his head. "But these . . . Oriani must believe that since they *look* like us, they *are* like us in whatever fundamental way that can be touched by reason. But they're not. Not yet," he emphasized, then frowned. "In some ways I suspect they're more outlandish than Lemurians. Even Grik." He sighed and looked squarely at Ciano. "But he was most determined, and I really did try to make him reconsider." Gravois wouldn't go so far as to call Ciano his ally, but they'd been through a lot together and he and his ship had shared Gravois's exile to this place. Ciano also shared his ambition for a more aggressive League, so he *was* an ally of sorts. That didn't mean he'd support everything Gravois intended, however, and he'd have to tread carefully, making sure *Ciano* got what he wanted out of their association.

"And most poignant of all," Gravois went on, "not only did Oriani name me his deputy in this endeavor, he fully supported all the plans we've made and every action we've taken. I believe I was on the threshold of a genuine rapprochement with the man."

"He should turn back," Ciano said, raising his binoculars and watching the boat near the dock. The waiting crowd was silent, but not respectfully so. More like a great predator preparing to pounce.

"Yes, he should." Gravois raised his binoculars as well.

The crowd opened around several men in red robes who harangued the people until they reluctantly gave way. Almost triumphantly, Oriani and his entourage stepped up on the dock. Nothing happened for a moment and it looked like Francisco was talking to the priests, but suddenly, at some apparent command, the crowd swept over the visitors like a wave. There were a few muffled shots but that was all. Then, like a receding tide, the mob withdrew, leaving no sign of the landing party. The launch and its crew remained untouched. One sailor recovered from his shock faster than the other. Gunning the engine, he turned away from the dock and raced frantically back toward the ships.

"An . . . interesting welcome," Gravois observed dryly.

"Damn you!" Ciano snapped. "We should shell the city!"

"Calm yourself. That's exactly what Oriani expressly forbade. And we can't just assume he's dead. All might still be well."

"'Well' for you, and your plans," Ciano growled. Gravois was mildly surprised by Ciano's reaction. Though he was Italian, he disliked Oriani even more than Gravois.

"*Our* plans," Gravois stressed. "And if the worst has happened, you and I will be in charge of the entire operation in this hemisphere."

"I don't want to be 'in charge' of anything but my ship," Ciano ground out.

Gravois looked at him coolly. "Surely you want *something* after all this is done, all you've been through? Flag rank, at least."

Ciano hesitated and finally lowered his binoculars. There was nothing to see. "Very well. Flag rank, possibly," he confessed, "but something personal too. If we fight the Allies—as you plan—I want to destroy *Walker*. With *Leopardo*."

Gravois blinked, surprised. He knew Ciano had been humiliated by the way Captain Reddy and his frail, dilapidated old destroyer forced them out of the Indian Ocean. It didn't matter he'd had a powerful auxiliary cruiser and hundreds of planes backing him up, it had been Reddy himself—and his decrepit ship—that drew Ciano's ire. Though not particularly pleased by the circumstances either, Gravois hadn't taken it personally. He had, after all, left Captain Reddy's wife in the hands of Hisashi Kurokawa. Gravois occasionally doubted his own sanity, and found that somehow reassuring, but Kurokawa had been utterly, barking mad. Fleetingly, he wondered if the charming Sandra Reddy was still alive. "You hadn't mentioned *Walker* for so long, I thought you'd gotten over that little episode," he said, then shrugged. "You know it's unlikely she'll make it this far, even if she's still afloat. And there's *no* possibility Captain Reddy will still command her. Our last reports revealed the 'Union' was building more ships like her. They'll be poorly made, no doubt, but he'll surely be in one of them, or something else we haven't seen." It was hard for Gravois to admit there were things he didn't know, but that was the new reality. The enemy was more careful with their communications, and since the mysterious loss of *U-112*, there'd been no direct observations in enemy seas.

"Nevertheless," Ciano insisted stubbornly.

Gravois secretly doubted he'd release *Leopardo* for combat of any sort when their reinforcements arrived. She was old, but fast and powerful, even compared to some of their newer destroyers. He'd have to see how things went. "Of course, Capitano Ciano," he said. "You have my word."

CHAPTER 4

////// Galk River
Grik Africa
May 5, 1945

Muddy brown water foamed alongside the low, beamy form of RRPS *Servius*, churning hard against the brisk Galk River current 120 miles north-northwest of Sofesshk. Dark smoke boiled from the ship's two funnels and her low freeboard bashed occasional packets of reeking spray over the armored deck as far back as the big, rounded, forward gunhouse. Nothing unusual in that. Princeps Class Republic monitors were wet ships, even for the harbor defense role they'd been designed for, and their shallow draft made them ideal for river operations. Many considered it something of a miracle *Servius* and *Ancus* both survived their open ocean voyage from the Republic city of Songze, however. And despite her best exertions, *Servius* was barely making five knots against the flow. Though bright and clear at present, the rainy season had begun and for the next couple of months, the river would only swell.

Above and behind the gunhouse, General Muln-Rolak, Colonel (Legate) Bekiaa-Sab-At, and Captain Quinebe stood on the comparatively fragile-looking flying bridgewing extending out to starboard of the heavily armored battle bridge. Quinebe, a tall, thin, dark-skinned human, dressed in the stark white tropical uniform of the Republic Navy, was staring ahead at a bend in the river. His mission was to provoke hidden shore batteries to reveal themselves, and perhaps even gauge their strength. The cover along the shore was too dense for planes to spot all the guns and they needed a better idea what they faced before planning any waterborne troop movements. Rolak and Bekiaa were Lemurians, both wearing faded camouflage combat smocks, standard for all Union and Imperial troops. Their helmets hung from their cutlass and pistol belts by their chin straps, since they fully expected to take fire at some point. They'd studied aerial photographs of the route ahead, but both had recently acquired a new appreciation for viewing the ground they had to lead their infantry across *from* the ground—or water, in this instance—and they were only here to observe.

Servius was alone on the water, but there were thousands of troops, Allied and Grik, fighting on both sides of the river less than a quarter mile off either beam. They couldn't hear the sounds of battle over the roar of machinery and rushing spray, but gunsmoke choked the woods on either shore. Rolak raised his Impie telescope and watched a V of Nancys drop incendiaries on a Grik position near the eastern bank ahead. A row of greasy orange fireballs rolled into the sky.

"Much haard work remains," he remarked somberly, looking at Captain Quinebe. "Whaat's the distaance to the great gates?"

It was only recently discovered by the Allies that the Galk River, flowing south to merge with the mighty Zambezi, was separated from a massive lake upstream by a series of enormous locks. They consisted, in essence, of monstrous movable dams, blocking a narrow gorge of living rock. They were, in fact, the only reason the lake existed at all. Grik considered them the "Gates of the Gods" and they might well have been, since the Grik certainly didn't have the technology to make such things. Maybe nobody did, now. And the fact they were quite obviously very, *very* old, possibly as ancient as the heavily eroded Palace of Vanished Gods itself, only added credence to the Grik belief.

Before he left for Alex-aandra, Courtney Bradford eagerly sought detailed descriptions and gazed (a little longingly it seemed, to some) at aerial photographs. An amateur naturalist, archeologist, anthropologist—interested in everything—the Australian had been a petroleum engineer in his former life and all his old passions converged on the Galk River locks. Once, nothing could've torn him away, but his dedication to winning the war surpassed all his previous obsessions. Still, he'd made a number of observations before he left. He was certain the gates were made of concrete, for example—something else the Grik didn't know—and the machinery operating them must be utterly stupendous. No one knew anything about that, since no machinery was exposed. Courtney decreed it had to be sealed inside the cliffs themselves. By all accounts, and perhaps most fascinating of all, an ancient and obscure . . . cult (for lack of a better word) of Grik devoted their lives to monitoring and maintaining the locks, but no one actually *op-*

erated them; they simply opened and closed *by themselves*. This was further evidence to the Grik that the gates moved with the lingering humors of the Vanished Gods, but Courtney solved that mystery at once. As soon as he learned the locks filled and flushed more frequently in the rainy season, sometimes remaining partially open for long periods, and perhaps only operating once a week or so when it was very dry, he concluded they were "quite practically and ingeniously" actuated by water levels or pressure, and water might even be the driving force.

They might never know who'd built them, and possibly other ruins as far as India, but Courtney had the utmost respect for their engineering skills.

Quinebe looked thoughtful. "Another hundred and sixty kilometers or so."

Rolak looked helplessly at Bekiaa, who blinked exasperation. It had been hard enough for her to learn miles and "standard" measurements, but to *then* have to learn metrics when she went to the Republic had nearly driven her mad. She had, though, of necessity, and could now convert them fairly quickly in her mind. "About a hundred miles."

Rolak blinked appreciation, but nodded as if to say "of course." "*Thaat's* where Esshk will make his staand," he mused. "He must. The lake beyond is where his laast heavy industries are, his laast resources for aarming and supplying his forces. His laast shipyards and waarships, for thaat maatter, though the ships caan be of little use—especially aafter Saansa Field is operationaal and our airpower moves up to mount a sustained bombing campaign. It might haave been nice of Cap-i-taan Reddy to leave us *one* carrier, to steam upriver this faar, at least," he added ruefully.

"I fear Cap-i-taan Reddy will need everything we haave that floats in the east, and it still won't be enough," Bekiaa said grimly.

"I know," Rolak agreed. "The League haas always interfered with our waar against the Grik—and still do, by drawing forces away." He grunted. "Enough reason in itself to oppose them, besides all else they've done."

They'd steamed beyond the front lines now and the fighting had begun to wane. There might be a few Allied patrols this far, but little else besides Grik—and other terrifying creatures, of course—for the better part of a continent. This was emphasized when a pair of white clouds blossomed on the shore and waterspouts rocketed up ahead of the ship. "Clear the deck, lock down, close all internal compartments!" Captain Quinebe shouted through the hatch into the battle bridge. 'Cats and humans, even a few

Gentaa, quickly rushed to comply. Gentaa looked like human/Lemurian hybrids. They weren't, of course, but had always kept themselves somewhat apart from Republic society, maintaining an influential and prosperous labor class. There'd always been a few in the navy, mostly youths rebelling against their culture, but those with the Army of the Republic had strictly adhered to a support and logistical role—until the desperate battles south of Sofesshk taught them it was time to join or die. They were "all in" now, finally choosing to support the Republic and Alliance in all ways. Even with their lives.

Bekiaa contemplated that, while the slitted battle shutters slammed over the bridge windows. *I wonder how maany cultures across this world haave been remade by this waar? It waas for the better in maany cases, but for others . . . We'll see.*

"How long would it take to reach the great gates?" Rolak asked.

"At this speed? Without obstructions, serious opposition, or anything . . . unforeseen, we might see them by dawn tomorrow." Quinebe paused, expression turning eager. "*If* we chose to push that far. It would empty our bunkers, but we have sufficient coal for a round trip. . . ." he prodded. Rolak nodded, saying nothing. More shore batteries opened up, one shot hitting the water close enough to throw spray on them. Quinebe frowned. "I'd recommend we step inside. This ship was never built for this latitude and it grows uncomfortable in there, over time," he conceded, "but it might become more so out here."

For the next two hours, Rolak and Bekiaa tried their best to see the land around them through the narrow slits in the stifling battle bridge while *Servius* pounded upriver, taking an increasingly heavy pounding in return. Quinebe continuously cautioned them to step back from the shutters as the incoming fire grew more furious. Lookouts in the fighting tops—dreadfully exposed positions—called in their observations and the ship's four 8″ guns punished the targets they designated. Sometimes they were able to get a plane or two to hit them, but most of those were dedicated to supporting the infantry. Damage reports started trickling in.

The boats were shattered in their davits, thin funnels perforated with holes. The wooden bridgewing they'd stood upon was shot away. Beyond that, *Servius* was just too tough for any Grik field artillery to harm. But the Grik had larger guns, and the dark water around the ship started spewing taller, heavier plumes. *Not so very long ago,* we *didn't haave aartillery,* Bekiaa mused. *Then we did and the Grik didn't. Even aafter they did, it waasn't very effective compared to ours . . . but the Grik get better at waar as well.* The battle bridge thundered with the deafening impact of a massive roundshot, and everyone inside the baking space flinched and closed their eyes and tilted their helmets against the stinging blizzard of thick paint chips.

Captain Quinebe was the first to inspect the deep new dent, protruding low down by the deck on the starboard side. "A big one," he said loudly, white teeth exposed in a grin. He actually seemed to be enjoying himself. "Probably one of their bigger naval guns, emplaced ashore. A fifty pounder, I shouldn't wonder. I'll have that position destroyed, if you please," he instructed his talker, a young Lemurian, who immediately spoke into a voice tube. The big round gunhouse on the fo'c'sle turned in response to instructions from the fighting top. Unseen, another turret tracked the same target aft. Moments later, four huge (if somewhat stubby) 8″ rifles roared. White smoke engulfed the forward part of the ship again, some seeping into the battle bridge. Everyone was so used to the bitter, sulfurous smoke by now, no one even coughed.

Rolak stroked the gray fur on his face and looked at Bekiaa and blinked the quizzical equivalent of a raised eyebrow. Bekiaa twitched her tail and returned a very human shrug. "Perhaaps, Cap-i-taan Quinebe, we've seen as much as we need to," Rolak said aloud. "We already knew the enemy has lined this stretch of the river with heavy guns. They'll only get heavier the faarther we proceed." He motioned at the new dent. "As you observed, whaatever threw thaat was probably originaally intended for one of their aarmored cruisers."

"I thought you wanted to see the locks."

"I do. Not only the locks themselves, but the ground rising to them. Third Corps"—he nodded at Bekiaa—"and Fifth Division haave fought their way upriver, meeting stiffer resistaance with every step. They caan't continue to slaam their faces against the wall. Neither caan this ship. The time will come when we'll need her too baadly, fit and ready to fight. We must all take a brief pause, I think. Wait for the rest of the aarmy, and make a coordinated plaan."

"*Servius* can take whatever those vile reptiles give her," Quinebe proclaimed proudly, just as more heavy shot banged against the superstructure behind them.

"I'm sure, for a while," Bekiaa told him. "We caan *all* take more thaan we think—until we caan't," she added softly.

Rolak quickly intervened, concerned as always that the brindled 'Cat beside him might've reached that point more than once. "I believe the Legate's point is this: At present, Third Corps and her division are fighting for inches instead of miles. Their, ah, 'bunkers' are empty aalready. *Servius* has endured quite a pounding today, laargely on a whim I haad; to test the enemy's river defenses and haave a look for myself." He hesitated. "One other thing as well. We've accomplished the first two goals and our next push will be in earnest, combined with air attaacks on those daamned guns, and enough infaantry to *flaank* the enemy out of their defenses. Along the river, at least." He chuckled. "And as long as we control the river, we only haave to attaack on one side, but the Grik still haave to defend *both*. Don't worry, Cap-i-taan Quinebe, we'll see the great gates soon enough."

Quinebe frowned. "But if we turn around, the enemy will think they bested us."

Rolak laughed. "Let them! All the better!" Quinebe bristled, and Rolak blinked consolingly. "I once fought for 'pride' and 'honor,' but this waar haas sucked those things awaay. Survivaal for our people, through victory, caan be our only consideration now. There are still faar more of them thaan us, so we sneak, we trick, to win." Another raspy chuckle was drowned by more drumming shot and the roar of *Servius*'s guns. "And thaat was the *third* purpose of my 'whim' today. I'd much raather the enemy be too confident thaan cautious. Much as my curiosity compels me, perhaaps the *worst* thing we could do would be steam paast everything they throw at us, look at the locks, then steam baack downriver. Turn around, Cap-i-taan Quinebe." He grinned. "Run awaay. The enemy's confidence will soar—and when we *really* hit them, it will shaatter into fear." He blinked something Quinebe didn't catch. "The Grik we fought at the Neckbone under Gener-aal Ign were cautious. They made *me* more thoughtful, and thaat's good." His grin faded and his eyes went unfocused. "But I prevented Gener-aal Aalden from shooting Gener-aal Ign when he haad the chaance, hoping we'd made him too careful to remain a threat. Thaat was a mistake, so I must always baalance my newfound caution with aagression. We *must* crush these Grik before Ign arrives to infect them with his competence. If giving them a little, temporary 'victory' at the expense of our—and your noble ship's—pride is the price we paay to sow overconfidence, it's cheap indeed."

Quinebe stared a moment, then shook his head. He'd been startlingly thrilled by the prospect of running the gauntlet all the way to the final great bastion of the Grik. And yes, the *honor* of that, for him and his ship, had fueled his enthusiasm. So maybe this aged, battle-scarred Lemurian was right, even if he sounded more like Inquisitor Choon than the great Allied general he was supposed to be. But Quinebe was just a sailor, relatively new to war, and Rolak *had* to know the strange minds of the Grik better than he. "Bring us . . ." He paused, looking at Rolak and Bekiaa. "We'll wait for another flurry of enemy fire, *then* come about and make all speed downriver." He forced a laugh. "With this current, we'll make twelve knots. It'll *look* like we're running for our lives!"

"Trust me," Rolak said, matching Quinebe's volume, "*Servius* will be baack, and it'll be the Grik who flee!" There were murmurs of approval and Rolak lowered his voice, looking at Bekiaa. "We'll *all* be baack. And with the Maker's help, it'll be the laast time."

CHAPTER 5

*////// **Alex-aandra***
Republic of Real People
Southern Africa
May 6, 1945

The reception greeting "General" Courtney Bradford at the brand-new train station on the southeast end of the Republic capital city of Alex-aandra actually embarrassed him. A band with lots of drums and strange horns erupted on the fresh timber platform in front of the wide, brick station house, even as venting steam from the locomotive gusted across the players. The music became chaotic for a moment before resuming its martial cadence. When Courtney saw Kaiser (sometimes still called "Caesar") Nig-Taak himself, surrounded by his retinue, he began to wonder if the train had hooked on another passenger car in the night. He'd slept through their stop at Kavaa-la, and perhaps some notable joined them there. The comfortable passenger car he was in, along with the heated boxcars, were full to overflowing with wounded from the battles to the north. *That's it, of course,* he decided. *Nig-Taak's actually a rather decent bloke, as semi-autocratic rulers go. He's here to greet the men, Lemurians, even Gentaa who fought for him against the demon Grik!*

"You *must* hurry, sir," urged his new aide, a young female Lemurian tribune named Nir-Shaang, whom General Kim had inflicted on him. "The Kaiser's waiting for *you* and they won't unload the wounded until you've been received." She turned to the soldiers blocking the aisle with crutches or legs in hard casts and barked, "Make way, there! Make way for the general!"

Courtney jumped up. "Yes, *do* make way," he said loudly. "Help these brave troops off the train, if you please," he called to the medical orderlies, "*then* I'll be able to pass." With that, he resumed his seat and utterly ignored Nir's fuming glare. Captain Nir-Shaang had been new to the front, fresh out of field-grade officer school, and from an aristocratic family. She'd joined Kim's staff ready to take over and win the war in a day. Kim thought he was doing everyone a favor by honoring her with the title of "tribune" and sending her off to take care of Courtney. Courtney didn't much care. He'd passed the point in his life where intense, officious snobbery (with which Nir virtually oozed) affected him. He'd seen and done too many momentous things to be personally disturbed by petty trivialities, but he'd taken a page from Matt Reddy's book and wouldn't abide their being scraped off on others.

"The Kaiser is *waiting*," Nir hissed at him.

Courtney looked at her. "Then he might be mildly annoyed that I delayed his appointment with some senator or other, but he won't really be angry with me." His eyes went wide, as if he was suddenly surprised by a thought. "But I wonder, what would happen to *your* career if I personally asked him for a different aide?"

The train quickly emptied. The hospitallers and Gentaa stevedores had learned from too much grim experience how to clear a train of wounded. Only then, with the band still playing and Nig-Taak's retinue still wearily holding salutes for the wounded at the Kaiser's command, did Courtney allow Nir to usher him down to the platform.

Nig-Taak stepped forward and heartily embraced him. *That* came as a surprise. Most Lemurians everywhere else were big huggers, but those in the Republic were more reserved.

"Welcome back to Alex-aandra, General Bradford!" Nig-Taak proclaimed.

"Thank you, Your Majesty, you do me great honor. But I'm not *really* a general, you know. I'm here again as ambassador from the United Homes, and those members of the Grand Alliance your nation joined, who entrusted me to represent them."

"Nonsense, my friend. You can be all those things *and* a General of the Republic! General Kim described in detail how you heroically led nearly half his army in the crucial campaign to seize the Zambezi River from the foe!" He glanced around and embraced Courtney again, this time whispering in his ear. "I truly do honor your valor, but as you might guess, it remains . . . politically expedient that you be a general. It impresses the people, and especially the Gentaa—largely thanks to you and Legate

Bekiaa—that we truly are 'all in this together.'" He chuckled, backing away and adding loudly, "You might even find yourself appointed praetor . . . uh, *admiral* as well, before much longer."

To Courtney's consternation, that happened in an elaborate ceremony two days later at the Kaiser's new War Palace (the new Imperator Class battlecruiser prototype), which gave Courtney another look at the type. He'd seen the finishing touches being applied to a pair of Imperators at Songze and they'd since sailed into the terrible, perpetual storm called "The Dark" off the southwest coast of the Republic. If they survived—no certain thing, even for a steamer (USS *Donaghey* was the only sailing ship known to have passed through from the east)—they should arrive any time. They'd sail again as soon as any damage was repaired. Courtney was anxious to see "the real thing" up close. The War Palace was an incomplete shell, unarmed and unarmored. He was also anxious to meet the Fleet Prefect of the Republic force marshalling to join its allies in the Atlantic.

His first act as Praetor was a visit to the dock where six new "destroyers" were clustered. They were quite long and narrow, looking shockingly like the first "torpedo boat destroyers" Courtney remembered from his old world. They'd doubtless been designed by men who came to this world aboard SMS *Amerika* in 1914. They were just as shockingly cramped, unseaworthy-looking, and poorly armed, each carrying only a pair of 3″ "Derby" guns on naval mounts, a couple of Maxim machine guns, and four measly torpedo tubes, two in the forward hull and two more in a twin mount aft. Courtney understood they were relying on their allies to supply torpedoes. The best comparison that sprang to mind was that they looked like the runt hybrid offspring of a liaison between USS *Walker* and a racing shell, or "fine boat," and he doubted they'd survive in heavy seas.

Courtney was polite to the young, enthusiastic Repub officers he met, and praised their efforts, while sadly predicting to himself they were doomed. He began to fear the much-vaunted Repub "battlecruiser" force might prove equally disappointing.

The next day, a wireless message brought by Nir (who'd seemed considerably less snotty of late) found him in the study/office of the villa he'd been granted by the Kaiser. The Imperator's coal smoke had been seen off Kavaa-la that morning, and they'd round the headland and enter Alex-aandra Bay by dusk. Though technically outranking the Fleet Prefect, by the Kaiser's decree, Courtney chose a delicate approach, instructing Nir to send a message that "Praetor Bradford requests the honor of informally calling upon the Fleet Prefect at 0900 in the morning, after the Fleet Prefect has docked his ships and enjoyed a full night's rest." An hour later, Nir returned and began reading the response. "Fleet Prefect Tigaas-Gaak—a *sister* of General Taal-Gaak, I believe—replies: 'Of course the Praetor is most welcome to call in any manner he sees fit, but wouldn't he prefer the full and proper . . .'" Nir stopped and blinked something amazingly like amusement—the first time Courtney saw such a thing occur on her face. "She doesn't know you yet. Be gentle."

Courtney Bradford, in the unadorned, cool-weather medium blue uniform of a junior officer, was piped aboard RRPS *Imperator*, the namesake of her class, and met by a strikingly tall 'Cat with bright yellow fur under a much grander uniform. After absently saluting the colors, something Repubs didn't do, Courtney exchanged salutes with his host. "Admir—*Praetor* Courtney Bradford, requesting permission to come aboard."

The tall 'Cat was taken aback by that as well. *They'd've had a band, and probably dancing girls, if I came aboard "properly," but a simple polite greeting like this is more customary—and* far *more important for what I must accomplish,* Courtney mused. "You're Fleet Prefect Tigaas-Gaak," he said before she could introduce herself. "I'd know you anywhere! The very *image* of your brother, except for your fur, of course, and you're much more attractive! Still, General Taal's a fine fellow, and a far better horseman than I!"

Courtney could tell by the pleased blinking that he'd scored some points. Despite the rank Tigaas had reached, Courtney intuitively guessed some things about her. First, she loved her brother, but felt in constant competition with him—especially with the "opportunities" he'd had to distinguish himself of late. This would be her turn. Second, she was very vain about her fur. . . . "This is Tribune Nir," he said, presenting his aide. "Would you kindly name your officers? Then I'd love to see your magnificent ship!"

Courtney's first impression of *Imperator*, and her sister *Ostia*, moored just aft (apparently the rest of the class were named for Repub cities), was that someone had practically taken them from drawings of a British Lord Nelson Class battleship. That wasn't necessarily bad. Nelsons were already obsolete when launched, but still pretty good. Just as important, it showed him the Repubs hadn't gotten overly ambitious for their "first try." And while their relatively small size and silhouettes screamed "Lord Nelson"—

to a degree—there were a lot of differences. Tigaas could've just turned Courtney over to the ship's captain for the tour, but she led it herself, answering Courtney's every question.

The first thing he learned was, though their hulls were built entirely of steel with considerable attention to reinforcement and watertight integrity, they were then planked over with four inches of a teak-like wood from the forests east of Colonia. Another layer of steel went over that, up to six inches of the best armor plate the Republic could produce, protecting vital areas. Courtney had no idea how well this "laminated armor" would defend the ships, but Tigaas told him trials were promising.

"Wood, though," he'd protested, "it's bound to get soaked and rot between the plates."

"Of course," she'd replied, "But there'll only ever be four Imperators, these two and the others at Augustus. We didn't make them to last forever. We didn't have time, and didn't know how. They only have to survive *one* battle, then return their crews to better ships." Tigaas and Kaiser Nig-Taak both soared higher in Courtney's estimation. The Repubs could've tried to build a modern battleship with all the dubious advice Matt, Spanky, Letts—who knows who all—had sent them, and they'd still be working on their very first hull.

"Well, when you put it that way, it makes perfect sense. And even rotting, waterlogged wood must provide *some* protection. Tell me about the engines, and armament!"

Imperators had sixteen coal-fired boilers with oil sprayers. Oil wasn't as plentiful in the Republic as coal, but the sprayers would give them a boost and extend their range. The boilers powered two triple-expansion engines that turned twin screws and drove each 15,000-ton ship at twenty knots, or eight thousand miles at ten. Also unlike the Lord Nelsons, they were "all big gun" ships, with three large gunhouses, or turrets. One was on the fo'c'sle, half under the bridge. Another was amidships, between the funnels, and the third was aft. Each protected two built-up 10″ rifles. They'd hoped to give them 12″s, but realized they'd never have them ready in time. For defense against smaller ships, like torpedo boats or destroyers—and aircraft, as an afterthought—there was a platform over the amidships turret packed with a cluster of 3″ Derby guns on dual-purpose mounts. Several more were scattered around the ships for a total of twenty, each.

The tour ended, they adjourned to Tigaas's spacious quarters for refreshments while the noisy, dusty job of coaling the ship began. Courtney wasn't disappointed. Twelve inchers would've been nice, to go up against the League's heavy hitters, but Imperators packed a lot of punch for such small ships. *And of course their size makes them harder to hit!* Smiling over the rim of a mug of excellent beer, he had to ask, "But why call them 'battlecruisers'? You must know the meaning of the name if you've heard it."

Tigaas smiled back, blinking mischief, and Courtney knew they'd be friends. "As I understand it, 'battlecruisers' were designed fast and light and powerful to catch anything they could kill, and escape anything they couldn't. Sadly, as proud as I am of them, I don't think that describes my Imperators very well." She made a very human shrug. "We chose to call them 'battlecruisers' for two excellent reasons. First was misdirection. We *know* the enemy has spies among us and we couldn't hide their construction, so why not sow confusion about their capabilities, if we can?" She laughed. "But the main reason was, it makes no difference to us what things were called on your old world, and many just thought 'battlecruiser' sounded good."

Even very junior officers exploded with laughter, and Courtney leaned back on the comfortable human chair Tigaas had provided him, smiling broadly. "Well, whatever you call them, I'm impressed." His smile faded lightly. "More so than I was by your new destroyers, I must confess. If they're to be used at all, I suggest they be used very carefully." He cleared his throat, getting down to business. "In any event, I'm anxious to sail for Augustus and join the rest of the fleet. After that, we'll train and train and make every effort to *appear* as though we're preparing to defend the Republic from League assault."

No one spoke, but he was surrounded by questioning, even somewhat angry blinking. These people were ready to fight, and that was good, but they had to do this right.

"How long will we . . . 'appear' to do this?" Fleet Prefect Tigaas tentatively asked.

"Until Inquisitor Choon's intelligence network tracks down all transmissions our movements inspire, and every League spy it can find. Then, if unforeseen events don't force us sooner, we'll begin our real mission." He held up his hand and looked steadily at Tigaas. "Let me be clear. I'm not here to fight your ships. I wouldn't even know how. But the Kaiser put me in *overall* command for a reason, and it wasn't just 'political,' as he implied to others. He knows *I* know Captain Reddy's basic plan, and I have a good idea what he'll do and need. So the ultimate purpose of the Republic ships under your command, Fleet Prefect Tigaas, is to lull the enemy and draw them out, then *lunge* to seize the opportunity I *know* will be presented." He smiled. "And be where Captain Reddy needs us, *when* he needs us, of course. That'll be the hard part."

CHAPTER 6

BLOODY BABY STEPS

////// El Palo
Holy Dominion
May 7, 1945

Fred and Kari had been treated with bemused cordiality by General Cox and his staff during the four days they'd spent with the NUS Army at El Palo. No planes were available to retrieve them, and *Donaghey* and the Repub seaplane tender/oilers had been busy escorting transports halfway down from Santiago. No warships came closer, for now. The Doms had no navy left and wooden warships were subject to destruction by *Leopardo* to no purpose. Yet transports loaded with munitions had to make the run, taking their chances with allied planes overhead to warn of the enemy's approach. *Donaghey* already had a new plane of her own, but it was busy with the scouts as well. Besides, it couldn't carry passengers *and* its own crew. So, specifically ordered by Captain Garrett *not* to risk passage on a returning transport, Fred and Kari were left to cool their heels in a somewhat . . . awkward environment.

Not only were they personal friends of the legendary "Captain Anson," they'd achieved a degree of celebrity as the first representatives of its new allies to make contact with the NUS. And they still—technically—had ambassadorial status. That made them tolerated, even amusedly welcomed by some when they dropped in to hang out in General Cox's headquarters from time to time. But they came from a different world—quite literally, in Fred's case—and were accustomed to friendly (if not actually *casual*) association with such luminaries as High Admiral Jenks and General Shinya, commanding the Allied forces fighting this way from the Pass of Fire, as well as *their* political leaders—and Captain Reddy himself. They behaved themselves, and treated General Cox and his senior officers with due respect, but may have also acted a little more familiar than was customary for Nussie junior officers. Their hosts didn't know what to think of that, and some probably resented them. Most simply dismissed them as a couple of kids, and no one took them very seriously.

"I'm gettin' tired of this," Kari groused quietly aside to Fred as a plate heaped with locally procured scrambled eggs, a hard biscuit from a cask, and something tasting like salted rhino pig was set before her. They'd been admitted to a junior officer's mess, a long hall once part of what had been the "palace" of El Palo's absent *alcalde*. Heavy beams supported plastered walls, and a ceiling of baked ceramic tiles kept the predawn drizzle off. A young local girl, once a slave in this very house, served those at their end of a long, central table.

"Not the accommodations, surely," a burly artillery captain named Giles Meder objected, chewing briskly, brown muttonchops flowing with the motion of his working jaw in such a way that suddenly riveted Kari. "Or the fare," he added lightly, raking in another mouthful.

"No, that's all swell," Fred agreed. He liked the sometimes profanely pious Meder who commanded "C" Battery—six guns—in the 3rd NUS Artillery Regiment. The Nussies employed a lot of rifled guns, mostly 10 and 20 pdrs, but Meder's smoothbore 12 pdrs were strikingly similar to those of the Allies Fred and Kari represented—which had been patterned after weapons derived from those first brought to this world by the Nussies. That fascinated Fred, particularly since all the refinements to the basic form they'd independently undergone left them virtually identical. That made sense, he supposed, since there was only so far a particular design could go. "I—me and Kari—just want back in the war. Back in the *air*," he emphasized. Meder had already offered to let them carry charges for his guns.

"I suppose that's a very fine thing," Meder allowed, "swooping about with a bird's-eye view of a battlefield, but I prefer to keep my feet firmly planted on God's good earth."

Fred started to point out they didn't just "swoop about" and Meder might not like how vulnerable he'd be to air attack, but let it pass.

Meder gestured at his food. "Eat. One way or another, I suspect you'll need your strength today. The God-damned Doms have worked their way all around us, and can't wait much longer to strike. The longer it takes them to destroy us, the closer your General Shinya comes."

Fred also refrained from reminding him that Shinya was still a long way off. Meder knew that as well as he did.

A bugle sounded "officer's call" in the darkness, its notes carrying through the open door. Meder, Fred, and Kari, and twenty other officers at the table, quickly wolfed down a couple more bites and chairs screeched and clattered on the stone floor as everyone rushed out into the clammy darkness. Caught in the middle of the hustling men, Fred and Kari were surrounded by the funk of stale perspiration permeating damp uniforms. It lasted only a moment since all the lieutenants quickly dispersed to their units. Only Meder and two other captains continued toward Cox's headquarters in El Palo's central temple.

The temple wasn't a pyramid here; the town was too small for such extravagance, but the square, two-story building boasted a tall, fat tower affording a fine view of the surrounding countryside. *There's never been a bell in that tower, like in a church back home,* Fred remembered with a queasy feeling, *only a big, bronze basin to collect the blood of human sacrifices.* They'd found evidence that T-shaped crosses were erected there from time to time as well, so victims could be burned alive. There were no crosses now, and the basin had been thrown to the cobbled street below as another grim reminder of their purpose here.

"Joining us again?" Meder asked, amused.

"Sure. Why not?" Kari challenged. "We got no plane so we're just observers here. You know a better place to waatch?"

Meder looked up at golden streaks beginning to color purple clouds. "This will burn off soon, I think. A fine day to do God's work and smite these soulless Doms," he said cheerfully. "If you don't want to join me with the guns, I can't think of a better place for you." A commotion was growing around them, more bugle calls sounded, and messengers galloped up and down the streets, horse hooves loud on the cobbles. Meder quickened his pace. "There's something going on. Best we hurry."

General Hiram Cox was tall and thin, his form exaggerated by the high collar and narrow waist of his dark blue frock coat. Bright red hair and whiskers were striking against a complexion as dark as any Dom, but that wasn't unusual on a world where every human population they knew of, the League excluded, was a result of generations of racial blending. A local servant wrapped a scarlet sash and buff sword belt around Cox's waist even as he listened to a steady stream of messengers. Fred and Kari saw one of them was an exhausted-looking Captain Anson, who spared them an ironic smile before stepping before the general.

"They have committed themselves," he said, summarizing the previous tidbits. "They're definitely moving into attack positions."

"Where?" Cox demanded, moving to a broad table with a large map laid out.

Anson pointed. "Mostly to the south, though a strong force seems prepared to shift *back* to the Camino Militar and press us from the east. We must be prepared for assaults from both directions . . ." He hesitated. "Possibly more. There's been no sign of their lancers, yet native scouts report they have a sizable contingent."

"Shock troops," Fred said, not meaning to, but Anson nodded. "Exactly. Prepared to strike where we're thinnest, at the worst possible time. I'd imagine that'll be from the east as well—or west."

"Behind us?" Cox questioned. Even with their backs to the sea, they'd taken to considering the direction Shinya and his "Army of the Sisters" would come from as "behind" them. In more ways than one, that was correct. There'd be no retreat by ship, and except for a further five thousand or so that joined the initial landing force of fifty thousand men, there'd be no more Nussie troops. Several thousand locals had been recruited, anxious to throw off the age-old blood-rite tyranny of their masters, but they had to be trained, armed, and clad—all the more reason why supplies had to keep coming—and watched for spies, of course. Most would make good troops, with time, the bulk of their training consisting of total immersion in existing units where spies were usually quickly identified by fellow recruits. Suspects tended to simply vanish.

But Shinya's army represented the only professional, battle-tested reinforcements they could expect. Another Dom army, a scratch-built force under General Mayta, stood between them, but it was close to three hundred miles away at El Henal. It was in no position to advance, and could only hope to block Shinya. Fred and Kari's assurance that Mayta would succeed in that on a "cold day in hell" was taken as gospel. Anson had met Shinya and corroborated their assessment. Still . . . "How could they have worked their way entirely around us without being detected?" Cox pressed.

Anson wearily shrugged. "This is their land." He glanced at Fred and Kari again. "One is tempted to consider the forest an impenetrable solid, but it's not like that at all. Besides, there's a web of interconnecting roads and paths beneath its canopy. We have limited mounted troops and can't watch every trail." He sighed. "Even if we did, they could *still* go 'round on horseback. Farther out, I daresay, than any local from *here* has ever ventured. Casual travel by the . . . lower classes between points in the Dominion isn't encouraged," he explained dryly, "nor is it safe. As you know, even our armed scouts suffer casualties to the forest predators." He pressed his finger on the map south of town. "But whatever else they do, the bulk of their troops are massing *here* and we must deploy to meet them. Except for the direction of the attack, it's all very straightforward. Too much so. I *strongly* recommend a respectable force be kept in the prepared breastworks facing east, and an equally formidable combined reserve be retained against all temptation to use it early, regardless of the apparent necessity or opportunity."

Cox leaned forward, studying the map and rubbing his chin. "Combined . . . I trust you mean infantry, artillery, *and* dragoons? Very well. Thanks to your efforts over the last days we've not been taken by surprise and are already prepared for much of what you advise." He looked up. "Colonel Prine, see to the organization of Captain Anson's reserve, if you please. Use the Fourth and Eleventh Infantry—they have no place in the line as yet—and Major Wolf's dragoons." He looked around and his eyes settled on Meder. The 3rd Artillery Regiment was near the southern defensive line, bolstering the incomplete breastworks, but Cox was enamored with the new rifled guns and considered smoothbores obsolete. "Colonel Hara," he said to Meder's commanding officer, "you'll pull your guns and join the reserve. If you're needed I expect the action will be close and your, ah, older weapons will still shine."

Hara visibly banished his flaring resentment and simply saluted before motioning to Meder and two other officers. "Of course, sir," he said. "In that case we'd best be moving so other guns can assume our positions." He glanced significantly at the brightening sky outside a nearby window, its heavy wooden shutters open. "Wouldn't want the enemy to catch us in the middle of that."

"Indeed. Dismissed."

Anson wore a troubled frown and Cox was quick to notice. "Your company is exhausted, Captain," Cox told him gently, misinterpreting Anson's unease. "You'll stay with me, your men nearby and ready to join the reserve at need."

Anson nodded distractedly.

"Whaat do you waant us to do?" Kari asked.

"Observe with the rest of us, from the tower overhead," Cox replied dismissively. There was easily room for a dozen up there and part of his staff would join him. A pair of field telegraph operators were already clambering up the spiral stairs. "I'm sure it'll be quite a show," he added.

The first threat to emerge from the distant tree line south of town stood on four legs, not two. Amid a rumble of crashing saplings at the edge of the wood, frightened mooing sounds, and the occasional hair-raising squeal, a number of gigantic sauropods seemed to almost *slither* into view. At first glance they looked and moved like momentous hovering snakes, long necks and tails weaving back and forth horizontal to the ground. Their coloration resembled copperheads, to Fred, and that added to the serpentine impression. Only a second glance was drawn to the massive pillar-like legs urgently churning beneath them. They seemed oblivious to the fact they'd been revealed, or to the different nature of their surroundings, and rampaged through the low standing crops of damp maize growing on the plain for eight hundred to one thousand yards around El Palo. Other creatures, large and small, joined them as they moved. Predator and prey ran together, heedless of one another. Whipping tides of birds and flying reptiles of all description flowed and fluttered above them all. No one in the tower spoke until Kari observed the obvious: "Somethin's pushin' 'em."

A thunderous roar announced the arrival of six huge bipedal predators like Fred and Kari had seen before. These were a different color: darker, like the herbivores, but otherwise identical and just as big. They kept themselves nearly horizontal as well, long tails whipping, shorter necks supporting great heads with steam-shovel jaws clearly designed to tear and engulf massive gobbets of flesh. They had no front legs or arms at all and their long back legs were almost as disproportionate as their heads. That made them look like giant, walking mouths, and that was essentially what they were.

"My God," Cox exclaimed. "I'd wager they're fifty feet long, and stand eighteen high! I've never seen their like."

In fact he had. There were similar monsters in North America, but none were used this way. Each beast was restrained on either side by chains secured to several of the biggest breed of armabueys known to exist. All armabueys looked like giant armadillos with horny shells and long, spiky tails, and Doms used those of average size as draft animals and to pull their largest cannon. Still tiny in the distance, and in comparison to the beasts they controlled, these were actually too big for that and each was surrounded by a cluster of men dressed in bright red breechcloths. *Dragon priests,* Fred thought, struck by their dress. *It's warmer here than it was at Fort Defiance—and they probably like to stay agile.*

"*We've* seen critters like 'em," Kari declared. "Call 'em 'Super-duper lizaards.' An' they pulled the same stunt on us." Fred and Kari had been busy elsewhere at the time but they'd heard about it. "They weren't thaat big a deal, just scaary as hell, is all."

"They are that," Cox agreed, noting the more urgent preparations in the unfinished breastworks three hundred yards away. Some outlying structures had been incorporated into the defense and fatigue parties were heaping stones and timbers in front of the line. There were almost twenty-five thousand troops down there, their numbers thicker in the middle, and national and regimental flags hung limp and sodden at regular intervals. There was considerable confusion behind the left flank of the rough crescent-like position as the 3rd Artillery scrambled to pull out and make room for a couple of batteries of 10 pdr rifles. Mounted couriers dashed back and forth and loud shouting could be heard. "No doubt their primary purpose is intimidation: to break our resolve before their assault," Cox surmised, then grunted, glancing at Fred and Kari. "I thought you said the Doms still enjoyed their penchant for pre-battle chats."

"They did with us," Kari confirmed, "but maybe they figger they did all the taalkin' with Nussies they needed to a hunnerd years ago."

Anson stifled a chuckle and Cox glared at him. "Be that as it may, perhaps we can reverse the effect they intend their monsters to make." He turned to the telegraphers. "Inform Major Alai he has some interesting targets for his twenty pounders."

"General—" Anson began, but Cox waved him to silence. Anson colored and brusquely raised his telescope to study the approaching beasts—and the forest beyond. "The enemy's unlimbering their guns at the edge of the forest, close on the heels of the monsters, and their infantry's beginning to form," he said in a "by the way" manner. It was obvious he thought the terrifying beasts were more a distraction than a genuine threat. And not only did the Nussie artillerymen have to deal with the monsters in any event, those at ground level couldn't see what the enemy was doing over the long mound of chest-high maize. "Should've cleared it away," Kari heard Anson mutter. "But just because our men can't see the enemy, doesn't mean they're safe." The NUS Army might be inexperienced but its artillerymen were well-trained at laying fire under the direction of observers.

Cox wasn't an idiot and he seized on Anson's hint. "The rest of our artillery in the southern line will commence firing at their predetermined ranges and fuse settings."

Each section of guns had been assigned a specific sector of the tree line, the range carefully surveyed. The idea was that adjustments would be made from the tower.

The first battery of six 20 pdrs was almost directly in front of them and all the guns roared together. A single enormous cloud of gray-white smoke billowed out toward the field and the concussion of the report slapped Fred and Kari in the face. Fred caught himself wishing for the earphones in his lost plane and Kari belatedly covered her ears. Another battery barked together, twenty-pound shells shrieking downrange with an urgent ripping sound.

The Nussie's rifled guns were probably as accurate as any modern artillery piece would be if it had to be rolled back into battery and re-aimed between each shot. And within their range limitations, of course. But they couldn't be traversed, elevated and aimed *through* the shot, like *Walker*'s 4"-50s, for example, so it was far more difficult for them to hit a moving target. Particularly when multiple guns relied on a single command to fire. Thus it was that at barely seven hundred yards, only one of the first dozen shots scored a hit on a "super-duper lizard."

The result was impressive to be sure, the heavy shell striking low in the abdomen and penetrating a couple of feet before the fuse exploded the bursting charge. The beast's intestines spewed out in a gout of smoke and the shattered ribs and head flipped back against the monster's rump as the whole thing collapsed in a lifeless heap. The surrounding armabueys, oblivious and undeterred, began dragging the flopping corpse. And the advancing wall of sauropods and other things weren't oblivious to the loud eruptions in front of them, quickly veering to angle away to the east and west. The battery fire resulted in that one advantage, at least, but Cox was outraged.

"Have that imbecile Alai release his gunners to fire independently," he fumed.

"And the rest of the artillery?" Anson prompted.

"At the discretion of the battery commanders. The enemy infantry and artillery will remain stationary a bit longer, I think," Cox replied.

But it didn't.

Even as the exploding case shot of thirty 10 pdr rifles and a dozen 12 pdr smoothbores still on the line flashed and raked the edge of the woods where the Dom artillery was setting up—a hellish experience for its gunners—the first division of Dom infantry, a tight formation half a mile long and six ranks deep, was already sweeping forward. The heavy morning air tended to a slight fog as the sun touched it, and without a wind, the thickening smoke made an increasingly opaque wall across the battlefield. The initial Dom advance was almost entirely masked.

Cox stood with his hands clasped behind him as one by one, the Dom's terrifying monsters were taken down. The last one fell barely two hundred yards short of the breastworks. Unfortunately, the armabueys continued, urged on by their keepers.

"Damn," Cox muttered, recognizing the threat. There might still be twenty of the brutes, and with the chains and carcasses stretched between them they could wreck his breastworks as easily as the great predators might've done. "All guns will focus on finishing those creatures. Marksmen will kill their handlers."

Anson relaxed a trifle. He'd been concerned Cox would order infantry volleys against the few dozen dragon priests. That would make short work of them, with rifled muskets, but would waste a great deal of ammunition.

A couple of artillery batteries were already engaging the armabueys. Their thick, segmented armor might protect them from the raking claws of predators, but couldn't stop a ten-pound shell traveling twelve hundred feet per second. They started dying in rapid succession, emitting loud rattling, gurgling sounds and flailing madly. Probably only the chains kept them from wrecking the breastworks in their death throes.

"We've done for them, at least," a major next to Cox commented smugly. Then his eyes widened in alarm just as one of the telegraphers pulled the metal-strapped earpiece off his head. "Sir!" he exclaimed. "A report from Colonel—"

"We see them," Anson interrupted. A solid wall of yellow and white uniforms was appearing in the smoke less than two hundred yards from the breastworks, stretching away to the left and right farther than they could see. Hundreds of their bloodred banners drooped listlessly above them, but that gave no real clue about their numbers. Most distressing, they were already twice as close as the Nussie's rifled muskets *should've* been hammering at them. At the same moment, a Dom case shot exploded behind the temple in the street, followed by a virtual storm of explosions all over town.

"All the light rifles will resume their bombardment of the enemy artillery!" Cox shouted. "The heavy rifles and smoothbores still on the line will engage the infantry with canister." Sharp, loud volleys started cracking along the breastworks as men in sky-blue uniforms brought polished rifle muskets to bear. "All infantry with the enemy in range to their front will commence firing," Cox belatedly ordered.

Fred and Kari had eased back from the wall at the top of the tower and were unconsciously crouching each time an enemy shell went off. "I like droppin' bombs a lot better thaan bein' under 'em!" Kari shouted.

"Me too," Fred agreed. "This doesn't look like it's going like it was supposed to."

Captain Anson must've heard because he laughed out loud. Stepping over, he spoke for them alone. "I believe that's beginning to occur to General Cox as well." He waved to the south. "This Dom commander is no fool. His monsters surprised me completely. Our scouts never discovered them. But I still suspect their attack was just a distraction to prevent us from ravaging his forces while they deployed. They're fine breakthrough weapons, but what's the point of a breakthrough without infantry to support it? Still 'General Dom' read the circumstances, ground, and weather perfectly, and already deployed to a large degree before he ever emerged from the forest. Then he used his monsters to distract us *and* advance his infantry. A brilliant move." He sobered as the sound of crisp volleys gave way to a rising roar of crackling musketry. "I fear the enemy has learned his art from your generals Shinya and Blair too well."

CHAPTER 7

*////// **SE of Monsu***
Holy Dominion

Despite how physically and emotionally hardened the newly promoted Colonel Blas-Ma-Ar had become, a few old friends still affectionately called her "Blossom." Some of her own troops, in the "Sister's Own" Division she commanded in all but name, called her that as well—behind her back. They did it with more irony than affection however, since they'd only come to know her after she'd "blossomed" into a ruthlessly effective combat leader. That didn't mean they weren't still fiercely loyal. On the contrary. Blas's troops had seen more action and suffered more casualties against the Doms than any other division, but Blas always led from the front and they *almost* always won. That was particularly important to a division largely composed of "locals," in a sense, with a very personal stake in the downfall of the Holy Dominion.

The Sister's Own was part of what had come to be called the "Army of the Sisters," in honor of Rebecca Anne McDonald, Governor/Empress of the Empire of the New Britain Isles; Saan-Kakja, the High Chief of all the Filpin Lands; and Sister Audrey, a young Benedictine nun who came to this world from a different Java. The division consisted of what was left of the 2nd Battalion, 2nd (Lemurian) Marines, Colonel Arano Garcia's "Vengadores de Dios," and now Colonel Dao Iverson's 6th Imperial Marines, all rather oddly under the nominal command of "Colonel" Sister Audrey.

The 2nd of the 2nd had few 'Cat Marines left, but had swelled to brigade strength by incorporating human rebels against the Doms into their ranks. These were "Ocelomeh" or "Jaguar Warriors" who'd been struck by the vague resemblance Lemurians bore to the feline manifestation of their deity. Most now accepted that similarity was coincidental, but they'd been trained, armed, and equipped by Blas's Marines and had taken the oath to the American Navy Clan. As far as Blas was concerned, they enjoyed full membership in the 2nd of the 2nd and would until the war was over and their obligation to a flag—the Stars and Stripes of another world—was at an end. She often wondered how many would stick, regardless.

The Vengadores were converted to the "true faith" by Sister Audrey and raised from the ranks of penitent Dom POWs after an abortive campaign on New Ireland (Oahu) against the Impies. Their ranks had swollen here as well, joined by other rebels whose adherence to a Christianity very similar to what Sister Audrey taught had resulted in bloody repression. Iverson's 6th Marines had been added to make good the losses they'd all sustained in the Battle of El Corazon. Blas personally didn't know how Iverson even survived the debacle under El Corazon's southeast gate, let alone could still muster nearly six hundred men from his regiment, fit to fight.

At the moment, however, Blas hardly cared, and didn't feel particularly "hardened" either. She'd been slogging through rainy forests and ankle-deep mud alongside her troops for three solid days. Ever since most of X Corps quietly landed at Monsu, a sleepy Dom town on the north coast of South America. Shinya was pushing them hard down narrow, thickly wooded tracks, south of the main "Camino Militar" the Doms maintained for rapid troop movements of their own. In contrast, this was a virtual game trail winding through passes between even more densely choked slopes, or switchbacking up and down actual mountains. The passage was probably sufficient for animal-drawn carts, but just barely managed their artillery and supply train, which only made the mud even worse. Blas wondered how General Tomatsu Shinya even knew these roads—such as they were—were here. *Probably squeezed it out of some officers that surrendered at El Coraazon,* she decided. *Or maay-be they were on maaps we caaptured?* Blas barely cared about that either. It was hard enough just sucking enough actual air past all the moisture saturating it.

With Admiral Lelaa-Tal-Cleraan's support, General Shinya convinced High Admiral Jenks they *had* to push troops through the Pass before the League closed it off with *Leopardo* or some other powerful, modern ship. But Jenks was right to be cautious. The League had shown its hand and *Leopardo* had proven it could destroy anything they currently had. He'd refused to allow direct reinforcement of the NUS landing at El Palo, fearing *Leopardo* might still be near, and he wouldn't take such a risk with the cream of Second Fleet's Allied Expeditionary Force. Besides, even if they got troops ashore at El Palo, they'd have the same problem supplying them that the Nussies were contending with.

Shinya proposed a compromise. They had two captured Dom ships of the line, USS *Destroyer* (formerly *Deoses Destructor*) and USS *Sword* (formerly *Espada de Dios*), that should be able to make a few runs before anyone got wise, and they still had four swift sail/steam Imperial frigates that could time their runs through the most perilous seas at night. ("Most perilous" in this case meaning those farthest east.) They'd land X Corps at Monsu, 190 miles west of where the Dom General Mayta would try to block them at El Henal. That would still leave them five hundred miles from El Palo and the Nussies, but it was closer than they were. And once X Corps was ashore, Jenks wouldn't have to risk any more ships in the Caribbean to supply it. The rest of the army under General Blair, whatever elements of XI and XV Corps Jenks didn't need to hold El Corazon, could be shipped southeast to the occupied town of Manizales on the *Pacific* side of the Pass. From there it could march inland across already pacified territory. Blair would have to push even harder than Shinya to catch up, and he'd bleed troops to the necessity of establishing security for the route, but he'd be on the Camino Militar for the bulk of his march. In any event, if all went well, X Corps would get its reinforcements and the whole army would have a secure, if lengthy, line of supply from Manizales.

The plan was working, so far. *It's strange how, the longer we're at this daamn waar, the more often thaat haappens,* Blas reflected. *Gettin' better at it, I guess. Better at fightin' thaan anything we ever done.* She pushed that thought away and focused on breathing again. Arano Garcia's Vengadores were trudging beside her, gasping just as loudly as her.

The Allied aircraft carriers, damaged in the battle for the Pass, carried XI and XV Corps down to Manizales on their way to the Enchanted Isles for repairs. X Corps' landing went off almost without a hitch. Most occurred in darkness over several nights and there was the inevitable confusion, but no opposition at sea by *Leopardo* or anything else. The first wave utterly surprised the inhabitants of Monsu and the town was taken with a minimum of bloodshed. Quite a few people escaped, no doubt, and General Mayta would quickly get word at El Henal but what could he do? He'd strengthen his defenses at the larger city sitting astride the Camino Militar and wait for them. What he didn't know, what almost nobody, even in X Corps knew, was Shinya had no intention of meeting General Mayta at El Henal. If Mayta wanted to fight, he was going to have to come to them.

"Colonel Blas," came a gentle voice, intruding on Blas's concentration. She looked up and blinked surprise at Sister Audrey and several others riding beside her on horseback. Audrey, as usual, was dressed like the rest in a long, tie-dyed camouflage smock held tight around her slim waist with a pistol and cutlass belt. Shoulder-length blonde hair spilled out from under a steel "doughboy" helmet. Blas knew Audrey's weapons were cleaned and oiled every night by her orderlies, but she'd never drawn one herself. Blas's own XO, Captain Ixtli, rode beside Audrey, followed by Captain Bustos, who served as XO for the Vengadores and Audrey's personal guard after the loss of Sergeant Koratin. Blas felt a stab of loss remembering the strange former "lord" of Aryaal. Bringing up the rear was First Sergeant Spon-Ar-Aak, better known as "Spook" for his white fur. He was doing the job of a lieutenant in Blas's 2nd of the 2nd.

"Hey," she said. "Yeah? Whaat's the maatter?"

"You didn't even know we were here," Audrey chastised her. "That's how people get eaten along this track—as you well know." She hesitated. "Did you even know where you were?"

Blas looked around. "Sure. Waalkin' with the troops. We all oughta do thaat from time to time," she added.

"You're with the Vengadores," Audrey pointed out. "Your Marines are up ahead."

"So? All these troops're mine, sorta."

"Of course," Audrey agreed. "But you *started* with the Second Marines. You're tiring." She didn't point out that Blas was short, even for a 'Cat, and had to take twice as many steps to cover the same ground as a man—and the Sister's Own was mostly human now. There were still female 'Cats in the 2nd, and female Ocelomeh too, but they didn't stay up half the night seeing to the division's business. Granted, Audrey, Garcia, Iverson, and their staffs all worked equally long hours—but they had the sense to ride. "You won't be any use to your troops if you drop dead from exhaustion."

Blas's tail whipped with annoyance and she blinked it at Audrey.

"Besides," Audrey blithely continued, "General Shinya wants us." Shinya remained near the middle of the column so he could react to reports from in front or behind.

"Who has the front?" Blas should've remembered.

"Colonel Garcia. Iverson leads the other column."

Finally, Blas nodded. "Okaay."

Spook hopped down from his horse, holding his Allin-Silva rifle high.

He hit the ground with a *splap*. "Don't worry, Col-nol," he said, grinning. "I'll shove these laaggards along!"

The huffing men managed a few good-natured groans. Oddly, Blas was pleased by that. All these men, original Vengadores or new recruits, had grown up under the menace of the Dominion. The slightest expression of discontent was liable to get them impaled, nailed up and burned alive, or "sacrificed" atop a stone pyramid. She'd never seen any of those acts performed and hoped she never would. She'd seen the aftermath, though, and done her best to instill a real sense of shared purpose and belonging in these men. Key to that was the time-honored tradition of allowing soldiers and sailors to share their discomfort, fear, or unhappiness by griping about their lot: spreading it around and having it confirmed by others. There were limits of course, and the troops themselves wouldn't tolerate whining, but it was the simplest way to let them vent a little steam before the pressure stoked it into genuine resentment. She was glad these men *trusted* her enough to let her hear a little grumbling.

She climbed in the saddle Spook had just vacated and plastered a false grin on her face as she called out, "So long, fellas. Enjoy the stroll. I'll see you in caamp tonight—aafter my baath!"

A few hoots followed her as she rode off beside Sister Audrey. Her fake grin turned to a small, real smile.

"You see?" Audrey chuckled. "You know more about this dreadful business of war than I will ever grasp, but there's one thing I can tell you. Oftentimes, those you lead don't want you around them all the time. They like it on occasion, and I spend a fair amount of time with them myself. But they *know* you have more important things to do than slog through the mud beside them, and they'd generally prefer that you do it."

They trotted back down the line trying not to splash the troops or throw too many clumps of mud their way. It took quite a while. There were roughly thirty thousand troops in X Corps, marching down two vaguely parallel tracks, each rarely wide enough for four to march abreast. Then of course, they had to stop and wait while batteries of guns creaked and spattered their way through clumps of mighty tree trunks too dense to go around. They finally joined a squad of dragoons approaching along an intersecting path and followed them to a full company of dragoons surrounding a group of riders plodding along in front of a line of wagons. One was larger than the others, covered with canvas on arched wooden hoops. It was Shinya's personal wagon, with a real bed and even a head—of sorts—inside.

Basically, it was just a seat over a hole in the wagon deck, but it was sheer luxury under the circumstances. Blas suspected it once belonged to some Dom officer.

Shinya saw their approach and urged his mount to meet them. In addition to the traditional long mustaches, full beards were now fashionable among Imperials—possibly because so many of the original destroyermen wore them—and Shinya had attempted one himself. It had been a poor, sparse thing, and he'd ended up keeping only a mustache. Otherwise he looked the same as always: trim and fit with dark hair and eyes, wearing the same helmet and combat smock as everyone. The men and 'Cats around him had to spur their horses forward. Blas knew most, but some had been members of General Blair's staff and Blas hadn't seen them before.

"Good afternoon," Shinya said, noting Blas's muddy, rumpled state. No one dismounted and the column continued on. "I hope the march hasn't been too taxing for you."

Blas blinked disdain and would've rendered an apparently universal hand gesture if they'd been alone. She'd almost hated Shinya once, but had learned to understand, even appreciate his brand of ruthlessness. Their relationship was still tense at times, but also somehow more relaxed, one-on-one, and Blas suspected they each recognized a bit of themselves in the other.

"It's been tiring for us all, I'm sure," Sister Audrey interjected wryly.

"Not too many dangerous animals?" Shinya inquired. "I've heard few shots."

Captain Ixtli cleared his throat. He and Captain Bustos were the best qualified to comment on local conditions. "Your riders—'dragoons'—help, casting about in front of the columns and along the flanks. They discourage the smaller predators." He was talking about creatures similar to Grik that roamed in packs, always fighting one another. And they wouldn't attack without an overwhelming advantage. That and the fact they seemed to recognize when their human prey was armed argued for intelligence of a sort. "None of the smaller grass or leaf eaters is a threat if left alone," Ixtli added, then seemed to consider. "Some of the larger predators might actually be *tempted* by the size of our force, and without air support only artillery can harm them." He shrugged. "But our numbers also frighten the larger leaf eaters away and the *hochiquatl*, ah, 'great dragons,' follow them."

"And no enemy scouts," Shinya concluded with satisfaction. "I doubt they imagine our purpose yet." He frowned. "But that won't last. We've only encountered a few small villages but their people are far enough inland and off the beaten path, far enough from . . . civilization"—Blas could tell he found it distasteful to associate that word with Doms—"that *any* strangers are cause for alarm. And a 'heretic' *army*?" He shook his head. "They're no threat, but I doubt we'll get many recruits. They may even send runners to warn the Doms. We could leave squads to sit on the villages but it would do no good. They can't possibly ensure that no one escapes, or find them if they did. This forest is their home."

"With respect, General Shinya, we *do* have sympathizers here," Bustos countered. "You should let some Vengadores—and a few Ocelomeh," he grudged, "scout with your dragoons. Warn the people before we march through. Explain we're here to crush the Dominion forever!" He paused significantly. "Other than accused dissidents and heretics, where do you think people in the cities get their slaves, their sacrifices?" He waved around. "Off the 'beaten path,' as you said. On the frontiers."

"He's right," Ixtli agreed. "You consider 'frontiers' to be faraway places, but each city in this land encroaches on one. Trust us. This forest harbors more hatred of the Doms than you would imagine, and more allies for our cause as well."

Shinya looked at Blas and Sister Audrey. Blas blinked agreement. "Worth a try," she said, blinking fondly at Ixtli. "Obviously, it's worked before." She straightened in her saddle. "But thaat's not why you sent for us."

"No," Shinya said, glancing back at a courier riding behind, then focusing again on Blas and Audrey. "I sent runners to inform Colonel Iverson and Colonel Garcia but in the interests of our . . . new understanding, I felt compelled to tell you face-to-face that, difficult as it might be, we must pick up the pace."

Blas blinked hot disagreement and her tail whipped menacingly beside her. "Thaat's aasking too much, Gener-aal. These troops're veteraans. More importaant, they're fightin' for a cause they believe in. Most won't just faall out when they caan't go on, like they might've once. They'll maarch theirselves to *death*."

"I know," Shinya said, and seemed genuinely sorry. "But that's as much your fault as mine, Colonel Blas. More so," he pointed out. Stung, Blas couldn't speak.

"General Shinya—" Sister Audrey began, but Shinya cut her off.

"And yours as well, 'Santa Madre,'" he snapped, using the title the Vengadores had bestowed on Audrey despite her constant complaints. "You might even bear the greatest blame of all," he added harshly, then his tone immediately softened. "And you should both be proud of that. But the fact of the matter is, our comm-cart"—he waved behind them—"has been picking up some rather garbled wireless traffic. It's these damned trees, you see," he explained, "but we've heard enough to know that General Cox and his NUS Army have a significant battle on their hands. Details are scant, but it sounds as if General Cox himself isn't sure what's going on. But that doesn't matter, and we haven't a moment to lose."

Blas had recovered from Shinya's brutal compliment. "But Gener-aal, we've only made about sixty miles from Monsu. It would take *weeks* to join General Cox even if we followed thaat main Dom road." She waved around. "In this? Whaat's the point? We caan't affect whaat haappens at El Paalo no maatter how faast we go!"

"We can," Shinya disagreed.

Blas blinked utter confusion.

"We've actually come about *seventy* miles. But the point is, General Mayta must know about our presence at Monsu by now. He doesn't have many professional troops and he'll fortify the city as best he can against our 'inevitable' attack."

"But we're not going there," Audrey pointed out.

"Exactly, and Mayta will discover that as well. He'll then be faced with some unpleasant alternatives. He can march on Monsu and attack our beachhead, but it's well protected by now and should withstand an assault. Mayta could lay siege, but eventually General Blair will arrive with two full corps. Mayta would probably learn he was coming but could only scurry back to El Henal by then."

"What else might he do?" Audrey asked.

"Believing Cox is weakened by his battle, Mayta might descend on him—but not only would that leave El Henal open to our forces, he'll know by then that *we've* moved southeast, toward their capital in New Granada City. I suspect the farther along we are in that direction, the more likely he'll be to chase us."

"And leave Cox alone," Blas guessed.

Shinya nodded. "He'd also, incidentally, wind up trapped between us and General Blair, or perhaps General Cox, coming up behind us."

"That's assuming Cox wins his battle, of course," Audrey interjected.

"I *am* assuming that," Shinya confessed. "I hope my trust isn't misplaced."

“Whaat do *you* think Mayta’ll do?”

Shinya frowned. “Honestly? My biggest fear is he’ll do nothing at all, and Don Hernan will spirit him away. I’m not worried about his little army at El Henal.” “Little” was a relative thing. It was believed Mayta had thrown as many as forty thousand men together, but against the veterans of X Corps, they’d collapse in a stand-up fight. “Mayta’s no fool,” he continued. “He showed us that before El Corazon. And then we showed him how *not* to defend a fixed position. I’m sure he took it to heart. On top of that, he survived Don Hernan’s wrath over the loss of El Corazon and the Pass of Fire. He’s either better connected than we can imagine in some way, or even Don Hernan believes he’s the best general they have. I’d much rather he chased after us so we can kill him.”

CHAPTER 8

////// El Palo
Holy Dominion

"This ain't lookin' good!" Kari-Faask shouted in Fred Reynolds's ear. He barely heard over the booming guns and crashing musketry. In spite of everything, the first wave against the south breastworks had been shattered, almost muzzle to muzzle, as Nussie troops shook off their initial terror and surprise—this was their first real action, after all—and their training and superior weapons began to tell.

Like the Doms—or maybe vice versa?—the standard NUS infantry weapon was .69 caliber, but there were profound differences. Even after finally discarding plug-style bayonets in favor of the socket type, Dom muskets remained smoothbore flintlocks that fired a loose-fitting one-ounce ball. They were wildly inaccurate past forty or fifty yards and very prone to misfires in high humidity. Still muzzle-loaders as well, Nussie muskets may not have changed much in appearance, dimensions, or rate of fire over the last century, but they were ignited by weather-resistant percussion caps and they were rifled. This and their ingeniously calibrated sights allowed them to accurately strike a man-size target with a 750-grain elongated, hollow-base bullet at three hundred yards with relative ease. They were thumpers, of course, but few soldiers really noticed recoil in the heat of battle.

Their long-range capability hadn't been an advantage here, but the fact they still worked and their heavy slugs could slam through two or three closely spaced attackers certainly had been. Regardless of their zealotry and the high-pitched haranguing of their surviving officers, the Doms fell back, stumbling over the heaped bodies of their comrades. The relaxing pressure allowed the troops in sky blue to really pour it in, and rifled cannon sprayed swathes of canister in thunderclaps of death. Rifled guns weren't good with canister, they blew their patterns all to hell, but at close range it hardly mattered and the Doms were turned to steaming mulch.

They'd hammered the Nussies hard, however, and the breastworks were clotted with dead and wounded. Worse, even as enemy case shot started bursting in the town again, the swirling fog of smoke revealed *another* wave of Doms. "My God!" Cox had exclaimed. "They're pushing the broken ranks of the first assault back forward, at bayonet point!"

"Sure," Fred confirmed, coughing smoke. "That's what they do. Doms that break keep fighting or die. If nothing else, they'll soak up bullets for fresh troops."

That's when Captain Anson's first prediction was confirmed and a large force rushed out of the forest to the east, quickly formed across the Camino Militar, and charged into the blocking breastworks there. From their elevated perch, they saw and heard the sudden explosion of fighting before the first reports came in, and that's what inspired Kari's gloomy appraisal.

"Don't worry about it," Fred replied, realizing his tone wasn't particularly encouraging. "We're used to watching battles from the air. Mostly," he quickly added, remembering their experience on the shattered deck of Captain Ruik's *Simms* at the Battle of Malpelo. "Everything always looks worse when you're in the middle of it."

"Not alwaays," Kari denied. "Sometimes you see *better* how much things is go to shit!" As usual, when she was excited, her English had begun to suffer. A shell burst on the roof of the temple below them and an officer shouting down at couriers in the street collapsed bonelessly by the telegrapher's station, the top of his head sheared off. Musketry on the south breastworks reached a fever pitch and Doms fell as thick as rain, but those behind were firing back, on the march. Accuracy was poorer than usual, but the volume of fire was sufficient to take a toll. Horns wailed from somewhere beyond the fighting and all the Doms flooded forward. Point-blank cannon blasts staggered the rush just before it hit, but in an instant, the fighting at the breastworks to the south *and* east had degenerated into a hand-to-hand brawl.

"General!" one of the telegraphers cried, "Colonel Roland urgently requests reinforcements for the Eleventh!"

Cox glanced at Anson, remembering his warning against committing reserves too quickly. "The Eleventh is in the center," he said, "where the heaviest blow has fallen."

"Then pull troops from the regiments around it," Anson suggested. Cox wavered, and Anson pressed, "Why else would the Doms attack so heedless of loss except to fix our attention? And where are their lancers? I'm *certain* they're coming from the west, against our weakest line."

"When?" Cox demanded.

Anson blinked, much like a Lemurian. "I'd do it *now*, if I were them."

Cox took a deep breath, gazing at the panoramic struggle, almost dazed by the titanic thunder of it all. He'd heard accounts of the unbelievable scope of some of the battles their Allies had fought and was honest enough to admit to himself that his imagination had failed him. This was the largest land battle the NUS had fought in a century and he hadn't been ready for it. No one could be. He looked back at Anson. "Very well. I hope to God you're right. I'll alert the reserves to complete the movement you suggested. Go. Take charge on my authority if you must, and we'll all pray whoever commands their lancers isn't as aggressive as you."

Anson saluted and turned toward the spiral stairs. Fred and Kari both rushed to join him, calling, "We're with him!"

"What're you doing?" Anson demanded, taking the steps two at a time.

"Goin' with you," Kari simply said.

"It'll be dangerous."

Fred laughed. "No more than squatting up in this big-ass target of a tower, if the smoke ever clears enough for the Dom gunners to see it better." He waved behind them. "Besides, there's nothing but a bunch of old sticks-in-the-mud up there."

Kari snorted. "An' when did we ever do somethin' *not* dangerous? Don't worry, we'll staay outa your waay."

The roar of battle was slightly muted on the west side of town. A breeze was finally rising from the northwest, starting to carry some of the noise away. And it was a kindly breeze for the Nussies already engaged, cooling them while blowing gunsmoke back in their enemies' faces. Anson and his Ranger company, accompanied by Fred and Kari, fell in with Captain Meder's battery rushing to bring up the rear of Colonel Hara's 3rd Artillery. The jingling, rattling clatter of six guns and limbers pulled by eighteen horses, surrounded by nearly a hundred more mounted men was almost deafening in itself. Up ahead, Hara's other two batteries were already unlimbering astride the Camino Militar on the outskirts of town, while columns of infantry raced at double time to form up behind them. Fred saw Lieutenant O'Riel trotting at the head of his company of the 4th Infantry and shouted, "Hi!" O'Riel either ignored him or didn't hear. Young face grim and pouring sweat, naked sword clenched in his right hand and resting on his shoulder as he jogged, he was focused on other things.

The teams pulling Meder's 12 pdrs, each horse carrying a crew member, dashed past the leftmost gun already in position and performed a wide turn to the rear. When they were even with the other guns on the line again, three men sprang from their cramped seat atop the limber chest, joined by half the men off the horses, and quickly unhitched the gun. The horses, relieved of all but three riders and the limber, moved a short distance to the rear. Fred was impressed by how seamlessly it all went and glanced past the arriving infantry at more teams pulling ammunition caissons. Anson shouted, "Good luck to you!" and led his Rangers toward a group of mounted officers clustered near the center of the forming line. Dragoons blew through it, racing west on the still empty road.

Looking at Kari, Fred urged his horse toward Captain Meder who was shouting at someone to "pull that God-damned handspike out of your arse and put it where it belongs!" Then he cupped his hands and bellowed, "Battery C! Take implements! Prepare for action to the front!" Noticing Fred and Kari, Meder grinned. "You decided to join me after all, I see."

"You *did* offer us a job."

"So I did—here, move your horses out from between the gun and limber. Better. The lads out there"—he gestured at the gun's crews, removing rammer staffs from the carriages and donning accoutrements handed out by men holding the lids of the limber chests only slightly open—"tend to take offense to that sort of thing."

"Whaat caan we do?" Kari asked.

Meder shrugged and quickly described the duties of the crew members at each position and how they used their implements. Then he asked a man standing behind a limber chest to open it wide enough for them to see how the ammunition was arranged inside. Reluctantly, the man complied. "That's a great, monstrous bomb, you see," Meder explained, "and that man, 'number six,' is justifiably hesitant to expose it—or himself—to the dangerous world around him."

"So where do you want us?" Fred asked.

Meder chuckled. "You're officers. Sit with me, watch the men. If the time comes when you're truly needed on a gun, you'll know better what to do. In the meantime, I appreciate the conversation. No one much to talk to." He nodded darkly at the officer behind the battery to their right. "That's Dukane. I call him 'Donkey,' of course, and he's an imbecile. He throws his roundshot true enough, but swears against all reason that one must fire *low* with canister. Says it's lighter and must therefore fly higher. Fool." He snorted and lowered his voice. "And a Jacksonian as well." He spoke louder. "All *proper* artillerymen are Whigs."

Dukane must've heard because he sent Meder a glare.

"I don't know whaat thaat means," Kari complained.

"Neither do I," Fred whispered back.

The sound of fighting behind them roared louder and Meder glanced that way. "I do hope we didn't scurry all the way out here for nothing. Worse, I'd hate to think the lads back there were in a bad way because of it." He nodded in the direction Anson went. "He seems a solid fellow and most speak well of him, but you don't suppose he misread *this* situation . . . ?"

As if to answer his question, puffs of smoke gushed from the forest at the dragoons advancing, spread out, up the road. A couple of men fell from their saddles but the rest started firing back, the *popping* of their carbines drifting to them seconds later.

"Caap'n Aanson usually knows whaat he's doin," Kari replied.

Heavy fire started coming from the trees and animals of all sorts darted across the road. More dragoons fell, but the rest wheeled their mounts and whipped them into a gallop. Almost immediately, a line of Dom lancers surged into the road, spearing men from their saddles. A few dragoons pulled sabers or pistols—large percussion six-shooters like Captain Anson carried—and tried to fight clear. Those outside the melee hesitated, but when more shots came from the forest, they continued their retreat.

"Lancers indeed," Meder growled. "Dangerous buggers. Well, we'll meet them with more than a few carbines if they've the nerve to try *us*."

Kari started to remark that the Army of the Sisters had pretty much rendered Dom lancers ineffective, but then again, Shinya's dragoons had *breechloading* carbines, shorter versions of the Allin-Silva rifle, that could fire fifteen rounds a minute.

The lancers had the nerve. Thick columns poured from the forest and galloped closer to the NUS position. The timber opened up at about eight hundred yards and they fanned out in a long, thickening line. About the time the dragoons returned, their horses white with foamy lather, the order came for the batteries to open fire.

"My God, what a lovely target!" Meder exulted, lowering his short brass telescope. "This is the day the Lord has made," he murmured softly. "Let us rejoice and be glad in it." Glancing around self-consciously he bellowed, "C

Battery, load case and hold! The damned wind'll be in *our* faces now," he muttered aside to Fred and Kari, then raised his voice again. "Elevation, one and a half degrees, fuses for two seconds!"

In less than half a minute, all six gunners—the men who aimed the pieces in Meder's Battery—were standing, fists raised, signifying they were loaded, on target, and ready to fire. But Fred had been watching how quickly the lancers' ranks were swelling. "First ones up, as usual," Meder proclaimed loud enough for Dukane to hear. "Battery C, at my command . . . *fire*!"

Six guns roared as one, smoke-belching muzzles dipping and clanging as carriages jolted back six or seven feet across the mushy ground. Even before they came to rest, their crews took hold to heave them back in place. Meder was watching through his glass. "Fine, fine," he murmured, watching shells burst over the enemy. Dukane's battery fired, blinding Meder with its smoke. "Damn that man," he groused. "Battery C, commence independent rapid fire, same settings, but listen for corrections."

All three batteries, eighteen guns, were pounding out shells as fast as they could as if the whole thing was more a competition among themselves than a desperate battle against a brutal enemy. A dense, impenetrable wall of white smoke towered in front and drifted across them, making it impossible to see. A young rider galloped up. "Colonel Hara's compliments; you've done excellent execution, but now you're firing long. Observers on the right report the lancers are moving forward with"—the kid gulped—"an estimated strength of around five thousand."

Meder arched his eyebrows and looked at Fred and Kari. "And us with two regiments, less than two thousand men in support. Things might get lively." He nodded. "Very well. We can't adjust fire in this smoke; we'll have to let it clear a bit."

"That was Colonel Hara's assessment as well. He wants you to know the infantry will begin moving up between your guns."

Meder turned back to his battery and yelled, "Load canister and hold!"

"Canister is for close up, right?" Fred asked.

"Indeed. And they might already *be* close enough, for all we know. Nothing for it."

Blocks of infantry about twenty wide and four deep double-timed up between the guns. Fred thought they looked sharp in their dark blue wheel hats and light blue uniforms with white crossbelts and polished rifle-muskets on their shoulders. He was glad to see them and thought the artillerymen would be too. Instead he heard cries like "How're we supposed to fight with these buggers in our way?" answered by variations on "You're not fighting now. Move, so we can." He shook his head and smiled. *Some things are universal,* he supposed.

But the artillery wasn't finished. The smoke had cleared just enough to see what appeared to be one great long mass of mounted men, coming at a canter, barely three hundred yards away.

"First rank!" shouted a young lieutenant commanding the troops between Meder's far right gun and Dukane's left. Fred was surprised to see O'Riel again. "Set your sights for three hundred. Present! Fire!" The small volley crackled among many others. "Second rank!" O'Riel cried.

Dukane's battery unleashed six loads of canister, consisting in this case of eighteen hundred half-inch balls. His gunners groaned when a gust of wind revealed only a score or so horses and riders going down. Almost all their fire had churned the ground a hundred yards short of the oncoming enemy.

"You're an idiot, Donkey!" Meder roared. "We haven't time for your foolishness now. Aim high!" Putting his hands on his hips he turned to the front and assumed a disdainful air. "C Battery! *We* shall not cast *our* seed upon the ground!" Even the nearby infantry exploded with laughter.

"Whaat does thaat mean?" Kari asked. Fred's face reddened and he shook his head.

"Fire!" Meder roared.

On any battlefield—on any world—no matter what kind of charcoal is in the gunpowder, what wood provides the sabot or sawdust that buffers the shot, gunsmoke billowing around canister always has a yellowish tinge. One is tempted to blame the brimstone in the powder, for its hellish associations, but if that's so, why doesn't the color exhibit when any other type of shot is fired? Perhaps it's because canister is so hellish, in and of itself.

Almost none of C Battery's canister went to waste. Men dropped their lances and threw up their hands as they tumbled from the saddle. Horses screamed and rolled, smashing and grinding their riders. A great swathe was torn from the cantering horde—just as the third battery savaged it just as badly. Rifle-muskets came into their own, keeping up a continuous fire by ranks and even the most dubious marksmen found it difficult to miss in such a press. But regardless of how many men and horses were shot or blown to the ground, there were more.

"Keep at it! Hammer 'em, lads!" Captain Meder cried, his own horse capering beneath him. *Poom! Poom!* went the big guns, canister shrieking away. *Poom-poom-poom-poom!* The rifles rivaled them and there was no pause as the infantry fired independently, men in the rear ranks crowding in around the guns even as artillerymen cursed and pushed them out of the way so they could reload.

A loud horn blared a long, piercing note and the enemy lances all came down, red pennants fluttering behind razor-sharp tips. Another horn sounded a different note that brought to mind the wailing shriek of a dying woman and the Doms finally charged. The sweat running down Fred's back seemed to freeze, the sheer weight of the thundering Dom charge as frightening as the Grik had ever been. He looked anxiously at Kari and she blinked something back he'd never seen before, like reassurance mixed with terror.

"Fix bayonets!" roared company commanders, punctuated by the bugle call confirming the order. "Guard against lancers!" Men in the first two ranks thrust their long muskets forward, trying to make an impenetrable wall of steel to discourage the horses. But the lances were longer. Meder calmly drew his revolver, another powerful six-shooter, and Fred nervously pulled his .45 out of its holster while Kari unslung her Blitzer. "Take care not to fire around a limber chest when it's open," Meder told them almost casually, just before the lancers struck.

Fred and Kari were never in a shield wall back in the "old days" after *Walker* first arrived, when 'Cats were fighting the Grik with whatever weapons and tactics they could throw together. But Fred imagined the clattering, screeching, booming crash they heard must've been what it was like for those who had. There were no shields here, however; all there was were bodies. Horses, men, and the weapons they held. Lances drove deep into the ranks, skewering men like shish kebabs before shattering and exploding under the strain. A terrible collective scream of horror, agony, and desperate defiance rose from the ranks, and not all of it came from human throats. Regardless of their training, horses are rarely as brave or stupid as their riders, and few will willingly bash their way through a phalanx of bristling bayonets. They may not recognize them for what they are, but they'll balk and slow in the face of roaring muskets, then instinctively recoil from the first searing pain of the sharp, wicked blades. And a 750-grain bullet traveling at 1,100 feet per second will wreck them. Yet the leading edge of such a charge can't escape the press from behind. Forward is the only way and even horses must subdue their pain and terror.

On the other hand, the courage and discipline required to stand and face the flashing lances and roaring avalanche of countless tons of horseflesh is beyond many men. Particularly when the ranks in front of them, several deep, have been wiped away, and no one stands behind them. Men will recoil from that as well, and it was in those places the lancers cracked the lines.

"Hold them, God damn you!" Meder roared as the block of men between his number three and number four gun shattered and spilled from the gap, heaved back by the sheer weight of the assault. Grim-faced Dom lancers, most now without their signature weapons, churned through the bloody break. A few fumbled for carbines while others swept heavy sabers from their scabbards and hacked at stubborn defenders. Men shot them or stabbed their horses with bayonets. The piercing screams of men and horses were indistinguishable.

Without hesitation, Meder kicked his horse to within six feet of a Dom and shot him in the belly with his big revolver. The Dom hunched over, dropping his saber to clutch the wound. Meder shot another man, charging through the smoke, then used his pistol to block a saber slash from a third. Fred and Kari exchanged another, different glance, and bolted after Meder.

Kari's Blitzer clattered loudly, sweeping men from their mounts. Fred hadn't shot a pistol toward anybody in a very long time, and then he'd only been shooting in their general direction—and hit his own plane. He suspected he'd killed a few Doms with a Blitzer once, when he and Kari sprayed a small boat full of them, but he'd never shot directly at an *individual* in his life. He did so now, popping at Doms pressing in on Meder. Almost immediately it seemed, his slide locked back, just as Kari's Blitzer emptied.

"Shit!" Fred squeaked, yanking at the magazine pouch on his belt. He might've hit a couple of targets; one fell off his horse. Still, with all the other shooting, it was hard to tell. He *had* drawn attention, however, and several Doms spurred toward him, sabers raised. Meder rammed his horse into one and cracked him on the back of the neck with his heavy revolver just under the flange of his plumed helmet. The helmet went flying and the man dropped away. Meder tossed the pistol. Either it was empty or the saber strike had damaged it. He drew his own saber.

Fred slammed a magazine home, dropped the slide, and shot at a rider right in front of him. The bullet hit the oncoming horse squarely between the eyes and it crashed like a stone, pitching the Dom forward and rolling on top of him.

"Whaat you shoot *horses* for?" Kari shouted angrily, finishing her own reload and sending quick, short bursts at the other men. Like most Lemurians, she rather liked horses. "*They* ain't tryin' to kill us!"

"I didn't mean . . ." There wasn't time to finish, and Fred shot another man. He knew he hit this one because he pitched limply from his saddle—but *another* Dom was close, saber already swinging. Fred ducked instinctively, hopelessly, but an artilleryman clubbed the Dom to the ground with a rammer staff and proceeded to beat him to death with it, screaming, "No damn horses in the gun line, damn you!" Kari blinked baffled relief—at the focus of the artilleryman's rage and that Fred was still alive—and shot two more Doms drawn to the preoccupied cannoneer. But the stream of riders gushing through the gap was becoming a flood. Guns still belched canister on either side of the breakthrough—double loads of the stuff—and the rifle-musket fire remained continuous, but Fred knew if this breakthrough wasn't contained, the line would eventually crack. And for all he knew, there might be *other* breakthroughs.

Despite the efforts of the infantrymen who'd been forced back, the lancers kept pushing to widen the opening, slaughtering gun's crews still feverishly working their pieces. Other Doms, maybe a couple hundred, simply galloped on, intent on striking deep. Fred thought he heard brisk firing behind, in the vicinity of the caissons. Inserting his last magazine—he'd only started with three, counting the one already loaded—he determined to make every shot count. Kari had more ammo for her Blitzer, ammo that would fit his pistol, but she was using it faster. *Better too,* he had to admit.

He caught a glimpse of Captain Meder, now afoot, shooting Doms with a revolver he'd apparently taken from a dead lieutenant on the ground.

"Let's cover him," Kari shouted. "He'll be empty soon, an' their pistols take longer to load." In unspoken agreement, they both dismounted and ran forward. Neither had been comfortable fighting from horseback, and though their mounts might've gotten them out if the line collapsed completely, what would be the point? They were stuck, like everyone else. If they lost this fight, there'd be no escape.

Suddenly, unexpectedly (they never even heard them coming over the roar of battle), about fifty of Anson's Rangers pounded through the clot of Doms, firing their big pistols and carbines directly into their enemies, almost touching their bodies with the muzzles of their weapons. Men fell all around them as they charged, as sudden and devastating as a bolt of lightning. And they didn't linger to mix it up as Fred expected; they simply galloped on, curving around, keeping their cohesion as if preparing to charge again. But *they* didn't charge. That was left to some fresh infantry surging in their wake, slamming the stunned, disorganized Doms with rifle fire. *They're hitting horses too,* Fred noted a little sourly, *and Kari's not griping at* them. They quickly joined Meder, and together, they added their fire to the infantry's.

Horses crashed and rolled and Doms tumbled to the ground. Others, wide-eyed, sawed at their reins, trying to turn their horses against the tide behind them. They were blown apart by heavy bullets blasting through brass cuirasses and the bodies within. The infantry streamed forward to fill the corpse-strewn gap and fire over the guns whose crews had died around them.

"Replacements forward!" Meder called, his voice hoarse and cracking. "Man those guns!" He looked at Fred and Kari as if just noticing them again. "Bring canister from the limber chests, if you please. To the left side of the guns, mind! Hurry!"

And so Fred and Kari did briefly join the artillery, until they themselves were replaced. By then, after just a few more hasty swarms of canister swept away the gathering mass of lancers poised to exploit the break, the pressure began to ease. Fred was relieved of the leather haversack he'd used to carry several heavy charges to a gun and almost numbly retreated to the limber where he found someone had tied his and Kari's horses to the splinter bar. They weren't likely to shift the limber, even in their excitement, since it was anchored by three of the six horses that pulled it, dead in their traces.

Kari joined him, wearily leaning against her horse, her Blitzer hanging from one hand. The fur around her eyes was wet with tears, but Fred's eyes were watering too, irritated by the smoke. The Doms were starting to break up and down the line, galloping away, but the fire chasing them only intensified. *Poom! Poom!* went the guns. *PPPPPoom! Ppoom!* Rifle-muskets raged and crackled. Part of Fred hated what they were doing. The enemy was finished, let them go. On the other hand, he understood why the Nussies would vent their fury on the fleeing foe. It had been a near-run thing and the Doms would've showed no mercy at all. Besides, sickening as he found the bloody math of war as General Shinya taught it, there was a terrible logic to it. Not only did the more Doms they killed today mean the less they'd fight again, it might also mean fewer would be *willing* to fight another day. And those who were might not stand as long or fight so hard.

"Dang!" Fred cried suddenly. "Look at that!" An orange ball of flame rolled up in the sky beyond the low-hanging smoke and he caught a glimpse of a Repub Nancy, a *Seevogel*, pulling away. Turning, he saw a pair of black toadstools rising in the sky to the south.

"At least *two* Naancys," Kari commented. "Wonder where they came from?"

"*Donaghey* and *Congress*, I bet. Maybe some others by now. Probably at the limit of their range when they heard what was goin' on."

"Still risky. Wish they'd come get us," Kari muttered.

"Yeah. Maybe they will, when things settle down."

"Load case!" Meder bellowed. "Prepare to resume firing at your initial settings! One and a half degrees, two seconds!"

At first Fred was mystified by Meder's order, then it dawned on him he either meant to rain hell on the retreating Doms, or make them pause in rifle range and under the firebombs of the aircraft. He looked at the artillery captain and saw his hat was gone, his sleeve torn and bloody, the buff saber belt around his waist stained a dark, blackening red. The longer hair on top of his head had fallen over his forehead in sweat-thickened strands but couldn't conceal the fury in his eyes. Raised to fear and hate the Doms but trained to keep his passions within professional bounds, this had still been his very first battle and his beloved battery had been decimated. All that was aside from the fact they'd very nearly *lost* the battle right in front of him. The cheerful warrior they'd joined just a short time ago was gone.

"Commence firing!" Meder roared.

The resuming barrage was quickly joined by other batteries and the stiffening breeze allowed Fred and Kari to see the effect this time. Exploding shells made a wall of smoke and slashing shrapnel that withered the farthest retreating lancers and confusion reigned behind them. Some tried to break south, but bugle calls sent dragoons sweeping around between them and the battle roaring in front of General Cox. Only a narrow band of forest separated them from the sea to the north. Whipped back and forth, with their number falling fast, and after a second firebomb dropped among them from an orbiting plane, few had any fight left in them when more bugles silenced the guns—and advanced the infantry. A lot of lancers seized the chance to bolt for the woods to the west, but most were simply too stunned, their horses too blown, to do anything but cast their weapons away and fall out of their saddles and lie on the ground when the vengeful infantry approached. Fred and Kari were just as stunned, in a way. As dreadful as the fight had begun, and as terrible as the ensuing one-sided carnage had been to view, they'd never expected to see so many Doms meekly surrender.

"Ain't thaat somethin'," Kari murmured softly.

Meder turned to her. "I thought you said Doms would *never* surrender on their own soil," he practically accused. That wasn't entirely true. The battle clearly lost, thousands of Dom regulars surrendered in El Corazon, even aiding the hunt for "elite" Blood Drinkers after they committed a particularly appalling atrocity. But no one had ever seen Doms just *quit* an open field battle.

"They never have, like this," Fred defended, mind racing. "Maybe news of what we did to 'em in the west spread farther than we thought. Especially that *we* don't murder prisoners." He hesitated, reluctant to voice another opinion, but couldn't help himself. "Or maybe on top of that, and the licking they just took, they're wondering why they should die for Don Hernan."

"I sure hope so," Kari agreed, blinking fervently.

By midafternoon, the Battle of El Palo was over. Even on the west side of the city where the fighting had been comparatively light, it took considerable time to check and organize prisoners and round up their animals. Fred and Kari could contribute little, so bidding farewell to Captain Meder, they rejoined Captain Anson and his Rangers. Anson was very busy too, sending and receiving scouts, and quickly questioning Dom officers before they had time to recover themselves. Dashing through the shell-torn town at the head of his company (the Dom bombardment had been haphazard but heavy), they quickly toured the eastern defenses and spoke to the commanders there. Other Rangers galloped up or charged away, bearing reports the entire time. Couriers came from General Cox as well, or from the telegraphers still atop the battered tower. Sometimes Anson issued curt instructions, but usually merely nodded and sent the messengers on their way.

Fred and Kari were two of very few who knew, "captain" or not, Anson acted under the express authority of the NUS president in various matters. General Cox obviously knew as well, which was why he kept him so meticulously informed, but this was the first time Fred or Kari ever watched Anson speak to majors and colonels like they were lieutenants—and saw them jump when he did so. They'd probably suspected he was more than he appeared all along.

"I always knew our pal was a big wheel," Fred muttered aside to his Lemurian friend, "but *damn*."

They finally ended their inspection of the battlefield at the south-central breastworks as the sun sank below the treetops. That's where they found General Cox. He and his staff were mounted, clustered together, rooted in place, surveying the ghastly scene. The bright green maize field had been trampled and scorched to the ground, and blackened bodies covered it all the way to the distant, blasted forest. Huge carcasses of super lizards and armabueys were everywhere (the Dom commander had sent more), and swirling scavengers, including feral Grikbirds, were feasting on their exploded remains. Smaller scavengers, frighteningly indistinct in the gathering gloom, darted through the stubble, tearing flesh from dead Doms. Occasional shrieks proclaimed that some weren't entirely dead, and Fred was glad to see armed parties bringing wounded in while dragoons scouted the tree line, screening their efforts. Occasionally, he watched a quick bayonet thrust, but supposed that was mercy of another sort.

As was apparent even before they took their position on the right, the fighting along the southern breastworks had been the most intense, where most of the NUS casualties were sustained. While clearly hoping his lancers would break through and wreak havoc in the city, it was here the Dom commander shattered his army, sending wave after wave against what he must've been certain were weakening defenses. Yet, Anson hadn't taken all the reserves and others had stopped serious breakthroughs here as well. On top of that, not only had the attack up the Camino Militar from the east been bloodily repulsed, it *had* been more a demonstration than a serious effort. Cox increasingly shifted troops from there as the battle progressed. Now, though obviously aware he'd won a major victory, it was equally clear Cox never dreamed how horrible it would be and he had no idea what to do next.

"Have we an estimate of the butcher's bill?" Anson asked quietly.

Cox seemed to rouse himself and shook his head. "Preliminary returns indicate as many as four thousand dead. Twice as many wounded." He sighed. "*One-fifth* of my army."

Anson waved at the field. "And the enemy?"

Cox glared at him. "I've no idea. More, I'm sure, if that's any consolation."

"It is," Anson stressed, voice still low. He paused before continuing. "General, I understand we took more than *three thousand* prisoners. They confirm the enemy general—Julio Quonik de Quito—attacked with almost seventy thousand men. My scouts, and other men they've captured, confirm that less than a third of that force left the field today"—he pointed east—"and the only ones to do so in reasonably good order were part of the force dedicated to the feint. *Not* the enemy's best troops. The rest are scattered, disorganized. And thanks to Colonel Hara's artillery on the right"—he nodded at

Fred and Kari—"and some timely support from the air, almost all de Quito's lancers are destroyed or captured."

"What're you saying, Captain?" a colonel sitting astride his horse next to Cox inquired.

Anson took a breath. "We must, of course, reorganize and regroup, see to our wounded, and replace lost mounts and draft animals. Fortunately, we captured more than enough horses to accomplish the latter. But then we should immediately press the enemy, push them aside from our line of march, and prevent them from reconsolidating behind hasty fortifications in our path."

Cox seemed stunned. "You're mad. We can't *advance*! What of our wounded? Our supplies?"

Kari snorted. "Whaat supplies, aafter this? Don Hernaan'll squall like a stuck rhino pig an' *Leopaardo*'ll haave to get off her ass an' do somethin'. Only supplies you'll get now're comin' behind Gener-aal Shinyaa—an' he ain't comin' *here*, is he?"

Cox looked at her and shook his head. "How do you know that? They just told us."

Kari flipped her tail. "'Cause Shinyaa goes for the throat—like you gotta do."

After a moment, Cox shook his head. "Impossible. Didn't you hear? We've lost twenty percent of our effective strength and used a quarter of our ammunition. We'd have to leave our wounded behind, and even if this was the biggest army the Doms could muster against us, General Mayta will follow. Anyone we left would be at his mercy and we might get caught out on the march. And what if our prisoners rise up?" he added, shaking his head. "We dare not abandon El Palo."

Unlike Fred or Kari, Anson had seen reports of what Shinya intended to do. "Two regiments will be sufficient to guard our wounded and prisoners from efforts to harass—or liberate them. And since there were no Blood Drinkers on the field today, I doubt many of our prisoners would much welcome 'liberation' in any event. They *did* lose, you know, and the enemy frowns on that. If it came to it, they'd probably defend this place from our enemies as desperately as we would.

"Otherwise, I suspect General Shinya's right. Mayta will have little choice but to pursue *him* or be evacuated to raise a new force to stop him, us, and the two corps that'll join us before we reach their Temple City."

Cox hesitated. Anson had obviously made his decision and might even *relieve* him if he objected too strenuously. Cox didn't know if his authority was quite that broad, but wasn't willing to press it. Just as important, he really was good at what he did and saw the sense in Anson's proposal. It was just so very risky! "How far must Shinya come?" he equivocated. "Perhaps we could wait for him here. March on the temple together."

Fred caught himself rolling his eyes, then studiously avoided Cox's gaze.

"With respect, General," Anson said mildly, "not only would that leave the enemy *you* broke here today too much time to recover, but General Shinya's already heading southeast. Such a change would require that he march all the way around Mayta at El Henal and back up here, adding *weeks* to his advance, to no purpose." His voice hardened. "We must join *him*, and do it quickly. The most important thing I learned while conferring with our allies," he said, referencing the time he spent with Shinya, Jenks, and Blair when Fred and Kari flew him across to do so, "is the Doms have learned how to fight. More than we did in this one battle." He looked south. "General de Quito's initial plan and maneuvers showed talent. He could've kept us pinned here indefinitely." He looked back at Cox. "Fortunate for us he was a little *too* aggressive, and just as inexperienced as we. We can't expect that again, and the longer we give the enemy to regroup, the harder and bloodier our advance will be."

"So you'd have *us* be 'too aggressive' in response," Cox suggested darkly. He held up his hand, conceding that pursuing a broken force was different from assaulting a fortified position. "But what of General Mayta?" Cox objected once more.

"Let General Shinya worry about him."

CHAPTER 9

/////// El Henal
Holy Dominion
May 9, 1945

Despite all his rationalizations, General Anselmo Mayta remained surprised he was still alive. He'd been appointed Supreme Commander of All the Armies of God by His Supreme Holiness Himself, but never personally enjoyed the presence of the Emperor of the World, and rather doubted the "Messiah of Mexico" had ever even heard of him. The appointment was based entirely on the good opinion of Don Hernan. And what had Mayta done to keep it? He'd lost El Corazon, the literal heart of the Holy Dominion in the northwest, and the enemy had complete control of the vitally strategic El Paso del Fuego. Without the aid of the League of Tripoli, the heretics could pounce at will upon any part of the Dominion. *Have pounced already,* Mayta grimly reminded himself, *at El Palo and now Monsu, and there's nothing I can do about it. So, stuck between two enemy forces, with mere militia and conscripts to command, I doubt Don Hernan has spared me sufficient thought to order my execution.*

Striding across the damp cobbles in the center of El Henal, he tried not to step in anything too unpleasant while avoiding the smelly mass of people—and all the beasts to feed them—they'd gathered from the countryside to bolster the defenses. His immaculate uniform coat and shiny, expensive shoes were the only things he'd brought from El Corazon, flying out on one of the greater dragons. He'd commandeered hose, trousers, and numerous shirts, even a replacement hat, but no one in the backwater city of El Henal could replace his shoes and coat.

With three greater dragons and two riders still at his disposal, he *had* managed a couple of worthwhile things. He'd dutifully sent a detailed report of the fall of El Corazon to Don Hernan, remaining as objective as he could. He'd accepted blame, of course, but bluntly hinted most should rest on the shoulders of the Blood Drinker General Allegria (one of Don Hernan's many sons). It had been his actions at the height of the battle that turned the city populace against them, and victory became impossible. He'd supposed that if he was to be impaled, he may as well tell the truth. To his astonishment, the dragon actually returned, its rider bearing a hand-scrawled note from Don Hernan that said, "See to the defenses at El Henal. General de Quito will deal with the heretics at El Palo." There'd been nothing about hanging himself or surrendering to the local Blood Priests to be burned alive. Nothing else at all. *He'll get around to it sooner or later,* Mayta had decided.

That was before Shinya landed at Monsu, however. He'd sent word of that as well, but there'd been no reply. He'd used his other rider and two greater dragons to scout the enemy as often as they were able. He knew from his own single, terrifying flight that dragons tired quickly and just hanging on and forcefully directing the recalcitrant beasts was exhausting for a rider. But he'd discovered the approximate size of Shinya's force—surely his veteran X Corps—and determined El Henal was his only possible objective. That was just as well. He'd begun improving the city's defenses the day he arrived and actually had more troops under arms than Shinya. That was small consolation, since he knew X Corps' quality (man and . . . beast) and had no doubt it could take El Henal with relative ease. But Anselmo Mayta could *bleed* X Corps and take comfort from that before he died like a soldier. *Far* better than shrieking and writhing on an impaling pole for hours, maybe days . . .

"My General!" came a wispy, breathless call behind him.

Mayta drew himself to an impatient stop and turned. "What is it, Colonel Yanaz?" he asked, harsher than intended. Yanaz was the startlingly corpulent *alcalde* of El Henal and fancied himself a military man. So much so that in the current emergency, he'd asked to be addressed by the traditional militia rank all *alcaldes* held. Mayta had to admit he'd done good work stockpiling supplies, and been as accommodating as possible when it came to defensive modifications to the city despite the cloud over Mayta's head. But he simply looked ridiculous. His tailored uniform fit well enough, even if it made him look like a yellow gourd, but the tails were too long, almost dragging the ground, probably intended to make him look thinner and more dashing. His sword *did* drag.

"General Mayta," Yanaz wheezed, trying to catch his breath. His voice was so quiet there was no telling how long he'd been chasing him, calling out. "Colonel Fuerte *insists* you make time to dine with him, and now I've been called upon by the Patriarca of the Blood Priests to intervene with you on Fuerte's behalf!" Yanaz sounded afraid, as well he might, but Mayta's expression turned to stone. Fuerte was a Blood Drinker. Anselmo Mayta remained devout in his belief that suffering was the price of entry to the afterlife, but he'd had an epiphany after El Corazon. If God truly required as much wanton suffering as the Blood Priests and their elite warriors claimed, and if He was truly on their side (a recurring, unbidden doubt he could *never* share), then He should've had His fill of blood at El Corazon—and Mayta would've won. He'd begun to suspect instead that God's *true* servants in this life, those most often called upon for sacrifice, probably earned sufficient cumulative Grace in their short, harsh existence without any help from the Church.

"I regret you've been disturbed, Colonel Yanaz. Please explain to the Patriarca, however, that it was a Blood Drinker—and his troops—who lost El Corazon, so I have little regard for them as soldiers. Moreover, since Fuerte has only a single company of Blood Drinkers here, he's of little utility and has no place in the command structure. I'm far too busy and poorly inclined to waste time staring at *any* man while he sips wine and chews his food just now."

Yanaz looked horrified. "I can't tell him that!" he blurted. Even an *alcalde* wasn't safe from charges of heresy by the lowliest Blood Drinker, and the Patriarca of a city could have virtually anyone "sacrificed" at whim. Anyone except Anselmo Mayta, it seemed, as long as he held His Supreme Holiness's commission. Mayta had developed an abiding hatred for Blood Drinkers and was perversely enjoying tweaking Colonel Fuerte. Particularly since it was understood that "dine with him" really meant Mayta should present himself. He'd never do that.

Mayta waved it away. "Of course not. Don't worry. If they press you again, tell them you passed the request," he smiled, "but even you had to chase me down to do it. I'm quite engaged in attempting to defend them, after all." He clenched his teeth. "I'll be happy to speak with Fuerte as well, if he can catch me as ably as you." He took a breath. "Come, I'll show you what we're working on today: a lovely entanglement that should funnel the enemy directly into our guns."

Walking slower so Yanaz could keep up, Mayta led him through the (apologetically when they passed) bustling crowd in the center of the city to an open courtyard behind one of the walls that was being strengthened on both sides to protect it from artillery fire. Men not working were training with shiny new muskets (of the older style) in the courtyard, learning to load them and clear misfires. They were peasants mostly, even a few slaves, donated by their masters. Mayta wouldn't trust any of them in isolated positions, but he'd made it clear what fate awaited if they didn't do their duty. He paused at the base of a sloping earthen berm, checking to see if it was packed hard enough that his precious shoes wouldn't sink before climbing to the top. There was a wide fighting position there, and masons were shaping stone-framed firing slits on the outer edge. He pretended not to notice Yanaz's huffing as the man labored up behind him.

"Excellent protection here for marksmen," he said, pointing, "and troops can move quickly from one point on the wall to another."

"But their flying machines drop bombs," Yanaz gasped.

"There'll be overhead protection, sloping away. Most of their bombs should be directed outside the walls." He tried to sound confident but both men knew there'd be no overhead protection for the city itself, and bombs dropping *behind* the walls would slaughter anyone near. *All the more reason for people to defend the walls,* Mayta supposed. *They might be the safest places.* "That said," he assured, "only a very few enemy flying machines have been seen at Monsu, and those must've flown across from Manizales. They probably positioned a little fuel and ordnance during their landing, but can't have a large reserve. Nor do they have many flying machines left," he added confidently. "They may prove a nuisance, but I wouldn't worry overmuch about them if I were . . ." His voice trailed off and he peered behind them to the east. At first he thought he'd cursed them with his assurances and two of the smaller enemy planes were swooping toward them. Then one briefly flapped its wings and he realized the shapes were greater dragons. "Clear the courtyard at once!" he bellowed below. "Dragons coming in!"

He didn't have to say it twice. All dragons were hungry when they landed, but those large enough to carry a man were even less patient than their smaller cousins and wouldn't hesitate to snatch the first thing to appear in front of their toothy snouts. *Even so,* Mayta considered with disapproval, viewing the panic with which the courtyard emptied, *a most unseemly display.*

The dragons flared out over the courtyard and descended with considerable commotion, stirring dusty gusts with their flapping wings. Handlers rushed in before they could light, each towing a pair of protesting goats. Swiftly slashing the animal's throats, they retreated to a safe distance. Immediately upon landing, even before folding their rather spindly-looking forty-foot wings, each beast seized a still thrashing goat and began chewing ravenously. The offering wouldn't sate their hunger but would put them in a more manageable frame of mind. It would also distract them while their riders dropped to the ground and hurried, wobble-legged, toward General Mayta and Colonel Yanaz. Gaining the fighting position, the flyers bowed, and one Mayta didn't recognize opened a leather tube hanging from a strap and handed him a scroll. He noted with familiar distaste that it was made of human skin, tightly rolled, and closed with Don Hernan's own elaborate seal. Trying to touch the macabre parchment as lightly as he could, he took the scroll but didn't open it. Instead, he turned to the flyer he'd sent to observe Shinya at Monsu.

"Why did you approach from the east?" he demanded.

"Actually, Lord General, I flew up from the south. Since no roads are visible beneath the cloak of trees, I had only my compass, the sun, and unfamiliar mountains to guide me. I struck the coast east of here where I met this other courier"—he nodded at his companion—"and we proceeded here together."

"South?" Mayta exclaimed, confused. "Whatever for? Your assignment was to view the enemy preparations at Monsu."

The flyer bowed again. "I did, Lord, and saw they've established respectable defenses facing east, toward us, and north toward the sea. Behind them they've started great pits and are gathering heavy materials to cover them. I imagine they're intended as shelters for troops and supplies against heavy bombardment."

Mayta nodded. Shinya had no reason to fear the Dominion Navy anymore, but he knew their greater dragons could drop a couple of bombs. And Los Diablos del Norte would certainly have informed him of *Leopardo*. Just as Mayta prayed for them, Shinya doubtless expected more League ships to arrive as well. The Shinya that Mayta had come to know without ever meeting him in person would take precautions against their powerful guns.

"What of the enemy army? Has it begun its advance?"

The flyer shifted uncomfortably. "Yes, Lord General, and it has made surprising progress."

Despite the damp morning heat, Mayta felt a chill. "How soon will it get here, do you think?" The flyer's face betrayed anguish, as if he feared Mayta's response to the news he brought. "Come now, our preparations proceed apace. It can't be that bad."

"My General," the man began, "I don't think the enemy is coming *here*."

Mayta simply looked at him and blinked. "Where else . . . ? I can't imagine . . ." He suddenly froze and his eyes narrowed. "Shinya has plunged into the forest, hasn't he? Angling southeast!"

"Yes, My General. It was difficult to tell for certain at first—the trees are so dense—but I caught glimpses of enemy movement as much as two hundred and sixty *leguas* almost due south of here."

"That's . . . a-amazing," Colonel Yanaz stuttered, and Mayta couldn't tell if he was alarmed or relieved.

"My General," interjected the other flyer, the one who'd brought the scroll. "I too have a . . . disconcerting report. It seems General de Quito fared . . . poorly in his battle with Los Diablos at El Palo. There was news of this at El Penon before I left, but I personally viewed shattered troops straggling along the shoreline." He shifted uncomfortably. "They appeared to be scrounging for dead fish on the beach." Mayta said nothing, but if that was true, de Quito's force had been broken completely and even his baggage was lost. The flyer continued relentlessly. "Overflying El Palo, it was clear there'd been a great battle and the city was still in the hands of Los Diablos"—he nodded at his fellow aviator—"but many of their troops were already gone. Based on the movement of wagons and those protecting them, I also got the impression they were moving south."

"Toward El Templo de Los Papas," Mayta murmured, suddenly blindingly certain, and he found himself strangely conflicted. Not only was he stunned by the realization, but also by the fact he couldn't help but admire the enemy's audacity.

"Then we have no choice," Colonel Yanaz began, his voice pitched high. "If the heretics have bypassed us, *you* must pursue them, General Mayta! They *can't* be allowed closer to the Holy City of Nuevo Granada itself!"

Shaking his head impatiently, Mayta tore the seal off the scroll and spread the tanned, crinkly skin. Everyone, even Yanaz, recoiled, clutching the jagged crosses they wore. It was considered sacrilege to allow sunlight to touch the written words of any Blood Cardinal, let alone those of Don Hernan. Such were to be read only by firelight in otherwise darkened rooms to simulate the heavenly underworld. Mayta ignored their reaction and quickly scanned the page. Finally, he grunted with surprise. Smiling oddly, he looked at Yanaz. "It seems I won't be with you much longer, and can't 'pursue' anyone." His smile grew broader. "Nor will the Patriarca have me for his fires or impaling pole. I've been recalled to Puerto del Cielo and ultimately the Temple City to prepare defenses there. By Don Hernan himself. I've no idea how he expects to move me," he added abstractly, glancing nervously at the dragons, but continued wryly, "yet, unhappy as he must be with me, I imagine he's even less pleased with General de Quito at the moment. And I did at least inconvenience the enemy a time or two. His Holiness 'prays I've learned from my experience.'"

"But what will we do here?" Yanaz demanded. Faced with Mayta's departure, his belligerent call to action turned to caution. "What if it's merely a ruse and the heretics come here after all?"

"They won't." Mayta rubbed his chin in thought and actually chuckled. "But you're right. They must be followed. Perhaps it *is* time I met with Colonel Fuerte and the Patriarca. We'll give them half your men, Colonel Yanaz. Only the very best, of course," he added with a veiled hint of sarcasm. "*They* will hunt General Shinya and Los Diablos down! I'm sure they'll enjoy it immensely." He caught the panicky look on Yanaz's face and formed a concerned expression. "No, no, Colonel, much as I know you yearn to join them, even command the expedition, I trust only you to hold El Henal when I depart. Objections will do you no good. Someone responsible must always stay behind."

CHAPTER 10

////// Lake Galk
Grik Africa
May 9, 1945

Wearing only a pair of ragged shorts made from his flight coveralls, "General of the Sky" Mitsuo Ando wiped at sweat gushing from his torso with his balled-up shirt, but all it did was smear the salty stream around. At least he was out of the sun, down in the cavernous armored casemate of Supreme Regent General Esshk's huge new flagship, supervising the loading of its primary weaponry. But the heat and humidity were still stifling. And the smell! The hundreds of Grik Uul workers under Ando's supervision relieved themselves wherever they stood, and he had to use other Uul solely to clean up the mess. It made little difference. He sighed, trying not to breathe too deeply.

The huge ship had been designed and partially built as just another ironclad "greatship of battle," festooned with monstrous muzzle-loading guns, but Ando and his four Japanese companions had designed new weapons called *yanone*, hopefully more lethal to the enemy than to the ship that fired them. *Yanone* were essentially a combination of enlarged, solid-fuel rockets like the Grik so profligately flung at aircraft, mated to remodeled versions of the flying bombs used earlier in the war, dropped from swarms of zeppelins. But the zeppelins were nearly all gone, and Ando and his people had come up with another way to deliver the weapons—and their suicidal pilots.

Yanone required large, stable launch platforms, invisible or invulnerable to marauding aircraft. And originally intended as offensive weapons, they had to be mobile. Offense was a forgotten dream, for now, but putting them in ships, open at both ends, remained the best way to move *yanone*, protect and aim them, even hide them from the air. And this was the second of only two *yanone* carriers Esshk was likely to have before he had to use them. Ando didn't think they'd be enough.

"Esshk is here," hissed Lieutenant Ueda. The youngster was Ando's XO, primarily (as far as they were concerned) of the little squadron of five Muriname-designed AJ1M1c fighter planes they'd brought over to the Grik. Ando and his four remaining people were still tortured by that choice and would un-make it if they could, but believed Muriname hadn't left them an alternative. Ando hissed, watching the tall, powerful leader of the Grik faction he "belonged to" approach. Esshk was surrounded by sycophantic courtiers, as usual, and despite a strange . . . benevolence he'd displayed around Ando of late, he looked as frightening as ever. Polished armor and a bright red cloak couldn't make the furry reptilian monster any less intimidating. He and his hangers-on surged through the working Uul, which immediately flung themselves to the putrid deck at their feet, and soon stood before Ando and Ueda.

Esshk was looking at the five *yanone* suspended overhead—only one remained to install—angled upward toward the bow. Sleek, lethal-looking little rocket planes pointed at the opening in the forward casemate. The exhaust funnels had been trunked and diverted and the framework bracing the launch tracks was tied directly into the knees once supporting the gun deck. This was more than ample, since in addition to the load of the deck itself, they would've sustained hundreds of tons of iron guns. Esshk swept his gaze back to Ando and his slit pupils narrowed.

"Almost loaded, I see," he said. "Is the ship ready to get underway?"

Ando nodded, a little hesitantly. "It is. Do you intend to move it?"

Both *yanone* missile ships were carefully concealed, snugged against the shore of an inlet on the east side of the lake where there were still plenty of trees. These had been pulled over on top of the ships and more branches brought in and tied all over them. And there were quite a few "decoy" ships, unfinished or unpowered but made to look operational, scattered around the lake, sure to focus the enemy's attention. Ando was sure the missile ships would be seen as well, eventually, as soon as the Allies brought their smaller planes close enough to linger over the lake and search at low altitude. But the big four-engine planes were too vulnerable to antiair missiles and had to stay high.

"I intend to *use* them soon," Esshk said.

Ando shook his head, uncertain he understood. "Against what? The enemy's First Fleet has departed. And no targets of consequence are in range."

"They will be," Esshk retorted darkly. "There are still at least *two* heavily armored enemy vessels, in addition to ours they've captured. *One* tested the river defenses and steamed almost close enough for a *yanone* to reach, had the carriers been in position on the south end of the lake." Esshk waved a clawed hand as if it were of no importance. "It was repulsed, and reports differ on how much damage it received, but it will come again, probably with its companion and other ships as well. When they do, we must be ready." He clacked his frightening teeth together. "I need not remind you of the consequences if the enemy passes the locks and gains access to Lake Galk itself. The Great Hunt and the Way of our race could be ended forever."

Ando didn't care what happened to the Grik race, but he'd given his word to serve Esshk and that was all he had left. "What of General Ign? Aren't he and General Halik hastening here?"

Esshk growled. "Ign still attempts to elude pursuit. He crossed Lake Nalak and evaded one enemy force, only to be blocked by another." He snorted. "Ign is my finest general, but he may be spent."

"And Halik?"

Esshk shifted, and from what little Ando understood of Grik expressions, he looked troubled. "He comes, as summoned," he said at last, "but hasn't openly declared for me. I don't understand," he complained. "And he only has a hundred thousands. I thought he'd bring more." Esshk appeared to brighten. "Then again, he's had to fight through numerous treacherous regencies. Why do that if he won't support me? Perhaps *that's* why he hasn't declared: to avoid combat when he can and bring me as many warriors as possible!" Esshk snorted and a string of snot arced out of a nostril on his snout, almost spattering Ando. He recoiled, but Esshk didn't notice. "Obedience to the Celestial Blood," his voice turned harsh, "even when it runs through a treacherous hatchling, is always blindest on the edges of the empire."

Esshk looked back at Ando, confident again. "Halik comes, but we must hold until he gets here. And I have to be ready to use the *yanone* against the armored ships, or any large enemy concentrations."

Ando glanced at Ueda and scratched his head behind his ear. The ship was infested with vermin. He was sure the *yanone* could smash the Republic monitors, or any other ships the enemy sent, but Esshk still didn't get it. Against infantry, they might slaughter a hundred troops if they were gathered close together—*if* the pilot saw them fast enough to aim himself at them—but they wouldn't break a regiment, much less an army. And not only did each ship carry only six, it took hours to reload them! He sighed inwardly. *We've been over this so many times, it's pointless to argue further.*

"Regardless," Ueda ventured carefully, "once you reveal the *yanone* and their carriers, the enemy will hunt them relentlessly. You'll only get to use them once."

If Esshk could've smiled, he would have. "Ah! Exactly why I'm here!" He gestured around. "Your task is complete and you're relieved of this burden I know you've chafed against; released back to your flock of flying machines!" His eyes focused on Ando. "You're my General of the Sky, after all, not an auger worm, boring through ships' timbers! When I use the *yanone, you'll* protect the carriers with your magnificent planes!"

Ando stared. *Protect them with my* five *planes.* They had plenty of fuel, not very good, but better than what had been available, carted down from Kakag where Muriname left a cache. But they only had enough 7.7 mm ammunition for *maybe* two loadouts, per plane. Even if he'd known how, it would've been impossible to recreate the industry Kurokawa established on Zanzibar. Again, with no other alternative, Ando bowed. "May I ask, Lord Regent General . . ." He licked his lips. "What if my few planes can't protect the *yanone* carriers? What if General Halik doesn't come in time? What if . . . despite all we do, all is lost?"

Ando had heard Esshk himself speculate about that before, but this was probably the first time an underling dared to pose the question. Esshk's shiny black crest flared above his head, but the tension eased just slightly. "I've given that thought, General of the Sky, and determined that, one way or another, *I will not lose.* Yours is not the only project to insure that," he added cryptically. "I prefer to reconquer the world as it was, and restore . . . *much* of what my race has been." His voice began to rise. "But if this regency, my final lair, appears ready to fall into the claws of the enemy—of *prey* . . ." He caught himself, calmed himself, and when he continued, his voice was flat. "I'll preside over the utter destruction, not only of the enemy and those of our race who collaborate with them, but of Old Sofesshk, the Palace of Vanished Gods . . . *everything* the Gharrichk'k to the south have ever been. I'll build a *new* Way, a new empire atop the bones of the old." He eyed Ando curiously. "You can be part of that. If you live."

Suddenly chilled beneath his sweat, Ando could only bow. He knew the *yanone* hadn't been Esshk's final bolt. He was a general, after all, and a fairly good one as Grik went. As soon as Sofesshk fell, he'd begun preparations for his final defense in a reasonable fashion that made good use of his position, as well as the bounty of heavy guns he'd stripped from otherwise useless ships. But Ando was mystified by this last revelation, and had no idea whether Esshk could really do it, or had finally gone entirely mad.

CHAPTER 11

////// *USS* Walker
Soonda Strait

Goddamn paperwork!" Chief Isak Reuben snapped at Tabby in his reedy drawl when she cycled through the airlock into the aft fireroom. With numbers three and four boilers both lit, the heat that struck her was oppressive, instantly wetting her gray fur with foamy sweat. An "ex-pat Impie gal" water tender named Sureen caught her gaze and rolled her eyes before glaring at Isak, who stood on the grating between the boilers like a scrawny troll, menacing her with a clipboard.

"No 'good morning, Lieuten-aant Tabby, how're you todaay?' Just . . ."

"Goddamn paperwork!" Isak repeated, belligerently whacking the clipboard against a fuel flow valve. Sureen sighed and inspected the valve. Like so many others, it was worn, leaky, and loose. Vibration alone was often enough to move it, alternately starving or overfeeding the boiler. The latter would quickly be noticed by lookouts above when black smoke swirled from the number three stack. Satisfied, the girl eased out of the path of Isak's wrath. Seeing Sureen in her virtually translucent sweat-soaked T-shirt brought Tabby an instant of nostalgic, bittersweet amusement, reminding her of when she first started working in the hellish firerooms with Isak and his half brother Gilbert. She'd been their student then, almost their pet, and they vicariously gloried in the way she tormented Spanky, who had her job then, by going topless. At the peak of the "dame famine," she knew she'd tempted him, but he'd resisted. Oddly, somehow, that made her love him. And he'd eventually come to love her too—in a frustratingly different sort of way. *All so long ago,* she lamented, *an' Spaanky figures it's settled—but I still feel the same.* She shook her head and prepared to receive Isak's rant.

"Look at all this," he snarled, ruffling the pages with grimy fingers. "Whaddaya even *need* it for? I tell you all the shit in here at quarters ever'day. I thought they made me chief 'cause I'm good at what I do, but all I *get* to do is scribble on these goddamn sheets while ever'thing falls apart! Better when I was just another snipe, fixin' shit when it broke." Tabby thought he might already be winding down when he took a PIG-cig from behind his ear and lit it, adding its acrid smoke to the steam, sweat, oil, hot iron, and bilgewater stink of the compartment. Unfortunately, he was just getting started. "We're buildin' ships, guns, stupid *airplanes*, fightin' half a dozen wars at once, an' some dope comes up with the bright idea to make flappin' *paper*, so half o' ever'body oughta be fightin' can spend all their time scratchin' on it! An' what good does it do?" he demanded. "We been steamin' without a break for the better part of a month an' can't really fix nothin'. Number two's cold, so we can work on it, but it's the queen, with the least wrong with it! These two bitches"—he whacked the boilers on either side of him—"ain't really mean." He paused thoughtfully. "Actually, they're in pretty good shape, considerin'. That last overhaul's holdin' up okay. They're just tired." His face clouded and he pointed at the fuel flow valve with his smoldering PIG-cig. "But there was a lotta little shit *Tarakan Island* didn't have for us—or didn't have *left* after they showered it all on that shit-heap *Ellie*." He sneered. "Oughta scrap that useless bucket an' start over."

Tabby was blinking exasperation and nodding, while inwardly amused by Isak's stubborn insularity. It wouldn't do for her to defend USS *James Ellis* by pointing out that, aside from some engineering issues (the only kind that mattered to Isak), *Walker*'s first "daughter" on this world was better than her "mother" in almost every way. A quarter century younger and more imaginatively framed—not to mention she hadn't been rebuilt from wreckage more than once—she was certainly stronger.

"I know, I know, an' we caan't secure another boiler an' still maintain twelve knots. Not an' make enough auxiliaary steam for all the other leaky, worn-out stuff, like pumps an' generators . . . I *know*, Isaak. An' the paperwork ain't my idea." She flicked her tail and confessed, "I caan only baarely read it myself. 'Course, thaat might be because o' your crummy writing," she teased with a toothy grin, but pointed at the clipboard. "Thaat's all goin' to the yaard apes when we get to Baalkpan. Think of it as a Kiss-muss list. Scuttlebutt is, *Ellie*'s gettin' new reduction gears, *Saavoie*'ll haave all her fire control issues sorted out, an' *we're* gonna haave *weeks* in dry dock. Every wish in your weird head is gonna come true." She blinked slyly and narrowed her eyes. "How'd you like to haave a braand-new *number one* boiler, instead o' thaat auxiliaary fuel taank in the forwaard fireroom?"

Isak blinked surprise in the Lemurian way. "I thought we was keepin' that damn thing forever, sacrificin' a few knots for range."

"Yaah, but despite how faar we haave to go, we won't need the range as much anymore. Mr.—I mean, Chair-maan—Letts's been sendin' oilers east for a long time. On top o' thaat, the Impies're gettin' oil from their colonies an' all their new ships burn it." Tabby shrugged. "Once we get through the Paass o' Fire, there's the Nussies. They already use oil, an' haave it at all their ports."

Isak sucked in a lungful of smoke and screwed his face into a thoughtful frown. "So the Skipper thinks we'll need the speed more than the miles. I like it, but I ain't sure I like why."

"Yaah." Tabby shifted to stand under one of the blower vents. "Look, you'll be able to give number three a rest pretty soon. Thaat make you haappy?"

Isak looked at her suspiciously. "Why?"

Tabby blinked. "Because we're almost there!"

"There where?"

"Jeez," Tabby said, shaking her head. "Don't you even know where we are?"

Isak blinked noncommittally. "Somewhere in the Indian—Western—Ocean?"

"We're in the Soondaa Straait! B'taava, by daark." She looked around at the single Lemurian and two Impies in the compartment. All were female and completely competent. *I wonder if Isaak even notices 'em?* she asked herself. *He was sweet on Sureen for a while, but I don't know if anything ever came o' thaat. Maybe he still is, an' just never told her—or he did, and she brushed him off? He* is *Isak, after all.* She shook her head, deciding. "C'mon up on deck. Somethin' neat you oughta' see. It's Sureen's waatch anyway, an' you're just buggin' your snipes." She patted him fondly on the shoulder. "You gotta get out more!"

The deck hatch opened under the motor whaleboat on the starboard side of the ship, between the amidships deckhouse and number one quadruple torpedo mount. Tabby luxuriated in the cool breeze evaporating sweat from her fur and clothes as she climbed on deck alongside the number three and four stacks. She wondered—again—how her people could stand living in the cramped, skinny ship. How did she? Lemurians were almost universally prone to claustrophobia, but none, given the chance, ever hesitated to serve in *Walker*, and now other ships like her. Granted, females did better belowdecks, but she'd always written that off to the fact they were smaller and there was less heavy work to do. Conversely, she'd known only a handful of Lemurian males to thrive in the engineering spaces. It didn't matter. The confines there never much bothered Tabby, and *Walker* always needed more hands topside.

Isak joined her, blinking like a mole, and they caught cooking smells sweeping back from Earl Lanier's galley under the deckhouse. Earl was a jerk, still somewhat obsessed with maintaining a small, battered, red refrigerator with "Coca-Cola" painted on the side. As far as Tabby knew, he never actually put anything in it. He could cook, though. Not that anyone would ever admit it, of course. "Not chowtime yet," Tabby said, doubting Isak had any idea what time it was, "but there's always saammitches. Waant one?"

"Nah." Isak was looking south to starboard, at a jungle-choked shore. A couple of mountains soared high and purple in the hazy distance, but the coastal land beneath the trees seemed relatively flat. "Big deal," he said. "I seen plenty o' jungle islands. Too many boogers. Too many goddamn trees. Who'd ever wanna go there? You'd get ate by somethin' before you took a dozen paces."

"Not thaat way, stupid," Tabby chided, leading to port, past the vegetable lockers, over the peak of the crowned deck, and finally past the portside torpedo mount to the rail. "There," she urged, flicking her ears northwest. Ten or twelve miles away, a dark, conical mountain rose straight out of the sea, thin brown smoke spiraling endlessly into the sky from a summit perhaps five thousand feet high. And ribboning its steep flanks, glowing bright as blood against the soot-black cone, rivers of lava flowed down to touch the water and form a misty shroud for the shore. It was so striking at first glance, only a longer inspection revealed smaller islands surrounding it. All except the monster in their midst were as green and lush as the shore to starboard.

"I'll be," Isak mumbled.

"Why, if it ain't ol' Isak, rose up from his steamy iron tomb!" came a loud voice, and Isak saw Dennis Silva, Lawrence, and Pam Cross approaching from under the deckhouse. Silva looked up and ostentatiously blinked his good eye, pretending to flinch from the sun. The fuzzy lizard around his neck did the same—but it always looked where Silva did. "An' it ain't even dark!"

"Can it, Dennis," Pam growled. "No wonder he never comes out, the way everybody pesters him."

Isak shrugged. He didn't care what people thought. "What's that?" he asked.

"A vol-caano," Tabby told him.

"I know *that*, but . . . damn, I never seen one *bleed*."

Silva spat a thick stream of yellowish Aryaalan tobacco juice over the side and grunted. "That ain't blood, you idiot." Pam poked him savagely in the ribs with her sharp elbow and gave him a harsh look.

"I know that too, you overgrown possum," Isak replied through clenched teeth. "I just . . . never seen its like."

"You will, though, what I hear," Silva told him, tone more serious. "There's another whopper on the Pacific side o' the Pass o' Fire. The strait's tighter than this there too, an' we're goin' through it. Gives me the quivers." He pretended to shake, then grinned and pointed. "On the other hand, you asked what that was, an' best I can tell from the charts, it's Krakatoa."

Isak gulped. Every sailor in the Asiatic Fleet had heard tales of Krakatoa's 1883 eruption; how it blew up bigger than all the bombs ever made, loud enough to be heard around the world, and sent tidal waves high enough to plop a Dutch gunboat a hundred miles inland on Java. Isak figured many of the tales had been exaggerated, but didn't know which ones, or how much. "So . . . if it blew up, what's it doin' here?"

Silva rolled his eye. "Different world, remember? It just didn't go off on this one . . . yet." He grinned again. "It's *way* bigger here too. When it does pop, I bet it's twice as bad!" He squinted. "Looks about ready, if you ask me."

"Oh, knock it off," Pam scolded, exasperated.

"An' how much farther is this joint we're headed?"

"We'll anchor in Soonda Bay, off B'taava. I don't know. Maybe eighty, a hundred miles?" Isak seemed to relax. "Which won't make any difference, o' course," Silva continued. "Wall o' water a thousand feet high? Ha! It'll wash us away like a soap flake in the tub."

"Not a gag," Lawrence said, voice flat, and Silva nodded thoughtfully. They'd survived a volcano-stirred tidal wave on Yap Island together, and Lawrence's people—they'd been Tagranesi then, not Sa'aarans—were virtually wiped out.

"No," Silva agreed. "Not funny at all, I s'pose." He nodded at the diminishing mountain of fire. "It prob'ly won't do nothin', an' we won't be at B'taava long. Just take on fuel. Maybe some grub. Skipper's whuppin' the horses hard. Ever' day it takes to get to Baalkpan is one less we have to get from there to wherever the hell else we're goin'."

"An' one day less we get in the yaard, I bet," Tabby agreed.

"Could be," Silva granted, "but I don't think so, this time. He's in a hurry, sure, but I get the feelin' he wants this old tin can readier to fight than she's ever been. Figgers she's gonna need to be."

Petey had raised his head, sniffing, probably smelling Earl's cooking. "Eat?" he inquired, almost politely.

"Not yet, dumb-ass."

Isak watched the exchange with interest. "You really talk to that thing," he said. "I mean, it understands you?"

Pam laughed. "Sure, a real meeting of the minds. An' he talks back too," she added with a measure of satisfaction.

"Almost as much as you, doll," Silva quipped.

"I used to talk to Grikky," Isak confessed, reminding them he'd once caught and partially tamed a baby Grik. "I thought he understood me," he added, glaring aft at *Savoie*, "until that bastard Laney murdered him." Dean Laney was *Savoie*'s engineering officer now.

"Let it go," Tabby advised. "Laney'll always be an aasshole, but he paid his bill in *Saanty Caat*."

Isak scratched the thin, scruffy beard on his chin, then looked back at Petey. "You let me watch him once, remember? But the only thing he ever said was—"

Pam stopped him. "For God's sake! Don't use the 'E' word! It's one thing if *he* says it and you shut him down. *You* say it, you'll wind him up and he won't quit till he, uh, gets to."

"But he throws out other words. I've heard him."

"Yeah," Silva agreed. "Mostly bad ones, like a parrot, er somethin', but he can tell you stuff too. I figure he's smart as a barn cat, or maybe one o' them stupid little dogs rich broads wag around."

"You think so?"

"Sure. I've even taught him some tricks."

Pam laughed louder. "Like gliding back to the ship after you throw him overboard?"

"Not just that. We're workin' on a new one, might be useful." Silva looked at Lawrence. "Ain't we, Larry?"

Lawrence snorted. "Yes. He'll ne'er do it, though. Not in 'attle. E'en you say he's a 'chicken lizard.' He'll just run a'ay."

"He's reformed," Silva defended, thumping Petey on the head.

"Reformed!" Petey adamantly confirmed.

"Maybe I oughta get me one o' them critters," Isak speculated. "I've seen a few on ships that stopped at Yap on their way back an' forth from the Empire." He lowered his voice. "Pickin' up thorns to make that 'killer kudzu' stuff." "Killer kudzu" was an insidious carnivorous plant infesting a large percentage of Yap Island. It quickly incapacitated its victims with a single thorn, then rapidly spread through their bloodstream and devoured them from the inside. The plant then burst forth from the corpse and spread in all directions, infecting anything it touched. Once considered a viable area denial weapon, the thorns had been carefully collected and various means of deployment explored. But Yap was the only known origin of the plant and the danger of spreading it across entire islands, even continents, ultimately prevented its use—all but once.

"I might buy one off some Impie," Isak continued. "Even if he didn't talk much, it might be like havin' ol' Gilbert around again."

The brow arched over Silva's good eye. "Better, I expect."

"Aw, can't you see Chief Reuben's lonesome?" Pam pronounced, patting Isak on the arm.

The skinny engineer tensed. "Am not!"

"Sure you are!" Pam argued, turning to Silva. "Why don't you just give him the little shit, Dennis?" When she said "little shit," her tone turned malevolent. She didn't like Petey. He knew it and cringed tighter to Silva's neck.

"Can't," Silva simply said. "He ain't mine. I'm just holdin' him for Lady Sandra, who was keepin' him for Governor-Empress Becky, if you recall." Petey did still—technically—belong to Rebecca Anne McDonald, ruler of the Empire of the New Britain Isles, and closest ally of the United Homes. "*Lady* Sandra"—he also stressed the title the Imperials gave Sandra Tucker Reddy—"don't want the gluttonous bastard hoverin' around little Fitzy—with good reason—so I'm stuck witheem."

"Stuck!" Petey boldly chirped at Pam before burrowing tighter around Silva's neck.

Pam blinked and Tabby said, laughing, "I think, like Silvaa, thaat daamn lizaard is smaarter thaan he lets on!"

"Gotta get me one," Isak agreed.

USS *Walker* entered Soonda Bay at dusk, still leading the small convoy of warships. Even though B'taava had once been a fairly prosperous Lemurian land Home, the Grik had swarmed it early in the war, practically exterminating its population, and none of them had ever been here before. An MTB pilot boat was waiting to lead them to the Navy Clan docks. A Morse lamp flashed in the gathering gloom, providing the recognition signal, the boat's number, and a request that *Walker* maintain her current course and speed while the boat came alongside to transfer a pilot.

"Gutsy to hop aboard at twelve knots, even for a 'Cat," Matt remarked when a signal-'Cat on the starboard bridgewing relayed the message.

"Chart says we're about eleven miles from the dock," observed Chief Quartermaster "Paddy" Rosen, looking at the red-lit chart table. "It's tricky water, though. Lots of little islands, with shallows and coral heads. I'd rather have somebody familiar with the place at the wheel, instead of just following a light."

"But why not heave to? Or slow down, at least," asked Commander Bernard "Bernie" Sandison, standing by one of his precious torpedo directors on the starboard wing. They were all reconciled to the terrifying additional hazard of living and fighting in a ship on the insanely predator-rich seas of this world, but why risk falling in the water for something like this?

Matt shook his head. "Probably for the best. Our ships are steaming at pretty tight intervals." That was so they'd never be separated, and less experienced watch standers would get used to close formations. Also because the League possessed *at least* one more submarine, and their fuel constraints had prohibited high speeds and zigzagging. He doubted a sub could operate this far from League support anymore, and the League was probably just as paranoid about losing it as he was to meet it, but if it *was* somehow around, and stuffed a few fish down—probably *Savoie*'s—throat, he wanted the rest of his ships close enough to help with damage control or take off survivors. And kill the sub, of course. "If we stop, we have to stop everyone," he explained. "No big deal, except for Captain Chappelle. His people are still learning how to handle that fat battlewagon. We're going to do a *lot* more maneuvering in formation drills," he resolved aloud. "Call the special sea and anchor detail," he told Minnie the talker behind him, "and have them rig a sea ladder."

Chief Jeek's bosun's pipe trilled on the fo'c'sle, working its way aft through the starboard side bridge hatch. Bare Lemurian feet thundered on the thin steel deck. ('Cats only wore sandals when the steel was broiling under the sun and always shed them after dark.) The MTB had made a wide turn and was closing on *Walker*'s starboard beam just as a wood rung rope ladder unrolled down her side, aft of the bridge. The MTB swept deftly in, and to Matt's surprise, a young *man*, not a Lemurian, snatched the streaming ladder and scurried up as nimbly as a 'Cat.

The MTB peeled off and raced ahead to take its leading position as surprised greetings on the deck below preceded the sound of shoes on metal steps behind the pilothouse. Matt stood to face their visitor and was surprised again. "My God, Nat! What're you doing here?" Lieutenant Commander Nathaniel Hardee, maybe all of seventeen, grinned and pulled his officer's hat out of his shirt and plopped it on his head before saluting. "Request permission to come aboard, sir," he said, smiling, his accent still very British. Of course, he *was* British. He and a bunch of other kids in the care of Sister Audrey had been snuck out of Surabaya in the old *S-19* before the Japanese could catch them. Whether arrival on this world could be considered escape was still debated by some, but not Nat. He and most of those kids had thrived. Abel Cook, about the same age, was a Marine major in Chack's Brigade.

"Of course you're welcome, Mr. Hardee," Matt said more formally, after returning the salute. Nat started buttoning his shirt. "I just wasn't expecting you. I thought you were heading to the Filpin Lands, to command MTB-Ron-5."

"I am, sir, but I'll get there soon enough if I can beg a ride with you to Baalkpan and catch a Clipper from there. My XO is good; she came off the old Fifteen boat. She'll have the newies whipped into shape before I arrive."

"I hope so," Matt said lower, "because we're probably going to need even more out of your new squadron than your old one gave at Zanzibar." Nat nodded. He'd expected as much. "But what're you doing here?" Matt repeated.

Nat grinned. "Right now, I'm your pilot. Shall I?"

"Sure." Matt turned to Commander Toos-Ay-Chil, who had the watch. Toos was a bear-shaped Lemurian, as big and muscular as "Ahd-mi-raal" Keje-Fris-Ar, Matt's best Lemurian friend. He was also the finest damage control officer *Walker* ever had. He was still a little ham-handed on the bridge, however. "Mr. Hardee has the conn," Matt announced.

"Ay, ay, sur. Mr. Haardee haas the conn," Toos replied. "Our course is one, five, seero, making turns for twelve knots."

Nat hesitated ever so slightly. He'd conned stranger things, such as the old *S-19* after her reconfiguration into a surface torpedo boat, but he'd never conned *Walker* before. "This is Mr. Hardee," he said. "I have the conn. Helm, maintain course and follow the stern light of the MTB ahead. Lee helm, stand by to reduce speed." He looked at Matt. "More MTBs will direct the other ships when we get closer to the Navy dock."

"Very well. Pass the word," he told Minnie. "Now, Mr. Hardee, why don't you explain yourself?"

Nat glanced around. "I don't know, sir. I'm on orders. Perhaps we ought to wait until we anchor and catch a private moment before you brief your officers, and those from other ships all at once."

"Orders?"

"Yes sir. From Mr. Stokes." Nat whispered the name, barely audible over the rumbling blower behind the bridge. Henry Stokes was a former Leading Seaman from the Australian light cruiser HMAS *Perth*, sunk with USS *Houston* during a furious night action with the Japanese in the very same nearby strait—on another world. He'd arrived on this one via a quite literally torturous route, as a POW in the hellish Japanese prison ship *Mizuki Maru*, and since become Director of the Office of Strategic Intelligence for the United Homes.

"Oh," was all Matt said. "Very well. Any reason not to gather everybody aboard *Savoie*? Her wardroom's bigger."

"No Leaguers left aboard her at all?" Nat asked.

Puzzled, Matt shook his head. "Not many stayed with her when Gravois gave her to Kurokawa. Any that did, and survived, got shipped back to Baalkpan."

"Yes sir. That's what I thought. Just double-checking. Shouldn't be a problem then."

Matt nodded, troubled now, and wondering what this was all about. Instead of pestering Nat, however, he looked out past the fo'c'sle. There was the blue glass sternlight of the MTB in front of them, but aside from the distant glow of the approaching city, which he couldn't get any sense of in the dark, there were almost no other lights. Not even lanterns rigged out on fishing boats to draw fish into their nets. That was very odd.

"Where's all the water traffic?" he asked. "I know B'taava hasn't been reinhabited long, but I thought the Sularaans were packing it with colonists from Saa-leebs. Ought to be more boats."

"Yes sir," Nat agreed lowly. "All the docks are closed until further notice, and the MTB squadron enforces it. Mr. Stokes authorized deadly force if necessary."

"Oh," Matt said again, eyes widening, and he wondered anew why, whatever was going on, he hadn't been informed by wireless . . . unless their codes were compromised, and *that* was what this was all about.

CHAPTER 12

////// *USS* Savoie
Soonda Bay, Jaava
May 11, 1945

USS *Savoie*, with the largest fuel reserve, was last to take her place at the fueling pier at the modest Navy Clan base at B'taava, Jaava. Most of those requested to meet aboard her gathered as the sun set on the island-dotted sea to the northwest and the closer, rebuilding city. All while woven, rubberized hoses snaked along the pier from tank batteries ashore and pulsed like massive arteries, filling the old battleship's bunkers with her black lifeblood.

"Attention! Captain . . . *and CINCAF* on deck!" called Commander Toryu Miyata, lunging to his feet from one of eighteen seats arranged around the long brown linoleum-topped table in *Savoie*'s wardroom. Compared to *Walker*'s, even *Fitzhugh Gray*'s similar compartments, this was practically cavernous. And though just as utilitarian in most respects, Matt noticed the nice hardwood cabinetwork had been refinished by the new, largely Lemurian crew since the last time he was aboard. *Those cabinets were probably for the ship's silver, looted by her French crew when they turned her over to Kurokawa,* he mused, following the BB's skipper, Russ Chappelle, in from the passageway aft. There were places on the bulkheads where plaques or paintings had hung, but those were gone as well. The only decorations were new curtains over the open portholes, finely embroidered in the Lemurian style and stirring listlessly in the faint evening breeze. There was also a large American flag, still the symbol of the American Navy and Marine Clan, hanging behind the head of the table.

Chairs for humans and stools for 'Cats screeched and clattered as others stood, joined by those at two smaller tables flanking the first, and even couches and cushions along the bulkheads. "As you were," Matt and Russ chorused and shared sheepish smiles. Russ had come a long way and was used to being top dog in his ship. Matt would *never* get used to being head of the entire Allied war effort. Sandra and her steward/bodyguard Diania followed them in, and Matt's own steward, Juan Marcos, stumped in last, peg leg thumping on the deck. Most in the compartment hesitated slightly before Sandra smiled and waved, exasperated. "Oh, sit down!"

Matt smiled too as everyone resumed their seats and he and Sandra took theirs at the head of the broad table—Juan and Diania standing behind them—and Russ went down to the other end. Looking around, Matt knew most of the faces. Bernie Sandison, Toos, and Nat, as well as Sandra, Diania, and Juan, of course, had come over with him from *Walker*. Spanky remained behind to oversee preparations for getting underway. USS *Mahan* was represented by her proud young female Lemurian skipper, Commander Tiaa-Baari, as well as her XO, Commander Muraak-Saanga. Matt didn't think there was a single human aboard the other old DD from another world. Commander Perry Brister, originally from *Mahan* himself, was there for USS *James Ellis*, along with his XO, Lieutenant Rolando "Ronson" Rodriguez, Gunnery Officer Lieutenant (jg) Paul Stites, and Engineering Officer Lieutenant (jg) Johnny Parks. Ironically, *Ellie*—the first Lemurian-built copy of *Walker* and *Mahan*—probably had *more* "old" destroyermen aboard than any ship in the navy.

Next in line had to be USS *Savoie* herself. Matt recognized Russ's XO, Lieutenant Commander "Mikey" Monk, as well as Surgeon Commander Kathy McCoy. His eyebrows arched when he saw Dean Laney, now Lieutenant (jg), and *Savoie*'s engineering officer. Laney was a born jerk, transferred out of every post he'd held on this world. Matt long suspected he'd have to banish him for his own good before somebody murdered him. He'd distinguished himself during *Santa Catalina*'s final fight, however, and there he was, neat and shaved, in a clean white uniform. He'd even lost weight. Next to him, but leaning away as if he didn't want to sit too close, was *Savoie*'s acting gunnery officer, a big, black-bearded "China Marine" named Gunnery Sergeant Arnold Horn. Many considered him a slightly better-behaved version of his old pal Dennis Silva. Sandra certainly approved of him, as did Diania, to whom he was engaged. Matt noted Horn was smiling at the diminutive "Impie gal" behind his wife—until he caught Matt's gaze. Some bright scars on his tanned right hand suddenly absorbed his attention.

The last *Savoie* crew member at the table, though there were others in the room, was Imperial Lieutenant Stanly Raj. The Empire of the New Britain Isles had rightly focused its manpower on the war against the Doms in the Americas. Only a couple of thousand Impies had directly fought the Grik, and most had been in Chack's 1st Amalgamated Raider Brigade. Raj was one of just a handful to actually serve in First Fleet ships. Another, a Marine (and bugler) was in *Walker.* Lots of Impies flew off Navy Clan and Union carriers, or served in other Navy Clan ships against the Doms, but Raj was a rare creature here and had become Russ's First Lieutenant.

Matt looked at the man who'd announced them, Toryu Miyata. Not only was he Japanese and a former enemy, he'd risen to command *Fitzhugh Gray. That's probably the biggest irony of all,* Matt supposed, *that we've entrusted him with the second-most-powerful surface combatant we have.* And Matt *did* trust him. *It's so weird how things turn out!* Seated by Miyata were his gunnery and engineering officers, Lieutenants Robert "Bob" Wallace and Sainaa-Asa.

Whatever new elements First Fleet gathered as it steamed east to face the Dom-League alliance, regardless of whether the NUS could really help or the Impies and Repubs actually added anything to their force, these people and their ships would be the most crucial. They'd be the point of the spear and had to form the core around which the rest could coalesce. They weren't ready for that. They were all veterans of hard fighting, in daylight, dark, storm and calm, open sea and even tight rivers, but they'd always had an edge. Their ships were faster, their guns shot farther, and they almost always controlled the air. That was probably over. Except for a very few—Matt's surviving "old destroyermen" who'd fought the Japanese in the Makassar Strait, Badoeng Strait, and of course the Battle of the Java Sea—few here understood what it was like to be outrun, outgunned, outfought, *outthought,* and utterly at the mercy of enemy aircraft. Matt bitterly remembered how that felt, and if the League came at them with what it might, the odds could be even longer than what the Americans, British, Dutch, and Australians faced from the Japanese before *Walker* and *Mahan* ever came to this world. That had been a disaster.

The good thing was, Matt had learned from that—and everything since. He still felt overwhelmed at times; how could he not, with so much riding on him? Only Sandra knew how haunted he was by doubt and crushing responsibility. Matt thanked God for her confidence, and frequent, even sometimes gently brutal reminders of bloody lessons he might've forgotten.

Those were the most important because he'd seen what *didn't* work. That gave him ideas that might, and he'd do his best to get these people ready to see if he was right.

But now there was the infuriating crap Nat had told him, on top of everything else . . .

"Well," he said, still smiling, as stewards distributed iced tea or coffee. (They'd laid in a healthy supply of real coffee before leaving Madagascar.) "I'm glad to see you all here. We have a lot to discuss and little time, but first I'd like to confirm some jabber you might've caught on the horn." Radio silent, none of his ships were transmitting, but that didn't keep them from listening. "First the good news. The Nussie General Cox won a big land battle against the Doms and is already marching south to link up with General Shinya, who's advancing independently. We probably won't know much more about what they're up to for a while." There was pleased applause, but Matt frowned. "The bad news is, the League's already building their forces in the Caribbean, preparing Martinique to support a *lot* of ships and planes. We're in a hurry, people, and that's one reason we'll be leaving as soon as *Savoie*'s refueling is complete, the same way we came in. In the dark."

There were murmurs of surprise, but some already suspected why. "I said 'one reason,'" Matt continued wryly, "but you might've noticed, aside from our Navy Clan comrades on the docks, our welcome here hasn't been as . . . enthusiastic, or even friendly, as we might've expected." B'taava had been liberated from the Grik and opened to repopulation, and the Grik had been pushed back across the Great Western Ocean to their source. Even if the final outcome of the war in Africa remained in doubt, the Grik couldn't threaten B'taava again for generations. The city and surrounding countryside were filling with colonists from Saa-leebs, the stone walls (unusual for Lemurians, and similar to those surrounding Aryaal on the other end of Jaava) had been neatly reconstructed, and the place, though still not packed, seemed to be thriving.

But there'd been no throngs of Lemurians lining the dock at daylight, no bands or speeches from the High Chief of B'taava. Some civilian yard workers seemed glad to see them, but resentful indifference practically radiated over the walls of the city. A lot of hostility probably resulted from the virtual blockade enforced by the squadron of MTBs, but Matt had been horrified when Nat explained why it was deemed necessary.

"It seems," he continued, "that not only are certain factions within the

United Homes growing weary of the war—understandable, because I am too," he quickly inserted, "but the Sularaans in particular, where many of the people here are from," he reminded, "want it stopped. Now." He waited while the resulting hubbub died down. Most Sularaans were fine folk, just like any Lemurians, and not only did Sularaan soldiers fight as hard as anyone, they had a special affinity for artillery. But a lot of their leaders had fled the Grik early in the war and come back to virtually empty cities and provinces whose populations either also fled or went off to fight. That left no one to challenge their return to power, or prevent them from grabbing more.

Perry Brister grunted and spoke in a raspy voice, ruined in battle, that didn't match his youthful face. "Sounds like we need to ship a few Sularaan regiments home to straighten things out. The Third and Fifth Sular are with Second Corps, right?"

Matt chuckled, a little darkly. General Queen Safir-Maraan's II Corps had been the hardest fighting force in the First Fleet AEF, and suffered commensurate casualties. Matt had finally pulled it—and its wounded CO—out of the line in Africa and sent it home to Baalkpan for a much-needed rest. He also thought he might need it against the Doms. "I'll see what Safir has to say. I doubt we can transport the entire corps to the Caribbean, anyway. But that doesn't solve our immediate problem. Chiefly"—he nodded at Nat Hardee—"Mr. Stokes believes that, not only is B'taava not necessarily a friendly port anymore, some elements here—and elsewhere—aren't just agitating for an end to all our offensive operations, but may be actively seeking a separate peace with the League."

"Holy smokes," muttered Mikey Monk. "That's crazy!" Realization appeared to dawn. "And nobody could've cooked that up if they weren't *already* in contact with the League." He also looked at Nat. "So you closed the port, afraid of spies?"

"*I* didn't close it," Nat objected, "it was already done. I just stayed here to tell you in person. *Nothing* about this goes out on the air. Nothing about anything anymore," he added with a glance at Russ Chappelle.

"We continue radio silence, maybe indefinitely," Matt confirmed. "Not even TBS. Flag or Morse lamp signals only."

"Sonofabitch," Russ hissed, glancing apologetically at Sandra and Diania, then Kathy McCoy and the female 'Cats as well, as if any cared. Habits die hard. "That's why no liberty when we got here, and why we're coming and going in darkness. Not sure what good it'll do." He rubbed his forehead. "We expected spies in the Republic and Empire, but if they're sneakin' around *here,* they'll be in Baalkpan, the Filpin Lands . . . everywhere. They'll know we've got *Savoie,* probably even the pigboat—*U-112.* Who knows what all. We won't have *any* surprises left to spring on 'em!"

Matt doubted that, but nodded. "We'll proceed as if that's the case; that when we finally meet the League in force, we won't have any *material* secrets left."

"What does that mean, sir?" Miyata inquired, rather boldly Matt thought. Miyata had never been comfortable with freewheeling discussions like this. They were so different from what he was used to. There was no denying they were effective, however. "What does that leave us?"

"We'll still keep a lid on what we have, in case the enemy *doesn't* have all the dope," Matt replied evenly, "but the biggest whammy we'll throw at 'em is something I doubt they'll prepare for." No one spoke, and he looked around the table. "As soon as we clear the Soonda Strait, and any time we're away from prying eyes, we're going to train like mad."

Commander Toos blinked inquiringly at him. "We train at daam-age control, gener-aal quaarters . . . maany things, every daay. Whaat more do you haave in mind, sur?"

Matt smiled grimly and leaned back in his chair, nodding for his wife to answer. Sandra leaned forward. "I learned a lot about the League while I was a prisoner on this very ship. I learned more from other members of the League on Zanzibar, and I had time to talk with the German defectors—Walbert Fiedler and Kurt Hoffman—before they shipped back to Baalkpan." Her lip twisted. "And I talked with 'Capitaine' Dupont before we sent him too. I'm sure Chairman Letts and Mr. Stokes've made the same conclusions I have, but one of our most valuable assets is, no matter how much they respect what we've accomplished—and they do—the League in general doesn't respect *us.* They're profoundly confident in their material, cultural, even racial superiority, and that makes them unwaveringly arrogant. Their commanders are professionals, but just as inexperienced at dealing with anything like us as we are them. More so," she insisted, and smiled at Matt, melting his heart with the love and support he saw in her eyes. "And they'll be stuck reading manuals, wondering what the hell we're up to, while we run around kicking hell out of them!"

There were shouts of approval, and Lemurians stamped the deck beneath their stools. Matt regarded Commander Toos, then gazed around the table. "So. While the League comes at us like an avalanche, secure in their awe-inspiring might, we'll practice maneuvers all across the Pacific and through the Pass of Fire, daylight and dark, rain or shine, until we can change formations in any conditions in our sleep." He looked at Russ. "And we're going to shoot the hell out of the sea. Until you get your new gun director sorted out, you can slave your main battery to the number two turret. It has its own range finder and director if I recall." His gaze swept across a thoughtful-looking Gunny Horn. "Put a good man in there and I don't think your salvos will suffer much at moderate range."

"What's 'moderate'?" Horn asked, then hastily added, "Sir."

Matt's expression turned grim. "As close as we can get," he told them, then looked back at Russ. "You'll save your armor-piercing shells for the enemy because I doubt the Baalkpan Naval Arsenal has matched them yet, but they've already tooled up to make common shells for *Savoie*'s big guns and they'll have plenty for you." He glanced around again. "Whoever's not towing targets will be shooting at 'em for the next twelve thousand nautical miles, and I don't care if there's only enough life left in your gun bores for one good fight when we get there, because that's all we're going to give those sorry League bastards. Is that understood?"

Matt was surprised by the enthusiasm behind the loud chorus of "yes sir!" and "ay sur!" and felt a little guilty, afraid he'd raised their expectations too high. Sandra's expression told him she understood how he felt, and there was no such thing as too much hope. "Very well," Matt murmured, then cleared his throat and repeated himself before glancing at the chronometer on the bulkhead and looking at Russ. "That took less time than I expected. Unless anyone else has something to say? Okay, it's only eighteen twenty hours, and we sail at oh one hundred." He grinned at Russ Chappelle. "You *did* say you were going to feed us."

Russ grinned back. "Absolutely. You remember Taarba-Karr?" Matt nodded and laughed. The young Lemurian had served as a cook in *Walker* for a time, under the abrasive Earl Lanier, and earned the nickname "Tabasco." Not only for obvious reasons, but because he and Juan Marcos had developed a concoction to sprinkle on Earl's food that unfailingly sent him to the head at strategic and embarrassing times. The conspiracy thrived long after Tabasco transferred to *James Ellis*, and though the treatment wasn't used as often (Earl had slightly mellowed), there was no indication he'd ever gotten wise. Russ bowed his head to *Ellie*'s skipper. "Captain Brister was kind enough to lend us Tabasco for the evening. I understand he's come up with something interesting"—he chuckled—"and maybe a little spicy, but otherwise completely harmless," he assured.

For a while, for more than two hours, a cheerful (if probably fragile) atmosphere pervaded *Savoie*'s wardroom, in which most of First Fleet's senior officers enjoyed a good meal and one another's company, and put their dread of what was to come to the back of their minds. It was the last such respite they'd have until they steamed into Baalkpan Bay, and Matt would make sure they'd be too tired to dwell on anything but training their ships and crews till then.

CHAPTER

13

*////// **Lake Uskoll***
Grik Africa
May 11, 1945

"Wonderful, wonderful!" the Celestial Mother exclaimed—as she had many times during the flight—while the big four-engine PB5-D Clipper banked into a rumbling, descending spiral toward a little Grik fishing village on the north shore of Lake Uskoll. The Celestial Mother had spent the entire trip up from Sofesshk gazing out the portside gunner's position in the waist, looking at miniature trees in the vast forest below, exclaiming how tiny even the most momentous sauropods and occasional large predators looked. Sometimes she scanned the sky, marveling at high, puffy clouds and the spare Clipper pacing them. Once, she chortled with something that sounded like an intermittent steam leak, but that Geerki assured them was glee, when she realized they were flying *above* a flock of large lizardbirds. Never once had she even seemed concerned.

Now her eyes narrowed and her crest rose a bit. "My head feels like I'm squeezing it," she announced. Pete Alden started to suggest she pop her ears, then wondered how to tell a Grik that. He was saved by Geerki, who'd flown before, and demonstrated by clamping his jaws and nostrils in his hands and blowing hard against them. Pete snorted himself because the technique made the old Grik look painfully constipated. When the Celestial Mother, Regent Champion I'joorka, and First Ker-noll Jash all copied him, Pete almost exploded with laughter and quickly looked forward to the elevated flight deck, where Mark Leedom and his copilot were. That put Inquisitor Choon and Sergeant Kaik in his line of sight. One was vigorously working his jaw, the other holding his nose and blowing as well.

"Everybody straapped in?" Leedom's copilot shouted back.

"Yeah."

"Good. We seen the signaal, but we gonna circle again before we set down." The world spun around them as Leedom continued his turn, scanning the area, looking at the trees, the sky, then the water itself, to insure there were no floating hazards.

"Okaay," the copilot cried. "We goin' in. Waater's smooth. Should be a snaap."

"Hold on," Pete cautioned the others. The plane steadied and the pressure in everyone's ears started to mount. Pete did laugh then, at the helplessly straining Grik. He couldn't stop himself, even though he was furiously working his own jaw now. A few minutes later, the big flying boat touched the water and the keel rumbled under their feet. The growing thunder was punctuated by a booming roar and a brief floundering sensation, and everyone lurched forward against their restraints. The plane quickly decelerated until it was almost motionless before Leedom advanced the throttles again and started moving toward a long, low dock, vacant except for a cluster of figures. Pete was surprised that the village beyond them actually looked more like a preindustrial Lemurian town than anything Grik, with wood and thatch dwellings elevated on tall tree trunks. *Sensible everywhere,* Pete mused, *that folks away from cities would want to sleep high up, away from predators.* Still quite humble, the place had a feel of relative prosperity, by Grik standards, and there were a lot of low-slung boats pulled up on the shore. None were alongside the dock, however, and Pete supposed they'd been cleared away.

"The other Clipper'll look around some more before it sets down too," the copilot assured. Before long, Pete felt the plane start to wallow as two engines quit. The others were idling when two 'Cats, the plane's only crew other than its pilots, climbed up behind the cockpit on top of the big wing above. Both carried coiled lines. Unstrapping himself and standing unsteadily, Pete looked out. There were no Grik villagers in sight and the shore on one side of the dock was lined with me-naak-mounted Lemurians. The beach on the other side, where most of the little boats were, was lined with 'Cats and men on kravaas. All were looking at the village and the dense trees beyond.

Three flags fluttered fitfully on the dock; a black and yellow swallowtail with a big red "5" in the center, a longer red and white swallowtail with a variety of embroidered devices, and a strange, upright blue banner supported on the top and leading edge. Beneath them stood half a dozen 'Cats in standard battle dress, three men—and two Grik!

"I'll be damned," Pete Alden said. "Halik's really here. That blue . . . flag, whatever, must be his. The others are Enaak's and Svec's."

"Of course he's here," the Celestial Mother said. "I summoned him, did I not?"

"Hmm." Pete looked back at the group and saw 'Cats catch the thrown lines. He recognized Halik now, his large, powerful frame, if not the new, surprising, short blue cape he wore. Grik generals always wore red capes or cloaks, but Pete didn't remember Halik doing so, at least not during their later meetings. Maybe he did now. *And what's with the color?* His eyes recognized Colonel Enaak, and Dalibor Svec's huge form and flowing beard were unmistakable. There was a smaller version of Svec as well. *His son, Major Ondrej, no doubt.* And there was "General" Orochi Niwa. *Damn Jap's done pretty well for himself,* Pete grudged. The last time he saw Niwa, he'd still been frail from a serious wound. Now he looked strong and healthy—and half-Grik himself, in brass-studded leather armor. *And who's that other Grik?* Pete wondered. He thought he would've recognized General Ugla, known to be with Halik's army. *And Shlook's still back in Persia.* He shook his head. *Maybe that* is *Ugla. Halik's easy to spot because he's so damn big, but otherwise it's always hard to tell the bastards apart. Hard not to focus on their damn teeth and claws, and* they *all look pretty much alike.*

Grunting, Pete opened the cargo door by the waist gunner's position and a ribbed gangplank—with safety lines!—was extended down to the plane. Obviously, no one wanted to risk the Celestial Mother falling in the water. Suddenly unsure of the protocol, Pete looked at Geerki, blinking a question in the Lemurian way.

"Her Magnificence will emerge at your signal," Geerki said primly in Grikish. Pete nodded, gesturing for Sergeant Kaik to stay behind as well, to make double sure the CM didn't fall. He looked at Jash, I'joorka, and Choon. "Let's go."

Gaining the dock, the first thing Pete did was assess its structural ability to hold them all. A lot of Grik construction was pretty haphazard. Not here. Like the elevated huts, presumably, the dock was built to last and take significant weight. The "crawdad" Grik living in tunnels burrowed in the banks of the lower Zambezi popped in his mind as an opposite extreme and he reminded himself once again that unvarying as Grik often seemed, in color, physiology, even general ferocity, there were distinctly different subcultures. And those differences were rapidly expanding as Grik were forced to diversify and embrace new concepts to cope with the whirlwind of change the war had stirred.

He warmly returned the salutes of Enaak, Svec, and their small escort, looking forward to a long conversation with his old comrades from the Indiaa campaign. Then he regarded Halik, Niwa, and the other Grik with a quizzical grin. "Well," he said. "Here you are."

"I was curious to see you again, after all that's passed," Halik replied somberly in Grikish, "and your invitation *was* rather compelling." He motioned to his companions. "You know General Niwa, of course, and this is General Yikkit. He joined me in Persia and was a champion in the battles there." He glanced at Choon, possibly surprised by his strikingly blue eyes, saw I'joorka, who even though badly withered by burns was clearly a warrior, then looked at Jash with open curiosity. "Who are you, consorting with our enemies?"

"First Ker-noll Jash, Lord General, commanding the Slasher Division." He tilted his head at Pete. "And these are not enemies, but saviors. From the vile traitor Esshk." His short crest fluttered irritably and he gestured at Enaak and Svec. "Aren't they *your* allies?"

Halik grunted. "Not allies. Perhaps . . . trusted adversaries." His own crest flared. "I see your point, however, and we're not here to bicker about the company we keep."

"I'm Inquisitor Choon, representing the Republic of Real People," Choon inserted impatiently, "and I respectfully disagree. The company we keep—or choose to join—is precisely why we must speak."

Halik glared at the diminutive Lemurian in the light tan jacket, waistcoat, and black and tan kilt. Then he nodded his snout at the plane. "And the Celestial Mother is truly here? To see *me*?" A tone of wonder had crept into his voice.

"She is," Jash confirmed, "but only because these you call 'enemy' preserved her from Esshk."

Halik grunted again. Niwa had been translating all that was said as fast as he could and Pete looked at the Japanese officer with an ironic smile. "I think we're all gettin' it. Glad to see you still alive, by the way." He was surprised that he meant it.

"As I'm glad to be," Niwa responded wryly. "If I'm not needed to interpret, I'll merely stand ready to correct misunderstandings."

"Fine." Pete whistled.

The great plane shifted slightly, and a large shape darkened the cargo hatch. There was no mistaking the distinctive coppery color or bright red cloak of the Celestial Mother when she fully emerged, stepping out on the gangplank that sagged under her still-growing bulk. With surprising agility, however, she quickly gained the dock, followed by Geerki and Sergeant Kaik, rapidly blinking relief. Mark Leedom came last, carrying a large, wooden crate.

For the briefest moment, Halik and Yikkit could only stare as if stunned. Then Yikkit hurled himself to the dock and lay on his belly at the Celestial Mother's feet. Instinctively, Halik almost joined him, but turned his movement into a deep bow instead.

"You do not prostrate yourself before your Giver of Life?" the Celestial Mother challenged.

"No, Your . . . Your Splendor," Halik replied softly, clearly using a title he fully endorsed, judging by the way his eyes consumed her. Pete knew she had a pretty coat, but Geerki and I'joorka assured him that her size, coloration, youth, and health personified the Grik ideal of female perfection. On the other hand, she'd been unambiguously cautioned against expressing the scent she controlled that would drive males of her species mad with lust. Halik was no hatchling and would literally sniff it out and back away. There'd be no possibility of trust after that. "It's ingrained in me to worship and respect you for who and what you are," Halik continued, "but I've learned the most honest respect is earned by and returned to leaders who allow their subjects to respect themselves."

"He won't make his troops squirm in front of *him* either," Enaak said lowly, "and look whaat he's accomplished."

"Good," the Celestial Mother said, clearly surprising Halik. "Please rise, General Yikkit." She waved at Jash. "I allow no one to prostrate themselves before *me* anymore," she added gently, "so it seems I've already been taught to think like you. I learned this from my conquerors, *our* conquerors," she added with soft emphasis, "and it's something I would spread to every member of our race." Her voice hardened. "Esshk wouldn't have that. He's the greatest traitor our race has ever known. He exterminated the Ancient Hij of Old Sofesshk, presided over defeats that set our race back a millennium, and actually attempted to destroy *me*. It's ironic that only defeat and conquest at the claws of what we once considered prey not only saved me from him, but might preserve our race." She straightened and her voice rose. "So that's why I'm here, come to *you*, to . . . ask, not command, that you join with me and your former enemies instead of Esshk—who *would* have you squirming at his feet!"

Halik's crest lay flat and anguish was in his voice when he replied. "You're my Giver of Life, and my foremost obedience must always be to you, but General Esshk made me." He waved at Yikkit, even Jash. "He made all of us, either by elevation, or through the creation of the Hatchling Host. None of us would have the minds to recognize the wrongs he's done you and our race if he hadn't allowed it. A portion, at least, of my loyalty must remain with him."

"Bullshit," Pete snapped. "Maybe Esshk didn't let them eat you when you started wising up, but that wasn't for *you*, it was for him. You made *yourself*, Halik, with a little help from a Jap." He shrugged and nodded at Enaak and Svec. "Maybe all of us, in a way. But then you helped your army, your new people, make themselves into what they are. Unlike Jash here, they weren't born and raised to it from the egg. You became what you are in *spite* of Esshk, who only wanted to use you and throw you away."

Still anguished, Halik shook his head. "Esshk summoned me from a continent away, and I came here knowing I'd face this terrible choice." He looked at the Celestial Mother. "To betray myself and my regency, and all it's become, or betray you and Esshk. Now I know the truth and it's only Esshk I'd betray, but the choice still lies heavy upon me. I'd . . . hoped to speak with him before making it."

"Sorry, but that ain't gonna work," Pete said flatly, shaking his head.

"I sympathize with your torment," the Celestial Mother told Halik, whose crest had begun to rise in defiance. "I experienced much the same—before Esshk tried to have me slain, and I began to understand our new allies really can be our friends, after all." She cast a proprietary glance at the hideous I'joorka, then her eyes flicked across Niwa. "I *know* you understand 'friendship,' Lord General Halik."

"I do."

I'joorka spoke up in very good, if somewhat raspy Grikish. "Do you think Esshk is your friend? Will he be grateful if you save him?"

"Who are you?" Halik demanded.

The Celestial Mother interrupted. "He's General I'joorka of the United Homes. My acting Regent Champion—in Captain Reddy's stead."

I'joorka bowed to her, then continued. "I got these wounds helping defeat Kurokawa on Zanzibar. Only now am I beginning to recover. Like too many, I'll never fully heal and I have more cause than most to prevent the suffering of others. If you believe Esshk will thank you, then you're not as smart as Colonel Enaak insists you are. With victory, you'd become Esshk's rival and he won't allow that. You've learned to lead, to rule a large regency you conquered yourself, and you *know* the old ways Esshk would restore are not the best for your race." He took a deep, ragged breath. "As acting Regent Champion of the rightful ruler of all the Gharrichk'k, and with her perfect agreement, I present you with three choices."

"There used to be only two," General Yikkit said, speaking for the first time.

"Times change," Pete murmured.

"The choices?" Halik asked, somewhat bitterly.

I'joorka raised one flame-scarred finger. "Go home. Back to your regency in Persia. Do that and we'll recognize it's yours forever—under the ultimate rule of the Celestial Mother, of course. There you'll control your population as you see fit, but never expand your borders. You'll also maintain peaceful relations with the people in Indiaa, whether they ever join the United Homes or not."

The plumage on Halik's tail flared but his crest didn't rise. "We've come a long way, just to turn around. The second choice?"

"Join us," I'joorka said earnestly. "Help destroy Esshk and change the world!"

"What else?" Yikkit asked, seemingly surprising himself. He glanced apologetically at the Celestial Mother. "What else would we get for that?"

"Little else," I'joorka conceded, "though in addition to what's promised in the first choice, you'll have a voice in the recreation of the Gharrichk'k."

"And the third choice?" Halik growled, already knowing part of the answer, and unconsciously flicking his eyes at a glowering Dalibor Svec.

I'joorka said nothing, and Pete shrugged, speaking up. "Colonel Enaak and Colonel Svec will escort you back to your army. That was the deal. You could argue I've exaggerated my advantages over you in the past, from time to time, but I've never broken our first deal, and I won't break this one. After that we'll be enemies again," he stated plainly, expression darkening. "Not the friendly kind, like now, but the kind that'll rip your guts out." He tilted his head at the Celestial Mother. "With her help."

Halik sucked air through jagged, yellowed teeth, eyes settling on Jash. "Were you given these choices?" he demanded.

"I was given three, slightly different—and no regency to rule—but essentially the same." He held furry-feathery arms out at his sides. "You see which one I chose: the one the Giver of Life preferred. So there really *was* no choice, in the end."

Halik looked at his friend. "General Niwa? What does *honor* demand?"

Niwa pursed his lips. "Only you can decide." He bowed his head toward Pete. "As you know, he and I were bitter enemies before we came to this world, and I advised you in battle against him. Yet I came to know him in India, and though he's used"—he smiled—"martial misdirection against us, there's no dishonor in that. He's kept his word." He glanced at Enaak. "*More* than kept it, and I . . . I do believe I trust him. Far more than I ever did Hisashi Kurokawa. *He* was the 'general' who 'made' *me*, in a sense, and to whom I've always rather compared Esshk in many ways. For that reason alone, *my* preference would be to work with General Alden against *any* such as Esshk, to whom I feel no obligation at all." He sighed. "Yet honor doesn't require 'preference.' My ultimate loyalty will always be to my emperor, but he's on another world and I can't know how he'd have me act. So you—who have been my lord, with honor given and received—will have my service no matter how you decide."

He pointed at the Celestial Mother. "But *there* is *your* 'Emperor,' and you know what *she* wants. I'd think honor demands that *her* desires should bind you tighter than those of a mad, rebellious general, as much a stranger to honor as Kurokawa ever was."

"General Yikkit?" Halik demanded. "You know Enaak and Svec, but have no opinion about Alden. What do you think?"

Yikkit clacked his teeth. "Esshk made me, Lord General, the same as you." He paused, reflecting. "But I thought he formed us to serve the *Celestial Mother*, not himself. We all may be his makings to some degree, but we *belong* to the Giver of Life. If Esshk rebelled against her, tried to destroy her and the Ancient Hij, then . . . I must oppose him. If any ever deserved the traitor's death, it's he."

Halik sighed. "And the army?"

"It will do as you command, as always," Yikkit assured.

"No!" Halik snapped, and Yikkit recoiled, surprised, while Halik made placating gestures. "I want my warriors to think for themselves!"

"They will," Niwa said softly. "They'll think whatever you decide is right, because you command their trust as well as their obedience." He smiled and looked at the Celestial Mother. "As she is attempting to do with you. So that's what it comes to, very simple. Can you really present your army to

Esshk for him to waste?" He nodded at Pete and the Celestial Mother. "Against him? Against *her*?"

Halik looked at every face, then stared at the rough-hewn timbers of the dock for several moments, clearly in deep contemplation. Finally, when the other big Clipper roared in for a landing, the sound seemed to snap his reverie. "No," he said starkly.

"'No' what?" Pete asked with equal severity.

"No, I can't do that," Halik specified, tone still harsh. "So I've decided to give *you* a choice." He paused, plucking at his cape and gesturing at his strange flag. "I've built more than just a far-flung regency. I've made a better Way for our race." He looked at the Celestial Mother. "A *different* Way than that which I understand you're trying to make, and I won't give that to Esshk . . . or you." He raised his snout in defiance. "You'll always be the Giver of Life to any who dwell in the lands of Persia and Arabia and they—and I—will serve you as faithfully as you could ask as long as you keep our trust. But we *will* remain different. If that's tolerable to you, my army will support you against Esshk. If not"—he tilted his snout northward—"I'll accept *your* first offer and go home."

"Goddamn!" Pete practically yipped. "Let me get this straight. You're saying you'll stay loyal to the crown, throne . . . whatever, and even fight for it, but you want to *secede*? Set up your own *country*?"

"Not exactly," Niwa denied thoughtfully, before Halik could reply. "At least I don't think so," he added warily, squinting at Halik. "We've discussed something like this, but he took even me by surprise. If I'm not mistaken . . . consider General Halik's, um, rather large regency as akin to Kurokawa's 'Sovereign Nest' at Zanzibar. Tied to the Grik Empire, but relatively independent."

"I'll be damned. Like Canada or Australia. On the loose, but still loyal to the British King."

"Essentially."

The Celestial Mother looked confused. "He requires a choice of *me*?" She looked helplessly at I'joorka, Choon, then Pete. "Does that count as one of the choices we gave *him*?"

Pete couldn't help but laugh. "Sort of." He became serious, thoughts spinning, wishing he could take a minute to talk to Inquisitor Choon alone. *Not a good idea right now. I gotta sort this out on my own, fast.* No matter what some might've hoped, most always knew they'd never wipe the Grik out, so they had to find a way to live with them. It seemed to be working with the Celestial Mother, but the former Grik Empire was so vast, it might take generations to pacify the various factions and glue the unwieldy beast back together. *And for what?* Pete wondered. *So we can keep the whole damn thing under our thumb forever? It'll never work. But* two *Grik nations—or more—no matter how closely tied, will still have increasingly different interests. Maybe that'll make 'em easier for us to deal with.* Helluva *lot easier to set against each other, if we have to,* he realized in a flash of practical cynicism.

He turned to the Celestial Mother. As he did so, he was pleased—and a little chilled—to catch Choon subtly blinking agreement and opportunity. "The main thing is, he'll fight with us against Esshk. And he'll support you." He looked sternly at Halik. "Right?"

"Right," Halik answered in English.

"Wow. Good." Pete clapped his hands. "So let's get on with it. We got a war to win. We can sort out all the other weird crap later." He looked at Leedom and jerked his head toward the village. The crate he'd brought contained one of the latest Grik army field horns, used in place of bugles or whistles to pass commands on the battlefield. It was actually a bellows incorporating several horns that produced different notes. It reminded Pete of a cross between a squeezebox and a giant chromatic harmonica since the notes could be varied or even combined by opening and closing various apertures with a sliding block. Leedom removed the device from the crate and handed it to one of Enaak's troopers. "It's already set on the old 'attention' call. Don't monkey with it," he cautioned.

"What are you doing?" Halik asked.

"I'm going to speak to the Hij and Uul of this village," the Celestial Mother replied.

Halik stood with his jaw hanging open. Clearly, the Celestial Mother had surprised him again. "You'd speak to *ordinary* Gharrichk'k?" he finally managed. "No Giver of Life has ever done that!"

"For the good of our race, I mean to do *many* things that've never been done," she told him haughtily. "What about you? You strive to elevate a regency. I must elevate a continent if we're to survive." She whirled in a flash of copper and red and walked after the 'Cat with the horn. Most on the dock followed, leaving only Pete, Leedom, Jash, Halik, Niwa, and two of Svec's troopers.

"Don't know what kind of crowd she'll draw," Pete mused aloud. "Who knows how far everybody ran? The Fifth Maa-ni-la and Svec's Czechs can be pretty scary on their meanies and kravaas." He looked at Halik. "But you know that. Still, I expect she'll be happy if half a dozen hear her. Word will spread."

"She is . . . not what I expected," Halik admitted.

"Me neither. But given what she's been through and what's at stake, she seems to be takin' this queen shit seriously."

Niwa had to turn the last part into something Halik could understand, but he nodded agreement.

"Kinda inspires you to want to help her, doesn't it?" Pete probed. Then he took a deep breath. "So. What're we gonna do?"

"I assume you mean our armies together?"

Pete nodded. "Sounds unnatural when you say it aloud, doesn't it?"

"Perhaps less so to me than you," Halik countered. "I've enjoyed the grudging assistance of Ker-noll Enaak and Ker-noll S'ec for some time." He stroked the slightly age-wattled skin beneath his jaw. "Esshk defends Lake Galk?"

"You know he does. With between three and five hundred thousand New Army Grik. Hard to tell for sure, since our air recon's been limited. Only the Clippers can make it that far until we finish our new airfield at Sofesshk, and with all the antiair rockets Esshk gathered around the lake, the Clippers have to stay too high for detailed observations. We do have some observers on the ground, believe it or not." He chuckled. "Ol' Geerki turned out to be one of our best assets. Gave me, Choon, and Rolak a couple hundred interpreters and spies he trained on Madagascar." Pete frowned. "Trouble is, *being* from Madagascar, they kind of stand out. A lot have been caught—or maybe just eaten by critters they've never seen before. Anyway, we know most of Esshk's forces are concentrated on the south end of the lake, defending the locks. They know we have to take 'em. Can't bomb 'em. Just think what would happen downstream, all the way to the sea, if the locks broke." He shook his head at the mental image of destruction. "Anyway, I'm coming up from the south with about a hundred and twenty thousand, you'll be coming from the north with a hundred thousand." He eyed Halik. "The overall strategy's pretty straightforward. The only real question will be one of trust."

"How so?"

"Easy. Either I attack Esshk and pin him to the south while you come up behind him and kick him in the ass, or you sneak up and draw his attention before I attack."

"And each of you must trust the other not to leave you exposed to Esshk's superior numbers," Niwa summarized.

"Yeah," Pete agreed.

"An interesting dilemma," Halik conceded.

"There is, of course, an alternative," Niwa said. "If General Halik openly declares for the Celestial Mother and makes no secret of our advance, Esshk will have to divide his force."

"Unfortunately, half his army might still stop us," Halik admitted. "Fighting our way across Arabia and half the sacred, ancient land you call 'Africa' has left us with . . . somewhat fewer than a hundred thousands now."

Jash was whipping his snout from side to side. "Lord General, if I may. Many more will swell your ranks after you declare." He looked at Pete. "The same is true for my Slashers."

Halik nodded. "Perhaps. Uul warriors of limited use for the most part, but better than nothing. Particularly given time to train and arm them." He looked at Pete. "I seized large stores of weapons in the regencies I crossed. The artillery is adequate, if overheavy, but like your paalkas and other animals, we've harnessed neekis—large, upright foodbeasts—to pull our guns. The small arms are not as good as what Esshk has now, such were not issued to frontier troops, but I can arm *many* recruits."

The first deep blast of the "attention" horn sounded, echoing dully back from the village and the dense forest beyond.

"Lord General," Jash resumed when the noise faded away. "It may be possible . . . I might secure additional *New Army* aid, if permitted to try."

Halik and Pete both stared at him.

"Where?" Pete asked. "How many?"

"How many do you believe General Ign has left? And how many of your own do you spend keeping him from joining Esshk?"

"Huh," Pete breathed, skeptically. "Well, as to numbers, Ign has fifteen to twenty thousand. Again, hard to say. He's in thick forest and rough country. Nancys off the river can reach him, and they bomb the crap out of him whenever he bunches up. The Repub Fifth Corps is short a couple of divisions, the Fifth for one, but it's got sixteen thousand, chasing him around."

Halik's eyes turned to slits. "Didn't Ign declare for Esshk?"

"Yeah," Pete confirmed, "and he's a tough old bastard. Could've thrown in the towel a dozen times but kept on going."

Niwa wasn't sure himself what "thrown in the towel" meant, but everyone seemed to get the gist.

"What else could he do?" Jash asked defensively, short crest rising. "Esshk 'made' him too. Worse, he made him complicit in his plot to eliminate the Ancient Hij and rule through a Giver of Life whom Ign assumed was a helpless hatchling. This when all he knew was falling apart and only Esshk seemed able to stop it." He hissed a sigh. "Ign knows what 'honor' is, even without a word for it, and must feel, like you"—he looked at Halik—"he owes some to Esshk. Conversely, he doesn't know the Giver of Life as we do, and can't imagine he can reverse his treason." Jash turned to Pete. "So as you say, he just 'keeps going.'"

"What's your point?" Pete asked.

"Only that I know him and he . . . respects me. I'd try to turn him from Esshk if I could."

Pete rubbed his eyes. "Shit. Look, Colonel Jash—I'm sorry, and no offense—but I'm not even used to *you* being on our side yet." He looked at Niwa, then Halik. "Them neither. Hell! We've all done our best to kill each other so long, I'll *never* figure out how I feel about this. But now you want to run off and try to get *Ign* to join us too? Just like that?" He snapped his fingers.

The thunderous "attention" horn sounded again and Pete looked that way. To his surprise, dozens of Grik had crept from the woods to stand in front of the frightening me-naaks of the 5th Maa-ni-la Cavalry.

"I doubt it'll be that easy," Jash admitted. "But *I* feel honor bound, as I understand the concept, to try. For you, for the Giver of Life, for Ign . . . even myself. I'm the most you'll lose if I fail, and Ker-noll Shelg can take my place commanding the Slashers."

"But . . . how the hell will you find him? Get to him in time to do any good?"

"Let him take one of those Grik zeps we captured," suggested Mark Leedom.

Pete was surprised, both by the proposal and its source. "One of those 'rattletraps'?" he goaded.

Leedom waved that away. "The lizard's *right*, General," he pressed. "I've gotten to know Jash better than you. Some of his guys're helping oversee the construction of Saansa Field, and I . . . well, he's all right by me. Besides, ask Rolak, Geerki, Chack—a hundred others. Grik don't break anymore, and they don't change sides just because they're losing, but sometimes they do when they know they've *lost*. We've seen it a bunch of times now, and the ones who've come over to us have stuck."

"It's true," Niwa said. "I saw the same thing in Persia." He took a quick look at his Grik friend. "Even General Halik was surprised when the remains of Shighat's army came over to him. I suspect it's an instinctive pack survival mechanism, long suppressed, since even their regency-on-regency wars always degenerate into harvesting meat for the cookpots." He frowned at that, but continued. "It's been so long since 'packs' have had the *option* of surrender, of joining those who beat them, they've forgotten how. Until now."

The horn blared a third time, and Pete saw the shore past the Maa-ni-los and Czechs had *filled* with Grik, patiently waiting.

"I want this over," Leedom said quietly. "I'm sick of losing people." He sighed. "And we've got a whole other war on the other side of the world. We've got to finish this, and Fifth Corps can help"—he nodded at Jash—"even if he only gets Ign to sit it out, like you said Halik could. That'll help by itself. Let him go."

Pete scratched his chin under his dark whiskers, then swept his hand across his beard to bring it back under control. "Okay," he finally said, looking at Halik. "Unlike our deal, which was already kind of agreed on, I'll have to let the CM, Choon, and General Kim kick it around. Fifth Corps *is* Kim's after all, and turning its back on Ign will be seen as a risk. But I think I can swing it." He glared hard at Jash. "Don't let me down . . . and don't get killed."

Halik shifted, seemingly uncomfortable. "Perhaps I should go to Esshk as well. Talk with him before attacking." He glanced at Niwa. "That would be the 'honorable thing,' would it not?"

Pete barked a laugh, then growled, "That's rich, asking a Jap about the 'honor' of a sneak attack." Niwa reddened, but Pete was looking at Halik. "Jash might actually have a chance, but if *you* tell Esshk to take a leap, to his face, he'll just kill you. Think where that leaves your generals, your army, all you've done in Persia, *and* your Celestial Mother. Besides, Esshk'll hear about it almost as soon as you declare against him. You won't be taking him by surprise. Matter of fact, the way things're set up, there aren't any *big* surprises left to spring on him," he added grimly. "He's on the defensive with an equal or greater force, and we have to go to him. Best we can do is throw enough little surprises at him to shake him up, spread him out, make him defend too much—then pound the ever-living shit out of him."

Halik flicked his crest, then sighed. "I must agree. That is how you once defeated me."

The Celestial Mother had begun to speak and everyone was interested in what she had to say, particularly Halik and Jash. "One more thing," Niwa said suddenly. "With our strategy outlined, basically attacking Esshk at Lake Galk from two directions at once, we have little need or ability to coordinate tactical movements—the 'little surprises.' We will, in essence, be fighting two separate battles so we don't even need to know each other's specific plans. We *must*, however, coordinate their commencement."

Pete nodded. "That's what those are for," he said, waving at three more wooden crates the Clipper's crew-'Cats had brought on the dock.

"And they are?" Halik asked.

Pete grinned. "Seems I remember you saying you could've beat me in India if you had decent communications." Halik's eyes went wide and his toothy jaws parted with pleasure. He had no idea how electrical communications—or even electricity—worked, he only knew it did. And the Allies' ability to talk over long distances had always amazed and filled him with envy. "Bullshit, of course," Pete went on, "but it would've made things tougher. Those crates contain batteries, an aerial, portable hand generator, and a single-frequency CW transceiver. There's earphones of course."

"Single frequency?" Niwa asked.

"One thing at a time," Pete replied. "You don't need to listen to everything. How's your Morse?"

"Rusty, but adequate," Niwa told him.

Pete scratched his chin again. "Well, it's mainly a backup anyway, for emergencies, so we'll have direct contact and you won't have to go through Enaak if you get separated. I'll have him loosen up what he tells you, and keep you in the big loop. I expect you to do the same for me, through him."

"Enaak and S'ec will stay with us?" Halik asked, surprised.

"Yeah. You need scouts, and Colonel Enaak'll have orders to cooperate with you more than ever before. Svec may not like it. Might even peel off. He's not really under my orders, you know. But I expect he'll stay. He still gets to kill Grik, and victory here is the best way to protect his people moving back into India."

Halik seemed almost overwhelmed. Finally, as they moved closer to where the Celestial Mother was making what sounded like a stirring oration, Halik managed to speak. "General Alden—" He stopped himself and started again. "*First* General Alden . . . I, I really don't know what to say. I always knew we'd meet again, but expected one or both of us to die when we did. That thought left me . . . disquieted. Now we *have* met, and"—he cast a look at Niwa—"my purpose is clear and pure at last. I feel like a great weight has been lifted from me. I'm experiencing unaccustomed anticipation, even pleasure, at the prospect of fighting for a shared purpose with you."

"Yeah? Well, I don't think it's gonna be fun, but I guess I'm sorta glad we're on the same side too." He snorted. "How weird is *that* shit?"

CHAPTER 14

FIRES ON THE HOME FRONT

////// ***USS* Walker**
Baalkpan, Borno
May 13, 1945

Under a stunning blue, late morning sky, almost exactly a year since she last steamed away, USS *Walker* prepared to return to Baalkpan Bay. A light northwesterly wind already filled the air with the . . . mixed aromas Matt had come to associate with home on this world: jungle flowers; spicy, open-air cooking; but also creosote, rotting wood, and dead fish. The hot, rancid smell of oil being rendered from the fat of great, whale-sized, predatory gri-kakka was no longer as strong, edged out by wood and oil smoke that contributed to a brownish, low-lying haze. Industry supporting the war effort, and the consequent explosion of the local population was the cause, of course, but Matt could summon little of the remorse he'd once felt over that. The reek of industrial and manufacturing pollution couldn't even remotely compare with the stench of death he'd so often endured, that once permeated the air here too.

Walker was bringing up the rear of the column this time, following *James Ellis* and *Mahan*, which trailed *Savoie* and *Fitzhugh Gray.* Matt thought it might be good for civilian morale if the biggest ships went first. In a nod to the pride and morale of his sailors, he allowed each ship to stream its big battle flag (Stars and Stripes over the League flag in *Savoie*'s case) and suitable colorful greetings from their signal halyards. Every ship was blotched and streaked with rust, and all but *Savoie* still wore scars from their last fight on the Zambezi, but Matt was proud of how smart they all still managed to look. Each line was taut or carefully coiled and the decks were as clean as they could be. Moreover, all their guns had already been carefully cleaned and aligned fore and aft, muzzles slightly up, after their predawn gunnery exercise off the southwest tip of Borno.

And despite how disfigured and insignificant she might appear compared to the rest of the ships, particularly *Savoie* and *Gray*, *Walker* still outshone them all in one respect. Never one to brag on himself (Matt was raised with a "no brag, just facts" personality), he'd long considered the busy collection of flags and silhouettes painted below the rails of *Walker*'s bridgewings almost comically boastful. They included Japanese, Dom, and Grik ships, Japanese planes—and did they really have to add *Grikbirds*?—as well as a League submarine. Enthusiastic 'Cats would've added all their "assists," extending the mural to the sides of the amidships deckhouse, but even Spanky had enough, declaring they'd "make the old girl look like some tin-pot dictator's suit." They might not've known exactly what he meant, but they got his drift. At the same time Matt was relieved by that, he understood the impulse. He was perfectly willing to brag on his old ship and her crew.

Things threatened to get out of hand, in Matt's view, when a grinning Sandra defiantly directed that an upended broom be lashed to the rail of the searchlight platform on the foremast when a lookout saw one go up on *Mahan*. Matt stifled an order to belay the display, based on the fact they had a *lot* of "sweeping" left to do, but realized that was irrelevant just now. All of First Fleet's people had been through hell and had a right to be proud of their ships and what they'd achieved. On top of that, they were *home. If they can forget, even for a time, that their greatest test still lies ahead . . . more power to them,* Matt determined. *I wish I could.*

"*Savoie*'s passin' Fort Atkinson," Spanky announced, peering through binoculars on the starboard bridgewing. "Joint's bigger now, and all the muzzle-loading guns've been replaced with dual-purpose five and a halfs."

"A new fort on this side," called a 'Cat lookout to port. "Not as big, but aarmed the same. An' lots more barraacks at the Baalkpan Advaanced Training Center," he mused, blinking thoughtfully. Sandra and Diania had come on the bridge, and Sandra stood by Matt's slightly elevated captain's chair, eye to eye with her husband. Unlike Matt, still in rumpled khakis, the two women already wore their best whites—as did most of the crew. "I can already tell a lot has changed," Sandra said quietly. "I wonder if we'll even recognize the city."

One by one, *Gray*, *Ellie*, and *Mahan* all passed the fort and entered the bay, but when *Walker* drew even with Fort Atkinson, smoke and fire started jetting from the 5.5″ guns. Moments later they heard the dull, windswept boom of the salute begin, and counted seventeen reports. Matt sank lower in his chair. "Good Lord," he muttered, "that's the salute for a full admiral. I *told* Alan—I mean, Chairman Letts—how I feel about that!"

"Hush," Sandra scolded. "It ought to be twenty-one, since as High Chief of the Navy Clan, you're technically a head of state. And what difference does it make, anyway? You still run around claiming to be a *lieutenant commander*, while giving orders to generals and admirals—even *other* heads of state, when it comes to military matters. Besides, don't you see?" She waved around the pilothouse where 'Cats were standing straighter, tails slightly arched, blinking satisfaction. "It's mostly for them, anyway. It makes them proud that our people—the people of the Union we all helped build and save—show respect and appreciation for you. You *represent* them, silly."

Matt cocked his head to the side with a crooked smile. "Yeah. I guess. Right, as usual."

"Of course I am," Sandra smugly agreed.

Two brand-new four-stacker destroyers met them shortly after, racing out with bones in their teeth and peeling in behind *Walker*. "Look at that, Skipper!" Bernie Sandison said excitedly. "The two new DDs that were undergoing trials while we were up the creek." He shaded his eyes. "First one's number twenty-four, so she's *Gerald McDonald*. We could call her '*Mick*,'" he suggested for the traditional nickname.

"Our Imperial Allies will be so honored," Sandra noted dryly.

"They should be," Spanky groused. "But Governor-Emperor McDonald was a good guy. He earned it."

"I was being sarcastic," Sandra pointed out. "And his daughter, the *current* Governor-Empress, may not be impressed by the flippant handle Mr. Sandison so casually hung on her father's namesake."

"She won't care," Spanky assured, though Matt thought she might. From all he'd heard, the little girl they'd left in charge of the Empire of the New Britain Isles had changed a lot.

"So the other must be *Tassat-Ay-Arracca*, DD-Twenty-Five," Bernie continued, then hesitated. "*Tassy?*"

Matt shook his head, remembering a terrible night long ago in the strait they just left. "*Tassat*," he said definitively. "Besides, we'll be counting on his daughter's carrier, USS *Madraas*, for air support. Better not aggravate her."

"Not to mention how thick she is with Keje," Spanky agreed with an exaggerated leer. "She gets him to pull *Big Sal*'s air support, we'll really be screwed!"

Matt nodded ahead as the bay spread out before them. Unlike Soonda Bay, this was packed with small, swift, sailing craft, jockeying to pace the warships in. There'd be an entirely different kind of welcome here. "Supposed to be another DD almost ready to go," he said. "USS *Adar*. I guess they're the 'dead leader' class," he added sadly.

"No, Skipper, still 'Wickes-Walkers,'" Spanky denied, deliberately misunderstanding, and trying to redirect Matt's thoughts. "The *next* class'll have the new DP five and a halfs, though. Same guns as *Gray*, only a little shorter so they'll train faster."

"They'll be heavier topside," Bernie warned.

"Nah," Spanky disagreed. "Well, maybe, but the whole ships'll be bigger. Genuine 'gold platers.'"

"Someday," Bernie pointed out, but then lit with anticipation. "*I'm* excited about our new Mk-7 torpedoes!" Bernie had been their chief torpedo engineer from the start, but he'd only been able to go so far, basing his designs on the crummy American weapons he was familiar with. But they'd not only gotten their hands on some excellent Japanese fish, salvaged from *Hidoiame*, but some of her torpedomen as well. *They'd* been happy to escape Khonashi nooses that went around most of their murderous officers' necks, and set about redesigning Bernie's weapons, within a 21″ diameter constraint. Bernie stayed "current on practical field applications," as he put it, and oversaw the program from afar. Long before the current radio blackout, he'd blessed the production of the new Mk-7 since it was supposed to outperform the Mk-6 in every respect; range, accuracy, and lethality—but at a cost.

"Oh yeah," Spanky groaned. "I forgot. Your new fish're gonna be charged with *oxygen* instead of just air. Probably stored in big tanks scattered all over our ships, just waitin' to blow the hell up."

Bernie shook his head. "We won't need much. Just enough to top off leaky air flasks on the fish in the tubes." He looked at Matt. "Unless we carry reloads?"

Matt shrugged. Who knew what they'd have to do?

"What difference does that make?" Spanky demanded hotly. "A single little hit that cracks a fish'll blow the whole ship in half!"

Matt cleared his throat. "We may be facing battleships," he reminded.

"No such thing as a 'little' hit. So you're right. What difference does it really make? Stow it." He nodded out past the fo'c'sle, off the starboard bow, as Baalkpan itself began to come in view.

They hardly recognized it. The entire shoreline, almost from Fort Atkinson itself to the jutting peninsula where the "new" fitting-out pier used to be was nothing but heavy timber cranes and docks, backed by massive warehouses and other big buildings. Few were easy to identify, but one stood beside another new dry dock, bringing the total of such permanent structures in Baalkpan to three. Matt didn't know how many floating dry docks there were; he saw two at once, large enough to accommodate even their biggest carriers or seagoing Homes. The old wharves for the fishing fleet had been replaced by shipyards containing a cluster of still *more* new destroyers under construction. None looked more than half complete, but the 'Cats in Baalkpan had certainly learned the art of large-scale mass production. Three of the shapes were a little different. Two would be the 1,500-ton "gold-platers" Spanky dreamed of, as much like a Sims Class as he'd been able to remember when helping with the initial design. Rising among them was another dream for the future: a proper cruiser incorporating many of the features USS *Gray* had lacked. Sadly, none would possibly be finished before Matt desperately needed them.

There had to be new wharves somewhere, judging by the number of fishing boats, and the exponentially greater numbers of mouths they had to feed. Maybe they docked somewhere up the bay, or on the other side beyond the ATC. Perhaps the most striking differences of all, however, were that the great open-air bazaar they found so charming when they first arrived, as well as the gun-bristling earthen berm they'd helped build around the city were both entirely gone. The bazaar had been a bastion of Lemurian culture and Matt regretted its absence, but the missing wall actually troubled him more. A lot of 'Cats had died defending it when the Grik came here, but it also protected against large jungle predators. Before it was built, armed, and garrisoned, all dwellings had to be constructed on high wooden pilings to keep their inhabitants safe. Despite the haven Baalkpan otherwise was, its furry people lived with danger every day. Now, not only was the wall gone—and most of the riotous *color* of the city, Matt noted as well—only the oldest buildings were elevated. *Maybe that's the reason for all the unrest and war-weariness on the home front,* he reflected. *People feel too safe. Not only from their own land, with the worst predators hunted out or pushed into the darkest parts of Borno, but from the Grik we slaughtered back to another continent and out of their nightmares.*

"Look there," Sandra said excitedly, pointing northeast to the interior past a smaller peninsula that used to be the "old" fitting-out pier. Alone of all the docks they'd seen, there was space at that one, apparently awaiting them, because it was absolutely packed with humans, Lemurians, even a few Grik-like Khonashi. And there was plenty of color *there*, at least; flags of every member of the Grand Alliance waved and fluttered, as well as red, white, and blue bunting lining the dock itself. A tall white mast stood behind the dock with the predominantly white "stainless banner" of the United Homes streaming out from one halyard under the cross spar. It was adorned with the symbol of the Great Tree, surrounded by representations of all the member states in the Union. Flying from the other halyard, at an equal height on this day at least, was the Stars and Stripes of the American Navy and Marine Clan. In Matt's mind, it would always be the flag of the nation he'd sworn to defend. Of course, the same was oddly, indirectly true for every member of his "clan."

But Sandra was pointing at something else: the *real* Great Tree, towering over the heart of Baalkpan. Matt hadn't known what to expect. The huge tree, hundreds of feet high (though still not as tall as its ancestral parents on Madagascar, Matt now knew) had burned during the battle here, as had the Great Hall it supported like a gigantic treehouse. The Hall had been rebuilt and the tree was just starting to recover the last time Matt saw it. Now the new Great Hall looked like a continuous structure all the way to the ground, but the tree itself had expanded even more grandly, thickening and branching out and almost literally scraping the sky. Matt had the impression it was trying to spread its comforting shade across the whole city and he caught himself smiling at the thought.

MTBs were maneuvering around them and a signal-'Cat on the bridgewing called in. "They requestin' permission to direct our ships to moorings."

Bemused, Matt nodded. "Very well. Honest to God, I wouldn't know where to put 'em." There were a lot of ships at anchor in the bay. Most were "heavy haulers," essentially freighters based on enlargements of the old Scott Class frigate design, but there were even bigger things too, like they'd never yet seen in the west. There were ships that looked like "proper" freighters and oilers, indistinguishable from some Matt would've seen in any port on the old world, except these were a little smaller and old-fashioned-looking. And they apparently had wooden hulls, of course. None of the SPDs (self-propelled dry docks) were in residence, nor, sadly, any of the carriers. The SPD *Tarakan Island* had already sailed east, as had USNRS *Salissa* and USS *Madraas*. Matt would've loved to share this homecoming with the carriers' commanders, Keje and Tassanna, but they would've arrived weeks before and, as soon as *Big Sal* completed swift dry dock repairs, steamed east as well. They were just too slow to waste time waiting around, and were probably in the Filpin Lands by now.

There were other unexpected guests. Two of the big Grik ironclad battleships lay at anchor in the roadstead, and neither was *Sular*—the one they'd converted to a semi-armored troopship. *She* was just coming out of a dry dock farther north, barely visible through the jumble of hulls and forest of masts. At second glance, however, the other two seemed to have undergone similar conversions. Both had only two funnels now, and their old armaments had been removed.

"I wonder where they got those?" Bernie asked.

"Madraas," Toos replied at once. "Before I, ah, raan off to help Commaander Tiaa build a new bow for *Mahaan*, I waas stuck raaising and fixing those naasty Grik things to send baack here."

Matt was watching the MTBs signaling for *Savoie* and *Gray* to anchor among the other large ships sharing the roadstead west of the docks and had a sudden thought. "Any comm traffic?" he asked Minnie. She promptly queried Ed Palmer below in the radio shack. A few moments later, she reported his response in her small, high-pitched voice. "Not a peep, Cap-i-taan, other thaan normaal chaatter from scout planes. Nothin' about us at all."

"Huh," Matt murmured. "As much as 'Cats love to gab, they're taking Mr. Stokes's radio silence pretty seriously."

James Ellis was the first to approach the dock, gliding straight in until she kissed it, and line handlers quickly secured her. *Mahan* was next, with an equally easy approach. The lane had been cleared, and they wouldn't have to twist and turn through any obstacles.

"Take her in, Mr. Toos," Matt commanded. The burly Lemurian nodded, blinking nervously. He knew his limitations, and if it had required any squirming around, Matt would've taken the conn himself, or asked Spanky to do it. He secretly suspected Sandra or Diania would do a better job, but Toos had to gain confidence with experience. As it was, he came in a little fast, reversed too much, and left Matt sitting white-knuckled in his seat. But by the time he nervously cried "All Stop!" he'd brought *Walker* to a halt within a dozen yards of the dock, an easy throw for her lines. The thunder of the blowers dwindled to a faint rumble—before Matt realized the crowd alongside was roaring.

"Liberty, Captain?" were Spanky's first words.

Matt nodded and stood. "For once, we're not sinking and nobody's shooting at us. Just a skeleton watch tonight, Mr. McFarlane," he added formally. "But have everybody back aboard by the forenoon watch. I'll have an idea what's what by then and we can arrange some real leave for our people. He stood and grinned at his wife. "My God, do you realize what we're about to unleash on this city?"

She chuckled. "Besides the obvious?"

"Yeah. Silva."

Sandra's eyes widened.

"I say lock his ass up," Spanky instantly suggested.

"Maybe . . . that's not such a good idea," Sandra countered, frowning. "He'd probably wreck the ship breaking out, and after all he's done for us, I wouldn't blame him. Besides, we need him too much. Can't let him hurt himself, or do something serious you'd *have* to lock him up for. Hmm . . ."

"What?" asked Matt, suspicious of the mischievous expression growing on his wife's face. She smiled reassuringly. "I think I've got it covered. Don't worry about it." Coughing politely, she gestured behind him. Matt turned to see Juan Marcos frowning disapproval at his khakis. He sighed. "Right. I know. It'll be a few minutes before they rig the gangway. I'm heading down to my stateroom to change right now."

"Better hurry, Skipper," Spanky said, nodding outside. Anxious dockworkers were already positioning a new wooden gangway, its fresh-cut planking bright and crisp. "Do you need help with your sword and pistol belt?" Juan asked. It wasn't as much a question as a reminder. Nat Hardee also told them that Chairman Letts wanted senior Allied officers to go armed at all times, even in Baalkpan, until they learned the extent of the suspected conspiracy against the Union. Such a precaution would've seemed ridiculous once, but there were so many new people in the city, from all over, it was impossible to be sure of each and every one. "I can manage that," Sandra replied. "And I'll make sure he puts it on too."

Walker's crew was already streaming down the gangway and boats were motoring in from the anchored ships when Matt, Sandra, Diania, and Pam Cross gathered by the brow. Sandra was clutching little Fitzhugh Adar Reddy close and Matt noted she'd added extra padding to his bundle, in case they got jostled in the mob. They were quickly joined by Spanky, Bernie, Tabby, Toos, Ed Palmer, and Nat Hardee. Sonny Campeti would remain in charge of the ship while Silva and Lawrence escorted the gaggle of officers. Chief Bosun Gray had once proclaimed himself head of the "Captain's Guard," choosing its members by steadiness, its number fluctuating with the circumstances. Silva had unconsciously assumed Gray's role after his death (when he was available to do so), but figured there wasn't much he and Lawrence couldn't handle. Of course, none of the officers they were guarding—except maybe Palmer—was helpless in a fight.

Before they could leave, a small party of Lemurian yard workers pushed past the dwindling flow. Their leader, carrying a writing slate, didn't salute, but he was grinning broadly. "I'm haappy to be first to welcome you home!" he said. "I'm the overhaaul supervisor, an' dis is my evaal crew. You got lotsa work for us, an' Chairmaan Letts waants us right on it."

Matt looked apologetically at Tabby and Toos. "Get the general schedule worked out, then take off. But make sure the new boiler's at the top of the list."

"Ay, ay, sur," Tabby and Toos chorused. The rest proceeded down the gangway and the boisterous cheers and cries of jubilation redoubled at the sight of them.

The dockyard had turned to bedlam as long-absent Lemurian sailors found their mates and squealed with happiness. Many hoisted new younglings for the very first time. But even if they'd never seen them themselves, all of *Walker*'s officers—and Matt and "Lady" Sandra in particular—had become iconic figures across the Grand Alliance, and especially in Baalkpan. The roar of approval for all they'd done resounded thunderously, seemingly spreading away from the dock to encompass the entire city. Matt felt Sandra's free hand clutch his and appreciated the contact. He even smirked slightly as the historian's voice rose within him, reminding that successful Roman commanders were supposed to have had someone, maybe a slave, constantly telling them "remember, you're mortal" during their triumphal processions. He didn't need anyone to remind him of that.

A square of Lemurian troops in standard (if fresh and unfaded) combat dress, armed with immaculate Allin-Silva rifles, opened before them, revealing a group of dignitaries. Matt was stunned to realize he only recognized a few, and didn't think he knew *any* of the Lemurians. That bothered him a lot. There was Henry Stokes, though, standing to the left. His wiry frame beginning to spread a little, and he wore Imperial-style weskit, coat, knee breeches, and tall brown boots. Matt wondered if that was typical human attire in the Union now. On the right, to Matt's surprise, was a similarly dressed Ambassador Bolton Forester. He'd been planning to retire and return to the Empire long ago. Had he stayed out of necessity, or just because he liked it here? Then there were Alan and Karen Letts, of course, both grinning hugely while trying to manage their children. Karen held a human toddler, Allison Verdia, while Alan tried to keep an even younger 'Cat named Seetsi from squirming out of his grasp. "Sandra" was their oldest adopted Lemurian daughter, named after Matt's wife and Karen's friend. Wearing a bright dress she'd contrived to streak with mud and creosote, she scampered boldly forward to peer at Matt and Sandra's son. "He's *pink*, just like a baby mouse!" she cried delightedly, without any accent at all.

"Yes, he is," Sandra agreed, laughing, and kneeling to embrace the precocious Lemurian child. "My name is Sandra too! I'm so glad to meet you at last."

"C'mon," the little Sandra said, tugging Matt's wife forward. "The sooner you meet my parents, the sooner we can get out of here and I can play!"

Silva leaned over and muttered at Lawrence, "Kinda how I feel."

"That's enough, young lady!" Karen scolded her impatient daughter, but now she was hugging her old friend and their two human children had been mashed face-to-face. "He stinks," remarked Allison Verdia, wrinkling her nose.

Matt solemnly shook Alan's hand. "Glad to see you . . . Mr. Chairman."

Alan shifted a wide-eyed Seetsi to the crook of his left arm and crisply saluted Matt. "Am I ever glad to see *you*, sir—and that rusty old bucket you rode in on." He shrugged, indicating the high-collar white uniform he wore, which was the same as Matt's. "And 'chairman' or not, as long as I'm in this, I'm under your orders. Not the other way around."

Matt smiled and shook his head. "*Not* the way it's supposed to work."

Alan shrugged again. "I guess. Too bad." Then he grinned. "Of course, if you *agree* you have to do what I say, that makes things easier. For example, I can make you accept some . . . revisions, shall we say, to the way you do things."

Matt stubbornly shook his head, suspecting where this was going. "Not if it's combat, or Navy Clan business."

"Maybe not," Alan conceded, "but I can make you take on a real, honest-to-God staff, for a change. Call 'em my representatives if you want, but you need to spread the work around, let others help you plan. This war went beyond what one man can handle a long time ago." He waved his arm around. "Believe me, I know. It's a miracle you've done as well as you have."

"I *have* a staff," Matt objected, glancing at Spanky. "All the officers and skippers under my command, and the land force officers too."

"It's not the same," Stokes denied, "and you bloody well know it." He glanced around, but there was no way anyone could hear what they said with all the noise. "Things aren't only bigger now, they're *different*. It was bound to happen eventually, mashed together as we were, but with the war pushed back farther than most can see it, the glue you used to hold things together is startin' to get wet."

"Mr. Hardee mentioned your suspicions."

"A bit more than 'suspicions' now," Stokes glowered, "but this isn't the time or place."

"Yeah."

"You *will* need a staff, though," Forester reemphasized with his deep, kindly voice, returning to a point they'd apparently agreed to hammer. "Not only for the obvious reasons, but to help . . . integrate developments you may not be aware of," he added, smiling conspiratorially.

"I assume you've already started thinking about how we're going to lick the Dom-League alliance," Alan stipulated.

"Sure. I started thinking about that as soon as they started killing our people."

"And with a good idea of what they have, you know you can't do it with what you brought home today."

"I've been stirring things around," Matt hedged, "based on what we have—and what we hope to. That's given me an outline to work from." He wouldn't mention that his overall strategy was already well established, discussed in depth with Sandra, Spanky, and Courtney Bradford. Given Stokes's concerns, he probably wouldn't add many to that list for a while.

Alan grinned even more broadly. "Swell. I'm sure it's a good one. But that's all the more reason you need a dedicated team to help put flesh on the bones of your outline." Matt could only blink at him, and Alan explained. "God knows how much we've been able to keep secret from the enemy, but something must be working because even *you* don't know about some of the fun toys you're going to get, do you?"

Completely taken aback, Matt shook his head. "I know about the new DDs, and torpedoes. There's more?"

Alan, Stokes, and Forester all laughed. Some of the Lemurian representatives behind them started making impatient noises. They were ready to be introduced and couldn't hear anything. "A lot more," Stokes confirmed. "You think the handful of tanks we sent you in Africa is all we've come up with? In a *year*?" He grinned wickedly. "Or all the specs we sent on what our allies are building—and you complained so much about—were real?" He shook his head. "Too many chances for them to be intercepted. I think you'll like what everyone's really been up to."

"And how better to fool the enemy than by duping me?" Matt mused. "Sneaky. And annoying. Costly too," he accused, wondering what they might've given him to save lives against the Grik—or to High Admiral Jenks against the Doms! "But effective," he granted.

"And necessary," Stokes stressed. "But now isn't the time," he repeated as the commotion behind him increased.

"All the more reason you need knowledgeable people helping you," Forester insisted. "Quite a few, in fact, including myself, of course. To help complete your 'outline.' Perhaps rearrange it a bit, as well."

"Maybe so," Matt finally grudged, fully aware that consenting would probably also mean accepting what all this was really aimed at: getting him out of *Walker*. He understood the rationale, but even discounting his personal feelings on the matter, he wasn't sure it was right. He had no illusions about his old ship's capabilities and doubted she—or *Mahan*—even belonged in any more fights. But she was where all his people, human and Lemurian, perhaps the entire Grand Alliance, *expected* him to lead from. *Walker* was their talisman, far more than him, he believed: a dilapidated but tangible symbol of past victories and hope for the future. And maybe her very decrepitude was an asset, in an "if *she* can still swing it, we can too" sense? Finally, ultimately, if his old destroyer wound up in the final fight, where the hell else *could* he be? He'd have to ponder that.

Alan turned, letting the first wave of Lemurian ministers, assemblypersons, and their deputies through, and their enthusiasm momentarily banished Matt's sour mood. These were politicians, but enough of them proudly shouted the names of battles and places they'd been, and a one-armed female stepped in front of him with an awkward, left-landed salute, proclaiming she'd been in *Mahan* at Second Madraas. Matt was struck by that because he now knew it was a League torpedo, not an errant one from *Walker*, that blew off *Mahan*'s bow—and this former sailor's arm. She knew it too, and most of these people were with them to the end. The others . . .

Stokes tugged on his sleeve and pulled his ear down near his lips. "See that ugly striped bugger over there?" he asked, indicating a rather surly-looking knot of Lemurians that hadn't advanced.

Matt thought he saw the 'Cat Stokes meant. "The one in black and red, with white whiskers?"

"That's the one. Deputy Assemblyperson Giaan-Naak. From Sular. Deputy in name only, since his boss never leaves Saa-leebs." Stokes chuckled darkly. "I think Giaan knocked him off. All them Sularaans've gotten pretty pushy, but Giaan's the real croaker. Watch out for him."

"You said there was more than just suspicion . . . ?" Matt asked tentatively.

Stokes hesitated. "You remember *Savoie*'s old skipper, exec, whatever the hell he was. Named Dupont?"

Matt's lip curled. "Yeah. Why?"

"We squeezed him as tight as we could, an' even Fiedler an' Hoffman had a go at him when they got here. You'll see Walbert Fiedler tonight, by the way. I want him on your staff. Anyway, Dupont'd clammed up by then, an' we'd actually kind of lost interest in him. Then, about a month ago, an' about right when a lot of other stuff started happening, somebody broke him out. Killed two guards."

Matt grabbed Stokes's coat. "What the hell?"

"Later," Stokes stressed, pushing away.

"Come! Come!" Alan shouted. "Let's move out of the press!" Misunderstanding Matt's suddenly furious expression, he added apologetically, "We've set up a reception at the Great Hall. You know how that'll be. Music, stories, dancing—though you'll find it a little different from what you remember. Stay for a while, then go see your home for the first time in a year!"

"What about us, Skipper?" Silva asked, jerking his thumb at Lawrence, and almost poking Petey in the eye. "With all Chairman Letts's troops around, you think you'll need us?" To Matt's surprise, Silva didn't sound like he was trying to bug out. He'd obviously *like* to, but he'd stick without complaint.

"Take off," Matt said, still fulminating, but knowing there was nothing for it at the moment. "Have fun," he added more cheerfully, then reminded, "but be back at the ship before the forenoon watch."

A gap-toothed grin appeared on the big man's face. "Count on it, Skipper. C'mon, Larry!"

"One thing!" Sandra shouted before Silva and Lawrence could disappear.

"I want you to help Diania find Gunny Horn, then escort Lieutenant Cross to the hospital where General Queen Safir-Maraan is staying. You should find Chack there," she added more softly. "I'll be along directly myself, and you *will* wait for me!" She suspected seeing so many wounded comrades and friends might have a cooling effect on Silva's revelry. Especially with Pam along. She couldn't *order* Silva to pay attention to Pam, or stick by her all night, but she could make sure they spent a little time together. And maybe they wouldn't fight in a hospital. . . .

CHAPTER 15

*////// **Baalkpan, Borno***

How's Colonel Chack?" *Savoie*'s acting gunnery officer, Arnold Horn, almost had to shout the question as he slid onto a bench across the scarred, rough-hewn table from Silva and Lawrence. They were seated in the open-air fringe of the Busted Screw, Baalkpan's oldest and hottest nightspot for Navy and Marine personnel. Lawrence managed benches by straddling them, but that forced him to twist awkwardly sideways to plant both elbows on the table. He sat like that now, hands wrapped around a large brass beer mug while his long purple tongue darted in it, nonstop. Silva had a pair of pitchers and two mugs, one for Horn, but the first pitcher was empty, the second almost so. Petey seemed jumpier than usual, and eyed Horn like he'd never seen him before.

The place was particularly packed that night—understandably—and even out from under the broad, colorful awning protecting the central area (including bar, bandstand, dance floor, and about half the tables) from near-daily rains, Silva and Lawrence had been lucky to find a spot. And that was only because some awestruck young 'Cat Marines from the ATC across the bay graciously (and a little fearfully) relinquished theirs. The Marines-in-training didn't leave, they only backed away and sat cross-legged in the sand a little farther out, staring at the "heroes."

"Chackie's in a funk," Silva answered Horn, carefully enunciating his words while dribbling the remains of the second pitcher in his friend's mug. Holding the large vessel over his head, he signaled for a refill. "He's *still* 'our Chackie,'" he defended, "but Gen'ral Queen Safir gettin' conked, kinda drew his fires. Sure, she's his mate an' all, but . . ." He shook his head. "Drink up, ol' buddy. Lady Sandra kep' me an' poor Larry coolin' our heels at the hospital for *hours*. Don't know why—'cept so Pam'd have plenty o' time to rag me. It was swell seein' Chackie an' Safir," he reflected, "an' there's other right guys in the joint I was glad to see alive, but Chackie didn't wanna talk, an' Safir fell asleep. Even Pam's turntable wound down by the time Lady Sandra showed, an' we took off."

He blinked and squinted his good eye at the big clock over the bar as a smiling, scantily clad ex-pat Impie gal took both empty pitchers and set a full one on the table. Silva smiled appreciatively, recognizing yet another way Baalkpan in general, and the Busted Screw in particular, had changed. The Screw was in a pretty rough district now, and not only were there waiters and waitresses of both sexes and every species in the Alliance, they clearly focused on the most receptive groups . . . and occasionally disappeared. Female sailors and Marines went off with male waiters, or vice versa, and the pairings weren't always members of the same species. *Weird,* Silva thought, a little blearily. *Not that I'm the king o' morality. An' me an' Risa might've even started* that *sorta stuff. But nobody here ever cooked up pay to play before the war. Before we came. Wasn't no need.* He blinked. *Oh well. Things were pretty damn weird in Subic an' Shanghai, once upon a time.*

He looked at his companions. "But the little hand says we only got two hours to soak in these suds, so let's get at it." Regulations posted on the gate to the bar area plainly spelled out how much beer or liquor could be consumed (and within how many hours of expected duty) by military personnel. Only those with a "leave card" punched with at least two days remaining were unlimited. Silva didn't have one of those, and everyone knew when those who'd arrived with First Fleet had to report. For that reason—and others—despite all the back pay they'd accumulated, they hadn't been given much money to spend. They'd get more when they got leave, but even though the new economy was thriving in the United Homes, most of First Fleet's Lemurian sailors had been gone so long they didn't understand it, and few had any idea what their money was worth. It would be tabulated for them in savings accounts until they got the hang of things. Still, technically, Silva, Horn, and Lawrence could each have two pitchers of beer—as long as they were served before 0100 hours. It was 2205 now.

"How much have you already had?" Horn asked suspiciously.

"Just three," Silva defended, punctuating his statement with a loud belch. He appeared satisfied with the volume and Petey seemed astounded. "My two, an' some o' one o' Larry's. He's still on his first mug." He looked owlishly at his Sa'aaran friend. "Though he's been givin' it hell. Cryin' shame he can't drink like regular folks."

"I could, it in a *dish*," Larry reminded, annoyed. "You get I a dish?"

Silva solemnly shook his head. "Wouldn't be right, little buddy. Nobody drinks beer like that. They'd throw us out." He added a little to Lawrence's mug, then refilled his own. "Don't worry. Me an' Arnie'll keep up your end, so it don't look like yer slackin'. Besides, you ain't used to it. Like as not, you'd just spew an' waste it all. 'Cats always made pretty good beer," he told Horn, filling his mug as well. "This is even better'n San Miguel," he judged benevolently. "Pukin' it up'd be a sin!"

"Sin," Petey piously agreed. He didn't demand something to eat, for once, and Horn saw his proud little belly was probably painfully swollen. Silva noted his gaze and shrugged. "Just about ever-body in the hospital tossed somethin' at the little mooch."

Drums thundered and music began to play. There was a fair number of old-world musical instruments, or copies of them, the former including a pump organ of all things. But many Lemurian instruments remained and they'd interwoven with the others to create some very unusual sounds. The combinations had evolved over time and didn't clash as much, to Silva's murky ears, and he caught himself enjoying the result. Even so, it took him a while to recognize a tune, quite popular from where he came. "I'll be damned," he muttered, incredulously. "That's 'Two Sleepy People,' just runnin' faster! Ha!" He then exploded in laughter when a female Lemurian's clear, high voice replaced Fats Waller's jaunty, slightly scratchy singing. That earned him some annoyed blinking and stares. The dance floor started to fill. "Ain't this a hoot?" he demanded of Horn before emptying his mug again.

"So how was General Safir?" Horn asked, practically shouting in Silva's ear. "Is she going to be okay?"

"Sure. She's a little dopey 'cause they keep her seeped up pretty good. Got her whole right eye socket caved in, after all. Way worse than me"—he poked a finger at the patch over his ruined left eye—"an' this *still* smarts from time to time."

"I heard she got shot too."

"Yeah. Twice. But that breastplate she always wears flattened them Grik musket balls an' slowed 'em down. They took one outa her left boob, big an' flat as a silver dollar. I seen it. The other . . ." He frowned.

"Is the real reason the general heals so slo', and Colonel Chack stays so close and sad," Lawrence said, hunkering closer to his beer.

Horn would've sworn he looked morose. "What did it do?" he demanded.

"Not my place, Arnie," Silva said, waving it away.

"If it involves Colonel Chack, it *is* your place to tell *me*. After what we went through with him!" Horn insisted.

Silva looked at him as he refilled his mug, took another swallow, then wiped his mouth. "I s'pose. But this ain't nobody *else's* business, see?"

"Of course, you idiot."

Silva grunted, then continued in the lowest voice Horn could hear. "Seems General Queen Safir-Maraan was pregnant, an' that second ball ended it. Might've ended it forever, if you get my drift. Now the poor kid not only figures she's too ugly for Chack"—he pointed at his eye—"but since she might never have kids, she don't want him stuck to her, neither."

"Shit," Horn murmured, and took his own long gulp.

"Yeah. *That's* why Chackie's leeched out. Not only lost his kid, but his wife, mate . . . whatever—who he's stupid for, dents an' all—wants to throw him off for *his* own good. They can do that, y'know." He snapped his fingers. "Just like that."

"But why? I still don't get it. Why run him off if he doesn't want to go?"

"I ain't real sure," Silva confessed. "Partly, maybe *mainly* for why I said, but there's more. There's way more to a *lotta* things than there used to be," he lamented. "Goddamn politics. Remember, Safir ain't just Second Corps' gen'ral, she's the friggin' *Queen* o' Aryaal an' B'mbaado. Chackie wouldn't never be king or nothin', but their kids could'a been. Best I can tell, listenin' to her talk with Lady Sandra, she's gotta have an heir or Aryaal an' B'mbaado might split an' start fightin' again."

"So why not adopt? 'Cats don't care about blood."

"They do in Aryaal an' B'mbaado." Silva looked at Horn as if trying to decide whether he was still only one of him. "You weren't here yet when we first met 'em, but folks on those two islands fought all the damn time." He pounded his finger on the table. "An' they care about that shit in the Filpin Lands too. More than you'd think."

It finally dawned on Horn. "And Chack isn't from there."

"Nope." Silva topped off their mugs, draining another pitcher. "Let's see if I can get this straight. Seems even if Safir can't have kids, but her hubby has the right blood, he can rake one up off some other highborn broad.

There's your heir. Folks'd know, but they'd sit still for it. Might even make things tighter if her new mate's from Aryaal and the broad's from B'mbaado. Safir caused enough ruckus when she mated with Chackie in the first place, but she—and he, to be fair—were admired enough at the time that nobody cared as long as *her* blood kept flowin' through their kids. Got it?"

"That's crazy."

"Yep. And stupid. Personally, I don't see how their . . . acristicrissy—is that the right word?—even matters now. The gooduns stayed and fought, an' most got ate by the Grik. The turds slunk off—like the honchos from Sular. Now they're slitherin' back. *I* think they oughta hang 'em, but Safir's worried they got enough support to keep things rocky. More'n anything, she wants the war *over*—if it's ever over. Not more damn fightin' amongst theirselves."

"That's . . . tough," Horn finally said, brows knitted, thinking. "A real shitty deal for both of them. I hope they sort it out." He was suddenly very glad his beloved Diania wasn't royalty of any sort. As far as she knew, she didn't even have any living family in the Empire.

They drank in silence for a while, listening to the music and watching the rowdy spectacle on the dance floor and elsewhere, even cheering with the rest when a couple slipped away. Once, both men would've joined in without thought, even going off with a girl. (Silva had identified the "madam": a large Dutchwoman behind the bar, who'd come to this world in *S-19*, supposedly helping Sister Audrey with the children in her care. She hadn't been much good at that, but was apparently thriving now.) But Horn was devoted to Diania and would never break her trust. Silva was . . . connected to Pam, in kaleidoscopically confusing and ill-defined ways, despite how much they fought. And he knew where she was, right then, waiting for him. They wouldn't fight when he joined her later.

"Look!" Lawrence said, nearly knocking his beer mug over and pointing with his snout. It was only the second time he'd spoken—and his tongue stopped lapping—and he appeared a little bleary-eyed. It dawned on Silva that, far from being "used" to it, he'd *never* seen Lawrence drink before. His little Sa'aaran buddy might be drunk. *Well, so'm I,* he acknowledged. *Empty belly, no booze in months . . .* He looked where Lawrence indicated, and there, storming toward the bar with grim purpose in their eyes, was a very unlikely trio. The massive Earl Lanier was plowing through the crowd, effortlessly displacing patrons with his great, mushy mass. CPO "Pepper," Lanier's original partner in establishing this bar, and now Chief Bosun on

USS *Fitzhugh Gray*, came on just as belligerently, if less intimidating. Finally, and probably least menacing of all at a glance, but most outwardly furious, was *Walker*'s scrawny Chief Isak Reuben. *If they ain't scared o' him, it's because they don't know the little shit,* Silva thought, especially when he saw the baseball bat Isak carried. *An' they don't know how he can hit!* The music screeched and tooted to a stop as the 'Cat and two men crashed past the players and sent the singer skittering behind the organ. To their credit, the big Dutchwoman and a little black and white 'Cat, colored a lot like Pepper, stood their ground behind the bar. "C'mon," Silva said, rising. "We need a ringside seat for this!"

"Get the hell out from behind my bar!" Earl thundered, shattering the general hubbub and creating a stunning near silence. Silva was grinning, a little wobbly himself, as he and Horn pulled a tottering Lawrence through the crush of spectators.

"*Our* baar," Pepper stressed, but his glare was on the 'Cat.

"That's Pepper's cousin," Silva whispered through an uncharacteristic giggle. "He must have five hunner'd of 'em, but that's the one Pepper left in charge o' the joint when he shipped out in *Gray*!"

"Speaking of *Gray*." Horn nodded into the gloom. A fair number of 'Cats in whites were following the confrontational trio. They weren't all from the light cruiser either. There were some of Lanier's assistant cooks and mess attendants as well.

"Hoo boy," Silva said.

"The Busted Screw belongs to me!" roared the Dutchwoman, slamming a heavy club on the counter, knocking mugs onto the dance floor. "I legally purchased a majority partnership from Kanaak-Uraa." She tilted her head toward the Lemurian by her side.

"Well that's odd as hell," Lanier rumbled, "'cause it wasn't his to sell. Pepper left him in charge of it"—he rolled his eyes when Isak yanked on his sleeve—"an' other of our interests, when he went off to protect your sorry, thievin' asses from the murderin' Grik."

The Dutchwoman—Silva couldn't remember her name for the life of him—simply shook her head. "According to Law number One Eighteen, passed by the Union Assembly and signed by former Chairman Adar, 'any property, improved or bare, deemed necessary to the war effort and having been abandoned, may be utilized by anyone who proves they will continue providing a necessary service, or construct facilities to provide other services agreed to be essential to the general welfare or prosecution of the war.'"

Lanier's eyes bulged. "What the hell? They cooked that up to keep shit runnin', or build shipyards an' such on land a buncha fat, chickenshit 'Cats ran off from. Tryin' to get *away* from the Grik!" he bellowed louder. "Not goin' to *fight* 'em! An' it don't say shit about you stealin' my goddamn bar!"

"*Our* goddaamn baar!" Pepper corrected emphatically.

"An' me an' Pepper an' Gilbert's PIG-cig factory, neither!" Isak added loudly, screechy voice breaking with fury. That's when half a dozen large men, Impies by the look of them, with long, braided mustaches, came out through a curtain behind the bar and quickly rounded it to stand in front of the outraged trio.

"Bouncers, huh? Hired thugs," Lanier growled, looking up at a man who seemed to tower over him. "We never needed none o' them, did we, Pepper?" he asked aside, then glared at his nearest adversary. "How're you supposed to scare me when you're too yellow to fight the Doms?" The man never had a chance to reply, because Lanier's fat fist slammed the bottom of his jaw and teeth exploded outward like bloody chips of ice. The man went down like he'd been poleaxed—but there were more.

"Always knew Earl was strong!" Silva hooted. "Have to be, to heave so much lard around!"

Isak shrieked like a rhino pig being eaten alive and his bat cracked against another bouncer's thigh, knocking his legs out from under him, but it rebounded and shattered when it hit a rigidly planted stool. His weapon wrecked, Isak jumped on the man like a grasshopper, pummeling the sides of his head with sharp-knuckled fists. Pepper emitted a keening cry and went for his cousin over the bar. One big man tried to grab him, another went for Isak. *Two* big Impies started pounding Lanier's well-padded belly.

"*Here* we go!" Silva roared with glee, shoving a reeling Lawrence toward Horn. "Get our little salamander outa here, Arnie! He's never been in a fight for fun. Drunk, he'll prob'ly kill somebody!" With that, he turned and grabbed the man trying to pull Isak off his comrade. The guy was fast and spun with a fist, connecting with Silva's right cheek. Silva saw what looked like sparks jetting from a funnel and took another heavy blow to the mouth while shaking the first hit off. His assailant paused and blinked when Petey hissed and assumed an aggressive posture on Silva's shoulder. He seemed even more surprised when Silva only spread a bloody grin. "I'd say 'you hit like a girl,' bub, but I been hit *harder* by girls! You fellas don't know what you've got yourselfs into. We're straight back from whuppin' the *Griks* all the way back to Old Sofesshk!" With strength and reflexes honed in deadly combat at similar quarters against foes that could tear him apart and eat him, Silva's fist flattened the man's nose flush with his face. Blood sprayed like the red yolk of a shattered egg—and that was about the last thing Silva remembered with any certainty.

Others would recall what came to be known as "The Battle of the Busted Screw" in lurid detail, though their descriptions evolved with the telling. Many witnesses became participants themselves, after all. So like any great battle, specifics quickly grew murky. Testimony to the shore patrol did reveal a few consistent facts and impressions, however. These were taken into account when Chairman Letts himself was summoned from his sleep to render summary judgment on those apprehended at the scene. Bleary-eyed and resigned (he'd been expecting something like this and left word not to trouble any of First Fleet's officers without his say-so), Alan Letts arrived at the brig closest to the waterfront in a robe and soft moccasin-like slippers.

Acting Gunnery Officer Arnold Horn and an unusually loquacious (if oddly incoherent) Lawrence stood as witnesses to the altercation, and representatives for one faction. It was a pretty mixed bunch, but the locals that didn't need medical attention were left to sleep it off in the brig, and the First Fleet sailors were taken (or carried) back to their ships. That left only Earl, Pepper, and Isak.

Horn stipulated that Earl Lanier struck the first blow. Earl wouldn't deny it (in fact, he couldn't, since he wasn't conscious), and there were plenty of witnesses, in any case. Most agreed there'd been extenuating circumstances, however. Chief Isak Reuben was accused of assaulting a civilian with a weapon, but Horn claimed he was merely demonstrating the proper use of what turned out to be defective sporting equipment. Isak said nothing in his own defense, having been counselled not to speak at all. When queried about Chief Bosun Pepper, Horn denied he'd been trying to drown his cousin in a barrel of seep, but had, in fact, attempted to pull him out after he fell in, headfirst. That's how it looked to Lawrence too, though he hadn't seen how he got there in the first place.

"Okay," Alan said tiredly, shifting a page on top of the report aside, "but how'd an ordinary bar fight turn into a riot?"

Horn seemed to wince. "Sir, there were a lot of *Gray* and *Walker* sailors there, already hot about what they'd heard about the Busted Screw—you didn't know about that?"

Alan levelled a narrow-eyed glare at a scruffy, sticky-looking Kanaak-Uraa, the three bloody Impie bouncers able to stand, and the intimidatingly large, disheveled, makeup-smeared Dutchwoman he remembered was named Serre Kloet. He'd thought she was one of Earl's partners too. "No, I didn't," he said sourly. "Get on with it, Mr. Horn."

"Yes sir. Best I can tell, a few local patrons probably just started out trying to break it up, but the cruisermen and destroyermen thought they were piling onto their shipmates." He glared at the Dutchwoman. "Some were. Looks like *she'd* been expecting trouble, and laid in a lot of extra bullyboys."

"The sailors attacked like fiends!" the Dutchwoman accused.

"That's enough, uh, Miss Kloet. Sounds like everybody went a little nuts, and the fight took to the streets." He waved a page. "There's reports of damage up to a *quarter mile* from the Screw!" He took a long breath and wiped a crackle from the corner of his eye. "And what about Silva? One account describes, and I quote"—he looked at another page—"'A one-eyed madman, roaring like a gri-maax'—you know that's a 'super lizard,' right?—when he single-handedly waded in and beat three men half to death." He glanced at Kloet. "The bouncers trying to kill Earl, Pepper, and Isak, I take it? Don't know whether to give him a reprimand or commendation for that," he mumbled, then looked back at Horn. "But he was last seen sitting on the bar in the midst of the spreading melee, throwing 'Cats around by their *tails* and paddling the rump of a woman as big as him." He raised his eyebrows at Kloet. "Who in turn was thundering like a wounded brontosarry and tearing the counter apart beneath them so she could beat *him* with a board!"

"The man is a *beast*!" Serre Kloet seethed. "And certainly no gentleman," she added, tilting her nose up.

"Who you tried to murder with a 'weapon' of your own?" Letts countered.

"And *you* ain't no *lady*!" Lawrence ejaculated happily and belched, tugging on Arnold Horn's sleeve. "I told a *joke*, Gunny! A *good* joke! Ha!"

Alan Letts blinked resignation in the Lemurian way. "My God. The biggest fight this city's seen since the Battle of Baalkpan and I'm sitting in a robe at three in the morning talking to a drunk lizard." He sighed and appraised Horn. "So where's Silva? He seems to have caused the most damage, as usual."

Horn looked pensive. "I'm sorry, sir, I honestly can't say. And *I* didn't see Silva do anything. He was there with Lawrence and I, for a while, but I understood he had other plans for later."

Letts was surprised. "Are you telling me it wasn't him? How many one-eyed maniacs do you know?"

"More than one, sir," Horn answered truthfully. "It's been a tough war." Alan started to ask if Horn knew more than one with a lizard-shaped parrot crawling on his head, yelling as loud as he was, but decided to skip it. Horn stroked the dark whiskers of his beard and asked, "Did *anyone*—besides Miss Kloet—positively identify Silva? Maybe he just left when the fight started."

Alan rolled his eyes. "Oh, please."

"And even if it *was* him," Horn hurried on, waving at Pepper (Lanier was still stretched out on a cot, like a sleeping walrus), "the *actual* owners of the Busted Screw don't want any damages from him."

Alan steepled his fingers in front of his face, like he'd seen Matt do so many times. "Which brings up another subject, doesn't it? Chief Bosun Pepper and Earl Lanier did, unquestionably, establish the Castaway Cook, AKA the Busted Screw. I remember." His eyes turned frosty. "Their departure for active duty in no way constituted abandonment. Law One Eighteen was never intended to serve as a vehicle for such underhanded usurpation. Kanaak-Uraa, at least, is liable for damages and lost revenues he appropriated from the absent partners." He looked at Serre Kloet. "Maybe he snookered you too, but that's for a more in-depth investigation to determine." He turned his chair toward a 'Cat Marine with an "SP" band, for "Shore Patrol," on her sleeve. "Take Kanaak-Uraa to a separate cell, for now. We'll put his case before the City Justice, but taking advantage of those off fighting for us is about the worst thing you can do, right up under treason."

"An' he swiped my PIG-cig factory too!" Isak chirped, unable to contain himself any longer. "You know how hard it was for me an' Gilbert to figure out how to strip that waxy crap off them leaves they grow in Aryaal?" he whined.

Alan glowered. "He might've done you a favor. Hard to make or not, your tobacco's the next thing to poison, and you've got half the Alliance hooked on it. Me too," he admitted. "They've got *real* tobacco in the NUS, which you don't have to wash with brontosarry piss. Partner up with the Nussies after the war and make cigarettes that won't tear people's lungs out." He looked at Horn. "Get 'em out of here so I can go back to sleep."

"But sir . . ." Horn began frantically. Just as Silva had been supposed to meet Pam—he guessed that's where the big destroyerman vanished during the brawl—he was supposed to see Diania again. *Not that we'll* do *anything until after the wedding, but still,* he thought wistfully. "Sir," he repeated, "they're not from my ship."

Alan grinned. "You defended 'em. They're your responsibility."

CHAPTER 16

////// Baalkpan, Borno
May 16, 1945

Surrounded by trusted guards and a cluster of hangers-on, Deputy Assemblyperson Giaan-Naak swept in through the elaborately embroidered curtain entrance to the Sularaan section of the Saa-Leeban Consulate. The large new wooden building was one of the first nonmilitary or industrial structures in Baalkpan to stand on a concrete foundation. It was situated south of the Great Hall with the momentous Galla tree towering up within it—now home to the Union Assembly Hall on the ground floor, in addition to numerous ministerial offices above—and separated only by a kind of park where the old parade ground used to be.

The park no longer hosted drilling and maneuvering troops, and hadn't since the Baalkpan Advanced Training Center was established across the bay. It simply wasn't large enough anymore. Instead (and ironically, to Giaan-Naak), it now hosted only an ever-increasing number of dead, unnaturally *buried* in the gentle shade of hundreds of young trees. Giaan hated it. No Mi-Anakka had ever imagined such a gruesome fate for their remains before the destroyermen came with all their deviant schemes and weapons. But more and more *People* chose to be planted (when possible) alongside their rotting comrades instead of rising to the Heavens, tenderly shrouded in the smoke of their funeral pyres. The very thought of the cemetery was enough to turn Giaan's stomach, for spiritual as well as personal reasons. He knew many had come to see it, complete with proud memorials to countless names—actually buried there or not—as a place for quiet reflection, remembrance, even healing. He regarded it as a slap at the Heavens, but also tasted intimate rebuke in the unfair glorification of those who'd made the ultimate sacrifice . . . while he and many like him ran away.

He preferred to think of it as a place for alien ideas to molder with their corpses.

“The Assembly won’t see reason,” he declared lightly as Nau-Pir, High Sky Priest for the entire Saa-Leebs delegation, strode across the ornamental rug to greet him. Much like that impossible Keje-Fris-Ar and the unlamented Adar, Giaan had known Nau-Pir since they were younglings, both being groomed for high status in their Home clans. They’d shared their fears and ambitions all their lives, but now shared the same “taint” of having evacuated to the Filpin Lands in the face of the first terrifying Grik Swarm that fell upon these islands. Giaan was glad the Grik were gone, of course, but those who remained to fight had left Nau, and particularly Giaan, looking rather bad. Even Sular wouldn’t send such a blatant “runaway” to head its delegation to the Assembly. Giaan had been fortunate to be chosen as a deputy. He’d done great things in that position, however, especially since the official assemblyperson had been old and often absent. Now he was gone forever. Giaan knew Henry Stokes suspected him of murder, but the old fool had simply died. Giaan wasn’t a fool, and knew he’d never be chosen to take his superior’s place. Better to pretend he remained on holiday—who would ever know?—and continue as before.

“Most unfortunate,” commiserated Nau-Pir. “And relentlessly provocative. Ships from Sular have actually been turned away from B’taava. There can be no question now that it’s under blockade: a direct act of war by the Amer-i-caan Navy Claan against another ‘sovereign State.’ By all the United Homes, if they don’t disavow the Navy Claan’s actions!” He blinked amusement. “We managed that quite well. Poor Minister Stokes is like a youngling cast adrift on a very small timber when it comes to this sort of thing. Now to make the most of our advantage.”

Giaan handed his embroidered vestments to a servant, revealing the bright yellow-gold smock he preferred to wear around the consulate. It was the “national” color of Sular and went well with his dark brown, tan-highlighted fur. It also contrasted less sharply with the silver-white fur surrounding his face. “It’s just as well you managed to”—Giaan lowered his voice. Even here, not all were privy to their subversive efforts—“make Gener-aal Linnaa-Fas-Ra, ah, ‘retire.’ His dawdling served us well in Indiaa, but he’d earned too much enmity. If we’d made him High Chief of B’taava, as he demanded, it would’ve raised doubt about our commitment to the Union.”

“Never fear,” Nau assured, “Gener-aal Linnaa’s outrageous expectations and hints of betrayal were well-rewarded.”

Giaan accepted a mug of seep and gestured for all but a few of his closest attendants to leave him. "And as you say, with so many who prop up the unnatural 'Union' now in Baalkpan, poised to drag Sular into yet *another* disastrous conflict, the time to act decisively has come." He downed his seep and gazed at Nau. "I'd like to speak to our 'guest' once more."

"Of course."

Capitaine Bucge Dupont was a bitter man. He'd been a listless convert to fascism in the tumultuous years when Europe embraced it, but made all the right noises to secure his advancement. He should've thrived, especially after the great Confédération États Souverains task force meant to wrest Egypt from Great Britain somehow wound up on this strange world and formed the League of Tripoli, but he'd been tied to *Savoie* and the politically suspect Contre-Amiral Laborde. At a time when the young League was busy subjugating a primitive Mediterranean, *Savoie* was sent on a lonely "show the flag" mission primarily intended to gather information and prevent external intervention in the Med with a show of irresistible might.

The mission evolved and lengthened as the Med grew more secure. Outposts were established in far-flung places to detect potential adversaries, and the League advanced its policy of deterrence through intimidation and subversion. Flexing its muscles, the ruling Triumvirate sent *Savoie* to overawe the Republic of Real People with an eye toward eventual conquest. The Republic was full of subhuman species, but its strategic position and potential industrial capacity was attractive. When faced with a credible threat that might crack the League's aura of invincibility, however, Laborde chose to depart Alex-aandra. Instead of being recalled, *Savoie* was sent to the Indian Ocean in support of Victor Gravois's mission to subvert the Allies by propping up Kurokawa (and the Grik). That didn't work either. Not only were *Savoie*—and Dupont—involved in a singular atrocity, they were shuffled off to Kurokawa's direct control to deny League culpability. Ultimately, *Savoie* was beaten and captured at the Battle of Zanzibar, and Bucge Dupont became a prisoner of the Grand Alliance.

He still wasn't a devout "Leaguer," but painfully wounded in the leg by Gunnery Sergeant Arnold Horn (a former prisoner of his own), and even more painfully humiliated by Captain Reddy and his imprisonment by animals, Dupont wanted revenge. He knew others had told his enemy all they really needed to know about the League so he saw no reason to resist at first. He only became obstinate when he noted some of his animal captors from a place called "Sular" on the Island of Celebes were actually *encouraged* by it, as well as the hatred for the Alliance he showed them. He deftly played on that, as well as their fear that League vengeance would be swift, irresistible, and complete. It developed that they represented a discontented faction that already believed that, and he gladly stoked their anxieties. After he convinced them only he could protect them from the League's fury, they broke him out and brought him here.

He was still in a "prison," of sorts, secured on the third floor of the "Saaleeban" Consulate. He'd thought it ridiculous to keep him there and expected swift recapture, but the animal named "Nau" who'd arranged his escape (and yearned to believe they were friends) had sworn no one would violate the sanctity of the consulate and particularly his own quarters. He was a "Sky Priest," whatever that meant, but it seemed important to him. Apparently it was to others as well, because Dupont had been on the loose, in the very capital of his enemies, for over a month. He had few visitors and not many even knew he was there, but his quarters were fairly large, his comforts seen to, and he'd been supplied with a workbench and tools to prepare "devices" he promised would be useful when the time came for Sular to distance itself from the Union and Grand Alliance. With his single small window, he could also now clearly see *Savoie* riding at anchor in the bay. The time for vengeance was at hand.

There came a tapping beyond the curtain separating his stateroom from the hallway beyond. He didn't respond, but quickly raked his hair with his fingers, sculpted the long, unkempt beard on his face, and tugged at the uniform they'd tried to clean for him, but shrunken terribly. Straightening on the chair they'd given him—he hated stools and couldn't abide the cushions he'd first found there—he sat upright and rigid, except for his still-painful leg, which he propped on a crate. Without a word, three Lemurians pushed the curtain aside and entered. Others probably waited outside to ensure they remained undisturbed. It was always like that, and he'd been cautioned never to speak or make excessive noises without such preparations. He immediately knew Nau and Giaan, but didn't recognize the other.

"Good afternoon," he said in English with a false, friendly smile. "What can I do for you?"

"No doubt you've noticed *Saavoie*," Giaan said, gesturing at the window, his manner abrupt. Unlike the others, he always kept a haughty tone and pretended not to be afraid when Dupont described the might of the League.

"Of course," Dupont replied. "Even with her bizarre new 'dazzle' paint scheme, her outline is distinctive. And I assume the rest of First Fleet's principal ships and officers are present as well?"

"They are," Nau confirmed. "More importantly, this one"—he indicated the Lemurian Dupont didn't know—"is one of our spies at the Allied airfield named 'Maacky.' They haave others, as you know, but there are two even we aren't supposed to know about. It's believed they experiment with new things there, but not only haave we never been able to get anyone in for a look at what they're doing, we've never even found them." He looked suddenly anxious. "We've sent *everything else* we know to contaacts we developed in the Empire," he assured. "They'll get word to the Doms and eventually the League, now thaat they're allies. With the blaackout, we caan no longer risk raadio."

"I'm sure the League will understand," Dupont soothed, "as long as it's clear you've done all you can to undermine the Union and the Alliance it supports." He shook his head sadly. "I can't stress enough how important that is. If you feared the Grik . . . They were a pestilence, to be sure, but were simply incapable of anything like the destruction the League can inflict. And the Grik could be sated for a while. The League will be relentless, exterminating all life in their path. Nothing will be spared . . . except those who gain their favor by helping them win more quickly."

"We will," Giaan stated sharply, letting some of his haughtiness slide.

"So," Dupont said, his smile returning, "tell me why this . . . person and the airfield are important."

"Chairmaan Letts haas collected advisors for Cap-i-taan Reddy, in addition to those he already relies on," Giaan began breathlessly, but visibly calmed himself. "This one"—he also indicated the other Lemurian—"says they'll all soon journey to one of the hidden airfields aboard the bizaarre new aircraaft we described. You might haave even seen it." He pointed at the window.

"Yes," Dupont agreed. He'd seen the thing a week or so before First Fleet arrived, ponderously nosing about over the bay. It was impressive and had numerous applications, but he doubted it would be much use in a confrontation with the League. He also nodded at the young Lemurian. "And it'll depart from Mackey Field, where he works?"

"Exaactly," Nau enthused, sounding relieved. "He caan't make the flight, he isn't allowed, but he caan board the aircraaft prior to its departure." He blinked excitement and nodded at the devices scattered on the workbench in various stages of completion. "If he placed one of those aboard, Cap-i-taan Reddy, Chairmaan Letts . . . who knows who all *else* might no longer be our concern! Surely the League would look with favor on those who helped accomplish thaat!"

Dupont turned to gaze speculatively at his devices and hide the gleeful expression on his face. *Parfait,* he thrilled. The devices were bombs, of course. They weren't very large, but they didn't have to be. Not only would he have his revenge, there'd be almost no risk to him. He had the perfect buffer. Giaan and Nau were cowards. Fearing the League, they'd do all they could to protect him, and fearing discovery by their own people, they'd quickly silence the *imbécile* who placed the device. And the bombs themselves were assembled from components from all over the Alliance! The battery, as bulky as the explosive, was from here, as was the wire, but the dynamite was from the Filpin Lands and the clockwork from the Empire. That appealed to Dupont's sense of fate.

He frowned. But the clockwork, taken from the ubiquitous, if overlarge Imperial watches, troubled him. They kept good time if they were wound every few hours to keep the springs tight, but that would be unworkable. And the longer they went without winding, the slower they went. He'd love to have one explode right over a secret airfield, wrecking its target and spreading destruction in all directions, but not knowing where the airfield was, timing for that was impossible. Second best would be if the aircraft went down in the middle of the predator-rich jungle, far from civilization. That he might manage, with a reasonable itinerary.

He turned back to his Lemurian co-conspirators. "Find out whatever you can about the schedule for this flight. Timing will be crucial," he stressed, then paused, looking back at his workbench. "We *should* only need one device, but two are ready, as you see. Both would be better, but that would double the risk of detection. I leave to your discretion how many to use." He glanced at the unnamed Lemurian. "All that remains is to set them—and place them, of course. Both of those things must be done with care."

CHAPTER 17

*////// **Baalkpan, Borno***
Mackey Field
May 22, 1945

"Wow," was all Matt could say, gazing up at the huge dirigible floating over Mackey Field, its nose anchored to a tall tripod mooring mast. He'd already seen it from a distance, of course. It was impossible to miss, shuttling passengers and payloads across the bay. And he hadn't had any anxious flashbacks to the times they'd been mobbed by countless Grik "zeps" and their "suicider" bombs because this airship was strikingly different. Not only was it painted a pleasant medium dark blue like all Allied aircraft (except Republic planes), its rudders and elevators sported the reassuring red and white stripes. The roundel "target" was composed of the blue, white, green, and gold of the United Homes instead of the white star with a red dot in a blue field of the Navy Clan, but it wasn't a Navy Clan airship. Yet even aside from the color, the biggest differences between this and the dirigibles Grik had made were that it looked a lot "cleaner," more finished, and it mounted four radials instead of the five horizontally opposed "flat" engines. It was also bigger.

"Her name's *Fueen*—'Cat for 'Union,'" Alan Letts told Matt and Silva. The translation was unnecessary, but Alan's warning tone prevented Silva's ready crack about another common, literal, usage of the word.

"Damn thing's half again bigger than any Grik zep," Silva said instead, echoing Matt's thoughts. "Can I fly it?"

"It's over four hundred and fifty feet long, and no you *can't* fly it," Alan replied, voice rising incredulously. He caught himself before he went off on a rant about the big man's destructive potential, however. It had been almost two weeks since “The Battle of the Busted Screw,” and Silva didn’t show much damage as a result. It was possible Matt wasn’t aware of his participation. *Better to keep it that way,* Alan thought, and consciously lowered his voice. “Trust me, the controls are different from what you’re used to.”

Silva shrugged, upsetting Petey. “How hard can it be? ’Specially with somebody to show me the knobs. Never had that before.” Silva had become the first dirigible pilot in the Alliance when he swiped a Grik airship and literally learned to fly it . . . on the fly.

Henry Stokes chuckled. “Later, mate.”

Lawrence, hanging back—he wouldn’t be joining them—made an amused *kakking* sound. Silva glared, then peeled Petey off his neck and tossed him at his friend. Petey’s gliding membranes deployed just long enough to correct his trajectory before little claws dug in and Lawrence yelped. “Take care o’ the little booger. He hates to fly as much as you.” He grinned. “*Feed* him somethin’.”

“Feed?” Petey inquired, tasting the word, then looked at Lawrence with demanding eyes. “Eat!” he cawed.

“But why build it at all?” Matt asked, focusing back on the airship and thinking of the materials and labor it must’ve taken. “We already know how vulnerable the damn things are—and I guess it’s full of hydrogen.”

“I asked myself the same question when I saw it,” Lieutenant Muriname began, conversationally, but Matt frowned at him. The balding, bespectacled Muriname had been “General of the Sky” for Kurokawa and the Grik, designing zeppelins (and other things) for the enemy. He’d finally come over to the Allies with the remains of a squadron of pretty good torpedo bombers during the First Battle of the Zambezi. Matt didn’t like him and his presence on this trip was probably why Sandra decided to stay and work in the hospital. But Stokes and Letts had vouched for him, and the League defector Walbert Fiedler, who Matt both trusted and respected, seemed to be Muriname’s best buddy now. Matt sighed. *Like it or not, the Jap’s part of the new “staff” they hung on me, along with most of the other people here.* He glanced around at those waiting to board the airship while Muriname kept talking, apparently oblivious to the look Matt gave him.

Muriname and Fiedler were on his “strategic consulting team” as air advisors, and somewhat whimsically as specialists on League tactics. More importantly, the latest dope was that Victor Gravois might actually be formulating League strategy in the Caribbean and they knew the French lunatic better than anyone else. Other members of Matt's new team included the Lemurian General Mersaak, once commanding Safir's fabled "600," and now in acting command of II Corps. Several other 'Cats were in, as experts on new systems and goodies they'd get. Many more would come and go, as usual, including all Matt's senior officers. The "permanent" staff would be heavy with bigwigs, like Ambassadors Doocy Meek from the Republic and Bolton Forester from the Empire. Both were smart guys, dedicated to the cause, but also frustrated by the fact they'd sat the war out, so far. They wanted in at the end. Matt's former coxswain, now "king" of North Borno, was an exception to that. Not only was he painfully crippled, he was absolutely terrified of the water. And there were thousands of miles of it between Borno and their destination. He'd go because he thought his human and Grik-like Khonashi troops deserved his support in the, to them, unimaginably distant fight. They'd probably have to add more Impies, Repubs, and even Nussies as time went by, Matt supposed.

"Actually rather simple to make, utilizing the ingenious laminated and diagonally braced Baalkpan bamboo for framing," he heard Muriname say admiringly as he tuned back in. They were ascending tall stairs to the top of a movable platform pushed against the belly of the airship. A hatch loomed open and exhaust washed around them from the muttering engines, their propellers spinning flat. Variable-pitch props were only one of many innovations Matt had apparently missed. "And the design is stronger, more efficient, and less labor intensive than anything I was able to accomplish," the Japanese officer went on. "You'll note only a single gondola, forward, where the flight crew navigates and operates the controls, but the passenger/cargo compartment we're entering is not only spacious enough for impressive loads, it avoids the drag of additional gondolas!"

"Looks like a midget version of the *Akron* and *Macon*. You remember what happened to *them*," Matt said aside to Alan.

"Sure, but we didn't build her to do all the crazy crap our old Navy wanted. *Fueen* is *not* a flying aircraft carrier, for God's sake, and anybody with planes—especially the League—makes her useless as a bomber. Like you said, we proved that against the Grik. She'd probably be a decent long-range scout," he conceded, "but still practically helpless if she got caught. We don't need her for that, anyway. We can put plenty of scouts in the air from carriers and AVDs. What we *do* need is a way to quickly haul heavy loads relatively short distances—she'll fly nearly seventy miles an hour—and get in and out of places there aren't any roads. She's a flying transport, period."

"The Republic's promised land locomotives," Doocy Meek said, ducking through the hatch behind Bolton Forester. "An' ye'll get 'em too. But current priority's on extendin' rail lines ta support the war in Africa. That, an' powerin' our own warships, o' course."

"Everybody's been busy with other things," Tony Scott conceded, limping into the passenger compartment behind Matt, Alan, and Silva. The stairs had been hard on his mangled leg, brace or not, and he quickly found a seat near a small open window. The others joined him, finding chairs or cushions. Matt and Silva walked around, looking at the little decorative touches—typically Lemurian, even for a glorified cargo bay—and glancing out more windows. "We couldn't use the locomotives if we had 'em," Scott added. "Haven't even started clearing the roadbeds yet. What for? With our shipbuilding program in such high gear, we can't spare iron for the rails." He arched his brows at Matt. "You remember the hell we had making our first pipeline cut."

A crew-'Cat ushered the last Lemurian specialists in and latched the hatch behind them. Matt noted that the hatch and frame around it looked like molded plywood. Mere moments later, the deck seemed to shift and angle slightly upward toward the stern. There was a bumping lurch and the massive craft began rising, yawing a little in the early morning breeze, before the idling engines increased power and their props began to bite. The subtle vibration they'd felt since they boarded grew more insistent. Still gazing outside, Matt saw the airfield slide away beneath them and *Fueen* seemed to surge, fluidly accelerating like a great startled fish swimming in the sky. Belatedly, Matt craned his neck at the window, trying for a glimpse of Baalkpan from the air. That was something he'd never had.

"Sorry, Skipper. Not much to see on this heading," Alan apologized. "Mackey Field's still on the edge of town. Not much past it but jungle. You can go down in the gondola when we come back, if you want. Have a good look."

"I'd like that," Matt agreed.

They flew east for a while, then turned due north for the better part of an hour, the rays of the morning sun washing through the starboard windows. To Matt it felt like they were gently climbing almost continuously, the impenetrable greenness below losing all features but those betrayed by mountain and valley shadows. After remarking on this, and various other things of interest, Matt determined now was the time to question Henry Stokes about his suspicions. This was the first time they'd all been sequestered from potentially prying ears, and the first time Stokes was trapped, unable to make a cryptic hint and bolt.

"Suspicions." Stokes glowered. "Hell, there's no question now." He took a breath and seemed to contemplate where to begin. "You'll remember that nobody liked General Linnaa. Had no bloody experience at all. But former Chairman Adar appointed him Commander o' Sixth Corps to make Sular happy when we were tryin' to ratify the Union Charter. Didn't like his draggin' arse around Indiaa when you needed Sixth Corps in the south either, but he always had excuses. It wasn't until you discovered he'd been slowin' iron an' steel shipments from Madraas, an' sittin' on repairs to *Mahan* an' those salvaged Grik BBs, we realized he was doin' it on purpose. That got him sacked, an' good riddance. You got Sixth Corps." He smiled. "An' *Mahan*. We started gettin' a flood o' good iron an' steel from Madraas. Those Grik BBs too. Speakin' o' which, they're all re-engined. *Sular* too. You saw her comin' outa dry dock the day you got in. 'Sular,'" he snorted. "There's bloody irony for ya!"

"Indeed," Bolton Forester agreed somberly, "but never forget, Sular itself is not to blame. Most of its people are loyal to your Union and its namesake ship has given good service."

"They all have the same engines as Fleet Carriers now," Alan supplied. "Their old guns are gone, but they still have some armor. They make decent protected troopships and they're faster now."

"I've been thinking about a couple more modifications I'd like done to them, if there's time, but for now let's get back to the point," Matt suggested.

Stokes nodded. "Yeah. So all the while we're gettin' yanked around by Linnaa, Sular's sendin' colonists to B'taava an' Raan-Goon. Sinaa-pore too. It wasn't long before B'taava had enough people to join the Union with full representation in the Assembly. Other places won't be far behind, an' it's obvious Sular's tryin' to pack the Assembly with a voting block that's in their pocket. That'd be bad enough, puttin' politics over the war effort, but it gets worse." His voice hardened. "They haven't just been puttin' themselves first, they've been workin' to throw the rest of us to the flashies."

"Those lousy sons o' goats," Silva seethed.

"Why?" Matt asked, genuinely perplexed. "How do you know?"

"It started comin' together when we looked closer at Linnaa. On top of everything else he did—or didn't do—in Indiaa, we found his name on orders refusing supply requests by Colonel Enaak an' Dalibor Svec, off chasin' Halik, citing 'emergency priorities' elsewhere. Since he wasn't *actin'* on any other 'emergencies,' I turned a pack o' OSI snoops loose to chase down where Enaak's supplies wound up. Take a guess."

"B'taava?"

"Right. Raan-Goon too. OSI dug deeper. Seems there'd been a lot of CW traffic outa Linnaa's HQ. In unapproved code," he stressed. "Signal-'Cats didn't know what it was, but a general tells you to tap somethin' out, you do what he says. Apparently, there was never any response except from some of our other stations asking 'what the hell was that?'"

"I wonder who it went to?" Doocy Meek murmured.

"It could haave been anyone with a receiver," General Mersaak spoke up, "but my guess would be Sularaan aaccomplices . . . or the League."

"One or both," Stokes nodded. "Chairman Letts an' I put the finger on Linnaa for treason instead o' just incompetence. When he was arrested in Madraas, he objected that the Navy Clan had no authority over him 'cause he was a general o' Sular. More important, he was gonna be the next High Chief o' B'taava."

"Payoff," Matt surmised.

"Right. OSI sweated him in the brig on Andamaan Island. With what we had on him, the Sularaans couldn't have the people in B'taava 'spontaneously' acclaim him High Chief, an' we damn sure *do* have authority over Union officers! He never squealed, though, which is actually kind of funny, since when we finally had him shipped back here for trial in an old Nakja-Mur Class APD, the ship stopped at Aryaal for fuel." He chuckled. "Not only was Linnaa discovered to be missing before the ship docked, several sailors the ship took on at Andamaan went AWOL in Aryaal. The skipper said their service jackets showed 'em all from Maa-ni-la, but they sounded like Sularaans to him."

"They bumped him off," Silva said wonderingly, looking at General Mersaak. "I can count the number o' 'Cat murders I've heard of on my fingers."

"The proof's still circumstantial, and none answers 'why,'" said Matt.

"The *real* proof we've been gettin' lately gives us 'why' enough, Cap'n Reddy," Stokes countered grimly, then seemed to go off on a tangent. "Y'know, even before hardly any of 'em knew how to read or write, 'Cats *loved* the regular mail runs you started, early as 'forty-two. So many'd gone to the Filpin Lands, not just 'runaways' but families o' those who stayed behind, 'er 'Cats you'd trained to teach Maa-ni-los to make things or fight . . . Hell, they drew *pictures* to one another if they couldn't write. 'Cats ain't shy either. They don't care if somebody else looks at what they write or draw. Most just fold a page over an' put a name on it. Even now there's envelopes, hardly anyone uses 'em. They cost more than half a dozen regular sheets o' paper! Anybody who springs for one won't seal it so you have to tear it either. They'll send it back and forth until it wears out."

"So the Office of Strategic Intelligence has been reading people's mail," Matt guessed.

"Right. Especially if it's sealed."

Bolton Forester stirred in his seat. "More specifically if it's sealed in a diplomatic pouch from the Sularaan Consulate, on its way to the Empire of the New Britain Isles. You can be sure Her Majesty's government is investigating the addressees."

"I wonder who gave them that idea," Matt speculated.

"Doesn't matter," Letts replied. "They might as well have put 'Read me! Incriminating shit inside!' on the label. It has been incriminating too. We now know *somebody* in the Sularaan Consulate's behind almost all our leaks, and a lot of the subversion of the war effort from the start. We just don't know *who*, exactly. My money's on Giaan because I don't like him, but it might be their senior assemblyperson and all this is why he's made himself scarce."

"How much have they spilled to the enemy lately? And you still haven't told me why, damn it!"

"As to the first, we don't really know," Stokes answered uncomfortably. "We believe we caught the first reference to *Savoie*, but can't be positive. There've been no more unauthorized code transmissions from here, and we're probably catching all their letter mail now. Moreover, we don't *think* they know about *U-112* because Captain Hoffman"—he nodded at Fiedler—"and the submarine he and his crew defected in, never came to Baalkpan. There's a static floating dry dock at Tarakan Island now—strictly Navy Clan territory—and that's where she was taken for overhaul. *U-112* actually remains our best source on League dispositions, as a matter of fact. You may remember Hoffman said he was still listening to their transmissions?" Matt nodded. "What you may not've realized was his boat had an ingenious cipher machine to encode and decode 'em, along with a key and various sets of—Hoffman called 'em 'rotors'—to randomly change the codes. For proof positive how arrogant the League is, and how sure they are his boat was lost, Hoffman says they've changed their rotors a time or two, on schedule, but not the bloody key. He's *still* reading their mail!"

"Which could all be bullshit, of course," Alan sighed, encompassing Fiedler and Stokes with a gaze. "We've spent a lot of time with Hoffman and I'll vouch that he's on the level. He didn't like the League anyway, and then the way Gravois just abandoned him and his boat . . . But there's always the chance the bad guys know he turned and are feeding us a bunch of crap. I don't think so, but we have to watch where we step."

"As to 'why,' well, I'd say that's bloody obvious, now," Stokes continued. "Our . . . homegrown enemies think the League'll beat us. To improve their lot under the fascist conquerors"—Stokes's lip twisted—"and ensure their sovereignty over lands they control—another reason for their colonizing blitz—they've promised their help. To show good faith, they've sent intelligence, of course, and 'rescued' Captain Dupont." He frowned. "They also promise to sow as much dissent as they can, and ultimately 'confusion at the highest levels,' whatever that means." He nodded at the pistol and sword belt Matt was wearing. "We've no idea how far they'll go."

"Why not just raid the consulate?" Silva demanded incredulously. "Shut 'em down. That's prob'ly where Dupont is, anyway."

Forester smiled at him. "Tempting as that is, I repeat that not all Sularaans are bad. Most would be appalled to learn what we know. And what if Giaan, objectionable as he is, isn't to blame? What if Dupont *isn't* in the consulate? I speak only as an interested ally, but might not precipitous action, without proof, only intensify the rift in the Union that *some* Sularaans have worked so hard to achieve? Might it not 'sow' the very 'dissent,' create the very 'confusion' they've promised the League?"

"He's right, Dennis," Tony Scott said, then smirked. "You have to think about bigger stuff, when you're king."

"I'll try to remember that, ol' buddy," Silva growled back dryly. He looked at Matt. "So what do we do? Just keep spyin, an' hope for the best?"

Matt rubbed his upper lip. Finally, he took a deep breath and grinned at Alan. "Not my job, thank God. That's up to the Chairman of the United Homes." He looked around at the rest of his "staff." "*Our* job is to take the tools he gives us out to beat the Doms and League. Stay focused on that, every day, and help me figure out how. Like I said when we first got here,

I've got a basic plan, but I *will* appreciate a little help putting the pieces together." He pointed at Alan and Stokes. "It's *their* job to keep the wheels from falling off while we're gone."

"I sure miss our old 'torpedo day' celebrations," Alan said wistfully, "when we showed off our new gimmicks instead of hiding them. Things were so much simpler back then."

CHAPTER 18

*////// **Near Baalkpan, Borno***

Less than an hour and a half out of Baalkpan, the roar of the engines lessened and the steeper sunbeams shifted in the compartment as *Fueen* began a gradual turn. Matt peered out the window. Jungle-choked mountain peaks weren't far below, forming a vast, jagged-rimmed valley sloping down and away to the shores of two fairly large, squarish lakes. There was no evidence of habitation in any direction except for a tan, dusty X, hacked out of the opaque greenery by the east shore of the southeasternmost lake. The X quickly resolved itself into overlapping airstrips as the dirigible descended, the runways oriented north-south, east-west, and bordered by large, rough-cut hangars. Smaller buildings crouched, offset to the south, and Matt identified a sturdy-looking log-built mooring mast. Tiny figures raced to assemble around it. Oddly—and surprisingly—the only aircraft he saw exposed was Walbert Fiedler's old trimotor Ju-52, sporting a new blue paint job and wearing Navy Clan colors. The last time he'd seen it was on Madagascar, and it looked like hell. He supposed the new planes he'd been brought to see were in the hangars. "I guess we're here," he said.

"I'll be damned! It's Jumbo!" Silva declared, descending much cruder stairs than those they'd used at Mackey Field. Looming above a gaggle of Lemurians, a couple of humans, and a handful of what looked like Grik-like Khonashi, the newly promoted Lieutenant Commander Walt "Jumbo" Fisher grinned back, saluting the officers. "How'd they ever get you outa those fat, flyin' whales—an' why'd they plunk you down out here in the middle o' nothin'?"

"Easy, dumb-ass," Jumbo called back, "they gave me something more aggressive to do. I'm sure you can appreciate that." He looked seriously at Captain Reddy and saluted. "Sorry, sir."

Matt chuckled. "That's okay. If there's one thing I've learned, some things take precedence over propriety. As I understand it, the last time you laid eyes on our one-man wrecking crew, he was jumping out of your Clipper over Old Sofesshk."

"Yes sir. Figured that would finally be the end of him. But like a bad penny . . ." He shrugged. "I'm also sorry you caught us almost *gone*," he added, waving back at the hangars. "I've only got four ships left to look at, doing some last-minute testing."

Matt looked alarmed and cast a glance at Alan. "I thought the new planes and weapons had already been thoroughly tried."

"They have, sir. They work swell," Jumbo assured. "We're just . . ." He hesitated. "Pushing things a little, is all."

"Why don't you just show him, Commander," Alan said, "and tell us what you're up to while you're at it. I'm afraid we don't have all day. The Assembly convenes this afternoon and I have to be there. You don't have much time yourself." He turned to Matt. "You approved him as COFO of the Eighth Naval Air Wing, but he lollygagged around and missed USS *Madraas* when she sailed with the rest of his planes and pilots. He needs to join her before she leaves Maa-ni-la in less than a week. That's a long way."

"My new ships can make it without even stopping for gas," Jumbo said proudly, then added lowly, "almost. We'll refuel on Palawaan to be safe. Hell—I mean, 'shoot'—sir, we could still catch *Madraas* a couple days out at sea to the east, almost as far as Yap Island. . . ."

"Big as *Madraas* is, she'd still be harder to find than the Filpin Lands," Alan retorted dryly.

"An' you don't wanna wind up on Yap," Silva added darkly.

"We'll make it," Jumbo promised. "I just want a couple more days to sort things out. C'mon, let me show you."

The big hangar doors were open but the bright sunlight made the interior difficult to see until they stepped into the shade.

"That's . . ." Matt began, staring at a fairly large (by the standards he'd learned to accept on this world) twin-engine aircraft with fixed landing gear. He guessed the wingspan at fifty feet, the fuselage almost forty, from nose to tail. The engines were protected by cowlings and faired-in to the leading edges of the wings. The plane obviously utilized a lot of the thin, molded plywood he'd seen in the dirigible, and if it weren't for the flat glass panels framed in around the fully enclosed cockpit and bombardier's station in the nose—and the fixed landing gear, of course—it would've looked like an utterly modern aircraft. It shared a few essential characteristics with Muriname's torpedo bombers, but clearly wasn't based on them. There hadn't been time to copy them if they'd wanted to. It bore a more than passing resemblance to the wrecked Bristol Beaufort they'd found on Madagascar, but they would've had to be working on this before they got many of the Beaufort's pieces to look at. Matt knew an engine, complete with supercharger and variable-pitch prop, had been sent back at once, but a lot must've been started from drawings.

"Our newest baby," Jumbo proclaimed proudly. "One of 'em, anyway," he corrected. "The new pursuit ships're being built in the Filpin Lands. You saw the trainers at Mackey Field?"

Matt nodded.

"Good. Chairman Letts or . . . Lieutenant Muriname, I guess, can fill you in on those when you get back. This is the TBD-2." He assumed an expression that made him look like he'd swallowed a bug. "No fancy name for 'em yet, like 'Devastator' or 'Avenger,' and some of the fellas started calling 'em 'To Be Determined.'" He rolled his eyes. "I'm calling 'em 'Twos' for now." He shrugged. "Muriname came up with the first torpedo bomber on this world and he's on our side now . . . right? Anyway, *all* our new planes have the same double-stacked radials we're building here. They're stout enough to take single-stage superchargers now, and the whiz kids at the Navy Clan refinery on Tarakan Island have come up with better fuel." He shook his head. "Don't ask me how. That's a bigger secret than the planes, since we know the League hasn't done it yet." He nodded at Fiedler and Muriname.

"Excuse me," Doocy Meek interrupted, "but I'm still not sure what a 'supercharger' does."

"Me either, exactly," Matt confessed. "I'm no aeronautical engineer like Ben Mallory—and all the pupils he's scattered around"—he smiled—"but I imagine it serves the same purpose as a forced-draft blower for a ship's boiler." He knew Meek was familiar with those. "Increase the airflow and you can burn more fuel to make a hotter fire. More steam."

"Not a bad analogy, Captain Reddy," Jumbo agreed. "The upshot's an increase in power. A single-stage supercharger doesn't give you much when you go really high, but we're figuring the League's crappy gas'll keep 'em low, anyway. What Fiedler says about League light bombers"—he glanced at the TBD—"these babies should give 'em a run for their money. They've got welded tube steel framing the fuselage, wing spars, engine mounts, and undercarriage, all underlying our usual laminated Baalkpan bamboo. Still a lot of fabric covering that, but good plywood stiffens the high-stress areas. They don't weigh near as much as their League counterparts, but they're just as strong. Might even take *more* light damage an' keep flyin." He frowned. "No armor for the crew, and they won't carry quite the load," he stipulated, "but they're probably more maneuverable, and damn near as fast."

"What can they carry?" Matt asked.

Jumbo grinned. "A ton of bombs, or a full-size torpedo."

"Full size . . ." Silva muttered appreciatively.

"That might prove very useful," Matt mused. "They're awful big, though. Will they fit on a carrier?"

"Barely," Alan Letts grudged. "They were designed to launch and recover on carriers—see the tailhook?—but the wings don't fold so they take a lot of space. *Big Sal* can carry thirty, packed pretty tight, with room for enough pursuit ships to cover her. The smaller Fleet Carriers can carry twenty. Just as well, since we've only got about eighty so far." He chuckled. "You'll notice the wingtips are kind of squared off?"

"Sure. I guess that's to stow them closer together?"

"Yeah, but only accidentally." Alan glanced fondly at some of their Lemurian tech advisors. A couple were blinking embarrassment. "All their miracles aside, seems anybody can goof. In this case, nobody thought to measure the elevator clearance on our carriers until *after* we started production. Had to trim a few of the first ones, then adjust the wing-framing jigs."

There was a moment of levity, the 'Cats laughing as loud as the rest.

"All the same," said Jumbo, "they are pretty big. If the Nussies build the airstrips we asked for and we base 'em ashore, that'll free up the carriers to carry more planes." Matt's response was drowned by the thundering rumble of two TBD-2s blasting over the hangars. Everyone stepped quickly outside to watch them bank out over the lake and begin a wide turn, bright sun flashing on glass canopies and new paint.

"What're they doing?" Matt asked.

"Pushing things, like I said," Jumbo replied. "About half my flight leaders are still here, working on dive and torpedo bombing. All of 'em are old Nancy pilots, by the way. Best way for them to get their flyers up to speed is to get as good as they can be. And going up against the League, no matter how you slice it, they're going to be flying into ack-ack like they've never seen. We're trying to come up with the very best speed, range, and angle of attack for them to release their weapons to maximize hits and survivability."

The two planes roared almost directly away from them toward a large silhouette target they hadn't noticed till then. "The trouble is, there really isn't an answer," he added grimly. "Even assuming calm water, you still have to fly straight and level long enough not to throw a hook in the fish before you drop it. And the livelier the sea, the closer and slower you have to go to keep the fish on target."

Shiny brass cylinders dropped away and splashed, the waterspouts almost as high as the planes that banked and sped away. Jumbo looked at Matt. "So basically, all these guys are learning is that if you want to kill a League ship with a torpedo from an airplane, you have to make yourself a perfect target for way too long."

Matt was nodding thoughtfully. "Against moving ships, certainly," he said. "And in the daylight," he added cryptically. He turned back to Jumbo and stuck out his hand. "You're doing swell. Keep it up. I won't see you again until we catch up with *Madraas* and *Big Sal*, but I'm damn glad we came out here today. I see now why we had to," he added with a grin. "This isn't the kind of training you do over Baalkpan Bay!"

He and the rest shook more hands, including—to Matt's surprise—another one of Muriname's Japanese defectors, two from Hidoiame, and one of Muriname's surviving Grik pilots who had to be coaxed out of the shadows. They stayed long enough to watch the two planes touch down and taxi toward the hangars trailing dense clouds of dust.

"That's it," Alan said, glancing at his watch. "We have to go. I hope you liked the show?"

"I did," Matt told him. "Very much. And just to think . . ." He shook his head. "Do the new pursuit ships perform as well? What're they calling them again?"

"P-5 Nighthawks—though some wags're already calling them 'Bull-Bats' or 'Bugeaters.'"

Silva was vigorously shaking his head as if to say "not me, this time."

Matt chuckled. "Inevitable, I guess. I've only seen the trainers, but they look slick. Like 'Fleashooters' still, but more"—he shrugged—"everything.

Longer, more streamlined, enclosed cockpits . . . They look kind of like Curtiss P-36s with fixed landing gear. My question is, how will they stack up against the League's Macchi-Messerschmitts?"

"Ben says about how they look, maybe almost as good as a real P-36 against a Messerschmitt or Zero. Not so hot," he conceded, then brightened. "But *way* better than a Fleashooter would, and we should have the numbers." He paused. "You know Ben loaded the last two P-40Es we had here on *Big Sal*, to join his two beat-up survivors?"

Matt nodded. "The last four modern planes we have. I hope we don't need 'em—and I hope my Cousin Orrin'll forgive me."

"Why?"

"Because I'm giving him one. He'll still be *Makky-Kat*'s COFO, but he may have to leave her." He snorted. "We've only got *four* experienced pilots left fit to fly a P-40 in combat: Cecil Dixon, a 'Cat named 'Shirley,' Ben Mallory . . . and Orrin Reddy. The real sticker's going to be when Ben and Orrin open their orders." Alan looked back blankly. "Ben's still CO of all Army and Naval Air," Matt explained, "but I want Orrin in charge of the reconstituted Third Pursuit Squadron when they fly. He's more experienced in P-40s—or anything else—and he's the best chance they have of coming out alive."

They boarded *Fueen* and headed back for Baalkpan. The sun crept overhead and clouds started to form while they talked animatedly about the new planes and how to use them. Finally, Alan smiled and announced, "We're about twenty miles out of Baalkpan and we've squeezed you enough about your thoughts on the TBDs. Why don't you go down to the gondola for a look?" he asked Matt.

"What about me?" Silva demanded. He thought he'd behaved himself rather well throughout the trip.

"Sure," Matt said. "Just don't touch anything. Anybody else?"

"I believe I'll join you," Henry Stokes declared. That started a rush of 'Cats and humans rising from their seats. "Enough!" Alan laughed. "You've all seen it before, and three's about as many as we ought to inflict on Commander Noor during his approach." He grinned apologetically at Matt. "We'll get together again, with the rest of the CINCAF's 'staff,' after the Assembly meeting."

A 'Cat sailor, with aviation machinist's mate insignia, opened a hatch forward and Matt, Stokes, and Silva found themselves creeping along a narrow, deceptively rickety-looking catwalk, clutching rails between great rubberized canvas bladders full of hydrogen. "No smokin', surs," the 'Cat said idly, obviously something he repeated to everyone. Soon they reached a broader, more substantial deck surface and their conductor opened a square hatch at their feet and stood aside while Matt, Silva, and Stokes descended a ladder inside a boxlike structure. Reaching the bottom, they stepped out into *Fueen*'s control gondola. Half a dozen 'Cats were there, one standing at a big brass wheel behind a compass binnacle, peering through the forward windows. To his left stood another 'Cat, poised by an engine order telegraph with four handles and dials. Except for another wheel on the starboard side, with a fore and aft inclinometer behind it on the bulkhead, the arrangement looked just like *Walker*'s pilothouse, down to the talker and speaking tubes at the back of the gondola. They were met by a 'Cat in whites, with three stripes on his sleeves. *Fueen* might not be a Navy Clan airship, but she had a Navy Clan crew.

"I'm honored to haave you aboard, Cap-i-taan Reddy, Mr. Stokes," he said, then blinked surprise at Silva, who'd already stepped past him to look at things. "I'm Commaander Noor-Kai," he continued. "I flew with Cap-i-taan Jis-Tikkar off *Salissa* until aafter Second Madraas."

"Then you flew with the best during a damn tough time. The honor's mine, Commander," Matt replied. He gestured around. "You have a beautiful ship. I don't mean to intrude, but I've never seen Baalkpan from the air. Chairman Letts said you have a great view."

"Truly," Noor agreed, blinking pleasure. "I believe we haave just enough time to make a loop around the city before returning to Maackey Field. Please, make yourselves at home."

"Thanks, we will." Matt saw Silva start opening access panels and finely finished storage locker doors, peering inside. "Within reason, of course. Chief Silva," he added sharply, "I told you not to touch anything."

Silva assumed a wounded expression. "I ain't, Skipper! Honest. Nothin' that *does* anything. Glory be, Mr. Letts was right. This thing's differenter from a Grik zep than a Model T from a 'thirty-six Caddy limo! Me an' Gunny Horn—an' that dipshit Laney—sorta . . . sat in one o' those once. In China. Might'a b'longed to a Chinese mob boss 'er Dutch diplomat." He shrugged dismissively, as if there was no difference. "But it was near as big an' fancy as this, with little doors on ashtrays wherever you looked; column shift synchromesh, V-16 . . . Boy, it could almost fly too!"

Matt started to ask how he knew that if they only "sat" in it, but changed his mind. There were rumors that Silva, Horn, and to an ill-defined lesser extent, Dean Laney had—against strict orders that the US 4th Marines had bitterly resented—somehow participated in the vicious 1937 Sino-Japanese fighting in Shanghai. Nobody knew more than a fraction of the story and even now, when it couldn't possibly matter, Matt hesitated to press the trio for details. All he was sure of was that Silva and Horn had apparently acted true to form and an airplane, Silva's missing tooth, a little Chinese girl, and a lot of dead Japanese had solidified the unlikely friendship of an Asiatic Fleet sailor and a China Marine—and left them both highly contemptuous of Laney. He now knew a 1936 Cadillac limousine had been involved. He shook his head and stepped forward to look out the windows as Baalkpan Bay rose shimmering out of the jungle.

It took a few minutes more to see Baalkpan itself. Few buildings, even the older style on pilings, rose higher than fifty feet, but the Great Tree was the only mature specimen of its kind on Borno and it dominated the coast, signifying the center of the city as surely as the Colossus must've marked Rhodes on another world. Closer still, huge cranes were visible and the huddled mass of shipping off the docks became individual vessels and not just a dark, blurry island. They flew onward, decelerating and descending, finally rumbling down to less than five hundred feet and almost crawling through the sky. Matt could see everything now, beneath the lizardbirds fluttering and flowing around them in their colorful multitudes: all the shipyards, lumber and mast yards, cable walks, machine shops, woodshops, steel fabrication factories . . . A lot of the really heavy industry had been moved out of the city, for room and security, but Baalkpan was still jumping with activity. New housing for all the imported workers sprawled beyond where the old defensive berms had been and looked a lot like similar suburbs Matt remembered around Manila, though it was probably laid out better here. The "inner city" retained some of its picturesque, prewar charm, though it was considerably diminished. Much along the waterfront had been knocked down to make room for industry, warehouses, and repair yards, but a large cluster of older buildings around the Great Tree and Hall, and surrounding the Parade Ground Cemetery, remained largely unchanged. Like the new construction, however, thatched roofs had been replaced with baked-clay tile shingles. Not only were they more durable, they were less susceptible to drifting embers spouting from stacks above wood-burning boilers and furnaces that still ran a lot of things, particularly smaller, nonferrous foundries.

Looking out at the bay, Matt saw transports and tugs crisscrossing the water, patiently avoiding the fishing feluccas coming and going from the sea. The far jungle horizon on the west side of the bay was smudged with the smoke of more industry, crowding right up against the Baalkpan ATC. He thought he'd had a good idea about how much had changed before, but the true scope had eluded him from the ground. Looking down, he caught a quick glimpse of *Walker* as *Fueen* turned to parallel the "old" fitting-out pier before steering east again, and was struck by how small she looked compared to *Savoie* and *Gray*, and especially the converted Grik BBs. *And she looks so old and tired,* he thought with a pang, compared to her newer "daughters," gathered around her and *Mahan* as if paying their respects or seeking hard-won wisdom.

He blinked and stepped to the starboard side of the gondola, avoiding Silva, who'd stooped excitedly to lift the cover of yet another access panel in the deck. "I never seen so many places to hide . . . I mean stow stuff," the big man murmured admiringly. He looked at the wheel, then back down. "These're the control cables for the rudder?" he asked.

"Yes," Commander Noor replied tolerantly. He knew of Silva's previous airship exploits and understood his fascination. "You'll see turnbuckles we caan use to adjust their tension from here, if necessaary. There are maany such around the ship, of course, but we like haaving extra, convenient ways to do a thing if others fail. . . ."

"Prob'ly shouldn't be nothin' else in here then, huh?" Silva interrupted brusquely, bending down. "'Specially just floppin' around loose."

Noor blinked annoyance and approached. "Certaainly not! Any loose object might bind or chafe the cables."

Matt was gazing out at the top of the Great Tree, seemingly just below to starboard. Its broad, rounded crest looked like an island in the sky. He was amazed by the variety of lizardbirds and other flitting things infesting it, and wondered if a few of Petey's relatives had jumped some westbound ships and moved in. They lived in trees on Yap, after all, gliding from one to another or branch to branch like flying squirrels. Either way, now it had recovered, the Great Tree was more alive than he'd ever imagined from the ground. As the central symbol of the United Homes—the leading military partners in the Grand Alliance—he found a kind of comfort in that discovery.

"What the hell?" Silva abruptly shouted, and Matt turned to see what caused his outburst. He'd opened a leather satchel in front of Commander Noor and both were staring incredulously at an object he'd fished out. Even at a glance, it was obviously a bomb. Two sticks of Sa'aaran dynamite wrapped in red wax paper tubes were affixed to one of their newest Bakelite battery boxes small enough to fit in a "Double E-8"–style field telephone pack. An uncased timepiece with exposed brass workings was secured to a sliver of wood, glued to the battery. Wires went from the battery to the timepiece to the explosive. The instant of confusion wasn't due to the identity of the object, only utter astonishment at its presence.

"Throw it out!" Noor commanded, trying to snatch the bomb.

"In the middle 'o town?" Silva countered, pulling it away.

"Better thaat, fool, thaan if it brings this ship down on the city!" Noor roared.

"Relax, Commander." Deftly, Silva unscrewed the wingnut on one of the battery terminals and lifted the wire. "I just pulled its plug. Safe as a tub toy now." He glanced at Henry Stokes. "Not that I ever *had* a tub toy . . ."

Noor didn't relax. "All aahead full! Helm, make your course seero, six, seero!" he cried, tail twitching spastically. "Staart your descent," he added to the 'Cat at the wheel controlling the elevators. "Level off at forty tails, then take us right down to the ground as soon as we cross the Maackey Field threshold." He lunged past the talker by the aft bulkhead, telling him to repeat what he said next, in the clear, to Mackey Field Control. Uncovering the entire cluster of voice tubes running all over the ship, he pitched his voice to carry like Lemurians did so well, ensuring it would resonate through every tube. He also managed to subdue any hint of alarm, though his next words doubtless inspired a great deal. "Gener-aal quaarters, gener-aal quaarters, all emergency paarties maan your posts. All haands—and honored paassengers—this is Commander Noor. I regret to inform you thaat we just discovered an explosive device in the gondola. It haas been disabled but there's no question it was placed deliberately in an attempt to damaage or destroy the ship. I've increased speed to return to Maackey Field, but since we caan't be certain there waas *only* one device, all haands without emergency posts will immediately search for more. I aask our paassengers to do the same. Look everywhere. . . ." He paused. "Everywhere something the size of a pair of hu-maan shoes might be hidden. Report any suspicious objects at once!" He took a breath. "Paassengers be aadvised: We won't make for the mooring maast. We'll go as low as we caan when we reach the field and you'll evaacuate down the emergency laadders. A detail will jettison the haatches, deploy the laadders, and aassist you. Thaank you. With the Maker's help, we'll all soon be safely on the ground."

Noor stepped back, took another deep breath, and exhaled. Matt was impressed by his quick, decisive action, as well as by what his orders implied about the professionalism of the Union's fledgling Airship Corps. Outside, the engines roared at full power and *Fueen* was beginning to accelerate. Stokes had taken the bomb from Silva and was looking at it with interest.

"Bloody crude," he pronounced, hauling his own Impie-made watch out of a vest pocket and glancing at the time, "but all the more effective for it—if the timer hadn't wound down." He sighed and looked at Matt. "It's still tickin' but it's lost time. The contact point shows it should've blown about forty minutes ago. Even if we survived the crash, we'd be in the jungle about fifty miles from here, with little more than a few pistols among us."

"Scout planes would find the crash site soon enough," Matt said.

"Yeah," Stokes agreed, "but with only the one airship, how would they get us before the bunyips an' super lizards?"

That was a sobering thought. "You think Giaan's responsible for this?" Matt asked.

"Yeah. Him an' Dupont, maybe. Who else? An' how better to get what they want? They knock us all off at once, but mainly you an' the Chairman, the *least* they get is your war plan outa whack an' the Union in confusion when she can least afford it. Giaan'd shout 'traitors in our midst!' an' use that to justify pullin' outa the Union to their people back home, *and* in our armies. Even if people think they did it, why should they care? They'd act offended an' use that to the same effect, sayin' 'after all we've been through, they accuse *us*?'" He shook his head. "They put their heads together on this, which makes me wonder why they'd leave it all ridin' on one Impie watch. . . ."

Matt's eyes narrowed. "Maybe we ought to go help look for more."

Stokes shook his head. "No. We'll be over the field in minutes. But I think they oughta jettison the hatches on both sides of the cargo/passenger compartment in case the blokes back there need out in a hurry."

That never happened, nor would it have helped. Giaan's saboteur wasn't in the Navy Clan, or the Air Corps. He was a civilian ground crew 'Cat, employed for airfield maintenance and to wipe bugs off airplane wings. Professing a fascination with the airship, he'd recently joined the crew of line handlers who helped stabilize it at the mooring mast, but was never granted access to *Fueen*'s inner structure. The army and navy aviators who flew and maintained it were picky about that. He'd occasionally been allowed to enter the gondola and passenger/cargo compartments, however, to keep things "tidied and polished," and that's where he'd hidden his two devices. During the frantic search following Noor's announcement, Alan Letts and Bolton Forester quickly found the second bomb—also under a deck access hatch, and running almost three-quarters of an hour behind—just as it suddenly detonated.

CHAPTER 19

*////// **Baalkpan, Borno***

Deputy Assemblyperson Giaan and High Sky Priest Nau had crossed the Parade Ground Cemetery and mounted the steps to the Great Hall and Assembly building surrounding the base of the Great Tree a little early. They had every confidence in their plan and knew it wouldn't take long for a scouting Nancy or training flight to spot a distant tower of smoke and investigate. It probably wouldn't be long at all before *Fueen*'s crash site was discovered and the grim news reported. There'd be pandemonium, and they wanted to be seated inside the Assembly room, chatting amiably with colleagues when that occurred.

They were both surprised to see the great, blue cylinder rumble in from the northeast, apparently intent on overflying the city, and they stood and watched in fearful disappointment.

"It didn't work!" Nau hissed at Giaan, his words submerged by the delighted babble around them. It seemed they were the only ones who loathed the unnatural monstrosity that mocked the Heavens. Airplanes were bad enough, but wings were like sails so they vaguely understood them. The great sails on seagoing Homes were called "wings" after all. But nothing seemed to suspend *Fueen* and that touched an inner terror in some, particularly those already prone to terrors of every sort.

Giaan tried to remain calm. "Either Dupont's devices didn't work, or they were discovered—and the finger of suspicion will point at us."

"It cannot *touch* us, though," Nau countered, as if trying to reassure himself. The airship was almost overhead now, largely obscured by the broad branches of the Great Tree. It seemed to be circling, as if already pointing its own finger down at them.

"Our infiltrator was dealt with?" Giaan asked anxiously.

"Yes. When he went to the appointed place to receive his reward, he . . . accidentally slipped and fell in the bay. The terrible fishes took him at once."

Giaan didn't respond. The great airship was invisible now, completely shrouded by the leaves above, but it was definitely turning. It soon reappeared, and he was startled to hear its engines roar thunderously, louder than they ever had over the city.

"It seems they are suddenly in a great hurry," Nau lamented, sure this was proof their plot had been uncovered. Most around them only chattered more enthusiastically, appreciative of the display of power.

"Put it out of your mind, brother. It never happened," Giaan said. "If they even reveal their discovery, we'll be as shocked and outraged as any other. We might still shape even that to our advantage. Come, let's be seen inside. Be cheerful. Relax." He glanced once more at the hated symbol of the Union he loathed as it accelerated away, descending rapidly even as it gained speed. It was already several hundred tails away when he saw a curious, smoky flash in its fat belly. He clutched Nau's arm. "Look!" he cried.

Smoldering streamers of debris and at least one windmilling body fell from a jagged, smoky opening that had appeared in the bottom of the airship. It seemed a tiny wound, hardly noticed, and the thing surged onward. A few concerned cries rose up, but most of the gathered assemblypersons seemed oblivious. Still watching intently, not knowing what to expect, Giaan saw an abrupt stalk of dark smoke gust upward at the sky, as if from the thing's broad back, followed almost instantly by a mushrooming ball of orange flame wreathed in an ugly black cloud. Simultaneously, he felt giddy with glee and dread. The crowd wailed in comprehending horror as the flames rapidly bloomed and spread. Imperceptibly at first, but quickly gaining speed, *Fueen* began to fall. The ship would crash in the city, there was no help for that, but for the first time, Giaan felt genuine regret for his actions when a furtive glance revealed the most likely impact point. Almost directly below the dying dirigible was the Baalkpan Naval Hospital—the largest hospital in the city. "Maker forgive us," he murmured.

Colonel Chack-Sab-At knew he was in a "funk," as Silva accused, and he'd been neglecting his duties as well. Particularly to his Raiders. But aside from the fact he'd been in almost constant combat for far too long, lost too many he cared for, and now an unborn youngling and possibly the mate he adored, Majors Enrico Galay, Abel Cook, and Hamish McIntire had thoughtfully made it easy for him to focus on Safir's well-being—and frankly, his own misery. They'd reorganized the First Raider Brigade and brought it back to Baalkpan, billeted it at the ATC with a big chunk of Safir's II Corps, and were feverishly bringing it back up to strength. In their concern for him, his officers had left him little to do except mope, and haunt his increasingly frustrated mate.

His wounded mind and spirit got jolted back in gear that day, with the abruptness of a popped clutch on one of the new tanks. Safir had sent him to get some air—*and probably out of her sight for a while*, he'd grimly reflected, and he'd joined some ambulatory wounded lounging in the open air on the hospital grounds. It was mostly clear, but starting to cloud up a little, preparatory to the daily squalls, and he'd been talking to Pam Cross and a few wounded Raiders when *Fueen* flew over the city. They were still there, talking a little less and watching the great airship thundering lower toward them when it suddenly exploded and began to fall. Mind reeling in horror, Chack first thought it would drop on the hospital, but even as the malignant flames raced fore and aft to consume the huge ship, pulsing with fire and a sky-blocking billow of smoke as hydrogen bladders erupted, he saw its rudders had kicked hard left and it was starting to turn to the north. That only helped because *Fueen* fell rather slowly at first. Despite her immense size, she was comparatively light, and the very heat of her immolation and the gusting flames encompassing her withering bones slowed her descent.

That could only last so long, and the flame-wreathed carcass fell the last hundred feet or so with a gathering, sparkling rush. By then it was clear she'd miss the hospital—barely—but she collapsed under a last monstrous fireball right on top of the neighboring traders' district: old-style, more inflammable dwellings, built down to the ground to accommodate the little shops and stores of Baalkpan's evolving mercantile class. The people there might not be as helpless as wounded in a hospital, but they were just as vulnerable. Many of the shopkeepers were either too old to fight or work in the factories, or had already been handicapped by the war. And as a class, they'd taken in more orphaned younglings than any other.

Even as *Fueen*'s crackling skeleton settled and sagged barely two hundred yards away and her own flames began to die, others licked at the trees and buildings beneath and around her. That's when Chack saw Pam already running toward the wreck—and Chack became himself again.

"Sound the gener-aal alarm!" he shouted at a 'Cat orderly standing nearby, even though the hollow bronze gongs were already ringing throughout the city. They were used to warn against everything from fires to air raids, and people would organize appropriately. Reserve troops, civil "damage control" parties, and fire brigades would be assembling, their destination obvious. "Who here is fit for aaction?" Chack added loudly, addressing the convalescents nearby. Most stood or stepped forward, even as Sandra Reddy, Karen Letts, and Diania led a flood of doctors, nurses, sick berth attendants, and other walking wounded out of the hospital. "Good." Chack raised his voice so the newcomers could hear. "Our first priority is to rescue *Fueen*'s survivors and get civilians out before the fire takes hold. Let's go!"

Karen caught his arm, eyes wide, almost wild. "Alan was in that thing!" she cried. Chack looked at Sandra's determined, anxious face. "I know," he said. He knew *Fueen*'s entire passenger list, in fact. Matt had asked if he'd like to go and he'd declined. He couldn't imagine how his presence would've made any difference, but the knowledge shaped another barb to prod him back to his duty. "Let's go find him," he said, turning to lead the first rescuers into the nightmare that fell out of a midday sky.

An hour or so after the disaster commenced an escalating calamity, 'Cat soldiers and sailors with MP or SP bands around their arms reinforced those already guarding the entrances and exits to the Assembly room under the Great Hall. Politely but firmly, they made it clear that no assemblyperson would be allowed to leave until further notice—for their own safety—and any who hadn't come or had already left were brought back. A few were indignant, but most understood. They were allowed upstairs onto the spacious veranda wrapping entirely around the Great Hall so they could view what many grimly thought looked like a "Second Battle of Baalkpan." The black smoke plume from the crash had been momentous, but fires hadn't seemed like much at first. They quickly grew and spread, however, and the black smoke turned dark gray to match the thickening clouds. More smoke than usual chuffed from the waterfront as industrial boilers diverted steam to pumps, supplying seawater to the strategically placed hoses the fire brigades quickly deployed. Industrialized as it was, Baalkpan's architecture was a crowded mishmash with a flavor of everything from tropic island huts to nineteenth-century wood frame and siding—with some startling concrete and masonry thrown in. Its vulnerability to fire had not gone unnoticed by Chairman Letts—or Adar before him. Steam billowed where water drowned the flames.

Even so, the unusually heavy afternoon squall that lasted until after dark did more to turn the tide than the puny efforts of men, 'Cats, and Khonashi. They'd have prevailed in the end, but it would've taken longer, and many more lives. By 0040 the next morning, there was only the smell of charred wood and wet smoke and a hazy red glow east of the Great Hall. And though there'd been constant reports on the progress of the firefighting effort, there'd been little word on casualties. Many assemblypersons were concerned for friends and family in the area. Others were just generally concerned. A few picked at the refreshments they'd been brought while others sat thoughtfully, but they all stayed close and conversed in worried or angry tones. Giaan, Nau, and other members of the Sularaan and B'taavan delegations sat pensively by themselves, disconcertingly avoided by their usual associates.

"They can't possibly suspect," Giaan hissed at the others.

"No," Nau agreed bitterly, "but this has turned into a *Union* catastrophe and bound the rest together. We're seen as outsiders. We've *made* ourselves seem so."

"Why are they keeping us here?" demanded the B'taavan assemblyperson, a female with white and gray fur.

"Why should they not?" Giaan asked reasonably. "This is the safest place in the city." He considered. "And soon they'll need us all in one place," he added very low.

At that moment, the big double doors at the entrance swayed open, and to Giaan-Naak's amazement, General Queen Safir-Maraan paced into the room. She was resplendent as always in a silver-washed cuirass, black kilt with silver strips, and a midnight-black cape swaying behind her. In a deliberate contrast to her ebony fur, a sculpted silver cup covered her ruined right eye. Giaan was flabbergasted. It had been known that Safir-Maraan was recovering from terrible wounds, but all reports had her bedridden. He thought he detected the slightest wince as she stepped up on the podium in front of the base of the Great Tree, but she moved more like a predator than an invalid. Giaan felt a chill seize his tail in a frozen grip and crawl up his spine. Especially when he saw the procession that followed her. Unlike Safir, her attendants looked like hell: tired, hurt, and those in white uniforms or shoregoing rigs were darkened and smeared with soot and blood. Yet all but one were on their own feet. The last was in a wheelchair, pushed by a bedraggled-looking civilian human. One by one, they lined up behind Safir, except for a fur-scorched 'Cat in a Marine combat smock, and the man in the wheelchair. They took places beside her. A late arrival hustled in, not quite as soiled, and Giaan recognized "Commaander McFaarlane," Captain Reddy's second in command. He also joined Safir.

"Aassemblypersons of the United Homes!" Safir called loudly, strongly. "As you've seen, our Union suffered a terrible traagedy today. The UHAS *Fueen* craashed and burned in the city, causing more fires on the ground. Thirty-two of the forty aboard her died in the craash, and most of the survivors were gravely injured. We don't know how maany died on the ground, but I fear the number will rise into the hundreds. Whaat I *caan* tell you is this was not an aaccident," she added coldly, "but a deliberate, premeditated, *treacherous* assault on our Union. And not by an enemy we knew, but a hidden, sneaking enemy, crouching in our midst!" Her silver eye seemed to fasten on Giaan before it passed by, and the ice in his spine sent frigid tendrils down his legs. She motioned to a big, grim-looking man with his own eyepatch, standing next to a ferocious-looking Sa'aaran. Giaan irrelevantly remembered he'd intended to propose that they, and their Khonashi relatives, not be allowed in the Assembly room. The man's beard was singed and his clothes were practically shredded. Absurdly, a small, colorful reptile . . . thing was perched protectively on his shoulder.

"Chief Gunner's Mate Dennis Silvaa, Cap-i-taan Reddy, Minister Stokes, and Commaander Noor discovered and disaarmed an explosive device of *domestic* maanu-faacture in the control gondola moments before another exploded in the paassenger compaartment. Chief Silvaa and Mr. Stokes"—she nodded at a second civilian Giaan knew only too well—"barely maanaged to pull two unconscious crew members"—she took a long, relieved sigh—"and Cap-i-taan Reddy, out from under the collaapsing structure above. Cap-i-taan Reddy suffered burns and other injuries, but stayed to help coordinate rescue efforts in the city until *caarried* to the hospitaal by order of Minister of Medicine Lady Saandra." She flicked a quick glance at Silva. "Saadly," she continued, voice turning hard again, "everyone else in the gondola burned alive. The story was similar in the paassenger compartment. Chairmaan Letts and Ambaassador Forester discovered another explosive, but it detonated. Thaat's whaat ignited the lifting gaas and brought the ship down." She placed a hand on the shoulder of the man in the wheelchair. He was shaking with anger and seemed to be suppressing tears. "The Maker waas waatching over King Tony Scott and Ambaassador Doocy Meek, both shielded from the blaast by cushions they were searching under." She looked at Meek, his own beard singed nearly off. "Ambaassador Meek simultaneously pulled King Scott and a baadly wounded Waalbert Fiedler from the wreckage. The Maker gave him strength indeed." Her voice turned to stone. "There were *no other* survivors in the paassenger compaartment, and only one other crew-'Cat maanaged a miraculous escape. She was unhaarmed."

The Assembly room erupted in angry shouts and gasps of realization. They hadn't added it all up yet, or come to the suspicion that terrified Giaan, but they finally knew the real reason they'd been sequestered. Safir was shouting and gesturing for quiet, and for the first time her flagging strength seemed to show, but Silva finally silenced the room with a thunderous "Shut your faces, goddammit! Let the lady talk!"

A horrified, almost murderous noiselessness ensued. "Thaank you, Chief Silvaa," Safir whispered, then spoke louder. "As you've guessed, it's my saad duty to inform you thaat Chairmaan Alaan Letts is dead." Her voice cracked ever so slightly on that final word, but she relentlessly forged ahead. "Our constitution clearly states thaat, in such a dreadful case, a new chairman must be acclaimed at once. Nominations may be made by heads of the severaal member states or Homes in the Union, or by their duly elected or appointed representative assemblypersons. As Queen of B'mbaado and Aryaal, I nominate—"

No one would ever know who Safir was going to name, but Tony Scott beat her to the punch. "Safir-Maraan!" he shouted.

"Second!" cried the female assemblyperson from Maa-ni-la. Safir looked taken aback, and Chack reached over and grabbed her fingers.

"Call the roll!" Spanky growled.

Nau couldn't contain himself and bolted to his feet. "Who do you speak for, hu-maan! *You* haave no voice in this assembly!"

"Damned if I don't," Spanky roared back. "My 'high chief' is flat on his back, sedated, and I'm his second in command. Piss off!"

Angry laughter silenced Nau, and more than angry looks started drifting toward the Sularaans as people began to think.

The Maa-ni-la assemblyperson looked a lot like Safir, with her black fur. Of course, she looked a lot like Saan-Kakja too, and was probably related to the high chief of the Filpin Lands. She started calling out the names of states or Homes. "Baalkpan!"

"Ay!"

"Austraal!"

"Ay!"

"North Borno!"

"What do you think?" snapped Scott. "I nominated her, didn't I?"

By the time all fifteen were called, even Sular had given its "Aye." What choice did Giaan have? Only Safir herself abstained, and when she was formally acclaimed with a thunderous, hopeful cheer, she seemed to slump a little. Chack supported her. "You know you're stuck with me now," she murmured in his ear, blinking a kind of sadness. "Even the oldbloods of Aryaal and B'mbaado would never defy the Chairmaan." She snorted. "They still remember the threat Cap-i-taan Reddy once made, and I caan aask him to fulfill it if they don't behave!" She straightened and her blinking turned savage as she addressed the assembly once more. "This is no time to celebrate! We're in a crisis. We're *attaacked* here, and the waar still rages. We must face *all* our threats. My first aact as Chairmaan is to appoint Minister Henry Stokes, Chief Silvaa, and Col-nol Chack to detect and arrest the traitorous murderers." Her one-eyed gaze fell remorselessly on Deputy Assemblyperson Giaan-Naak. "I believe they'd like to speak to members of the delegations from Saa-Leebs, and Sular in paarticular. Gentlemen, perform your duty."

A limping Henry Stokes gathered Giaan and Nau, each by an arm, and together with the others, roughly ushered them away to the very brig where Alan Letts had come down in his robe to basically bail his old shipmates out. Chack and Silva never even touched them, but their fury alone was sufficient to induce Giaan and Nau to squeal. Armed with what they spilled, Silva, Chack, Lawrence, Spanky, Henry Stokes, and a dozen of Chack's Raiders who "happened" to show up with Gunny Horn marched across the Parade Ground Cemetery and stormed the consulate for all the delegates from Saa-Leebs. Their guards didn't resist, though the Sularaans tried to bolt. They were caught. Pounding up the stairs and into a hallway of curtained chambers, Silva, Lawrence, Chack, and Gunny Horn drew their pistols and went straight to the room they'd been directed to. Capitaine Bucge Dupont was comfortably arranged on his chair, leg propped up, idly fussing with loose items on the table under the light of a fish oil lamp. He looked up, unsurprised, as if he'd been expecting them.

"Well," he said amiably, "you've caught me at last. I suppose I'm to be your prisoner again?"

"Nope," Silva said. "You killed our friends."

"Prison's for prisoners, not mad bombers," said Horn.

"Not assaassins," agreed Chack.

Lawrence said nothing, but joined the other three when they emptied their magazines in Dupont's chest.

"Co'ander S'anky get angry at us?" Lawrence asked as Dupont slipped to the floor with a lifeless thump.

"Naw," Silva said, pointing at the table. "We'll telleem the bastard came at us with them tweezers. *Had* to kill his ass."

Ultimately, Giaan-Naak's long scheme had cost the Alliance a lot, and his final plot most dearly of all, killing the two men (counting Lord Bolton Forester's stabilizing influence) who, along with Adar, had done more than any to build the Union in the first place. But Alan Letts's greatest accomplishment had been ensuring the Union could go on without him, and Giaan's actions only strengthened it in the long run. He'd also decimated Matt's infant "staff," but that was of little account since his real staff would always be the officers under his command. So in the end, all Giaan and his accomplices really did was destroy an airship, kill a lot of people, and add more graves and monuments to the cemetery he hated so. Giaan's soul would never ascend to the Heavens in a gentle twist of rising smoke, however. Weeks later, after his trial, and as soon as he was cut down from the gallows, his corpse was unceremoniously carted down to the dock and dumped in the bay for the flashies to feast upon.

CHAPTER 20

////// Puerto del Cielo
Holy Dominion
May 29, 1945

The orange morning sun revealed that the League presence off Puerto del Cielo had grown. The latest additions were another small oiler and a smart-looking Churrucca Class destroyer, contributed by the Spanish contingent. Her captain presented himself with the dawn and Gravois was quite taken with the lines of his ship, not to mention that she'd nearly doubled his combat power. The rusty old oiler that had dogged *Leopardo* so far and long was laboriously raising steam. She'd weigh anchor and proceed to Martinique, pump her remaining fuel stores into one of the newly constructed storage tanks, and finally steam back to the League. Gravois and Ciano, sipping tea on *Leopardo*'s port bridgewing, wouldn't be sorry to see her go. Another destroyer, a newer oiler, and the departure of that old slug seemed to imply things were finally starting to happen.

There'd been no communication at all from shore, however, except for the usual bumboats bringing fresh fruit, meat, vegetables, and water. Nor did their handlers confess any knowledge of what happened to Oriani and his escort. Gravois was certain they were lying. He'd been confirmed in his post as Gouverneur Militaire du Protectorat des Antilles in a radio dispatch after reporting Oriani had "disappeared ashore," and was feared "attacked by something," or had simply "gotten lost." To the Triumvirate, anything beyond the Strait of Gibraltar was darkest wilderness and getting lost on land and probably eaten was only to be expected. Gravois doubted his confirmation came easily to his superiors, but not only had it been Oriani's wish, he was the resident expert on the Dominion and the face of the League in their eyes. Besides, the French General Faure—remarkably still "first among equals" in the Triumvirate—had been reluctant to appoint Oriani to the governorship in the first place. The Italians were far too cozy with the Spanish and were gaining too much power in the League. He might not personally like Gravois, but at least he was French.

"Capitano," murmured one of the bridge officers after responding to a call from the lookout. He nodded toward shore.

"I see it," Ciano replied. A gaudy bireme, Don Hernan's personal barge, was shoving off from a dock near where Oriani was taken. Double ranks of oars churned the brown river fan and the vessel backed, turned, and headed for *Leopardo*. Gravois had ordered her tucked in behind *Ramb V*, and the Churrucca anchored astern of *her* when she arrived. That left the ships arranged in a line opposite the fort on the east side of the River of Heaven—and unmasked all their portside guns. Don Hernan knew what those guns could do and would recognize the threat implied his allies weren't pleased. That the bireme now approached *Leopardo* instead of the bigger *Ramb V* also meant he knew where Gravois was. Obviously, the bumboat skippers weren't only sent to deliver supplies.

"I rather expected a visit after our new arrival," Gravois said with satisfaction. "Assemble a side party," he ordered.

Ciano looked at him sullenly. "To greet that *sporco bastardo*, or arrest him?" he demanded.

"Let's keep our options open, shall we?" Gravois responded, raising his binoculars. Don Hernan was indeed standing on the high poop deck under a gauzy awning and flapping red flags. He was unmistakable in his long red robe, trimmed in gold, and the bizarre white hat standing tall on his head. As usual, his features, sharpened and lengthened by a graying mustache and pointy chin whiskers, looked utterly benign. Gravois was surprised to see another, shorter man beside him, dressed in the rumpled, looser-fitting uniform of Contrammiraglio Oriani. "Well," he said, his tone perturbed, "I didn't expect to see *him* again."

"Good morning, my dear Gravois!" Don Hernan greeted him, then beamed at the men of the side party standing at tense attention with their weapons. "Good morning to you all!" To Gravois's astonishment, Don Hernan boarded without his usual entourage, accompanied only by Oriani. The man looked . . . destroyed, in some undefinable way. It wasn't anything obvious to a stranger, though he was less rotund. He was cleanly shaven and if a bit untidy, his uniform was clean. There were no obvious signs of mistreatment at all, in fact. But the arrogant light—*any* light—in his eyes had been extinguished, and he practically quivered at the sound of Don Hernan's voice.

"Thank God you're safe!" Ciano said, taking a step toward him. Oriani cringed and retreated, uttering a small squeak. Ciano stopped in surprise and spun to face Don Hernan. "What have you done to him? What have you done to the others?" he demanded.

Don Hernan regarded him with wide, kindly eyes. "*Done* to him? Why, nothing that might be considered *abuse*, as you imply. Rejoice! He and his fellows have been *cleansed* by the grace of God, as any must be who set foot upon our holy soil! Most now bask in the glow of their newfound faith and will be returned to you to spread the light when they're ready. Even the most perfunctory cleansing can be mildly tiresome," he explained, then paused. "And I fear some have been . . . more difficult to purify than others. The filth within them runs quite deep. But I will *never* forsake any who are worthy, and will continue my efforts until all corruption has been banished from their souls." His expression turned mournful. "Unfortunately, a very few were far too malignant to save. No doubt they were infected by demons and simply couldn't be made clean regardless of the grace lavished upon them. You wouldn't have wanted *them* back, I assure you," he murmured darkly. Then his voice brightened again. "Most were quite fortunate, however, and embraced their rebirth with the same enthusiasm as this fine man!" He gestured grandly at Oriani, who'd begun to drool.

"Fortunate also that divine providence guided some of His Supreme Holiness's priests to the vicinity at the exact moment your people stepped on our sacred ground, unannounced and uninvited," he added sternly, looking at Gravois. "There's no doubt they saved their lives." He looked reflective. "Most of them, at any rate. Two men were killed by the mob, rightly angered by such impious trespass."

Ciano and some of the side party looked stormy. "You . . ." Ciano began, taking another step toward Don Hernan.

"Dismiss your men," Gravois barked at Ciano, looking closely at Oriani. He simply didn't appear to be *there* anymore. "And take Contrammiraglio Oriani to the infirmary. Do it yourself. Everyone else, make way." He looked around distractedly as the men reluctantly dispersed, his face darkening with fury. *How dare this . . . creature . . . treat our people this way?* He didn't care about the people *themselves*, per se, but it was the principle of the thing. The sheer arrogance. *And then he comes here, alone, daring me to do some-*

thing about it! He raged to himself. "Clear the fo'c'sle," he snapped. "I want everyone aft of the bridge, and no one in the pilothouse. Don Hernan and I have a great deal to talk about. Your Holiness?" he seethed, gesturing perfunctorily forward.

"You're a monster," Victor Gravois stated flatly. It had taken longer than he wanted to achieve the open-air privacy he needed just then—there was no way he'd enter a room alone with this man—and he'd felt a painful blaze burning just behind his face the entire time he'd waited. Now he and Don Hernan stood on the foredeck in front of the splinter shield protecting the twin 120mm guns.

"I've been called worse," Don Hernan agreed with a snort and Gravois was surprised to see his act drop away so quickly. He didn't think Don Hernan's *faith* was an act, not entirely at least, but his over-the-top performance as its compassionate steward certainly was.

"What did you really do to those men? To Oriani?"

Don Hernan sighed. "I'm sure you'd say I tortured them," he answered simply. "For the good of their souls, of course. One can only achieve grace through suffering and God decreed that this land cannot bear the tread of heretics. . . ." He paused. "And it truly was the only way I could justify sparing them. My own Blood Priests might've turned against me if I neglected the cleansing." He gestured enthusiastically. "And Oriani embraced the true faith much faster than I expected. Such a clever man! I believe I sensed in him almost a kindred spirit. Once his mind absorbs the rigorous toil it has performed, it will be as if he was reborn."

"He has no 'spirit' left!" Gravois almost exploded. "What could do that to him, without even leaving a mark?"

Don Hernan peered at him strangely. "You didn't see? He's marked forever inside. Perhaps I'll show you how it's done someday."

Gravois shuddered.

"But not now, we have work to do," Don Hernan continued, touching the whiskers on his chin and looking at the Churrucca lying aft. "I confess, I also indulged my . . . curiosity during the procedure, to learn about Oriani the man, as well as his understanding of the League's plans here." He glanced at Gravois. "Oh come now, don't look so shocked! You've gained information from those distracted by discomfort yourself." He smiled. "As has Oriani. Many, many times. Perhaps that's why he revealed it so readily. He knew he could never resist." He shook his finger scoldingly at Gravois. "But as for the League's plans, it seems you omitted certain details from our earlier understanding."

Gravois suddenly found himself on the defensive. "It's not set policy in the League, only the ambition of a sizable faction I—and Oriani—happen to support. But it meshes perfectly with what we discussed! It's the essential part. You and I *talked* about joining our people together and I never implied it would only happen in Europe. It must be here as well."

Don Hernan turned to face the fortress walls. "That will not be easy." He chuckled. "The cleansings alone will take considerable time. Unless that's part of our faith you intend to 'subvert.'"

Gravois impatiently waved that away. "I told Oriani that, for his benefit, as well as anything else you may have learned from him against me. You're smart enough to know that. But yes, *that* will have to change. You and I already discussed the need to make religious adjustments that would be acceptable to all our people." He was growing angry again. "But all that's for the future. None of our ground troops will be committed here and you'll have plenty of time to reconstruct your priesthood."

It was inconvenient that Gravois couldn't even supply a few modern weapons, since he'd also have to provide men to show the Doms how to use them. Sending men to be tortured, however briefly, would undermine his position when it was inevitably discovered. *And perhaps it's for the best? We don't have* that *many troops or modern weapons to spare. And if what I hear of the forests of this land is true, our armored vehicles would be of little use. They could move well enough, by all accounts, but couldn't see far enough for the range advantage of their guns to provide significant benefit. Ultimately, it's better to let Don Hernan's army spend itself against the enemy.* He did wish they could build an airfield here, and at other places on the continent. It would make things easier, and he could disperse his airpower as it arrived.

That wouldn't happen. Not only would his priceless air and ground crews be subject to Dom mistreatment, the Dom's own "airpower," their various large flying creatures, couldn't be counted on to discriminate friend from foe in the air. Some of the League's aircraft might be damaged to no purpose. He'd have to be content with the airfields at Martinique, and eventually other islands. Don Hernan had little interest in islands and had magnanimously "given" Gravois any that he wanted.

"And I'm sure you've already begun to identify and surround yourself with a few more flexible priests, in any event," Gravois concluded.

Don Hernan's eyes grew wide. "Of course, and just imagine their surprise—and gratitude! Not long ago they would naturally have expected that very doctrinal elasticity to be . . . corrected."

"I'm sure," Gravois agreed ironically, "but as I said, all this is irrelevant at present. Our forces are rapidly building at Martinique, but I've had no word at all from you regarding your strategic situation. The information exchange between us has been amazingly one-sided of late, particularly since it seems you have the conversation between myself and Oriani verbatim."

Don Hernan's eyes narrowed. "My 'strategic situation'? As you so succinctly summarized to Oriani, El Paso del Fuego and my navy are gone and I'm assailed on land by all our mutual enemies. I imagined that was all you needed to know. Now, however, not only have the western heretics and their bestial allies landed a large force on *this* side of the Pass, Los Diablos have been able to supply their forces sufficiently to defeat General de Quito at El Palo while your powerful ships wallowed lazily at anchor. That's what's most *immediately* 'relevant' to you from my perspective," he inserted cuttingly before resuming. "Worse, since the cream of my professional army was lost in the west and at El Corazon, and now de Quito has squandered much of what remained, I have little in position to prevent *all* the heretics from marching overland toward the Temple City of Nuevo Granada itself," he seethed.

Gravois raised his brows. This was the first he'd heard that the western allies had a ground force in the Caribbean, or the oh-so-confident Don Hernan had lost a battle to the NUS.

"The land itself will rebel beneath their heretic feet," Don Hernan added with more hopefulness than confidence this time, "and God will set the monsters of the forest upon them. But I never dreamed they'd be so bold. A sane man would naturally expect any direct threat to El Templo would necessarily have to run the gauntlet of forts lining the River of Heaven."

That might be true, Gravois mused, though he often doubted Don Hernan's sanity. At the same time, however, even Don Hernan should've realized by now that *this* enemy would usually do what was least expected.

"Now the garrisons of those forts have no purpose and I must send them to defend our Sacred City." Don Hernan paused, expression dark. "So believe me, I fully understand how much I 'need' you."

Gravois nodded solemnly, though inwardly delighted by Don Hernan's admission. *Perhaps now we can move forward with minimal obstruction.* "We apparently need each other more than ever before," he said, "and the time for these ridiculous games is past," he added firmly. "How could I steam away and fight for you while you toyed with our commander?" He pointed at the city. "Do you realize I've been urged by my superiors almost daily to *blast* those forts to rubble?" That was a lie, but Don Hernan couldn't know *that.* "Your war, our alliance, and all our plans have been put in jeopardy because of your obsession with secrecy and because it amused you to torture a man *who was on our side*! We must coordinate more closely, with real trust between us. If you'd asked, I would've told you Oriani was no threat. He had great value, in fact."

"Value to *you*, as *cover,* in case things go awry," Don Hernan countered. He paused, regarding Gravois again. "I'm surprised by your naiveté." No one had ever used that word to describe Gravois before and his ears burned hot. "I learned that from Oriani as well, of course," Don Hernan explained. "He knew it himself and it wouldn't have worked. He wanted the prestige this posting gave him but not the responsibility. He endorsed your strategy because he had none of his own and was prepared to take all the credit for success—or blame you if it failed." His smile turned benevolent once more. "Of *course* I 'toyed' with him to discover if you'd betray me. I'm more confident now that you won't and that allows me to invest a measure of genuine trust in you at last. Not only because our interests intertwine, but because, committed to your strategy now—at least the part they know about—your League will certainly hang you if it fails. Finally . . . well, we both got what we wanted. You're now in charge of all your people and ships in this entire region. What more could we desire?" He waited a moment while that sank in, that he'd *engineered* it that way.

"But . . ." Gravois stammered, knowing he sounded foolish, "how did you know Oriani would go ashore as soon as he got here?" Even as he asked, it dawned on him. Dom ships had ventured to Ascension Island several times. Some had been lost, but delegates who survived the round trip would've reported everything the Blood Cardinal needed to know about the man.

Don Hernan nodded at Gravois's comprehension. "Kindred spirits, as I said. Of a sort," he qualified. "I probably would've done much the same myself in his place." He took a long, deep breath. "Now, as we both agree, we have work to do. Our scouts report the allied force under their 'General Shinya' is marching south from Monsu but its depot is vulnerable on the coast. I want it destroyed, along with whatever ships are carrying *his* supplies. I wonder also if it's possible for one or more of your ships to penetrate El Paso del Fuego and bombard the source of their supply effort at El Corazon?"

"Go *into* the pass? Even beyond?" Gravois briefly considered the newly arrived Churrucca and its dual-purpose guns. Then he shook his head. "Not until we're stronger. Primitive as the enemy's aircraft are, they remain a threat. And the numbers they could sortie so close to their *new* base of operations might be overwhelming." He couldn't resist reminding Don Hernan that if he'd allowed *Leopardo* to defend the Pass in the first place, from the open water on the other side, there might not be a threat from that direction. "I don't believe they can hit anything we have that's free to maneuver at speed, but their bombs *can* damage our lighter vessels in confined waters. We'll have to wait before attempting something so ambitious."

"I suspected that might be the case," Don Hernan conceded with surprising ease, but then his expression hardened. "So in the meantime, the very first thing I require is that you *stop* all resupply of heretic forces on this side of El Paso. I also want you to retrieve General Mayta from El Henal. He can achieve nothing of substance there." His eyes narrowed. "He failed me badly at El Corazon, but he's the best we have. I cherish high hopes that he learned a painful lesson. He'll teach it to our armies gathering at the Temple City."

"Very well." Gravois nodded. He only had two ships to send, but they didn't have to seek the enemy. The transports would come to them. And within weeks he'd have *more* ships, larger and more powerful than Don Hernan could imagine. He was amused by the thought of the impression they'd make. "Our new arrival must refuel and I'll top off *Leopardo*'s bunkers." He quirked a brow. "I'll remain here in *Ramb V* so we can continue to plan together, at last. Ciano can take the destroyers out, to vent his frustrations on our mutual enemies." He paused, suddenly curious. "What happened to Oriani's chief of staff? Roberto . . . something. I could use him if he's not too, ah, damaged."

Don Hernan beamed. "Ah! Roberto Francisco! You'd never believe it, and I'm not sure myself if he's not my finest achievement. After only a day of cleansing, not only did the priests assigned to his purification declare it complete, he petitioned to take the first rites required to enter the priesthood himself. I'm amazed!" Don Hernan frowned. "But of course you may have him back if you need him."

Roberto a Blood Priest, and him a Carlist. Gravois felt a chilling ache of foreboding and shook his head. "No, you keep him," he said, wondering who would ultimately subvert whose faith.

CHAPTER 21

////// In the Wilderness of Nuevo Granada
Holy Dominion
June 6, 1945

Colonel Blas-Ma-Ar and Colonel Sister Audrey were riding with Captain Ixtli and Lieutenant Anaar-Taar at the head of 'C' Company, 2nd Battalion, 2nd Marines as the column, wider now, on a better road, marched easily down a wooded slope five hundred miles from Monsu, and two hundred miles from the coast. The forest canopy remained thick overhead, covering the road entirely, but there was still little undergrowth and except for the humid morning haze, the ground level visibility was only limited by tree trunks and the meager light filtering down from above.

Blas still marched with her troops from time to time, and she'd grown as lean and well-seasoned to the hardships of the trek through the seemingly endless forest, river crossings, and winding mountain roads as the humans and 'Cats under her command. But Sister Audrey's words were never far from her thoughts. Consequently, she spent most of her time on horseback now.

They'd lost some people to accidents and the occasional ambush, but enemy resistance had been sporadic and poorly coordinated at best, always quickly dealt with by her veteran troops. More people were killed or injured by vaguely Grik-like predators—particularly at night—and those attacks seemed to come in spells, as if coinciding with their entry into tribal territories of some kind. That's what the locals told them. And there *were* quite a few natives, inhabiting a surprising number of villages tucked away, almost invisible to the rare aerial observations by the few planes they had operating out of Monsu. The people weren't always supportive of the invaders, but were appreciative of the benign treatment they received and acted as if keeping them well fed was a small price to pay to see the army pass. This was confirmed by refugees describing how Dom troops razed villages in the path of NUS forces marching down from the north to prevent their sustenance. This gained them enough recruits who, while not immediately fit for combat, made excellent guides, foragers, and escorts for the trickle of ambulance wagons carrying the army's injured to the rear, or freight wagons full of supplies pushing ahead of the vastly more cumbersome XI and XV Corps. In any event, X Corps was tired, but generally healthy, and there were no stragglers.

The objective for the day was a relatively large village under an open sky for once (they were all looking forward to that), about eleven miles ahead. The NUS Army, less well-supplied and facing stiffer resistance had nevertheless pushed hard and Shinya intended to await it there. A battalion of dragoons and two batteries of guns had occupied the village the day before, in case the enemy tried to burn it and slaughter the inhabitants. By all accounts, the people were grateful. They'd been getting refugees as well, and knew what had been in store for them at the hands of their own troops.

"Idiots," Shinya had remarked at the previous evening's officer's call, outlining his intentions as well as warning them to be extra vigilant. "A scorched-earth strategy can be effective at denying forage to an enemy, but murdering all the people as well only weakens your support."

"The goddaamn Doms don't care," Blas had replied. "'Least Don Hernaan an' his sort don't. Anybody sees us an' lives, learns they don't *haave* to put up with the crazy shit the Blood Priests dish out—so they *caan't* let 'em live. The only 'support' thaat maatters to them is in the places they caan defend: the cities."

Here near the very front of the column, vigilance was always necessary, not only for the enemy, but the beasts. Predators weren't the only dangerous animals. They'd been seeing more and more creatures similar to armabueys, only these were flatter, with hard, spiked shells. They also had powerful spiked tails that they wielded with surprising agility considering their awkward appearance. They were generally seen near deadfall, rooting under or destroying rotten trees for the insects infesting them and they reacted aggressively to being disturbed. Blas figured their eyes weren't very good and if you got close enough for them to notice, you were too damn close.

Blas suddenly cocked her head to the side, listening. Despite the currently semidry nature of the track and soft covering of leafy needles lying inches deep upon it, the army made a lot of noise. Men and 'Cats chattered, canteens and other accoutrements bumped and clattered, and hundreds of nearby feet made a low rumble no matter how mushy the ground. There was also the ever-present pop and creak of the giant trees, but Blas thought she heard another kind of popping, muffled by distance and the forest, but wholly familiar to her. "Somebody's shootin' at somebody," she declared, nodding to the northeast. "Thaat way, pretty faar." Audrey didn't hear it but took Blas's word.

"Riders coming in," Lieutenant Anaar observed, flicking his ears forward.

"I see 'em," Blas replied. "An' put your daamn helmet on." Falling limbs were always a hazard too. Anaar reluctantly complied. There was little or no breeze and helmets got hot.

A pair of Impie dragoons pulled their horses to a halt and saluted Blas and Audrey while four more dashed down the column, showering Marines with pointy brown leaves and clods of damp earth.

"What's happening?" Sister Audrey asked.

"There's Doms ahead, barely half a mile. "They dragged up some dead trees an' hunkered down behind 'em, across the road."

"How many?" Captain Ixtli demanded.

"Three hundred, maybe more. Must've moved in last night. They can't stop us, but seem set on slowin' us."

Blas was still staring northeast. "I wonder why?" She pointed where she was looking. "Any idea whaat's haappening thaat way?"

The dragoon trooper looked, then shook his head. "Nothin' I know of, Colonel. Maybe some o' our other scouts tangled with more Doms."

"This is so frustrating!" Audrey exclaimed. "I became spoiled by our airpower, I'm afraid, always knowing at least vaguely what the enemy was doing. Now, even when our planes do venture overhead, they see almost nothing. I feel too much like I did back in the old *S-19*, creeping about beneath the sea. The enemy had difficulty finding us, but we couldn't see them either."

"I bet it's them Nussies," First Sergeant Spook declared, stepping out of the column while it moved past them, "an' them Doms that've been snaappin' at 'em are tryin' to slow 'em up. The ones across our front're just there to keep our attention."

"Thaat's not possible, is it?" Lieutenant Anaar asked, blinking concern. "Laast we heard, the Nussies were still fifty miles north."

"And our planes caan't see 'em any better thaan us," Blas countered. She was sure the volume of distant fire was picking up. "Word is, they ain't gettin' supplied as well as us. They caan't turn baack, they'd never make it, so all they *caan* do is push haarder to meet us." She paused. "I bet them Doms're goin' all in to stop 'em, or bleed 'em so baad they won't do us no good." She looked at the senior dragoon who'd reported. "Tell Gener-aal Shinya whaat I said."

They heard a rush of horse hooves and Shinya himself appeared with a small escort, accompanied by Colonel Garcia, whom he must've called along from his position with the Vengadores behind. "I'm sure you already know why I'm here," he said.

"Doms're fightin' Nussies close enough to hear," Blas replied.

Shinya nodded. "So it seems. Scouts aided by local guides just reported from the northeast." Cannon started rumbling, shaking condensation from above, even at this distance. Everybody heard them now.

"How far?" Audrey asked.

"About six miles. The scouts saw two Dom regiments preparing a position across the north-south road I showed you on the map we've been compiling. Chances are, there are twice that many, but it's likely the largest organized force they have left. No NUS forces were seen before the report was dispatched, but there can be no doubt who they're fighting. If we crush the Doms between us now, we'll not only relieve our allies, but should eliminate the last major obstacle between us and the Temple City."

"We?" Sister Audrey asked wryly.

"Well, the Sister's Own Division, of course," Shinya replied with a smile. "The rest of us will smash the distraction ahead and proceed toward the village. I'll expect you to join us there no later than tomorrow." He looked at Blas. "Speaking of 'distractions,' bear in mind the enemy has their attention focused elsewhere just now. If you can remain undetected long enough to strike them from behind . . ."

"We got it," Blas replied, turning to Garcia. "Shake the Vengadores an' Colnol Iverson's Impies out. We'll maarch in three columns as faast as we caan through thaat"—she pointed at the trees—"an' won't go into line until we're behind the Doms." She looked at Shinya. "You'll give me the scouts that saaw?"

"You'll have all you need."

"An' some o' those little caannons? I like those."

"Of course."

"Good." She addressed the others. "For now, then, I guess we maarch to the sound of the guns."

It took three hours to navigate through the woods, being careful to maintain visual contact between the three columns, and it was early afternoon before they shook out into lines behind the Dom position. Blas sent several scouts to pick their way around the battle and try to contact the Nussies. "Tell 'em not to waste men on a frontal aassault, an' for the Maker's sake, cease firing when we hit 'em!" She hoped they'd get through. More scouts scurried back and forth, reporting the dispositions as best they could, drawing pictures in the soil and speaking excitedly with Arano Garcia. Blas shifted her entire division slightly to the right before she was satisfied. She still couldn't *see* the enemy, the gloom and smoke under the trees was just too great, but she was assured they'd arrived completely undetected less than three hundred yards behind the enemy works.

"Wish we had a few *real* caannon," First Sergeant Spook muttered loud enough for Blas to hear. She was still mounted and intended to stay that way. As far as she could recall, she'd only ever ridden into battle once before. Spook was obviously referring to the two batteries of 12pdr "mountain" howitzers unlimbering in the ranks. They were relatively tiny things, each pulled by a limber hitched to a single horse and requiring half the crew of a full-sized gun. But Blas had used them to great effect in confined places. They were short-ranged, but that didn't matter in a forest.

"In all these trees?" she scoffed. "Anything but caanister, we'd probably just bounce right back in our laaps." Glancing back at Spook she was surprised to see him grinning at a 'Cat named Captain Aakon commanding one of the batteries. He'd been with them at El Corazon and replied with a grin of his own—and a lewd gesture they'd picked up from the Impies. Blas shook her head. Spook knew what the little guns were good for.

"You'll advaance with the infaantry, Cap-i-taan Aakon," she ordered. "We won't fire until the enemy notices us, but when they do, I waant you to lay into them!"

"Ay, Col-nol."

Blas noted that Aakon's guns were already loaded, the charges in the barrels pinned in place with the vent picks. *Not* the safest way to transport them, but all his gunners had to do to fire was insert a friction primer and pull the lanyard. All the infantry had breechloading Allin-Silvas and Blitzerbug SMGs. They were already loaded, she knew, and as she watched, the order quietly spread to fix bayonets.

"Another bloody fight," Sister Audrey said beside her. Blas didn't know if she was referring to the ongoing battle or the part they were about to play.

She supposed it didn't matter. "There won't be many more, you know," Audrey continued in a strange tone. "Probably one last big one, after this," she sighed. "Then we can rest."

"I don't know about thaat," Blas retorted. "I doubt it. These daamn Doms're crazy."

Audrey looked fondly at her. "We've all gone a bit crazy in this war, I'm afraid. You did, for a time," she reminded. "But you recollected yourself and that gives me hope others might be saved from insanity when this is done."

"Well maybe," Blas grudged, "but we're gonna haafta kill a heap more of 'em to save a few—an' some *need* killin' before the rest'll haave a chaance."

Audrey patted her shoulder. "You know, Dennis Silva once told me almost precisely the same thing. You remind me too much of him at times. You're just as lethal and just as necessary to the cause." She smiled. "On the other hand, there are very distinct differences between you. You're more pleasant to look upon, of course, but you also take your role in this far more personally. Maybe too much so."

Blas was surprised. "Don't *you* take it personaal? I'd figure you would more thaan most."

"Actually, I don't. Usually," she qualified. "I try not to. I oppose the enemy behavior, not them. Just as that behavior insults the God"—she bowed her head—"the *Maker* they profess to revere, not me . . ." She frowned. "Though I suppose I *do* take it personally on *His* behalf." She sighed again. "Oh well, so much for that. At least I'm honest about my inconsistencies."

Blas grinned. "Thaat's true. Now, why don't we go do a little 'opposing'?" She turned to Captain Ixtli. "Quietly now, paass the word: the division will advaance!"

The line bulged slightly as the 2nd of the 2nd Marines moved first, but the Impies and Vengadores had been expecting the order and quickly caught up, keeping the line as straight as possible in the maze of trees. There were stack-ups and breaks in places but they magically vanished moments later. These troops knew what they were doing and Blas spared an instant of appreciation for the apparent longevity of the mighty trees and big armored rooters (probably other things as well) that kept the ground so clear of deadfall.

She didn't like keeping her troops so bunched up, though. That was a tactic the Allied armies had abandoned with their shields and had cost the Doms horrifically in every engagement. But if surprise was achieved, their first devastating fire and concentrated mass could be decisive. Still, the movement was incredibly loud to her and as they drew closer to the enemy—near enough for her to glimpse the color of their uniforms now—she couldn't believe they'd remained undiscovered. *Surely they had pickets out behind 'em?* she thought. It seemed not, and even though the Doms didn't have many cannon, they were maintaining a steady rate of fire, deafening them to all else and focusing their attention. *Must haave everybody with a musket concentrating on the Nussies,* Blas realized, and that's when she knew Sister Audrey was right; this *was* the last serious resistance the Doms would mount for some time to come.

"I wonder if the scouts we sent to the Nussies got there," she said aside to Captain Ixtli, "an' got believed."

They'd know soon enough. At barely a hundred and fifty yards behind the busy defenders, she saw a man in a yellow coat hurrying to the rear, possibly to secure more ammunition for his comrades. Seeing them, he stopped for a moment and simply stared. Then he pointed and gave a panicked cry. A gathering of officers turned to look, also hesitating in disbelief before they scattered, roaring commands.

"Pity we can't seize this opportunity to demand their surrender," Audrey said low, almost pleading, but she knew better herself.

Blas made no reply, instead raising her voice in that peculiar way Lemurians had of making themselves heard across vast distances. "Sister's Own! Halt!" She took a breath while the order was repeated and the division ground to a stop, dressing its lines as best it could into three jumbled ranks. "Prepare to fire by raanks! Commence firing!"

The Vengadores constituted her heaviest brigade and some on the far right didn't have targets, but the brigade composed of her Lemurian and Ocelomeh Marines and Iverson's Imperials joined those that did in delivering what constituted a single, long, aimed volley. It was punctuated an instant later by the rolling booms of twelve little howitzers, spraying canister. Even before the last cannon fired, another rolling volley roared, followed by a third. The first rank's breechloading Allin-Silvas would be ready to fire again by now, but the smoke hanging in front of them was so dense Blas didn't think anyone could possibly see a clear target. With supplies still only trickling across such a long and perilous route, and so far still to go, now was no time to waste ammunition. She nodded at Captain Ixtli, who shouted at his bugler to sound the charge.

The 2nd of the 2nd and half the Vengadores swept forward, shouting and trilling their high, sharp, terrifying cries, and Ixtli urged his horse to follow. Captain Bustos started to join him before remembering his duty to Sister Audrey and pulling back.

"You're not going with them?" Sister Audrey asked Blas, somewhat surprised.

"Not this time," she replied, blinking commiseration at Bustos before raising her voice again, shouting to pass the word for Colonel Garcia to stand by. The rest of the Vengadores would follow the first assault and Iverson's Impies and his own understrength battalion of Maa-ni-los would stand in reserve.

"Why not?" Audrey pressed. There was return fire now, and a few musket balls whizzed past. One struck a tree nearby with a dull *thwok!* showering them with fragments of bark.

Blas blinked respect at the blonde-haired nun, sitting unconcerned in her saddle. "You told me a while baack—again"—she flicked her tail—"the Maker knows how *maany* times you've tried to tell me, thaat my troops don't always need—or waant—me by their side. Maay-be there *is* times I haave more importaant stuff to do, like waatchin' their tails an' staandin' ready to send reserves if they need 'em." She looked back to the front. There was another ferociously sustained crackle of rifle fire before the distinctive clash of steel on steel amid piercing screams. Almost immediately, the shooting and yelling began to taper off. Blas still couldn't see anything through the smoke but her ears told her everything. "*Our* troops know I'll be with 'em aat the end, just like you," she continued, "but this ain't it. How stupid would I be to get rubbed out now an' not be there when they really need me?"

Cheers started drifting back through the wall of smoke, joined by the ululating cries of exultant Lemurians. There were a few final shots, then the forest erupted in a triumphant roar.

"Sounds like more thaan we sent into aaction," Blas observed.

"It does," Sister Audrey concurred, just as Lieutenant Anaar galloped back. The fur on his neck was matted with blood where a ball had grazed him but he was grinning hugely. "Cap-i-taan Ixtli begs to report the enemy works haave faallen. He's securing prisoners now." He blinked amazement. "There's a *buncha* prisoners. He also aasks if you'll come forwaard an' meet a Lieuten-aant named 'O'Riel,' er somethin', who led some guys over the breastworks from the other side right when we were hittin' the Doms." If it was possible, Anaar's grin got bigger. "Says he's a officer in the NUS Aarmy, an' mighty glaad to see us."

Late the next morning, under a clear blue sky that left everyone squinting as they finally entered a broad clearing in the sea of trees, Colonel Dao Iverson and his 6th Imperial Marines escorted almost thirteen hundred Doms into the picturesque river valley village of Neri. The village was built entirely of local stone, roofed with sawn timbers covered with living sod. There'd be a church, of course, but no pyramid-shaped temple could be seen. All around the town, stretching as far as the distant trees, was a grassy landscape covered by dingy, mildew-blackened canvas tents showing the hard use of a long, damp campaign. Colorful regimental flags fluttered in a woodsmoke-hazed morning breeze, and the flags of the United Homes and the Empire of the New Britain Isles flew in front of a larger tent at the center of it all, just outside the village. The company streets seemed to radiate outward from there.

Joining Iverson at the head of his column were Blas and Sister Audrey, accompanied by General Cox and half a dozen of his senior staff. All but one were dressed in their dark blue finery, complete with gleaming brass buttons, tall shakos, and gold epaulettes. The sixth member of their party, riding between Cox and Sister Audrey, wore only a dark blue shell jacket and sky-blue trousers (both much the worse for wear), a wheel hat, sword and pistol belt, and the shoulder boards of a captain.

Even before the troops and prisoners, equally bedraggled in dress if not mood and bearing, reached the outer tents, a group mounted in front of the command tent. "That'll be Gener-aal Shinya," Blas stated simply. Curious soldiers, gravitating into the streets between the tents to see the new arrivals, scattered as their commanders' horses galloped through.

"Column, halt," Iverson commanded, and he and his companions urged their horses into a trot. All the riders met in the open, just shy of the first tents—and a quickly forming line of rough-looking troops.

"Take charge of the prisoners," General Tomatsu Shinya called behind him at the man leading the ready soldiers. "There's a large stockade for some of the more boisterous local livestock on the other side of town," he explained with a smile. "It'll be crowded and smelly, I'm afraid, but I never expected so many prisoners and it's far better treatment than we could've expected from them." A strange insight struck him as he spoke, regarding just how far he'd veered from that impossibly distant culture he sprang from. Not only was he glad to see so many prisoners, he suspected from *their* cultural perspective it might've taken more courage to surrender than fight to the end. No one he'd ever known, steeped in the code of Bushido, would've entertained a notion like that.

He nodded at Blas, Audrey, and Iverson, saying simply, "Well done," before turning his attention to their NUS Companions. "An historic meeting, gentlemen," he proclaimed, "between friends united in a worthy cause. Welcome to our camp, and I'm honored to have you join our campaign."

The captain edged forward. "Thank you, General Shinya," he said. "Perhaps you remember me?"

"Of course, Captain Anson, though the circumstances and geography have changed considerably."

Anson smiled and bowed. "Indeed. Allow me to present General Hiram Cox, commanding all NUS forces on this continent."

Shinya nodded, waiting for Anson to name the other officers, and the salute he'd been told to expect. Anson cleared his throat and Cox finally, somewhat reluctantly, raised his hand to the brim of his shako, palm out. The other NUS officers followed his example. Shinya let the hesitation slide, knowing how hard it would be for him if the roles were reversed, but it had been agreed ever since Fred and Kari flew Anson across to meet him and Jenks that they had to have a unified command if they ever combined their forces. Moreover, since the Union and the Empire of the New Britain Isles had the larger force in theater and greater resources in terms of modern weapons, and had borne the heaviest burden in terms of casualties and experience gained, it was only reasonable that Shinya take the lead on shore while Jenks did so at sea.

"I'm honored to represent my country and join my army with yours for the duration of the momentous undertaking in which we're jointly engaged," Cox said somewhat stiffly, as if he'd rehearsed the lines.

Shinya thought he probably had. "Excellent," he said, returning the salute, and getting straight to business. "How many men do you have, fit to fight, and what do they need?"

Cox appeared perplexed, probably having expected a longer exchange of ceremonial sentiments.

"Around thirty thousand, after yesterday's action," Anson supplied at once, "though not all are entirely fit. In addition to the wounded, they're tired and hungry and there's been some disease. They should begin arriving with the rest of Colonel . . . Sister Audrey's troops before the end of the day." He glanced apologetically at Audrey before continuing. "The first thing they'll need is a safe place to lay their heads and recover for a time. And food, of course, if you have any to spare. The League's been shelling our outpost at El Palo from the sea and has made it impossible for supplies to get through. And since the Doms left us no forage on the march, our only provisions have been those our local friends in the vicinity of El Palo sent behind us. Not enough, I'm afraid, and our men have been on half rations. Reaching you here consumed the last of our reserves."

"Of course. We're somewhat weary from our advance as well," Shinya replied, "and we'll linger here until our united force refits. We won't wait for the arrival of Eleventh and Fifteenth Corps." He gestured around. "There simply isn't room, and our combined movements might be too cumbersome and obvious, not to mention taxing on the locals. But for now, rations aren't a problem and our hospital corps should be able to return many of your sick and injured to duty."

General Cox finally seemed to relax a bit. "That's a great relief, General Shinya, and I apologize for coming before you like beggars, hat in hand as it were. . . ."

"Nonsense. We knew the enemy would control the Caribbean, for a time at least. They've struck at our beachhead near Monsu as well. We *do* have an alternate line of supply, however, though it's considerably longer and more vulnerable than I'd prefer." He rubbed the thin whiskers on his upper lip. "I assume you're short of ammunition as well?"

"It's not yet a crisis," reported another NUS officer. "Colonel Prine," he reminded them. "We laid in a considerable stockpile before the Battle of El Palo. That took a bite out of it, but we received more before the shipments halted. Our campaign to reach you consumed a great deal as well, but we have a sufficiency for at least one major engagement. Perhaps two."

Shinya considered. "We can't help with your rifled artillery, but ammunition for your smoothbores shouldn't be a problem. Through luck, or Captain Reddy's"—he chuckled—"historical foresight, our field artillery shares a common bore diameter. The strength of our gunpowder may vary from yours but your gunners should be able to compensate. As for small arms, we carried extra crates of breechloaders with us and more will continue to arrive. I propose that we begin arming your men with them. If we're able to provide enough for your entire force, you can consign your current arms to our native recruits."

Cox was speechless, unable to believe anyone, even allies, would just give them such advanced weapons.

Shinya misinterpreted his reaction. "I assure you, our Allin-Silva rifles are quite accurate and their shape and general function is virtually identical to the weapons your men are used to. I only caution you that their chief advantage comes with heavy, rapid, *aimed* fire, and they consume a lot of ammunition very quickly. We have supply problems too."

Cox shook his head and actually beamed. "No, General Shinya, you misunderstand. I . . ." He stopped, still smiling. "Thank you. Thank you very much indeed."

Shinya pulled his reins to the side, turning his horse. "Why don't you join me at the HQ tent for refreshments while we wait for everyone else to get here?" he said. "As I mentioned, we'll remain here awhile, but we need to begin planning our next move at once. We're less than three hundred miles from the Dom capital, but I'm told there's difficult terrain ahead. And though I don't expect serious opposition until we get closer to New Granada City, I could be wrong." Dom prisoners were already moving by, guided by men they were clearly terrified of. The others joined him and Iverson's troops finally stepped off again, heading toward a part of the field already laid out for them to camp.

"We appreciate your hospitality," Cox said, "and your priorities. It reminds me of one I've neglected. I must bring the behavior of two of your officers to your attention: Lieutenant Fred Reynolds and Lieutenant Kari-Faask"—he glanced at Blas—"of the, ah, 'Lemurian' people." To Cox's surprise, Shinya burst out laughing and Sister Audrey chuckled. "What? Did I say something . . . ?"

"No, no, it's just the way you said it," Sister Audrey replied. "Though there are many races in the Union, and Republic as well, most consider themselves one 'people.'"

"It's the same in the NUS. How could it not be?" Anson interjected. "But I think General Cox was unsure if the same applied among the various *species* and didn't want to offend." He looked at Cox. "It does," he stated flatly. "But I think he was more startled by your amusement."

"That had more to do with the way he began his statement," Shinya explained. "Those of us who know young Mr. Reynolds and Miss Faask couldn't help wondering what they've gotten themselves into now."

Cox blinked. "Oh. Ha. I see. Yes, their general behavior is somewhat unconventional. But I meant only to commend them. Not only did they provide timely warning of General de Quito's movements before their aircraft was lost, they supplied us with much-needed insights regarding our enemy—and our friends. They also fought gallantly in the Battle of El Palo. I regretted it when they were finally recovered by one of your larger flying boats—such an enormous machine! At any rate, I confess I've rather missed them."

"As do I, General Cox," Shinya agreed, and saw Anson nodding. "I'll pass your compliment along. Personally, I wish they were still with you, to better coordinate our airpower with our movements, but I doubt they'd have much to do for a while."

They were riding among tents now, down a company street already dark with mud, and the HQ tent was ahead. "I don't think we're gonna get much air this time, Gener-aal Shinya," Blas suddenly said, speaking for the first time. "The waay things're goin', I expect our planes'll be mighty busy over waater, an' we're gonna miss *all* our flyboy friends."

CHAPTER 22

////// Ando's Airfield
East Shore of Lake Galk
Grik Africa
June 9, 1945

General of the Sky Mitsuo Ando banged angrily through the rickety wooden door of his "headquarters" building, near his rough, narrow airstrip. Hundreds of Uul laborers had pulled up thousands of stumps and levelled the ground as best they could at the edge of the receded forest so his five meager planes could enjoy a little cover under the trees. The problem was, timber to build so many now virtually useless battleships, even the *yanone* carriers they'd never finish, had been cut so far back, the airfield was rather inconveniently distant from Esshk's commodious HQ villa by the lake. Messages came quickly enough by pennant or reflected lights, but round trips for personal meetings took more than an hour, riding an un-sprung rickshaw pulled by a pair of trotting Grik.

And Ando's HQ was rather pretentiously named. By Grik standards, it was rather opulent, maybe once belonging to some mid-level Hij in the Galk Lake regency. To Ando and the four other Japanese pilots, it was a low, 10′ x 30′ rock and adobe shack full of bugs, still reeking of feces and the rotting bones they'd thrown out. Their beds were vermin-infested blankets and grass-stuffed pallets under a tree-limb-beamed roof that sagged under rotting, leaking thatch. If it wasn't for the frequent rains and packs of vicious little predators roaming about (mostly feral young Grik in these parts), they would've lived better in the open under the trees with their workforce.

There was another problem with that, however. Lake Galk was very big, but with so many Grik packed in around it, the fish were quickly depleted and wildlife was scarce. There'd been no supply from downriver for months, but now nothing came from upriver either and food was getting low. As usual, Grik began eating one another, the oldest, weakest, and injured first, but they'd soon start picking their fare at random. Ando and his flyers were officially immune from making such . . . contributions, but their workforce and virtually useless ground crews, unfit for anything other than fueling planes and pushing them around, were mostly mindless Uul. They were aware enough to know they'd be killed and eaten if they harmed the Japanese aviators, but an agonizingly empty stomach sometimes spoke louder than consequences. Something Ando and his people were beginning to realize as well.

Lieutenant Ueda rose from his pallet and hopefully asked, "Did you see Esshk?" Ueda was young and strong, but there hadn't been any fat on his unusually big-boned frame and he was taking hunger worse than the rest, face narrowing and eyes beginning to sink into his brows and cheeks.

"Our Lord remains indisposed," Ando snapped sarcastically. "It seems he took General Halik's declaration against him very hard. Even with the enemy pushing ever closer, he hasn't spoken to his generals in days. Doesn't seem to think their dispositions will make any difference."

"Then he expects defeat?" one of the other flyers asked.

Ando shook his head, puzzled. "No. He *does* talk with the vice-regent, who I saw, and who told me Lord General Esshk remains supremely confident in Second General Ign coming to his aid, the *yanone* we made—and whatever else he's prepared." He held his hands out at his sides. "I have no idea what *that* might be. As for the rest, I know nothing of Ign, but the *yanone* alone can't win his war." His expression darkened. "But even if there is, as yet, no fighting north of the locks, Esshk is slowly losing. Through starvation and self-consumption, I think his army is already weaker, perhaps even fewer, than the enemy. He has a strong position in the south around the locks, but with Halik coming up behind us now . . ." He shrugged.

"But what about the food?" Ueda asked desperately. "Did the vice-regent give you food?" That had been the primary reason Ando went to see Esshk. They'd eaten well, for a while, better than most, with regular deliveries of wild game carcasses, fish, even some of the few vegetables Grik apparently cultivated. That changed after the *yanone* were completed and there was almost nothing left, even with rationing. Ando's men weren't just a little hungry anymore. He grimaced. "The vice-regent told me we should eat dead Grik like everyone else. Even gave me leave to slaughter as many of our own as we cared to."

Ueda stared at him, scratching a sore on his stubbled jaw. "That's it? Even if we did . . . If we start killing and eating *them*, they'll eat us."

Ando nodded. "That's what I said. I also told him that just as our planes need fuel to fly and fight, to protect the *yanone* carriers, so do we. He said he knew nothing of that, but couldn't imagine they needed much protection. He's not a warrior and hasn't seen . . ."

"Only Esshk would understand, and he won't talk to you," Ueda mumbled mournfully.

"We should've gone with Muriname," another pilot muttered bitterly, and to everyone's surprise, Ando actually nodded.

"It's probably too late for that, but yes. That was my mistake, and I don't deserve the loyalty you showed by staying by my side." He frowned. "But neither does Esshk anymore. Our obligation to any lord is contingent upon his to us—the least of which is to *feed* us, and acknowledge the honor we give him." Making up his mind, Ando straightened. "Our oaths aren't broken, they've been cast aside, and our service here is ended."

"Where will we go?" Ueda asked helplessly. "Even with full tanks, we can't make it back to Kakag with the terrible fuel they've given us."

"What purpose would that serve, anyway?" another asked.

"It would put us behind Halik. Perhaps he'd take us in."

Ando was shaking his head. "Even if he would, I've had enough of Grik. You can all do as you choose, but I'll fly south when the time is right."

"The Americans and their allies will kill us," Ueda stated flatly.

"They might. Or we might seek asylum in the Republic."

"What can we offer them?" asked the youngest pilot, who hadn't spoken yet. "Their planes are better than ours."

"We'll tell them about the *yanone*," Ando said, shrugging, "and that Esshk has another unpleasant surprise."

Ueda dropped back down on his filthy mat with a frustrated snort.

"What?" Ando asked. "Don't you agree?"

"Oh, yes," Ueda said. "The problem is, it won't work." He sat back up. "How will you *tell* them?"

"I speak sufficient English," Ando retorted. "Even Esshk understan—" He stopped. "But my plane has the only radio, and the power tube failed.

We have no spares, and can't make any." He looked around at the men, his friends now, all looking to him. "If we fly south to warn Esshk's enemies, to join them, they'll simply shoot us out of the sky."

Ueda's sour expression suddenly turned thoughtful. "Probably," he agreed, "but there may be a way to give them pause."

CHAPTER 23

////// 80 miles west of the Galk River
Grik Africa
June 12, 1945

It was clouding up to rain as it did nearly every day this time of year; starting clear and hot and damp, then building to dump strong showers on the strange, sturdy trees and rocky hills northwest of Sofesshk by early afternoon. The Grik airship First Ker-noll Jash was riding really needed to be down and secured by then, or to climb above the pounding rain. In that case, it might as well turn back and attempt its mission another day. Though crude in many ways, Grik zeppelins were tough, but even they could be shredded by the vicious winds often accompanying the sudden storms. And finding a concentration of General Ign's forces—and hopefully Ign himself—would become impossible in any case.

To make matters worse, they weren't sure where to look. The forest here wasn't impenetrable, but Ign's veterans were accustomed to hiding from telltale rumblings in the sky. His *screening* warriors were in contact with Fifth Corps' probing scouts, which had even picked up a few lamed or exhausted stragglers. If they knew where Ign was, they wouldn't talk. Ordinary Uul laborers in the region, instinctively responding to the Celestial Mother's general summons, reported seeing warriors—in their infantile, almost incoherent way—but couldn't tell them where. Their most reliable guide came from increasingly numerous Nancys flying off the river behind the advancing Allies. But they were marauders, attacking whatever they saw with incendiaries and further dispersing Ign's force. Jash wasn't sure he'd *ever* locate his one-time mentor and deliver the Celestial Mother's benevolent offer, but he had to try.

Standing in the forward open-air gondola, eyes watering against wind, he peered intently at the forest below. There were gaps in the trees, even the occasional cart path, but nothing moved. *That itself is significant,* he supposed. *The forest harbors many large creatures. Only the passage of something they fear—like an army—could leave it so apparently empty.* He squinted and tried to discern ground disturbance in the openings. He thought he did, but it could've been made by herds of beasts. With Ign's army spread out, there'd be no distinctive scars on the land made by columns of troops.

The wind gusted harder and Jash blinked, wiping his eyes with an absorbent white cloth—booty from Zanzibar given to him by General Alden. Slitted shutters could be lowered over the glassless openings for long-distance travel, but they hindered observation. The aft gondola, designed to carry bombs, was empty and buttoned up. The vast, rigid envelope above, enclosing cells of lifting hydrogen and supporting engines and gondolas, was painted black. That identified the airship as one reserved for the nighttime transport of General Esshk or his messengers. The fact it was day and nobody shot it down as it crossed over country Ign would know was infested by the enemy might raise suspicion, especially since Saansa Field was now operational, despite the daily rains. Allied fighter planes like P-1C Mosquito Hawks and Repub Cantets increasingly prowled these skies. Suspicious or not, however, Ign wouldn't shoot. Esshk didn't care about the lives of aircrews, but airships were getting scarce. He wouldn't risk one without a reason and Ign would want to know what it was.

Jash looked at "his" aircrew, all Grik, despite the fact a few Lemurian Shee-ree had volunteered. Shee-ree had been the first to operate a captured Grik zep and tended to recruit their own when it came to training others to fly them. But this wasn't like the prearranged meeting with Halik and there was every chance Ign would kill them, especially if they showed up with enemies. Interestingly, though, all six aviators *chose* to accompany Jash and he sensed a . . . difference in the way they behaved toward him. *Strangers* who looked to him like his own Slashers did. He guessed that came with the favor of the Celestial Mother, or perhaps his reputation as a warrior, and wasn't sure if that gave him satisfaction or discomfort. He watched the aircrew perform their duties awhile longer, enduring their occasional respectful glances, before peering back over the rough-hewn rail with a hissing sigh.

"A smoke!" cried an observer on the starboard side of the gondola, and Jash paced quickly across to see. A large white gush of gunpowder smoke, torched in a cauldron, was rapidly dissipating downwind from the center of a medium-sized clearing where a number of figures had appeared. It was a brief, unmistakable attention signal like Jash had seen numerous times. It wasn't very useful on a battlefield, obscured by cannon and musket fire, but like this . . . The smoke was discreet, yet quite visible to someone looking for it, and it quickly vanished. At night, the flash of the powder had the same effect. Jash turned his head to the side to gaze through an Imperial telescope he'd been given. The clearing was half a mile away, but the figures—clearly Gharrichk'k warriors, with a pair of signal pennants—leaped into focus and appeared very close. He watched the pennants a moment, then collapsed the telescope, briefly marveling at it once again.

"Come around downwind of the clearing and approach with care. Do *not* tear the envelope on the trees," he cautioned. If things went poorly, he doubted they'd escape, but if the meeting went well, he didn't want to walk out through the trigger-happy lines of Fifth Corps to make his report.

"Of course, Lord First Ker-noll!" the dirigible's captain cried loudly. Leaning on the large steering tiller before him, he shouted at others to adjust the throttles on the five engines and aimed the ungainly craft down at their destination. "Release the mooring lines!" he called.

They couldn't spill much hydrogen if they wanted to rise again, so they'd literally fly down to the ground; a dangerous maneuver under the best of circumstances. Here, it was potentially catastrophic, with tall trees on the other side of the clearing waiting to crash them to shreds. They'd only survive one approach. Furthermore, there was no mooring mast and Jash had no idea how they'd hold the airship stationary. This mystery was solved when a hundred warriors burst from the trees pulling six heavy cannon. They were arranged in a rough circle, their crews grabbing the dangling lines as the dirigible's captain flared out and ordered his crew to throttle the engines back. Jash felt the gondola deck jerk and dip as the lines were made fast to the guns. The captain looked at him, snout lowered in regret. "We cannot accompany you, Lord. Even tethered thus, we must fly the ship against the wind and it will take us all."

Jash jerked a diagonal nod. "I always meant to go alone." He paused. "How long can you . . . stand above this place?"

"Four handspans. Perhaps longer—or as soon as the rains come hard. They should release us if that occurs and we'll return as soon as we can." Unspoken, of course, was that the scratch ground crew *might* release them—if they weren't ordered to kill them.

Jash moved to the trapdoor in the deck at the front of the gondola. A long, rough rope was coiled beside a winch standing over the opening.

Raising the trap, he tossed the rope out, watching it unroll about 150 feet to the ground. “If conditions warrant and they don’t release you, slip the mooring lines yourselves. Likewise, if they try to haul you down or behave in any way hostile, or you hear nothing from me in . . .” He paused, considering. There was no guarantee Ign was even near. “Give me as long as you can,” he said, “but don’t linger if you sense aggression.”

“As you command, Lord First Ker-noll.”

Jash grasped the rope and started down, footclaws catching in the fibers from time to time to slow his descent. He was halfway to the ground, spinning enough to make him queasy, before realizing the airship captain called him “Lord,” as if he was a general! He shrugged it away. Technically, he commanded more than enough troops to be called “General,” and even Ign once said he’d have raised him to that status if he could. Yet as of now, Halik was the only Gharrichk’k general serving the Celestial Mother and Jash suspected that was for the best, for now. He knew as well as anyone how much needed to change, and the hierarchical bickering of generals jostling for dominance would only slow the process. He’d even caught a taste of it in the air between General Alden and General Kim. It lasted only a moment, and Alden quickly tamped it down, but it was clear he hadn’t entirely approved of Kim’s dispositions. Particularly how he’d practically ignored Jash and Shelg, and relegated their Slashers to a rear-area role. The Celestial Mother wanted her race in the fight for this new Way. How else would they have a voice in it? General Alden seemed to agree with that—or at least believed letting Gharrichk’k fight Gharrichk’k would preserve his own warriors. Either was a position Jash could respect, and both led to what the Giver of Life desired.

An even greater loyalty toward First General Alden surged in him as he touched the ground, not even because he wholly trusted him, but he did trust his focus on doing whatever he must to win. Crushing Esshk was part of that, but so was supporting the Celestial Mother, because the Gharrichk’k and the various races Alden protected could only live in peace someday through *her. And through me, at present,* he suddenly realized as dozens of scrawny, bedraggled warriors—once *his* warriors—gathered around.

There was surprised hissing and a lane opened for a skinny, rough-looking officer. Weather-faded devices painted on once-gray iron and leather armor, now soiled and rusted to a mottled reddish brown, were those of a Ker-noll, and Jash recognized Naxa, once his second in the Slashers.

“First Ker-noll Jash?” Naxa demanded, tone betraying wonder. “How can you . . . In Supreme Regent Esshk's own airship? We thought you destroyed with the rest of the Slashers at Old Sofesshk. How did you escape?"

"You haven't heard?" Jash asked, equally surprised to see his former subordinate, especially looking so haggard. "I thought everyone would know by now," he murmured thoughtfully, then raised his voice. "Clearly, General Ign keeps much from you." He paused, considering. "Or Esshk's *Dorrighsti* 'Night Hunters' do. Are there many of them among you?"

Naxa angrily clacked his teeth and others gurgled disapproval. "Some were with us from the start, as you know—such arrogant creatures!—and now that the Celestial Mother is lost, they assume liberties beyond their rank. More come down from Supreme Regent Esshk's stronghold with every airship bearing dispatches, urging us to 'greater efforts' to join our Lord—as if we weren't already marching on our anklebones!" he added resentfully. "Three tens of them now guard Lord General Ign." This statement carried a note of injured betrayal. "I doubt they considered *your* survival consequential enough to inform him of it."

"Perhaps not that, specifically," Jash agreed enigmatically, "but a great deal else, I'm sure. Where is Ign? I must . . . confer with him at once!"

Naxa waved behind, then glanced at the hovering airship, obviously concerned it would mark the area for air attack. But the clouds were darkening and soon nothing would be flying. "Not far. He maintains a minimal headquarters. The prey keeps us moving and we can't mass." Naxa's short, grungy crest lifted slightly. "If our last report reached the Supreme Regent, you know we lost more than *half* our force evading General Al-den. We disengaged at last, but were set upon by *another* force, of the Other Hunters from the south! It's been . . . an unpleasant time." He stopped, taking a breath, then finally managed to look like he was glad to see Jash. "But tell me, how *did* you break free, with the enemy rampant all around Old Sofesshk? And since you live . . . Esshk must've found you blameless for the violation and death of the Celestial Mother?"

Jash regarded Naxa with wide eyes. He truly *didn't* know. "Take me to General Ign at once," he repeated. "But I'll tell you this; the Giver of Life is safe and sound . . . because I never *left* Old Sofesshk."

Naxa scratched at the stained leather doorflap of a ragged marquee, erected under the broad-topped trees, and Second General Ign almost immediately stepped out. He'd no doubt heard the commotion as Jash was recognized and startled troops began to gather. Jash wondered why Ign didn't just have him swept quickly inside, out of sight, and just as quickly dispatched. If Naxa knew nothing of Esshk's treachery and the Celestial Mother's oft-repeated plea for allegiance and offer of amnesty, neither could anyone else—other than Ign and the *Dorrighsti*. Why allow a spectacle, or Jash a chance to speak? Then Jash got his first look at Ign. He wore no armor, just a filthy tunic that ordinarily padded it and covered his midriff. He'd also drawn the now faded and tattered red cape of his office around him. Just as worn down as the rest of his troops, he also looked positively ancient. Not because he was frail; he'd lost all the flab he'd accumulated over his muscles through the years, and was probably a match for the powerful warrior he'd been when he was younger, but the feathery fur down the sides of his snout, around his eyes, and halfway down his neck had gone pure white. The impression of age stopped at his eyes. They looked tired, almost melancholy, but also keenly interested to see Jash. Wary too, betraying complete understanding that he and Jash, master and apprentice, were now on opposite sides.

"There's water. I have no other refreshment to offer," Ign said gruffly.

Jash bowed. "With my deepest respect, Lord General, I require nothing of that sort from you."

Ign's eyes narrowed and his crest rose in defiance. "So. Straight to your purpose, then. Do tell us all precisely what you *do* 'require.' Let me guess; that I and my army throw down our weapons and become the laboring Uul of the conquering prey?" He turned to those around them and pointed at Jash. "That's what *he's* become, he and the warriors he betrayed into submission to those we still defy!"

A steaming hiss of horror and outrage jetted through the teeth of every warrior and they started to surge forward as one.

"Untrue!" Jash roared, hand moving to rest on the pommel of his long, back-curved sword. The furious mob paused in astonishment. Jash was known to most of them and his voice carried the same tone of confident command they'd heard on the battlefield. His reputation and, frankly, the shock of such a brazen denunciation gave him the seconds he needed to say the words that would guarantee they heard him out. "The Celestial Mother still lives and rules all the Gharrichk'k *despite* Esshk's attempts to murder her!" he yelled. Now there was a sound like breaking surf as gasps of dismay and confusion swept around, expanding outward. "The Slashers and I fiercely fought the enemy—until we discovered we had the same goal: to *save* the Giver of Life from Esshk's *Dorrighsti* assassins who'd already slaughtered most of the Ancient Hij of Old Sofesshk! It's true!" he roared louder into the growing howls of disbelief. "Only with the *assistance* of the enemy *we provoked* did we save the one we revere. The 'enemy' no longer comes to destroy us, but would save us from Esshk, who elevated *himself* to Supreme Regent through foul endeavors and profane massacre. They work *with* the Giver of Life to preserve and unite our race.

"To that end, the Celestial Mother has summoned you, *all loyal Gharrichk'k*, to join her in this effort. . . ." Slowly, he turned to face Ign. With deep regret, he pointed. "And he knew."

The tumult then was shocking, growing, as word spread of what Jash said. There were probably four hundred warriors around them now, and some started bashing bayonets against musket barrels like they would before a charge, but they didn't have a target. Jash had made himself one of them and they trusted him, believed him—but Ign was one of them too. Look at him, he even bore the same miseries now . . . but had he also *brought* them those miseries? And Esshk! Could he actually have attempted what Jash so resolutely claimed? It was too horrible to contemplate.

There's no telling what would've happened next; about half wanted to slaughter Ign for leading them astray, the other half, even if they believed Jash, felt almost compelled to destroy him just for telling them, leaving them so suddenly rudderless in a sea of uncertainty. In an instant, however, the dynamic changed, crystallizing and focusing on Ign's *Dorrighsti* guards, who surged into the wavering mass. Hindclaws raked and flashed, gouging legs to the bone and severing arteries. Teeth ripped throats and bellows of rage at this unexpected betrayal turned to blood-spewing gurgles. Blades hacked and flailed, cleaving heads, chopping arms and necks in a welter of more spraying blood that painted Grik troops yards away and gave them startled pause. Most of the *Dorrighsti* fought their way through to surround the general they'd been told to guard—and watch. Others, perhaps a quarter, tried to smash through to the visitor who'd exposed them and their master.

Jash was as surprised as anyone and cursed himself for a fool even as he whipped his sword from its scabbard. He'd seen the black and red slashmarks painted on the armor of nearby troops and knew what *Dorrighsti* were capable of. *Perhaps I just never expected to live long enough to concern myself with them*, he confessed to himself, his sword clanging upward to meet a blow meant to split his head. Bodies already covered the ground and a lot of troops were pulling back in confusion, trying to arm themselves or just figure out who to fight. For the moment, that left Jash and maybe twenty regular, half-armed troops outnumbered by the unusually skilled and suicidally murderous *Dorrighsti*.

Jash moved to spin inside and slash his attacker's throat with his claws, but there was another *Dorrighsti* sword, lunging for his belly. He arched his back to draw away, but his attacker had the reach. He steeled himself for the punch to the gut that would begin his death. The sword dropped to the ground, the red-streaked arm on top of it, and Jash saw Naxa finish the attacker with a stroke from a second sword in his other hand. *I never saw him fight with* two, he realized. Then he had no time for thought. The *Dorrighsti* had received some sort of ancient sword training even New Army soldiers lacked. Moreover, they had even less regard for their lives than their master did and they fought with wild abandon, widening the circle around Ign and filling it with severed limbs and corpses.

On the other hand, regardless of their skill, this was the first time they'd used it in earnest. The hard-earned experience of the veteran troops, warriors who'd survived the most grueling combat imaginable, quickly adapted to their unconventional, almost artistic technique, and began to turn the tide with brutally efficient blows and blocks. And when other troops returned with bayonet-bristling muskets, snatched from tripod stands, a different type of artistry went on display. Very quickly, a meager semicircle of seven gasping, bleeding *Dorrighsti* remained around Ign, who stood, crest high, snarling furiously.

Then, without warning, he snatched a *Dorrighsti* blade from the blood-muddy ground and roared "Enough!" So accustomed to his voice of command, his soldiers drew themselves back, even Jash—and the *Dorrighsti* were on them, stabbing, hacking, biting and clawing. "Enough, I said, you miserable, slinking scum!" Ign bellowed, swinging his sword and completely decapitating a *Dorrighsti* in front of him. It spasmed and leaped in the air amid a spraying fountain of blood. Crashing down on the ringing troops, it knocked several, including Naxa, to the ground. "You're Esshk's reeking turds, hatched from his arse-slit!" Ign ranted. "You'll kill no more of my army!" With that he struck again, hacking down with a blow that nearly cut one of his guards diagonally in half, but his sword lodged and he couldn't pull it free.

"So you broke at last, old one," snarled a *Dorrighsti* with a white claw painted over his slashmarks. He spun from Jash, now heedless of his opponent. "My Lord Esshk always thought you might."

A half instant before Jash's slashing blade swept deep across the back of the *Dorrighsti*'s neck, knocking its helmet away and severing the spine, the guard turned assassin thrust its sword between Ign's ribs. The general gasped, recoiling from the blow, but then straightened and looked down at the protruding sword.

Naxa and the nearby troops swept across the last few *Dorrighsti* and literally tore them apart. But in the bloody space in front of the battered marquee where only Jash and Ign stood, time seemed to slow within an incredibly fragile, soundless bubble, and the two regarded each other as they always had, with deep respect and a bond neither could describe, but Jash had heard called "friendship."

"I apologize," Ign said, his voice still strong and gruff. "I knew the terms offered by the Giver of Life, and the *Dorrighsti* were here to ensure I didn't join her—and you. They would've destroyed me and taken my army straight to Esshk. Not that it would've survived bashing through the enemy that blocks it. None of that mattered, you see. Lives *never* mattered to Esshk, or the Celestial Mothers of the past." He coughed blood and swayed slightly, but managed to straighten. Still, the bubble around them seemed to burst and the tumult surrounded them once more.

"Silence!" Ign roared, orange froth spraying from his teeth. "First Kernoll Jash has brought the truth. Esshk *did* betray the Giver of Life. The old enemy is our enemy no more." He looked back at Jash. "I sacrificed one army in front of General Alden. I . . . I couldn't do it again. Not for Esshk. So I've dawdled about in the wilderness, fighting only to keep from being destroyed, while ever *seeming* to move toward Esshk to satisfy my masters." He said the last with contempt and hawked a gobbet of blood on a *Dorrighsti* corpse. "*You* would've seen it in an instant, had you been with me. I'm sure Naxa suspected as well. But these . . . *krikau* had no idea." He looked back at Jash and when he spoke again, his voice gurgled, blood ran down the white fur on his throat, and his breathing was quick and ragged. "I did it all to save as much of this army as I could. I even denounced *you* to gain more time." He shook his head and looked down, blood drooling from his jaws. "Foolish of me. I should've known, together, we'd overcome Esshk's assassins, but . . . perhaps I still wonder if this new Giver of Life—little more than a hatchling—and her enemy supporters we've fought so hard, are really any better. *Worth* further sacrifice by those I lead."

"She is. They are," Jash assured gently.

Ign coughed rackingly, spewing blood, and finally sank down on his haunches. Jash and Naxa knelt beside him, as did many others, amazingly moved for Gharrichk'k. Of course, none were *ordinary* Gharrichk'k anymore. "Very well, First Ker-noll Jash," Ign finally managed, as formally as he was able. "*You* command this army now—such as it is. Take it to join our old enemies and destroy our old world." He coughed again, long and hard, then gagged, blood going everywhere. When he tried to talk again, his voice was a hoarse whisper. "I'm rather glad the responsibility is lifted from me. I'd like to see the new world you'll make, but there'd be no place for me. I'm as blameworthy as Esshk."

"No, Lord General," Naxa denied.

"He is," Jash disagreed softly. "Not for the attempt on the Celestial Mother, but he knew all else that Esshk was doing. 'Truth in all things' is the new motto of the empire—and perhaps the harshest commandment our Giver of Life has made."

Ign looked at him in wonder. "Indeed?" he croaked. "Good. It's unattainable, of course, but a commendable ambition. The worthiest aspirations can never be fully achieved, but knowing that and trying anyway is perhaps the very purpose of life." He suddenly grasped Naxa's arm. "You'll support Jash?" he gasped.

"I failed to once," he confessed, "and Esshk was the cause of that too. Never again."

Ign squeezed his arm, then panted, "In that case . . . I'll say no more." It was as close as he'd come to a plea to end his suffering while he still controlled it.

Nodding solemnly, Naxa grasped the sticky, red-washed sword hilt protruding from Ign's chest. "Farewell, Lord General," he whispered, and drew the long, curved blade out. Blood gushed after it and Ign shuddered, eyes clenched shut. Then, with a rasping sigh, he lay down on his side and died.

Jash stood, staring at the body that was somehow no longer Ign. "Don't eat him. Our former enemies memorialize their notable slain in various ways. We should as well. Perhaps mount his skull in the Palace of Vanished Gods?" He shook his head. "Ign always wanted to be remembered," he explained. "Let's see that he is, for the right reasons."

The sky was very dark and raindrops had begun to fall. "I must return to the airship," he said, raising his voice to carry. "Ker-noll Naxa will command, for now. He'll wait two days for me to ensure all is arranged, then gather the army and march to meet our allies, designated 'Fifth Corps' in this area. Part of the Army of the Republic. I'll try to meet you there. Even if I can't, they won't shoot. Flying machines may watch your movements, but they won't attack. Do *not* fire at them!"

"It'll be . . . difficult to just stop fighting the prey," Naxa reflected, then he had a thought. "What'll we call *our* army now, Lord General? If this prey . . . 'allied' army has a name, so should we."

"I'm no general," Jash retorted, "but I'm the only 'First Ker-noll.' That should suffice. As to a name . . ." He considered. "You were a Slasher once. So was I. So is the force I still command. We're *all* Slashers now, the 'Slasher Corps.' Number the divisions in . . . the 'Army of the Mother' accordingly." He looked around at the gathered troops, the bloody bodies, and the dead general. "We have much to prove to our new allies—other hunters who defeated us—and there'll be hard fighting ahead. Perhaps hardest *of all* for us, since I mean to reach Esshk first . . . and rip him apart."

CHAPTER 24

////// **USS Savoie**
Scapa Flow, New Scotland
Empire of the New Britain Isles
June 29, 1945

The Union fleet anchored off the Imperial naval base at Scapa Flow was more impressive than anything these waters had ever seen. From his vantage point in *Savoie*'s pilothouse, Matt reflected it was even fairly "modern-looking" at a glance, and wouldn't have seemed particularly out of place in the nearby Pearl Harbor on the world he came from. *Savoie* vaguely resembled *New York* or *Texas*, and *Gray* looked just as much like an Omaha Class CL. Then there was *Gray*'s Filpin Lands–built sister, USS *Maa-ni-la* (the only one like her that would ever be built there either), and the growing shoal of "4-stacker" destroyers accompanying them. These included *Walker*, *Mahan*, *Ellie*, *McDonald*, *Tassat*, and *Adar*, of course, joined by the Maa-ni-la-built USS *Daanis* and USS *Steele*. USS *Sular* was anchored near *Savoie* among a pack of the fast oilers and freighters, with II Corps' 6th Division and Chack's Brigade embarked.

They'd had a pleasant cruise out of Baalkpan, just what they needed after a whirlwind stay marked by herculean effort in the yard, unrestrained revelry ashore by some who'd kept the cork in too long, and the tragedy and grief resulting from treachery, of course. And to Matt's surprise (with the exception of a single episode he'd caught lurid rumors of), Silva conscientiously behaved himself the entire time they were there. He and Lawrence, or a detail of their minions (representing every ship in the fleet), shadowed Matt and Sandra wherever they went. Chack stuck with Safir, of course. Her performance the night of the disaster had been masterful, if exhausting, and she still needed rest before fully assuming her new duties.

At least she was "herself" again. So was Chack. With his heart secure, and half of II Corps' veterans—including the remnants of Safir's own "600"—remaining at Baalkpan to protect everything he left behind, he was ready to fight again.

Matt and Sandra had been at a loss as to what to do with their son. Matt hadn't even tried to suggest that Sandra remain behind, but they were agreed young Fitzhugh must stay at Baalkpan. Karen Letts provided a solution by insisting she and her children would care for the infant on the very day they buried her husband. Matt hadn't been keen on that, worried her offer had been impulsive and inspired by grief still fresh and sharp, but Sandra believed her friend and their son would benefit from the arrangement. She was probably right. And ultimately, if something happened to them, Karen was the obvious choice to raise the boy, anyway.

First Fleet found just as many ships under construction at Maa-ni-la as Baalkpan, but in addition to many planes and MTBs (all their MTBs were made in the Filpin Lands), time had only allowed the completion of the one CL and four "modern" DDs. Two destroyers, USS *Araina* and USS *Sineaa*, had already proceeded west toward the Pass of Fire, screening the carriers USNRS *Salissa* and USS *Madraas* (loaded with new planes); self-propelled dry dock USS *Tarakaan Island* (packed with MTBs); the other two ex-Grik APDs, *Saa-Leebs*, and *La-Laanti*, as well as another herd of replenishment ships. All were under Keje's command, though the APDs had veered off toward the shipyards at the Enchanted Isles for modifications Matt requested.

There'd been a near riot on their last night in Maa-ni-la, after the final game in a series in which the new light cruiser's baseball team humiliated all comers. Baseball had become an obsession in the Filpin Lands, and USS *Maa-ni-la*'s team was *good.* Fights broke out near the navy yard bars and radiated through the city. The resulting damage was shocking, and the Lord High Sky Priest Meksnaak, still reluctantly in charge during Saan-Kakja's absence, had been enraged. Matt was unconvinced all, or even most, of the damage was caused by "his" people, but Meksnaak didn't care. He'd finally become a convert to the necessity of their cause, but still—understandably—hated what it was doing to his city and its culture. He'd been ready to make an example of every Navy Clan member the SPs rounded up. *Only* the fact they were steaming away to a real battle where "maany of the miscreaants might earn proper punishment" allowed them to sail with full complements.

The wind built to near strakka force and the sea kicked up from there. The DDs rolled their guts out and couldn't refuel underway. Even *Savoie* took a beating and heavy water coursed over her fo'c'sle. By the time they made Respite Island, the Empire's westernmost outpost, the DDs were gasping on fumes. The fleet spent two days recovering and making repairs and some of the hardier souls even went swimming in the island's crystalline lagoon. As far as Matt knew, Respite was the only place on earth you could swim in seawater in relative safety. Watching hundreds of Lemurians splash in the shallows, nervously at first, then with growing excitement and hilarity, was quite a sight.

Matt and Sandra spent their days with the charming Governor and Emelia Radcliff, touring the vivid, rocky island in a comfortable coach drawn by a four-up team of burros. They rarely discussed the war, but Emelia gave them her impressions of how High Chief Saan-Kakja and Governor-Empress Rebecca McDonald had been changed by it. The two leaders had made a visit before backtracking to the main Impie Isles. Matt and Sandra spent their very pleasant nights in the same beach bungalow where they'd enjoyed their brief honeymoon. Though they missed their new son even more than they'd expected, it was their first opportunity to really relax, entirely alone, and fully enjoy each other almost since they were married on that very island. After all they'd both been through since, it did them a world of good.

They steamed out of Respite, rested and healed. And though the air turned hot and sultry and the ship's crews took to sleeping on deck again, they enjoyed unchallenging seas the rest of the way to the main Impie Isles. Matt took the opportunity to practice maneuvers again, and the destroyers rehearsed dashing out of line to make torpedo runs in the blink of an eye. The sea rumbled with the thunder of gunnery exercises on alternating days and nights, shredding targets towed behind racing DDs on the horizon. *Savoie*'s new fire control computer might not be as good as the one taken from her, but it worked well enough. More important, her people were getting very good indeed. All the crews were, and the fleet that put in at Scapa Flow was small, but confident.

"Motor launch comin' over from thaat dopey-lookin' Impie crooser by the dock," called a Lemurian lookout. Matt and Captain Russ Chappelle raised their binoculars. Scapa Flow was a wonderfully broad harbor on the south of a larger, craggier, single island where Molokai and Maui should've been. And like Baalkpan and the Filpin Lands, it had been transformed by war. Already the main naval base of the Empire of the New Britain Isles, it still possessed a restrained, picturesque atmosphere the last time Matt was there. No more. If anything, it looked like "progress" and the industrial requirements of a near-global war had corrupted the beauty of Scapa Flow even more profoundly than Baalkpan and Maa-ni-la. *The haze doesn't help,* Matt supposed gloomily. *Impies are just now shifting to oil for their ships, now they've got it coming from their colonies, but their industry's still coal-fired.* Even the brisk sea breeze couldn't sweep the brown haze away. And though plenty of lizardbirds swooped and crapped all over the ships in harbor, few fluttered over the city.

There weren't many large, dedicated sailing ships left in Scapa Flow either. They were principally employed hauling crucial cargoes from Maa-ni-la and raw materials from the Empire's colonies in North America, and never lingered long in port. A few remained for interisland commerce, but the forest of tall masts once inhabiting the place was gone. There were still plenty of sailing fishermen, and swift Imperial couriers came and went, their extreme hulls slashing through swells and spray under clouds of sails, but almost every other ship in view, of any sort, was a dedicated steamer, boasting the same "dazzle" paint scheme the rest of the Allies had adopted.

The new Impie warships, all eight of them, had been started at the same time, following the same lines. Finishing up just as news of the Battle of the Pass came in, they were christened *Mars*, *Centurion*, *Mithra*, *Hermes*, *Diana*, *Ananke*, *Feronia*, and *Nesoi*, in honor of ships lost there. Matt finally knew their proper particulars now, as he did the details of the "battlecruisers" the Repubs were contributing.

"I guess we ought to be impressed, considering where they started from," Matt told Chappelle after scrutinizing one of the "protected cruisers." He redirected his binoculars at the approaching launch and felt a thrill to recognize familiar faces. "Stand by to receive dignitaries," he said. "Assemble an appropriate side party."

"Aye, sir. The accommodation ladder's already rigged." Chappelle hesitated, motioning back at the ships they'd been looking at. "They look kinda like the old *Olympia*," he said encouragingly, "except without that ram, or whatever it was, poking out forward. And she did pretty good."

Matt frowned. "Sure, against inferior ships. That's not what we're up against. And they're almost *exactly* like her: about six thousand tons and three hundred and forty feet long. Four eight-inch guns in twin turrets, and ten five-fives like we put in *Gray*. The five and a half inchers are okay, but I wouldn't count too much on the eights. Strictly close-range jobs, like on Repub monitors." He considered. "I don't mean to sound so critical," he confessed. "They're a hell of an achievement. I'm just trying to figure out how to plug them into the 'Big Plan.'" Russ had been added to the carefully growing list of those who knew how Matt hoped to face the League. "So, on the plus side," he continued, "they have five inches of case-hardened armor, so they might hold up under light fire. And they can make twenty-five knots, flat out, so they can keep up with *Savoie*. They've even got four twin 25mm mounts, like all our new DDs, so they might help brush off some planes. Probably should've given 'em more of those instead of that quad torpedo mount between the stacks."

"Maybe, but we're getting a *lot* of fish," countered Russ, the former torpedoman. "Might as well use 'em. And if the Leaguers are expecting the ones we used to have, they're gonna be in for a nasty surprise. One good thing came of not hangin' all the Japs we caught," he added philosophically. "They make good torpedoes."

Matt nodded. "Yeah. C'mon. Let's go meet our guests."

The launch was just hooking on when Matt and Russ joined the others gathered around the side party. Matt wasn't surprised to see Sandra, Diania, Juan, and Gunny Horn already there, or Silva and Lawrence either. He hadn't realized how many had already come over from other ships, however, like Spanky and Tabby from *Walker*, and Chack, Abel Cook, and Major McIntire from *Sular*. Others were there as well, all anxious to greet their guests.

The first up the steps, looking a lot older than the last time Matt saw him, was Sir Sean Bates, the one-armed Prime Factor to Her Majesty. He was grinning hugely through his monstrous, graying mustache, and crisply saluted the colors aft, the young 'Cat CPO of the deck who greeted him, then the rest of the waiting party. With a wink at Silva and an anxious-looking Abel Cook, he stepped quickly aside. Bosun's whistles trilled and Governor-Empress Rebecca Anne McDonald and Saan-Kakja, High Chief of Maa-ni-la and all the Filpin Lands, ascended the stairs together. Rebecca wore an unadorned dark blue uniform of the Imperial Navy, long blonde hair uncovered and tightly braided down her back. Saan-Kakja was dressed in traditional black leather armor with gold trim that reflected her mesmerizing eyes so well. They were small enough to take the steps side by side, arm in arm, and when they reached the deck, all reserve fled and a spontaneous cheer erupted. Casting decorum aside, both young females dashed forward and embraced Sandra in a shower of happy tears, then started hugging all the men and 'Cats, who tried in vain to stand stoically straight.

Matt endured his own crushing embrace while Rebecca's elfin face looked into his with pleasure and satisfaction. "You've returned at last," she proclaimed. "At long, *long* last." She pulled back and gestured exuberantly around. "With a mighty fleet! Together with what we've made to join you, we'll end this dreadful war!"

"I'm sure of it, Your Majesty," Matt lied.

She'd already turned away, caught up in the joyous reunion, anxious to greet others. "My word! Lawrence, my old friend! I hope you're quite well?"

"Just shot again, now and then," he replied a little hesitantly, glancing at Silva. Silva himself simply reached down and picked Rebecca up, holding her at arm's length. "My li'l sis," he murmured softly, eye suspiciously bright. Matt started to shout at him to put the Governor-Empress *down*, but saw the look of almost worshipful gratitude the young lady gave the big man. *And she* is *a young lady now,* Matt realized, watching Saan-Kakja squeal, "Col-nol Chack!" and enfold the battle- and soul-scarred 'Cat, pressing close. *They both are. Just as important, they've both been to hell and back—and still love us as much as we love them. This is the soul of our Alliance; it's what'll keep it strong in the time to come, win or lose. We're not just allies of convenience and necessity, we're friends who* like *each other, and have* helped *each other in the toughest times imaginable. How else—if they didn't trust us completely—could two heads of state let themselves act like a couple of kids again, with so many people watching?* Then suddenly Rebecca wasn't a kid anymore. She'd found herself facing Abel Cook: the boy she'd endured so much beside, who'd become a man far too young. Matt noted they didn't embrace, but only stood looking at each other, holding hands.

Silva broke the spell, crouching between them. "Got another old friend o' yours, still alive an' raisin' a ruckus. Say 'hello,' Petey!"

"Hello Petey!" the creature cawed and blinked at the girl without recognition. Rebecca laughed, a trace of her reserve returning. "I fear he's forgotten me. Understandable, since I suspect he was very young at the time. As was I," she added with a furtive glance at Abel Cook, "and quite given to impulsive sentimentality. Probably just as well."

"No, it ain't. You saved his goat-sniffin' ass—'scuse my Grikish—an' I've carted the little mooch along all this time just ta' bring him back ta you. Why, Pam would'a tossed him in the wake, or ol' Larry would'a *ate* him if it weren't for you."

Rebecca gently patted Petey's head. "Then our association wasn't wasted. But you're clearly much attached to him and his life has taken him far from me. He'd find the Governor-Emperor's palace like a cage after his adventures, and I'd never dream of separating you. Or confining him."

Abel Cook abruptly turned and vanished in the growing crowd of onlookers. Rebecca stared after him, face torn.

"Huh," Silva grunted. "I think Mr. Cook figured you was talkin' as much about him as Petey."

"Perhaps I was," Rebecca whispered.

Silva stood. "Then you're even sillier than you was when we was trapped on Yap," he pronounced. "There ain't a braver, *better* kid than him, an' he's been sweet on you ever since. You waitin' on a better deal in an arranged match? Shit. Cook's like a son to Cap'n Reddy an' Courtney Bradford. Chack too. An' *he's* mated to the new Chairman of the United Homes an' Grand Alliance now."

Matt had moved toward Sir Sean, but he'd seen the exchange. "Why don't we adjourn to the wardroom where we can talk a little easier?" he suggested loudly. "Or perhaps somewhere ashore? I appreciate you meeting us out here, and it means the world to the fleet's crews, but maybe you had a different venue in mind for our planning sessions?"

The smile on Bates's face vanished. "Hardly. Especially not after what happened in Baalkpan. These islands've always been infested with Dom spies. They don't attempt much disruption because it draws attention to them, but since I expect we'll be underway quickly enough to outrun their reports, they may try something unpleasant." Another man had ascended the ladder, and Matt recognized Ezekial Krish. He was a captain now, but obviously still the Governor-Empress's aide. Matt shook his hand. "We'd just as soon stay aboard here while we discuss our movements," Bates continued, then grinned at Russ Chappelle. "I'm sure this monstrous thing has sufficient space to host all our commanding officers? We'll bring things from shore to contribute to your kitchen, of course."

Sandra and Pam brought Rebecca and Saan-Kakja back over. Matt looked at the two leaders, but spoke to Bates. "You said 'we' when you mentioned getting underway. I'm sorry, but we're *not* taking the Governor-Empress and High Chief of the Filpin Lands *back* to the war. They just returned, and I had to order High Admiral Jenks and General Shinya to send them!"

"Of course not," Saan-Kakja said. "We gave our word. No more fighting for us. I'll remain here, as represent-aative of the Eastern United Homes—

which will give my poor Lord Meksnaak a fit of some kind, I'm sure—but you, or he, haave no further need to concern yourselves for us."

"I'm going this time," Sir Sean told him firmly. "Just me, but I must."

"And I'm only here to see you, and support all our brave sailors and Marines," said Rebecca, with a quick glance at Chack. "I'll certainly never question your plans." She hesitated, smile dissolving. "I did enough of that to High Admiral Jenks. I only have a single question and I pray you'll answer truthfully. I know we could beat the filthy Doms. They teeter on the edge of collapse even now. But all that'll be for naught if you can't defeat the League. I must have your honest answer. Can you do it?"

Matt looked into her earnest eyes and caught himself rubbing his chin. Then he looked around at Chack, Horn, Sandra, Pam—everyone around him as his eyes passed theirs. Finally, he glanced at the distant docks lined with what he skeptically thought of as the "half-assed cruisers" the Empire was contributing, but he nodded slowly. "Yeah," he said. "I wouldn't risk it if I didn't. I hated the Grik for what they did, and with God's help, we've nearly got them licked. Funny thing is, I don't even hate 'em anymore because, as bad as they were, it dawned on me they're not really *evil.* All this time, they were just being what they are. Couldn't help it. Maybe that'll change, now. The Doms're worse than Grik because they know better. That *makes* 'em evil, in my book. Some of 'em, anyway, and I'll hate 'em until they're through.

"But the League may be the worst of the lot because of what they stand for. I won't go into fascism and all that, even if it's the same thing we were fighting on the world we came from. Feels like we've come full circle," he mused, then continued. "But the League's killed our people and made the wars we were already in a lot bloodier than they had to be. Worse, it knows what the Doms are and is willing to help 'em, anyway. What's more evil than helping evil flourish? So yeah, we're going to beat 'em because we have to, and as complicated as the final operation'll likely be, the strategy's as simple as I can make it." He shrugged and looked around. "In a nutshell, we're going to poke 'em in the eyes, then rip their guts out. It may cost every ship and plane we've got, and they might even 'beat' *us* in that sense, but we can make *more* ships and planes, faster than they can. They'll never make it through a second round."

CHAPTER 25

////// ***USNRS* Salissa**
El Paso del Fuego
July 20, 1945

"Hell of a thing," Matt said sincerely, gazing out at the panorama of the western mouth of the Pass of Fire.

"It is," agreed "Ahd-mi-raal" Keje-Fris-Ar, moving to join him by the rail surrounding part of USNRS *Salissa*'s superstructure "island," all that remained of her old Great Hall. The two, both wearing whites, were still a study in contrasts. One was tall, lanky, clean-shaven. The other was short, burly, and covered in rust-colored fur. Still, they couldn't have been closer friends, and they were alone together for the first time in months, sharing a brief companionable moment and taking in the sights while the cyclone of their greatest challenge mounted beyond the horizon. "Our fellowship haas been full of wonders I never could haave imaagined, from the moment I first saaw your skinny little ship, all the way to the present. Some haave been terrible," Keje stated matter-of-factly, then blinked wry amusement, "but none haave been tedious. I've seen great suffering and the end of the life I knew and loved," he conceded, "but I've also seen the Ancient Grik Enemy beaten baack." He chuckled and waved to starboard, to the south, toward the captured city of El Corazon. "And here I staand on the very 'bottom' of the world, without falling off! I miss the . . . sweet simplicity of my old life, but it does now seem thaat it was raather . . . tiny in comparison to whaat it haas become."

"You might be kinda short, Keje, but nothing about you ever struck me as 'tiny,'" Matt told him, also looking at the fallen Dom city.

El Corazon was beginning to recover, but signs of the desperate battle remained everywhere. The high walls were scorched and blackened, still rubbled in places, and many buildings on the west side of town looked battered and misshapen. Those to the east had burned. The local population, now indiscriminately mixed with freed slaves and even former Dom soldiers, were hard at work completing the teardown so they could rebuild and Matt was gratified to see that a lot of stone was being taken from the abominable pyramidal temple in the center of the city. He was of two minds about that. On the one hand, the temple was ancient and had significant historical value. On the other, however, it represented a *current*, not historical, cultural depravity that had to be erased while the ruin it wrought was still running with blood.

"Look at all those bones!" Keje exclaimed, pointing at sun-bleaching skeletons beginning to collapse in the shallows. Most were smaller, but some of the ribs looked large enough to frame ships as big as *Salissa*.

"Yeah. Amazing." Matt looked at Keje. "That was Orrin's idea, by the way. Got all the mountain fish hanging around the mouth of the pass stirred up into a stampede that shattered the Dom fleet. Nobody knows how many of the *fish* died in it. Hundreds, maybe. I bet you didn't see many on your way out here. We didn't." He snorted grimly. "Courtney'll be furious when he finds out, if he hasn't already. Probably go on about the ecological imbalance it caused, taking so many predators off the top of the heap. And I imagine he'd be right. Probably be a lot more flashies and gri-kakka in the seas for a while."

"He did the right thing," Keje said with certainty. "You would haave done the same. One trait you share is the aability to think quickly, ruthlessly, and make big decisions. They may not always seem *right* to you, aafterwaard, but they're generaally for the *best*." Keje blinked thoughtfully. "You aare a good person, my brother, so I know such things hurt your soul, but you haave a taalent I do not. I think too ponderously in baattle, the way we both do when we plaan. I try to think of everything. But when the plaan shaatters, as it often does, there's no time for thaat. When suddenly faced with *no* good choices, you quickly choose the best baad one—more often thaan not—before it even occurs to the rest of us." His large, thoughtful eyes gazed in the distance where herds of big, bizarre animals had returned to graze on the slopes of high, peaceful mountains beyond the city. The great volcano brooding to the north of the Pass of Fire was never entirely peaceful, but it was invisible from where they stood.

Matt was looking closer, at the vast assemblage of ships anchored nearby. First Fleet and Second Fleet were no more. All Union and Imperial ships, and whatever the Nussies might contribute, had been gathered under the umbrella of "United Fleet" for the duration of the coming operations, and would be divided into task forces. The Republic Fleet might or might not consider itself part of that inclusive organization, but had agreed to fall under Matt's overall command "when the time came" (whatever that meant), and be attached to other Allied task forces.

But the force gathered here was already more powerful than anything Matt ever expected to scrape up to face the League. There was the battleship *Savoie*, of course, as well as two Gray Class light cruisers, eight Poseidon Class Impie protected cruisers, and nine "modern" destroyers, including his old *Walker* and the patched-together *Mahan*. The SPD *Tarakan Island* held a swarm of MTBs he hoped to make good use of, and USS *Sular* probably carried the best troops in the world. On top of that was the logistics train: oilers and cargo ships to keep his combatants fueled, fed, and armed. These were yet another legacy of Alan Letts, and Matt felt a familiar pang of loss when he remembered the easygoing, almost lazy kid he'd been, turned into an organizational marvel by the love of his wife.

These things alone probably left the United Fleet about on a material par with the Asiatic Fleet when it faced the Japanese Imperial Navy in the Java Sea—the closest thing to a League analog Matt could imagine—but he had several advantages. First, there was a genuinely unified command and no significant language barrier to communications. Nearly all Navy 'Cats spoke some English now, and comm- and signal-'Cats had to be fluent. Next, he'd trained this fleet himself, to do what he wanted when he wanted it, and it was very good. The Impies had learned what was expected of them on the long voyage from Scapa Flow. A lot of his crews were newies, but they were leavened by veterans. Few had ever experienced anything like what they might this time around, but they'd been tested.

Probably most significant, he had something the Asiatic Fleet never had, and neither did the League as far as he knew. He'd be bringing *four* aircraft carriers to the fight: *Salissa*, *Madraas*, and the hastily repaired *Maaka-Kakja* and *New Dublin*. Half were actually overloaded with older planes, for various reasons, and they'd soon reshuffle the mix, but Matt intended to relentlessly exploit his air advantage, and his very first priority was to keep it.

"I'm still not sure whaat you mean to do with those," Keje said, pointing at two strange shapes. They were the former Grik BBs Matt diverted to the Enchanted Isles, where the Impie's first 8″ guns, recently sent there as shore batteries, had been hastily installed. The rest of the modifications he'd asked for had been mostly cosmetic, including mock superstructures meant to resemble *Savoie*'s.

"They're the rest of our battle line, along with the Impie cruisers," Matt replied with a straight face. "I considered asking them to do the same to *Raan-Goon* when I heard they'd never get her new flight deck finished in time." He shook his head. "We'll have to watch for those big dragon bombers. They really did a number on her. Doesn't matter, though. She's probably too big to pull it off. Besides, we might need her. Can't risk *all* our carriers in one throw."

Keje grunted and blinked skepticism at the awkward-looking ships. "Those things won't fool anyone. They look ridiculous."

"Maybe. But if we're lucky, the Leaguers still don't even know we have *Savoie*. *Three* of her showing up might give 'em a fit—make 'em think she's somewhere she isn't. I'll take what I can get." He shrugged. "And if we're not lucky? I doubt they'll believe we already made two more like her, but those things *might* fool 'em on the horizon, or from the air. And the whole idea is to disperse their attention and their fire."

"*Draaw* their fire, you mean."

"If you want to look at it like that. Their crews know the score and they're all volunteers. Honestly," he added bitterly, "that's pretty much how I'll probably have to use the Impie cruisers too."

Keje blinked at him. "You see?" he asked softly. "You've already made a 'best baad' choice before our operation even begins. I could never do thaat. But even as you described it, I knew it waas one."

Matt shook his head. "Maybe not. I *really* don't want it all to come down to a daylight punching match, and we've still got a few stray aces up our sleeves." He lowered his voice, though there was no one around to hear. "As you know, *Adar* and *Sineaa* punched through the Pass yesterday evening with the tidal race, escorting two tankers, two cargo haulers, and High Admiral Jenks's last two sail-steam ships of the line, USS *Destroyer* and USS *Sword*. Both of those are ex-Doms and might be useful. Anyway, they're all making for Cuba, and there's not supposed to be anything in their way. *U-112* went through to skulk it out a week ago, and was ordered to squeal if she saw anything. We're not going to be able to keep radio silence much longer, and they'll be expecting to hear *something* coming from this way anyhow."

"*U-112*," Keje growled, blinking skepticism anew.

"Yeah. Hard to believe we've got a Kraut pigboat on our side," Matt admitted, somewhat wonderingly. "Sure wish I could've talked to her skipper more, but Alan did the right thing sending her to Tarakan for overhaul. Fiedler spent a lot of time there, and I guess Hoffman got a good dose of 'Cats and the way they think while they were refitting his boat. Fiedler believed in him. So did Alan, after they met." He sighed. "I wish Fiedler hadn't been so banged up in *Fueen*'s crash. We sure could've used him out here. But just like I guess not every Kraut on my old world could've been a hardcore Nazi, they aren't all Leaguers here. And even if Hoffman wanted to betray us, we swiped most of his submariners for other stuff. I don't think he's got enough left to run the boat without the 'Cats that took their places, and *they'll* kill him if he turns." He blinked philosophically in the Lemurian way. "He might come back to bite us on the ass, or he might save the day. Who knows?"

A door opened and Sandra stepped out on the deck they stood on, eyes twinkling. Their time on Respite had been too short and they'd had little time alone in the Empire, but Matt knew he loved her more now than he ever had. "Sorry to interrupt you guys," she said, "but I think everyone's waiting on you."

"They're all here at laast?" Keje asked her.

"You saw the Clipper set down, and Miyata brought *Maa-ni-la*'s skipper over with him."

Matt nodded. Everyone might be waiting on them now, but they'd been waiting on others first. One of the big four-engine flying boats had arrived about half an hour before, flying in from the east. "Okay. Let's get this done." He glanced at Keje. "I don't think the Nussies're going to like it much."

Salissa's Great Hall was less than a quarter as large as before the massive seagoing Home was smashed at the Battle of Baalkpan and rebuilt into the Allies' first carrier. Even then, its remnant had been partitioned into many compartments, including staterooms for visitors and Keje's own quarters. There was still a spacious conference room, however, entirely unique in the Alliance. Growing up through it, rooted in the ship's very keel and carefully directed to the side and upward as it also recovered from the ship's near destruction, was the flourishing remnant of the Galla tree that served as a living symbol *Salissa* remained a Home and not just a warship. That was important to her people. After the loss of *Humfra-Dar*, then *Arracca*, *Salissa* was the only carrier boasting a shady canopy between her forward superstructure and exhaust funnels, so in addition to her many accomplishments, that made her a precious symbol for the Alliance as a whole. Matt—and Keje, of course—was uncomfortably aware that, though her great size kept her more capable than smaller, newer, purpose-built carriers, she and USS *Maaka-Kakja* (CV-4), built to the same dimensions, were also slower and more vulnerable to a modern opponent. They'd have to keep that in mind.

A soft carpet of fine, silvery-green Galla leaves reappeared each day that the overhead awning wasn't rigged and they added a pleasant sense—and scent—to the chamber even when it was packed. Like now. Everyone stood from stools and chairs as Matt escorted Sandra to the broad head of the massive, hand-carved table, where they were joined by Keje and Tassanna, as well as High Admiral Jenks and Admiral Lelaa-Tal-Cleraan. Matt noted that Silva (without Petey, thank God), along with Lawrence, Diania, Juan Marcos, and several of *Salissa*'s Marines, stood behind where they'd sit. All the warship skippers (Spanky was there for *Walker*) and division commanders of the auxiliaries flanked the table. Nat Hardee and his XO of MTB-Ron-5 were standing by *Tara*'s skipper. COFOs Tikker and Orrin Reddy were with Ben Mallory, Jumbo Fisher, and a tiny 'Cat Matt remembered was called "Shirley." Chack was down the table with representatives of their land force, flanked by Abel Cook and Enrico Galay. So many more faces, so many friends—*so many legends, now,* Matt realized, *and so many gone.* It dawned on him then that Doocy Meek and Sir Sean Bates were the only members of his "staff" that wouldn't've been there anyway, but he thought differently about that now and delegated a lot more. Commanding something this size, he had to.

Standing between Meek and Bates at the far end of the table were their visitors, and Matt gladly recognized one immediately. Commander Greg Garrett was *Walker*'s gunnery officer when she came to this world and distinguished himself commanding one of the first sailing frigates they built to oppose the Grik. Like *Walker*, USS *Donaghey* had endured terrible maulings and outlasted all expectations. Reliant only on the wind, she and her gallant skipper and crew had been the perfect choice for an indefinite scout into the Atlantic to make formal contact with the NUS. Their adventures along the way had made them icons of the Union, and in many ways, set the stage for the current operation.

Matt didn't know the two men with him, both shorter, wearing dark blue uniforms with the only apparent difference being that the older, gaunter, gray-haired man's coat was closed with more brass buttons than the younger, blond man's. Both wore black cravats that seemed to be trying to escape from behind tall, stiff collars.

"Captain Reddy, Admiral Keje," said High Admiral Jenks, "may I present Admiral Robert Semmes and Leftenant Tomas Perez Mole of the New United States Navy." He smiled. "You remember Commander Garrett, of course."

"You bet," Matt said, smiling. "*Well* done, Greg. And I'm very pleased to meet you, Admiral Semmes. Lieutenant Mole. Have a seat, everybody. Coffee? Iced tea?"

While 'Cat stewards filled mugs, Matt watched their visitors thoughtfully. "Congratulations on your promotion, Admiral," he said. "My last report had you a commodore."

"I wasn't raised on merit, I fear, only survival," Semmes replied cheerlessly. "Admiral Sessions is still military governor of Cuba and in charge of our overall effort against the Doms, but General Cox has the army and I've got the fleet—such as it is." He nodded at the young man beside him. "Your reports may also have mentioned my aide—and future son-in-law."

Matt blinked confusion, but realization dawned as Greg explained significantly. "He was *Atúnez*'s only surviving officer."

"Really? That League destroyer you sank with *Donaghey* and your prize, *Matarife*?"

Greg chuckled, glancing apologetically at Mole. "Yeah, and I don't mean to laugh. It wasn't funny. What tickles me is how mad he was at the time—rightfully so, I guess—but how fast he switched sides when he got to know the Nussies . . . and Admiral Semmes's daughter. She's a dish, and poor Fred Reynolds was sweet on her too. He might've moved quicker if he knew Tomas was after her."

Mole smiled a little shyly and spoke in near-perfect English. "It was you who taught me to act so decisively and irresistibly, Captain Garrett. At the same time that I . . . regret the violence of the lesson and resulting loss of life, I've come to consider it a blessing of a sort." He looked at Matt. "I understand if you're suspicious of me; we discussed this beforehand and I'll wait elsewhere while you talk if you wish. But please understand two things. First, the NUS has a long history of converting—perhaps 'rescuing' is the better word—prisoners they take from the Dominion. It requires little effort, really." He waved in the general direction of El Corazon. "As you've already discovered, a little kindness and a glimpse of a better way instead of the life of daily abuse they endure, or atrocities they're taught to expect from us, works wonders."

He paused. "Yes, 'us.' I'm an officer in the NUS Navy now, wholeheartedly, because I was saved in much the same way. Most soldiers and sailors of the League are young men like myself who came of age under the fascist oppression and brutal intolerance of what became the League. They know nothing else, and without the examples I've been blessed with, they think theirs is the better way." He hesitated. "They'll fight for it rather mercilessly, and you can hold nothing back. They won't. All I ask is that, if the opportunity presents itself, you'll show individuals the same mercy I was given. You'll only grow stronger with each one you save."

Matt rubbed his chin, thinking about Walbert Fiedler, Kurt Hoffman, and all his submariners. There was truth in Mole's words. *Then again, what about those like Dupont?* he thought darkly. He'd always preferred to think of things in terms of black or white, right or wrong, but experience had taught him everyone harbors varying shades of gray in their soul. Over time, they'd encountered good and bad 'Cats, Japanese, Doms, even Grik. Now Leaguers. There'd been bad men in *Walker* and *Mahan* when they first came here, and if Silva wasn't the "grayest" thing alive, he was a turnip. All you could do was oppose the darker streaks when you found them. In yourself as well as others.

"No, Mr. Mole, please stay. I assume your assignment as aide to Admiral Semmes is based on more than your engagement to his daughter?"

"Yes sir. I'm aware you discovered, at least roughly, what the League can bring against us, but based on my own experience and . . . clandestinely gained knowledge of what's arrived and what's still due at their forward base on Martinique, I'm prepared to advise you as best I can. I was astonished to see *Savoie* anchored among your ships, by the way. I can only hope the enemy will be equally surprised."

"We can all agree on that, and I'm anxious to hear anything you can tell us." He looked around. "Well then. Let's get started."

As it turned out, Mole was as good as his word and the first half of the lengthy conference developed into a polite but fairly intense interrogation of the young man, interspersed with comments and observations by Semmes and Garrett. Mole knew the League's capabilities, and a lot of other intelligence had been gathered by spies and careful aerial observations made by a slowly growing Allied scouting force. As they'd suspected, the League had bases in the Azores and Cape Verde Islands, as well as a small outpost at Ascension. *Matarife* settled this, posing as a Dom frigate again. They'd actually felt fairly safe doing that, doubting the Doms would've reported her capture to their allies. They were right, and she'd sailed close enough to also confirm the bases were little more than way stations, supply and fuel depots, and none were strongly held. Apparently, they relied on the ships trickling through to Martinique for protection.

Martinique was another matter. Its impressive anchorage had been dredged and *Atúnez*'s wreck was righted and moved, for later salvage, no doubt. Docks, storehouses, and fuel tank batteries had been built on ground hacked from the snake-infested jungle by five thousand Spanish troops, and at least two airfields had been completed with antiaircraft guns emplaced around them.

"Jesus!" Spanky exclaimed. "What've they got on the water?"

Semmes took a folded page from his coat pocket and began to recite from a list in a somber tone. "Arrivals have accelerated over the last few weeks, but as of our latest direct observations, there appear to be five of what you call battleships, six cruisers, and six destroyers anchored rather closely together in the harbor." He looked up. "It's fairly large, but not terribly deep. Other than *Leopardo* and another destroyer still based at Puerto del Cielo—which have harassed our positions at El Palo and Monsu—three destroyers are usually at sea around Martinique on patrol, but they haven't ventured far." He handed the sheet to Mole, who continued for him.

"I'll be happy to give you the particulars of each ship to the best of my knowledge—" He stopped and his face turned glum. "But it's a very powerful force. And if our information is correct, it'll soon be joined by another battleship, two cruisers, and several more destroyers. They're currently en route, perhaps already at the Azores."

Matt kept a straight face. He—and a very few others—knew all that, courtesy of a surveillance report Hoffman left with Jenks before proceeding through the Pass. He also knew the bulk of the League's oilers were accompanying that force. He was actually somewhat relieved by this ultimate corroboration of Hoffman's . . . if not necessarily "loyalty," at least "commitment" to the Allied cause, and wondered if there was anything Courtney Bradford could do about those reinforcements. The oilers in particular were critical to his plan.

"Shit," Spanky breathed in the near silence. He knew what Matt did, of course, but was more focused on the lengthening odds.

"Airpower?" Ben Mallory practically barked.

"Fifty aircraft altogether, split between what you call medium bombers, dive bombers, and fighters. They may get more," Mole added doubtfully, "but that's already more than half the modern aircraft the League possesses. Their own efforts at local construction don't yet match your first planes."

"Still, altogether, a *little* more tonnage than we'd really hoped to face," Matt confessed dryly.

"Actually, more than anyone did," Mole agreed, "and perhaps more than the League can afford to send. I can only wonder what new imperative aroused the Triumvirate to support Gravois's scheme so vigorously. Perhaps the Pass of Fire was more important to them than we imagined?" He bit his lower lip. "Regardless, they've certainly sent more than they can afford to *lose*. I pray you have a plan to make them see that."

"Maybe we do," Matt said slowly, cutting his eyes at Sandra while clutching her hand under the table. Of all his "staff," she was still the most important. Not only did she know his plan, she knew his fears and helped him figure out ways to minimize them. "First, let me get this straight; everything they have so far is at Martinique?"

"Everything on this side of the Atlantic, at any rate, except a large auxiliary named *Ramb V* and a small oiler lingering near Puerto del Cielo, possibly as tenders for *Leopardo* and her consort."

"How often do they sortie?" Matt asked.

"Every few days," Greg Garrett replied, "but not always to haunt the sealanes. Sometimes *Leopardo* runs up to Martinique."

Matt grunted. "*Leopardo*, huh? Interesting. We've met her before. I wonder if Gravois is still in her?"

Mole cleared his throat. "Given time, the League forces will disperse, likely seizing the rest of the nearby islands, probably even Puerto Rico and Hispaniola once open hostilities commence. They must, since the Dominion still won't allow 'heretic' air bases or port facilities on their soil."

"Stupid of the Doms—and stupid of the League to put up with it—but good for us if we can move fast enough." Matt shook his head and looked at Admiral Semmes. "*All* the airfields we requested are under construction?"

"Virtually complete, though I remain somewhat mystified why you want to conceal some and not others. Particularly those closest to Santiago."

Matt drummed his fingers on the table and replied starkly. "Because Santiago's going to take a beating. Nothing for it. The League'll eventually pound it to rubble from the sea and air if for no other reason than it's your principal city and seaport on Cuba. You might even say I'm counting on it. . . ."

Semmes's face clouded. "I protest, sir! Admiral Sessions will protest! As our ally, you should help us *defend* it for that very reason!"

"We can't."

Semmes looked shocked.

"Look," Matt said, "did Admiral Sessions agree to follow my lead in this or not?"

"He did," Semmes agreed cautiously. "He had little choice."

"No, he didn't. And you need to get it through your head that we're *all* going to take a beating." His gaze swept the other faces around the table. "And we're going to lose a lot of planes—our older ones—on the ground around Santiago. Is this starting to make more sense?"

"So . . . Santiago—and your planes—will be a lure so you can strike while they're spread out?"

"Sure. A lure to split them up—they'll never send their whole force to Santiago—and hopefully a way to reinforce their arrogance. They can't know we brought every plane we could lay our hands on, airworthy or not. Some are wrecks and some've never even been assembled, still in their crates, stashed in freighters. But our newer planes'll be on our carriers or at other fields. If they take out some—quite a few, I expect—and think they've hammered all our land-based air, they might not look for the rest. In the meantime, though, we're going to hit them on the move, at anchor, in daylight and dark, to keep them running in all directions. What we absolutely *can't* do is let their whole force bunch up and box us in, see?"

"I think so."

"Good." Matt frowned. "And to do that, we have to scatter for a while as well. You can't imagine how much I hate that," he confessed, "and we can only do it because of your help." He couldn't mention *U-112* and her contributions. Their visitors would be heading back. If they were shot down and captured . . . "We now have a pretty good idea about the enemy's strength and disposition, as well as one very critical material deficiency," he added cryptically. "Just as important, it's starting to look like they don't know near as much about *our* strength as we were afraid they did, and when they finally catch sight of some of our elements, I hope their compositions and positions will only add to their confusion." He paused and looked at High Admiral Jenks. "That brings us to assignments. We don't need a CINCEAST anymore, so you'll be in charge of our battle line: Task Force Jenks."

To his credit, the Impie admiral started to protest that he had no notion of the tactics they'd devised for the new cruisers, and certainly not *Savoie*, but Matt waved it away. "Rely on Russ Chappelle and his staff to bring you up to speed, but in the meantime you'll focus on the logistics requirements of the overall strategy. We're all going to split up and bunch up from time to time, and you'll make sure the independent elements stay supplied." Matt saw another concern cloud Jenks's expression and guessed what it was with a smile. "Don't worry. You'll keep Admiral Lelaa, in one of the fast carriers." He turned to Lelaa-Tal-Cleraan. "You'll turn *Maaka-Kakja* over to Tex Sheider and shift your flag to *New Dublin*. *Makky-Kat* will stick with *Big Sal*, forming Task Force Keje." He didn't say they had to keep their two biggest, slowest carriers together—and hidden as well as possible—for a time. He chuckled at a sudden thought. "You might as well transfer Gilbert Yeager back to *Walker* before you go. I doubt *Makky-Kat* needs him anymore and I'm sick of reading his requests. Guy writes like somebody inked a mouse's feet and chased it across a sheet of paper."

He looked at Tassanna. "*Madraas* and *Gray* will stick with TF-Keje until all the planes we're putting ashore have been dispersed. After that, they'll form the core of TF-Tassanna and head back toward TF-Jenks's operating area. But don't join. You're our semi-independent reserve and I want you to disappear. Stay close enough to Jenks that your planes can keep you in contact and you can support one another if you have to, but otherwise keep your scouts up and stay as far from anything as you can." He looked back at Jenks. "Is that clear to you, High Admiral?"

"Perfectly."

Matt gathered the rest of the faces into another long gaze before fastening it back on Semmes. "Now that's settled, and I've told you how we keep from getting caught and slaughtered, here's how we're going to *win*. . . ."

CHAPTER 26

////// West of Nuevo Granada City
Holy Dominion
July 23, 1945

"I confess, General Shinya," General Hiram Cox of the NUS Army remarked quietly, gazing intently east at the dazzling white city of Nuevo Granada and the Templo de los Papas. "I never truly believed we'd make it."

Tomatsu Shinya had been watching a pair of "greater dragons" kiting overhead, spying on the army's progress. They never attacked or came close to rifle range and he suspected that meant there weren't many nearby. He looked at the city again as well. This was a comparatively highly populated, affluent region, with scenic villas and estates on the slopes below a vast tabletop mountain, or *tepui*, overlooking the capital city of the Holy Dominion roughly eleven miles away. The Lago de Vida, or "Lake of Life," shimmered beyond it, bordered by forest, its far shores beyond his view. A great stepped pyramid, larger than the one at El Corazon, rose from the center of the city, and he got the impression numerous smaller pyramids were arranged geometrically around it at different points. And it *was* a city, much like descriptions he'd heard of Alex-aandra in the Republic, which was the biggest, oldest, and most . . . interesting city—from a somewhat classical architectural standpoint—in the Grand Alliance. From a distance, Nuevo Granada gave the distinct impression of civilization, yet that sense warred with what Shinya knew of its inhabitants and he realized he had to adjust his preconceptions. The Grik had a civilization of a sort as well, but that didn't mean they were "civilized" as he defined the term. The same applied here.

The environs were deserted now, the great estates empty and stripped of valuables. Likely the only reason they hadn't been destroyed as the Allied army approached, as happened around El Corazon, was that their owners were richer and more influential—and there'd probably been a general disbelief the "heretic horde" would ever really reach this far. But the crops hadn't been burned and there was a lot of livestock running loose, easy to catch. *This will do,* Shinya decided.

Looking at Cox, he reappraised the man. He was even thinner than when they met and his red whiskers had bloomed into a full beard. His dark blue frock coat had faded to a kind of sickly light purple, and the once immaculately white sword belt had turned a grubby gray. He smiled slightly. "I never doubted *Tenth Corps* would get here, but after we met and I took the measure of your men, any reservations I had about them—or you—quickly vanished." Cox nodded appreciation and Shinya wearily slid from his saddle, performing a couple of deep knee bends while Cox and their respective staffs dismounted and handed off their horses.

The big HQ tent was swiftly rising amid a cacophony of tent stakes being pounded in the ground. The 'Cat Marines assigned the detail had done it so often that it only took a few minutes and even fewer words. Looking around, Shinya watched as row after row of wedge tents sprouted as quickly, like dingy brown mushrooms under an overcast sky, while columns of troops snaked up out of a wooded ravine to the north and marched to join those already present. Sheer, jagged cliffs jutted from the carefully terraced and cultivated detritus of eons of erosion and stood high above several nearby villas and the encampment growing around them.

Shinya had considered using one of the lavish homes for his HQ, but after everything he'd been through with X Corps he finally had a sense his troops considered him "one of them" and he wouldn't undermine that. Just as important, the NUS soldiers and most of their officers had quickly accepted his authority and combined with the already blended army as seamlessly as anyone could've hoped. There was some friction, and even the occasional altercation, but the various peoples and species of the allied force had more similarities than differences, in addition to their common cause.

Still, as Cox implied, just getting here had been an achievement, and if the Nussies hadn't come quite as far, they'd all endured endless miles of hostile wilderness, privation, exhaustion, terrifying monsters, and occasional combat of varying intensity. They hadn't faced a serious engagement since the armies met, but their supplies had abruptly ceased when a force out of El Henal cut the line and commenced a half-hearted pursuit. That alone made Shinya doubt General Mayta still commanded the Dom force. When the enemy was, in turn, cut off and destroyed by General Blair and leading elements of XI Corps, his suspicion was confirmed. Prisoners told them Mayta had been recalled some time ago, and might even be waiting for them here.

"Now we only have to decide what to do next," Shinya said, looking at the *tepui.* It was called something like the "Footstool of God" in the local tongue, and was one of the northernmost of what he believed were the "Guiana Highlands." Imposing as it seemed, it wasn't the most impressive example by any means, if some of the cooperative locals were to be believed. And Shinya did believe them. Not only was that consistent with what he remembered of "old world" geography, they'd been right when other things weren't even close.

A high-pitched cry, like a hawk with its mouth full, echoed off the vertical, rocky cliffs and Shinya looked back up at the dragons. Following his gaze, Cox frowned. "Are you sure this plateau is the best place to establish our base? It's exposed to observation, and might be isolated by the enemy."

"The same is true for anywhere in this unfamiliar land," Shinya agreed, "and if we do become isolated, better that it's on high, defensible ground. Besides"—he waved at Nuevo Granada—"not only do we have a fine view of the enemy capital, they can clearly see *us* firmly established here. I *want* to be 'observed.'"

"That seems counterintuitive," Colonel Prine objected. "It limits our movement options and might further anger the enemy."

"I certainly hope so," Shinya snorted. "I hope it drives Don Hernan, or whoever commands over there, even crazier than he already is and makes him come to us. Let's be clear; we *will* probably have to assail the walls of Nuevo Granada at some point, but our similar experience at El Corazon was a bloodbath. I expect if General Mayta's here, he's learned to make such an assault even costlier. I'd rather he came out after us so we can meet him in the open and bleed *him* first."

His words were punctuated by popping sounds a half mile down the slope where Rangers probed a wooded creek bed and the Sister's Own were digging into a protective line. The *thump* of muskets was answered by the crackle of rifles.

"How long will we wait?" Prine asked, apparently oblivious. "While it's true the army is well fed, and reasonably well-armed and supplied with ammunition, our tents are threadbare shreds and our uniforms are disintegrating rags." He looked back the way they'd come. "And we've picked up so many camp followers . . . We aren't a very formidable-*looking* force."

Shinya took a calming breath. "Our logistics train is almost a *thousand miles* long, stretching all the way to Manizales. It has focused on the essentials, for obvious reasons. And the 'camp followers' aren't only refugees that our presence here created, they're the source of most of the supplies that keep us so well fed. Their men—and not a few women," he reminded sharply, "have become soldiers and scouts, risking worse treatment than our own people, if caught. They have a vested interest in our success and we couldn't have more important support."

"Perhaps . . . for the most part," Prine conceded sourly.

"For the most part," Shinya allowed, sure there were spies mixed in. Some had even been identified and might be used. "But how our troops *look* won't affect how they fight, and we'll wait as long as it takes. An assault on the city without General Blair and Eleventh and Fifteenth Corps would be pointless."

"Skirmishers," Cox finally observed as the firing down below increased.

It suddenly struck Shinya as very odd that he was standing here arguing about clothes, and his orderlies and the 'Cats erecting his tent were calmly carrying tables, chairs, and his personal effects inside—while men and 'Cats were shooting at one another, being wounded and killed, just a short distance away. Two clouds of gray-white smoke blossomed out of the forward line and moments later they heard the *Poom! Poom!* of field pieces.

"That's Captain Meder's battery supporting your Lemurian Marines and Sister Audrey's Vengadores," Cox remarked. "Good man. He wouldn't waste ammunition without a good target." He glanced at Prine. "The combination of all our artillery using common ammunition into mixed battalions attached to divisions instead of infantry brigades has eased their supply and administration, while allowing them to be deployed more efficiently. And the creation of a common reserve that can be quickly massed where necessary was a master stroke."

"Not my idea," Shinya demurred. "Captain Reddy's. And you already had fine artillery."

"For a naval man, your 'Captain Reddy' has a strong understanding of land warfare."

"Better than he thinks," Shinya agreed, "and it's informed by his interest in history. He had the benefit of hindsight to preserve us from the problems you had with your previous system."

"He sounds like a remarkable man. I hope I meet him someday."

"So do I," Shinya said.

The firing down by the creek bed was almost constant now, more than a few skirmishers would justify, and a couple of cannon had joined the action on the other side, drawing a response from Meder's entire battery.

"Perhaps we've made Don Hernan angrier, more quickly, than we were prepared to," Colonel Prine observed wryly.

"Possibly," Shinya agreed. "General Cox, would you be kind enough to send some of your men to support the Sister's Own?" The closest arriving troops were Nussies.

"My pleasure, General Shinya." He spoke to a rider and the man galloped to a nearby column. Their once-sky-blue uniforms were now a dingy gray, but their weapons were clean and bright. They'd had a long march, like everyone, but were still in formation. Officers and NCOs shouted and the troops double-timed down the slope behind their regimental flag and deployed into line behind Blas and Sister Audrey's division. Almost immediately, the firing reached a crescendo and then began to wane.

"The enemy's not quite ready for a meeting engagement, it seems," Cox said, sounding a little disappointed.

"Apparently not," said Shinya, "but I expect they'll reinforce and attempt to contest the creek crossing—maybe every mile, all the way to the city. That's good."

Cox looked at him strangely. "Good?"

"Of course," Shinya assured.

Captain Anson and a squad of Rangers thundered up, throwing clumps of grass and divots of earth in all directions. When they halted near the command tent, Shinya saw Blas and Captain Bustos had accompanied them with a prisoner.

"Get down, you," Blas said sharply and Bustos translated. The prisoner complied, quickly taken in hand by a couple of Rangers while everyone else dismounted. The Dom was young, a junior officer, and though his face was dark, his hair was almost as yellow as his uniform. The coat was remarkably clean and bright except for a smudge of dirt on the shoulder and a bloodstain where his sword belt had been. Shinya was surprised by how obedient he was, despite a defiant air.

"What have we here?" he asked.

"A goddaamn hu-maan *Grik*!" Blas raged, yanking on a line she still held, securing the man's hands behind him. The Dom apparently understood what Shinya expected of him and calmly proclaimed himself to be "Teniente Paolo Chavez, *a su servicio*."

"Murderin' baastard!" Blas seethed.

Shinya looked at her. "What did he do?"

"Some o' my guys were down in the creek, haulin' out brush an' limbs to throw on the trench we're diggin' when he an' his buddies showed up. Shot two o' my guys down. One was still alive an' I saaw *him* shooteem in the head an' cut off his tail!" Blas gestured at the bloodstain on the man's coat. "Tucked it in his belt." She nodded appreciatively at Anson. "Him an' his Raangers scooped him up with haaff a dozen others when the Nussies baacked our line an' the Doms across the creek—prob'ly brigade strength—skee-daaddled."

Bustos's tone was as hostile as Blas's when he translated Chavez's reply. "He said he did it, and doesn't understand our reaction." He nodded at the bloodstain. "Says it was a trophy taken from an animal, nothing more."

Cox and some of his officers were visibly shaken by that, not only the act, but the casual confession. "I begin to see the . . . different dimension to your conflict with the Doms," Cox told Blas. "None of my men expect mercy if captured, but this—"

"Doesn't make any difference," Shinya interrupted coldly, still looking at the prisoner. "Ask him how many men defend Nuevo Granada City," he instructed Bustos, and to their growing amazement the young man apparently unreservedly told them everything he knew. According to him, there were roughly 140 thousand troops in and around the city, but the militia was training and could probably supply forty or fifty thousand more. They wouldn't stay there either; they'd advance and drive "all the invaders from this holy soil, given by God to the Emperor of the World."

"Disconcertingly confident, don't you think?" Colonel Prine murmured uncomfortably.

Clearly disgusted with Prine, Blas rounded on Bustos. "Aask him *why* he's so sure—an' why he don't lie."

After a rather lengthy exchange, Bustos summarized it. "He says it's a sin to lie, and why should he? Everyone breaks under torture, and he'd just as soon avoid the discomfort. Besides, this conflict, even our presence here, was foretold by God long ago—convenient that the Blood Priests of Nuevo Granada only recently revealed that," he said aside. "But it was also foretold that the 'heretics' would be entirely destroyed and 'cleansed from the earth, root and branch.' They can't lose, *we* can't win. All is preordained by God, so nothing he reveals is of any consequence." He shook his head.

"A true believer," Shinya concluded, "and not even a Blood Drinker, but just as bad. I'm afraid we'll see more like him, at least among their officers." He gestured at the city. "This is the very heart of their twisted faith, after all." He rubbed the scant stubble on his chin. "Ask him who commands here."

Chavez replied, and Bustos reported, "Technically, a 'Capitan General Maduro' commands all the forces in this part of Nuevo Granada Province, including in and around the Temple City, but he takes orders from a new man named Mayta, the 'Supreme Commander of All the Armies of God,' recently delivered by His Holiness, Don Hernan." Bustos sighed sarcastically. "He gushed on about what a 'hero' Mayta is, and how he 'slaughtered demons and heretics up and down the west coast of the continent.'"

Shinya was nodding, unsurprised. "Thank you, Captain Bustos. Please join Captain Anson in choosing one of the prisoners to carry a message to Mayta for me."

That startled everyone, but nobody spoke except Blas. "Whaat about the rest?"

"They'll be sent back to Neri to join the other prisoners guarded by our local allies."

"An' *him*?" Blas demanded hotly, yanking the line again.

"Please translate once more, Captain Bustos," Shinya requested, eyes narrowing at the prisoner. "You may be surprised to learn, Lieutenant Chavez, that *we* are the 'demons and heretics' General Mayta 'slaughtered' in the west. Perhaps you'll reflect on that and other inconsistencies the Blood Priests have fed you—while you choke on the end of a rope." He turned to the others when Chavez's eyes went wide and he began to struggle. "Any Doms who mistreat our people in their hands will be hanged. The messenger will witness the punishment before he departs."

"Good. Give 'em a taste of their own," Blas smoldered.

Cox gave her a cautious glance. "What will your message to Mayta say?" he asked Shinya.

"Only what our new policy will be," Shinya stated. "No quarter for Blood Drinkers or those who commit atrocities. And civilian 'militia' caught under arms and out of uniform will be summarily executed. Those were the rules where Captain Reddy and I came from," he added. "That might only strain their supply of uniforms when word gets out"—he flicked a glance at Colonel Prine—"but it *will* get out. We'll ask our 'camp followers' for volunteers to infiltrate the city and spread the word." Incongruous with his expression, he chuckled then. "Oh, and my message will also decline in advance any request Mayta makes to meet before battle. As far as I'm concerned, the battle has already begun."

"Very good," Cox approved cautiously, "but if everything else that man said is true"—his eyes settled meaningfully on Chavez, now being dragged away—"the enemy has nearly two hundred thousand men. Our combined forces, after casualties, sickness, and all the outposts we've established to protect our supply line, have been winnowed to less than fifty thousand over the course of the campaign."

"Eleventh and Fifteenth Corps will double that, and we have over fifteen thousand local troops under arms or in training," Shinya countered.

"Excellent," Prine inserted, "so we're only outnumbered two to one."

Blas blinked impatiently. "So whaat do *you* wanna do? Quit? Go home? We've haardly ever *not* been outnumbered, so whaat's the big deal?" Prine bristled but Blas ignored him, blinking anxiously at Shinya instead. "*Unless* we're gonna baang our heads against the city waalls again . . ."

"No," Shinya denied. "At least not until it's time," he added vaguely. "As I said, I expect Mayta to come to us. He *has* to try something different. Not only will he be reluctant to risk a repeat of El Corazon, we're encamped in full view of the city. Regardless of what the Blood Priests tell them, the people will be afraid. Perhaps more afraid of us than the Blood Priests, for the very first time." He shook his head. "Mayta has the numbers and he'll be under pressure to keep us at a distance and destroy us at once."

He looked around at the gathered officers. "Don't underestimate Mayta," he warned. "He's capable and audacious. He showed us that already. So we'll continue to improve our position here, for now. I believe we have the strength and the ground to hold." He smiled. "We also have more experience, and *far* more historical guidance to borrow from."

"Then we stand on the defensive at present," Cox approved, "but what exactly is your ultimate plan?"

Shinya waved that away. "It's impossible to tell you *exactly* just yet, but if Mayta does as I suspect he must, once Eleventh and Fifteenth Corps arrive, we should be able to combine certain historical operations Mayta can't expect and I've always admired. We can't count on any air support of our own," he lamented, glancing up at the circling dragons, "but unless those things see better in the dark than I've been informed, we should still be able to apply a few tactical improvements." He looked back at Anson. "Better maps of the area are essential: every road, trail, ravine, and promontory.

There's also a river somewhere ahead, and we need its exact course, and any fords and bridges."

Anson pursed his lips but nodded. The information Shinya wanted might be costly to obtain.

"Whaat then?" Blas pressed.

"Then, Colonel," Shinya replied, expression hardening, "we'll amuse General Mayta with an escalating *series* of engagements unlike anything he's ever seen."

CHAPTER 27

////// **Leopardo**
Puerto del Cielo
July 25, 1945

"Capitano Reddy has come through the Pass," announced Capitano di Fregata Ciano, almost dashing into the wardroom where Gouverneur Militaire du Protectorat des Antilles Victor Gravois sat alone in the compartment under an oscillating fan, legs crossed, drinking a kind of spicy local tea. He'd just arrived from Martinique in *Ramb V* that morning, after further tedious consultations with all the officers now under *his* command. (It still amazed him that all his machinations were finally bearing fruit.) He'd only be here a couple of days, pumping Don Hernan for information from his spies in the vicinity of the Pass of Fire, but he'd immediately shifted back to *Leopardo* for the duration of his stay. *Ramb V* was larger and more comfortable in every respect, but the presence of Oriani's living corpse, sequestered in his stateroom, bothered Gravois almost as much as it seemed to disconcert *Ramb V*'s crew. He'd thought getting them away from here might help them—and it did—until they had to turn back to Puerto del Cielo. Now he glanced up from the report he'd been writing for the Triumvirate and saw the Italian officer slapping a yellow sheet of paper in his hand.

"Indeed? And how can you possibly know for certain?"

"Because our Heron *saw* him off Jamaica!" Ciano exclaimed indignantly. The Heron was a CANT Z.506, the only one of its kind on this world. It had been sent out on one of the cruisers now at Martinique, and Gravois was stunned the Triumvirate (and Field Marshall Messe in particular) had been willing to part with it. He'd been pleased, of course. With its three engines, long range, and heavy construction, it was arguably the best scout plane the League possessed.

"*Saw* him? Don't be ridiculous. What was he doing, walking on water?"

Ciano clenched his teeth. Gravois was in one of *those* moods. He waved the yellow paper. "It reported seeing two enemy destroyers screening several other ships, heading north, clearly bound for Santiago!"

Gravois frowned. "Then perhaps it's true. *Just* two destroyers? Our latest intelligence gives the enemy at least one, possibly another copy." He sniffed. "Then again, the Americans will have had to rely on their animal friends to make them, as well as their supposed new 'cruiser'! Ha! Perhaps they couldn't complete the voyage. What else did the Heron report?"

Ciano almost enjoyed telling Gravois the rest, if only to see the look on his face. "That it was under air attack by swift little blue planes. Without floats," he stressed. "The transmission was cut off, mid-sentence, so we must assume the Heron was destroyed."

Gravois stiffened. Derisive as he might be about Allied shipbuilding, he recognized and respected what they'd done in the air. He'd even tried to get the Triumvirate to authorize converting one of their precious cargo ships into a carrier. They still might, eventually, but there was little point at present. They had no carrier planes. But he'd been persuasive enough about the threat to get a lot of the League's airpower sent to counter it. "Carrier planes," he stated flatly. "Here, in the Caribbean. It must be their '*Maaka-Kakja*,' already repaired. Survivors from the dragon raid said she was least damaged."

"What if they sent another one?" Ciano asked.

Gravois shook his head dismissively. "They couldn't have. We know for a fact the war against the Grik still rages in Africa, and victory there has always been their primary focus. I'm surprised enough that Captain Reddy would abandon that other front. No choice, I suppose, with us here, but just as well in the end." He stood, beginning to smolder. "But as instructed, I've waited and waited for all our forces to arrive before doing more than interdicting NUS supply ships down to El Palo. I've waited long enough! Our force is already irresistible, and frankly, we can afford to lose a ship or two, if required."

"Perhaps," Ciano granted, "but our fuel reserves still limit our movements. Those fat battleships are far too thirsty. It would've been better if they sent only cruisers and destroyers. They could easily deal with anything we'll ever face here."

Gravois touched his right index finger to his chin, visibly calming himself. From a practical standpoint, Ciano was right, but he'd *asked* for the battleships. His expressed purpose was to overawe the League's adversaries (and allies), but his primary, secret objective was to take them from the Triumvirate for himself. "I've proceeded with utmost caution to this point," he said, glancing at Ciano, "in *all* our endeavors. More fuel and forces are on their way but we must move boldly and decisively now. If Captain Reddy *is* here with his modern ships and a carrier, *he* will certainly do so. As I've said many times, we mustn't underestimate him. He's an amateur, but a gifted and aggressive one." He paused and looked at Ciano. "Aggressive to a fault—like you, my friend. Tell me, what would you do in his place?"

Ciano shrugged off the comparison but stepped to the chart pinned to a panel on the wall. "He must first secure a base of operations, as we have done, while at the same time protecting his carrier. Galveston or Mobile on the North American continent would serve well enough, but he *is* aggressive and they're too far for his planes to fly. Santiago, Cuba, is the only place near enough to suit him, I think, with a good anchorage and fueling facilities. He'll use that as a base from which to harass us with his destroyers," he pronounced with growing confidence, "and put many of his planes ashore before sending his carrier out of our reach in the Gulf."

Gravois was nodding. "I believe that's *precisely* what he'll do, and that makes our course plain. We must prepare to sortie the fleet and every bomber with sufficient range to utterly pulverize Santiago. It'll take some days to prepare, but that's to the good. It'll give Captain Reddy time to begin unloading his planes and commence necessary maintenance on his ships, but not enough time to use them, or prepare any surprises for us. Perhaps we'll even catch Captain Reddy and his precious *Walker* tied to a pier, and blast them to oblivion." He chuckled. "Whether we're that lucky or not, the devastation we unleash will give the NUS pause to wonder if they should oppose us further."

Gravois sat back in his chair. "Summon the Heron to take me to Martinique. . . ." He paused, grimacing. "I suppose not. And I dislike flying in those smaller scout planes. You'll take me to Martinique in *Leopardo*," he decided.

"Of course," Ciano said, glad as always to move his ship away from Puerto del Cielo. "But speaking of the other scouts, I think you should confront Don Hernan and insist he allow at least some to be deployed on his coast. They can do nothing bottled up at Martinique. They haven't the range. And the probable loss of the Heron is like losing one of our eyes."

Gravois was shaking his head. "I'll speak to Don Hernan, and stress the critical nature of the situation." He smiled wryly. "He's increasingly concerned with the progress of the enemy armies in the vicinity of New Granada, and has gotten *much* better about coming out when we signal him." He turned almost giddy. "I wonder what 'His Holiness' would think if he knew I couldn't possibly care less about the fate of his filthy capital. Not even whether it stands or falls. The armies there will slaughter one another and it'll make no difference in the end. All is starting to fall into place for us, Capitano Ciano! We have our fleet and the blessing of the Triumvirate to dominate the Caribbean. Now, Captain Reddy has offered himself up for destruction. Once that's complete and the Pass of Fire is retaken—by us—we can dictate terms to the NUS and turn the Dominion to our will with or without Don Hernan. We'll be *awash* in fuel, slaves, raw materials . . . all the things so precious in the Mediterranean, and we'll *own* this hemisphere, secure against any threat. Even from the Triumvirate," he added lower, his voice bitter.

Ciano smiled. For the first time it seemed Gravois's grand scheme really couldn't fail and he cast all but practical, everyday reservations aside. "You amaze me, sir," he said truthfully. "But do you think it wise to leave *Ramb V* and the Churrucca alone here with the oiler? And what about the planes?"

"The Churrucca will accompany us to Martinique for repairs." She'd been mobbed by floatplanes when they shelled Monsu, and taken some surprisingly serious bomb damage. "The other ships can take care of themselves. *Ramb V* alone is nearly as heavily armed as the enemy light cruiser—that probably never made it here. Perhaps I'll send them upriver?" he mused. "Don Hernan has hinted he'd like to return to New Granada, which means he's desperate to do so. I'm sure he'd enjoy the accommodations aboard *Ramb V*—and I might use that to gain some leverage to make him relax his tedious proscriptions against our people on his soil." He shook his head. "But I don't intend to strip the cruisers and battleships of their scouts just yet. They might need them when they sortie."

CHAPTER 28

////// Upper Galk River
Grik Africa
July 28, 1945

Colonel Enaak sopped foamy sweat from the top of his furry head with a ragged, dingy brown bandanna, once a bright yellow. The high-elevation afternoon sun dried the lather almost at once, turning the fur stiff and bristly. Tucking the cloth in the pistol-cutlass belt around his middle, he plopped the hot helmet back on his head and took a quick sip from his canteen. Still lukewarm from the morning's boiling pot, the water wasn't very refreshing. And the sweet-sharp bite of seep was as acutely absent as a cherished friend.

The purplish, rather pear-shaped polta fruit provided essential nutrients when eaten or its juice consumed. Aged and mysteriously (to Enaak) prepared polta paste eased pain and prevented infection when applied to wounds. Just as important to many, the juice was rendered into various . . . recreational libations, the strongest and most popular being seep, and the army and navy could hardly function without it. Not for its intoxicating effects—use for that purpose in the field or at sea was strictly forbidden—but mixing roughly one part in ten was usually sufficient to kill the harmful bugs lurking in streams of foreign lands where they filled their canteens and water butts. Other than the obvious ones they filtered out, along with sticks and other debris, Enaak couldn't *see* the bugs—Svec called them "germs"—and assumed they were invisibly tiny infant versions of the ones he could. Every type looked perfectly capable of eating somebody from the inside out and giving them a terminal case of the runs. So "seeping" water was a regulation practice unless, like Enaak's and Svec's, one's forces had outrun supply and all the seep was gone. In those situations, the manual—*Flynn's Tactics*—prescribed boiling all drinking water.

"Let's go," he called behind, briskly whipping Aasi's reins. The naturally armored case covering a me-naak's spine, head, and vitals was insensible to a rider's legs and even spurs were useless, so rein movements and tension, both visual and felt—particularly when communicated to a spiky rowel on the bridle under the more sensitive lower jaw—were the primary means of control. Exceedingly well-trained and long-service me-naaks, like Aasi and the rest in Enaak's 5th Maa-ni-la Cavalry, were sufficiently attuned to their riders by now that some thought they read their minds. They certainly understood various voice commands, unless drowned in the roar of battle. That didn't mean they always *obeyed*. They were apparently fearless and never shirked a fight, but might refuse paths with unsure footing likely to cause a fall that would injure them and kill their rider. *In thaat respect, they're prob-aably smarter thaan we are,* Enaak suspected. Aasi accelerated into a smooth-gaited gallop, up a low rise on the spur of a near naked mountain. The second of four battalions—the 5th Maa-ni-la was over strength—flooded up the grassy, stump-dotted rise behind him in a long column of fours, the clatter of their carbines and harness sounding very loud in the still air and sprawl of mountain roots.

Nearing the crest, Enaak pulled up, joined by Major Nika-Paafo. Nika was young and relatively inexperienced, coming to the 5th only after it shadowed Halik all the way across Indiaa and Persia. He'd matured a lot in the saddle, over Arabia and a good chunk of Africa, and finally earned his place as commander of the 2nd of the 5th and Enaak's XO. The standard bearer drew to a stop beside them, the shot-torn black and gold swallowtail fluttering high. "Lower thaat," Enaak cautioned, as the rest of the battalion flowed into double lines to either side. It was a fluid, effortless maneuver, honed by countless repetitions before fights and skirmishes too numerous to count, across a distance Enaak could hardly imagine. "Scouts ahead," Enaak called. Three troopers loped forward another sixty yards before dismounting. One 'Cat held the animals and two crept to the peak of the ridge.

Nika mopped his sweat-thickened fur as well, and sighed. "I thought it was supposed to be *cold* in the mountains," he mock complained. "Pilots always say the higher you fly, the colder it gets."

"We're not high enough, appaarently," Enaak said. "And I don't think it would make much difference here. They also say we're right on the middle of the world, where the sun comes closest when it paasses overhead. The 'ee-kwaay-taar,' they caall it." He paused and blinked confusion. "Or it's where the world spins closest to the sun. . . ." He shrugged. "I forget, and I'm no Sky Priest to understaand such things, or really much care. Either way, it seems only naturaal thaat the higher you go, the *hotter* it will get."

Nika said nothing and Enaak suspected he knew the answer, but didn't want to embarrass him. He'd had more contact with Impie scholars, not to mention "old" destroyermen he'd taught with at the Maa-ni-la Advanced Training Center while recovering from a wound received during the New Ireland campaign, his only great action. But while Nika had been essentially repeating to recruits what he'd learned from *his* inexperienced instructors, Enaak had amassed a vast trove of practical battle wisdom. Probably the most important thing Nika had learned since joining the 5th was to shut up and listen when Enaak and Colonel Svec talked.

Now they watched the two troopers ahead go to their bellies, tails consciously lowered, and peer beyond the ridge. One glassed what he saw with an Impie telescope, dark with tarnish, while shielding the lens from the sun. The other scratched notes on a scrap of wood with a charred stick. Finally, they slithered backward and jogged to their animals, then galloped the short distance to Enaak and Nika.

"Whaat did you see?" Enaak asked.

"Griks, sur, lots of 'em," the trooper with the glass told him, but he was blinking uncertainly. "No works, no formation. They just . . . down there, in a mob."

Blinking surprise, Enaak urged Aasi forward, followed by Nika. Together, they reenacted the movements of the troopers until they too gazed down the slope. The north end of Lake Galk spread before them in a great ragged V, from where the river emerged from a gorge to the west. The bright sun made the water hard to look at, and flanking mountains were blurred and purpled behind rising haze. Looking closer they could see there *were* a lot of Grik, among maybe thirty haphazardly placed banners. They'd been told each vaguely Japanese-looking flag represented the Grik equivalent to a company, roughly two or three hundred warriors, but there wasn't anything like the nine thousand Grik the banners indicated. Maybe five? Both Lemurians extended their telescopes, covering them as the others had.

Enaak focused. Like the trooper said, the Grik weren't doing much. They weren't stacking breastworks or digging, or acting like they had the slightest care. There *were* a lot of smoky fires under the ubiquitous copper cauldrons all Grik armies carried. Nika gasped.

"What?" Enaak asked.

"*There* sir, near the middle. Look at all the *bones*!" Enaak did. The pile of bones with the meat boiled off was huge and bright, easily mistaken for a heap of stony mountain rubble like they often saw—if it weren't for all the Grik gathered around, cracking bones for the marrow. "It . . . looks like they fought a baattle and they're eating all the slain!" Nika continued. "*We* didn't haave anyone . . . ?"

"No," Enaak replied with certainty. No one was out beyond the 2nd of the 5th.

"Not even Col-nol Svec?" Nika pressed, though he knew the Czech Legion had been detailed to lead a brigade of Halik's troops across the river. They'd find a good place for the brigade to set up a blocking force and leave a couple of companies themselves, before rejoining the rest of the army's push down the east side of the lake—where most of the Grik were supposed to be.

"No," Enaak said again, tail twitching behind him like lice were crawling on it. "Those're Grik eating Grik. Eating their *own*, on a fairly laarge scale." He rolled over on his back and started to slide away.

"But . . . they alwaays do thaat, don't they?" Nika asked, emulating his superior. "Even Haalik's army eats its dead," he added with disgust.

"True, though not as much anymore. I don't know if thaat's because they're changing, or just well fed." He tilted his helmet back at what they'd seen before standing up in front of Aasi. "Those Grik are 'New Aarmy' soldiers. You saaw their flaags. Respect-aable opponents if properly led, and better aarmed thaan Haalik. But you saaw their numbers and disaarray. I think they *did* fight a baattle—among themselves for *food*. They must be very hungry indeed." Looking down the mountain spur they'd ascended, into the wooded valley below, they saw the leading columns of Halik's army snaking through more great boulders bordering a minor stream that fed the Galk. From this distance, they looked like ants streaming to a meal of their own. "And if they know we're coming, they don't much care." That seemed inconceivable. They'd met a lot of refugees, for a while. Halik let some pass, enlisted others, and probably ate a few, but surely they'd been observed as well, and reports sent back? Enaak snorted when the truth came to him. "I saw no discipline among those Grik, so they prob-aably ate their officers. We might really be unexpected." He jumped on his me-naak, grabbing the reins. "I think we should report to Gener-aal Haalik, and Gener-aal Aalden as well; Esshk's army is staarving, and I think it's time to finish him."

Nika was confused. "Well . . . if thaat's the case, maybe we should hold off. Let them *all* staarve."

Enaak shook his head. "Won't work. You don't think *Esshk* will staarve, do you? We wait too long, he'll slip awaay again and thaat caan't haappen. As long as he's alive, he's a threat. But as long as he's got an aarmy"—he flicked his tail and grinned, exposing sharp white teeth—"he caan be surrounded."

CHAPTER 29

OPERATION NOOSE

////// Galk River
Grik Africa
July 30, 1945

The conference room aboard USS *Liberator*, an armored Grik battleship captured on Lake Nalak, was right behind the pilothouse—and had probably been a meeting area for those who built her as well. Still, like all things Grik, the space was gloomy and tight, with insufficient lighting provided by smelly fish oil lamps. Side bulkheads were part of the armored casemate, sloping and narrowing toward the low overhead, and heavy skull-cracking beams supported a final deck above that would've mounted dozens of big antiair mortars. *Liberator* had never quite been finished, her cannon never mounted, and she still carried no armament—other than most of First Corps, which crammed the cavernous interior to overflowing. The rest, along with a division of General Kim's IV Corps reserve, was embarked aboard another former Grik BB named USS *Raanaisi* (basically "Protector," in Lemurian). Little more than Colonel Will's Consolidated Division of Maroons and Shee-ree and Ker-noll Shelg's 2nd Slasher Brigade remained to guard their rear, Sofesshk, and the Celestial Mother.

There were no chairs or cushions for the corps, division, and brigade commanders gathered in the space, only a long map table, and First General Pete Alden had no intention of letting things run long enough for anyone to need to sit. For one thing, even though it was evening and an uncovered grating and mushroom vent provided modest ventilation, it was hot as hell. The smell of sweaty 'Cats, humans, a few Khonashi and Grik, even the leather they wore, preserved by various—some quite disgusting—techniques, was almost unbearable. Besides, the time for rest was over.

"I'll keep this short," Pete said loudly, silencing the muffled roar of conversations, and everyone focused their attention on the aft end of the table. Second General Marcus Kim was on Pete's right. Even glowering down at the map, eyes slitted, he exuded an air of excited intensity. Choon was close to him, somehow seeming fresh and cheerful in a red waistcoat and kilt, and fluffy white cravat. His only concession to comfort was that he'd removed his jacket to reveal black-and-white-striped shirtsleeves. There weren't many other senior Repubs, since almost all were in the field. On Pete's left stood Seventh General Taa-leen of the 1st (Galla) Division; Ninth General Minja-Kakja, cousin to Saan-Kakja, and commanding 2nd Division; and Colonel Saachic of the 1st Cavalry Brigade. Most of his troopers were up north, screening Rolak, and he'd be glad to get back with them.

Crowding around the far end of the table on the other side of I Corps brigade commanders were those responsible for naval and air elements of the operation. Captain Quinebe of RRPS *Servius* represented the Repub monitors, the most powerful ships they had. Captain Mescus-Ricum commanded the up-armored and rearmed old DDs USS *Bowles*, *Saak-Fas*, *Clark*, *Kas-Ra-Ar*, and *Ramic-Sa-Ar* of Des-Ron 10. MTB-Ron-1 was under Lieutenant (jg) Arai-Faar-Ar, probably the lowest-ranking officer present. Her mission would be to scout ahead for obstacles, even mines, the Grik might've placed. Finally there was Mark Leedom, who'd just arrived at this forward staging point about halfway to their objective in a Nancy he flew up from Saansa Field.

"This operation, 'Operation Noose,' is gonna be as simple as it gets," Pete said, then added wryly, "which I'm sure will come as a relief to many. Just remember, though, sometimes the simpler things seem, the more damn near impossible they turn out to be." He slapped the '03 Springfield he always carried slung, even here. "This is pretty complicated compared to the Allin-Silvas half our troops carry, but the magazine spring breaks, you can still shoot it single shot. Mainspring snaps on an Allin-Silva, you got nothin' but a club."

"And a daamn fine spear with the baayo-net fixed—as you well know, Gener-aal," Taa-leen reminded, bright canines bared.

"Well, yeah, smart-ass," Pete growled, "and everybody's got pretty good at stayin' on the crapper in a heavy sea or they wouldn't be here now."

"Keeping their heads when all about them are losing theirs," Kim paraphrased and Pete looked at him, wondering where he got that. *Probably from captured Brit sailors that came over in SMS* Amerika, he supposed. Though he didn't sound it and rarely showed it, Pete had been a reader as a kid. Unfortunately, he'd let it slide. Then, when he'd been in USS *Houston*'s Marine detachment, his CO loaned him some Kipling while he was sitting in the brig, saying "read this through and I won't take your stripes. If it sticks, I won't ever have to." He'd been right. Pete felt a twinge, remembering that officer was now most likely on the bottom of the Sunda Strait—on another world.

He cleared his throat. "Right. Just don't forget that 'simple' don't always mean 'easy.'" He picked up an iron Grik ramrod and smacked the map east of the Galk River just short of where the locks were depicted. Those and their environs had finally been photographed from the air and the painted map was particularly detailed in that area. "We've pushed the Grik all the way back to here." He whacked the map again, then moved the rammer northeast. "General Rolak and Third, Sixth, and Twelfth Corps are here, spread out to here"—he glanced at Kim—"along with Legate Bekiaa's Fifth Repub Division, of course. Most of the Grik our air has seen are bunched up in front of 'em, well protected in some damn rough terrain." He nodded at Leedom. "Our air's been giving 'em hell, now that Saansa Field is up. Sunk everything they could find on the lake too, but we all know that don't mean shit. It's a big lake, with a rough shoreline. Lots of hiding places." He slapped the map, close to the locks. "But this looks like the toughest nut, and they're dug in tighter than ticks."

"And bombing can only do so much, I assume?" Kim asked.

"Right. The screwiest problem is where they're most heavily concentrated: right on top of the locks. On both sides, actually. They know we can't get up on the lake with our monitors and transports without the locks, and they've pulled out all the stops to hold 'em. Worse, they've *opened* all the lower gates so not only can't we use 'em as we take 'em, only the last big innermost gate is holding that whole giant-ass lake in by itself." He shook his head. "The strain must be incredible. Whoever built those things back at the beginning of time really knew what they were doing. Anyway, you can see the problem. We can't risk bombing too close to that damn gate. Hell, I'm scared to even shoot *artillery* around it. We shake anything loose, the gate busts, and we lose everything on the river—including us—all the way down to the Zambezi. Hell, maybe to the sea. Sofesshk, Saansa Field . . . nearly the whole population of 'allied' Grik, loyal to the CM, is back in drowning distance of the river. Prob'ly a couple million of 'em."

"Not to mention the CM herself," Inquisitor Choon pointed out.

"Not to mention," Taa-leen murmured, leaning closer to the map.

"Point is, Rolak's gotta take those heights the old-fashioned way. I was exaggerating a little about artillery and air support, at least until he gets close to the *last* gate, but moving guns up there in the teeth of *Grik* gun emplacements is gonna be a nightmare. I don't know if Rolak has the weight for it, even with three whole corps." He shrugged. "That's why we're taking him another one."

"What about the Grik on the west side of the locks?" General Minja asked.

Pete nodded. "That's our first ace in the hole. As far as we know, the lizards think all we've got on that side of the river is the Repub Fifth Corps, under General Tiaan-Kir, and he can't punch through by himself. But they're still expecting General Ign to join them." He smiled grimly. "He will. Or rather, First Ker-noll Jash will, with the Army of the Mother. Fifth Corps will come in behind him."

"It . . . might work," the Repub brigadier said, scratching her furry ear, blinking yellow eyes. "If this . . . 'Jash' can be trusted."

"He can," Inquisitor Choon assured, "especially with the stakes downriver to consider. That brings us to our final 'ace,' does it not, First General Alden?"

Pete nodded. "Yeah. Halik." He looked around. "It looks like the back door's wide open for him, and that's why we're all moving now. The Grik on the north end of Lake Galk are starving. Maybe they all are." He snorted. "If it seems those in front of us have plenty of fight in 'em, it might be because we've been killing enough to keep 'em fed. The ones up north are killing *each other* to eat." He rubbed the dark beard on his chin. "I sent Halik the 'go' order an hour ago, and he'll be starting his show any minute. So will Rolak. Hopefully by tomorrow morning when we steam upriver, Rolak'll have the heights leading to the locks and Halik'll be galloping up Esshk's skirt with a hot poker in his hand. No way to know how far he'll get before somebody stands up against him, but I don't think it'll make much difference." He sighed at the skeptical faces and doubtful Lemurian blinking. "Look," he said, "I know this lizard pretty well. Fought him once, long and hard." He shrugged. "Sometimes it seems, you butt heads with somebody long enough, you get to know 'em better than yourself. Anyway, it's hard to explain why, but I trust him. More important, he knows we beat him, the CM's on our side, and we *will* beat Esshk—eventually—with or without him. If he wants to keep what he's got, save what he's made of his army . . . and just rear up on his hind legs and look us in the eye someday—that's damned important to him—he's *got* to do this, and do it with style. Same as Jash. If I'm wrong and they screw us, actually *turn* on us—" A lopsided grin appeared in his beard. "Then I guess we're screwed. But I ain't wrong."

CHAPTER 30

THE BATTLE OF LAKE GALK

////// North shore of Lake Galk
Grik Africa

General Yikkit had been granted the privilege of leading the first assault on Esshk's final stronghold around Lake Galk. Standing in a neekis-drawn chariot in the gathering gloom on the flat alongside the valley stream, he watched the setting sun pour its dying light on the mountain above the spur Enaak explored. Enaak was up there now, in fact, with Halik himself, and would signal the advance of Yikkit's twenty thousand warriors with two batteries of the little mountain howitzers, positioned on the near slope of the ridge. Just as the line of creeping darkness passed over the stubby guns, piercing whistles trilled and all twelve weapons vomited bright balls of fire into the twilight. Yikkit could actually see the exploding case shot arc over the spur in their high trajectories, flame-jetting fuses spinning or tumbling as they vanished from view. About the time they would've exploded but before he actually heard them, Yikkit pointed at the signalers and they pumped the bellows of the battle horns. The sound started with a wispy *brap*, but quickly rose to a rumbling roar echoing in the valley.

The first line of ten thousand warriors, half a mile wide and four ranks deep, burst forward at a ground-eating trot. The line bowed back on the left as those troops came to the base of the spur and had to break into a run to keep their alignment but they managed it magnificently. Yikkit growled with predatory satisfaction and pointed at another crew of signalers, who joined the roar of the first horn with a slightly different note. The next four-deep line advanced, and Yikkit whipped his neekis forward to follow the first.

* * *

"A slaughter," Halik murmured, his tone a mixture of satisfaction and disappointment. He stood in his own chariot with an aide as they watched Yikkit's first line smash into the disorganized camp below, trying to steady the scene in the Impie telescope Enaak handed him. The constant uncomfortable shifting of his own neekis, acutely aware of the hungry, speculative scrutiny of Enaak's cavalry mounts, made that difficult. Still, it was obvious that without defenses of any kind, the brief shelling had decimated the enemy and induced an initial panic. The survivors rapidly formed a ragged, bayonet-bristling firing line, even managing a volley sufficient to stagger Yikkit's center for a moment. There was no second volley as the tide of Halik's army swept upon them, only a rising roar of independent fire that quickly dwindled. A few Grik, probably less than a thousand, broke for the rear, but they'd been waiting for that. Dalibor Svec and his Brotherhood of Volunteers had worked their way around the mountain to the east and positioned themselves in a scrubby creek bed. Now they thundered down on the fleeing Grik, their big kravaas bashing through the mass, goring and trampling, troopers firing carbines and pistols or laying about them with cutlasses.

Enaak slapped the telescope shut when Halik handed it back. "A slaaughter indeed. I'll be surprised if a single survivor makes it paast Svec. You complain?"

"No," Halik denied. "I'm proud of my army, proud of Yikkit, but I suppose . . ." He snorted. "General Alden beat me in India, yet Esshk has given him considerably more trouble. Perhaps I just expected more of these other New Army troops Esshk made."

Enaak blinked amused irony. High on the spur, there was still sufficient light for Halik to see. "You wanted a tougher opponent? Don't worry. We haave a long waay to go and I'm sure you'll get one." He pointed below. "You *will* note thaat, probably even without officers, they were well enough trained to pull themselves together, however briefly, and relatively few aactually fled? And thaat waas prob-aably just Esshk's version of a picket to waarn of our approach. Now, with luck, we'll caatch his *next* line equally unprepared. Sooner or later, though, you'll meet troops thaat're ready for you. Svec and I caan't stop all the runners. When thaat haappens, you'll prob-aably haave the fight of your life—and better appreciate whaat Generaal Aalden's been up against."

"Limber up the guns and let's go," he called aside. "Time to push paast Svec and stick *our* necks out!" he added cheerfully. The 2nd of the 5th had followed Svec around the mountain, broken into scouting companies, then pressed on. They'd stay high, for the most part, where Grik didn't like to go—and wouldn't be expecting an advance at any rate. Barring a report from Nika, Enaak would take the 1st of the 5th across the flat to contact. Svec's Legion would finish up below, then reform into a heavy flanking force. "So long, Gener-aal Haalik!" Enaak said, whipping his reins. The me-naak under him trotted forward and two double lines of troopers flowed into column behind him. "Don't daawdle, if you please," he called back over his shoulder.

Halik harrumphed, then turned to a me-naak-mounted 'Cat. Enaak had left him a company of the 5th to act as runners, and another company to operate (and protect) the main comm-cart. The smaller sets on pack me-naaks had limited range in the mountain-bound bowl of Lake Galk. "My regards to General Niwa," Halik told the 'Cat, "and the grand battery will advance." That was essentially Yikkit's artillery, backed by ten thousand of Halik's longest-serving (and oldest) Grik. Yikkit was supposed to move as fast as he could and stay as close behind Enaak as possible. When he ran into something he couldn't run over, his artillery and heavy reinforcements would be close, able to deploy at a decisive point. At least that was the idea. "General Niwa will follow, with General Ugla close behind." Niwa and Ugla each had thirty thousand troops and a third of their artillery.

The 'Cat sketched an ironic salute and dashed down the slope, his me-naak throwing gravel at Halik's command staff with its feet. Halik looked below. It was getting very dark down there and all he could see of Yikkit's force was a dark line moving south across a desolate plain between the mountains and the water. Closer, Enaak's column was already skirting the demolished camp. A few scattered fires still flickered there, but otherwise it looked like little more than a lumpy stain in the gloom. Halik gestured to another 'Cat. "Hurry to your radio cart. Have its operators inform General Alden we've engaged the enemy and are pressing south, as pledged. Operation Noose has commenced."

CHAPTER 31

///// ***Southeast of Lake Galk***
Grik Africa

More than two hundred cannon flared half a mile behind them in the night, spurting sparkling spears of flame, quickly dimmed by enveloping smoke. The gunline of 12 pdr smoothbores at the edge of the forest bordering the base of the escarpment was a mile long here and the blasting thunder and ripping-sheet shriek of projectiles reached them roughly two and a half seconds after the first bright flash, pounding and echoing off the cliffs as the first case shot began crackling over Grik positions above. A blizzard of hot iron casing fragments and balls sleeted down on the defenders. The Grik had already been firing on the gun line they saw begin assembling before dark, especially after it loosed a few ranging shots of its own, at roughly equal intervals, but as the light faded and their aim points vanished, Grik fire became desultory. Now, almost immediately, Grik cannon opened back up, pouring shells and solid shot back at their counterparts. *More* cannon responded from the Allied line, spitting brighter, sharper tongues of flame. These were Repub "Derby" guns, 75mm rifled breechloaders that could slam out three times as many shells a minute, faster than even the veteran Allied "Napoleon" gunners, and hit exactly what they were aiming for at this range. Though at near maximum elevation to reach this height, they fired at the muzzle flashes of Grik guns, wrecking them with direct hits or shredding their crews with shrapnel.

Enemy cannon didn't much concern Legate Colonel Bekiaa-Sab-At at present, though it certainly had throughout the long, bloody slog upriver. Right now, her 5th Repub Division and most of Rolak's III Corps were all "under" the guns: too close and too low for them to bear. The Grik had never developed hand grenades, or if they had, they'd never made enough to field, and the closest thing they had was lit case shot, dropped from above. This was a menace, and quite a few 'Cats and men were wounded by flying iron, but the bulk of the infantry remained just outside the lethal blast radius. Well-concealed Grik infantry was doing more harm, blindly firing muskets down at them as the assault force prepared itself. Bekiaa swore as one of her runners shrieked and fell beside her. Even before she could call for a Repub *medicus*, the man went silent and still. "We need some daamn air support," she fumed.

"They can't do it. Not in the dark," Bekiaa's aide, "Optio" Jack Meek, reminded reasonably. The son of Doocy Meek, Jack was more than just an optio and he'd become Bekiaa's most devoted and trusted assistant. "We're too close," he continued. "Like as not hit us." He nodded forward and up. "They're dumpin' plenty of incendiaries farther back, though, burnin' Grik that're tryin' ta move up from behind." He grinned and waved behind at the rapid-fire cannonade. "An' our guns're doin' well enough, Legate." It was true. As much as Grik artillery had improved in this war, their crews had only begun to gain a proficiency Allied gunners had two years ago—and had steadily improved upon. Even at this range, their direct fire was good enough to shoot over their heads—usually—and push the Grik down or blast them apart. The effect was already apparent and the musket fire was dwindling.

Meek watched the exploding shells rippling and flaring redly on the heights with a critical eye. "Even with their old smoothbores, Union gunners're daamn good. P'raps they tend ta shoot a bit long. . . ." He chuckled. "But with our precious bodies in front of 'em, I reckon that's better'n short! But how 'bout them Derby guns!" he added proudly. Sometimes called "sniper caannon" by their envious allies, the Repub 75s were rapidly suppressing Grik counter–battery fire.

"They're swell," Bekiaa conceded, "but still too slow. Time for us to get in on the aact. Staand by, Mortaars," her voice trilled loudly, carrying farther than one might expect in the overwhelming din. Bugles and whistles took up her command, radiating outward. Mortar men and 'Cats poised finned bombs over pre-registered tubes. "Commence firing!"

The unmistakable *tunk! T-tu-tu-tun-tuuunk!* of mortar bombs rising from hundreds of smoky tubes quickly sounded, and Bekiaa knew others would be doing the same out of sight and hearing for *miles* to the right. Just as other gun lines, equally long, were punishing more Grik in front of additional attackers. The cloudy night sky to the east-northeast was glowing and flashing continuously, like some great, terrible storm on the horizon.

This was the heaviest bombardment of the war to date, incorporating every field piece in the combined Allied armies on the continent. Over eight hundred guns were firing as fast as their crews could serve them and there'd probably never been so much metal in the air on this world at one time. The earthshaking noise of it all was overwhelming, and soon would come the largest coordinated advance against a single objective. Three entire corps, each composed of between twenty-five and thirty-five thousand troops, would make the initial assault, followed by half the Repub IV Corps and eventually I Corps and the rest of IV Corps when they arrived. They were the only *real* reserve they had, since the overall strategy was simplicity itself: overwhelm the enemy with fire, fury, determination, and—if Enaak was right—superior numbers. There was no fallback, no "plan B." They'd carry the heights and secure the locks and win the war . . . or be repulsed. If that occurred, all they could do was assume the defensive and think of something else.

The boulder-strewn base of the cliff was about two hundred yards ahead, and the jagged crest a hundred and sixty to two hundred feet above was backlit by constant flashing, smoky strobes of light as mortar bombs burst. Slides of gravel and stone, mingled with the wet thud of Grik bodies blown from their defenses were already falling in front of them, and this deluge of rock and flesh only intensified. Able to fire and adjust the mortars themselves, Bekiaa's infantry could drop them much closer. An entire gun tube slammed into the rocky ground with a loud iron *crack*, splitting when it hit.

Then again, Bekiaa mused, *Gener-aal Aalden doesn't think he'll* haave *to think of something else. At least he hedged one bet.* She tilted her helmet forward to ward off settling dust and gravel. This far back, she shouldn't be hit by anything large, or any parts of Grik. *Despite his trust in Haalik and Jaash, we'll be facing the first when he meets us. If he double-crosses us, he caan't threaten our flaanks with the mountains on one side and lake on the other. As for Jaash, he might eat the Repub Fifth Corps, but he caan't get at us across the lake or river.* She had no inclination to trust *any* Grik and wondered how General Alden could. *'Course, he'd know a lot of folks feel like I do,* she realized. *Prob'ly rigged it so none of our tails'll be flaappin' in the breeze exaactly so we* won't *worry about 'allied' Grik when we already got the rest to think about.*

She hauled her Impie watch out of a belt pouch and studied the hands, well lit by flashing shell bursts. *Four minutes,* she told herself.

"Good evening, Legate Bekiaa," came a cheerfully urbane voice beside her.

"General Rolak!" she exclaimed with surprise. Her corps commander, indeed the commander of all three corps about to storm the cliffs, was surrounded by aides and runners as well as his personal guard platoon of the 1st Marines, members of the famed "Triple I." Rolak wore the same battle dress they did and carried an Allin-Silva rifle slung over his shoulder. "Whaat're you doin' here?"

Rolak blinked amusement. "I'm in chaarge. I caan do whaat I waant." He chuckled at her disapproval. "In truth, as you know, no one will be in 'over-aall commaand' very soon, yet everyone, down to our most recently arrived replacements, knows exaactly whaat to do. Those new arrivaals maay not yet know *how* to do whaat we expect of them, but thaat's whaat NCOs are for. My point is, there's no subtlety here, no . . . aart, and now it's been set in motion, none of us caan materially affect the outcome of this baattle except by fighting as haard as we caan. I mean no disrespect to Gener-aal Aalden with the 'aart' craack," he hastened to add. "His plaan is raather beautiful in its simplicity and I applaud him for it. *He* might affect the outcome, depending on where he puts First Corps, but this will be a Grik hunt for the rest of us."

He drew himself up and for the first time in quite a while Bekiaa remembered the old Lemurian general was taller than she was. "We haave excellent communications and if all goes well, the Aarmy HQ will quickly be hopelessly distaant from any direct observations I might make in any case." He looked around at the Repub troops nearby, their flash-lit human expressions and Lemurian blinking showing astonishment at his presence. "I've fought alongside you, Legate Bekiaa, but never with Republic forces. It's high time I did." He gestured at the cliffs. "Paarticularly since you're the aarmy's left on this side of the river, and will likely face the stiffest opposition."

"But . . . Gener-aal Rolak! If you faall . . ."

"I'll be ably replaced by Gener-aal Faan." Rolak blinked enjoyment at Bekiaa's discomfiture. "I'll never be a *modern* gener-aal," he told her, lower. "I could never abide all thaat ridiculous bookkeeping, the little details." He blinked amazement. "Gener-aal Faan thrives on thaat! No, I'm just an old waarrior, ready for my laast baattle." He paused, taking in the maelstrom of fire they were about to enter. "I used to love to fight, you know," he murmured conversationally, barely audible, "but I've never much enjoyed this waar. It was faar too serious for my taste." He looked intently at her. "I fully intend to enjoy *this* baattle, however, and I won't be denied." His eyes narrowed and his tail whipped dismissively as he raised his voice to carry. "And as Gener-aal Aalden personaally led the aarmy out of its defenses at Tassanna's Perimeter, *I* will lead this attaack. With you and your division, Legate."

Bekiaa barely heard him add "It's my turn" over the sudden spreading cheers that rivaled the bombardment. Of course, there was a reason why she heard him at all. She glanced back at her watch. The cannonade was beginning to lift, and it was time. "Graapnels," she roared. More mortars sounded, reports oddly heavier as they lofted hundreds of four-prong hooks up the cliff, lines uncoiling like mad jumping spiders spraying strands of silk.

"Up and at them!" bellowed Prefect Bele, an amazingly tall, black-skinned Repub and Bekiaa's XO. Hundreds of Repubs, human and Lemurian, surged forward to grasp the dangling lines and start racing up. There was no return fire from the shell-shocked Grik—not yet—but it would come.

"Very well, Gener-aal Rolak," Bekiaa growled, then glared harshly at his Marines. Many probably knew her from old. "But *you* better keep him safe," she told them. "My people will be too busy." She looked back at Rolak. "And though you *are* my gener-aal, you'll obey me in any close fighting!"

Rolak smiled. "Of course!"

"Optio Meek!" she called loudly.

"Aye, Legate."

"You bear witness?"

"Heard it all an' wrote it down. Even signed it meself," he chuckled, holding up a notepad. "He'll not get *our* arses on the block for his foolishness."

The grapnel lines were black with figures now, and muskets were starting to thump down at them. Marksmen had been detailed to shoot at the flashes above but there'd soon be too many if they didn't get a foothold. Even as they watched, a line must've been severed and men and 'Cats fell screaming like beads off a broken necklace. Those lowest to the ground might've been fine if half a dozen more hadn't landed on them. "Stretcher-bearers!" came the cry. Bekiaa looked up. With the big guns and mortars quiet, the only illumination came from fires they'd started and the increasing rifle and musket fire. She realized then that there *were* rifles at the top, which meant some of her own must've made it already.

"No time like the present," Rolak challenged.

Bekiaa nodded. "I'm going up, Prefect Bele," she shouted over the firing. "I'll signaal when the lodgment's secure. Only then will you allow Generaal Rolak to ascend. You'll staay with the reserve until I send for you, and keep pushing up supplies. Hopefully there're already other lodgments along the line, but Grik'll focus wherever they are and counterattaack. I'll waant maachine guns first, to keep them off us, then mortars to push 'em back."

CHAPTER 32

/////// ***West shore of Lake Galk***
Grik Africa

General of the Sky Mitsuo Ando and his skeletal pilots were checking their planes one final time. They hadn't flown in months, and the worst abuse for complicated machines is disuse. Their inspections were awkward because the only light came from torches held by sullen Grik. This was disconcerting for a variety of reasons. First, the proximity of open flames to their fueling operation was enough to give them all the creeps. Second, they'd watched as Allied aircraft methodically destroyed nearly everything left on the water over the last few days, with virtually no resistance from antiair rockets. Ando didn't get that. There'd been a *lot* of the things hereabouts. Granted, they'd stopped production when he began the *yanone* project—they could only make so much gunpowder for the fuel—but there should still be plenty to make it rough for Allied planes. In any event, the land around Lake Galk was darker than he'd ever seen it, utterly blacked out, and other than a couple of charred ship carcasses still smoldering in the shallows, theirs were the only visible lights. Ando could occasionally hear the engines of the smaller Allied floatplanes prowling over the lake and expected air attack at any moment.

Finally, there were the Grik themselves. Looking at them. Whether the half-starved creatures believed Ando and his men were preparing for a mission for their Supreme Regent or not, their greedy eyes and drooling jaws betrayed their thoughts: supper was getting away.

"Ready?" Ando demanded.

"All ready," Ueda agreed briskly, voice belying his weakness.

Must be using up the last of his reserves for this, Ando thought. *He looks barely able to stand. I hope he can fly.*

There came the sound of trotting feet, lots of them, preceding the grinding rumble of iron tires on gravel. A Grik-drawn vehicle was coming. Ando could hardly remember the last time a supply cart came, but the sound of its solid wood wheels and two plodding Uul was nothing like this. Only coaches carrying Esshk's important messengers made the noise he heard, and Ando's heart shriveled.

"Let's go now!" Ueda hissed. "They'll stop us!"

"We *can't*," Ando breathed back, nodding at the Grik around the planes. "Without torches marking the runway, we'll hit a stump or something. The strip's too narrow! We'll just have to bluff a little longer. They'll leave and we'll go."

A hundred harnessed Grik, all warriors, pulled the tall, narrow carriage up in front of the planes. Two Grik jumped down from the back and opened a door. To Ando's amazement, Esshk himself stepped out, followed by two other Grik generals.

A wild temptation seized him. He and Ueda still had Nambu pistols holstered on their loose belts—their only protection from the ground crew. The urge quickly faded, damped by the fact they only had the rounds in their magazines and it usually took at least two, sometimes three, of the small-caliber bullets to stop a single Grik. They had no chance against this many. Even if they killed Esshk, they'd be shredded in seconds. *Still, it's almost worth it,* Ando mused. The only things that stopped him were his responsibility to his men, and the fact he *had* made an oath to Esshk. He was ready to abandon him, but couldn't quite kill him.

"Extinguish those torches at once," a general bellowed, "and show your obeisance to the Supreme Regent!"

Ando's Grik quickly dropped their torches in ready water buckets before flinging themselves to the ground. One would've had to take a couple of steps to the closest water, so he simply dropped on top of his torch and smothered it with his body. There was a sizzling sound—the ground crew wore no armor, of course—but the creature made no cry.

Esshk stepped forward. With his night vision destroyed, Ando could barely see him—*can't tell if* he *has missed any meals,* he thought darkly—but when Esshk spoke, his voice didn't sound any different from when he last heard it. "You prepare your flying machines?" he demanded.

"Yes, Lord," Ando replied. There was no point denying it.

For a long moment, Esshk said nothing. Finally, he grunted. "I would counsel you not to show lights at night, General of the Sky, but I approve of your diligence. Particularly now. You've doubtless seen what happened on the lake, and watched the approach of our enemies as well." For the first time, as his eyes adjusted, Ando *did* see flaring flashes far to the north, amid a long line of large fires. *Burning lumberyards, shipyards, maybe villages,* he thought. Closer, firecracker flickering of massed musket fire was interspersed with longer, brighter pulses of artillery. Obviously, a great land battle was underway on the other side of the lake, just short, it seemed, of the bay where the *yanone* carriers were hidden. Turning to his right, following the line of the mountains to the east by the way they blocked the stars, he saw more pulsing light to the south, beyond the distant lock he could barely see in daylight. "Yes, ah, yes, Lord," he stammered. "They appear closer than they did when we first noticed. Don't they, Ueda?" he prompted.

His frail XO started, but quickly caught on. "Yes, they do. Much closer."

Esshk sighed. "And you prepare to meet the threat. Of all who've served me, *you*, at least, are loyal," he murmured bitterly through teeth almost clenched. "It's unfortunate we've been . . . unable to communicate as closely as before, but I've been pressed by other matters. As you might've guessed, the force in the north is General Halik. He makes me pull reserves from my defenses around the lock"—his voice turned to a snarl—"which the *real* enemy has suddenly, so coincidentally, chosen to assail in force." Dark arms emerged from under the cape Esshk always wore and he waved them in the night. "I'm *hard*-pressed," he confessed. "General Ign may yet join us, but the rest of my army is fighting for its life, for the life of our race." If he realized he'd included five beings he once considered lowly prey in his use of the word "our" he made no sign. "But though the army remains loyal and strong, it *has* grown more . . . fragile of late. And for the first time in this war, perhaps ever, combat attrition and . . . supply issues have reduced the numbers of a Gharrichk'k army, an entire *swarm*, below those of the enemy."

He's outnumbered, Ando translated to himself, *and has no idea how to deal with it.*

"We still grasp the advantage firmly in our claws," Esshk assured. "We hold difficult ground around the locks and neither of the *yanone* carriers have been detected. At this moment they're responding to my command that they steam out of the bay threatened by Halik's advance and position themselves near the center of the lake."

"Do they have a target?" Ueda asked.

"Scouts declare the armored enemy ships, and others bearing more troops, no doubt, will approach within range sometime after dawn." He hesitated. "Perhaps later, but certainly sometime tomorrow."

"Sometime tomorrow," Ando frostily echoed in English. "You know the enemy will see the carriers as soon as the sun comes up."

"Yes," Esshk agreed. "Probably almost at once, and they'll attack very quickly. They can't know what the carriers *do*, but will doubtless assume it's dangerous. They've proven they're not fools."

"No," Ando agreed. *Unlike you,* he told himself, *trusting us so completely after you've nearly starved us to death.* A thought came to him. *He can't see us in the dark so maybe he doesn't even* know. *Would he care if he did? It makes no difference now. It never should have,* he added bitterly.

"You and your pilots *must* protect the *yanone* carriers!" Esshk stated adamantly. "I know you'll be at a . . . disadvantage, considering the numbers of enemy flying machines. . . ."

Disadvantage! Ando snorted to himself.

"But you need only protect them until they launch their weapons," Esshk continued. "There will be no opportunity to reload them."

"*How long* will we have to defend them?" Ueda pressed. One of the generals gurgled a growl, but for a wonder, Esshk didn't snap at what even he had to recognize as insubordination.

"The pennants will pass the warning as soon as the enemy ships are sighted," he answered evasively.

Ando sighed, stepping in front of Ueda. "It will be done, Lord," he said forcefully. "We'll do all that *can* be done," he added cryptically, then hesitated. "I do have a question, if you'll permit me?"

"Ask."

"What happened to the antiair rockets? I expected to see them rise against the enemy planes. Have you been saving them to help us protect the *yanone* carriers?"

"Lord Supreme Regent!" one of the generals objected indignantly, glaring murderously at Ando. "You've already been more gracious than this creature deserves. It's not entitled to know *anything* beyond what you require of it!"

Esshk waved him away. "Actually, General of the Sky Ando's loyalty has entitled him to more than I can give, and there's a simple answer to his question." He looked back at Ando. "There *are* no more antiair rockets. The *yanone* project was very expensive in terms of materials, particularly gunpowder—which we desperately need for muskets, cannon, and . . . other things. The rockets were wildly wasteful, as you've remarked yourself. We simply repurposed various of their components."

Ando bowed, mind racing. *Other things?* "If there's nothing else, then, My Lord, I'll resume preparing my planes."

"Of course. Avoid making more lights, however," he warned. "I can't spare you to air attack and dawn will be soon enough for you to take to the sky."

All five aviators could only stare as Esshk's carriage vanished in the darkness and the dust its passage stirred. Ueda broke the silence. "We're . . . we're not going to do as he asks, are we?"

Ando looked at him. "He didn't 'ask,'" he replied sarcastically, then grinned at their startled, forlorn expressions. The moon was beginning to rise and he could see them better now. "Of course not! Esshk can eat shit!" He gestured at their Grik ground crew. Somehow, the one who'd dropped on his torch was suddenly dead and the others were carrying him away. "Bring them back. Tell them they'll have all they can eat tomorrow, but I'm afraid we simply *can't* avoid making just a little light. Supreme Regent Esshk has given us such an important mission, we have to properly test our planes." He glanced at the sky, listening. There were no telltale engines droning overhead, at present. "Two torches, one on either side at the end of the runway should be enough. Let's get out of here."

"Maa-chine guns, there and there!" Legate Bekiaa roared, pointing at a gap in the back of the second Grik defensive line. The first had been surprisingly easy to overcome, in 5th Div's sector at least. The surviving Grik on top of the cliffs had been so stunned and disoriented by the furious, concerted bombardment, they simply couldn't mount a vigorous defense. Localized counterattacks drove against some of the first troops up, but those were wrecked or driven away by savage, well-disciplined, continuous rifle fire even before the first machine guns were hoisted to the heights.

Just as Bekiaa's troops—and she prayed to the Maker others as well—quickly expanded their toehold and flooded the first pulverized, flesh-mulched trench, Grik boiled out of their *second* position and charged through the broken remnants fleeing back past them. They'd been met by even heavier fire, augmented by the first wave of dozens of cart-mounted "light" machine guns: Baalkpan Armory copies of water-cooled 1919 Browning .30 cals. The

Repubs had good machine guns of their own, based on 8mm Maxims, but with the production bottlenecks in Baalkpan now gone, there were more .30s. To simplify logistics, they'd be used exclusively in this assault, and the Repub Maxims had been sent to V Corps and Jash on the other side of the river.

Tracers chewed the swarm of Grik thundering out of the dark, heralded by heavy musket fire and roaring war cries. Bright orange lines of death swept across it in a riotous, stuttering roar, ricochets flaring and bouncing high. They were quickly dimmed by dense smoke created by rapid rifle fire, better-organized companies even managing volleys by ranks, their metronomic *Ccrack, Ccrack, Ccrack!* sounding like cannon. Like the .50-80 Allin-Silvas of their allies, the 11.15mm bolt actions used by Repub troops were still only single shots, but they loaded just as fast and were comparably lethal. Growing banks of gunsmoke and the night vision–shattering ripple of muzzle flashes made it difficult for marksmen to pick specific targets, but it was nearly impossible not to hit something in the dense enemy press, and nothing could live long in that barren, rocky space under such a deluge of flying lead. The Grik attack shattered and scattered like a window struck by a flurry of stones.

Bekiaa often had to remind herself that Grik only recently began learning the concept of "defense," and if the works they took were any indication, they were getting better at the physical preparations. But defense required a mind-set as well, and with the exception of Halik's and Ign's—now Jash's—forces, Grik didn't do retreats, so there were never many veterans to steady new forces no matter how well-trained or dug in they might be. All Grik instinctively knew how to attack, but if the thrust failed, returning to the defense wasn't instinctive at all and confusion often reigned.

"Up and at them!" Prefect Bele had roared again, and 5th Division, touching and joined by III Corps' 10th Aryaal, charged forward at once and quickly fought their way into the second Grik trench. A lot of Bekiaa's men and 'Cats fell in that rush, mostly to a rushed blizzard of canister, it seemed, until it was discovered quite a few simply plunged down in connecting trenches and advanced under cover. The enemy guns were overwhelmed, their vents spiked, and solid wooden wheels shattered with axes. Bekiaa hated wrecking the guns; they were decent, well-bored pieces. But they were heavier than they needed to be and supplying crews and turning them would take time. Advancing them would slow her down. And with even *more* machine guns joining them by the moment, and light mortars too, they really didn't need them.

"Commence firing!" Bekiaa said, and the two weapons she'd just directed opened up on the *next* charge, coming from the third Grik line. The firing spread outward and met the enemy in the same old way.

"It makes no sense!" Bekiaa shouted at Bele, crouching under the *vooping* warble of returning musket fire. The big man was sitting in the muddy ooze beside her while a Lemurian *medicus* split his sleeve and wrapped a bandage around a shallow, bloody gouge caused by a Grik musket ball. Even sitting, the giant man was nearly as tall as Bekiaa. "Why did they even dig trenches if they're just gonna jump up out of 'em an' run at us to die?"

"I can think of two reasons," Bele said, stifling a grunt of pain as the *medicus* worked. "As *we've* discovered, a 'fighting withdrawal' is one of the most difficult things for even experienced troops to accomplish. I'm told Halik once managed it, and Ign as well, but regardless how well-trained and armed they are, a *conventional* fighting withdrawal is beyond Esshk's Grik." He shrugged.

"So they attaack to slow us?" Bekiaa asked. "Couldn't they do thaat better under cover?"

"Of course. Unless, after the initial bombardment, they see the trenches themselves as death traps. And they will be in daylight when our planes are overhead."

"The other reason?" Optio Meek asked, still gasping from his sprint from the first Grik position. Bekiaa was glad to see he had a rifle, even if it was slung over his shoulder. She couldn't gripe. She still carried her precious 1903 Springfield the same way. "Booms're rigged to hoist supplies, ammo, even our own cannon should we want 'em, by the by," Meek told Bekiaa. "General Rolak's compliments, an he'll be joinin' us directly," he added neutrally.

The repair to his arm complete, Bele answered Meek. "The other reason might well be to blood us, scratch us—and pull us onward. Get our entire army on the heights, with the cliffs at our backs, and mount a major counterattack." Despite the warm humid night, a chill raced down Bekiaa's spine. That made a terrifying kind of sense, and though wasteful, it *would* be consistent with Grik thinking.

Optio Meek kicked a Grik corpse, half buried in muck at the bottom of the trench. It twitched feebly but wasn't a threat with most of its head blown away. "Did ye look at these damn things? Really *look*? Colonel Enaak was right. Look how skinny this one is." He waved around. "They all are." He had to raise his voice over the growing machine-gun and rifle fire. The whine of musket balls was louder as well. "Maybe there's another, simpler reason. Maybe they've finally just had as bloody much as they can take? We know they're smart enough to realize they're *it*, the last thin line between us an' their precious, bloody Esshk. Half-starved an' dyin' in the dark, could be they don't feel much inspired by Esshk's management, or even legitimacy, anymore. If they've just had enough, there's nothin' for 'em but charge er run away."

"And in the waay of Grik, they might first do one, then the other," Rolak agreed, joining them out of a communication trench through which he and his Marines had moved forward. Dipping his furry, almost bearded chin at Bele, he confirmed he'd heard the entire exchange when he continued. "Whether the Prefect is correct or not, however, whether the enemy *plaanned* it or not, his theory represents a significaant risk we must guard against as we push on."

They chopped up the attack out of the third trench much as they had those before, though it took longer this time and a staggering remnant of Grik took a significant toll from the Repub 5th Division and the 10th Aryaal before they fell, virtually at the muzzles of their rifles. And this time, Rolak chose to wait until reports returned that every division under his command had achieved similar results before resuming his advance behind a curtain of mortars. There were no more trenches or steep cliffs, but the terrain rose rough and abrupt ahead, strewn with boulders and jutting monoliths of stone that hid clusters of defenders. Both disrupted Rolak's advance, as did a small, rocky mountain in front of VI Corps, right in the center, where a lot of fleeing Grik had gathered. The whole assault bogged down while General Faan's 9th Division stormed the slope and evicted the Grik in the costliest fighting so far.

By the time the army was ready to push on, everything it could want in terms of supplies, including ten batteries of 12 pdrs and three of Derby guns, had joined it. So had the dawn, however, and as the hazy gray of morning shifted to a reddish gold, splashing across dark gray stones protruding from damp reddish soil, Bekiaa found herself much higher than she'd been at nightfall, with a stunning view all around. Only then did she truly grasp the scope of the battlefield they'd fought over.

Miles to the south, down the rugged slope and 9th Div's bloody mountain, were the gore-choked stains of the Grik trenches they'd overrun. They were ragged and cratered, and barely resembled lines anymore. *The shelling* really *pasted 'em, faarther baack thaan I thought,* she realized. Beyond the red-gray edge of the cliffs was the green of the forest they'd fought through for months. *The Grik* down there *learned to baack up fightin',* she remembered bitterly, *but most prob'ly never got up the cliff.* She felt a grudging respect for them, and a surge of outrage at Esshk for not *providing* for the escape of such troops. *If any did make it out, he prob'ly fed 'em to the 'fresh' ones we killed laast night.* Now the space between her and the cliff fairly worked with moving figures and marching columns. There wasn't any cavalry—no way they'd hoist me-naaks up with ropes!—but Colonel Saachic was advancing on the far right, through passes in the high mountains silhouetted against the rising sun. He was supposed to link up with Enaak or Svec and join Halik's push. Bekiaa wondered how that was going. She could just barely see a swatch of the big glittering lake to the northeast over a final rise ahead and there might've been smoke in the distance.

Deliberately looking northwest now, as if she'd been saving it for last, Bekiaa caught her first glimpse of their objective. She hadn't seen the open locks they'd already passed in darkness, hadn't even seen the narrow canyon they stoppered, when closed, off to 5th Division's far left flank. She'd heard the torrent of water thundering down the gorge, however, not recognizing the booming roar for what it was at first. Now she saw the source and it filled her with a sense of supernatural awe. A massive wall of water, perhaps two hundred feet high (she couldn't see the bottom and the rising mist would hide it anyway) and twice that wide, stood like a titanic, surging wave, miraculously restrained, about half a mile ahead. She knew the enormous inner lock that held Lake Galk like a trembling dam was somewhere under the cascading overflow caused by the rainy season downpours, but wished she could see the thing itself, get a notion of its construction. That was impossible.

She did see another structure, however: a wooden suspension bridge of rough, if intricate design, arched high over the falling water from one side to the other. It was packed with Grik, funneling over in front of them.

"Look," Rolak huffed, pointing southwest. Bekiaa looked at Rolak with concern instead. The whole army was tired after its uphill fight, but Rolak was *old.* Examining him, Bekiaa saw only fatigue and turned her gaze where he indicated. Other works, like those they'd stormed, stood across the river. They were full of Grik, and were the source of the reinforcements. Below the cliffs they guarded, another great force was streaming out of the forest across the open ground. "Thaats Jaash," Rolak said with certainty.

"How caan you be sure?"

"The enemy is. Sure enough to send help over *here*—to whaatever force awaits us beyond the crest. Our air should tell us soon, if the Grik don't announce themselves first." He grinned wickedly and blinked sarcastic sorrow. "Won't the enemy be embarrassed when Jaash attaacks after they just weakened themselves!"

"Won't do *us* much good," Bekiaa grouched, staring at the bridge again.

"No. Pity our planes caan't just bomb it. But who knows whaat even a concussion in the waater, so close to the lock, might do? I'm sure our aviators will work on them, however. Strafing runs, perhaaps?"

That would probably happen soon. Bekiaa could hear the sound of engines, even over the rumble of thousands of troops marching forward deployed into lines. Even now, as the front slightly narrowed, they were relatively loose lines compared to those the Grik still used, but they were deep. Not knowing what was ahead, Rolak *had* to advance in battle formation. Glancing behind, he blinked relief. "Ahh. It seems all the pieces we have any control over are now in place." Bekiaa looked as well.

She was certain of *this* smoke, thick and black, chuffing from the coal-fired Repub monitors *Ancus* and *Servius* struggling around a final bend in the swift-running Galk River about six miles to the south. Little dots trailing white water identified the MTBs scouting ahead amid tall shell splashes made by thus far lightly molested Grik shore batteries on the west side of the river. *Ancus* and *Servius* systematically smote them with their big 8″ guns as they revealed themselves, as did more dots swooping from the sky, dropping an endless stream of incendiaries. They blossomed into orange spheres of fire that roiled black into the sky before turning a dirty gray.

"*Liberator* and *Raanaisi*, screened by Des-Ron 10, won't be faar behind," Rolak remarked. "I wonder where Gener-aal Aalden will laand First Corps? Will he reinforce us or Jaash? We won't know if we need him until we see whaat's ahead."

"I wonder where General Alden *is*," Optio Meek speculated aloud, moving up slightly to march alongside his commander. He was huffing a little too.

"He'll be at the front of it all, no doubt," Rolak answered sourly. "Probaably on the lead monitor, now." He sighed. "He really should look to the future. My life belongs to Cap-i-taan Reddy," he reminded them, "and whether I faall in baattle or not, it's nearly spent. But regardless how this baattle goes, Cap-i-taan Reddy, the Union, the entire Graand Alliaance, will need Gener-aal Aalden for years to come." He chuckled. "Even if he only commaands our aarmies from a desk, as he so fervently dreads." He paused a moment and watched curiously as a Lemurian Marine sprinted toward them from the creaking comm-cart four men were pulling nearby.

"Sur," the 'Cat cried breathlessly, "COFO Leedom's respects, sur. All his strikes an' recon birds is in the air." They knew that. The motors they heard and the mayhem underway across the river were sufficient evidence. Rolak gave a hurry-up gesture, like he'd seen Captain Reddy do many times. "Ay, sur. COFO Leedom confirms there's a 'aabso-lute shitload' o' Griks in front of us." Rolak nodded. He expected that. The Marine continued. "Whaat's weird is, the air corps haas . . . took custody o' some Jaap planes an' pilots, who spilled some o' Esshk's plaans." His eyes went wide and he blinked alarm. "COFO Leedom fears 'the shit's fixin' to hit the faan'!"

Rolak's response was interrupted by several things at once. First, as good as his word and having gained the heights across the gorge to "join" Esshk's defenders, Jash immediately attacked. The trenches erupted in confusion, fire, and rising white smoke. The stream of warriors crossing the bridge must've heard the strident recall horns because it began to jam up and stall—just as a flight of blue and white Mosquito Hawks roared up the gorge at Rolak's eye level. Unheard in all the noise of engines, renewed battle, and the smoky, tumbling torrent of water, their machine guns slashed the vulnerable Grik. As if that had been their signal, more horns blared, seemingly mounting into their hundreds, as countless Grik banners rose into view beyond the crest Rolak's army approached. And louder than everything all together was a sound like continuous thunder, getting louder overhead. Looking up, they watched a solid white streak of cloudy smoke, high above, draw a stark line from north to south across the brightening sky. It looked like a Grik antiair rocket, only much, much larger—and another was rising to follow from somewhere out on the lake.

"Whaat *are* those things?" Bekiaa breathed.

Rolak didn't reply, startled when the first smoke line abruptly ended and the larger part of the rocket tumbled away. He thought the thing had malfunctioned, like so many Grik rockets did, but a flash behind the smaller front section preceded another line of smoke, thinner, more erratic at first, but it quickly straightened and started down. "Whaatever they are, they're aimed at our ships on the river, under some kind of control. . . ." He blinked astonishment. "Like suicider bombs Grik used to drop from their airships! A waarning to Gener-aal Aalden at once!" he told the runner, who immediately bolted back toward the comm-cart. "Not thaat it will arrive in time,"

Rolak added almost conversationally, drawing his cutlass and pointing it forward. Thousands, *tens* of thousands of Grik were marching over the crest ahead, shoulder to shoulder. Bright musket barrels and bayonets glittered above seemingly endless ranks extending as far to the east as Rolak could see, easily matching the length of his own three-corps line. And the fluttering banners were all the same, so similar to the Japanese flag of Kurokawa's they'd fought so long, with its bloodred rising sun. The only differences were that the flaring rays were less numerous, the field a dusty tan, and the center circle was embraced by a pair of distinctively Grik swords. *Esshk's own flaag,* Rolak thought. *Gener-aal Aalden would find it remaarkably appropriate, I think.* He also suddenly knew, somehow, that Pete should've been here, and he should've been on the water with I Corps after all.

"I think COFO Leedom waas incorrect," he stated dryly. "The shit already *haas* 'hit the faan'!" Tail high, he whirled to the Repub bugler and the runners drawing up around him, speaking quickly. "Signaal Gener-aals Faan, Ra-Naan, and Mu-Tai to prepare for a gener-aal ad-vaance behind four-raank volleys." He shuddered inwardly at the thought of the cost of reverting to linear tactics, but they might have no choice. "They must keep their alignment at all costs, allow no breakthroughs, so they may haave to close their raanks as well. Aartillery and maa-chine guns to the front, mortaars behind. Fourth Corps will remain in reserve." He gazed east-northeast, and saw the army's distant right flank crawling up the denuded slope of a mountain that grew quite steep. He couldn't see the far end of the Grik line yet; it was still cresting the rise. But the mountain would anchor his right, the gorge his left. "I believe I'll move more to the middle," he told Bekiaa apologetically in their native tongue. "May the Maker of All Things watch you closely this day."

With that he trotted away, followed by more than half the runners. Bekiaa turned back to the front. The Grik had halted at the crest, less than half a mile away. The horns went silent, but then the Grik began a roaring drone of their own. It was an awesome thing, a *hungry* thing, punctuated by a thunderous, staccato thumping sound, like a great beating heart, as they slammed the butts of their muskets against the ground.

Machine guns and cannon took their places in the line, troops moving aside for them. The cannon crews looked particularly exhausted after hauling their guns all this way themselves, like Grik, but they shoved their weapons into battery with a will, quickly taking implements and making ready.

"I hope ol' Rolak hurries," Optio Meek murmured worriedly. "Be nice if we were already hammerin' the buggers. How come our *planes* ain't hittin' 'em, all bunched up in the open?"

"I suspect they're suddenly preoccupied looking for the source of these new rockets," Bele said, pointing up. Two more of the things were racing across the sky.

"It's okaay," Bekiaa said softly. Everything else was forgotten, the strange rockets, the battle already raging on the west side of the river. Her whole attention was focused on the Grik in front of them. "We got time. Grik're still gettin' their shit in the sock. Us too." She blinked . . . anticipation, something Meek never would've expected, no matter how well he thought he knew her. "We all gotta be good an' ready for whaat's comin' next," Bekiaa almost whispered.

Trilling whistles swept the line, joined by bugles, even drums, and ten batteries of "Napoleons," three of Derby guns—almost sixty cannon in all, minus those damaged hoisting them up the cliff and others that broke down on the way—thundered and vomited fire and shot at the numberless horde before them. Exploding shells snapped and sprayed lethal iron amidst dirty gray rags of smoke. As far as Bekiaa-Sab-At was concerned, the real battle, the *retribution* she'd longed for since Flynn's Rangers were massacred on North Hill in Indiaa, had finally begun.

CHAPTER 33

////// **RRPS *Servius***
Galk River
Grik Africa
July 31, 1945

"What the hell," Pete murmured, looking at the message form a Repub sailor brought Captain Quinebe, and Quinebe immediately passed to him. After "irresponsibly indulging himself" (Captain Reddy's scathing words) leading the breakout from Tassanna's Perimeter, Pete decided to command Operation Noose from the safety of RRPS *Servius*, the best-protected ship in the Allied river fleet. At the moment he was standing on the repaired starboard bridgewing with Quinebe, the ship's engineering officer, several lookouts, and a Maxim gunner—and Sergeant Kaik, of course. *Even bein' extra "conscientious,"* he'd told himself piously, *since all the roundshot from the shore batteries is hittin' the* port *side of the ship. But I'm missin' Jash's big change of colors! I can barely see it from here, but he* is *doin' it.* He felt somewhat vindicated. He'd never really doubted Jash would keep his word, but a lot of people had. *Bet that gives old Esshk the droops.*

Then, of course, the message form arrived. "What does it say, if you don't mind my asking?" Quinebe prompted. To his credit, he'd only glanced at the heading where it said TO FIRST GENERAL ALDEN.

Pete frowned. "It's from COFO Leedom, commandin' air ops from a PB-5 Clipper." He pointed up and added sarcastically, "Bein' 'responsible,' like me. Says those five Jap planes Ando had squirreled away just showed up over Saansa Field at first light. Could've raised a lot of hell if they wanted to, and Leedom's got egg on his chin even if his CAP bounced 'em fast." He shook his head. "Our fighters knocked two down on the first pass, but the Japs didn't scatter. Didn't do *anything* but roll over on their backs, flyin' upside down. The reporting flight leader said it was like they were wavin' their wheels in the air like legs. Smart—and gutsy, after we already killed two of 'em."

"And?" Quinebe pressed.

Pete snorted. "Bastards'd painted 'Don't Shoot' on the bottoms of their wings! Leedom's fighters rounded 'em up and pushed 'em down. Soon as they stopped rollin', three starvin' Japs jumped out and took to yammerin' that Esshk had ships about to shoot *guided rockets* at us. Maybe some other shit."

"Guided rockets?" Quinebe said, eyebrows rising, equally incredulous.

"Yeah," Pete murmured, his own brows knotting. "Leedom's plane—two of his Clippers—have Jumbo Fisher's first torpedo mounts under the wings. We all thought we'd see the last Grik ships when the balloon went up, and Leedom wanted to test the rig in combat." He shook the page. "But if this is on the level, he has to get those rocket-shootin' ships *fast*. He's already heading over Lake Galk, an' pulling damn near every plane we have after him to hunt 'em down."

"That seems . . . excessive, and it'll leave us with no air cover of our own."

Pete shook his head, then tilted his helmet aft, where *Liberator*'s bulky form was rounding the bend, attended by the comparatively small armored DDs. "No choice. All our ships could be sittin' ducks for somethin' like that, and most of First Corps and part of Fourth Corps are packed in those big tubs like scum weenies in a can. We gotta get 'em ashore."

"What's a 'scum weenie'?" Quinebe inquired.

"Never mi—"

"Gener-aal! Cap-i-taan!" Sergeant Kaik cried, pointing at the sky over the gorge, just as the lookouts in the fighting top started shouting through the voice tubes. They saw the same white streaks that Rolak had, though his warning hadn't yet arrived. Even as they watched, a smaller section jetted away from a powerless, tumbling cylinder and streaked downward at an impossible speed.

"Those're suicider bombs—with rockets up their ass!" Pete ground out with certainty. "Maneuver your ship, Captain Quinebe. Message to the transports: head for shore. Ground your ships if you have to. All other ships will scatter." His orders were superfluous. Quinebe was already bellowing for full speed ahead—there was almost *no* room to maneuver here, where the river narrowed at the base of the first open lock—and the dual-purpose guns on the DDs started booming at the sky independently, trying to put a curtain of iron in front of the descending rocket plane. Their skippers were all veterans of the battles of Madraas and probably recognized the threat faster than Pete. Not fast enough.

The first suicider was heading straight at *Servius*. But either the Grik pilot misjudged his angle of attack or *Servius*'s sudden acceleration threw him off and he quickly chose another target. Almost faster than they could see, with tracers uselessly crossing the sky behind it, the big flying bomb slammed into the river close alongside RRPS *Ancus*. With a loud, dull blast, a huge geyser of smoky water towered high, heaving the ship aside and splashing down across it. Pete was no navy man, but he'd been in plenty of actions at sea. He knew even a near miss that size would cause a lot of damage. How much was immaterial, since a *second* suicider immediately crashed *Servius*'s sister right behind the pilothouse. A great explosion shook the ship, blowing her funnels down and tilting the bridge structure forward. An instant later, a cloud of scalding steam enveloped *Ancus* amidships. Flames leaped skyward and the stricken monitor swirled away in the rushing current.

"More comin' in!" a Lemurian lookout cried. They saw two more, clearly going for *Liberator*, just now turning for shore. The first went straight and true, right into the massive ex-battleship's side. The blast blew armor plating away like sheets of crumpled black paper and smoke belched out of a gaping hole that appeared at the bottom of the casemate, extending down to the waterline. The fourth flying bomb overshot its target and the pilot tried to correct. Stubby little wings fluttered away and it went out of control, blasting up a pillar of river water in front of USS *Bowles*. In all the confusion, none of the lookouts on *Servius* ever saw the fifth and sixth suiciders coming in, both of which hit USS *Raanaisi* almost simultaneously. The huge ship convulsed under the dual hammerblows, both high and almost straight down. Funnels toppled and steam jetted from all the empty gunports aft. A relatively small internal explosion jolted the massive vessel and she lost way, starting to settle by the stern. 'Cats were pouring out of the big troop doors they'd built into the forward casemate and scrambling out on the fo'c'sle.

"Jesus!" Pete gasped, seeing the carnage inside the sinking ship in his mind. "All DDs to *Raanaisi*'s aid!" he shouted past Quinebe at a signal-'Cat. "Get our people off her!"

"Right full rudder!" Quinebe shouted abruptly. Distracted, he'd nearly forgotten his ship was still charging toward the lower locks. The great gates stood ajar, high above her now, and the water was swifter, increasingly rough, splashing back over *Servius*'s fo'c'sle and swamping the base of her forward turret. Pete glanced up at the improbably huge structures, apparently concrete, though they were so old and eroded, it was impossible to distinguish them from solid rock. His horror and urgency were momentarily touched by wonder at the sight of the ancient feat of engineering. *How the hell? And they've gotta be supported on the bottom, somehow. All that weight . . .* He shook his head. *Not the time.* "And tell COFO Leedom to *kill* whatever the hell's shootin' at us *right damn now*!" he roared.

Over Lake Galk

"I'll be damned, there they are!" Commander Mark Leedom agreed when his Lemurian copilot pointed at a surprisingly large gathering of ships near the middle of Lake Galk. His four PB-5D Clippers and the 4th Pursuit Squadron protecting them had actually been first to arrive. The rest of his Clippers were scouting and observing elsewhere and all the closest attack planes, venerable Nancys and Repub Cantets, had expended their ordnance and were returning to base to refuel and rearm. Captain Araa-Faan's 8th Bomb Squadron, just up from Arracca Field, was close behind. "Where'd they get 'em all?" Leedom murmured as they closed the distance. Twelve improved "Azuma Class" Grik cruisers were anchored in a circle. Azumas were lightly armored wooden-hulled steamers about 300 feet long, normally armed with everything from 40 to 100 pdr guns. Tougher than Allied sail-steam frigate "DDs," even after the latest modifications, they were slower and their guns didn't have the range. Still, they were small enough that the Grik had obviously been able to hide them from prowling Allied planes along the convoluted shoreline. It was harder to credit how the Grik concealed the two huge ironclad battleships the cruisers now surrounded.

How didn't matter now, only that they had, and the bigger ships weren't ordinary BBs. One was wreathed in sufficient smoke, trailing off to leeward, that it almost looked afire. Leedom doubted that. The smoke was gushing from open bays, fore and aft, and he knew these were the things Ando described, that had launched the rockets raising so much hell downstream. Even as he watched, white smoke billowed out the back of the casemate of the second ship before it spurted out the front, chasing another suicide rocket bomb streaking off to the south.

"Shit!" Leedom shouted. "They spit out another one! We have to hit 'em now."

"Whaat we do?" Leedom's copilot challenged. "Only two of our Clippers got torpedoes, an' them croosers is aanchored too tight to the taargets. How our fish get through?"

Leedom grimaced and pressed the Push to Talk button on his radio microphone. "Captain Araa, this is Black Cat One, over."

"This is Cap-i-taan Araa," came the female Lemurian's sometimes frustratingly husky voice. "Whaat happened to 'raadio discipline'?"

"In the crapper, and we don't have time. Just split your squadron and attack from east and west. Blast those Grik cruisers and make lanes for me and Black Cat Two to stuff our fish in those big bastards' guts." Black Cat 2 was the other Clipper carrying a pair of Mk-6 Baalkpan Naval Arsenal torpedoes. "Black Cats Three and Four will follow you with their bombs, if they're needed, but we need a clear shot for our torpedoes."

"You alwaays take the good jobs," Araa-Faan mocked lightly, but she wasn't really kidding. "Why not my Naancys go for the missile ships?"

Leedom's voice hardened. "Because you're not carrying AP bombs and those bastards are armored. You might get lucky, but we don't have time to screw around. You can take the cruisers with whatever you've got, even incendiaries."

There was a moment's sullen pause. "Wilco, Blaack Caat One," Captain Araa replied. Another rocket blasted away from the second ship. "Shit!" Araa snapped. "We attaacking now!"

The four lumbering Clippers flew over the formation of enemy ships, at about three thousand feet, and started to circle while Araa's Nancys dove on the cruisers. White puffs of smoke appeared in front of the attacking planes, as antiair mortars lobbed exploding shells in the sky. Those could be very dangerous, making a curtain of musket balls and iron fragments that could shred fragile planes and pilots. It was nothing unexpected, however, not like the sudden violent explosions that blew two cruisers completely apart before Araa's planes even got close—or the heavy gush of smoke that engulfed four more as they spat *eighty* antiair rockets into the sky, lancing straight at Leedom's Clippers.

"Break right! Dive!" Leedom shouted in his mic, turning the leather-bound wheel before pushing the yoke to the stop. Heavy explosions, much bigger than the mortar bombs, bounced the big plane around, and there was a drumming sound as fragments tore through wood and fabric—and flesh. A pair of wind-whipping holes appeared in the side of the cockpit by Leedom's copilot and the side of his face was splashed with blood, sticky and hot. His copilot lolled forward against his restraints, eyes staring, jaw slack.

"Maker!" cried one of the 'Cat gunners in the waist. "The Maker-daamned lizaards get the Two plane!" Leedom saw it—almost hit it—as its ravaged, folding, burning wreckage plummeted past the nose. "They get the Three plane too!" shouted the other gunner. "Is pullin' awaay, two engines smokin!"

"Shit!" Leedom roared.

Pulling up at about eight hundred feet, he banked back to the left. The plane responded slowly, the controls mushy, and the yoke rattled in his hands. Now he could see what was happening, at least. Most of the 8th Bomb Squadron had gotten through and only globes of fire and smoke marked where a couple of Grik cruisers had been. *Probably hit before they launched their rockets,* Leedom thought grimly. Two more cruisers were burning fiercely and the rest were in disarray. The big BB he'd first seen smoking was getting underway, trying to turn west. "I bet that one shot its wad and is tryin' to scram," he growled. That wouldn't do. It might reload. He spoke into his mic.

"Captain Araa, I want you and your remaining bombers with anything left to throw at the bastards to go after the missile ship trying to retire. Go with 'em, Black Cat Four. Looks like the damn thing's open on both ends. You ought to be able to get something inside. Fourth Pursuit? You're with me—or I'm with you—and we're going after the one still launching missiles. Get in low and fast and shoot 'em up. Maybe they'll waste their antiair mortars on your faster planes. I'll come in behind you."

The six swift little Mosquito Hawk "Fleashooters" did as directed, running interference for the PB-5D, but it seemed all the Grik mortars were waiting for Leedom. Shells burst all around his big, slow target, buffeting, tearing, stripping its lift and power, particularly when the number one engine was torn off its mount and tumbled into the lake. Still Leedom bored in, going lower, lower, and the missile ship grew in front of him. It started lofting its own mortars then, from the peak of the casemate, and they cracked in front of Leedom, sleeting metal through his plane. *Good shooting,* he grudged through gritted teeth, wincing as the windscreen disintegrated, spraying his face with shattered glass.

At five hundred yards, he pulled briskly back on two brass levers with red-painted knobs, and—probably miraculously, considering how battered his plane now was—both torpedoes dropped in the water less than thirty feet below.

"They runnin' hot, straight, an' normaal!" came the cry from aft. *At least one of my gunners is still alive,* Leedom thought bitterly as he pulled back on the yoke. "*C'mon*, you fat whale!" he urged. "Get *up*!"

Even with the weight of the torpedoes gone, the three remaining engines, battered and spewing oil, barely had the power to drag the plane over the looming funnels ahead. They managed it, somehow, and Leedom let out a breath he'd been holding—just as more exploding shells burst in front of him. He had no idea if they came from the missile ship or a cruiser, but he felt a savage pounding in the right wing. Then there was a terrible ripping, cracking sound, and the plane started going over. It all happened so fast, Leedom was still fighting to level out—impossible, of course, since the wing had torn away entirely in a smear of burning fuel—when the rest of the plane struck the water and exploded in a splash of spume and roiling black smoke.

An instant later, two torpedoes slammed the side of the missile ship, their blasts communicating to the three remaining weapons, waiting to be fired. A massive thunderclap jolted Lake Galk for miles around and the nearby cruisers were swamped when not only the flying warheads but the huge gunpowder engines that propelled them all detonated at once.

Supreme Regent Esshk watched the destruction of his *yanone* carriers from the arched timber loggia on the second level of what had been the local regent's villa. The regent had grown increasingly anxious, even querulous, as the prospect of this confrontation neared. Tiring of the distraction, Esshk had him destroyed, along with all his guards and half his collection of females. The guards had been necessary, of course, but the females—charming as they were at appropriate times—had been indulged to a dangerous and unprecedented degree. Always allowed free reign of the villa, and even to *speak*, they'd made a nuisance of themselves as the great battle loomed. The five he'd preserved (properly sequestered) were all of The Blood, however, and would be essential to establishing Esshk's own dynasty. Particularly now that it seemed he had no choice but to wipe the slate entirely clean.

He mildly regretted destroying the regent for one reason: he had no one left to talk to. General Stragh was competent enough; he'd designed the defense on the eastern heights above the inner lock and that, at least, seemed to be going as planned. The enemy army—under their Lemurian General Rolak, *Dorrighsti* spies reported—had fought its way past credibly stiff resistance, lured by success, into the combined waiting strength of three-quarters of Esshk's remaining force. Opposition to Halik had been all but abandoned so Stragh's deputy could beat Rolak before turning on Halik from the heights. It was a fine, straightforward battle design, and Rolak's advance had been slammed to a bloody halt. Unfortunately, Stragh didn't know Halik. *Nor do I, it seems,* mused Esshk, still watching dense smoke tower up in the midmorning sky from the final ruin of his once mighty fleet. Instead of marching his army cautiously down the east shore of the lake, Halik—guided by his perverse alliance with the thrice-cursed enemy cavalry—was practically *sprinting* south. General Stragh had just admitted it was "possible" Halik might strike his army in the rear before it finished with Rolak. Of course, Stragh wasn't at the battle, he was here—where any proper general would be—saying nothing to Esshk but what he must. He was saying little enough to anyone, in fact, except the signalers communicating with his army by pennants. Exciting as that innovation was, pennants could still be tedious, and in rapidly developing situations, reports were often obsolete before they were received. Doubly so before responses or orders returned. Esshk only now fully appreciated General Ign's insistence that he command his army *with* the army.

And what of General Ign now? Esshk thought sourly. He—or whoever commanded his army—had attacked the forces protecting Esshk himself, just a few miles away. With the enemy concentrated on the east side of the river to the south and the lake to the north, Esshk thought he'd be perfectly safe in the regent's villa on the southwest shore no matter what occurred. It was even difficult to see from the air, protected by a great, overhanging slab of stone. The enemy had destroyed the airship mooring mast a quarter of a mile away, and all the nearby buildings, down to the smallest hut. But the villa had remained unmolested. That would change when Ign's troops came. And they would.

Glaring at the smoke billowing from his shattered fleet, and beyond at all the distant docks, warehouses, and industrial capacity he'd so carefully hoarded, he could actually gauge Halik's advance by the fires of what he destroyed. General Stragh's "possible" was almost a certainty now. All that remained, at last, was to enact his "restoration contingency" after all.

He made a small sound that would've betrayed a mix of amusement with despair if anyone heard him. And "betrayal" was a word much on his mind. Though it was unclear *how*, he felt that Regent Consort Tsalka had somehow betrayed him long ago, when the war first began. Of course, Kurokawa had betrayed him repeatedly. That was the nature of the creature, and Esshk had expected it. But he felt betrayed by the old Celestial Mother as well, primarily because she'd never taken the threat of "prey" seriously, then allowed herself to be killed by them, leaving Esshk to be betrayed again by her daughter. But that wasn't all. Even the Chooser—dead now, by all accounts—who'd essentially started Esshk down his present course in the first place, had turned on him in the end. Now even Ign had betrayed him, either directly, or by allowing another to take his place. Halik's betrayal . . . moved him the most because he'd been his first creation, and lavished so much hopeful trust upon him. He'd always thought of Halik as the spear-point of the New Way he wanted to make, and it never dawned on him Halik would find a Way of his own.

Still, ironically, Esshk probably felt most disconcerted by the betrayal of General of the Sky Ando. He didn't know why. Perhaps it was because he knew the "Jaaph" hated and feared him, yet gave excellent service and advice regardless. *Perhaps Ando and his men might've been treated better,* he grudged, *at least as well as other generals in my service—Stragh has missed no meals!—but after Kurokawa, I believed it best that Ando never presume to consider himself an equal. A mistake, it seems—but must I think of everything?* Regardless, the simple rare honesty of their association left Esshk entirely surprised when Ando's five little flying machines did *not* swoop in to sacrifice themselves in defense of the *yanone* carriers.

He found dark amusement in the content of their final conversation. He'd been entirely truthful when he told the aviator he had other uses for the antiair rockets, one of which actually had nearly saved his carriers. But revealing that to Ando might've made him hesitant to defend them closely. Moot now, of course. He'd also been truthful, if again vague, when he'd said the explosive fuel and components of hundreds of rockets would be used for other purposes, this plan born of a growing certainty he'd ultimately been betrayed by the moods of the Vanished Gods themselves. *How else could things have come to this?* he silently protested. *I've waited as long as I possibly can, to feel the slightest contrary stirring, taste the feeblest mood of denial. I don't* want *to do this!* he practically wailed inside. The only response was a rumble of bombs falling on his troops on the heights. With nothing else to distract them now, the enemy flying machines were free to concentrate on Esshk's warriors once more.

"Lord Supreme Regent!" General Stragh cried urgently, striding closer as a messenger darted away. "General Halik's advance forces are near the bluff behind your main army on the left. He'll soon be up in force. General Ign has driven a wedge through your lighter forces on the right"—he gestured up the very slope the villa was built into—"and *prey warriors* stream through after him, rolling up our defense from the center!"

"No matter, General Stragh," Esshk murmured. "I'll have my satisfaction. Even at the expense of the Vanished Gods themselves," he added darkly, glaring at one of his *Dorrighsti* guards, a First of Fifty, standing attentively nearby. "Have the coaches prepared," he commanded. "One for the females, and—" Turning his head to General Stragh, he almost drew his sword and hacked him down. But Stragh *was* competent. Esshk might need him to build another army. "The other for us. And my closest guards, of course. We go to the forest beyond the Jaaph airfield where an airship lies concealed. We'll wait for the end of this terrible day, then—if we still must," he inserted cryptically, "we'll fly in darkness to the western regency of Engunu. We're not . . . unsupported there." He faced another *Dorrighsti*, the leader of the detachment protecting him. "It's time," he hissed. "To the pennants! Signal the pack with special instructions to perform the task assigned." He considered, then added, "All will be given names, and I'll commit them to memory, reciting them to myself each morning when I wake! One day, *all* our race will chant their names before undertaking any task!"

This *Dorrighsti*, a nameless First of One Hundred himself, stared at him in awe. Earning a name was the first ambition of any Grik warrior, unusual for a First of Fifty, even One Hundred, untested in battle. There'd been exceptions for New Army troops, recognized for excellence in learning new weapons and tactics, but most of those had died under Ign in the horrific battles around the *Nakkle* leg. Warriors here, even New Army troops, had generally not conspicuously distinguished themselves in training, nor had many seen combat before the final enemy push up the Galk River from the Zambezi. Many Gharrichk'k would earn names today or in the days to come. The *Dorrighsti* hoped he might. But having one chosen by such as Esshk was beyond any expectation. What he promised now . . . !

"Yes, Lord Supreme Regent! At once!"

"Come, General Stragh," Esshk said, whirling toward the stairwell, tail plumage and long, red cape sweeping a cloud of dust in the air. "We must go. It may not be safe, even here."

"Indeed. The enemy could arrive at any moment," Stragh agreed.

Esshk glanced at him. "I'm not concerned about the enemy."

CHAPTER 34

////// *Lake Galk—Inner Lock*
Grik Africa

The great gates of the ancient locks that made Lake Galk and allowed ships to pass between the high lake and lower river seemed to open and close by magic. Externally, nothing was visible save the tremendous eroded gates themselves, and that's all anyone ever saw move. Yet a great deal *did* move, deep inside the cliffs of the gorge on either side. Down long passageways, cunningly cut in the living rock and accessed by steps rounded by eons of trampling feet, huge underground chambers enclosed monstrous mechanisms made by the Vanished Gods themselves. Whoever or whatever they'd been.

The mechanisms would've resembled titanic clocks, for the most part, if viewed by anyone familiar with such things. Huge, toothy cogs of age-crusted bronze turned other great gears, smaller to larger, extending or retracting fat rods the size of battleship rifles connected to levers even longer and more immense. An ancient order of Holy Hij claimed the Vanished Gods had commanded them to provide constant ceremonial maintenance, such as they could. None understood how the mechanisms worked, and they were religiously forbidden to try to learn (no one can know the minds of the Vanished Gods), so their ritualistic duties consisted almost entirely of frequent lubrication, or wiping white powder off tarnished green surfaces as tin slowly leeched from the bronze. Yet despite their unknowable age, the workings were so robust they didn't need much more than that, and unlike the gates themselves, might've lasted another millennium. Unfortunately, the cavernous chamber in which the mechanism controlling the east gate of the main inner lock tirelessly labored was much more crowded than usual.

There were the bones, of course, of the Holy Hij that tried to bar entrance to Esshk's *Dorrighsti.* They were scattered all over the place, gnawed and tossed aside weeks ago. Then there were the *Dorrighsti* themselves, that had endured boredom and hunger just as long, but now stirred from their excruciating wait into frantic motion by a runner bearing word of the signal pennants. Inflamed to an anxious eagerness beyond words by Esshk's astonishing promise, they raced to recheck preparations and rushed to assume their places among the eleven hundred tin-lined wooden crates, stacked everywhere they wouldn't interfere with access.

Few of the crates contained a precise weight of gunpowder. They'd been built to transport bagged artillery charges but now were filled with rough, dusty chunks, broken and crumbled out of its solid form in the rocket engines so the crates might weigh anywhere from a hundred and ten to a hundred and thirty pounds apiece. So roughly sixty tons, all told.

A single device should've been enough and the *Dorrighsti* First of Fifty in charge would've gladly killed all his warriors for the privilege of performing the act himself—if the Supreme Regent's promise hadn't included them all. As it was, each hefted their heavy packs, carefully opened leather flaps, and unrolled short lanyards hooked to friction primers inside. One by one, they signaled their readiness. The First of Fifty was just as excited as the rest—they were all about to live forever, after all. He had no idea how that could be, after their bodies ceased to exist, but young as he was, he already knew he didn't know very much. Nodding benevolently at each companion, and with profound anticipation, he wondered by what name *he* would be remembered and gently tightened his lanyard.

"Rear rank, fire!" roared Prefect Bele. Two hundred rifles cracked as one, though it was hard to distinguish the report from the continuous firing along the miles-wide front. Bekiaa and Meek had drifted to the right, more to the center of her division, directly behind the 14th Legion. Colonel Naaris had the 1st again, and though Bekiaa still considered the 23rd "hers," Major Khun was in direct command. "Three steps forward!" Bele cried, his order reinforced by a bugle sounding the 14th's prefix, then the command. The 1st and 23rd had already moved. The whole line was rippling like an enormous snake slowly rolling itself uphill. "First rank, fire!"

Bekiaa had never seen anything like it. The closest was the open field battle on the plain of Gaughala, but that was a terribly disorganized affair, the Republic Legions meeting the Grik for the very first time. Here on the heights above the south end of Lake Galk, the ground was rougher, more broken, but the lines never lost contact as they faced the Grik just as openly. They had to, to advance—which both sides were—and the space between the roughly forty thousand men and 'Cats of III, VI, and XII Corps deployed in the great Allied line, and the probably seventy thousand Grik opposing them, had dwindled to less than four hundred yards.

Cannon snapped and recoiled back, spraying canister, while mortars *tunked* incessantly, throwing gouts of pink dust and body parts in the sky. Nancys and Repub Cantets swooped, braving the little antiair mortars Grik troops carried, to drop load after load of incendiaries. Great whooshing, roaring toadstools of flame engulfed the Grik, accompanied by horrible squalling shrieks. Few cannon returned their fire. Bekiaa supposed the Grik were finally getting low on powder, or they'd abandoned most of their guns back at the top of the cliffs. She wondered at that. If Bele was right and the plan had been to suck them here all along, why waste their cannon, short of powder or not? *Maybe they thought maassing their guns would point our air at their trap?* She preferred to hope Esshk was an idiot and never expected they'd get this far. *An' they do haave a buncha' firebomb throwers,* she added darkly to herself.

The Allies hadn't faced those, basically wheeled catapults, or "mangonels" as Bekiaa remembered Courtney Bradford calling them, in a long time. They launched rope-reinforced clay jars full of flammable liquids that burst and burned on impact. They'd disappeared from the battlefield because they were easy targets for cannon, didn't have near the range, and the big ones were even harder to move. They were back now, throwing endless streams of their destructive payloads in fiery arcs, struggling to get the range. Only a few had landed in the Allied lines, but they were getting closer. . . . The planes had orders to concentrate on them.

The great Grik line disappeared behind a fire-stabbed, rippling cloud of smoke, and a storm of musket balls whizzed all around, kicking up plumes of dust, *spanging* off cannon, and thumping into bodies, knocking men and 'Cats to the ground. Grik muskets weren't accurate at this range, but they were lethal. And even with the Allies' looser formation, it was impossible that a lot of them wouldn't hit somebody. Most hit were Lemurians, of course, being thickest in the line, and their screeching wails of agony tore at Bekiaa's soul. *This is it,* she told herself, over and over again, praying to the Maker it was so. *The laast time! One more time!*

"Legate Bekiaa!" Rolak cried, rushing to her, surrounded by his Marines. He pointed to her left. "Your First Legion is getting too faar ahead. I know they're aanxious," he added drily, "but they must wait for the rest of us."

"Haard to keep creepin' at this pace, Gener-aal," Bekiaa snapped back bitterly, "when they're choppin' us to bits. An' it seems like *haaff* the enemy's shootin' at the First Legion! They're gettin' creamed."

"You maay haave noticed, we're 'chopping' them up worse. But a regiment from Fourth Corps is already moving to join First Legion. They're our left flaank and the enemy *must not* get between them and the gorge when we come to grips."

Bekiaa blinked confusion. "But why're we even *doin'* this? Why not just chaarge 'em an' get it over with, or dig in an' kill 'em from here?"

Rolak blinked understanding. "The first, as you know, would be faar too costly. Cap-i-taan Reddy would haave me haanged—rightfully so—for ordering such a thing! As for the second, however, I fear they *wouldn't* come. If we stop advaancing and take the pressure off, they might notice thaat Gener-aal Haalik is, even now, preparing his assault up the slope in their rear."

Bekiaa blinked surprise and her tail arched behind her. "Already? Thaat's . . ."

"Impossible? No." Rolak grinned. "Amazing? Most certainly. But apparently, he's faced little opposition." He gestured before them as another whirlwind of musket balls passed like a terrible swarm of bees, striking dozens down around them. A long, rumbling stutter of cannon belched canister in return and Bele's hoarsening voice yelled, "Third rank, fire!"

"Thaat's all they haave left, Legate Bekiaa!" Rolak almost crowed. "'Esshk's laast ace,' as Gener-aal Alden would say!"

Only it wasn't.

Suddenly, the very earth seemed to lurch beneath their feet. An instant later, it came up and slammed Bekiaa in the face.

"Leedom's gone," Pete murmured, crumpling the message form in his fist. "*Shit!*" he snapped, raising his head to stare up the gorge ahead. "Another hour's warning and we would've *had* those missile ships! Now a good kid and three-quarters of his aircrews are gone, *Ancus* is a wreck, and both our troopships took it on the chin."

"There *is* a bright side, General," Captain Quinebe reminded. "The missile ships are both destroyed and *Liberator* is fast aground, conveniently close to the bank."

Sergeant Kaik nodded. "Haaff her troops're already ashore, along with Inquisitor Choon. Gener-aal Taa-leen an' the Triple First is cuttin' trail for the rest." He blinked satisfaction. He'd been one of the earliest members of that unit. "They'll be climbin' the cliffs behind Rolak soon. They've lost much of their equipment—aartillery an' aammunition—but Rolak should be able to supply 'em." He gestured back at the river bend. "True, *Raanaisi* haas sunk, but she's in shaallow waater. Gener-aal Kim says the troops aboard are in no danger an' the DDs'll ferry 'em ashore."

Pete nodded but his expression remained bitter. "Yeah, I'm glad they're okay, but they'll be so mixed up they won't be worth a shit today. It may take *days* to get 'em sorted out. Esshk just rendered half a corps—at least—combat ineffective right when Rolak needs 'em most, without even laying eyes on it. *My* corps!" he stressed fiercely. Rolak had commanded I Corps for a long time, but Pete built it and it had always been his baby.

The glass in the pilothouse windows rattled violently, like a roundshot from a heavy Grik shore gun just smacked the ship close to the bridge. Jash's Slashers and the Repub V Corps were reportedly already through the enemy works on the heights to the west, rolling the Grik up, but they'd ignored isolated Grik positions on their side of the river.

"Return fire on that gun emplacement!" Quinebe called in the voice tube to the fighting top where the gun director for the forward 8″ turret was. For a moment, there was no response, then came a high-pitched, almost panicky Lemurian cry. "Wasn't a shore battery, Captain. Look up, off the port beam!"

Servius had been turning back downriver to cover the ships taking troops off *Raanaisi*, so the gaping lower lock gates and long, narrow gorge was on their left. Pete, Quinebe, and Kaik all raced out to join the lookouts on the port bridgewing, where they looked up—and up—at the towering wall of smoke and debris rising high in the air about six miles to the north. Where the inner lock was. Even before the ear-splitting boom and long, echoing roar came down the gorge, Pete knew exactly what happened. "Crazy damn lizards *blew the goddamn lock*," he ranted.

Quinebe knew it too. Instantly, he raced into the pilothouse, roaring, "Make your course one, six, zero, all ahead full! Close all internal and external hatches! Seal the ammunition hoists in the turrets and clear the crews out! Signal 'seek high ground' at once!" He punctuated that by pulling vigorously on the steam whistle cord three times.

"What the hell are you doing?" Pete demanded hotly.

"Trying to save this ship, though I can't imagine how," Quinebe replied bitterly. "We're about to be swamped by a lake the size of a small *sea*, moving *very* fast." *Servius* had almost completed her turn and was beginning to accelerate as the swift current took her.

"What about my corps?" Pete challenged.

Quinebe laughed, almost hysterically. "What about it? Don't you understand? *We can do nothing.* Not for them, or probably ourselves. Even if we survive the initial burst of water, as soon as the speed of the river exceeds the thrust of our screws, we won't even have steerageway! No control! We'll be like a leaf in a whirlpool!"

"Beach her. Some might get off," Pete suggested.

"Are you mad? We have minutes, perhaps only *seconds*! And the 'beach' will soon be miles away, or over our heads!" The more he thought about it, the more his expression betrayed mounting resignation. "No use," he murmured. "It's hopeless."

Pete looked at *Liberator* as *Servius* raced past her. There was a little panic among the troops on the beach as they realized what was happening, but Pete was proud to see how many were streaming up the bluff beyond, and how orderly that stream appeared. And as far as he could tell, none of his beloved troops had cast away their weapons. "Professionals to the last," he whispered as his heart cracked open. Snarling, he turned to Quinebe. "So what're you gonna do, roll over and die?" He fumbled at the flap on his holster. "If you've already given up, I'll shoot you right now. *Damned* if I'm gonna get drowned in the last *land* battle with the goddamn Grik!"

Jolted back to himself, Quinebe roared back, "I'm doing what I can!"

Nodding, Pete turned to the signals officer. "If it's the last thing you ever do, get a message off to Sofesshk and Saansa Field. Everything that'll fly gets in the air, down to Arracca Field. Every*body* gets to high ground. And Major I'joorka *will* get the CM the *hell* out of there!" He blinked, shrugged. "I guess that's it." Turning, he strode out on the bridgewing as *Servius* churned past the sunken *Raanaisi*. He was startled to see the ships of DesRon 10 already shoving off, turning downriver, stuffed to the gunwales with 'Cats and men wearing camouflage smocks and mustard-brown uniforms. He had no idea if they'd be any safer, but the DDs had taken a lot of troops aboard.

More remained behind. The old mortar deck at the peak of *Raanaisi*'s casemate was packed, mostly with 'Cats, but a few men as well. One caught his eye and Pete recognized General Marcus Kim, face expressionless other than his perpetual frown. Suddenly, he clenched his fist and slammed his chest in a Republic salute. Pete took a deep breath. *Goddammit!* he seethed, and did the only thing he could. Standing stiffly at attention, he rendered the finest, sharpest hand salute he was capable of, performed a parade ground about-face, and marched back into the pilothouse.

Three minutes later, a great moaning wind roared out of the gorge, instantly erasing *Servius*'s smoke and whipping her signal and battle flags taut with a crackling rush that sounded like rifle shots. Moments later, the tight gorge ejected a chaotic explosion of water as high as the cliffs. The front of the tumultuous wave quickly collapsed as it spread, racing across the width of the river, but it was still higher than *Liberator*'s casemate when it slammed her, spinning her sideways, then rolling her over. In seconds, she was gone, tumbled into a thousand fragments that joined the cataract racing downstream. Hundreds of 'Cats were swept off the bluff and no more would possibly join those already at the top.

Servius saw none of this, not even her lookouts in the fighting tops. Engines racing, twin screws spinning faster than they ever had, the Repub monitor had already rounded the bend. Those aboard heard the rapidly mounting thunderous din, however, and many staring aft actually saw *Raanaisi*'s sunken carcass consumed in foam—before all twenty-odd thousand tons of her was lifted and hurled onto what had been the west bank of the river. The great ship smashed like a sack of eggs and the cluttered flood's first inclination was to carry its trophy of wreckage straight on, flattening the forest across the countryside. Much of it did. Most, however, still spreading and shedding height as it came, made the turn and cascaded greedily up the wakes of Des-Ron 10 and RRPS *Servius*, just slightly ahead.

General Pete Alden faced through the pilothouse windows as the side hatches were dogged and battle shutters came down. The swift torpedo boats of MTB-Ron-1 were also covered with clinging troops. *Hauling ass too,* Pete appraised approvingly. The little boats, combined with the river flow, were probably blasting along at forty knots when they disappeared around another slight bend. *Maybe* they'll *make it, at least,* he thought grimly.

The ground was still shaking when Bekiaa opened her eyes. Rolak was beside her on his hands and knees, coughing and spitting reddish-brown mud. She couldn't hear him. Couldn't hear anything but an endless, rolling roar. Looking around, she saw most of the 14th Legion was doing the same: rising under a layer of chalky pink dust and pebbles, acting stunned. Larger rubble, some bigger than wagons, had fallen as well—some still did, with ground-jarring impacts—and she realized many of her Repub troops would never rise again.

Widening gritty eyes, she saw a stupendous, opaque curtain of dust drifting west on a fitful breeze, and far above it stood a terrible gray cloud, reaching for the sun. *A vol-caano!* she thought with certainty. *We're fighting on a vol-caano, and the baattle stirred it to life!* The roar grew louder and she cringed, expecting the beast to belch again. There was only one Maker in her faith, but many Changers, terrible beasts of nature the Maker unleashed to reshape His world. Their efforts were generally beneficial in the long run, but Changers resented their constant labors and could be spiteful at times. The sea was one Changer, and though quick to take offense, was usually benign, even helpful. It provided the People with its bounty and confined its many monsters. The wind was a more capricious Changer. It moved ships and stirred the air so it was always fresh, but bored easily, shifting on a whim. It also reveled in provoking the short-tempered sea to a frenzy. The earth was the laziest Changer, least likely to stir. When sufficiently provoked, however, its temper was most malevolent, venting its fury by throwing wide the gates of Chik-aash, where the flaming spirits of evil dwelled. They often returned to the world with a bang.

"*Not* a vol-caano!" Rolak was yelling as if he read her mind, or started with a similar assumption. His voice was muffled, buzzing, but Bekiaa saw him pointing to her left and she looked. The river gorge still had a ragged east rim, but it was closer now. Enough so that only part of the 14th Legion lay sprawled on the ground beyond her. The rest of the ground, as well as Colonel Naaris and the entire 1st Legion, were simply gone. Bekiaa whipped her head around to gaze ahead. It was hard to tell through the lingering dust and rising fogbank of spray, but she finally saw not only was the bridge over the inner gate of the lock entirely gone, the unnaturally flat-topped wall of water had taken on a jagged, concave aspect. Escaping water was the cause of the ongoing rumbling roar. "Maker in the Heavens," she murmured, barely hearing herself as she blinked horror and amazement. "The Grik blew the lock."

"Up! Up! The Grik are coming! On your feet!" Rolak bellowed. He was right. Bekiaa stood, whipping dust away in a drifting cloud. Down the line, far to her right, the battle was slowly resuming. A ragged volley slashed, then another. A half dozen cannon fired. The closer they were to the scene of the catastrophe, however, the slower the stunned army responded. No doubt the Grik had been just as terrified by the unprecedented blast—probably the biggest nonnatural explosion this world had ever seen—and far more of them were killed by it too. But they'd seen the signal pennants and were warned what was coming. None could've actually been *prepared* for such a thing, so far beyond their imagination, but they'd been ready for *something* terrible, and recovered more quickly—to a degree. They'd never reform their ordered ranks or keep alignment on the move, but that didn't much matter right now. Despite how much they'd changed, Grik would always remain consummate predators that instinctively knew, whether they were truly ready or not, the very best time to strike their prey was when it was hurt and reeling. Amid blaring horns, the entire right half of the Grik battle line rose up and charged, en masse.

Right at Bekiaa, it seemed to her. Men and 'Cats scrambled to rejoin their firing lines, shoulder to shoulder now, to better support one another in what was to come. Bekiaa prayed her wobbly troops would stiffen before the Grik slammed into them. Four loose ranks jostled into two tighter ones, and the confused 20th Legion from IV Corps that had—lucky for it—just arrived to back the 1st, quickly spread out to form a third line behind what remained of the 14th and 23rd.

The sun was almost directly overhead, the column of smoke and dust leaning away. The dust in Bekiaa's sweat-foamed fur was starting to thicken, but she was so caught up in the spectacle before her she barely noticed. She knew the blown lock would result in untold calamity downriver, but simply couldn't contemplate that now—beyond hoping someone at a comm-cart or flying overhead would pass a warning. Her entire world, her whole *life*, narrowed to focus on the ravening Grik horde. A stutter of shots pecked at it, but Bele and others roared to stop them. Cannon belched smoke and fire, and mortars started lofting. Machine-gun tracers swirled wildly before settling down to peel bloody layers off the running Grik. Now Bele bellowed, "Front rank, volley fire, present! *Fire!*" A creditable *Craaack!* resulted, throwing out a long, dirty white screen of smoke.

The Grik responded with a single, prolonged, unaimed avalanche of musket fire, and dozens of men and 'Cats fell screaming, or pitched backward out of line.

I doubt they'll even shoot again, Bekiaa thought. *Caan't load muskets on the run.* She noticed Optio Meek by her now, helmet gone and blood washing down his face. At least he had a rifle. "Just like old times!" she shouted at Rolak over the roar of guns, Grik, and the agonies of a dying lake. She was trying to project confidence, but thought her voice only sounded tiny and desperate in the heart of the tumult.

"Indeed," Rolak replied, turning his gaze on her. He'd been staring south, blinking despair for Pete Alden, I Corps, and all that lay behind. But when he spoke again, his voice was strong. "As if we've come full circle. Once more, they come at us with teeth, claaws, steel . . ." He forced an unconcerned grin and blinked disdain. "No maatter how haard we try to teach them, they never really learn."

Bekiaa knew that wasn't true, but nodded anyway. Her tail rose behind her. "Between volleys, fix bayonets!"

CHAPTER 35

////// Sofesshk
Grik Africa

Acting Regent Champion I'joorka, formerly of the 1st North Borno Regiment in Chack's Brigade, was practically running, hissing with pain as tight, burn-scarred skin tried to flex to match his haste. And though it probably made him look more presentable, covering the patchy, rust-colored feather-fur sprouting like moss on purple bark, the rough fabric of his tie-dyed combat smock chafed annoyingly. The stairwell from the entry/audience chamber loomed intimidatingly before him. *At least it's well lit,* he thought gloomily, imagining how hellish it must've been for 'Cats to fight their way up it in the dark. Without pause, he hurried on, surprised (and slightly triumphant) to hear Centurion Ione, one of his female human Repub aides, huffing to keep up. *And she much younger and fitter than I,* he reflected. Every sign that he'd pushed beyond expected limitations after his frightful wounds was a victory. Of course, his long convalescence had left him dreadfully out of shape and he was literally gasping by the time they reached the top of the turning stair and stepped into the more private audience chamber the Celestial Mother of all the Gharrichk'k had been allowed to consider hers alone. Centurion Ione was still only huffing, and probably would've been after ten times the distance.

"You must leave this place at once, Your Highness," I'joorka snapped without preamble, more harshly than intended.

Here, the Celestial Mother lounged on a larger, more "appropriate" saddle-like throne, attended by her new "Sister Guards." All but one of these was Khonashi, sent from I'joorka's own village in North Borno by King Tony Scott. Khonashi females, though never truly warriors, could at least fight. A single Sa'aaran female, from Lawrence's tribe, had joined them not long ago.

Thus the Celestial Mother had her proper guards and the Allies could keep an eye on her at all times. As it happened, that appeared increasingly unnecessary, and she treated her new "Sisters" more like advisors and friends than guards. It seemed she fully appreciated—and embraced—her new role in the world and the Grand Alliance, and her insistence on truth and transparency was sincere. By all accounts her guards even liked her. *Very* interesting, since one had been I'joorka's own mate twice, and he respected her opinion. *Still,* he realized, catching his breath, *none of that will matter if we don't move quickly!*

New attitude aside, the Celestial Mother was clearly annoyed by I'joorka's brusque manner and Ione's intrusion. "What's the meaning of this?" she demanded. "Leave? Whatever for?"

"My humblest apologies for barging in unannounced and uninvit—" I'joorka began, but the Celestial Mother waved that away.

"Never mind. I've already learned you wouldn't do so without good reason. What has transpired?"

There was nothing for it. No way to soften the blow. *Nor should I,* I'joorka realized. "Esshk has destroyed the inner lock holding back Lake Galk. We tried so hard to avoid damaging it ourselves. . . . With the vast majority of the population endangered by its loss being Gharrichk'k, it never occurred to us *Esshk* would destroy it deliberately. He has."

The Celestial Mother was stunned. "So," she murmured sadly. "I fear our campaign has been too successful. Finally realizing he can't reconquer the empire and rule it himself, Esshk has chosen to ruin it. How?" she asked, very quietly.

I'joorka waved his clawed hands. "A mine, probably. A very *big* bomb. Reports from Generals Rolak and Alden were brief, and in Alden's case, cut off."

"First General Alden was on the river, with parts of First and Fourth Corps," the CM guessed. Clearly she'd been keeping up and knew who was where.

"I'm afraid so. Fortunately, we've had further reports from aircraft so we know the battle on the heights still rages—if less . . . coherently than before. But much of the force we had on the water"—he sighed—"and likely First General Alden and Second General Kim, have all been lost. Along with virtually every remaining warship we had."

"The battle . . . ?"

"Remains in the best possible, um, 'claws.'" Grikish was similar to

I'joorka's native tongue and came easily to him, but he struggled with many expressions. "Third General Rolak, General Halik, and First Ker-noll Jash were pushing Esshk hard. Probably, as you say, why he did what he did. Now?" His tone became urgent once more. "The battle can no longer concern us, nor can we even influence it from the air. All planes here, or at our forward base farther upriver, must fly to Arracca Field on the coast. Hopefully planes now engaged can make it here"—he waved in the direction of Saansa Field across the river—"and refuel before the flood."

"The flood will come so far?" asked the Giver of Life, rather weakly.

"Yes."

"How bad?"

I'joorka hesitated. "I've no idea how fast or high the water will rise, but Saansa Field and everything we've built where New Sofesshk once stood will surely be swept away. The river now runs at its seasonal peak and the airfield is barely six or seven feet higher. On this side of the river . . . You must expect Old Sofesshk to flood as well. Rather deeply, in fact."

The ramifications of that were obvious. Hundreds of thousands of Grik Uul had filtered back, commanded to come swell the ranks of Jash's army, clear rubble from the battle, or work on the airstrip across the river. There was little shelter for them, but hunters and fishers kept them fed. They were helpless in the face of what was coming, however. "And there are no ships to save my subjects—or all *your* people here?"

"No. And ships may be of no use in any case. Thousands, perhaps *many* thousands will drown, and I must get you away." I'joorka was surprised, but heartened as well, to witness something like anguish displayed in the Celestial Mother's expression and posture. "There should be time for you to sound the attention horns and instruct the few thousand Ancient Hij still living in Old Sofesshk to rush for high ground or climb atop the tallest buildings. Across the river, our people are already sending yours southwest, into the hills. Most should reach safety. But *you* must go, and there's little time." He motioned for the Sister Guards to prepare the Celestial Mother to move.

"Will merely climbing buildings save them? There *are* no heights within several miles of Old Sofesshk," the Celestial Mother insisted, "and no means of quickly crossing the river. The last of the Ancient Hij will perish."

Despite the damage sustained elsewhere on his body, I'joorka's crest had grown back fairly full. It rose now. "That can't concern *me*, I'm afraid. My primary duty is ensuring your safety—"

"And cooperation," the Celestial Mother hissed.

"Of course," I'joorka agreed reasonably, "which I can't secure without your safety." His tone turned hard. "You *will* come away from here. There's a Clipper waiting in the water by the dock. So summon your Hij and send them on their way. Some may be saved. And every moment you argue might cost many lives."

There came a gasping sound from the stairway behind I'joorka and Ione, and Hij Geerki finally tottered into view. He was trying to speak but it took the somewhat feeble old Grik a moment to catch his breath. "Bring," he wheezed, "bring them in the Palace," he managed at last.

"Of course," the Celestial Mother said at once. "Why didn't I think of that?" She looked at I'joorka. "Will they be safe here, in the upper levels?"

I'joorka held his hands out again, calculating. He knew a little more than he'd let on, but not much, and that was based on guesses. Lake Galk covered roughly five to seven thousand square miles, but without knowing its depth, they couldn't estimate its volume. And at least the lock gorge ensured its drainage would be relatively slow. The whole lake wouldn't just *dump* out in a single massive gulp, and it would spread out as it came. So . . . the initial surge, here, might be anywhere from ten to thirty feet, depending on too much I'joorka didn't know. But a respectable percentage of that first gust might be sustained for a while. I'joorka desperately wished Courtney Bradford was here to help sort this out! "In the upper levels, perhaps," he conceded. "This one and above. I really can't say. . . ."

The Celestial Mother turned to Geerki, gesturing around. "Then that's what we'll do. You could . . . tightly pack a thousand Gharrichk'k in this chamber alone. There are five more above it—considerably smaller, granted. . . ." She paused.

"We could quickly rig platforms outside," Centurion Ione suggested, startling I'joorka with her enthusiasm. "Drag the temporary floating docks up the sides of the Cowflop—I mean, the Palace—and support them with cables. There's plenty of cable."

"But is there sufficient labor?" one of the Celestial Mother's Khonashi "Sisters" questioned. "With enough Uul it would be a certainty, but—with respect"—she glanced at the Celestial Mother—"smarter or not, most 'Ancient Hij' don't even know how to *hold* a rope."

The Celestial Mother stood abruptly, decisive. "They will after today, if they want to live. Hij Geerki! Sound the Great Attention horns—no, no, send someone else. You'll die if you take those stairs again so quickly."

Geerki bowed, then briskly tugged a colored cord that would ring a bell to summon messengers. The Celestial Mother turned a defiant gaze on I'joorka. "I'll call all our people close enough to come, and allow them the *choice* to flee, or join us in—or on—the Palace." She surprised him even further by blinking determination in the Lemurian way. "And we'll stay with them, you and I," she decreed. I'joorka's eyes bulged and he opened his mouth, but she cut him off. "Your 'Captain Reddy' wants me to be a new kind of leader for my people, so I shall rule as he does: by example, and by sharing the peril of those I lead. How can I be what he—and *you*—want me to be, if I flee in the face of risk to my people and my Allies?"

I'joorka just stared. The centurion at his side started to speak, but he shushed her. "No," he said, "she's right." Then he surprised everyone by rasping a toothy chuckle. "But by all the Gods of the Alliance, if we don't all drown, Chairman Safir, Captain Reddy, and King Scott will fight over who gets my crest for a flyswatter."

A pair of Repub soldiers topped the stairs. "Go!" I'joorka cried in English. "Sound the Attention Horn. 'Ut do not stray," he cautioned. "There's a great deal else to do."

"How long, do you think?" Centurion Ione asked, her voice slightly nervous.

I'joorka replied in Grikish for the Celestial Mother's benefit. Working in the Palace so long, Ione had learned it fairly well. "Based on reports by some of our flyers"—he paused—"two hours. A bit more, perhaps, but we must act as if it's less."

CHAPTER 36

*////// **Southwest shore of Lake Galk***
Grik Africa

It had been necessary for Esshk's airship to take off into the stiffening breeze, heading east, or the wind would've raked it across the jagged treetops on the other end of the clearing. And heavily loaded with extra fuel, a full crew, six fat females, a dozen *Dorrighsti* guards—most in the aft gondola with far too much baggage—as well as Esshk and General Stragh, of course, the airship's five little engines roared and strained just to get the thing aloft, nose angled frighteningly high. After its initial reluctance, however, the zeppelin rose fairly quickly and Esshk was astonished by what he saw.

The plume of dust thrown up by the great bomb still stood over them like a malignant reddish-brown cloud. It was finally beginning to disperse, it seemed, but other clouds were darkening the sky. Typical of the season or not, these afternoon thunderheads touched Esshk with superstitious dread. He imagined they were the moods of the Vanished Gods, gathering to view the desecration he'd committed against them.

Looking at the dying lake itself, it seemed as if it had already noticeably dropped. Just a few feet, perhaps, but enough that small boats dragged up on shore leaned higher and drier than before. Esshk shaded his eyes and tried to see the battle on the rocky summit east of the gouged and frantic gorge. Dust obscured much, but smoke still rose amid a horribly congested, miles-long melee, with banners—his, and various enemy emblems—chaotically intermingled.

It had been so long since he'd dared fly in daylight he couldn't help but absorb the view, and for several long moments he gave no orders for the steersman to turn away. Sickly fascinated, he saw dull columns of enemy troops on the long slope to the south, rushing to join the ferocious fighting near the crest. Worse, the lead elements of Halik's army, only lightly opposed, were scaling the craggy rise behind his own forces. To his surprise, his unique vantage point left him no doubt his army still outnumbered its attackers. And it was a *good* army, probably the best he ever made, if slightly less experienced and well-equipped than he would've preferred. But it couldn't see what he did. All it would know, very shortly, was that it was locked in a battle more savage than anything it ever imagined—before it was suddenly assailed from the rear! He was virtually certain that would break it.

Nothing I hadn't already known, he reflected with a terrible sense of gloom, *but to actually see it, to witness the end of all my efforts with my very own eyes . . . Oh, Halik!* he almost wailed to himself. *How could you do this? Together, we could've had all the* world *in our claws!*

"Supreme Regent!" General Stragh cried out, pointing down. Esshk tore his gaze from the battle on the heights just a few miles away, and peered over the rail of the forward gondola. A few hundred feet above the trees they'd found a capricious void in the surface winds. During his distraction, the airship rumbled out in the clear over Ando's airfield—and the ground below practically seethed with warriors. Esshk squinted. Most were obviously Gharrichk'k—but their banners weren't his. And look! Mingled with them, in somewhat better order, were clusters of humans and Lemurians in yellow-brown uniforms. Most horrifying of all, none were fighting, and all were looking at him.

"It's Esshk! It *must* be Esshk!" First Ker-noll Jash roared at the top of his lungs. Jash's Slashers and the Repub V Corps had fought together amazingly well, considering they'd been bitter enemies such a short while before. But General Kim, possibly even Rolak, would've been surprised by the depth of Pete Alden's cunning, in maneuvering it so *only* Repubs directly supported their new Grik allies on the left—and Bekiaa in particular, *especially* commanding Repubs herself, would be nowhere near them. Repubs had fought the enemy as hard as anyone, but even sharing a continent, they'd remained historically isolated from the Grik and hadn't fought them nearly as long. And it was the duration of the struggle that had scarred those like Bekiaa so deeply, perhaps *too* deeply to even contemplate cooperation in the heat of battle. Pete hadn't been concerned that she—or anyone in his AEF—would disobey orders, but with timing so critical, they might've enjoyed the spectacle of Jash's spearhead assault, with Grik killing Grik right in front of them, just a little longer than was wise.

As it was, V Corps swept into the gap the Slashers blew through Esshk's lighter defenses on the west side of the gorge at precisely the right moment, adding needed weight and inertia to the attack. Still, the Slashers and V Corps had been wildly disorganized by their lightning crash through the Grik positions and a lot of them were still fighting there, widening the breach and rolling up the lines. They were even calling for and accepting *surrender* from large contingents in ways Halik told Jash had worked for him. Bekiaa, for one, wouldn't have even considered that. But Jash and Naxa, and two legions of V Corps, had stormed onward into the enemy rear, falling on what had to have been Esshk's primary HQ on this side of the lake. The sacrificial defenders, all *Dorrighsti*, put up a furious fight, but they'd had no chance and hadn't much slowed Jash's vengeful rampage.

Now they all saw the distinctive black airship, already five or six hundred feet above, clawing for the sky. Not quite three hundred feet long, its dark shape still looked huge against a remaining patch of bright blue sky. Almost frantically, Jash looked around, hoping to spot an Allied plane, swooping to shred the monster with its guns, but there was nothing.

"There might be one of those big four-engine beasts up there," gasped the Lemurian Repub Legate named Pol-Heena, trotting up to join him. He obviously knew what Jash was thinking. Pol had traveled farther than Jash could imagine, and knew the wider war. And though new to the fighting here, he was a competent commander and had diplomatic experience. It hadn't surprised Jash at all when Pol brought two Repub legions to join his push. "But all the other aircraft have been pulled back, to get ahead of the flood," Pol reasoned, just as frustrated as Jash. His big eyes suddenly went wide. "That thing is held up by hydrogen!" he exclaimed. "I don't think we can light it, but we can let it out!" He spun to his troops. "Shoot it!" he roared. "Open fire at the airship!"

The thing was seven hundred feet up now, but still less than the three hundred meters from which any Repub rifleman was expected to hit a stationary target the size of a Grik. None of Pol's roughly eighteen hundred troops could possibly miss—nor could many of Jash's three thousand Grik, armed with Allied rifle-muskets.

The ground fire began sporadically but quickly intensified, a startlingly high percentage of projectiles crashing through the thin planking of the deck under the forward gondola where Esshk stood. Almost at once, General Stragh squealed and fell amid a blizzard of splinters, as did—very quickly—two of the throttlemen on the starboard side. Instinctively, the steersman, crest low and eyes narrowed to slits, leaned on the big tiller to bring them around, back over the forest. "No!" Esshk screamed. "You'll take us right back over them! Fly over the water and outdistance their weapons before we turn." Even in the time it took to speak, dozens more holes appeared in the deck; a *Dorrighsti* screeched and flopped, drumming his feet; and splinters swirled. Esshk could only imagine what it must be like in the aft gondola—or up in the envelope where the rubberized skin bladders enclosed the lifting gas. . . . An engine, a cylinder probably dented by a bullet, seized and died. "To the throttles, you fools!" Esshk roared at his two remaining guards, both bleeding. "Open them all the way!" All the regular throttlemen were down, and only the extra layers of wood and bracing supporting the tiller had preserved the steersman. The *Dorrighsti* rushed to comply, and the engines roared louder. Slowly, slowly, the thundering impacts dwindled as the airship climbed over the lake. By the time they stopped completely, all lay dead except one *Dorrighsti*, the steersman, and Esshk himself.

Esshk had no idea how he'd been spared. Actually, he hadn't, entirely. Noting a throbbing ache in his foot, he looked down, expecting to see splinters in his feet. For a moment he could only stare while blood oozed and dripped through a hole where his right middle toe had been.

Even in his terror, the steersman knew his business. One of the "oldest" airship pilots, he'd been elevated and trained by Muriname himself and remembered the heady days when Grik airships filled the sky. For all he knew, this was the last one left, but he wouldn't've been Esshk's personal pilot if he wasn't the best and didn't know how to get the most from his machine. A machine he knew was dying. "Hold this, just so!" he cried to the last guard, lurching from the tiller without even waiting for the wounded *Dorrighsti* to take it. Scampering around the gondola, he pulled vigorously on tight, colored chords. Esshk noticed, through his growing pain, that many already hung limp. "What're you doing?" he demanded.

"Dropping weight, Lord Supreme Regent," the steersman replied. "We're losing lifting air." Esshk understood "lifting air" was hydrogen, though he only had a vague idea what *that* was, or how it was made. He knew all the large works that manufactured it had been bombed and destroyed long ago, however, and only small, tediously operated field facilities—such as the one in the clearing they just left—remained. Perhaps the steersman knew where others were? That creature, after pulling all the colored cords, dashed to a speaking tube and shouted into it. There was no response. "No one answers in the aft gondola," he reported, crest lying flat again. "I was going to have them throw the bodies out."

"Return to your post," Esshk commanded, limping forward. "My guard and I will do it. Tell us what else must be done." Despite the now searing pain in his foot, Esshk was still strong. He lifted General Stragh over the rail and dropped him by himself while the guard started tossing the others. Looking down, watching Stragh fall, Esshk estimated they'd reached about a thousand feet, but even with the engines running full out, they weren't climbing anymore. "Empty the other gondola," he ordered the *Dorrighsti*, who, without a word, climbed the ladder to the envelope above, where he could work his way aft. Esshk turned to the steersman. "The truth," he rasped. "If we turn west, even avoiding further damage, we can never reach the Engunu Regency." It wasn't a question.

The steersman lowered his snout. "No, Lord."

"Are there places we might seek repairs along the way?

"Yes, Lord . . . but they're too far. I doubt we can make ten miles before we strike. We're already beginning to fall."

Esshk considered that, looking back, stomach roiling and blood roaring in his earholes. Turning west, they'd probably fall into the trees *within sight* of the force that fired on them, and they'd be quickly killed or taken. Esshk snarled loudly. He'd *never* spend his final hours running crippled through the woods like wounded prey. Spinning back swiftly—painfully—to the front, he fixed his gaze on the battle raging on the heights east of Lake Galk's gushing wound. "We can reach *there*," he snapped, "can we not? Set me down in the broken heart of my army. I'll die with it." He tilted his head back at an angle, one of several Grik gestures comparable to a shrug. "And perhaps if I rally those troops, we might yet win."

CHAPTER 37

////// South Shore of Lake Galk
Grik Africa

A bit to the northeast, beyond the desperate, bloody, seething line, Legate Bekiaa-Sab-At caught a glimpse of a descending zeppelin—actually, it looked to be crashing—and witnessed the enormous fireball climbing in the sky a short while later, near where it must've come down. But she and those around her were too busy to do more than notice, and it was soon forgotten. Despite the horrific mauling they gave it, the sheer weight of the Grik charge had severely cracked the reeling Allied left. It was holding—barely—but it was clear to Bekiaa that both armies, probably for the very first time, were equally conscious of the battle's significance as they stubbornly spent themselves to end the other. And the balance was teetering in favor of the Grik.

Machine guns had been overrun or pulled behind the line. A few Blitzers still stuttered but they couldn't be easily reloaded in the desperate press, so rapid fire lost its advantage and brute strength and steel—and teeth and claws, of course—became the dominant weapons. Grik were bigger than 'Cats, as heavy as a man, and though not really stronger than Bekiaa's seagoing brethren, could often overpower Republic 'Cats. Theirs had been a longer-settled land, affording them a more civilized, somewhat easier existence. And if Repub 'Cats weren't "softer" anymore, they were still generally smaller. So her human troops, and recently—surprisingly—self-integrated Gentaa, were forced to the forefront to blunt the tide of death. They were tiring and dying fast. Battered 'Cats supported them as best they could, shooting and stabbing past them with bayonets, but the Grik didn't seem to tire and they just couldn't kill enough.

And yet the Gentaa were magnificent, Bekiaa thought. Nearly as big as a man, with all the agility of a 'Cat—both of which they resembled so closely—they fought like absolute furies. That had surprised Bekiaa the first time she'd seen it, but had utterly astounded her Repub troops who'd wondered anew about the large population of prideful but standoffish, outwardly pacifistic people they'd harbored in their midst so long. However this battle, this war, turned out, and whether they wanted to or not, the Gentaa had thrown off their aloof detachment and would have to assume the full responsibility of citizens of the Republic. First they had to win, though, and things were looking grim.

Not for the first time, Bekiaa nostalgically wished her troops had shields—*anything* to push Grik back while riflemen shot them to pieces. But shields were heavy, and lugging them in addition to the rest of their equipment, solely for their rare utility in situations like this, was ridiculous. *And daamn it,* Bekiaa raged, *we weren't* supposed *to be fighting like this anymore!* "Supposed to" had no meaning in war.

"There!" she cried, seeing a pack of Grik slam through between the 14th and 23rd Legions and start sleeting in behind them. "Follow me!" Optio Meek and half a dozen runners, as well as a clot of Gentaa apparently devoted to protecting her, rushed at the growing mob. It appeared momentarily disoriented, as if surprised it made it through and didn't know what to do next. General Rolak himself, and his dwindling company of the Triple I, raced to support her.

Bekiaa shot a Grik with her Springfield, quickly worked the bolt, and slammed her bayonet in the side of another that never saw her. Like the rest, it was turning to take the defenders it just broke through from behind. Its squeal alerted others.

"Fill thaat gaap!" Rolak roared, physically shoving his Marines, then launching himself after Bekiaa and her Gentaa again—even as humans and 'Cats fell back from another Grik surge that hammered a bloody breach through the 23rd. Bekiaa watched Optio Meek go down under the ravening crush, and in an instant she was surrounded. Stabbing and slashing, shooting when she could, she fought like she never had. Part was desperation, part for Jack Meek, yet another friend this terrible war had taken. All thought of anything but survival vanished, however, as the mass of Grik around her only grew and her breath turned to gasps and her rifle got heavy and slow. Sickly, she thought the entire line must've collapsed. *Discipline and couraage are all thaat's saved us this long,* she realized bitterly, *and they caan't laast forever.*

A Grik, very close, just a musket barrel away, lunged and missed her with its bayonet. Without thinking, Bekiaa leaned against the blade to roll inside and smash the butt of her Springfield in the thing's face. The muzzle of the musket spat a jet of fire, snatching her left arm away from her rifle. Her right hand still held the weapon by the wrist and she slammed the whole thing forward like a poorly balanced spear. Sheer luck guided her bayonet, gouging along the Grik's snout, into its eye, and out the back of its head.

It stuck. Her left arm wouldn't work at all, and still holding her precious rifle with her right, the falling Grik pulled her over. Others raised their weapons, jaws agape . . . and that's when Bekiaa saw something amazing. Without question, General Lord Protector Muln-Rolak was one of the finest leaders in the Grand Alliance. And despite his age, he'd still been reckoned the greatest warrior in Aryaal, possibly all of Jaava: an unusual land of Lemurian warriors even before this war began. The funny thing was, Bekiaa suddenly realized, no one she knew had ever actually seen him fight.

Rolak had discarded his rifle. He still had his pistol in its holster but never touched it. His hand held only a cutlass like the one Bekiaa wore, but he started doing things with it that she'd never seen. And he didn't attack the Grik as much as he seemed to *dance* among them, with all the fluid, predatory grace of a flasher fish, or a lizardbird snatching insects from the sky. The cutlass darted and slashed as he leaped and twisted and rolled, tail high and tucked tight to his back, never parrying blows, only avoiding, redirecting, smoothly slicing throats and piercing ribs in such a way that he never broke his lethal rhythm, not once. And in no way did his deadly strokes undermine the elegance of the dance. The blood that fountained all around only painted the art with color; the screams and squeals were music.

In spite of everything, Bekiaa was mesmerized, and any Grik could've killed her then, but with a thundering roar, another of IV Corps' reserve legions swarmed around her, slamming the Grik back and reinforcing the staggering 23rd. It *hadn't* broken, she saw with pride, even holding in place with fighting behind it! Heavy firing and the bark of cannon had never faltered elsewhere, but now it resumed here once more.

Rolak, huffing now, and a pair of surviving Gentaa were at her side at once, dragging her away from the dead Grik. There were bodies everywhere, of all kinds, but that had seemed important to them. Now they ripped battle dressings from pouches, doing things with her arm. She noticed how limply it flopped beside her, had seen similar wounds a hundred times. The Grik musket ball would've pulverized the bone to salt and only torn flesh was holding it on. It didn't hurt.

"I never knew," she told Rolak loudly, over the renewed roar of battle. His face was very close, eyes sheened with tears, rapidly blinking sorrow, rage—too many things at once.

"*Medicus!* Corps-'Caat!" he shouted desperately aside.

"Don't worry, Gener-aal, I ain't gonna die," Bekiaa assured him, "but you'll haave to teach me whaat you did." She flicked her eyes at her arm. "Haave to fight one-handed now."

"An outdated style, from a time when waar was . . . fun," Rolak lamented. "It takes too long for aarmies to learn and is really only suited to single combaat. Doesn't fit our current taactics," he added ruefully, voice now the same as always: stoic, urbane, unflustered, but the tears were starting to spill.

"Still useful," Bekiaa countered. "It saved me. You did."

"No," Rolak denied. His tone hadn't changed but he was blinking bitter regret. "I used you up, at laast."

"Lizaardshit, Gener-aal," Bekiaa snapped, angry now. "Nobody used me up but me, an' I ain't done yet!"

Miraculously, Meek was suddenly by her. He'd retrieved her Springfield and it was absolutely washed in sticky blood. So was Meek, for that matter, and a long gash split the center of his face from forehead to chin. It had to have been a claw that did it, and his right nostril was nearly gone. Somehow, it skipped his lips and he didn't seem otherwise hurt. "I got her, Gen'ral," he said. "They're callin' for ye." He nodded to the right, toward the comm-cart, then cocked his head. "Battle sounds different. Somethin's goin' on."

Rolak gently touched the blood-caked fur on Bekiaa's cheek, then considered the battle line while half a dozen of his guards from the Triple I filtered back to join him. Most were wounded and gasping with exhaustion and pain, but their tails were high and they blinked satisfaction. Volleys by ranks were starting to sound again as the relentless pressure eased, and a section of 12 pdrs poked blackened snouts through the press and spewed screaming canister. An endless stream of stretcher-bearers had been carrying crates of ammunition forward and wounded to the rear. A tired-looking pair, hardly more than younglings, laid their blood-soaked stretcher by Bekiaa. Aided by the two Gentaa and a harried-looking Repub *medicus*, they gently lifted her on it. "Take care of her, Optio Meek," Rolak said.

"Legate Bekiaa haas done more thaan her paart and Prefect Bele haas our left flaank firmly baack in haand." With that, he turned abruptly and jogged away to the right, followed by the remnant of his guards.

"Did you see whaat he *did*?" Bekiaa asked Meek, sitting up before the stretcher-bearers could raise her. She winced. The pain was starting to come.

"Lay back!" Meek scolded. "See what? I got trampled!" He pointed at his face. "A *toe* claw did that, for the love of God! Me looks an' marriage prospects ruined forever in the biggest battle against the Grik—by the flick of a bloody toe!"

"Help me up," Bekiaa demanded.

Meek sighed, unsurprised. "Ye'll bleed ta death."

Bekiaa glared at the *medicus*. "Then bind me up. Or cut the daamn arm off and *then* bind me up. I'm not leaving now! Not aafter . . . so much."

A musket ball whizzed over Meek's head. He barely twitched. Originally set to essentially spy on Bekiaa, she'd inspired greater loyalty in him than anything or anyone else in the world. He desperately wanted her safe. But she was right. If this was the end, whichever way it went, she of all people deserved to be there.

"She needs more treatment than I can give her here. I won't be responsible," the *medicus* stated flatly.

"Aye, ye will!" Meek snarled. "Give her some seep an' do what ye must, an' be quick about it too. I'll take care o' her after that."

A comm-'Cat captain from the 8th Baalkpan quickly summarized the situation for Rolak, who was beginning to feel increasingly awkward for having neglected his primary command responsibility. Especially with Pete Alden almost certainly lost. *Another long-suppressed relic from my past life,* he admitted contritely to himself. *Once aactually* in *the battle . . . it's difficult to stop killing when there's so much killing still to do.* He was sure Dennis Silva would understand. And he—and Bekiaa—had been needed on the left. He'd somehow recognized that would be where the most critical moment would come. He'd never foreseen the great blast that shook it so terribly, but like Pete Alden during the breakout from Tassanna's Toehold, he'd known where he had to be.

But things were changing. The captain quickly briefed him on reports he'd compiled from runners, field telephones wired in up and down the line, and all the way back to their starting point. There were radio reports from a Clipper still orbiting above, Colonel Enaak's cavalry, screening Halik, and as far back as the Palace at Sofesshk.

Everything downriver was being engulfed by the flood, now fanning out beyond the river. Saansa Field was being evacuated and all the Grik workers sent into the hills. The Celestial Mother had summoned those on the north side of the river into her palace. Rolak didn't know if that was brave or stupid. He hadn't spent much time around the chief of their allied Grik and didn't know her well, but now he respected her. Stupid or not, she'd made a decision to safeguard as many of her people as she could, and was sticking with them. If any survived, they'd remember.

But the most critical news had been that General Faan was dead. That hit Rolak almost as hard as Bekiaa's injury. Faan—and his III Corps—had always been a rock. The only consolation was that his subordinates were just as steady and III Corps was in good hands. XII Corps' General Mu-Tai on the far right seemed just as steady, but his Austraalans were still relatively inexperienced. They'd fought well during the breakout but they'd never been pushed. They weren't now. The Grik seemed most concerned with holding them in place. That left VI Corps in the center, which despite also performing well before, had spent most of the war on garrison duty in Indiaa. Composed largely of Lemurians from Saa-Leebs, and Sular in particular, the troops themselves were fine. Especially after Matt Reddy and Pete Alden relieved some of its more . . . political officers and put General Grisa in command. But Grisa was killed in the breakout, and General Ra-Naan, from Maa-ni-la, had taken his place. Now Ra-Naan was dead. That left what Rolak considered his shakiest corps right where the Grik seemed to be concentrating, near where Rolak saw that black zeppelin go down. *Esshk haad to be in it,* he thought, *and I bet he got out before it burned.*

There were only two pieces of really good news. First, General Halik, combined with a lot of Enaak's cavalry, had finally smashed into the Grik rear on their center left, across from Mu-Tai. *Probaably whaat's taking the pressure off III Corps on* our *left, and why the Grik are flocking to the center,* Rolak mused. *And all the more reason to believe Esshk himself was in thaat airship. Whyever he came here, he'll waant protection now.* The second bit of good news was that a little over half of I Corps had survived the deluge that shattered *Liberator*, and General Taa-Leen had linked up with Colonel Saachic's 1st Cavalry Brigade, which had squirmed around and worked its way up on the heights from the east. Riding double, sometimes triple (very awkward on a me-naak), Saachic was bringing Taa-Leen and most of his 1st Division forward. They'd arrive ready to fight instead of utterly exhausted.

"Very well," Rolak said. "Send to all commaands: Mu-Tai's Twelfth Corps will stop sitting on its aass and *attaack*. We didn't come all this way to stop and hold our ground. Mu-Tai will link up with Haalik, then sweep the Grik to the center. *All* of Fourth Corps will join Third Corps and push the Grik on the left. I expect they'll eventually peel to the center as well." He blinked grim decisiveness. "Thaat's where I'll be, with Sixth Corps, and thaat's where I waant Gener-aal Taa-Leen and Col-nol Saachic to join me." He looked at the communications officer. "I mean to roll the Grik into a big, faat baall, then smaash it like an egg."

CHAPTER 38

////// South Shore of Lake Galk
Grik Africa

For all the remainder of the day, as clouds gathered thicker and light rain washed the smoke from the sky, the grand Allied army literally hacked and blasted the increasingly desperate Grik back down the slickening reverse slope to the shrinking lake. Many fought even more ferociously than before, and survivors of various Allied units would later relate grisly descriptions of those hours in haunted tones.

Somewhat controversially, Halik left a small gap through which brighter Grik commanders might take less shattered units, squirting through the tightening cordon to the east. But the rest, some thirty-five thousand, slowly recoiled from the bristling, fire-spitting, Allied hosts, down around the charred remains of the dirigible, until their packed, jumbled mass roughly resembled the battered egg-shape Rolak had desired. Precarious as the Allied supply line had been, its wagons and beasts of burden (mostly paalkas, but also Borno "brontosarries" brought in for the task) had made it firmer and surer than the Grik's—until today, of course—and they'd hoarded plenty of ammunition for this fight. They hadn't actually expected to *use* so much, relying heavily on airpower for the real killing, but despite the absent planes, Rolak adapted and they had enough.

The Grik, on the other hand, had nothing left. The lake had been their only means of tactical resupply and nothing floated on it. Besides, the only munitions ever made at Lake Galk had been gunpowder for rockets, then *yanone*, most of which Esshk cannibalized for his great bomb. All the Grik artillery had been overrun at the escarpment cliffs and by that drizzly evening, the final remains of Esshk's New Army had been pinned against, partially *into* the bleeding lake. Its warriors were exhausted, bloody, half-starved, and hopeless, and probably didn't have five thousand musket rounds among them. That's when Rolak directed that every cannon, machine gun, mortar, and rifleman he had left should form a crescent around the prostrate force.

Bekiaa joined him and General Taa-Leen on the corpse-choked crest they'd fought so hard to win, half supported by Meek, with Prefect Bele at her side. Her arm was gone, the stump bundled in bloody bandages and strapped against her side. Inquisitor Choon had arrived with Saachic and Taa-Leen, and was fussing over her enough that, half drunk on seep or loss of blood, she was getting annoyed with him. He could hardly hear her objections. Even with the fighting paused and hardly a shot now fired, the noise of this dreadful dusk was tremendous. A panicked tumult rumbled among the ruined remains of Esshk's last horde as it milled and jostled, tightly packed, still dying as water monsters snatched shrieking warriors into the shrinking lake. Those closest to the water tried to surge away but others cut them down. Blood fanned out, drawing more predators. Above all that was the constant death roar of the murdered lake. Bekiaa only cared how that affected her own people downstream, and had no concern for other Grik, allied or not. The noise struck her as appropriate somehow, and her eyes were alight with satisfaction.

A short column of me-naak cavalry loped up from the right, not Saachic's. That was clear at once. The riders looked more threadbare and weathered than any one battle could've made them. And then there were the kravaas, carrying men as well as 'Cats. Bekiaa knew only one force that rode those tall, frightening beasts, and she owed them her life. Behind the columns, in front of others, came several bipedal hadrosaurs like Bekiaa had seen in Indiaa. They were pulling wide-axle chariots, each bearing two or three Grik.

"Col-nol Enaak! Col-nol Svec!" Rolak called in greeting. He sounded tired, old. Not the same 'Cat who'd done what Bekiaa saw earlier at all. A moment later he added, "And Gener-aals Haalik and Niwaa, I see as well."

Bekiaa actually hissed, and Rolak blinked surprise at her. "You forget," she reminded loudly, through tightly clenched teeth, "no maatter how . . . extraa-ordinary you and Gener-aal Aalden later found them to be, I only ever met them in baattle—on Saay-lon, in Indiaa, in the Rocky Gaap"—she took a harsh breath—"and on North Hill, where Flynn's Rangers died." Seeing the Japanese officer up close for the first time as he, Halik, and another Grik stepped down from the first chariot, she omitted her suspicion that she'd been the one who shot and wounded him at Flynn's Lake. Svec and

Enaak, their columns halted, dismounted as well. Enaak crisply saluted Rolak and Taa-Leen, but Svec continued forward, exhausted eyes fixed on Bekiaa and flaring with concern in his grimy, bearded face. To Bekiaa's complete astonishment, the huge man knelt and very gently embraced her.

"My dear child, bravest of the brave. It breaks my heart to see you so, yet I'm glad to see you at all." He straightened, then shrugged somewhat wryly. "I understand how you feel. No one ever hated Grik more than I, yet here I've come in company with them, having fought *beside* them almost since you and I parted!"

Halik, Niwa, and the other Grik looked as tired as everyone, their arms and leather armor crisscrossed with cuts and caked with drying blood, but Halik heard Bekiaa and replied in Grikish. She didn't understand, but Niwa translated for her. "It's true. And General Prime Regent Halik would apologize for much, but it's *Esshk* who earned the blame. Esshk made him what he was—made *all* of us what we were for a time, I suspect," Niwa added as softly as he could over the racket. "But we've remade ourselves and traveled far, in more ways than one. Thousands of miles, and even further in our thinking."

Halik stepped up to Rolak, who straightened now himself. To Bekiaa's further astonishment, the powerful Grik *saluted* the old 'Cat. "Third General Rolak," he said in English, then continued in his own tongue. "It's been a great long while, and I greet you now as my master in this common Hunt, instead of my very worthy foe. May I present General Yikkit?" He gestured at the other Grik—who also saluted! Bekiaa thought she must be delirious. "And where is First General Alden?" Halik asked.

"Lost, I fear," Rolak replied grimly, blinking remorse and twitching his tail toward the broken lock, "along with . . . maany more downriver."

"And the Celestial Mother?"

"She wouldn't evaacuate Old Sofesshk, and took refuge in the upper levels of the Palace with the remaining Ancient Hij of the city. The flood reached there some hours ago and we lost contaact. We caan only hope they stayed above it."

"Indeed," Halik brooded, turning to face the booming cataract a few hundred yards to the west. "I was favorably impressed by the Giver of Life when I met her, and her devotion to her subjects only raises my appraisal." A sigh rattled through his teeth. "In any event, you command," he stated simply, turning to the Grik below. "What are your intentions?"

"Kill 'em all," Bekiaa snapped harshly, as if challenging Halik to object.

"We can do that," he agreed. "Rather easily now, and with few further losses." He waited a moment while that sank in, then added, looking at Rolak, "Or you can give them to me." He gestured at the chariots. "Taking a lesson I learned from you, I brought signal horns"—his frightening jaws parted in an evil Grik grin—"and willing converts who'll sound a combination of notes meant to call troops to attention—and cease fighting. It's a new signal, intended to end an accidental attack on a friendly force in the confusion of battle or darkness. If they obey, I believe I can secure a kind of surrender."

"A *kind* of surrender?" Inquisitor Choon demanded. "First Colonel Jash surrendered completely to Captain Reddy."

"That was an extraordinary circumstance, and Captain Reddy had the visible support of the Celestial Mother. We do not."

"An' if they roll over, what'll you do with 'em?" Bekiaa challenged suspiciously.

Halik looked at her. "Save them, as I've been saved, and take them back to Persia. The Celestial Mother will always be Giver of Life to my regency, but it's *my* regency and I must finish winning it." He tilted his snout at the warriors below. "They can help."

Rolak was blinking undecided interest. "If they yield, how do we feed them? With our supply lines cut and the scope of the disaaster downriver unknown, I don't even know how we'll feed our own aarmy."

Halik snorted something that might've been amusement. "*My* supply lines, though tortuous, are intact. And when the outcome of this battle is known, none of the regencies I passed through will oppose us. With your wagons and other transport added to mine, and if you can subsist on what Enaak's and Svec's troops have, we should be able to procure sufficient provisions for all." He waved around. "And after today, I believe there'll be plenty of . . . rations for my troops, our prisoners, and your me-naaks as well. For a while, at least."

"No *waay* he gets Esshk, if he's down there!" Bekiaa objected, then accused, "An' if he didn't sneak off through the gaap he left." She'd been particularly worried about that.

Halik blinked at her. "He did *not* 'sneak off.' Those who did were carefully watched and will be given the same 'offer' to join *my* Hunt as the rest. As for Esshk, his fate belongs in the claws of the Celestial Mother"—he hesitated—"and yours as well, as the people he most grievously harmed."

"First Ker-noll Jash should have a say," Choon murmured. "It was he who flushed Esshk out of his lair and shot him down. Otherwise, he would've escaped and remained a persistent problem. I wish we could get him over here."

"He'll haave a saay about Esshk, I'm sure," Rolak said, suddenly decisive. "If Esshk is truly down there, still alive, and we get him," he qualified, "I haave no doubt *everyone* will haave something to saay. But ending this baattle—" He glanced at Halik and a note of wonder entered his voice. "Ending this *waar* at long laast is up to me." He finally nodded. "Very well, Generaal Haalik. See whaat you can do. But commaand any who surrender thaat Esshk must be spared for us, and not allowed to destroy himself. Moreover, if he's already dead, he must be identified. We caan't be chasing his despicable spirit—if he haas such a thing—for the rest of our days."

General Supreme Regent Esshk survived the crash, and a ragtag gaggle of Grik officers, about half *Dorrighsti*, had dragged him from the wreckage of the airship before it burned. The steersman, pinned in the collapsed gondola but otherwise unharmed, was abandoned to the quickening flames. Esshk felt an instant of remorse over that, but he'd been groggy and disoriented after the impact, even if his only real injury remained a missing toe.

His wits returned as the battle on the ridge above reached its peak, however, and though he could do little to direct it from where he was, he thought his presence had actually turned the tide. He was right, in a way. As his frustrated officers began to hear he was there, many felt justified in pulling their wavering warriors back from the murderously unyielding enemy lines they simply couldn't break. They were sure Esshk would excuse their faithful desire to personally defend him. Esshk personally *slew* the first such officers to make their obsequious reports, while their troops fell back in disarray and the enemy relentlessly advanced. Still, a contraction of that sort, on such a vast scale, takes time, and Esshk summoned all his energies to stop it. He sent his improvised staff racing in all directions carrying direct commands that the army stand, no matter what. Keeping only a handful of officers and *Dorrighsti* around him, he ranted and raved through the thickening mob, hacking down every messenger from officers swearing to "save" him. Eventually, the messengers no longer came, or if they did, they didn't approach, and the fatal retreat continued. How could it not? Whole blocks of troops left the fight at random, leaving others unsupported. Better commanders, recognizing the disaster in the making, tried to cover the gaps, but the enemy was pushing harder now and their thinner ranks couldn't hold. They melted into rivers of blood, and finally, shattered fugitives.

This is the end, Esshk understood at last, as the sun, long hidden behind dripping clouds, must've disappeared entirely beyond the western mountains. *And such an ignominious end!* He silently seethed. *Impenetrably encircled by my enemies, surrounded by warriors turned prey.* "Not acceptable!" he bellowed aloud, his voice stifled by the din of defeat. "I've accomplished too much. . . . I'm too *great* to end this way!" he railed. Only those closest heard him, and his tone was tinged with madness—and the plaintive bleat of cornered prey. Even his remaining *Dorrighsti* bristled at the sound. Then there came another sound, rising to a thunder from the heights around them.

It was the "attention" note, roaring from many horns. Since it was preceded by no unit prefix, the whole army paused to hear. The call was immediately followed by the relatively complex "cease fighting/firing, no enemy" tones Esshk had concocted himself so his own warriors wouldn't kill one another in the confusion of battle. It had seemed a good idea at the time.

"No, no, no!" he screeched, doubly tormented that something *else* he'd created had turned against him, as the second call repeated again and again. "Sound the 'attack' horns at once!" he squawked breathlessly, slamming through the milling troops, trying to reach a lone pennant section nearby. There'd be horns there. A few *Dorrighsti* tried to make way for him in the press. "Attack, attack!" Esshk chanted with every step, voice firming, starting to earn some echoes. Then he bashed against the back of a young warrior with a very short crest, helmet gone, eyes wide. Pure reflex spun the warrior around, lashing with a musket butt that crashed into Esshk's lower jaw, snapping bone and scattering teeth.

Esshk stood a moment, stunned and drooling blood, before being carried forward by a *Dorrighsti* who pushed him against the back of a Kernoll, judging by the full crest and elaborate leather armor. The officer's response was the same as the young trooper's, however; only he turned with a sword stroke that nearly severed Esshk's left arm. Esshk shrieked . . . calling another kind of attention to himself: the sort hungry predators pay to wounded prey.

"I'm Supreme Regent Esshk!" he tried to roar, but to his horror, his broken jaw turned the grand pronouncement to a meaningless bleat. He realized then that few nearby would recognize him anyway, seeing only blood and weakness. A dispassionate fatalism washed over Esshk. He sighed and blood bubbled. *So after everything, it will be like this,* he thought. He drew his sword.

Even wounded, he was powerful, well-trained with swords, and he'd killed many hundreds over time. But those were all mere executions. He'd never actually had to *fight. It'll be interesting to see how I fare,* he thought, *in this final battle against warriors I made.* He never really found out. Confused and starving, half-"prey" themselves, the closest warriors swarmed him, tearing him apart just like others by the water were shredding those trying to escape it. Esshk's composure fled with the first cuts and slashes, and before he died, screaming like countless others he'd sent to die, he was aware the soldiers he'd created from nothing—even one of his *Dorrighsti*—were already feeding on his flesh.

Esshk wouldn't escape, nor would his spirit wander as Rolak feared. His gnawed bones and armor and the shredded remnants of his cape would eventually be definitively identified by that very *Dorrighsti* in exchange for beheading, instead of the traitor's death. Anything was better than being chained down and consumed by hungry hatchlings. And since it was reserved only for Hij, or those elevated enough to understand their crime, not only was the traitor's death dreaded as lengthy and painful, it was humiliating as well. But even Halik wouldn't allow *Dorrighsti* to live; they were all traitors to the Celestial Mother. Most suffered fates ironically appropriate and similar to Esshk's. Though adults, of course, every *Dorrighsti* had been *his* hatchling, after all.

CHAPTER 39

THE CURTAIN RIPS

////// *USS* James Ellis
Santiago Bay, NUS Territory
The Caribbean
August 3, 1945

Lieutenant Rolando "Ronson" Rodriguez leaned on the rail of USS *James Ellis*'s fire control platform, just above her pilothouse, watching the sun creep over the horizon and bathe Santiago Bay in golden morning light. It was a beautiful anchorage, filled with clear, greenish water, bordered by white sandy beaches, well-kept docks, and semi-surrounded by a bustling city of whitewashed stone and stucco. The scent of flowers and the contrasting rancid stench of gri-kakka oil wafted on the morning breeze. (Like Lemurians, Nussies hunted gri-kakka—pliosaurs—for their oil and meat.) There were probably only a couple dozen ships anchored in the broad bay, in addition to the freighters *Ellie* and *Adar* escorted in, but they took him back a little since all were either sailing steamers or dedicated square-riggers.

"How about the dope out of Africa? You believe that?" said Lieutenant (jg) Paul Stites, joining Ronson by the rail. The coded news they'd picked up of events in the west was triumphant but very confusing. It *sounded* like victory over the Grik, and Esshk was confirmed dead, but not only had the casualties been appalling, there was a stunning number of missing—including General Alden. "Yeah, crazy," Ronson replied, not sure how he felt. He should've been jubilant but only felt . . . drained. He nodded at Santiago to change the subject. "Pretty place."

"I guess. Wish we were the hell out of it, though." Stites was *Ellie*'s gunnery officer, good at what he did, but he hadn't changed much from when he'd been one of Silva's troublemaking gunner's mate minions aboard USS *Walker.* He still seemed grumpy all the time and given to a pessimistic streak. Ronson had to agree with him now, however. Santiago was picturesque, but it wasn't really *right.* He'd been in "old" Santiago in the '30s. Not only did this one look a lot different, it wasn't even in the right place. He didn't know why that bothered him, but it did. Or maybe it was just that *Ellie* and *Adar*—pretending to be *Walker* and *Mahan*, of course—stuck out like sore thumbs among all the older-style ships and couldn't really stretch their legs to avoid the air attack they knew was coming.

The warning came from a pair of Repub *Seevogels* that'd been watching Martinique for days without even being pestered by the impressive air armada they'd reported growing there. It was like the Leaguers *wanted* them to know what they were up against. They'd signaled when they saw *Leopardo* and another DD come in two days before, and that seemed to stir things up. Then, that morning, word came in that it looked like somebody shot a hornet's nest. Ships—even a trio of battleships—were getting underway and planes were taking off. Shortly after, there'd been a short, frantic "mayday" from a scout plane. There was only one place all that power could be heading—there'd been League scouts over Santiago Bay as well—and Ronson felt helpless, too much like when they'd all been waiting for the inevitable Japanese attack on Cavite.

Worse, Ronson knew Captain Reddy *wanted* the enemy to see them. The scouts had already spotted them, but it was important the Leaguers be certain that they, and possibly Captain Reddy himself, were still there. The good thing was, there'd be no enemy fighters—they didn't have the range—and the bombers couldn't stay long. The enemy fleet couldn't arrive before late the next day at the earliest, and *Ellie* and *Adar* would be long gone by then. They didn't have to just sit and take it when the bombers came either. Both destroyers, like all the new DDs, had dual-purpose guns, and *Ellie* had been upgraded with the new standard *four* twin 25mm mounts, as well as five twin-mounted water-cooled .50s. Two flanked the gun director near where Ronson and Stites now stood, another pair was on the amidships gun platform, and one was right behind the aft deckhouse. They were better armed against air attack than any 4-stacker destroyer ever was before.

The roar of an engine came from aft, almost drowning the impulse charge of the catapult rigged to port. Smoke swirled and a PB-1F—the newest type of Nancy floatplane—was ejected over the water and rumbled into the sky. "Well, we're stuck here for now, with all the sacrificial lambs ashore," Ronson said, referring to the scores of old P-1B Mosquito Hawk "Fleashooters" they'd used to bait the airfield. Some had been flown down off the carriers, but more were unloaded from the freighters and literally rolled through the streets to their final destination. "We even reported in, that we're ready as we'll ever be," he added. "Actually feels kinda weird just to make a routine radio transmission after we've been blacked out so long," he reflected. "Sneakin' around without comm has really been a pain, but I get it. The enemy learns stuff from our wireless traffic even if they can't break our codes."

"Like what?" Stites asked.

Ronson twisted his big mustache. "All sorts of things. Approximately where we are, for one thing. The League's got radio direction finders, same as us. And if everybody's jabbering away, they can even get an idea about the size of our force and how it's distributed. Now they know where we are, though, we can squeal all we want."

"Nobody'll answer."

"Nope. Not for a while. I guess it won't matter, once the balloon goes up, except for the task forces still sneakin' around. They'll keep their traps shut until the Leaguers get wise."

With their planes gone, *Ellie* and *Adar* got underway and the growing breeze was almost cool. This was the farthest Ronson had been from the equator in a long time and it was refreshing. Together, the destroyers slowly steamed back and forth in the outer harbor inside the long eastern breakwater.

"We gonna have anything in the air to meet 'em when they come?" Stites asked grumpily, still focused on the expected attack.

Ronson noted several 'Cats listening closely, blinking nervous curiosity. "A little," he replied. "Not all the planes they strung out on the fields were wrecks. Probably could've done some good with 'em against bombers if we had time to train Nussies to fly 'em. No sense wasting *our* pilots in 'em, now we've got better planes."

"So some of our new pursuit ships're here? Be neat to see how they do."

"Just a few," Ronson warned. "Most're still on the carriers, or with Ben Mallory."

"Flyboys," Stites grumped, and launched a brown stream of real tobacco juice over the rail. Not a single drop touched the deck below before it splashed in the foam alongside. "I hope they kick the shit out of 'em."

Seepy Field
Puerto Rico, NUS Territory

The lush, grass airstrip named "Seepy Field" on the northeast end of Puerto Rico—the third largest of the NUS-occupied "Isles of Cuba"—was wide and flat and bounded only by the sea and a modest cluster of mountains to the southeast. Dense trees bordered it on the lower slopes of closer hills, providing cover for Jumbo Fisher's thirty TBD-2s, twenty-two P-5 Bull-Bats (the nickname had stuck hard) of the 7th Pursuit Squadron under Ez "Easy" Shiaa, and Orrin Reddy's four P-40Es, all under Ben Mallory's overall command. Particularly observant enemy scouts might've seen lines in the grass where planes had landed, but the aircraft themselves were well-hidden. Only one enemy scout ever overflew the place in any case, a three-engine medium bomber Ben identified as a "Kingfisher." Its crew was probably equally impressed by the area's future utility as an airfield, but apparently found nothing amiss.

Preparing the airstrip hadn't required much effort by the Nussie labor battalion sent to perform the task. All they'd done was mark its boundaries, remove a few cartloads of stones, fill some holes, set up tents and other necessities under the trees, and keep the strange, hadrosaur-like "cattle" chased away. Virtually the entire sparsely populated island was given over to ranching since there was fine grazing and few predators. Preparing for the logistical requirements of Ben Mallory's Army/Navy air corps detachment was another matter, however, taking weeks. The most frustrating aspect required gathering nearly three hundred wagons and draft animals. Horses were rare, so "dillos" had to suffice. These were somewhat stunted (compared to their continental cousins), but still gigantic, armadillo-like "armabueys." They also needed about half the remaining population of the island, mostly women and children since their men were off with the army or fleet, to converge at a little fishing village called Port January, about where San Juan would be on a different Earth. When the SPD *Tarakan Island* backed into the docks and offloaded her burden of fuel barrels, bombs, and torpedoes, as well as Ben's ground crew personnel and all the stuff they needed, the real work began. By morning, *Tara* was gone, empty except for the twenty-four boats of Nat Hardee's MTB-Ron-5. Directed by the ground crews, women and kids loaded hundreds of tons of fuel and ordnance on the wagons and laboriously hauled it all seven miles east across streams and stretches of swampy ground until they reached the new airfield under cover of another night. The delicate, dangerous freight was unloaded and concealed in hastily built bunkers under the trees by the bulk of the labor battalion. By the time Ben's planes started landing, already loaded with fuel and munitions, most of the locals had dispersed. Ben was impressed by the civilian effort in particular and came down hard on anyone he heard denigrating Nussie devotion to the cause. So did the ground crews who'd helped them.

Not that there was much time for reflections of any sort, as it turned out. They'd barely gotten settled in, a mere two days after their arrival, when the radio squawked the warning they'd been waiting for and Ben passed the word to sound the scramble alarm.

"What's the dope?" Orrin asked, running up with Jumbo.

"League bombers, headed for Santiago. No fighters, and even the bombers must be carrying extra fuel, but it looks like they're sending all they have. Maybe about twenty three-engine jobs, and ten twin-engine."

"Then it's time for us to paay them a visit as well," Shirley said grimly.

"Still not sure I ought to go," Cecil Dixon grumbled, staring at one of the last four P-40s in the world, dark and mottled in the shade of the trees. "Always been a better wrench than a pilot." Nobody thought he was afraid, but he'd made it clear that he believed the plane was wasted on him.

Ben growled, exasperated. "You may not've had a commission in the old days, *Lieutenant* Dixon, but you taught an awful lot of guys to fly P-40s. My money's on you showing us again. C'mon, let's get going."

"My Far—I mean, TBDs—are loaded with bombs. No change?" Jumbo asked. The new torpedo bombers had finally been designated "Banaakaai," basically Lemurian for "Thunderer." The pursuit pilots immediately, probably inevitably, changed that to "Farter," and the bomber crews—understandably proud of their new planes—had simply reverted to calling them "TBDs," or just "Twos," again, in an effort to suppress the slander.

Ben shook his head. "No. Even if we had time, the word is about half the League fleet sortied too. You'll get your chance with torpedoes later."

"Don't forget, Colonel," called Orrin, splitting off toward his own plane. "You may command our little wing here—hell, you're in charge of *everything* with wings, when it comes down to it—but when we're in the air today, we're in reserve. If we have to jump in, you're supposed to follow *my* lead."

"No arguments," Ben called back. "My one and only tangle with Macchi-

Messerschmitts, they nearly ate my lunch." He nodded at Shirley, grinning. "She's way better than I am—as long as her feet don't slip off the rudder pedals." Shirley was very short and had to sit on two parachutes to see through her gunsight. She also wore special thick-soled sandals instead of the wooden blocks she'd once used just to *reach* the rudder pedals. The sandals made it hard to walk, however, so her ground crew laced them on her and hoisted her into her plane.

Orrin grinned at the sight as he vaulted up on the wing of his own P-40 and settled into the cockpit. "Come to think of it," he shouted back at Ben while his Lemurian crew chief strapped him in, "I've spent more time *out* of these crates than I ever did in 'em, and it's been a while since I mixed it up with Japs over the Philippines. I'm a little rusty. Maybe you better watch *my* ass!"

Ben snorted to himself. Regardless of his past, Orrin had been dogfighting Grikbirds in Nancys and Fleashooters. They were slower, but way more maneuverable. All he'd ever asked about the enemy's Macchi-Messerschmitts was whether he could turn with them or not. Impressed by Orrin's grasp of something so fundamental, he'd said, "Yeah, barely." Orrin had only nodded.

The four P-40E Warhawks fired up easily, blue smoke swirling and jetting away, their healthy exhaust sounds a testament to the loving maintenance they'd received. Shortly afterward, with Orrin's plane flanked by Ben's, and Shirley's by Cecil's (Dixon *was* rusty, despite the reorientation flights they'd made back at Baalkpan, and would follow Shirley's lead), they taxied out on the grass field and thundered into the sky. Once airborne, they orbited while the TBD-2s joined, followed by Easy's P-5s. When their formations were sorted out, fifty-six aircraft, loaded with bombs, bullets, and precious aircrews, slanted off to the east-southeast.

CHAPTER 40

////// League-Occupied Martinique
The Caribbean

The die was cast, and Victor Gravois, Gouverneur Militaire du Protectorat des Antilles, was enjoying a splendid early lunch with Capitano Campioni aboard his enormous 46,000-ton Littorio Class battleship *Impero*, while they waited patiently for news of the grand air and sea attacks Gravois ordered against Santiago. His and Ciano's suspicions had been confirmed by a recon plane launched off a scouting cruiser; Captain Reddy's destroyers *were* in Santiago Bay, and a large number of aircraft had been gathered on nearby fields. There was no news of Reddy's carrier, but they were doubtless right that it had retired into the Gulf.

There'd be a much longer wait before they learned how Ammiraglio di Divisione Bruto Gherzi's three battleship, four cruiser, and eight destroyer bombardment raid went, but that should be anticlimactic since its target was two aged, dilapidated destroyers, a helpless fleet of sailing ships at anchor, and the city of Santiago itself. In any event, the bombardment element's primary purpose was more intimidation than destruction—though it would certainly perform a lot of the latter. How better to accomplish the former? But now that the final curtain had been raised, Gravois felt almost giddy, anticipating a most pleasant wait.

Impero was the newest and arguably most powerful ship in the entire League fleet, rushed to completion just months before the fateful operation that brought them to this dreadful world. As such, she was Ammiraglio Gherzi's flagship in the Antilles. But Gherzi left her behind for his sortie, shifting his flag to the Lyon Class *Tourville*, an elderly but powerful and highly modernized French battleship. He was under Gravois's operational direction, but held orders directly from the Triumvirate never to risk *Im-*

pero in unfamiliar waters. That was fine with Gravois, since the rotund Gherzi was a slave to his stomach and his table in the spacious flag officer's suite was exquisite.

The company wasn't bad either. Ciano was there, *Leopardo* anchored nearby, and Capitano Campioni was an old friend and enthusiastic convert to Gravois's scheme. Campioni worried about Gherzi, who was neither terrified of the OVRA, nor as deferential to Marshall Messe as he probably should be. Campioni believed Gherzi's primary loyalty was to his duty to carry out orders, period, and thought he'd follow Gravois's when the time came. If not, Campioni would be happy to take his place. Gesturing gently at a window with his half-filled wineglass, Campioni now indicated the other ships remaining at Martinique. "I wish we all could've gone," he said wistfully. "I understand our fuel constraints, but another battleship, four more cruisers, and five more destroyers—including yours, my dear Ciano—would've made the impact"—he smirked—"even more profound. And I suppose we could've even towed that loathsome old toad out there along. Whether she can move or not, her guns still fire." He was referring to the only other BB still sharing the harbor, the old Spanish dreadnaught *Espana*.

"Come, come," Gravois chastised. "She's in little worse shape than some of our French battleships, I hear. Their maintenance was too long neglected."

"True," Campioni grudged, but his face wore a sneer. "*Espana*'s engineering problems aren't severe, she's just . . ." He sighed. "So poorly manned. A *proper* crew would have her seaworthy in hours, not days. Or weeks. The Spaniard is a fine soldier," he granted begrudgingly, "more experienced and ruthless than my Italian brethren, but I fear his seamanship has declined precipitously in recent centuries."

"Well," Gravois said, "then it's fortunate we have so many of them for land operations, while the French and Italians carry the League at sea!"

"What of the Germans?" Ciano questioned.

"What of them?" Campioni countered harshly. "They have but a single cruiser here." He was referring to KMS *Hessen*, still anchored as well. Her sister, *Elsass*, was the only other large German surface combatant, and she'd been kept in the Med. Always dissatisfied with their subordinate standing in the League, the German contingent was growing increasingly rebellious and Marshall Messe didn't trust them. Gravois intended to use that to his advantage. "And their single remaining submarine is at home, under repair," Campioni complained.

"At least they have one," Gravois pointed out, remembering he'd abandoned another—*U-112*—in the Indian Ocean. He cared nothing for its crew, but the submarine would've been handy now, parked in the mouth of the Pass of Fire. Then of course, there was that lone French submarine that wasted itself in a premature attack on their current enemy. . . . He took a sip of his wine. "Come," he admonished again, "I know you would've enjoyed some action, but you'll soon have it. In the meantime let's enjoy our meal"—he also gestured at the window—"and the scenery."

Campioni stared at him, agog. "Scenery? With respect, sir, you've not been ashore on this miserable island. The deadly snakes are so numerous they could only be sustained by the multitudes of vermin and insects that infest the place."

Gravois's voice turned hard. "At least you've felt dry land beneath your feet, Capitano. I can't remember when Ciano and I last did. Our 'allies' won't permit it. Just as well, because your view is *much* more pleasant than what we've endured at Puerto del Cielo for so long. You can't imagine the depravity we've witnessed. . . ." He shook his head. "Believe me, Capitano Campioni, Don Hernan and his Blood Priests would make your serpents and vermin blush. Enough of your complaints."

"Then why do we tolerate them?" Campioni asked, genuinely curious.

Gravois sighed. "Because Don Hernan and I have an understanding, and he's currently occupying *all* the enemy armies in this hemisphere. Despite our naval power, do you think we could hold this outpost with a mere five thousand troops—Spanish or otherwise—if he wasn't?" He shrugged. "And since Don Hernan trusts me, I can topple him whenever I wish." Ciano would know that was a boastful simplification at best, especially since Don Hernan trusted no one, but if their analysis was correct, he'd soon be utterly dependent on Gravois.

They felt more than heard a quick, staccato thumping, like someone jumping up and down on the deck overhead. Then a speaker on the bulkhead crackled and a bugle call blared through the metal grill. Gravois wasn't familiar with Italian alerts, but Campioni and Ciano knocked their chairs over jumping to their feet. "I must go to the bridge," Campioni called behind as he bolted through the hatch.

"What is it?" Gravois demanded of Ciano.

"*Air attack.* I must return to *Leopardo*!"

Gravois's mind reeled. *How?* he demanded of himself. Then he knew. *Captain Reddy's* Maaka-Kakja *must've slipped past our scouts, somehow.*

"No," he snapped. "You'll never reach her in time and you must stay with me. Let's go out on the flag bridge and observe."

The first thing they saw was a cluster of heavy smoke plumes rising like black towers against a bright green mountain. Gravois hadn't been ashore, but knew where the island's two airfields were. One, at least, was catching hell. A junior officer rushed up behind them, probably sent by Campioni, and Gravois snatched his binoculars. Focusing on a flitting shape, he gasped. "Those are bombers! *Real* bombers, with two engines!" he exclaimed. He'd seen the aircraft Muriname made for Kurokawa on Zanzibar, but these weren't the same at all. He wondered what other surprises the enemy had conjured since the League's intelligence-gathering apparatus was eviscerated by their expulsion from the Indian Ocean.

"There are quite a few of them," Ciano stated grimly, "and some are heading this way," he added, voice rising.

Gravois watched ten blue, twin-engine shapes arrowing toward the harbor. Dark clouds blossomed around them as ground-based antiaircraft batteries finally opened up. The surprise had been so complete, he was frankly amazed the gunners reacted so fast. A ball of orange fire rolled into the sky about where the other airfield was, but Gravois saw some of their own planes taking to the air. *A few would've been aloft already,* he consoled himself, *and they'll be coming soon. Quick enough?*

"On your tail, Cecil! Seven o'clock!" Orrin Reddy shouted in his mic. Any need for radio silence vanished when A-Flight's ten TBD-2s swept over the first, largest airfield. Each dropped two of their four 250-pound bombs. The dirt strip erupted in massive, dusty brown stalks that cratered the runway. Then the bombs started finding planes and fuel storage tanks and those explosions were much more colorful. B-Flight's bombers had more trouble finding the smaller, better-hidden airfield farther from the harbor, and fighters were already rising before they turned in on it. Others already in the sky were going after them. A section of Easy's pursuiters dove, and just as a Macchi-Messerschmitt riddled a TBD-2 with holes and sent it plunging into the jungle to sear the trees with flames, a pair of "Bull-Bats" got their first air-to-air kill, exploding the same "Macchi-Mess." But there were more, and Orrin quickly realized, surprised or not, League pilots were pretty quick on the draw.

The Bull-Bats held their own, in pairs, keeping League fighters off their bombers pretty well. As the confusion of the dogfight spread them out, however, they started falling to the swifter, more heavily armed planes. New explosions gouging the second airfield diverted some defenders and Easy's pilots reorganized to chase them. The sky over Martinique started to resemble a giant spaghetti pile of smoke trails, streaming tracers, and white vapor streaking from radically maneuvering wingtips. League fighters fell to earth, but so did Bull-Bats and TBDs. Orrin cold-bloodedly figured the exchange rate at three to one in favor of the League, but the Allies could afford that. And it was actually better than he'd cynically predicted.

C-Flight, each plane carrying two *500*-pound bombs, charged toward the harbor, low over the trees, with a mixed gaggle of Macchi-Messers—*and freaking Stukas!*—after them. All of Easy's 7th Pursuiters were occupied.

"Third Pursuit! Tallyho the bandits after C-Flight!" Orrin had called, peeling over and starting his dive. He'd just taken the little squadron of P-40s in its overwatch position away from Ben Mallory—and Ben away from himself. To his credit, Ben hadn't squawked, and he, Shirley, and Cecil immediately followed Orrin in.

They downed several planes in their slashing dive, and most of the pursuit—all but the slower Stukas—broke away from C-Flight in confusion. The bombers carried on through a growing barrage of AA fire from the ground and ships at anchor. Some staggered from hits and started to smoke as they separated and went for specific targets. The sudden appearance of Orrin's modern planes seemed to draw every League fighter on the island, however, and the 3rd Pursuit quickly found itself almost as outnumbered as the enemy had been by Bull-Bats.

Two overriding questions that had haunted Orrin, Ben, Shirley, and Cecil were answered very quickly in the savage free-for-all that ensued: P-40s *could* turn with Macchi-Messerschmitts, at least at low attitude. More importantly, "rusty" as they might consider themselves, they'd all been flying *something* in combat against challenging opponents of various kinds ever since they came to this world. The mighty League air force had never been tested in the air. Their pilots were a lot rustier, and it cost them.

Cecil Dixon flipped his plane into a tight left bank and Shirley swooped and shattered his attacker with her six .50s. Small chunks fluttered away, followed by the entire left wing. The fighter crashed into a camouflaged storage building that erupted with secondary explosions like a fireworks show. Orrin caught a tightly turning Macchi-Mess with a difficult deflection shot and it disintegrated into dozens of flaming fragments. That brought his rapidly rising total to four League planes, so far. Then he spotted a pair of Stuka dive bombers pulling away, either lured by easier targets or repelled by the growing hurricane of flack directed at the Allied bombers. Despite being warned, Orrin was still surprised to see their distinctive, unchanged, gull-wing shapes. *Junkers must've gotten through whatever made Willy Messerschmitt merge with Macchi,* he mused, as a burst from his guns sent a Stuka tumbling into the trees. Ben got the other one and they pulled up, looking for more dangerous game. It wasn't hard to find.

Despite the stress of combat, even the fear, Orrin felt a kind of inner peace he'd rarely experienced since the Philippines. The enemy was different, even the world was, but the circumstances were the same. He was fighting for his life over mountainous jungle in a desperate battle against planes at least as good as his. And the League reminded him of the Japanese. They were fascists with a mighty fleet, here to conquer. But he was back in a P-40, flying like he was built with it, exhilarated by his skill, the raw power of his plane, and even the fierce nostalgia of the moment. More significantly, as much as he'd enjoyed working with Admiral Lela, he'd never liked the responsibility of being *Makky-Kat*'s COFO. He suspected Matt knew that, and was probably even a little disappointed he hadn't stepped up more vigorously. But he'd done his best, damn it. And as much as he—mostly secretly—admired his cousin for taking charge of . . . everything, it seemed . . . Orrin wasn't made that way. He was just a fighter jock at heart, never cut out to wear the heavy brass. He knew Matt probably felt the same way and bucked under the weight, but he had the *will* to carry it. Orrin didn't. Now here he was, doing what he was best at, only part of a team he wasn't really in charge of once again. Even over a backseater in a Nancy. And for the first time since he lost his last P-40 over Luzon, he was having fun.

"Intel was right," Orrin heard Ben's stressed voice say as he chased a Macchi-Mess in front of Orrin's guns. The sleek shape with the mottled paint scheme started smoking and dived away. Another took its place almost instantly and Orrin didn't even have to maneuver to blast it out of the sky. "*All* their fighters are here," Ben continued. "Shit!" he chirped.

Orrin saw tracers flaring past Ben's plane and remembered he *was* responsible for helping his squadron mates, and protecting Ben in particular. *Matt would never forgive me for blowing that.* Instinctively, he kicked his rudder left to bleed some speed before cutting right again to point his nose at Ben's attacker. Six .50s rattled in his wings and the Macchi-Mess in front of him came unzipped amid a cloud of aluminum confetti and fell away in two large, burning pieces. An instant later, the fun ended when Orrin's plane shook again—and he wasn't firing. Pain lanced up his legs and the windscreen in front of his gunsight started going opaque. "Oil!" he shouted, disgusted voice tinged with shock and fear. "I'm hit and blowing oil, goddammit!" Acrid smoke boiled up under the instrument panel, immediately followed by a gust of flame. For an instant, as the burning agony engulfed him, he thought he'd jump and take his chances with the Leaguers. *Stupid,* he just as quickly realized, as the flames seared his face around his goggles. His shattered, burning legs wouldn't *let* him jump—and he'd never be a prisoner again. Gritting his teeth and closing his eyes, he pushed his stick forward.

As low as he was, he only suffered for four more seconds before, entirely by accident, his burning plane slammed into the fueling pier serving one of the tank batteries the TBDs hadn't hit. The crash that killed Orrin Reddy, Second Lieutenant, US Army Air Corps, wasn't particularly spectacular and the nearby oil tanks weren't ruptured, but the wooden dock was demolished and fueling lines ignited, leaking burning oil into the clouding water of the bay.

Victor Gravois was stunned by the scope of the disaster, and how quickly the serene certainty of his grand scheme was threatened. A constant stream of messengers brought him the latest reports and he digested them as best he could, but what he saw with his own eyes was bad enough. Tall columns of gray-black smoke stood over both airfields, joined by steamy tendrils rising from the jungle. Almost *half* his precious fuel reserves around the harbor were burning, and flaming oil was spreading on the water, hindering firefighting efforts. The raid had been a complete surprise, but the quality—and quantity—of the aircraft was just as unexpected. The little fighters had been no match for his modern planes, one-on-one, but they'd brought enough to more than occupy the League fighters that took off before many were slaughtered on the ground. And they weren't the pathetic little things he'd seen before either. These were probably less than a decade behind the best planes he had, and perhaps that far *ahead* of anything the League could make with its current priorities. Their numbers had made the difference, falling like flies, but felling or repelling most of the defenders as well. The appearance of four modern planes (one of which, at least, was lost) had been almost superfluous, except for how they covered the bomber approach to the harbor.

And those bombers! Not only were they nearly as fast as his own, they flew through more than enough concentrated fire to have blotted them all from the sky. Half of the first ten *were* blown apart before they reached their targets, but the rest wreaked enough destruction to justify the loss of them all. Tank batteries and docks, along with three precious, irreplaceable freighters tied to them, were blasted by what behaved like 250kg bombs! Other bombers, apparently finished with the airfields and still armed, came in as well. *Impero* and one of the newer cruisers savaged them with their heavy AA artillery suites and remained untouched. *Leopardo* as well, because she was so close alongside. But even though more than half the attacking bombers were shot down, they damaged *every other* ship to various degrees. Most were badly shaken by near misses, but one of those ruptured a destroyer's hull and sank her. Another destroyer was gutted by a hit directly amidships and sank in flames as well. Most critical, in Gravois's opinion, a French Suffren Class cruiser was horribly mauled and disabled by bombs that smashed her aft engine room and a forward turret. A fire consuming ammunition in the hoists still endangered her.

Perhaps most dramatically, the poor, immobile *Espana* was utterly destroyed. Her formidable appearance and weak AA must've drawn the bombers and she suffered hits on her fo'c'sle and amidships before *Impero*'s fire damaged a plane (apparently still carrying at least two bombs) that crashed into one of *Espana*'s aft gunhouses. The bomb blasts and wash of burning fuel somehow reached an aft magazine and the detonation was stupendous, shattering the ship's stern and sinking her at once. Every window on *Impero*'s starboard side turned to shards of flying glass, causing dozens of casualties. Gravois was lucky to escape serious injury himself, and even then he could barely hear over what sounded like constant, screeching brakes in his ears.

Reports told an even grimmer tale. Of the four bombers held back from the raid on Santiago and the twenty fighters and fifteen dive bombers Gravois had at dawn, *half* of everything had been destroyed on the ground. Eight fighters and seven dive bombers had apparently been shot down, and many of the survivors were damaged or destroyed trying to land on cratered runways! It was a catastrophe. His once mighty air arm had been whittled down to a single fighter, five Stukas, and two medium bombers fit to fly—other than those still winging toward Santiago, of course. His fuel reserve, already meager, was burning up around him, and a lot of his ordnance stores ashore had gone up in flames as well.

Ciano returned from inspecting his ship and joined Gravois and Campioni on *Impero*'s bridge. "Perhaps"—he hesitated—"perhaps we should recall Ammiraglio Gherzi and the airstrike," he suggested.

Gravois rounded on him. "To what possible advantage? The enemy planes at Santiago could *not* have made it here. The attack had to come from the enemy carrier. And as bad as our losses were, theirs were more severe. Their carrier is virtually disarmed! We can't allow the planes at Santiago to go to her." He fumed. "And we'll need some time to make hasty repairs to at least one airstrip so our planes can land when they return." A thought struck him and he turned to Campioni. "Our remaining planes can still take off, can they not?"

"Carefully," *Impero*'s captain hedged.

"Good. Then I want them all back up at once, every seaplane we have as well, searching for that enemy carrier. I want it found and *killed*, do you hear?" He was looking out at the harbor, suddenly aware of a glaring flaw in his dispositions: the destroyers that had picketed the approaches to Martinique—and might've given warning of the raid—had been dispatched with Gherzi's task force, and hadn't been replaced. "I want ships out searching as well."

"Most should make repairs before putting to sea," Campioni objected, "though one cruiser and two destroyers can sail at once."

"Very well, send them. But I want *everything* out searching as soon as possible, even if that leaves only *Impero* and *Leopardo* to protect our remaining oilers and cargo ships until Gherzi returns."

"It'll be costly in fuel," Campioni warned, "something we're suddenly far shorter of."

"And what of Gherzi?" Ciano pressed. "His sortie was designed to overawe the enemy. You don't really think he'll catch Captain Reddy at Santiago."

"What's your point?"

"He's burning fuel as well, for little return. We can't afford such extravagance now. He should be recalled."

Gravois considered that. When he spoke, his voice had lost a lot of its heat. "You're right, of course. But we can't remain confined in this harbor, and much of Gherzi's fuel is already spent. To recall him now will just ensure it was all wasted. Besides"—he tried to cheer them—"we'll soon have more. The supply convoy remains sensibly silent, but it must've left the Azores by now."

"Escorted by *another* thirsty battleship, two cruisers, and four destroyers," Campioni pointed out. "They'll suck the oilers dry by themselves."

Gravois frowned. He *wanted* those ships for his ultimate plan. The stronger he was, the easier it would be to defy the Triumvirate—and win converts to his defiance without a fight. But Campioni was right. He had to get through the current crisis first. "Send a priority message to the commander of the reinforcement and supply convoy informing him . . ." He paused. He couldn't let the slightest hint of what had occurred escape. "Tell him fuel constraints still concern me, and limit our operational flexibility." He managed a wry shadow of a smile. "That much is true, and no secret to anyone." He looked back at Campioni. "Continue that we have sufficient large combatants to achieve our goals and no fuel for more." He glanced outside at the still-burning cruiser, tempted, but shook his head. "Two destroyers are quite enough to escort the convoy the rest of the way to Martinique. The other ships would merely be a drain on our resources and must turn back."

CHAPTER 41

////// **USS** ***James Ellis***
Santiago Bay, NUS Territory
The Caribbean

"Here they come!" came the cry down from the crow's nest on the foremast, high above the fire control platform. Even as Ronson heard the piercing Lemurian shout, *Ellie*'s general quarters alarm sounded and her crew raced to their battle stations. The same thing was happening on *Adar*, but even though bells started ringing all over Santiago, Ronson saw little activity in its streets. A few people were running for cover, some loose animals wandered, but that was it. The same was true for many of the ships in port. They looked fine from a distance, and a few had even been quickly disguised to resemble Nussie warships, but most were old, run-down merchantmen, not even fit for sea. Santiago was where they'd ended their commercial careers due to age, disrepair, insolvency of their owners, or any number of ordinary, mundane reasons. But with Santiago's real maritime power and wealth and many of its people already evacuated, its fleet of derelicts would serve a final upright purpose.

Ronson redirected his binoculars at the sky to the east. Three Vs of planes, bigger than anything they had but Clippers, were dark against the high, white clouds. Again he was reminded of Cavite and the Japanese bombers that blew it to hell. Two formations seemed to be edging toward the airfield and the city and one was coming straight for the harbor. "This is it," he told Stites. "I gotta get aft." He paused and looked at the man with the bulging cheek and scruffy beard. "I know you don't have an antiaircraft director for our four-inch-fifties, but the Skipper's counting on you to be on your toes about ranges and designating targets. The 'Cats on the twenty-fives and fifties can take care of themselves. Good luck."

With that, he slid firehouse style down the ladder to the signal bridge behind the pilothouse where he heard Captain Brister barking orders in his scratchy voice. Bounding down the metal stairs and racing aft past the galley under the amidships gun platform, he waved at Tabasco, who was sending mess attendants off to carry ammunition to the guns above. "Don't let us vapor lock if we have to step on the gas," he called good-naturedly to Johnny Parks, *Ellie*'s engineering officer, as the big man squeezed down the hatch to the forward engine room.

"Don't let 'em put any holes in us, and I'll try," Parks replied.

Ronson kept jogging past the searchlight tower and cluster of 25mm guns. He finally reached the aft deckhouse and clambered up. A 'Cat talker was already waiting by the auxiliary helm controls. The number four 4″-50 crew was training their gun out to port and raising the muzzle to the sky. Ronson nodded at the talker.

"Auxiliaary conn, aaft aantiair baatteries, an' number four gun maaned an' ready," the 'Cat reported. White water was churning up through the propeller guards as *Ellie* increased speed. Ronson raised his binoculars again. Bomb blasts were marching across the airstrip in the distance and antiaircraft bursts from the two 4″-50s they'd emplaced there were popping in the sky. He caught a glimpse of a cluster of swooping shapes and saw a bomber cough black smoke and veer out of formation. A couple of parachutes opened before it exploded in a greasy slash of orange flame. Another simply dipped its nose and powered straight down.

"Yes!" Ronson exulted. "Our Bull-Bat jockeys're havin' a swell time!"

That wasn't entirely true. Ronson quickly realized there were only about a half dozen pursuit planes in the air, and they were chewing on targets that could bite back. Smoky tracers from dorsal gun positions on several planes converged on a Bull-Bat and it went into an impossible spin after a wing folded up. Another exploded and flaming debris fluttered down. A third staggered and started to smoke. But the fighters were through the bombers now, pulling up to hit them from below. The League bombers had guns there too, and more tracers sizzled across the sky. With half their number damaged or destroyed putting on a spirited performance, the Allied pursuiters broke off. The airfield already lay at the mile-wide base of a towering plume of smoke in any event.

The next to catch it was Santiago. Streams of bombs tumbled from the bellies of the strange-looking tri-motors, impacting near the middle of the city. Black geysers crowned by rubbled white masonry smothered the commercial district, pounding remorselessly right across the classically impressive-looking Government House. Ronson didn't see if it was hit or not, the dust and smoke just seemed to swallow it, and it was quickly obscured even further when bombs exploded along the waterfront, shattering docks, ships, and fuel storage tanks. Ronson couldn't watch anymore, because now it was *Ellie*'s and *Adar*'s turn.

"All guns, fire at will!" came the order from the bridge. Since there was no centralized antiair fire control, like for surface targets, all they had was local control and the skill of the 'Cat gun's crews. Fortunately, like everything else, they'd practiced for this, shooting at target sleeves towed by aircraft all across the Pacific. It was no real substitute, but it was better than nothing, and keen-eyed Lemurian gun captains had developed a knack for calculating where their target would be when their shells got there, and set their fuses accordingly. *Ellie*'s four main guns started hammering in rapid fire, throwing a wall of dirty brown-shrouded iron fragments in the path of approaching League planes. One of them, a twin-engine job, was hit almost at once, right on the nose. It pulled violently upward, fell on its back, and spiraled down. Another was hit by *Adar*, a blast ripping its tail, and it fell out of formation. Rolando was startled to see a couple start to smoke or burn for no apparent reason, then realized they were taking hits from fragments falling from higher bursts. The deafening roar of the portside pair of twin 25mms started pounding his ears and he roared down at their gunners. "Cut that shit out! They're too high, and you're just wasting ammo!"

"Bombs, Commaander Ronson!" cried his talker, before shouting the report in his mic. Ronson looked up, first surprised by how many planes seemed to be shying away from their aerial barrage, but also by how many bombs were wobbling downward, starting to straighten out. . . . The crowned deck slanted beneath his feet as *Ellie* turned hard to starboard and white water churned up around him as the ship went to emergency flank and the stern crouched down. Towering white jets of spray erupted all around, but mostly in their wake. One hit barely twenty yards to port, however, throwing up enough water that it pounded him when it fell. There was a loud clanging as iron splinters sprayed the ship, and screams rose from the gunners he'd just yelled at.

A quick glance at *Adar*, now a quarter mile off their beam, showed she was enduring a similar dowsing . . . until it changed entirely. A ball of fire engulfed her amidships deckhouse and black smoke and steam jetted from her two center stacks. She wallowed to a stop almost instantly, as if she'd run hard aground. More geysers shot up around her, joined by another indistinct dark blast that shook her somewhere forward. Guns still pounding, *Ellie* was shrugging off the latest cataract, her deck awash as far forward as Ronson could see, when he chanced a look up. The planes were peeling away, probably satisfied they'd killed *Adar*, at least. They flew to join their comrades still working the city over, or starting to hit the rest of the anchorage.

Ronson noted *Ellie* was still accelerating, still heeling to port in her hard starboard turn. The talker's mic was soaked, so Ronson removed the cover of the voice tube to the bridge. Shouting into it, even as the ship's guns kept hammering, wildly shifting to compensate for the moving ship and targets, he got no response from the pilothouse. "Shit!" he shouted, opening other tubes. "This is Mr. Rodriguez, I'm taking the conn, aft. Corps-'Cats to the bridge, on the double. Damage control parties report to the auxiliary conn!" He turned to the 'Cats moving to their conning stations. They were blinking concern over their popular skipper. "Rudder amidships. All ahead one-third." He looked forward and thought he saw wisps of smoke peeling back from the pilothouse. "Can't see a goddamn thing. For all I know, we're about to hit the breakwater! Left standard rudder. Bring us around toward *Adar*."

The League bombers broke off their attack. Even if they saw *Ellie* slow and start easing toward her burning sister, they didn't pay her any more attention. They'd received quite enough *from* her, and there were easier targets in Santiago Bay. They had limited time over target in any event and Martinique was a long way off so they focused on bombing and strafing the cluster of wooden ships, which, like the airfield, docks, and Santiago itself, they set afire before winging away to the east.

Ronson conned *Ellie* as close to *Adar* as he dared, ordering boats in the water. The other destroyer was listing and burning from her amidships deckhouse forward. Firefighting parties sprayed water on the flames and steam rejoined the malignant black column standing over her. On *Ellie*, excited 'Cats chattered and boasted they'd hit ten enemy planes, distracting and engaging wounded shipmates as they carried them down to the wardroom. Ronson thought they might've hit half that many—still pretty good—and *Adar* could've hit a few. The pursuit planes definitely got a couple. Eight to ten, all told, was a respectable score, and a damaging percentage of the whole.

Still, the price was high. *Ellie* had suffered seven dead and five wounded.

Except for those in the portside 20mm tubs, most of the casualties were on the bridge, also slashed by bomb fragments. Captain Brister was only slightly wounded, catching a few small iron splinters and knocked cold when a severed conduit conked him on the head. His helmet saved him. There were plenty of little leaks that needed attention as well: popped rivets, opened seams, more splinter wounds. Generally speaking, though, considering they'd been hit in broad daylight in restricted waters by a helluva lot of planes, *James Ellis* came out pretty well. Her pilothouse needed work, but she could steam and fight. *Adar* wasn't so lucky.

Nineteen of her crew were dead and twenty-three badly wounded. Injured and nonessential personnel were taking to the boats *Ellie* sent, and *Adar* was dead in the water, leaning heavily to starboard. Signals flashing from a Morse lamp aft detailed her damage. She was taking water in both firerooms and all but her number one boiler was out. Worse—and they could see this for themselves—the water pressure was beginning to fail. On the other hand, her captain, Lieutenant Commander Pina-Ta-Biaa—aft now, like Ronson—was optimistic her ship could be saved if *Ellie* would join the firefighting and pumping efforts.

With the help of a couple of 'Cats, Captain Perry Brister joined Ronson atop *Ellie*'s aft deckhouse. His trouser legs had been cut away and he wore bandages on his legs, but he seemed to have recovered from the blow to his head. Ronson was torn between concern for his skipper and relief he was no longer in charge. "Tell Commander Pina to abandon," Brister rasped. "Our freighters are coming and we have to scram. The whole League fleet's on its way and we can't get stuck in here."

Leaving the freighters in the harbor that brought a lot of the planes to the sacrificial airfield—along with some other things—had been High Admiral Jenks's idea. Since they had to stay close, he'd proposed they'd draw less attention stationary, near shore, covered with brush laced into netting, than if they'd been underway. They'd nervously watched the attack from as far away as they could get from anything else on the west end of the bay, but now they were coming.

"Caap'n Pina . . . strenuously objects to your order, sur," the signal-'Cat said diplomatically. Brister barked a laugh. He'd seen the somewhat insubordinate response himself. "Nevertheless, repeat that it *is* an order, and she needs to hurry it up."

It took an hour to complete *Adar*'s evacuation, her wounded coming aboard strapped in long baskets. Ronson was sickened by the mixed smells of burnt oil, flesh, and fur. By the time Pina herself climbed up *Ellie*'s side, the freighters were closing. And though *Adar* was burning from stem to stern, she wasn't noticeably lower in the water. Still, Pina had lost a lot of her own heat by then, and joined Ronson and Brister (for whom a chair had been provided), on the aft deckhouse. She noted *Ellie*'s starboard torpedo mount had been trained out over the side, pointing at her ship.

"We caan do nothing for her?" she almost pleaded.

"Just one last thing." Brister's gravelly voice managed to sound amazingly gentle. "I'm sorry. *Adar*'s finished and the League fleet's coming. Their ship-mounted scout planes might be overhead soon and we need to be gone." He shook his head. "I don't know why, or even how they might recover *Adar*, but we won't be here to stop 'em if they try and I'm damned if I'll leave her for 'em." He nodded at the torpedo tubes. "Lay your ship to rest, Captain Pina."

Back in *Ellie*'s pilothouse (her wheel and EOT were intact), a Nussie pilot took her out, carefully threading a specific channel. The two freighters dutifully followed in line abreast like a pair of oxen sniffing a cheetah's tail, but they had another final chore. Still on the aft deckhouse, physically and emotionally exhausted after the long morning, Ronson Rodriguez watched the smoke of Santiago Bay merge with the haze of early afternoon. *Adar*'s smoke had quickly vanished when the single torpedo broke her back and put her on the bottom.

Raising his binoculars, Ronson caught occasional splashes aft of the large, wooden-hulled freighters as they filled the gap in the minefield they laid when they arrived. He knew, even if these mines were essentially just anchored depth charges, their magnetic influence exploders were fairly sophisticated. Industrious 'Cats had been inspired by (but absolutely didn't copy) the Mk-6 magnetic torpedo detonators that proved so useless against the Japanese and that Bernie Sandison abandoned in favor of contact exploders. The mines required no electricity and worked just fine, if they didn't leak. And if a steel-hulled ship passed close enough.

Ronson hoped they'd blow the bottom out of a few Leaguers but wasn't optimistic. The enemy would have to come close in, almost into the mouth of the bay, and why should they? Their BBs could churn the rubble of Santiago from here. *Maybe we should've left* Adar *afloat as bait,* he thought to himself, as USS *James Ellis* headed south to link up with TF-Tassanna.

CHAPTER 42

////// Impero
League-Occupied Martinique
The Caribbean
August 5, 1945
0012

It was just after midnight in the flag officer's suite aboard *Impero*, but nobody slept as messengers scurried in and out with new dispatches every few minutes. Gravois was exhausted, but dutifully digested each new piece of information before relating it to the small, vocal mob that had become his staff. He'd never felt the burden of command on such a scale, particularly when failure entailed such daunting personal consequences, but after a couple of profoundly frustrating days, things seemed to be looking up.

Most of the planes had returned from their raid on Santiago where—they claimed—they'd destroyed the enemy airfield entirely, inflicted heavy damage on the docks and city, as well as a large number of NUS warships, and sunk one of Captain Reddy's modern destroyers. So at least they were even for the enemy raid on Martinique. With fuel more suddenly precious than ever, however, Gravois had directed Ammiraglio Gherzi to proceed into Santiago Bay and attempt to replenish his bunkers there before bombarding the city. He'd considered that a brilliant stroke. To his dismay, Gherzi almost immediately reported that three of his ships struck underwater mines. A destroyer sank immediately with great loss of life, another would have to be scuttled, and a battleship had been damaged. A mocking backhand by the fickle fates had left it bleeding oil from a ruptured torpedo blister and slowed by a damaged propeller shaft. The effort had proven worse than useless and Gravois ordered Gherzi to haul off, shell the city, and begin making his way back to base. All his fuel hopes now rested on the convoy coming from the Azores.

On the other hand, there'd been no more enemy air raids. Even better, he now saw, looking at the latest dispatch from the cruiser he'd sent scouting with two destroyers, its seaplane had discovered the enemy carrier at last, barely two hundred miles to the north.

"*Two* carriers, in point of fact," Gravois declared with new enthusiasm, "though I can't imagine where the other came from. They're in company with what may be a Republic seaplane tender and two enemy destroyers, one slightly larger than the other. . . ." He glanced up and murmured, "The bigger one *must* be their new light cruiser, if two destroyers were at Santiago. But how could the survivor have joined so swiftly?" He shook his head bemusedly. "And the pilot *swears* he saw our own *Savoie* in company with the enemy!"

This elicited an astonished explosion of voices, mostly proclaiming its impossibility, but Ciano silenced them. "It's *quite* possible. We know little of the events surrounding *Savoie*'s engagement with Captain Reddy's forces at Zanzibar, but he's here so he must've won. It follows that he could've taken *Savoie* from Kurokawa. She was . . . less than properly manned, if you'll recall. Yet even if the enemy captured her intact, she'll be little use to them." He glanced at Gravois. "We disabled her fire control apparatus ourselves. She might be dangerous at very close range," he qualified, "but they still have only animals to crew her."

Gravois refrained from pointing out those "animals" had stymied them quite effectively so far, and ravaged their air bases and oil storage here on Martinique. Just as bad, even if most of their bombers safely returned from the attack on Santiago, the gasoline stockpiles were sorely depleted as well. And the crash on the fueling pier was proving more problematic than first suspected. It was nearly impossible to refuel their ships from what remained onshore until repairs were completed. At present they were utterly reliant on four medium-sized tankers, and they were sucking them down like ticks.

"Regardless," Gravois said, "we're gifted with an opportunity. We've found what can only be the entire remaining enemy fleet. We'll launch an air strike immediately, vectored by the scout ships, which will attack in concert."

"In the dark?" *Impero*'s XO asked, incredulously.

"When better?" Gravois countered. "In spite of the fact there'll be little moon, the phosphorescent wakes of the enemy are quite clear. They're like lighted roadways in this sea, that stretch for miles." He raised the message in his hand. "That's how our scouts discovered them. Besides, we have no fighters left to protect the bombers and the new enemy fighters are more effective than expected. A night attack will be safer."

"We'll have no fuel left for our planes when they return," groused the Italian colonel in charge of air operations. "None."

"If they're successful, they won't need more before replenishment arrives," Gravois argued reasonably. "Those are my orders. We attack at once!"

Another messenger arrived, looking more harried than the others, and a little nervous too. "Sirs," he said, not waiting for the printed words to make their rounds, "there's been a sudden explosion of radio traffic. Most is coded, of course, but some is in the open. The animals . . . Lemurians . . . seem incapable of maintaining proper procedures, especially when they've been quiet so long."

"Have you determined the direction of these transmissions?" Campioni questioned.

The messenger actually shrugged. "They seem to be coming from everywhere, sir, but the voice transmissions are in the southwest. It's impossible to say how far, but they made mention of our bombardment force."

Gravois slapped the table with his hand. "A ruse, no doubt, to distract us from their force to the north."

Ciano was shaking his head. "I refuse to accept they're that cunning, and Lemurians *are* loquacious. They may be stalking Gherzi. We know they watch him with scout planes, probably from steam-powered sailing ships they use as seaplane tenders."

"Stalking him with what?" Gravois asked.

"I don't know . . . but they already surprised us with one air strike—and mines. Perhaps they've gathered a number of those seaplane tenders and mean to make an air attack. I don't know!" he repeated in frustration.

Gravois steepled his fingers, elbows on the table. "Gherzi is still about eight hours out. Have him reduce speed to conserve fuel, but scout his surroundings as best he can." He frowned. Gherzi had lost five of his six seaplanes. Some may have simply gotten lost and gone down, but at least one was probably destroyed by surviving fighters out of Santiago. They now knew those could even be a threat to modern fighters. A floatplane would be helpless against them. He looked up. "As to the other transmissions . . .

clearly, the enemy is preparing an attack of his own from the north. Why else is he so close? We must beat him to it."

KMS Hessen

The lookouts on the starboard side of the big German cruiser KMS *Hessen* were bored out of their minds. The ship was anchored in one of the deepest parts of the bay, but there was nothing beyond her to the south but three tankers and four ammunition ships clustered where nothing could get at them without going through *Hessen* first. A fourth tanker had been moved alongside *Impero* to top her off, and stand ready to replenish the bombardment force when it returned. Past the isolated ships to the south, however, coral heads came up abruptly and there was nothing but the snake-infested jungle to look upon. It was inevitable the lookouts' attention would wander.

That's when there was a sudden disturbance in the water directly alongside and the bridge lookout gaped. Instead of the sea monster he was certain he'd see, the even more unexpected shape of a submarine conning tower rose, dripping, almost silently into the night. Water sluiced from around the hatch, which clanged open even as the boat's big deck guns rose into view. That was about as high as she came, her main deck awash, and the lookout redirected his gaze at a man climbing out of the hatch, followed immediately by other people . . . creatures . . . that even Leaguers called "Lemurians" now. The lookout fumbled at the holster on his belt and gathered his voice to shout the alarm.

"Don't!" the man called, already pointing a pistol of his own. The Lemurians were armed as well. "We mean you no harm and I'm only here to have a quick word with my old friend Willie. Kapitan Dietrich, I mean," he added with an encouraging smile. "Tell him Kurt Hoffman has come to call. Quietly, if you please."

The lookout above seemed even more shaken, but nodded and disappeared.

"This is stupid," growled Andy Espinoza. The former *S-19* sailor was *U-112*'s chief of the boat.

"Perhaaps," said Hoffman's 'Cat XO, Lieutenant Eno-Sab-Raan. He'd been *Fitzhugh Gray*'s torpedo officer, detached for this assignment. "But I believe Cap-i-taan Hoff-maan. So did Chair-maan Letts, who gave him permission to try this if the opportunity presented. And this is a chaance worth taking. On the other haand . . ." he began.

Andy nodded. "The charges are ready to go."

Moments later, a half-asleep face peered down at them, blinking incredulously. "Kurt?" he called. "Is that you? What're you doing here? You're supposed to be dead!"

"Supposed to be, yes," Hoffman agreed. "But as you can see . . ." He held his hands out to his sides, glancing toward the entrance to the bay. "As to how, I must say it wasn't easy. I'm afraid I scratched my bottom paint. Why?" His voice turned hard. "That's simple enough. After Gravois abandoned my people and I in the Indian Ocean, we chose to change our allegiance."

Dietrich was looking at Eno and the other 'Cats who'd followed the first ones out. "*Those* aren't your people," he stated flatly.

"They are now, Willie. As much as you." He shook his head. "There's a lot wrong with this world, from our perspective, but there's more wrong with the League *because* of its perspective. You *know* this," he urged. One of the things, besides being German, that had made the skipper of KMS *Hessen* "socially unacceptable and politically unreliable" was that he'd applied to marry an "indigenous" woman on the Italian peninsula. Liaisons were encouraged, for procreation, but actual *marriage* to the "degraded" humans of this world, for this generation at least, was barely tolerated and required permission that was rarely granted. Dietrich ran his fingers through his hair but didn't comment. He did notice a growing number of sailors lining the rails to stare. "Then *what* are you doing here, Kurt?"

"I came to warn you as a friend and countryman that there will soon be . . . a great deal of noise and activity here." Kurt frowned. "There's nothing I can do about that, but Kapitan Reddy understands the . . . awkward status of the German contingent and every effort will be made to spare you." He frowned more deeply. "Unless you join the rest of the fleet in active operations, of course. If you do, I'll sink you myself."

Dietrich was still looking disbelievingly at the sub, Kurt, and the gathered Lemurians. "You want me to change sides?" he demanded. "Join *them*?"

Hoffman sighed. "Why not? They're on *our* side, you fool! The side that opposes the Dominion, the League, and the Triumvirate." He'd raised his voice so others could hear. "This is, literally, the chance of a lifetime. There won't be another if we fail, and the League will always be what it is—only worse, with the dark influence of the Dominion."

"What about our families?" came a cry from nearby. Dietrich wasn't the only one who had one, or considered himself "married," for that matter.

"There's always risk when great things are at stake, but if we win, our friends won't be forgotten. Their families either." Kurt looked at his watch. "I have to go now and there's little time. Either say goodbye or shoot me, Willie. You won't have another chance."

Kapitan Dietrich seemed to be trying to speak, but ultimately said nothing at all as Kurt, Andy, Eno, and three other 'Cats dropped down through the conning tower hatch. But he didn't shoot at them as the sub flooded down and crept slowly away.

CHAPTER 43

////// *USNRS* **Salissa**
East of Antigua (N-NE of Martinique)

Matt and Sandra Reddy stood with Keje, Sir Sean Bates, Captain Atlaan-Fas, and his XO, Commander Sandy Newman, on USNRS *Salissa*'s bridge as Captain Jis-Tikkar's 1st Naval Air Wing thundered off the big carrier's deck into the damp, drizzly dark. The sea was getting up, which went hardly noticed by *Salissa* or *Maaka-Kakja*, even the Repub seaplane tender/oiler, but the converted Grik BB, *Saa-Leebs*, was rolling heavily. Her kind had always been prone to that, and even with all her older heavy guns removed, the new additions—particularly the high top hamper to make her resemble *Savoie*—had made her more unstable. Matt pitied her small, intrepid crew, but pitied himself a little as well when he saw *Walker* and *Mahan* bounding exuberantly through the sea, seeming to spend as much time under the waves as over them. He remembered the old destroyermen joke about how they deserved flight and submarine pay too. But the *Walker*s and *Mahan*s were used to it and few probably even noticed it anymore.

Matt desperately missed his old ship, and even if he'd left her in the best possible hands—Spanky's—he felt like a traitor for not remaining where he felt he most belonged. But Alan Letts and Henry Stokes had been right. If he was going to be in charge of an operation this complex and far-flung, he had to stay back from the fight with people who could help him coordinate it.

"Jumbo and Ben have lifted off from Seepy Field with the planes they have left," Newman told them. Matt felt a fresh spike of sadness for Orrin's loss, particularly regretting he hadn't *made* him hold still long enough for them to have a real visit before they came through the Pass of Fire. But Orrin hated the very idea that Matt might be seen to show him favoritism, and probably dreaded being put on the spot even more. Still, Matt had always thought his kid cousin was indestructible. Pete Alden too. The first jubilant news of victory over the Grik was increasingly leavened by sadness. So many had been lost! And they might never know what happened to many, like Pete and General Kim. . . . But Rolak seemed to be getting along with the "allied" Grik around Lake Galk, and it looked like the fighting might really, finally, be finished. I'joorka's reports from Sofesshk were equally promising. The death toll there had been much lower than initially feared, and the Celestial Mother not only survived, she was now seen as the *true* "mother" of her people.

"Tikker's First and Second Bomb Squadrons're up," Newman continued, "and the Third's taking off now. Captain Sheider's Seventh and Tenth Pursuit Squadrons are about to lift off *Maaka-Kakja*."

It dawned on Matt that they were about to have more than half their new planes in the air at once. The smaller *New Dublin*, attached to Jenks, had bombers but few new pursuit planes. Tassanna's *Madraas* had pursuiters but no new bombers—and he didn't know if TF-Tassanna had joined Jenks yet or not. "What about Nat and MTB-Ron-5?" he asked.

"Closing in on Martinique, easy as can be. They're being careful," he assured, "but *U-112* reports no pickets outside, and just one DD stirring in the bay. Seems they're not much worried about a surface attack." He hesitated. "Hoffman also said he made contact with his 'friend' inside, but isn't sure how that turned out."

Matt sighed. "Very well. Radio silence—for us—is about to go in the crapper anyway, so pass the code word to Tikker and Nat not to shoot at *Hessen* unless she shoots at them." He frowned. "She'll be lucky to get out alive, anyway."

"A big risk ye're takin," Bates observed.

"I know. This whole operation's chancy. I wish I could've thought of something better. . . ." He sighed. "I never was 'high command' material. I'm just a destroyer skipper and my only training at grand strategy came out of history books about battles fought in another age." He shook his head apologetically. "Not complaining, just reminding you who you signed on with."

Salissa's signal officer dashed onto the bridge from the comm-shack aft. "Cap-i-taan Tikker sends thaat he spotted wakes of three ships approaching from seero, six, seero, relaa-tive our position, twelve miles! He aalso blew paast enemy planes, lower thaan him. At least a dozen. Maaybe twenty!"

"Sound gener-aal quaarters!" Keje bellowed. "Staand by for air *and* surfaace aaction!" He looked at Matt and blinked dark amusement. "Planes. We expected to be seen, aapproaching close enough thaat *our* planes would have the fuel to carry on to Seepy Field, but I'd hoped the enemy wouldn't haave maany left. It seems they do. And better scouts as well." The latter was certainly true since, except for a meager pair of overworked Clippers that were too vulnerable to allow near known enemy concentrations, they'd necessarily relied on Nancys and *Seevogels* for reconnaissance. Not only did their open cockpits make observations difficult in drizzly conditions, the sea was running too high to operate them safely.

"Have *Makky-Kat* expedite getting her fighters in the air. Their new target is the incoming planes," Matt ordered. "The Third Bomb Squadron's loaded with torpedoes, right? They'll go for the enemy warships"—he hesitated—"joined by *Saa-Leebs*, *Mahan* . . . and *Walker*."

The action that ensued was a nightmare of confusion. League bombers arrived before half the fighters were in the air, though two were turned into flaming meteors by the desperately climbing defenders. Two more, almost miraculously, were illuminated by their falling comrades and were shattered as they dived. *Salissa* had a relatively impressive antiair armament, consisting of six DP 4″-50s and four twin-mounted 25mm guns. All sent tracers slashing at the attackers and several veered away, their bombs throwing up geysers of spray beside the massive ship.

Maaka-Kakja was still heavily armed against primitive surface threats, with fifty 50pdr muzzle-loaders, but had only two of *Amagi*'s old 4.7″ DP guns to defend against aerial threats. Compounding the problem, though their boilers and engines had been improved to the point they could make sixteen knots in an emergency, both giant carriers were just too big and ungainly to maneuver radically enough to spoil the enemy's aim. Still, *Maaka-Kakja* had the fewest teeth and suffered for it first when a string of bombs marched across her flight deck, blasting gaping craters in the heavy timbers and exploding the half dozen planes still waiting to launch. Burning fuel poured down onto her hangar deck and ignited flammables there. More bombs quickly found her, but fortunately didn't fall through any of the previous holes and only blasted her flight deck into further ruin.

Keen-eyed Lemurian pilots in their new fighters took a vengeful toll on the bombers then, as they tried to reform for another pass. Regardless how modern their aircraft were, League pilots simply couldn't match their tormentors' vision and most never knew what hit them before they were plummeting into the sea. Only five planes survived to complete their final run on *Salissa*. Two missed her entirely, and one of those was shot down by a stream of 25mm as it thundered low over the flight deck. The others, bombs tumbling in erratic strings, managed three hits each.

Everyone on *Salissa*'s bridge was thrown to the deck by a nearby concussion and sprayed by flying glass. Matt looked to Sandra first but saw Sir Sean had shielded her with his powerful frame. His back was a mass of cuts but he seemed not to notice as he helped Sandra to her feet. She immediately crouched over the helmsman, who was spewing blood from an artery in his arm. Corps-'Cats arrived and took the casualty in hand before she could do much but get blood all over her. "You next," she shouted at Matt, ears likely ringing from the blasts, but Matt was staring down at Sandy Newman, *Big Sal*'s XO. He was covered with cuts, like they all were, but didn't look that bad. Nevertheless, when Captain Atlaan stood from beside him, his mournful blinking confirmed that the former gunner's mate 3rd from USS *Walker* was dead.

"Oh no," Sandra murmured, then shook her head and resumed her inspection of her husband, who couldn't say anything at all.

The blaze outside was already dying. There'd been no planes on *Salissa*'s deck and the bombs hadn't penetrated like they might have if dropped from a higher altitude. Hoses and *Salissa*'s constantly upgraded sprinkler system were quickly extinguishing the flames. The flight deck had been fearfully blasted, however, and splintered holes gaped wide—over the armor they'd installed after the loss of *Humfra-Dar*. Repairs would be fairly simple for a yard, probably complete in a month, but *Salissa* wouldn't be operating any planes till then.

Maaka-Kakja looked much worse. Her flight deck was an inferno and flames were gushing out her sides from the hangar deck below. Occasional explosions shook her as fuel or ordnance went up.

"Cap-i-taan Sheider says his fires are out of control," reported a messenger from the comm shack.

"Very well," Keje said, stricken, wondering if he could make such a confession if it was *his* ship. His Home. *Maaka-Kakja* might not officially "count" as a Home as such things were reckoned; unlike *Salissa*, she'd been built for war. But did that make her any less a home to her people? He didn't think so. *Walker* was as much Matt Reddy's home as *Salissa* was his. "We'll maaneuver upwind and begin taking her people off," he said.

"Wait," Matt ordered. He'd crunched across the broken glass to *Salissa*'s far bridgewing, looking to the south. There were bright flashes there, and it wasn't lightning. *Walker* and *Mahan*, even *Saa-Leebs*, in her way, were fighting a cruiser and two destroyers by themselves. He literally ached to be with them. "What's going on over there?" he asked. "If they're taking a beating, we'll have to go."

"Matt! You can't!" Sandra exclaimed, horrified.

He turned to her and replied, voice rough, eyes red. "Of course I can. I have to. Our first responsibility is to *Salissa* and the Repub ship with us. We have to get them out of harm's way—and can't wait long to do it."

USS Walker

Commander Brad "Spanky" MacFarlane heard from Ed Palmer and the lookouts aft what happened to *Salissa* and *Maaka-Kakja*, and knew exactly what Matt was thinking. He had to make this quick. They'd started trading salvos with the enemy at ten thousand yards, primarily targeting the cruiser, and even *Saa-Leebs* was firing her Impie-made 8″ guns. In this sea, both sides would be lucky to hit at half that range, and *Saa-Leebs* had no chance at all. She was just putting on a show, her bigger guns in local control only, but blooming *much* brighter than the destroyers'. The Leaguers wouldn't know that, though, and if they recognized her silhouette, it had to make them edgy. Regardless, until now, Spanky had just been trying to make the enemy cautious and slow their approach. That wouldn't work anymore.

"All ahead full, make your course one, eight, five. Tell Mr. Palmer to get on the TBS and signal *Saa-Leebs* and *Mahan* to do the same. We and *Mahan*'ll start zigzagging to avoid enemy fire and so *Saa-Leebs* can keep up." He paused. "Tell Mr. Campeti to continue targeting the cruiser, but keep his eyes on the DDs and watch for torpedoes. Mr. Sandison?" he shouted across the bridge. "Prepare our own torpedo batteries." *Saa-Leebs* couldn't zigzag and Spanky figured the enemy would focus all their fire on her, at least until they got closer to the wounded carriers, but that couldn't be helped. "And find out what's the status on our planes. Are they gonna give us a hand or not!"

"Ay, ay, Commaander Spaanky!" Minnie replied. She'd been following him as he paced, relaying his orders, the wire to her headset trailing behind her. Now she spoke urgently into the microphone, her squeaky little voice lost in the roar of the blower and bark of *Walker*'s 4″-50 guns.

As the range rapidly shortened, salvoes fell closer, churning phosphorescent plumes high in the air, collapsing in a glowing froth on *Walker*'s fo'c'sle. A cluster of six- or eight-inch shells straddled *Saa-Leebs* and one struck a glancing blow, throwing bright sparks off the side of her armored casemate. *Those old Grik BBs are tough,* Spanky thought uneasily, *but wouldn't even stop a square hit from our* four-*inch armor-piercing stuff.* Campeti reported that the League DDs were racing ahead and Spanky told him to target them, but instructed Bernie to keep tracking the cruiser. Three of *Walker*'s 4"-50s started hammering even faster, tracers arcing out, converging on flatter trajectories. Splashes straddled a distant, flashing shape, and a red flower of flame blossomed in its superstructure.

"We hit her!" exulted a 'Cat lookout on the port bridgewing.

"Range to cruiser?" Spanky demanded.

"Six thousand!" Bernie Sandison shouted from the starboard wing where he was tracking it with his torpedo director.

"Crow's nest reports enemy torpedoes in the waater!" Minnie cried, her small voice suddenly very loud.

"Beat us to the draw, did they? We'll see about that." Spanky growled. In spite of their maneuvering, *Walker* and *Mahan* had outpaced *Saa-Leebs*, which was starting to take some damaging hits. The tripod mockup simulating one of *Savoie*'s most prominent features had been knocked askew. "Left full rudder. Make your course zero, nine, zero. Signal *Mahan* to follow our lead and fire all starboard torpedoes on my command." Spanky considered ordering *Saa-Leebs* to turn as well, but feared she'd only make a bigger target for the fish already speeding at her.

"Third Bomb Squaadron's making a torpedo run on the taarget!" Minnie cried out excitedly as *Walker* heeled into her turn. Incoming shells churned the sea behind her and they were close enough to see the sudden frantic twinkling of the cruiser's antiaircraft batteries drawing weak yellow lines in the sky. Paddy Rosen spun the big brass wheel back to center and announced they were on course as *Walker* steadied.

"I have a solution!" Bernie reminded anxiously.

Spanky held out a hand. "Hold your horses, let's see this."

The League planes that struck *Salissa* and *Maaka-Kakja* must've missed the flights of SBD-2s the carriers already launched and gave no warning at all. The cruiser's panicky air defense only downed one plane—the only one those on *Walker*'s bridge ever saw in the dark. Five more successfully, almost leisurely, dropped their Mk-6 torpedoes from a range of less than six hundred yards. (Planes didn't need the new longer-range fish.) Despite the heavy sea, three struck the cruiser in quick succession, the glowing cataracts of water seen before the knocking *boom, boom, boom* was heard. There was the slightest pause before a titanic explosion ripped the sea and the League cruiser simply ceased to exist. Spanky thought he saw one of her forward turrets tumbling end over end atop a fiery cloud of molten debris.

But the torpedoes weren't finished. Purely by chance, one that missed went on to strike the closest League destroyer, retreating behind a futile, wind-whipped smokescreen after loosing its own weapons. Passing to port of the deathly pall of the demolished cruiser, it was enveloped by another towering stalk of sickly lustrous spray.

"I guess you'll have to wait another turn to play with your new fish, Mr. Sandison," Spanky deadpanned.

Minnie spoke. "Mr. Caam-peti says the other destroyer, the one we hit, is retiring under smoke. We go aafter her?"

Spanky never had to decide. All the League torpedoes had passed astern of *Walker* and *Mahan* when they turned, and *Saa-Leebs* had only presented a target a hundred feet wide. Practically the eye of a needle under these circumstances. One torpedo threaded the eye and hit *Saa-Leebs* square on the cutwater, blasting her bow apart in a torrent of spume and tumbling timbers.

"Shit!" Spanky snapped, then blew out a breath. No Grik-built BB could live for long with damage like that. The four transverse bulkheads the Allies installed weren't watertight; making them so in the crudely built ships was practically impossible. All they were meant to do was slow flooding with the aid of pumps until repairs could be made or the crew taken off. They might've killed a cruiser, and maybe a destroyer, but it seemed like a pretty poor trade. There'd be no fixing *Saa-Leebs*, and *Maaka-Kakja* was still burning fiercely in the distance. "A hell of a mess," Spanky muttered.

"Our air strike got off okay, and Martinique's going to have other visitors tonight," Bernie Sandison consoled, stepping closer. "I'll tell you what Chief Silva told me once, when I had to get him out of the brig in Manila. In the old days."

Spanky blinked. "Wait. Are you about to try to *inspire* me with something that maniac said?"

Bernie shrugged. "Nah, just something to think about. He'd been in a fight ashore, a big one, and said *he* learned that no matter how beat and bloody and ready to quit you are, sometimes the other guy's even worse off, just as ready to throw in the towel. You only have to outlast him." He frowned. "On that particular occasion, it was *three* guys. Snipes off the *Canopus*. But I guess that's not the point."

Distracted, Spanky barked at the 'Cat by the EOT. "All ahead one-third, let's save some fuel." He turned slightly toward Minnie. "Have Ed inform Captain Reddy the enemy surface force has been destroyed or driven off and he's free to do whatever's necessary to aid *Makky-Kat*. They've probably been on pins and needles back there. Then get on the TBS and signal Commander Tiaa on *Mahan* to move alongside *Saa-Leebs* and take her people off." The giant ship only had a crew of forty 'Cats, and about twenty Impies to man her guns. "We'll stand off and keep an eye out in case that League DD comes sneaking back." Resting his eyes back on Bernie, he actually managed a laugh. "Silva's a maniac for sure. Lucky for him the war came along or they'd have had to hang him. But he's not an idiot."

CHAPTER 44

////// *RRPS* Imperator
440 Miles E-NE of Martinique

Courtney Bradford remained impressed by the Republic battlecruisers *Imperator*, *Ostia*, *Augustus*, and *Songze*, even after being aboard one almost continuously for three dreary, often frustrating months. And he was equally pleased with the progress of the sailors manning the Republic's first "blue water" fleet. He'd been right about Fleet Prefect Tigaas as well. Despite her growing impatience with him, and desire to "steam west and have at the League," she was as professional as his first impressions led him to believe and he liked her very much. He'd even grown close to his aide, Tribune Nir. This in spite of the fact his first two and a half months "in command" had been marked by stupefying monotony for his captains as they predictably patrolled back and forth between Colonia and Ascension Island (which they exuberantly bombarded each time they passed), and daily, exhausting drills for their crews while they waited for his promised "opportunity." In all that time, they'd seen no sign of League activity at sea, and even doubted the enemy had maintained its presence on Ascension. Worst of all, they'd "missed" the climax of the war against the Grik, and had heard almost nothing of the progress of the Allied campaign in the Caribbean.

All that changed quite suddenly, because Inquisitor Choon's intelligence service had been very active indeed, identifying a surprising number of spies by triangulating transmissions dutifully reporting the Republic Fleet's arrivals and departures at Colonia. Just after the fleet coaled, provisioned, and sailed the last time, intelligence agents swooped in and swept up every spy that had revealed himself, as well as several of their complicated cipher machines. The information bonanza was brief, at least until they could crack the new code that swiftly replaced the old one, but they did learn the details of a powerful, critical supply convoy gathering at the Azores for a run to Martinique. Interestingly, the departure date for the convoy had been delayed due to difficulties in amassing the ships and resources, but was now scheduled to intersect a course Fleet Prefect Tigaas carefully plotted . . . *if* her ships could make the crossing at full speed. They shelled Ascension Island again—why break tradition, and what if there actually was someone there to report?—but this time the Republic Fleet steamed on to the northeast.

They averaged fifteen knots for five thousand miles and it took them two full weeks (including two days of rare calm they spent hove to so they could refuel) before they reached their current position 440 miles north-northeast of the enemy base at Martinique. And the mostly unruly seas, taken at speed, had revealed a few complaints Courtney could legitimately make about Imperators. Their somewhat stubbly lines and low freeboard made them *very* wet. And probably because of the wood sandwiched between their plates, they were very loud as well, creaking and groaning in shocking ways Courtney had never heard. But the same conditions, not even real storms, had swamped one of their nine destroyers with all hands, and periodically scattered most of the rest. The current blow was the lightest they'd faced, yet only five destroyers were with the battlecruisers and their perfectly seaworthy support ships in the black early hours of August fifth—when bugles called *Imperator* to battle stations, and Courtney was politely invited to the bridge.

Excited, terrified, vengeful 'Cat voices crackled from a speaker on the aft bulkhead, and the bridge crew was listening, entranced. Courtney gratefully accepted a hot cup of *srass*, a pungent root tea from Trier that he liked, and looked questioningly at Tigaas. Still much farther away at the time, they'd caught similar, scratchy sketches during the Allies' first air raid on Martinique. This was clearer.

"There seems to be an air *and* surface engagement underway near Antigua, roughly six hundred kilometers away," Tribune Nir informed him. "The names '*Salissa*' and '*Makky-Kat*' have been spoken in the clear by Allied pilots."

Courtney nodded, still listening carefully. He'd heard similar traffic many times now, and had acquired a feeling for what went said—and unsaid. "It's a dreadful shame we can't let our friends know we're here," he lamented.

"Why not?" Tigaas challenged, somewhat angrily.

Courtney sighed. Once they'd detected the enemy supply convoy with scouts sent aloft from the seaplane tender/oiler accompanying them, its progress had been ridiculously easy to track by the massive glowing wake it left at night. And to their knowledge, the little *Seevogels* had never been spotted in return. One was watching the enemy now, prepared to drop flares and backlight the enemy as soon as they blundered within two thousand yards of the battle line that had been formed and waiting since dusk. Better, the plane the current scout replaced had confirmed a previous report that the battleship, two cruisers, and two of the four destroyers accompanying the otherwise helpless ships were no longer with them. It was possible they remained a threat, still advancing from a different quarter, but Courtney was convinced they'd turned around. They couldn't discount the two remaining enemy destroyers, but not only did it now seem possible the Repub fleet would survive (something Courtney honestly hadn't been able to imagine if they faced the original force), the convoy itself should be easy meat. Courtney waved impatiently eastward, out to starboard.

"Our objective—our 'opportunity'—is there, Fleet Prefect, almost in our laps. And I assure you its destruction will make a *far* larger contribution to victory than if we simply shout 'here we are' and turn and steam to the sound of the guns." He gestured at the speaker on the bulkhead. "Yes, there's a battle, but I hear the voices of a great many fliers, few of whom are fighting it—yet. I submit what we're hearing is but a skirmish, possibly even *invited* by Captain Reddy, and the greater battle is yet to begin. I'd listen for a lot more voices, from different sources, soon."

Tigaas blinked consternation. "But how do you *know*?"

Courtney shrugged. "Because I know Captain Reddy. I'm as sure what we're hearing is just his opening act as I am that he's trusting me, *all of us*, to destroy that League convoy whether he even knows about it or not." He paused, considering. "That probably sounds rather odd, but you must remember he's a *destroyer skipper*, and all such creatures are obsessed with fuel. The logistical preparations necessary to secure fuel for his old ship, then ammunition, new weapons, aircraft, more ships . . . All were born of that obsession, and it not only spawned an industrial revolution throughout the Grand Alliance, but a *logistical* revolution as well." He shook his head. "But I digress." Looking squarely at Tigaas, he continued, "As I said, I know the man. And just as you may be sure he brought plenty of fuel for himself, he'll mercilessly target the enemy's supply. So must we."

A string of bright red lights began igniting in the sky about two miles to the east, and the ghostly shapes of ships, already apparently washed in glowing blood, were revealed beneath the flares.

"Commence firing! All ships, commence firing!" Tigaas shouted. "Our destroyers will attack those of the enemy, but don't pass up opportunities to torpedo large ships."

Courtney winced at the thought of Repub DDs going against the League's, but they might at least keep them occupied. The ship shook when six 10″ rifles roared together, lighting the night with yellow-orange balls of fire. Courtney had opened his mouth to protect his hearing, but neglected to close his eyes. The afterimage would blind him for some time.

All four Imperators were firing now, and less than two minutes into the action, several ships were already afire and the first League tanker exploded. The destroyers and some transports, no doubt, were shooting back with light guns, but the slaughter was going as well as Courtney could've hoped when Tribune Nir shouted in his ear, "After all our waiting, work, and preparation, it seems almost too easy."

"All the work has made it so." He grinned. "And never complain when you have an advantage, just take it quickly before someone snatches it back."

CHAPTER 45

////// League-Occupied Martinique
August 5, 1945
0300

The atmosphere in *Impero*'s flag suite alternated between optimism and gloom, sometimes within minutes of each other. Apparently, all their precious bombers, except a handful of Stukas still here, had been lost in the raid. On the other hand, they'd reported catastrophic hits on *both* enemy carriers before they went silent. This was confirmed by the shadowing scouting force before it closed to attack as well.

They'd been assailed in turn by what Gravois thought *must* be *Walker* and the light cruiser *Gray*. (A visual report noted again that one was longer than the other.) They'd been excited then, thinking they could win it all that night—until *Savoie* made her appearance. There was no doubting her identity; she was the only Bretagne Class battleship the League ever had and her silhouette was distinctive. The scout commander was ordered to disable her with torpedoes before disengaging.

The following moments held all the tension of a bitter sporting grudge match, as salvos crossed and destroyers dipped under the arcing shells to launch their deadly primary weapons. The gloom deepened when the cruiser and a destroyer were blotted from the sea, the surviving destroyer captain beating a hasty retreat, unsure whether enemy torpedoes or *Savoie*'s 340mm rifles had smashed his consorts. Oddly, he'd seen the cruiser firing furiously at the sky just before she was destroyed, but no planes were observed.

On the bright side, *Savoie* had definitely taken at least one torpedo, and the enemy destroyer and probable cruiser had gone to her aid. The carriers were badly damaged and burning, and even if the cruiser had been shooting at planes from them, they'd have nothing to return to. They might make it to Puerto Rico or Hispaniola, but where would they land? How could they refuel and rearm? There were still some primitive floatplanes about, but everyone was sure they'd seen the last of the enemy's more dangerous aircraft. So the men in the quarters Gravois borrowed from Ammiraglio Gherzi were in a buoyant mood when several catastrophic events occurred at once. First, a panicky messenger burst in with a report that the relief convoy was squealing madly, in the clear, that it was under attack by *four capital ships*! Before they could attempt to digest that, they felt the first trembling thumps of powerful detonations, and alarms bugled in the ship.

Everyone raced out to see what was happening, even Capitano Campioni. The tanker moored alongside partially blocked their view, but there was the unmistakable roar of airplane engines and tracers already flailed the sky. The airfields were blazing again, glowing in the distance over the tangle of trees, and as they watched, their remaining fuel storage tanks ashore were wracked by bombs that blew them open and ignited their contents in swirling, orange-black sheets.

Campioni produced a speaking trumpet and bellowed down at confused men on the tanker, just standing and staring. "Take in your lines and shove off! Get that thing away from my ship!" Searchlights snapped on, stabbing at the dark, long, bright beams whipping in all directions. *Stupid,* Gravois thought. *They'll draw planes like moths.* He was right. A pair of enemy bombers, blue paint purpled by the flames, roared by at Gravois's eye level, toward a cruiser anchored aft of *Impero*. Two long objects dropped from their bellies and splashed in the sea. The planes pulled up, barely clearing the cruiser's wireless aerial, chased by tracers all the way. Gravois looked down and saw yellowish wakes streaming toward the cruiser's side.

"*Savoie* didn't destroy our scout ships, these planes did!" he exclaimed over the thunder of torpedoes hitting the cruiser. Underwater flashes blasted spray as high as the planes had flown. "They were already coming *here* when we found their carriers!" More than just planes had come. A frantic searchlight swept past speeding shapes on the water, then fastened on a trio of zooming boats. They were relatively small, but considerably larger, beamier, and *much* faster than any motor launch. Several machine guns mounted on them sent tracers back at the searchlight and it was quickly shattered. Not before Gravois noted their primary armament, however.

"Torpedo boats!" he cried in mounting, barely suppressed terror. "The boats carry torpedoes too!" Another cruiser was hit by at least three of the weapons, and the first was retching flames in the sky and heeling onto its side. Its crew fought one another for the few bobbing boats about to be crushed by the descending, fire-shrouded superstructure. Their panic was understandable. Many who'd instinctively jumped to avoid the flames were already being shredded by teeming flasher fish, and the water around all the stricken vessels boiled with pinkish foam. The defensive fire was frenzied now, utterly wild, and if some managed to destroy a few enemy boats and planes, more was probably hitting friendly ships. Gravois's devious mind could plot and scheme, but it was never trained to deal with such calamity, on such a scale, all hurled at him at once. It was finally just too much, and all he could do was watch, transfixed, as his meticulously laid plan was enveloped in fire and burned to ash.

Ciano grabbed his arm. "We must go," he shouted urgently over more booming explosions, casting a meaningful glance at the tanker still secured alongside. Its crew was dashing to comply with Campioni's command and its boilers had never gone cold, but it would take long, precious minutes before it could move. *Impero* shuddered violently as bombs or torpedoes struck her aft, and Campioni bolted for the hatch, presumably heading for the bridge. Summoning his last reserves to reassert his affectation of imperturbable poise, Gravois shook off Ciano's hand. "Why? *You* go. It's just as well that I end here. My plan has failed."

"Then make another," Ciano snarled, grabbing him again and dragging him into a passageway filling with smoke and running men. "You're the only one who can," he continued, suddenly hoarse, "and frankly, we've been together too long for me to disassociate myself from you, even if I left you here or shot you as a traitor. We're linked, damn you. If you fail, I fail, and the Triumvirate will just as surely stand *me* up against a wall."

Gravois shrugged. "Where will we go?"

"To my ship—if she hasn't sunk." *Leopardo* was on the other side of *Impero*.

Out in the open, racing against a tide of running men, the horror was even more profound. Smoke and flames were everywhere and the air was filled with roaring engines, tracers, and exploding flashes of antiaircraft shells. A bomber caught fire and staggered in a flaming turn before disintegrating in a sparkling, expanding shower. Ciano and Gravois were knocked to the deck when the tanker beside *Impero* blew up and washed the great battleship's superstructure in sheets of burning oil. Ciano dragged Gravois to his feet and they reached the accommodation ladder at last. *Leopardo* lay untouched, darkened, un-firing, ready to get underway.

"You *ordered* that *Leopardo* be kept in this condition," Gravois accused as they boarded and hurried to the bridge.

"Of course. You've been associated with *me* long enough to know I like to be prepared. I didn't expect this, but my crew has standing orders never to draw attention to themselves under air attack, day or night," he confessed.

"A wise precaution, it would seem."

"Cast off all lines!" Ciano called out. There was no one on *Impero* in a position to release them, and the current would pull *Leopardo* away from the battleship. Suddenly, an absolutely titanic blast erupted in the inner harbor a couple of miles away, backlighting the German cruiser *Hessen* with a flare like a star fallen to earth.

"That'll be the munitioning ships and our last oilers," Ciano said darkly, just before the ear-splitting thunderclap and window-shattering blast wave struck. "*Damn* them!" he shouted as his bridge crew picked themselves up. Flames roared to the heavens, lighting the clouds above. *Hessen* was still there, but her silhouette didn't look quite the same. She wasn't firing anymore either. *Then again,* Ciano thought in passing, *I haven't seen her fire at all.* He shook it away. She'd probably, wisely, been lying low just like *Leopardo*—not that it did her much good.

"If it's any consolation," Gravois observed, hands shaking as he patted his tunic pocket for his cigarette case. Remembering it was empty, he dropped his arms to his sides. His tone had reverted to its normal, sardonic tone, however. "I imagine whatever dropped or launched the fatal stroke couldn't have survived it."

"High-speed boats, coming in to port," called a lookout. "Zero, nine, zero relative, range eight hundred meters!"

"Surface action port, commence firing! All ahead flank!" Ciano shouted. Eight 120mm guns and clusters of 20- and 40mm pom-poms opened up, thrashing the sea and the oncoming MTBs as *Leopardo* crouched and sprang. Two attackers spat torpedoes before they were blown to matchsticks, but they missed the accelerating *Leopardo* aft. They didn't miss *Impero.* Blasted by three torpedoes—right where *Leopardo* had been—plumes of flame and smoky water rose to the sky. Her aft engine room pounded open to the sea, *Impero* started to list.

"Capitano!" cried a signalman on the port bridgewing, "one of our destroyers reports *sailing ships*—perhaps steamers too—coming into the bay! They were just suddenly *there*, out of nowhere. The destroyer is taking accurate fire from heavy guns and trying to open the range."

"That'll be NUS warships, full of troops, no doubt," Gravois said. "As you know, they're fragile targets for our weapons, but their rifled guns are quite large. Very dangerous at this close range." He sighed. "Signal all remaining ships that can get underway to break out to sea. Do *not* linger to engage the enemy, just get past them." His voice hardened. "The Spanish infantry ashore will defend the island to the death!"

"You have a new plan already?" Ciano asked.

"It's not complete, but one thing's obvious. We must join Ammiraglio Gherzi and head for Puerto del Cielo. Our supply convoy is certainly doomed. *Four* 'capital' ships? They had to be those things the Republic calls 'battlecruisers,' which were *supposed* to be eight thousand kilometers away! In any event, the oiler with *Ramb V* is now our only source of fuel."

"But the oiler accompanied *Ramb V* upriver, to deliver Don Hernan to New Granada."

"We can await its return at leisure while I formulate a new strategy. The enemy has no more carriers, and with Gherzi's force around us, they can't challenge us on the open sea."

***USS* Donaghey**

Commander Greg Garrett had no business bringing his old sailing frigate (technically DD-2) USS *Donaghey* into the bay of Martinique at the head of the NUS battle line. She was old in experience and increasingly frail after her long, solitary voyage, not to mention some pretty rough scraps. Even when new, her wooden sides and 18pdr smoothbores were no match for anything here, though she'd once faced—and sunk—a League ship in this very harbor.

On the other hand, COFO Tikker's surviving bombers were leaving, bound for Seepy Field, and Nat Hardee's marauding MTBs were taking little fire now. League sailors seemed primarily occupied saving themselves and their flooding ships—practically every one of which had been damaged by the combined air and sea attack that *again* caught the enemy by surprise. Greg was satisfied with that. He probably hated the League more than anyone in the Navy Clan and United Homes, but knew its commanders had no monopoly on hubris or incompetence. He remembered how effortlessly the Japanese devastated the equally unprepared Clark Field and Cavite *after* everyone already knew about Pearl Harbor.

But this fight wasn't over, and Admiral Semmes was anxious to do his part. *He thinks the NUS is showing thanks and respect to* Donaghey *by giving her pride of place, leading his fleet with the Stars and Stripes of the American Navy Clan,* Greg thought ruefully, looking around in the dark at his loyal, long-suffering, mostly Lemurian crew. They *think so too. I'd've just as soon declined the "honor" if not for them.* He mentally shrugged. *At least* Donaghey*'s still faster than the Nussie sailing steamers behind her, and we won't get jammed up if someone in front of us gets hit.*

She almost threw the line into confusion herself, however, when machine-gun tracers suddenly arced into her from a League DD sweeping out of the smoky gloom two hundred yards away. *Donaghey* replied with a broadside of canister (the only thing she'd loaded), which swept the enemy's decks and gun's crews before Captain Willis's heavy screw frigate, NUSS *Congress*, heartily hammered the ship with his big rifles and sent it reeling into the darkness. Deeper in the harbor, another machine gun stuttered from shore. *Donaghey* blasted more canister at the area and her Maxims chattered. After that, searchlights started snapping on, aiming bright beams straight up at the sky in a token of surrender. The shooting all but stopped and there were only the rumbling explosions of burning, sinking, capsizing ships; the roar of the spreading inferno in the jungle; and the whoosh of flames eating oil spilled across the water.

"It looks like a lake in hell, for sailors," murmured *Donaghey*'s balding gunnery officer, Lieutenant (jg) "Smitty" Smith.

"It does," agreed Lieutenant Mak-Araa, Greg's Lemurian XO. He was blinking horror at the sight, tail swishing nervously. "Chik-aash for baad ships and the evil people they serve."

"Leaguers ain't all evil," Smitty objected. "An' all the fight's blown out of these. Most o' the poor bastards're just tryin' to save themselves."

That wasn't entirely true. A flurry of firing erupted near the rear of the battle line and a large, speeding destroyer was identified by the flare of her snap-shooting guns. They landed some hits too, but she was quickly obscured by the falling damp darkness as she raced out to sea.

"One o' the rats scurried off," Smitty conceded. "Still prob'ly just tryin' to save his ass."

"Whaat about on laand?" Mak asked. "Ahd-mi-raal Sessions only coughed up two thousand troops, with *muzzle-loaders*, to send against *five* thousand Leaguers gaarrisoned here."

"It was all he had," Greg defended, scratching the black stubble on his chin. "Besides, the Leaguers don't have much choice but to quit. Who's going to feed them? We've been here before, remember? Not much to eat on shore. Snakes, I guess." He raised his voice. "Helm, come left ten degrees. Make for that big ship backlit by the fires. I need to have a talk with her skipper." He looked at Mak. "And signal Fred and Kari that it's safe to set down." *Donaghey* had launched her Nancy to get it off the deck when she came in. "I don't think anybody else is going to shoot at us. Tell 'em to be careful, though. There's lots of junk in the water."

At the mercy of hot, swirling winds fed by the flames, Greg Garrett's ship wallowed a little and had to tack before carefully drawing alongside the big German cruiser. The MTBs and SBD-2s had been ordered to leave *Hessen* alone, as long as her guns stayed silent, so Greg was surprised by how beat-up she looked. He was even more surprised to see *U-112* snugged up beside her. And nothing astonished him more than the furious hostility with which Kapitan William Dietrich and several bedraggled-looking officers met him, when he, Mak, and Smitty went aboard.

"You nearly destroyed my ship!" he exclaimed. "I didn't fire a shot, yet you nearly sank me when you blew up those ammunition ships anchored inshore!" He pointed accusingly at the flaming wreckage in the shallows. Nothing even remotely resembled a ship anymore. "My hull is buckled and leaking and there's serious damage all over. I also lost six men killed and almost a *hundred* wounded!"

Greg was taken aback, totally unprepared for this reception. Kurt Hoffman, the sub skipper whom Greg only met when he arrived on station, then a few days before when he came alongside for diesel, seemed a little abashed. The Dominion Navy might've been essentially destroyed, but it still operated a few dedicated sailing ships. *Donaghey* and her prize, *Matarife*, posed as such to carry fuel and supplies to the sub.

"I'm sorry, Willie," Hoffman said. "You *know* no one fired on you. Frankly, I'm surprised, under the circumstances. Accidents are very common in night actions. But you also knew what was in those ships. Perhaps you should've . . . moved farther away?"

"And how could I have explained that to my superiors?" Dietrich flared. "I know! The ghost of my old friend in *U-112* appeared to me and *told* me to!"

"It would've been true."

Dietrich's face reddened further and Greg held up a hand. "Cease firing, gentlemen." He quickly introduced himself and his officers, prompting Dietrich to do the same. It seemed to calm him a little. "Look," Greg said, "I'm just here for a couple of reasons." He stuck his hand out to the German skipper. Grudgingly, Dietrich took it. "First I want to thank you for your cooperation, and extend an invitation, in the name of Captain Reddy and the American Navy Clan, for you to join us. Second, if you do join up, are you seaworthy? Can you fight your ship?"

Dietrich grunted. "For good or ill, I've *already* joined you just by surviving this fiasco. The Triumvirate will certainly see it so. That I did nothing to prevent it might make it worse for me, if they knew, but the result would be the same." He pointed at Hoffman. "This man said you'll do all you can to save my family—and the families of my men?"

"That's correct."

"How?"

Greg hesitated. "I won't lie, it's a long shot," he confessed, "but we hope to wind up with a little . . . let's call it leverage."

Dietrich seemed to consider this, then sighed. "We're with you, then. We have no choice. I fear my ship will need longer to decide, however. She's in no shape to fight. . . . I may not even be able to keep her afloat."

"We have a self-propelled dry dock just a few days from here. If *Hessen*'s damage is that bad, we can put her in it." Greg turned to Smitty. "Go get Lieutenant Sori-Maai and all our pharmacist's mates and SBAs. Sori's our surgeon," he explained to Dietrich.

The German frowned. "What manner of . . . person is this officer?"

Greg's eyes narrowed. "He's a 'Cat. So what? I bet he's a better human doc than anybody you have."

"Perhaps so, and I mean no offense," Dietrich assured, "but strong prejudices exist among some of my crew, and they're difficult to cast aside."

"Mine are gone, Willie," Hoffman told him gently, "and I don't miss them. Your wounded will find it even easier to overcome racialism if their suffering's relieved."

Dietrich gazed at Mak-Aara a moment. The Lemurian hadn't spoken, but though the German knew the 'Cat's blinking meant something, he didn't know what it was. "Very well, then. Please. Any help will be appreciated." Smitty nodded and hurried to the rail.

Greg smiled gratefully at Hoffman, but asked, "What about you? Why're you even here? You were supposed to wait outside the mouth of the harbor and pick off the leakers. At least report which way they go."

"I meant to be there," Hoffman temporized, "and I would've been . . ." He glanced at Dietrich.

"You!" the man said, enraged once more. "*You* torpedoed the ships that nearly destroyed me!"

"They were, arguably, the most important targets here. I couldn't help myself," Hoffman confessed. "And my Lemurian crew—which has worked so hard to learn how—was keen to strike a blow." He waved a hand helplessly. "They're very excitable, you know, and I've grown quite fond of them. You have my deepest regrets, Willie. I never expected . . ." He took a long breath. "I saw no harm in it, and a great deal of good. I thought I'd wave you a cheerful farewell as I resumed my position. But the shock wave pounded us against the bottom and forced us to the surface." He sighed and looked at Greg. "I may need to visit the dry dock as well."

"Oh, boy."

"But I *do* know where the 'leakers,' as you called them, were bound," Hoffman added.

Dietrich nodded. "I as well. Gravois sent a message as he cleared the harbor."

"That was him?" Greg cursed.

"Indeed. A shame you didn't get him. But I can tell you where he went."

Twenty minutes later, just as Fred Reynolds and Kari-Faask were motoring their tired Nancy alongside, Greg reboarded *Donaghey*. "Get your plane gassed up and serviced," he told the two friends when they climbed aboard. "I've got some hot dope for Captain Reddy. I'll send it by wireless, but I want you to carry it too." He smiled sadly. "Back to *Walker*, finally, where you belong." The smile faded. "Fly due north about two hundred miles. From what you've probably heard on the radio, you can't miss her. *Maaka-Kakja*'s burning up, and *Walker*'s standing by."

CHAPTER 46

////// USNRS **Salissa**
East of Antigua (N-NE of Martinique)

"That's the last of 'em, Skipper," said Chief Gunner's Mate Dennis Silva as he, Lawrence, Tex Sheider, and Pam Cross reported on *Salissa*'s packed hangar deck. They'd just ascended under a ragged, cloudy dawn with twenty others (mostly officers) from the final boat to cross the choppy sea from the raging inferno that had been USS *Maaka-Kakja*. Silva and Lawrence, "with nothing else to do just then," originally took one of *Salissa*'s boats to transfer survivors. Pam hopped in at the last moment, as usual, to help wounded sailors. They wound up staying and doing everything from fighting the flames to flooding magazines and pumping oil on the water to calm the frisky waves for the boats. Ultimately, along with Tex, they remained until the bitter end. All were red-eyed, scorched and blackened, and looked done in. Even Petey was singed and exhausted, eyes half open. Tex probably looked the worst; he was losing his ship. Still *Admiral Lelaa's* ship, as far as he was concerned, which she'd confidently entrusted to him. It would never matter to him that there'd been no way to save her, he was still responsible. The weight of that wore heavy on his face.

Only the dozens of large, lightweight wooden rafts every ship now carried for rapid abandonment were left behind. Lacing those into a kind of undulating dock had been Tex's idea, and probably contributed to the near miraculous fact that no one was lost to the ravening sea during the rescue. Part of the shoal of bounding barges and motor launches—about half from *Makky-Kat*—would be abandoned as well, but most were being hoisted to the hangar deck by *Salissa*'s seaplane-handling cranes.

"You did well," Matt told them, standing with Keje, Sandra, and Sir Sean, shouting to be heard over the nearly eighteen hundred sailors from the dying carrier. "*All* of you," he added fiercely, gazing directly at Tex. "If anyone's to blame for this mess, it's me."

Keje blinked impatience. "Whaaat mess? Haaven't you read the reports from Maartinique? We forced them out! It is victory! There were losses," he conceded, "but all great things come with a cost."

"We could've sent our planes to Seepy Field, launched the whole raid from there. . . ."

"And Graavois would still wonder where our caarriers are. He *haad* to find us for our—*your*—next surprise to work."

"Maybe . . . but damn." Matt looked guiltily at his friend. "We could've lost *Big Sal* too."

Keje nodded. "And *Waalker*. Do you think I don't know why she and *Mahaan* were here to protect us?" Matt nodded, a complex expression on his face. The two destroyers had fought fires as well, as soon as they finished rescuing *Saa-Leebs*'s crew. They couldn't save the carrier, but they helped keep the flames pushed off her stern where all the survivors had gathered.

Sandra hugged her husband, trying to infuse him with her love and confidence. She knew more than anyone how cold calculations involving lives tore at him. And they'd lost *so many* over the last few weeks, here and in Africa. Sandra suspected, when the final tally came, their *military* casualties over the last six months would exceed those of the previous two and a half years. And the percentages were catching up with their closest friends and Matt's old destroyermen just as fast.

Cries of joy cracked the somber mood and they turned to see another pair of familiar faces as Fred Reynolds and Kari-Faask rushed to join them. They'd set their Nancy down at the edge of the same lee *Big Sal* formed for the boats, and a crane had just lifted them aboard. It had been a bumpy landing but there was no danger. Fred and Kari had lost a *lot* of planes over time, but never one that was undamaged. Kari, a mushy cigar clamped in her mouth (which Petey regarded with interest), embraced everybody in the Lemurian way before catching herself and stepping back alongside Fred to salute. They both looked tired but exuberant to be back among so many friends, and quickly gave an enthusiastic eyewitness account of the crushing raid on Martinique. That finally added an exclamation point to Tikker's, Nat's, and Garrett's dry wireless reports. Until then, the success of the operation had seemed vaguely abstract to many still absorbing the loss of *Maaka-Kakja* and *Saa-Leebs*. An excitement started to swell among them, even in Matt.

Keje raised a speaking trumpet toward the milling crowd of survivors. "Sailors of *Maaka-Kakja*! *Waalker* and *Mahaan* will come around to refuel as soon as the boats are out of the waay. If you caan help, you know how, but we must clear this area to extend the hoses." Willing hands joined the effort while others stayed out of the way. The last boats were brought aboard or sunk by a stutter of Blitzerbug fire in their hulls. *Walker* took station first (with four boilers now, she was the thirstiest), and fuel lines were rigged. As soon as oil was pulsing through them, Spanky came aboard and joined the group. He grinned at Fred and Kari, then shook his head back over his shoulder. "What a goat rodeo. With Gilbert back, *Walker*'s engineering plant couldn't be in better hands, but . . . well, you'd think him and Isak would be glad to see each other, after so long." Isak Reuben and Gilbert Yeager weren't only the original "Mice," they were half brothers. "Maybe they are, in their way," Spanky conceded, "but they went straight to bickering over who was senior—Isak for staying with *Walker* all along, or Gilbert for being Chief in a flat-top." He rolled his eyes. "Glad they're Tabby's problem."

The low-pitched, indignant roar of Chief Bosun Jeek reached them from the fo'c'sle below, countered by Tabby's equally distinctive voice, arguing over oil that splattered the deck. "Then there's *those* two. There'll never be another Chief Gray, but Jeek's the closest 'Cat equivalent. And officer or not, Tabby'll scrap with him when he gives her snipes hell." He looked ruefully at Matt. "I guess us old Asiatic Fleet sailors didn't set the best example for naval etiquette."

Matt laughed, and it sounded strange coming from him. He'd brooded over the complexity of the plan ever since they came through the Pass of Fire. Given the disparity of forces, it was complicated of necessity and he really hadn't expected all the pieces to fit so well. Now, despite their losses, and the even more dangerous phase they were entering, the big puzzle actually seemed to be coming together. "No, but I think the *fighting* example is the most important right now. We'll work on our manners after the war."

"Yeah. So what's next?"

"I'm sure you caught the gist on the radio, but Fred and Kari made it real. We licked 'em at Martinique and Gravois ran off in *Leopardo*. He wants Admiral Gherzi to meet him and they'll head for Puerto del Cielo together." Matt waited while his friends nodded appreciatively, then continued. "What most of you *don't* know is that we caught a single quick transmission from Courtney and the Repub Fleet. They rounded up and *smashed* a supply convoy meant for Gravois and Gherzi, which means not only are they more desperate for fuel than ever, that little oiler we've been keeping tabs on at Puerto del Cielo is the *only* resupply they have, and why they *have* to head that way." He shrugged. "We just have to figure out where they'll meet, and get there first. No sweat." He acknowledged the uncomfortable chuckles before adding, "One good thing: though Colonel Mallory couldn't hit Gherzi with his bombers, saving the few he had left for tonight, he hammered Gherzi's scout planes pretty hard with his last three P-40s, homing in on their radio signals while the enemy was still theoretically in range of our 'base' at Santiago. Even if the scouts squealed about the P-40s before they died, Gherzi won't worry about them now he's out of what he thinks is *their* range. So if he isn't totally blind, he can't have more than a couple planes left. It's a damn big ocean, and with luck, we should be able to get the drop on him.

"So now . . ." He sighed and looked at Keje. "*Big Sal*'s out of it. Take her to Port January and offload any supplies Seepy Field night need, then make for Mobile. The Nussies can't do much for our steel ships, but they can fix your wooden flight deck."

"A fine suggestion, Cap-i-taan Reddy," Keje agreed, "and I've already told Cap-i-taan Atlaan to do so. I'll accompaany you in *Waalker*, however. I aassume you'll proceed in her?" He blinked amusement when Matt guardedly nodded. "Then we caan shift both our flaags at once! *My* Home is safe, and you caan't leave me when you take yours into haarmful waaters again. I *will not* miss this," he added defiantly.

Matt didn't even try to argue. Whatever happened, Keje had earned the right to be there. He said nothing to Sir Sean Bates for the same reason, or even Sandra, though he desperately wished she'd stay with *Big Sal*. She'd made her feelings clear long ago and Matt refused to throw down the "who'll take care of our son?" card. He knew *she* thought about it every day. But young Fitzhugh Adar Reddy would be lovingly cared for regardless of what happened to them. In the end it came down to their commitment to each other. They'd started this odyssey together and would finish it that way. Sandra deserved to be there just as much as Keje. And where Sandra went, so would Diania. . . . Silva and Lawrence were a given, though Matt still hadn't decided whether to use them in *Walker* or send them to Chack in *Sular*. He blinked resignation in the Lemurian way.

"You can't leave us neither," Fred and Kari chorused. "We just got back! Though . . ." Fred looked askance down at the newer-model Nancy perched on *Walker*'s pitching seaplane catapult. "You think we might swap planes? We're kinda partial to ours. Just gettin' used to it, in fact. And I've never flown one o' those souped-up crates."

"We can give that one to *Mahan*." Spanky smiled. "She took a hit against the aft deckhouse that wrecked hers. Not much other damage, and only a few light splinter wounds to some of her people, but the plane was trashed," he added for Matt's benefit.

"Very well," Matt said lowly, "I guess everything's settled." He looked at Spanky. "Go back aboard *Walker*. Make room for our additions, then put Ed on the horn to Colonel Mallory and tell him all of Jumbo's and Tikker's remaining bombers that can make the trip will fly south to join TF-Jenks and TF-Tassanna. We'll squawk their positions after they respond to the code they've been waiting for. Ben'll have to stay behind with the fighters—and his P-40s. He'll hate that, but *Madraas* has her own fighters, and Ben has to defend Seepy Field and provide air support for Nussie troops going ashore at Martinique. Then?" He paused, considering. "As soon as I'm aboard *Walker*, we'll look at the chart and find someplace for everybody—and I mean *everybody*—to converge. Between the League fleet and Puerto del Cielo."

Spanky whistled. Everyone knew the object of all their operations so far had been to set up the very Allied "David" versus League "Goliath" scenario now in motion—after inflicting as heavy and blinding a preliminary beating on Goliath as they could, of course. The first part had succeeded, but now David must face his larger adversary, toe to toe. They could only hope they had enough sling stones in their poke to do the job. "That's a long haul for us, especially if we don't chase right up *Leopardo*'s skirt—which I wouldn't recommend. That would leave her, and probably Gherzi, between us and our guys."

Matt chuckled. "Not my intention. We'll steam west around Antigua before heading south, relying on scouting reports from Jenks and the other Repub seaplane tender's Nancys and *Seevogels* so we don't run into Gherzi by ourselves. Low on fuel as he should be, he's never run at high speed since he left Martinique so his heavies'll still have plenty for a fight," he warned, "but unless he's an idiot, he's had his destroyers sucking his teat so they won't run dry either. He'll stay slow." He looked out at *Mahan*. Now that the boats had all been taken in or disposed of, she was approaching aft of *Walker* to refuel as well. "How fast can she go?" he asked.

"Commander Tiaa says she'll make twenty-eight knots, after her yardwork at Baalkpan. Maybe thirty, if they don't look at her pressure gauges too hard. Not saying that's a good idea. . . ." Spanky hedged.

Matt smiled grimly. "And *Walker* can make thirty, standing on her head, with her new boiler. If *Mahan* can keep up, swell. We'll need her. But it's more important that one of us gets there in time than if neither of us does." He cocked his head at Spanky. "Remember when we went chasing those Grik ships that raided Baalkpan so we could catch one and look it over? Look the *Grik* over so we'd know what we were getting into?"

Spanky was nodding. "I talked you into backing down, just sinking 'em."

"Right. And your reasons were sound. You said that if we broke down, we were stuck. No spare parts, no way to repair the ship . . . hell, we didn't even have enough fuel left to run the pumps! You were right, then, and I'm glad I listened, but this time it's different. This is *it*, Spanky. We're all in, and we won't hold *anything* back for later."

CHAPTER 47

////// Leopardo
August 5, 1945

Leopardo sprinted due east after escaping Martinique. Ciano and Gravois agreed their first imperative was avoiding the planes and torpedo boats that suddenly swarmed the harbor. The planes would be gone by now, but after sighting the puny but numerous NUS ships—undoubtedly full of troops—they realized the NUS (and torpedo boats) was there to stay. Once *Leopardo* rejoined Gherzi, they could easily expel them, but the facilities at Martinique were wrecked and its utility was finished. They needed a new, more secure base of operations. Gravois decided that would be Puerto del Cielo—whether Don Hernan liked it or not. He was through tiptoeing around that madman's sensibilities, and they'd take the city by storm if they must. They'd lost their Spanish infantry, of course, but Gherzi had over a thousand Marines aboard his battleships and cruisers. Even sailors, armed with modern weapons and backed by naval gunfire, would make short work of Dominion troops. And who knew? Dom civilians had sometimes welcomed the NUS and their Allies as liberators. After the drumbeat of daily atrocities at Puerto del Cielo, perhaps its population would similarly welcome the League?

First, however, Gravois and Ciano had to get there in one piece. They remained confident in the overwhelming power of Gherzi's battle line, but they'd suffered too many unpleasant surprises to maintain their previous disdain for the enemy. Truth be told, they were rattled, and they craved the comforting embrace of Gherzi's armored ships. The trouble was, after being told to delay his arrival at Martinique, Gherzi had turned west, then south-southwest, to parallel the Windward Isles, and remained at an inconvenient distance.

"We just received a signal from *Canet*," reported a messenger. *Canet* was the Alsedo Class destroyer that first alerted them to the NUS arrival. "She took some damaging hits at close range, but managed to escape as well. She wishes to join us."

Gravois started to reply, but Ciano shook his head and interrupted. "What's the nature of her damage?"

"Forward fireroom. Her speed is reduced to twenty-four knots."

Ciano looked at Gravois. "I'm bound to you and will obey your orders, but leave the safety of my ship to me."

"Of course," Gravois granted.

Ciano strode to the chart table and traced his finger across it. "Ammiraglio Gherzi will rendezvous with us twenty kilometers west of the island of St. Vincent tomorrow afternoon. Advise *Canet* to make her way there independently. Use the islands as cover, and we'll give her more specific times and positions as we know them ourselves." He looked back at Gravois. "Alsedos are even less capable than we are against air attack. I don't want her attached to my hip if we have to maneuver briskly."

Gravois shrugged. "As you say, our safety is in your hands, though I'm confident the enemy has shot his bolt in the sky."

Ciano just gazed at him a moment before reminding, "That's what you said right before their planes ruined us at Martinique." He turned to the messenger. "Send it."

USS Walker

Under a still blustery but clearing morning sky, Ed Palmer marched triumphantly up the metal stairs aft. Longish hair whipping in the stiff breeze around his tanned, boyish face made him look like a teenager on a beach. Stepping up by Keje and Sir Sean, next to Matt's chair in the pilothouse, he proclaimed with savage glee, "We've got the sons 'o bitches!"

Immediately realizing what he said, Ed's eyes went wide and he took a step back. Matt's chuckle and "spit it out" gesture reassured him, however, and some of his enthusiasm returned. "*Hessen*'s still in the League radio loop, and Captain Garrett forwarded what they picked up."

"What's the situation at Martinique?" Sandra interrupted. She was sitting on a tall stool secured directly to the deck. Ed looked at her, torn, and Sir Sean laughed at his expression.

"Go ahead," Matt told him. "I want to know that, *whoever* we've 'got.'"

"Aye, sir. Well, a couple more destroyers that weren't hit skedaddled, no one knows where, but all the remaining ships except *Impero*—she's their flagship—have surrendered. Not much choice; they're sunk or sinking." His face darkened. "The NUS Admiral Sessions is already croaking about who gets salvage." He shook his head. "*Impero*'s half-sunk herself, low by the stern, with her screws and rudder on the shallow bottom. She can't move. But she isn't shooting either. Nobody knows if her main battery's operational. Probably is, since she's got steam, but she's also got plenty of secondaries. On the other hand, Nat Hardee's MTBs have her by the throat. He's got six of 'em idling abeam of her at five hundred yards, ready to slam her full of torpedoes if she makes a peep. He thinks her skipper will behave himself.

"Otherwise, there's some fighting ashore, but not as much as you'd think. A lot of League troops are surrendering. Seems they figure they're through, and . . . well, there's *lots* of snakes, that love hanging out in their fighting positions."

"Jesus," Spanky commiserated, stepping over from the port bridgewing. "Hardly any snakes anywhere else in the world we've seen, but Captain Garrett mentioned 'em in his report about the place. I get why nobody'd want to *die* for it."

"Especially since we don't eat or murder our prisoners," Sandra agreed. "So who—or what—have we 'got'?"

Ed looked back at Matt. "*Leopardo* and Gravois will meet Admiral Gherzi this evening, about ten miles west of St. Vincent Island."

Matt stood and went quickly to the chart table. "Show me," he demanded. When Ed did, Matt whistled. "Not sure who's 'got' who. Look at this." He pointed. "TF-Jenks and TF-Tassanna are here, and here. They can make it if they haul ass. We can too, if we refuel when we get there. Trouble is, as close as they'll be to Puerto del Cielo, we're faced with the exact *opposite* kind of action I wanted. I'd hoped to catch 'em at night and finish 'em in daylight, out of sight of their objective. The psychological effect of that would be particularly important, now. Besides, against those heavies, a night action's our only hope. The trouble is, if we wait for dark to engage 'em, things're gonna get tight and they could be *at* Puerto del Cielo by dawn. We *have* to stop 'em short of there, at any cost," he added grimly.

"What about Courtney and his Repub ships?" Sandra asked.

Matt shook his head. "They're on their way down to the general area and we'll forward the update, but I don't think they can get there before tomorrow morning."

"So we delaay them," Keje said simply. "Use *Madraas*'s and *New Dublin*'s planes."

"We need them to deliver our final kick in the guts," Matt reminded, "but Jumbo and Tikker might hit 'em a lick coming down to join us."

"Would'nae that reveal we've another carrier here?" Sir Sean asked skeptically. "Where else could the planes land?"

"Probably," Matt agreed, frowning, "but I don't see any other way to slow 'em down. . . ." He blinked suddenly, and straightened. When he spoke again, his tone was hard as iron. "Actually, I do. We *will* pick a fight in daylight. Evening, rather." He looked at the others. "They're scared of our planes, but not our ships. *Savoie* and her look-alike'll give 'em a start, especially since they probably think they already got her, but that whole fleet came all this way to hunt us down." He was warming to his argument. "They won't run when we show 'em what they want to see. Gravois won't *let* 'em! We've handed him a mess so far, and beating us decisively is his only way out. Give him a glimpse of *our* battle line, and he'll take the bait," he added confidently.

"'Bait'? For what? And depending on their gunnery, a 'glimpse' is all they might need," Spanky grumbled.

"We'll cross in front of 'em and invite a fight, then get 'em to chase us through those islands between St. Vincent and Grenada. They're supposed to be the 'Grenadines,' but don't look quite right." He shook his head. "Nothing new about that. I just hope the charts Admiral Semmes gave us are good, because that's tricky water." He looked up. "And that's why we'll lead 'em in. They get tangled up in those islands, they lose sea room and their range advantage—and keep burning fuel. Once it's dark and they're committed, focused entirely on us, our bombers'll take 'em from the unengaged side. *Then* we'll lunge in and turn the fight into a barroom brawl instead of a long-range punching match." He paused, thoughtfully. "I don't think anybody can plan what happens after that, but at least with islands around, crippled ships might run aground and keep their people out of the sea, away from the damned flashies." After a moment of contemplative silence, he spoke to Ed Palmer. "Send to all commands: I want every scout plane we have in the air, and real-time coordinates on all enemy ships. We don't want any of ours stumbling into them piecemeal at this point!"

"Aye, aye, sir."

Sandra gave his arm a gentle squeeze. She knew he sometimes worried that, in situations like this, he let his instinctive aggression get the better of him and cloud his judgment, but she couldn't see an alternative. And Matt's relationship with Spanky, Keje, Bates, or any of his senior officers was such that if anyone had a better idea, they'd speak up. No one did.

Keje's tail swished as he looked out at the fo'c'sle and the white-capping purple sea. *Walker* was surging through it, bounding and blowing spray. In most ways, despite the countless patches and makeshift repairs and the many miles she'd steamed since her last overhaul, the old ship was healthier than she'd usually been on this world. Even her normal creaks and groans were stifled by the anxious roar of her blowers and machinery. It was almost like she was *eager* to meet what lay ahead.

In contrast, the tails of the 'Cats of the bridge watch swayed as much as Keje's, if more erratically, betraying their tension. After the brief action against modern ships the previous night, they knew what they were getting into. At least they thought they did. They wouldn't have been sane if they weren't afraid.

"My friends . . . my faamily," Keje said evenly, blinking affection, "we haave dared maany desperate moments together. I'm no Sky Priest to entreat the Heavens as Adar once did, so I caan't be as sure the Maker will listen, but if you haave no objection, I'll offer the same prayer and perhaaps He will hear."

"By all means," Matt told him.

Turning to port, toward the morning sun, Keje spread his arms. All the 'Cats but the one at the wheel copied him unselfconsciously. "Maker of All Things!" Keje said loudly. "I beg your protection for myself—and all your people gaathered in this ship." He paused. "And do not forget the ship herself. She is as alive as any Home ever waas, and haas done your work here well." He took a breath. "But if it is indeed our Time, please light our spirits' paaths to their everlaasting Homes in the Heavens."

Crossing their arms over their chests, all the 'Cats bowed. Then Keje grinned. "And to those who haaven't heard it before, yes, thaat's it."

"I've heard it," Sir Sean assured, smiling, "but it's always struck me as rather broad."

"It's an inclusive prayer for the protection of maany," Keje told him. "I like to think the Maker hears our little selfish ones, as well. I'll be adding a lot of those over the next few days, I'm sure."

"Amen to that," Spanky said.

CHAPTER 48

MANEUVERS

////// *USS* Savoie
The Caribbean

The United Allied Fleet gathered and rearranged its might throughout the day. TF-Jenks had remained largely unchanged throughout its inconspicuous cruise, as had TF-Tassanna as soon as it came into being. Now, as they both swept east and gradually converged, Admiral Lelaa-Tal-Cleraan's carrier, USS *New Dublin*, and USS *Sular*, transporting Chack's Brigade and II Corps' 6th Division, fell back with all the fast cargo ships and all but one fleet oiler to join TF-Tassanna's USS *Madraas*. Tassanna's escorting destroyers, except for *James Ellis*, sped off toward TF-Jenks.

High Admiral Jenks now had the superdreadnaught *Savoie* (and her shadow, *La-Laanti*); the light cruisers *Fitzhugh Gray* and *Maa-ni-la*; Impie cruisers *Mars*, *Centurion*, *Mithra*, *Hermes*, *Diana*, *Ananke*, *Feronia*, and *Nesoi*; as well as the "modern" DDs *McDonald*, *Tassat*, *Daanis*, *Steele*, *Araina*, and *Sineaa* under his titular command. With *Walker* and *Mahan* racing down, virtually every Allied combatant, other than the Nussies busy at Martinique, and Courtney's Repubs on the way, would be gathered in one place. It was a formidable force on paper, the most powerful the Allies ever assembled, but even Jenks wasn't persuaded his own country's cruisers could make a significant contribution. Particularly in daylight, as it now seemed they must. He distracted himself by smoking his pipe and pacing *Savoie*'s bridge with Ambassador Doocy Meek and Captain Russ Chappelle while the latter ran low-impact gunnery drills to perform last-minute tests on equipment and polish the sharp edge his gun's crews had achieved through daily training across half the planet. Calling out imaginary targets to the talker, who relayed them to Gunny Horn in the armored but still dangerously exposed fire control platform above the bridge, they watched the massive turrets train out and their guns seemingly elevate of their own volition.

"I'm always amazed to witness that," Jenks proclaimed, twisting his long mustaches and exhaling a gust of smoke. "Similar evolutions on your cruisers and mine"—by that he meant the Impie's—"are quite impressive, but these things . . ." He gestured at the numbers one and two gunhouses forward. "They're of an entirely different order of magnitude. And you have *seven* of them to hurl their monstrous projectiles!"

"Wish we still had eight, because the Leaguers have a whole lot more," Russ complained. The left gun in *Savoie*'s number one turret had been badly damaged (by Horn) during the action in which she was captured. It was removed at Baalkpan and replaced by a gun from the number three turret, aft. It had been a big job, inspired entirely by Russ's preference for more firepower forward, but by then *Savoie* hadn't needed much more work. Most had been completed by *Tarakan Island* and her own crew on the long voyage home. The empty hole in the face of the number three turret had been covered by the last sections of *Amagi*'s armor plate they had left.

Russ brightened. "And don't sell 'your' cruisers short. Their crews've learned to operate seamlessly with ours and their main guns aren't that bad. Each ship can loft four 250-pound shells, and keep 'em pretty tight out to ten thousand yards. The five and a halfs we all use aren't much good past fifteen thousand." He didn't add that *none* of them would penetrate thick armor at that range. "And to be honest, I'd hate to catch Gunny Horn's eye that far with the new gear in *Savoie*, but it's not good enough for anything past that."

"And the enemy can be expected to hit us at what range?"

Doocy Meek spoke up. "That depends on how good *they* are—and frankly, how well they've maintained their equipment and ammunition. Fiedler said they didn't at all, for a while, and only just started trying to make new ammunition. They may not have any yet, and some of their old stuff could be unreliable. Worst case, I'd say about fifteen thousand too."

Russ nodded agreement, but frowned. "With *three* BBs, probably four cruisers—don't know how many are heavy or light—and maybe as many

DDs as us, if those that got out of Martinique join up . . ." He forced a grin. "I'm praying for a lot of duds."

USS Madraas *(CV-8)*

With the arrival of Admiral Lelaa in *New Dublin*, Commodore Tassanna-Ay-Arracca no longer commanded the task force bearing her name and was relieved in more ways than one. Their combined carriers, auxiliaries, and *Sular*, of course, now protected by Perry Brister's lone USS *James Ellis*, was a larger force than she was used to handling. It would also make an irresistible target, she thought. She was grateful for Lelaa's greater experience and reassured by her confidence they'd remained undetected. Their older Nancy scouts, which the enemy would hopefully attribute to outdated frigates the Allies had converted to seaplane tenders, had dogged Gherzi's fleet throughout its sortie. There were no other League ships—and their radios—anywhere around, and the scarce Dom ships discovered hugging the coast were destroyed by their prowling Dom prizes, USS *Destroyer* and USS *Sword*, under Captain Ruik-Sor-Ra. Otherwise, they'd stayed too far out to sea to be bothered by Grikbirds. Only Dom "dragons," with their ability to carry observers (and bombs) posed a serious threat, and their combat air patrol had easily killed the few of those they'd spotted. Either the enemy was short of them, or they were occupied elsewhere. Maybe both. Trailing TF-Jenks by only twenty miles now, Admiral Lelaa took TF-Tassanna pounding east-southeast behind the rest of the United Fleet at fifteen knots.

"Strike all but the ready fighters on the caatapults down below," Tassanna ordered. "Commaander Jumbo Fisher and Cap-i-taan Jis-Tikkar will be aarriving with their bombers this aafternoon." She was a little concerned about that. *Madraas* had unofficially been designated the "fighter carrier" for this operation, and had a full loadout of Bull-Bats, but she'd never even practiced recovering and launching the equally new, much bigger, SBD-2 torpedo bombers. The possibility they might have to learn in darkness was even more unsettling. "We don't know how maany they're bringing, or even if we'll haave space for them all, so Ahd-mi-raal Lelaa commaanded thaat we be ready to throw fighters into the sea." She looked at *Madraas*'s XO. "If so, we'll probaably haave to do it quickly, so aassemble details and haave them staand by."

"Whaat ordnaance for tonight?" the XO asked.

"Torpedoes."

Gherzi

Ammiraglio di Divisione Bruto Gherzi moved uncomfortably back to the plush chair provided for him on *Tourville*'s bridge. Groaning slightly, he sat, and glanced surreptitiously at the men at their stations. He was surprised again by the apparent lack of derision radiating in his direction. There'd been some at first, of course, when he (an Italian) hoisted his flag aboard the elderly, but mighty, and unusually well-maintained French dreadnaught. This was due as much to his nationality and the sometimes bitter rivalry between the preeminent members of the League as it was his rotund frame—and resultant, painful gout. Oddly, however, as the ill-fated sortie progressed, he noted a gradual softening in the resentment aimed at him, and was amazed to discover the padded chair awaiting him on the bridge the morning before.

He wondered about that. He hadn't gone out of his way to curry favor—quite the opposite. He'd made it clear what he expected—that their orders would be followed to the letter—then settled in to shoulder the initial hostility and his own misery without complaint. He avoided interfering with the ship's officers or business in any way, except insofar as its position in the formation and their pursuit of the objective was concerned. That was nothing special; he always operated like that. He was the *fleet* commander, and couldn't care less how the men in the engine room tied their shoes. Not an ardent fascist, his general competence, *obvious* lack of political ambition, and popularity-inspiring behavior was probably the only reason he'd survived the snake-pit intrigues and purges in the League.

His stoic, carefully polite personality may have cracked the ice, but his sincere obsession with saving every man they could after two of their destroyers, one French, struck mines earned the respect of *Tourville*'s officers. Truth be known, he would've done his best to save enemies in the water. This world's seas were no place for a man—or anything else—to die. *Tourville*'s Capitaine de vaisseau Michel Sartre in particular may've been just as impressed by the reluctant resolution with which Gherzi then completed his mission and mercilessly shelled Santiago into flaming rubble, once catching Gherzi mumbling, "Damn you, Gravois," under his breath.

Commandant Sartre made occasional probing observations after that, pertaining to everything from their place in this world in general, to his anxiety about the motives of Victor Gravois. Gherzi made no comment, but didn't upbraid Sartre either. He believed a man's thoughts should be his own. Besides, he privately loathed Gravois as much as Sartre apparently did. Somehow, this became understood. Maybe his face betrayed something when they learned of the attacks on Martinique, or he was less than discreet when it was reported they had no fuel to replenish their bunkers, and no port to return to. Regardless, the chair had appeared.

Now the silent, painful pacing he'd just engaged in had made clear to all his fury that his entire, oil-thirsty strike force was waiting off the east coast of the island of St. Vincent *solely* for Gravois to make his appearance and lead them to salvation. A lone ship had been seen approaching from that direction and they were waiting for it to identify itself.

"Ship is the Spanish *Canet*," announced a messenger from the port lookouts. His excitement ebbed when he continued. "She asks if the scout planes overhead are ours."

They weren't, of course. The little Allied floatplanes had pestered them all the way from Santiago. Most infuriating (and unnerving) was how they dropped bright flares at night, marking the formation's progress for all to see. Unfortunately, of all Gherzi's ships with aircraft catapults, only *Tourville* still had a plane, and it had been worked half to death. It was blowing oil and desperately needed maintenance. With no threat imagined between them and Puerto del Cielo, Sartre finally allowed his air division to begin necessary repairs.

"Tell *Canet* they are not," Sartre replied darkly, then said aside to Gherzi, "At least she escaped the debacle at Martinique. Now the world wonders, where's Gravois and *Leopardo*?" Gherzi frowned at the sarcasm, but remained silent. That might cost him someday, if word got out, but his orphaned strike force was in a bad way, its morale in the bilge. He wouldn't contribute to more unease.

"Message from *Leopardo*," a runner from the radio room almost immediately told them. "She sees our smoke and will round the island behind *Canet*."

"Very well, record the time in the log," Sartre told the man, glancing at the chronometer on the bulkhead beyond the helmsman. 1620.

"Commandant!" came the cry of another messenger. "Starboard lookouts report surface contacts on the horizon, south-southwest, bearing two, one, zero!"

Gherzi stood, wincing. "What? How many? What are they?"

Sartre quickly strode to the aft bulkhead and spoke into a voice tube himself. A tinny reply came from the foremast fighting top high above, built during a major modernization. Before it was installed, the ship had only a single mast, amidships, of very limited utility. Sartre was the only one who clearly heard the report and his tanned face paled. Looking at Gherzi, he spoke in a tone of disbelief. "It's difficult to tell at this distance, Ammiraglio, but the lookout is sure of more than a *dozen* warships, at least two of which strongly resemble this one . . . or more accurately, *Savoie*."

Gherzi blinked. "But . . ." They'd listened disbelievingly to the reports of the cruiser that engaged "*Savoie*" to the north, before its transmissions ended. But it was impossible that *two of her* could be here, especially if the surviving destroyer's account of torpedo damage was true. *And where was* that *destroyer?* "They can't be more of *our* ships, also escaped from Martinique?" Gherzi asked hopefully.

"No."

"Then only one possibility remains. Contact . . . Monsieur Gravois in *Leopardo*, and inform him the enemy fleet is in sight."

Sartre gave the order, and a messenger returned with Gravois's reply. It seemed almost as breathless as the man who brought it:

> CONGRATULATIONS AMMIRAGLIO GHERZI. DISCOVERY OF PREVIOUSLY UNEXPECTED FORCE—CONCUR IT MUST BE MAIN BODY ENEMY SURFACE FLEET—SOLVES MANY MYSTERIES. ENGAGE AND DESTROY AT ONCE. ALL OTHER CONSIDERATIONS SECONDARY.

"'All other considerations secondary,'" Gherzi quoted aloud, after passing the page to Commandant Sartre. An overt bitterness colored his tone for the first time. He took a long breath. "Signal the fleet. Form line of battle—cruisers leading the battleships, destroyers in line to port. Then we'll come about to the south on a course of one, eight, zero. Make turns for twenty knots."

Sartre relayed the order, then asked, "Destroyers on the disengaged side? Shouldn't we put them forward, to scout what we face? Perhaps make torpedo attacks?"

"Do we *have* unlimited torpedoes?" Gherzi asked. "I thought not. And not knowing what we face, we must scout with our better-protected ships. Unless your remaining scout plane can fly?"

Sartre shook his head regretfully.

"Not your fault, Commandant Sartre," Gherzi soothed gently, then the bitterness returned. "I wonder if Monsieur Gravois will be joining us in *Leopardo*? And I certainly hope our last oiler remains safe at our destination, or after we destroy the enemy, *our* mighty fleet will be so many aimless iron rafts."

USS Walker

Chief Gunner's Mate Dennis Silva and several 'Cats hurriedly disconnected the lines holding the end of the long, fat hose down in the fueling trunk on the fo'c'sle. He waved at a crew-'Cat on the big new wooden-hulled fleet oiler, USS *Mangoro*. The 'Cat waved back and raised his whistle. *Walker* and the oiler were steaming at fifteen knots less than fifty feet from each other, and Silva never heard the whistle over the swishing rush of the sea between the ships. The boom operators did, though, and the hose whipped up and away, drizzling dark dots on the deck. "Bear a hand there!" Silva bellowed at his detail. "Lick that oil up quick, 'er Tabby'll knot yer tails together an' give 'em to Chief Jeek for mooring lines!" He turned back toward the pilothouse and waved again. "All bunkers're topped off an' fuelin' trunk hatches are secure!" he bellowed. *Walker* immediately veered away from the larger ship and accelerated to catch *Mahan*, already speeding east past *Savoie* and *La-Laanti*.

"C'mon, fellas," Silva called to his number one gun's crew, gesturing back at the weapon. "Let's put that ol' hag through her paces once more. I know you can do it in yer sleep, with yer toes, but we'll be heatin' her up pretty soon."

"Eat?" Petey shrieked hopefully.

"*Heat*, dumb-ass," Silva told him, then rounded back on his gun's crew. "C'mon, chop, chop!"

The League fleet was hazy, barely visible on the northeast horizon, a little to the left of a large, equally hazy purple island. A wispy gray volcanic plume stood over it. More islands, smaller in comparison, littered the sea to the east. Silva had seen too many 'Cats just standing, staring at the enemy. Thinking. Not good. They needed something to do with their hands and minds. Jerked out of their pensive reverie by his order, they scampered to their places on the pointer's and trainer's "bicycle" seats while others prepared to handle ammunition.

Silva sensed the approach of Lieutenant "Sonny" Campeti behind him and abruptly announced, "I'm dead. Who takes over? Jump!" A 'Cat immediately took the gun captain's place by the breech and started running the rest through their drill. Turning, Silva arched the brow over his good eye. "What?"

"Skipper's not goin' over to *Savoie* to run this fight, is he?" Campeti asked without preamble.

"How should I know? He don't tell me everything. You're the gunnery officer."

"Yeah." Campeti shrugged. "Don't really need to ask, do I?" He started ticking points off on his fingers. "First, as soon as *Mahan* topped off an' we moved in, he sent three folks off on *Mangoro*; Larry, Pam, an' Mr. Bates."

"Sir Sean," Silva corrected imperiously.

"Whatever." Sonny held up another finger. "Him an' Larry probably went because *Mangoro*'s headin' back for the carriers and the troopship, *Sular*. They'll join up with Chack—to do whatever he's gonna do—while you stay here an' fight the ship for a change. Fine with me, so long as you stick to your job an' keep outa my hair." He held up finger number three. "Pam'll prob'ly sneak off with 'em. 'For the wounded,' o' course, but mainly to piss you off," he added sarcastically. Fourth finger. "Which brings me back to the start. Pam's gone, so Lady Sandra's our doc—and since she stayed, the Skipper's stayin'."

Silva looked at Campeti with mock admiration. "Figured that out all by yerself, huh? You'll get a medal for it, someday. Whenever somebody makes medals."

"It ain't funny, you big freak," Campeti snapped angrily. "Cap'n Reddy don't *belong* here right now."

Silva gaped. "You shittin' me? You want the skipper *off Walker*?"

"Of course I do, for now," Campeti grated through gritted teeth. "This is gonna be a shitstorm, like the Java Sea, an' we all *need* him somewhere safer than this tired ol' bucket. Who's gonna tell us what to do if he gets it, Admiral Jenks? He might be a swell guy, but he don't know shit about *this*."

Silva was shaking his head. "You *are* a idiot." He pointed at *Savoie* as they arrowed past her, shouldering aside rainbow sheets of spray colored by the dropping sun as they bounced across her long, rolling wake. "Scout planes say we're goin' up against *three* battlewagons, four cruisers, an' God knows how many tin cans. *Savoie* an' that poor ol' *La-Laanti*'ll be gettin' shot at by *every damn one of 'em*! So unless Captain Reddy goes all the way back to the carriers where he can't see shit 'to tell us what to do,' you tell me, is he safer on *this* 'ol' bucket,' or the biggest target we have?"

"Here we go, chargin' straight down the goddamn throat o' doom. Again!" Chief Isak Reuben groused at Gilbert and Tabby. They were near the throttle station in the forward engine room and he had to shout over the thundering turbines, reduction gears, steam generators, pumps, even the sea pounding against the thin hull plates. Tabby looked fondly at both odd men, the "original" Mice, who'd adopted her as one of their own and taught her much of what she knew. Neither resented her jumping past them in authority. If anything, they seemed most annoyed by the responsibility *they'd* been given . . . until they had to figure out which of them was senior to the other. Tabby settled it, she thought, by putting Isak over the firerooms and Gilbert over the engines. Both were firemen at heart, but Isak still basically considered engines useless leeches his precious boilers had to feed. Gilbert had been acting engineering officer in *Maaka-Kakja* long enough to expand his horizons. At least belowdecks. Ironically, Isak had seen more of the "outside world" since they parted. In some respects, they were vastly different from the achingly insular men they'd been, but their fundamental personalities hadn't changed. Tabby was glad, and she dearly loved them both.

"Thaat's right," she said loud enough for the other sweaty snipes to hear. It was still relatively pleasant on deck, especially with the breeze and the sun beginning to set. Down here, it was topping 120 degrees and she'd given permission for her snipes to strip their shirts. How could she not, when she used to do it herself all the time? Curiously, she noted that Sureen still wore her sweat-soaked T-shirt. It didn't hide anything, but she wondered about the sudden modesty—until she saw Isak looking everywhere *except* at her. *So,* Tabby thought, *he's still sweet on her. Better find out how she feels, and if she's waitin' for him to make his move. If thaat's the case, she'll wait forever.* "Things're gonna get frisky for a while," she continued, "but this is the best daamn engineerin' division in the fleet, on the best daamn ship. An' Caap'n Reddy's stayin' aboard. We already blew paast thaat faat slug, *Saavoie*."

There were cheers at that. After Matt went to *Big Sal* for a while, everyone just assumed he'd leave them now. Most were glad he hadn't. "We're gonna be okaay," Tabby assured, "an' we're gonna kick hell outa them daamn Leaguers once an' for all!" Suddenly, impulsively, she hugged Sureen, and all the other snipes in sight. She even embraced Isak and Gilbert, despite their squirming. She was stronger than they were, and held them tight. "You stink," Gilbert complained. Tabby burst out laughing. If Gilbert had bathed since he rejoined the ship, no one knew about it.

"This is gonna be a tough one," grumbled Earl Lanier, *Walker*'s bloated cook, heaping ladlefuls of scrambled akka eggs on slices of dark brown, pumpkin-flavored bread. Despite Juan Marco's general disdain of the irascible Earl, he was in the galley under the amidships gun platform helping him and his cooks and stewards build several mountains of sandwiches. The galley fires were out and there'd be no "proper" evening meal. Battle could be hungry business, though, and to Earl's credit, he'd always made sure the crew was fed. Whether they liked it or not.

"Gimme one o' them egg saammitches," called Chief Bosun Jeek through the open serving window over the stainless steel counter. His large eyes seemed to glow as bright as the cherry on the PIG cig dangling from his lips in the relative darkness of the semi-enclosed space.

"You don't want one of those," Juan urged, offering a rhino-pig sandwich he'd just made, pointing at two 'Cats cutting thick slices off a pair of massive hams. "This is fresher, better." He cast a disgusted look at Earl. "And I didn't drip my rotten, acid sweat all over it."

Jeek shrugged, scooping up the sandwich with dark dots on the bread. "I don't care. I like the eggs." He blinked regret. "I sure miss caatch-up, though."

"That takes tomaters an' proper sugar," Earl griped. "I could make some, with them things."

Jeek waved around as if to encompass the hemisphere they were in. "Scuttlebutt is the Nussies got . . . to-maaters." He looked questioningly at Juan, who rolled his eyes.

"Tomatoes," Juan corrected, then nodded at the vile-smelling cigarette. "They have good tobacco too." He grimaced when Jeek removed the offending tube, blew nasty smoke, and took a bite of the sweat-soaked sandwich.

"Enough reasons right there to make this goddamn fight," Earl proclaimed, slapping another egg sandwich together. "Good smokes now and then, good booze too, I hear, and the right ingredients to make proper chow. Maybe go fishin' whenever I want." He actually smiled, apparently imagining what that might be like.

"I'm glad you've finally settled on suitably lofty war aims, Earl," Juan told him sarcastically.

Earl's face reddened. "I don't need no lip from you! Shove off. I can finish here myself."

Juan shook his head. "I need to know which sandwiches are safe to take to the officers." His face brightened when he saw Fred Reynolds and Kari-Faask rush up to the counter. He quickly pushed a plate of his sandwiches toward them and smiled with triumph when they each took one. "You'll be flying?" he asked.

"Yaah," Kari replied. "Scoutin' an' spottin', but also just gettin' our plane the hell off the ship."

"Then be very careful, both of you," Juan urged seriously. "We've missed you very much."

Fred waved his sandwich. "Thanks, Juan. We missed bein' home." He paused, looking down at Earl's Coke machine. "Hey, they'll be soundin' general quarters soon. Better get that thing struck down below."

Earl shook his head, expression wooden. "Nope. I'm through with that. Damn thing has to take the same chances as everybody, now."

Kari blinked surprise.

"Well, c'mon, Boats," Fred told Jeek. "Gotta rig the catapult out. Skipper'll want us off the ship any minute." He hesitated, as if wondering if he'd ever see any of them, or the ship, again. "So long, fellas."

Matt lowered his binoculars. "Sound general quarters," he called back to Corporal Neely, who blew the long-familiar notes on his bugle over the ship-wide system. He couldn't see it, but he heard the halyards squeal as *Walker*'s big, shot-torn Stars and Stripes battle flag whipped up the foremast. The sound and what it meant stirred an odd mixture of sensations: pride, fear, excitement, even eagerness . . . more. Most everybody was already at their battle stations, but those who weren't quickly dashed to their places. With a reluctant handshake all around—no words were necessary—Spanky departed for the auxiliary conn, aft. "What's the range now?" Matt asked. *Walker* had quickly passed the plodding cruisers and taken station on the western end of the line of destroyers. *Mahan* would join on the eastern end of the eight DDs advancing in line abreast, six hundred yards apart. The eight Impie cruisers were swinging into a similar formation behind, with *Gray* and *Maa-ni-la* on either end. Bringing up the rear, able to shoot over everyone, came *Savoie* and *La-Laanti*. Matt could see the enemy had already formed a battle line, aiming slightly south-southeast.

"Eighteen thou-saand yaards," came the reply from the 'Cat at the chart table, tracing a line along a straight edge with a pencil, and listening to Campeti's ongoing reports from above.

Chief quartermaster Paddy Rosen relieved the 'Cat at the helm, and Bernie Sandison's 'Cats pounded up the stairs and started preparing their torpedo directors on either bridgewing. Minnie cried, "All stations report 'maanned an' ready'!"

"Very well. Pass the word to all ships with scout planes to get them in the air." Each DD had one, and *Gray* and *Maa-ni-la* had two apiece. None would be armed with bombs for two reasons: to extend their time aloft and prevent their pilots from making suicidal attacks on ships that could swat their slow-moving planes from the sky with ease. Matt briefly heard Fred and Kari's Nancy run up before the impulse charge on the catapult hurled it into the sky abeam. That gave him a sense of real relief, and not only because the highly flammable plane was off the ship.

He raised his binoculars to study the enemy again. "I'm kinda surprised they haven't already opened up on us," Matt said aside to Sandra. He hated—and loved—that she was here, but no matter how he cut it, there'd never really been a choice. Almost half *Walker*'s crew was female, and if it was still technically against regulations for mates to serve in the same ship, everyone knew "Lady" Sandra no longer had a strictly defined place in the chain of command. She simply wouldn't move quietly to the rear while other females—other *mothers*—remained in harm's way. And she'd be leaving Matt's side soon enough, heading to the wardroom, quickly being transformed into a surgery by pharmacist's mates and SBAs.

"They caan truly shoot this faar?" Keje asked, amazed.

"Yeah," Matt told him. "I forgot. You never saw *Savoie* practicing, and we were always at knife-fighting range with *Amagi*. Believe me, they can. Fiedler and Hoffman said they had two Lyon Class BBs. They never built 'em on our old world, but they're whoppers. Big as *Savoie*, with the same caliber guns, but each of their four turrets mount *four* thirteen and a half inchers instead of two. Together, they can throw four times as much metal as *Savoie*—and she's missing a tooth. That Italian wagon over there has eight *fifteen* inchers."

As if their speculation summoned the storm, a series of brilliant flashes obscured the largest distant forms, followed by massive billows of brown smoke, tinged with gold by the setting sun. Moments later, enormous red and yellow splashes shattered the sea, jetting two hundred feet in the air about eight hundred yards ahead. A rumbling shriek passed overhead and even taller green splashes erupted between the DDs and cruisers.

"God save us all," Paddy Rosen muttered to himself.

"Jee-zus an' the Maker!" gulped a 'Cat by the starboard torpedo director, blinking furiously.

"Why were the splashes so pretty?" Keje asked, amazed as much by the color as the size of the eruptions.

"Dye in the shells," Matt told him. "Helps those shooting tell whose shells fall where, so they can correct their fire." He took a deep breath and noted the time. 1655. "Very well. We've got a little more than an hour before dark. Let's see if they'll take the bait—and we can last that long. Pass the word to all ships to turn to starboard into lines by divisions on my command. The leading ships in each division will steer zero, nine, five. The rest will follow, increasing speed to twenty-five knots." That was as fast as their slowest ships could go.

Something still bothered Keje. "If they're so low on fuel, so desperaate to make Puerto del Cielo, and chasing us takes their advaantaage, why do it?"

"Because Matt's right," Sandra said, "Gravois will make them. He's always been contemptuous of us, but terrified too. Especially after the last few days, I'll bet. Our forces, 'pathetic' in his mind, have ruined all his plans. The only way he can salvage them"—she grinned—"he must be on 'plan C' or 'D' by now—is to finally, completely, *get us off his back*."

Matt nodded. "So that's it. If they chase us, we've set the hook. Our Impie cruisers and *Savoie* can't outrun 'em, so none of us can in a straight-up fight. But we get in among those islands, at close range in the dark, with *Lemurian* eyes spotting targets . . ." He smiled with predatory satisfaction and his green eyes took on that cold, shiny glint that sometimes made his friends uneasy. "I said all along our strategy was simple: poke 'em in the eyes, then rip their guts out. We did the first part at Martinique. With any luck we'll get the second part wrapped up tonight."

"And at worst, we may still haave them by the tail when Courtney Braadford finally aarrives," Keje said. "He'd be very disappointed to miss it all." He suddenly blinked anticipation. "And there *is* still Taask Force Tassanna."

Matt smiled at him. "Yeah. We're counting an awful lot on Admiral Lelaa . . . and your girlfriend on *Madraas*."

Another mighty salvo rumbled in, clustered closer to the cruiser column. Matt glanced at the time again, before gently touching Sandra's arm.

"Time for you to go below, sweetheart," he told her, then raised his voice. "On my command, execute the turn!"

The United Fleet had practiced this maneuver often, across the vast Pacific, and every ship quickly turned to the right, reforming from line abreast to line ahead and presenting their own broadsides to the distant enemy. "*Savoie* may commence firing, but remind Russ his first fire is supposed to look like half-salvos. Ranging fire, from two ships."

"Ay, ay, Cap-i-taan," Minnie replied, then picked up the TBS transceiver. Moments later, *Savoie*'s forward guns vomited their massive shells. After a pause, her aft guns fired. The half-ton shells screeched overhead like God's fingernails on the chalkboard of the sky.

"Green splashes, then red, about five hundred short," Campeti's voice bellowed gleefully down from above.

"Good shooting. Tell *Savoie* to keep it up. Maybe she'll get some hits. Poke 'em in the nose, they'll chase us for sure," Matt said confidently.

That wasn't necessary. On Gravois's orders, and against his better judgment, Ammiraglio Gherzi was committed to the complete destruction of the Allied fleet. Only death would turn the relatively mild, genuinely rather decent man from his appointed task. Steering southeast, he brought his mighty battle line booming down on a course to parallel and eventually overtake and smash those he'd been told were enemies of the League.

CHAPTER 49

BATTLE OF ST. VINCENT

////// *USS* Savoie

"I feel so . . . frustratingly useless!" High Admiral Jenks exclaimed. "I know little of this sort of war, and my common sense informs me we simply can't prevail. Yet my confidence in Captain Reddy assures me we have a chance, at least, or he wouldn't have invited this engagement!" The two battle lines had been trading salvos for almost twenty minutes, the islands ahead growing ever closer. So was the enemy. Despite the hurricane of shells falling around *Savoie* and *La-Laanti*, however, both had only been hit once, neither suffering serious damage. Amazingly, spotting planes informed them that *Savoie* had hit one battleship twice, and a cruiser once. Fred and Kari were speaking directly to Gunny Horn, helping correct his fire. And the cruisers were in it now, lofting their lighter shells from within a random forest of slightly smaller splashes. But the destroyers were making smoke, spewing a dense black cloud and hiding the cruisers from enemy sights. They couldn't see their targets either, but the spotting planes could.

Savoie's great guns, trained out to port and elevated at a high angle, salvoed again, first forward, then aft, and the great ship jolted alarmingly. Gigantic splashes geysered around her, and the 'Cat at the helm subtly turned the wheel as the Impie Lieutenant Stanly Raj (who had the deck and conn) directed, steering *toward* the splashes to foil the enemy's efforts to adjust their fire.

"You're wondering whether to trust reason or faith," Russ stated, matter-of-factly.

"I suppose," Jenks confessed.

"Me too," Russ admitted, "I always do. But the skipper usually comes through." He grinned. "I wasn't there, but everybody knows the story about when you and him had to fight a duel against professional assassins. Captain Reddy didn't know squat about sword fighting, except what little you taught him. How did he win?"

Jenks blinked and puffed his pipe, flinching when more green splashes collapsed on the fo'c'sle. The light was failing and it was harder to distinguish the colors. "Honestly? He didn't know the rules, so he didn't follow them. His technique was so unorthodox—there *was* no technique, in point of fact—that it utterly confounded his expert opponent."

Doocy Meek laughed out loud. "Sounds just like the man!"

Russ shrugged. "People forget *Walker* was his very first command, and he was just a lieutenant commander when all this started. Not only did he never go to any fancy navy college for admirals and such, he didn't spend enough time around big brass to learn much from 'em, good or bad. He's been wingin' it all along." He waved at the epic, violent panorama as *Savoie*'s angular shape battered through more shell-tossed swells. "He wasn't any readier for this than I was. Than *you* are. But he's been *getting* ready ever since we came to this world, so my reason tells me to have a little faith." *Savoie* shuddered violently under a pair of heavy hits, followed by a cluster of lighter ones. Her main guns replied almost immediately, proving nothing critical had been damaged.

"Guess they're getting the range," Russ quipped, listening to preliminary reports from damage control parties.

Jenks—who'd stood on wooden decks with deadly splinters and massive roundshot flying all around him—looked a little shaken. "I'm . . . impressed by your calm, under the circumstances."

Russ barked a nervous laugh. "Really?" He lowered his voice. "I'm scared shitless. But one thing about this old tub, she was built to take whatever she could dish out, and that's a lot."

An alarmed report interrupted him, reminding them all that, receiving just as much attention as they were, *La-Laanti* couldn't take it.

"She's lost her forward fireroom and is dropping baack," the talker finished.

"Damn!" Russ exclaimed, even as he knew it had been inevitable. As *La-Laanti*'s crew had known. "They'll *really* hammer her now, and we can't slow down."

USS Walker

"*La-Laanti*'s haad it," Minnie told Matt in her high-pitched voice. "She took another hit thaat jaammed her rudder while she was maaneuverin' an' she's circling *towaard* the enemy. They're throwin' ever'thing they haave at her."

Matt ground his teeth and nodded. "*La-Laanti* did her job. She's still doing it, by drawing fire. Those 'Cats had plenty of guts going into battle aboard what they *knew* was just a target. Hopefully, some'll get off." The fight was turning vicious now, with only the destroyers unable to reach the enemy with their guns. *Gray*, *Maa-ni-la*, and the Impie cruisers were firing furiously, aided by airborne spotters, but the League cruisers and battleship secondaries were saturating the sea behind the smokescreen with a blizzard of shells. *Mars* and *Centurion* had suffered serious damage, but were keeping up. *Gray* had taken a hit on her aft deckhouse that wiped out her number three 5.5″ mount. *Mahan* was getting a lot of attention too, since she was fully visible leading the line of smoke-belching destroyers. So far, she'd only been slashed by near-miss splinters, but that couldn't last. Matt desperately wanted to make a torpedo attack, but wouldn't risk disrupting the enemy battle line. Not yet.

"I'm not sure we aabsolutely *must* wait till daark to spring our surprise," Keje offered, as if reading his mind. Matt frowned. He'd just gotten word the "surprise" wouldn't be as big as planned. One of Jumbo's bombers must've taken undetected damage over Martinique and its landing gear collapsed when it set down on *Madraas*. The hook caught the arresting gear, but only tore the tail off. The front half of the plane careened forward, smashing into the other bombers gathered for the attack. Explosions wracked the carrier and most of the precious new planes went up in flames or had to be pushed over the side before they added to the conflagration. Probably only Tassanna's innate caution saved her ship, since (despite Jumbo's badgering) she'd refused to fuel or load torpedoes on the planes until the last one was down. The damage to the ship was amazingly light, and powerful hoses actually washed the flaming fuel and wreckage off the flight deck into the sea, but *Madraas* had no more bombers. She couldn't launch or recover aircraft at all until hasty repairs were made. That left just the fourteen SBD-2s from Admiral Lelaa's *New Dublin*, as well as three more that Captain Jis-Tikkar brought her. Not exactly the overwhelming strike force Matt had hoped for.

"Probably not," he agreed, as purple spume rocketed up off the port bow and shards of iron crackled against the hull. The League cruisers and battleship secondaries were groping for the screening DDs with a vengeance as well, but the color of the spray came from gathering darkness, not dye. "We do seem to have their undivided attention," he added wryly. "Very well. Captain Tikker's already airborne, correct?"

"Ay, Cap-i-taan. His orders were to hold northwest until caalled. You waant me to do thaat now?"

"Yes." Matt looked at the looming shapes of the islands ahead, praying again that the charted depths were correct. They'd be among them soon. "He'll attack from due north, and target only the enemy battleships and cruisers." He turned to Keje. "As soon as he hits 'em, we'll finally get busy ourselves."

Captain Jis-Tikkar learned to fly from Ben Mallory—sort of—in a battered old PBY Catalina they literally flew to death. After that, he'd become the first Lemurian aviator on the planet to "solo" in one of their early Nancys. He'd gone on to fly a P-40E and been awed by its power and capability, but the time came for him to shoulder the responsibility his status as "first" demanded, and he became *Salissa*'s COFO, training and commanding a seemingly endless succession of flight crews. Far too many of those were dead, lost in desperate actions across the Western Ocean, over Indiaa, and finally during the long nightmare over Zanzibar, Mada-gaas-gar, and Grik Africa itself. Most of the latter fell to ground fire, supporting Allied troops, so even if they survived their crash, they were probably eaten by Grik. He'd lost so many people, so many friends, he thought for a time that his soul had been eaten as well.

Then the war in the west turned, and *Salissa* not only went home, but they finally got new planes. And what a plane the SBD-2 was! It wasn't a P-40, but it was leaps beyond anything else they'd ever had. It was big and burly and fast, and could carry real weapons. It was, in fact, the very first plane they ever designed from the ground up to carry heavy bombs or a torpedo specifically for *attack*. It had beaten the League at Martinique almost by itself and he absolutely loved it. It wasn't perfect, and they'd lost a lot to enemy fighters and now to accidents, but it was probably nearly as good as those ugly League bombers—and could definitely outfight them! Without a bomb load, SBD-2s were faster and more maneuverable than League bombers, and the two .50-caliber machine guns in the nose (and two .30s aft for the navigator/comm-'Cat) could tear the hell out of them. It seemed like his joy of flying, of life itself, had been rejuvenated.

He realized as he led his flight of seventeen SBD-2s northeast, then south, low over the purple-black water, that he would've been almost blissfully happy if Jumbo and his planes were along—and his targets weren't killing people he cared about right then, making the success of his mission disproportionately critical once more. He also really missed Ben Mallory. He knew why his human mentor had to stay where he was—somebody had to—and Ben had never trained in SBD-2s. He still wished he were here, even as a passenger, to see the result of the confidence and patience he'd lavished on his first student on this world.

"Cap-i-taan!" came the voice of the 'Cat behind him. "Bombfish Eight sees a surfaace taarget, bearing seero, six, seero. Looks like a League destroyer. Maay be the one thaat got awaay from *Waalker* an' *Mahaan* laast night, up north."

"I don't care which one it is. It's not in the fight, or liable to be. My question is, did it see us?"

There was a short pause. "Bombfish Eight thinks yes. You waant him to attaack?"

"Don't be an idiot." Staring straight ahead and down, enemy silhouettes were clear even against the darkening water, betrayed by their long, phosphorescent wakes and lit by continuous gun-flashes and tracers. The shell tracers looked particularly odd, like bright, deceptively slow-moving flares, rising and falling, ending in distant flashes. He presumed the duller flashes were misses, the brighter ones hits. The latter were increasing in number as he watched. "Inform Cap-i-taan Reddy we may haave been seen, but are attaacking. I hope he'll be able to tell."

Tourville

"Now," Ammiraglio Gherzi ordered, tone still placid and collected despite the growing ferocity of the action. Capitaine Sartre relayed the command and seven destroyers immediately veered right to pass between the capital ships and charge south toward the enemy trailing their own growing plumes of smoke. He'd hammered the enemy dreadnaughts hard enough that one was a circling wreck and the other was firing more slowly. He then ordered his Italian battleship *Francesco Caracciolo* to focus on the enemy cruisers. He thought she'd destroyed several, though it was hard to tell past the enemy smokescreen. On the other hand, this had already taken longer than Gravois led him to expect was possible, and the enemy was far more capable.

He'd been incredulous when confronted by two "*Savoies*," and grew increasingly skeptical both could be what they seemed—especially when the incoming fire wasn't radically reduced when one was disabled—but sparse as it was compared to his own, the "real" *Savoie*'s salvos had scored serious hits. He was sure the loitering scout planes were most responsible for that and cursed the fact he had no reply. Planes were obviously correcting the lighter fire from enemy cruisers as well. It was surprisingly dense, increasingly accurate, and doing a lot of damage to his own cruisers and even the superstructures of his battleships. All were wreathed in numerous fires of varying concern—and the enemy was deliberately leading him into the dangerous waters around the islands ahead. He needed to end this quickly.

"In response to your earlier point, Commandant Sartre, I've been hesitant to risk our destroyers because they're so vulnerable, yet so useful, and we've already lost too many on this . . . bizarre operation. Their general utility to the League is actually greater than our mighty battleships." He frowned. "But our battleships are precious as well, and far more difficult to replace. Therefore, you'll instruct our destroyers to press their torpedo attacks aggressively. When their primary weapons are expended, they'll closely engage their enemy counterparts. Even if we lose *all* our destroyers, at this point, it'll be worth the sacrifice if we strip the enemy's away. Their heavier ships *can't* survive long without that damnable smokescreen!"

Perhaps startled by the intensity of Gherzi's purpose, in contrast to his tone, Sartre passed the order. Then, obviously just as concerned about the direction the battle was heading, he admonished the navigator at the chart table, "I know it's difficult under the circumstances, but you must keenly monitor our precise position. There are treacherous shoals ahead, according to the Dominion charts Gravois furnished." His lip curled. "I hope they're more exact than his estimation of the enemy!"

Shell splashes inundated the bridge and *Tourville* shuddered from a heavy strike near the waterline, followed by a gonging *boom* that shook the deck.

"Commandant!" cried a messenger from the radio room. "One of our destroyers rushing to rejoin from the north detected a formation of twin-engine planes approaching from that direction!"

Gherzi and Sartre exchanged horrified looks. *They* had no more such aircraft. "All ships!" Sartre shouted. "Prepare for air action, port!" With that, he and Gherzi raced out on the port bridgewing. They were almost too late.

Their destroyers were gone, of course, but antiaircraft guns aboard *Tourville*, *Francesco Caracciolo*, and two smoldering cruisers were already throwing tracers at more than a dozen dimly lit shapes barreling in low over the water. Gherzi and Sartre had never seen the enemy bombers and were surprised by how *modern* they appeared. They couldn't judge their speed because the formation instantly betrayed its intention to launch torpedoes—which also made them easier targets.

One must've been struck directly by a large gun because it simply disintegrated. Two more, in quick succession, drew converging tracers that set them afire. Both dipped their wings and cartwheeled on the sea, smearing the water with flames. Another staggered, shedding fragments, and nosed over into the waves. Gherzi was proud of how quickly his crews responded to the unexpected threat, but there was no way they could down every plane so fast. Ten survived to drop torpedoes, though two more were shot to pieces as they roared overhead. Gherzi actually felt the hot exhaust and blossoming flames of one that barely cleared *Tourville*'s bridge. He was shocked to see a Lemurian face, lit by fire, glaring at him as it passed.

Of the ten torpedoes that hit the water a couple likely went astray, diving too deep or porpoising off target. Three simply missed. One hit *Tourville* forward, under her number one turret, shaking the ship and enveloping her in spray. Two hit *Lille*, the other Lyon Class, one amidships and the other aft. Sparks spewed from her aft stack like fireworks in the twilight, quickly quenched by roaring steam, and the great ship veered sharply out of line. It seemed like two more torpedoes hit their most powerful cruiser, a French Algerie. It was impossible to tell for sure because the big ship, a thousand meters in front of *Tourville*, vanished inside an expanding ball of fire and smoke. Even this far away, Gherzi and Sartre were nearly knocked off their feet, and heavy debris started striking the ship.

"Commandant!" insisted a pained, frightened voice, reaching both men through their wounded hearing. "The destroyers are making a torpedo run!"

Well of course they are, thought Gherzi. Then realization struck.

USS Walker

Matt saw the results of the airstrike as *Walker*, *McDonald*, *Tassat*, *Daanis*, *Steele*, *Araina*, *Sineaa*, and *Mahan*, once more in line abreast and zigzagging among the shell splashes, sprinted at flank speed through the choppy waves and storm of iron. Aside from the immolation of one large cruiser, perhaps two, it was hard to tell how successful it was, and Tikker's curt transmission from his damaged plane reported only half his bombers survived it. But the damage and confusion inflicted caused a brief, critical reduction of incoming fire. Matt immediately ordered the cruisers to follow his DDs in under the shifting smokescreen.

The enemy destroyers were making a run of their own, closing at a combined speed of sixty knots or so. Charging head-on presented the smallest possible target and was the best way Matt knew to thread the wakes of the torpedoes sure to come. He hoped to get the cruisers close enough to inflict some serious damage with their 8″ guns, especially as the battle moved in among the islands.

"Range, twelve thousand!" called Bernie Sandison, tracking one of the heavies with his torpedo director as *Walker* chased incoming splashes slightly to port. The salvo alarm sounded and three of the ship's 4″-50s barked, sending converging tracers toward a closing destroyer. A ripple of flashes lit its fo'c'sle and forward superstructure and Campeti's roar of "no change, no change, rapid salvo fire!" drowned the initial cheering. After doing little more than making smoke for the last hour, it was *Walker*'s first blow against the enemy. Her guns fired as fast as they could be loaded and their crews could match pointers with Campeti's director.

USS *McDonald*, running to starboard, was bracketed, then hit, by a cluster of large shells and veered drunkenly toward them, spewing flames and smoke amidships. Losing speed, she quickly fell back. "All destroyers! Stand by to fire torpedoes from whichever side bears!" Matt shouted at Minnie, and she immediately repeated the order over the TBS. As much as the ships were twisting back and forth, there was no way to coordinate fire from port or starboard tubes. A shell blasted some of *Walker*'s wooden rafts and both her motor launches apart, spraying splinters all over her torpedomen. Several fell, but the rest managed to crank her starboard tubes out. "On target, Skipper!" Bernie said.

"Fire starboard torpedoes! All DDs, fire torpedoes!"

The ship lurched as impulse charges sent four shiny brass 21″ Mk-7 Baalkpan Arsenal torpedoes over the side, one by one. All were spewing steam, propellers racing, when they hit the water in great, concave splashes. Another shell hit *Walker* somewhere aft and exploded with a bright orange blaze. It was almost entirely dark now, so the hit—and the flurry of shells that struck the unfired weapons in USS *Araina*'s starboard torpedo mount and blew the ship in half—almost blinded Matt.

"Jesus!" Bernie gasped. The new oxygen torpedoes were very good, but also very vulnerable. It was a chance they all were taking.

"Come right, thirty degrees," Matt told Paddy Rosen. "Stand by portside torpedoes." *Walker* was still surging at thirty knots and her rudder quickly answered so the latest hit aft must not've wrecked anything. The guns fired again before Rosen announced "steady on zero, four, zero!" quickly followed by the 'Cat on the port torpedo director. "On taarget!"

"Fire port torpedoes!" Matt told him. As soon as they were away, he ordered that both mounts be reloaded with two of the four extra fish they'd stowed in the aft deckhouse.

"It'll be a few minutes," Minnie reported. "Commaander Too's daamage control paarty is put out a fire in the portside aft 25mm mount. Rounds is cookin' off." Then she added, "Torpedoes awaay from all ships thaat could fire 'em. *Daanis* has a casualty on her portside mount."

"Very well. The destroyer division will reverse course and let the Impie cruisers launch their fish."

Matt was pleased but not surprised by the alacrity with which all his surviving destroyers briefly turned broadside the enemy—hammering out rapid, scorching salvoes—before dashing to the rear. His eyes lingered on the broken, burning corpse of *Araina*, still drawing fire as wounded 'Cats struggled to get rafts in the water. They passed the charging cruiser division very quickly, their forward 8″ guns searing the darkness, and Matt was saddened to see only five of the original eight ships still in formation. The whole sea seemed littered with burning ships, in fact, and as soon as Minnie told him each cruiser had emptied its single mount of four torpedoes, Matt ordered his destroyers to come in directly behind them. Just in time.

Like other spotters high above in the little flock of Nancys, Fred and Kari were dazzled by the spectacle below. Miles of dark water were flaring with fires and white and red shell tracers crisscrossing as thick as flies. Kari was doing her best on the radio to describe the rough shape and bearing of the islands the battle now raged between (she thought they were called Mustique and Canouan), but even she could hardly see them against the black water anymore. Phosphorescent wakes, shell splashes, and burning ships were still visible, so their spotting remained critical, but Fred was getting impatient just watching. "Shouldn't we be dropping flares or something? Backlighting the Leaguers for our guys?"

"No. Cap-i-taan Reddy said to lay off thaat durin' the aaction. They ain't gonna use spotlights or them new star shells, neither. The thinkin' is, whoever lights up first is gonna make theirself a taarget. Besides, nearly all our gunners're 'Caats, an' we see better thaan humaans in the daark." She suddenly gasped loud enough that Fred heard it over the voice tube.

"What?" he demanded worriedly, thinking she was hurt. Then, looking down, he saw. There must've been a *hundred* softly glowing lines in the water, racing both directions. "Torpedoes," Fred called back to his friend. "Report inbound torpedoes. Jesus," he added worriedly. "The next few minutes are liable to be pure hell down there. Cross your fingers, pal."

He was right.

The first ships to die were the Impie cruisers *Nesoi*, *Hermes*, and the already damaged *Mars*. As much improved as Allied torpedoes were, the League's—those that functioned properly after hasty maintenance following years of neglect—were still faster, more accurate, and carried deadlier warheads. They completely shredded the cruisers' bows. Even then, they might not've necessarily sunk their victims. Despite being new and utterly unfamiliar types of ships, rushed into production, Impie cruisers were tougher than Matt gave them credit for and their designers had embraced the concept of watertight compartments. Also seizing on an "all or nothing" armor approach, however, they'd protected machinery and magazines against broadside shell strikes—but not underwater torpedo hits forward. All three ships were utterly destroyed within moments of one another when their forward magazines blew up.

Almost as an afterthought, another League torpedo blasted into *Mithra*'s side at the junction of her aft fireroom and forward engine room as she veered to starboard to avoid heavy, damaging debris raining down from her sisters. She vomited steam and flames and immediately heeled to port. Avoiding a collision astern of her, USS *Steele* was struck in her aft engine room and sloughed to a stop, her stern nearly severed. USS *Maa-ni-la* wasn't hit by a torpedo, but caught an unlucky shotgun blast of eight 15″ shells fired by *Francesco Caracciolo*. Two hit her. The first armor-piercing shell never struck anything sufficiently robust to set it off until after it angled down through the pilothouse, the forward fireroom, and out the bottom of the hull. *Then* it exploded, cracking her keel, and flooding the space immediately. A boiler burst, and every 'Cat in the compartment was scalded to death. The second shell exploded against the heavy reduction gear housing in the forward engine room, killing everyone in there as well.

The remaining League torpedoes sped relentlessly on. Long minutes later, *Savoie* endured a terrific blow directly amidships that blasted a massive hole in her port torpedo blister and caved in hull plates beneath her armor belt. Water rushed into one of her firerooms as well. Already badly battered by at least fourteen major-caliber hits, she slowed slightly and leaned a little to port, but fought gamely on, even steering to close the enemy—after Russ Chappelle and High Admiral Jenks saw what the *Allied* torpedoes did.

Those torpedoes were slower, less accurate, and comparatively weak, but Matt's destroyers and the Impie cruisers had put almost *seventy* of them in the water. One of the remaining League cruisers took two fish aft, scoring simultaneously. Already reeling from hits by *Savoie* and the Impie cruisers, she heaved to a stop, her stern wrapped in flames. The damaged *Lille*, struggling to steer on her engines and return to her place in line, was pummeled by no less than six underwater weapons. Roaring with flames from fuel oil blown all over her and wracked by secondary explosions, *Lille* heeled over to starboard and lay down on her side, sinking quickly by the stern. The big Italian battleship *Francesco Caracciolo*, probably least damaged so far, absorbed two torpedoes without apparent notice, other than the gigantic plumes of glowing water spouting up alongside. She immediately steered away, however, apparently turning north for the gap between what should've been the islands of Bequia and Mustique. *Tourville* took her licks as well, pounded by another torpedo hit forward, opposite the previous one, that dragged her heavy, blunt bow low. Another fish hit her amidships, causing similar, if slightly less damage than *Savoie* endured. The only large League ship untouched was the Italian Trento Class cruiser *Adige*, which began edging north to follow her bigger countryman. In mere moments, both proud fleets, however disparate they might've been before, were equalized by the weapons of their smallest ships, and now fire, misery, and inrushing water.

Yet those were trifles compared to what was at stake. Lying on the deck of *Tourville*'s bridge, Ammiraglio Gherzi had no illusions about who started this conflict, and how. He imagined the enemy was driven as much by a desire for a *reckoning* as by the threat a rampant League posed to their long-term survival. He did not, *could* not, question his own motives. His actions, as always, were ruled by orders and his duty to follow them. He had to wonder, however, what drove the architect of this unfolding disaster and decided Victor Gravois had probably hidden that even from God. Gherzi struggled to rise to his painful feet even as the Battle of St. Vincent turned to a melee. As the combatants circled and closed among the cluttered islands, the knives came out.

"Flood the forward magazines!" Sartre roared as an inferno roiled skyward from *Tourville*'s fo'c'sle, even as shell splashes gathered again, like moths to the flame.

"That will put our forward guns out of action," Gherzi objected, allowing a bloody sailor to help him up.

"Better that than we explode," Sartre replied. "*What is* Adige *doing?*" he practically screamed at his talker, suddenly catching a flash-lit glimpse of the cruiser turning. "And where is *Francesco*? Inform them both I'll fire into them myself if they run away! They'll return to their places in line at once!"

"Commandant, there *is* no line!" a sailor on the bridgewing cried desperately. It was true. For the moment, at least, *Tourville* was all alone. And though *Adige* responded and came about, *Francesco Caracciolo* didn't. All they saw of her were occasional sharp searchlight glares growing steadily farther as she visually checked her bearings among the treacherous islands.

A thought struck Gherzi. "Where's *Leopardo*, and Gravois?"

"He hasn't responded either, but all our destroyers joined the torpedo attack. I assumed *Leopardo* did as well," Sartre said. Gherzi looked to starboard. The sea out there was lit by enough fires that it might've been an army camp at night—except for all the chaotic movement. And the violence of it all, of course. Even as the battleships dueled at longer, but increasingly—ridiculously—close range, relatively speaking, all the destroyers were intermixed, dashing back and forth and firing at point-blank range. It was like watching a savage, Dantesque brawl to the death between burning and fire-breathing hellhounds. And beyond it all, *Savoie*'s smoke-shrouded, flickering shape came relentlessly closer.

"Did they all, indeed?" Gherzi wondered aloud, then pointed at *Savoie*. "Illuminate her with star shells and searchlights. I want all our remaining guns, and *Adige*'s as well, focused entirely on her."

USS Savoie

The night lit up with drifting flares and stabbing beams of bright white light. Gunny Horn and his 'Cat assistants on *Savoie*'s fire control platform, all somewhat dazed by overpressure and bloodied by splinter wounds, were dazzled and blinded by the carbon arc glare. Muzzle flashes blossomed in the night. "Shit," Horn said, "here it comes."

USS Walker

"Left full rudder, port engine, full astern!" Matt shouted when the glare of the spotlight revealed a League destroyer almost dead ahead that even his Lemurian lookouts missed. "All guns to local control!" With enemy—and friendly—destroyers all around, the fight was too hot and heavy and close to waste time on salvoes. And gunners had to choose and engage targets or identify friends in a heartbeat. A blast slammed the ship behind the bridge, around the amidships gun platform, spewing a cone of debris to starboard. Matt thought he caught the image of a 'Cat cartwheeling out over the water. "Get me a torpedo solution on that damn BB, Mr. Sandison!" he shouted at Bernie over the supersonic *crack* of more shells whipping past the pilot-house. The torpedo officer had rushed to take over the portside director when its crew was swept away by near-miss shell fragments.

"I'm trying!" Bernie raged in frustration. "We're squirming around too much. Give me twenty seconds on a steady course. *Ten* seconds!"

"*Holy shit*, look at that!" Dennis Silva roared. "No, *don't* look, goddammit, just take my word an' keep shootin at that tin can!" he told his suddenly rubbernecking gun's crew.

"Keep shootin'!" Petey screeched with more than usual emphasis. He'd been shrieking that with manic intensity throughout the action.

If anyone was truly in their primal element on that fiery, shot-torn sea around the Grenadines that night it was Dennis Silva, but even he almost despaired when *Savoie* suddenly lit up brighter than if she'd been bathed in sunlight. Not only because she made such a wonderful target, she also looked a wreck. Silva doubted she could take much more, and then where would they be? As if the fates were making up for all *Walker*'s previous maulings, she'd seemed charmed in this fight. She'd taken some heavy hits, but ugly as they were, they hadn't slowed her speed or gunnery. On the other hand, only one flame-cloaked Impie cruiser was still fighting with them, and judging by glimpses of hull numbers Silva caught as obvious four-stackers churned past, the eight DDs they started with had been whittled down to *Mahan*, *Sineaa*, and *Daanis*. All looked pretty rough. He thought the enemy had at least three DDs left, but his and the number three gun had taken the specimen they nearly rammed under rapid fire and were giving it hell. But what if the League big boys were free to turn their attention on them?

Then, out of the darkness, from the *west*, of all places, USS *Fitzhugh Gray* swept down almost directly alongside the remaining League cruiser, just ahead of the last enemy battleship. Their own lights must've blinded them to her approach. Stuttering flashes from all *Gray*'s remaining guns raked the cruiser from bow to stern, smashing her lights and igniting a string of fireballs, like glittering red glass beads, down her entire length.

"God*DAMN*, that's the style!" Silva bellowed exultantly. "How the hell did ol' Miyata even get *Gray* over there?" He grinned. "Who cares! Shit! Don't shoot *that* way, dumb-ass, train back to the right an' stay on that League tin can!" he added as heavy machine-gun fire drummed into the starboard bow, ricocheting off the anchor and bollard in a spray of shrieking fireflies. The gun swiveled as the trainer spun his wheel and stomped the firing pedal. The gun roared and spat a long spear of yellow fire. There was only the briefest whip of a tracer before the shell exploded at the enemy's waterline, blowing steam from the funnel and out across the water, squealing like a dying hog.

Gray was catching hell now too, from *Tourville*'s secondaries, as the Allied light cruiser tried to knock her lights out as well. She succeeded and the burning beams were quenched, but *Gray* was streaming smoke and flames as she galloped into the darkness to the east, astern of the big French battleship.

"This is friggin' *awesome*!" Silva roared as his gun's crew sent another 4″ shell into the floundering destroyer to starboard. An instant later, it sent one back, gouging the port bow just behind the anchor billboard and exploding in the chief's quarters. Twisted shards of deck plates blew off the fo'c'sle and sharp iron clattered against the gun's splinter shield. The 'Cats on the bicycle seats were shaken, but not badly injured. The rest were scythed down, most with ragged, bloody leg wounds. Silva was blown back against the bridge structure and found himself lying on the wet deck, throbbing head propped against the hard steel wreckage of a ready locker, good eye filmed with blood. "Friggin' awesome," he mumbled, before drifting away amid the crashing tumult of battle.

"Rudder amidships, all ahead full. Replacements and stretcher-bearers to the number one gun!" Matt ordered, staring at the League DD they'd nearly run into as it disappeared astern, spewing a final gulp of fire and steam as it went down. They'd only been in contact for seconds, it seemed, but they'd savaged each other brutally. *Walker* had been maimed, but the enemy destroyer—and probably all its people, in this sea—was dead.

"Fire in the waardroom, spreadin' aft from the chief's quaarters," reported a breathless messenger. "Commaander Toos says his repair party caan deal wit' it, soon as Lady Sandra gets the wounded out. They're workin' on thaat now."

Matt had to shove concern for his wife back into the leaky compartment he tried to keep it in. "What about the forward magazine?"

"Toos says we don't haafta flood it if he caan get the fire out quick. He thinks he caan."

"Pressure's droppin' faast in the forwaard fireroom," Minnie announced, relating what Tabby told her, "but Isaak got it bypassed an' ever-body's out. Some're burnt pretty baad. Prob'ly drop us to twenty-five knots. Soon as the steam's vented out, Lieuten-aant Tabby'll go in an' see if she caan get boilers one an' two baack online."

"Captain Miyata wants to know should he run alongside the enemy BB again," asked Corporal Neely, who'd taken the place of the wounded signal-'Cat on the port bridgewing. Behind him, the portside and aft 4"-50s had joined another Allied DD and the Impie cruiser in hammering another target. It suddenly seemed that the air wasn't quite as full of tracers as it had been, and there definitely weren't as many muzzle flashes.

"Negative," Matt replied. "Mr. Sandison?" he added urgently. The enemy cruiser *Gray* pummeled was dark except for her glowing fires, but the battleship—afire and low by the head, creeping toward a low, dark island through towering shell splashes at barely ten knots—still boomed away at *Savoie* with a single aft four-gun turret. *Savoie* looked even worse, virtually wrapped in flames, but Chappelle or Jenks was bringing her on regardless, both forward turrets still booming. It was an awe-inspiring, heartbreaking sight, like two old bulls with mortal wounds still goring each other as their lifeblood puddled around them.

"I haave never seen anything like this, my brother," Keje said, voice hushed. His blinking in the dimly lit pilothouse was an indecipherable blur. "The Maker help me, in all our baattles, I never even *imaagined* such violence at sea, on such a scale. Are all the sea baattles on the world you came from like this?"

"Pretty much all the ones *I've* seen," Matt told his friend dully, then was surprised to see Spanky appear on the bridge. He was scorched, smoke-smudged, wet, and bloody, and his eyes looked a little wild, but his voice was level when he spoke.

"We took a lot of hits aft, mostly small stuff, which killed half the 'Cats on the aft deckhouse, ripped out the voice tubes, an' knocked the wheel off the auxiliary conn." That explained his presence on the bridge. "Took some bigger hits too. The searchlight tower's gone." He shrugged. "Hell, the whole ship's a shambles from here to the fantail, but we've damn sure had worse. All the damage is above the waterline and the hull's tight, except for a few sprung plates. Aft gun is okay but it won't track with the director. All the wiring's burned out."

"Fires?" Matt asked.

"Under control. I helped fight 'em all the way up here."

"What about the League DD you were firing on?"

Spanky took off his helmet and ran his fingers through sweaty hair. "She quit. Turned on her searchlight an' pointed it up. Damnedest thing."

"What's left?"

Spanky nodded out toward the League battleship, still firing at *Savoie*. "Just her, far as I can tell. Looked like *Gray* was shooting at something a minute ago, northeast, but I don't know what it was."

They all turned to look at the last enemy combatant they could see. The cruiser was still out there, astern of the battleship now, but she wasn't shooting at anything. And just in the few seconds they'd been distracted, the situation on the battleship itself had badly deteriorated. It was barely moving, entirely aflame forward of the superstructure, with fires amidships as well. Ammunition for her secondaries was cooking off. Only her number four turret was still firing, very slowly, one gun at a time, and none of the splashes her shells raised came very close to *Savoie* anymore. Even as they watched, a 13.5″ shell punched through the armor of the number three gun house and flames spewed out of the face shield around the giant rifles.

"I have a solution on the target. . . ." Bernie prompted. "Range, five thousand yards. Ready to fire tubes one and three."

Matt took a deep breath, beginning to wonder, beginning to hope . . . could it be? He glanced at the chronometer and realized it was already? Only? 1920 hours. Barely two and a half hours since the first salvoes flew. That was hard to reconcile, since it seemed like only a few moments had passed, but each had been an eternity. He looked at Bernie and said, "Stand by. Minnie, instruct *Savoie* to cease firing, then have Mr. Palmer attempt to contact the enemy ship in the clear. You'll do the same on the Morse lamp," he told Corporal Neely, his voice hardening. "She has thirty seconds to stop shooting and respond or we'll put her down like a rabid dog."

Leopardo

"Cowardice!" Capitano Ciano seethed aloud in *Leopardo*'s otherwise silent bridge. She was sprinting south in company with the orphaned Alsedo Class destroyer *Canet*, which had warned of the gathering bomber strike on Gherzi's force. With the battle still flaring among the islands and gun-flashes silhouetting strange shapes in the gloom, the two ships actually exchanged hurried shots when they blundered into each other. They discovered their error before any damage was done when they flashed nervous messages. Now the battle was apparently over, the night sky lit only by burning ships, and having heard Captain Reddy's ultimatum to Gherzi, there could be little doubt who won.

Gravois regarded Ciano coolly. "Cowardice? As soon as the enemy planes were spotted I knew that we were doomed—and we'd never seen a *tithe* of what the enemy could bring against us. At least one more carrier, and another pair of battleships copied from *Savoie*—if she wasn't one of them herself." He shook his head. "I can't imagine how they did it, but the Allies, Imperials, the NUS . . . *all* have shown resources and capabilities beyond what we thought they could possibly possess." He frowned. "After you and I were effectively marooned, it was *Oriani*'s responsibility to gather this intelligence. *He* clearly failed, and we inherited the disaster he set in motion."

Ciano was stunned by how quickly and easily Gravois began to marshal arguments to deflect blame from himself. And he'd help, of course. At this point, if Gravois went down, so would he. But that didn't make it easier to stomach.

Gravois continued, his voice lower. "My ultimate plan for the two of us to control this hemisphere within—or apart from—the League has suffered a . . . minor setback," he confessed—Ciano snorted—"but now we know our enemy better, the *League*'s enemy," he added firmly, "and can begin more deliberate preparations to face him." He touched his chin and searchingly regarded Ciano. "But there was no 'cowardice' displayed, except by the Captain of *Francesco Caracciolo.* I take it there's still been no word from her? Joining that mindless melee in *Leopardo* couldn't have made any difference and would've only resulted in another wasteful loss. Not only of your fine ship and crew, Ciano, but you and I! Who else could bear the news and the *proper* account of this fiasco to the Triumvirate? Who else would have the *courage* to face them, *tell* them what they must do to prevail? We need new ships, new planes, and there must be a final end to the complacent lethargy that's infected the League too long. And it's even more critical than ever that we strengthen our ties to the Dominion." He made a moue. "Distasteful as Don Hernan certainly is, he must not be allowed to fall."

Ciano stared sullenly ahead. "You may be right," he conceded, "but how can fleeing from battle *not* feel like cowardice? How can it not be seen as such? How are we different from *Francesco Caracciolo*? And we might've destroyed *Walker* and Capitano Reddy," he added bitterly. "That alone would've been enough for me."

Gravois chuckled. "It's different because I say so, and for all the reasons I plainly stated. And don't be ridiculous. Capitaine Reddy is clearly more devious than I ever gave him credit for. He misled me—I mean Oriani—amazingly well, in point of fact. But he never would've fought that battle in his worn-out old ship, so don't be troubled by might-have-beens. You'll meet him again someday, I'm sure."

CHAPTER 50

////// *USS* **Walker**
South of St. Vincent Island
August 6, 1945

"I still can't hardly believe it," Matt confessed softly to Sandra, as they drank coffee with Keje and Spanky on *Walker*'s starboard quarterdeck beside the number one funnel. Keje blinked dismay at the taste since it was double-strong fireroom coffee. With the big refrigerator smashed, there wasn't any ice for the tea he preferred. Together they watched the cloudy, dreary dawn reveal the scattered, smoldering flotsam of battle south of St. Vincent and Spanky wearily murmured, "Honestly? Neither can I."

They'd gone into the fight expecting a mutually destructive brawl, but doubted they had the power and numbers to accomplish more than that. They'd never dreamed for a decisive victory, yet that's what they'd achieved—in a "last man standing" sense—because they still had a very few ships both willing and able to keep on shooting and their opponent didn't. To emphasize the point, coal smoke on the eastern horizon heralded the arrival of Courtney Bradford's powerful Repub squadron. It might be a day later than would've been ideal, but the Repubs had collected the fleeing *Francesco Caracciolo*, floundering among them in the dark. She quickly surrendered to surrounding gun-flashes after a few panicked salvoes. The victory *seemed* complete, but at what cost!

Matt couldn't help a hesitant glance at the closest, least example: the fire-blackened amidships deckhouse and the shredded galley beneath. Earl Lanier, Chief Bosun Jeek, and twenty other 'Cats had died in or on top of the structure, and their bodies had already been sewn into mattress covers and laid out on deck with the eight other fatalities the action cost them. One body was bigger, much rounder than the rest, and a miraculously undamaged Coca-Cola machine had been carefully placed at its feet, securely fastened to the cover.

Matt looked away and focused on *Walker*'s own motor whaleboat, bearing the enemy commander from *Tourville*'s wreck, just as another boat arrived from *Savoie*. High Admiral Jenks, Russ Chappelle, Doocy Meek, and surprisingly, a heavily bandaged Gunny Horn scaled the accommodation ladder. All saluted *Walker*'s big, ragged battle flag, then the officer of the deck, as they requested permission to come aboard amid the squeal of whistles. Seeing Horn, Matt asked aside, "How's Silva, anyway? Are you sure he was fit for duty?"

Sandra shrugged. "Slight concussion, maybe, and a bad surface cut on his thigh took some stitches. You know as well as anyone it would take more than that to keep him in his rack. If you don't keep him busy, you'll probably wish you had," she added philosophically, then turned to face her husband. "And what did you mean, you 'can't believe it'?" she gently mocked, trying to lighten the mood. "Didn't the whole thing go like you planned?"

Keje barked a laugh and Matt shook his head ruefully as they returned the salutes of their visitors. They'd heard the question and his wife had put him on the spot so he had to answer to them all. "No. I wanted to tear 'em up, run 'em out of fuel, and keep 'em away from Puerto del Cielo. I figured it might cost us every ship we had, but we'd lay 'em on a platter for Courtney. I never thought we'd really just . . . *beat* them like we did."

"We'll soon know if that's the case," Jenks said, smiling, "but I strongly suspect they were beaten at Santiago, Martinique, and off Antigua—in their minds and hearts—before we ever met them here. They simply never knew what to think of us." He sighed. "I certainly hope so. I'm no judge, but I doubt *Savoie* is in condition for an immediate repeat of last night."

"Not even if they came at us in a rowboat and whacked us with their oars," Chappelle stated emphatically.

"How's Diania?" Horn whispered at Sandra.

"Fine." She snorted. "She's changing a dressing on Silva's pet lizard, if you can believe it. Petey and Silva were both hurt, but Petey got the worst of it. A chunk of shrapnel clipped that furry membrane he glides with. I sewed him up myself, after all our other wounded were stabilized." She cocked her head to the side. "He took it pretty well, as long as he had something to eat. To distract him, I guess. Or maybe he doesn't have many nerve endings in there?" She shook her head.

"I believe that 'Gherzi' fellow is coming alongside now," Jenks interrupted significantly.

Matt glanced at his dead once more and frowned. He was impatient with this whole "surrender ceremony," with so much to do, and despite Juan's insistence, no one had even changed for it. They were exhausted, almost numbly so, and filthy with soot and blood. The sky seemed to threaten rain, but the breeze carrying the persistent volcanic plume from the island and smoke from mangled ships downwind was gentle and so was the sea. That was a major blessing.

Tourville had been sinking when she juddered aground in the coral shallows of a tiny island with no known name. *Savoie* wasn't in much better shape, and was leaning hard to port at anchor alongside the League cruiser *Adige*, which *Gray* had savaged more thoroughly than they'd realized. She was relatively sound, but virtually every officer on her bridge had been slaughtered by Miyata's furious fire. Joining them in the impromptu anchorage (most had been towed in during the night) was a collection of floating wreckage that included two League DDs; the Impie cruisers *Mithra* and *Ananke* (the only ones afloat); and USS *Gerald McDonald*, USS *Maa-ni-la*, and USS *Steele*. *Maa-ni-la* and *Steele* probably couldn't be saved, nor could *Mithra*. Their damage was simply too severe. Their crews were racing to stabilize them for a longer tow to Martinique, but Matt suspected he'd have to decide whether to beach them for future salvage or scuttle them in deep water. *Gray* herself was standing protectively alongside the big troopship, *Sular*, which was escorted up in the night by *James Ellis* (her skipper sullen for missing the fight). *Sular* had launched her landing dories to look for survivors—a search that was increasingly frantic.

More than a dozen ships had been sunk that night, and there were a lot of boats and rafts adrift, being swept along and scattered by the current. Even more critical, and frankly amazing, there were a lot of men and 'Cats *alive* in the water. Those coated in thick, black, bunker oil apparently weren't appetizing to the flashies—and other things—gorging on those who weren't, but oil would slowly wash away and 'Cats didn't swim. Nancys were already up, searching diligently overhead, and the dories and most of the relatively seaworthy Allied DDs—*Mahan*, *Sineaa*, and *Daanis*—were racing against time to save them.

Practically only *Walker* and *Ellie* weren't involved in the search, and that was because Ammiraglio Gherzi had urgently requested this meeting. Matt was annoyed and didn't care a hoot about the enemy commander. He wanted to be out looking for survivors himself, but High Admiral Jenks and Keje both thought it could be important. At the very least they might learn enough to help them decide what to do with their more helpless cripples. Besides, the carriers and the entire fleet train were coming up now. They'd comb the sea as thoroughly as possible.

In contrast to the Allies, the two enemy officers had taken pains to make themselves presentable, both wearing whites with medals and gold braid, but the sword belts buckled around their waists had empty scabbards. The shorter, rounder officer also wore bloused black trousers and high black boots and seemed to have difficulty walking without clutching the other's arm. They weren't met by whistles and salutes, only stony expressions and the angry blinking of 'Cats with frizzed and arching tails. The long line of shrouded corpses should've been sufficient explanation for that reception. On the other hand, Tabby, a slightly limping Silva, and an utterly filthy Gilbert Yeager (with two swords unceremoniously stuck in his own belt) didn't actually shove them aboard at gunpoint either. Four 'Cats, all armed, completed the escort detachment Matt had sent over.

The shorter man straightened unaided, flicking surprised glances at Keje, and particularly Sandra, before crisply saluting. "I am Ammiraglio di Divisione Bruto Gherzi, commanding the League force you so ably defeated, and this is *Tourville*'s commandant, Capitaine de vaisseau Michel Sartre," he announced in careful English. The salutes were returned just as crisply by Jenks, less so by the others. "May I ask to whom we have the honor of presenting ourselves?"

Jenks made the introductions, but Gherzi's wide, measured gaze now fastened on Matt alone. "As you might imagine, I requested this meeting to discuss terms of surrender."

Spanky laughed, drawing a withering glare from the French battleship captain, but Gherzi remained unfazed.

"Your destroyers and cruiser surrendered unconditionally last night," Matt countered sharply. "Your other battleship, *Francesco* . . . something, did the same when it met Republic forces steaming to join us." Matt gestured in the direction in which the ships themselves were now visible on the horizon. "And we just got word the holdouts on Martinique, *Impero* and your Spanish infantry, have given up. I'd argue so did you when you agreed to stop shooting before we sank you."

"Merely a cease-fire, I assure you, and agreed to under duress," Gherzi replied quite calmly.

"Shitfire," Silva blurted. "I may be a ignorant hick from Alabama—not that we're all ignorant," he qualified sternly, "but even I know war *is* 'duress'! Are all you Leaguers as slimy an' squirmy as that goddamn Gravois?"

For the first time, Gherzi's round face twisted with genuine anger. "No," he said flatly. "But though I cannot fight you, I do have something to bargain with."

"What?" Sandra demanded.

Gherzi smiled at her. "Information. I cannot tell you more than that before we come to terms, but I think you'll find it interesting."

"It's a pig in a poke, Skipper," Silva objected to Matt.

"Perhaps," Gherzi agreed, "if I understand the metaphor, but it's a very large, succulent pig."

Matt shrugged. "What do you want?"

Gherzi smiled again. "The Triumvirate appointed Victor Gravois 'Gouverneur Militaire du Protectorat des Antilles.' With him gone, administration of this region falls to me and I'm willing to negotiate an armistice, including a disengagement and mutual withdrawal of all our forces to their pre-hostility dispositions."

There were angry growls and Matt seemed about to explode before Gherzi held up a calming hand. "I had to try. I will certainly be *asked* if I tried," he added more darkly. "My realistic expectation is that you'll allow our seaworthy ships to embark all captured personnel and return them to the League."

Matt glanced at Keje, Jenks, then Sandra. "No," he said. "First, the only even marginally seaworthy ships you have left are warships, a couple cruisers and DDs, and you're not taking *anything* with guns on it back home. Period. Second, 'all personnel' won't work either, because they won't all want to go." He was speaking for the crew of *U-112* and *Hessen* when he continued. "If the League wants any of its people back, they can send unarmed transports to Martinique to get them. In return, they'll *bring out* the families of any who choose to stay."

Now Sartre nearly burst with anger, and Gherzi frowned. "I don't think the Triumvirate will meet that demand," he murmured. "People mean less to them than our hoard of machines, ships, and weapons. People can be more easily replaced on this world."

"That's where they're wrong," Sandra said hotly. "You think we beat you with our *machines*? We did it with the people who came to this world on this rusty old ship. They taught others what they knew, who taught others and others, until we *built* enough machines, *here*, to kick your ass." She looked at Matt and sighed. "If we were smart, we wouldn't let the League have *any* of you back because there'll never be peace between us until your stupid, fascist Triumvirate falls apart. We'll be right back at all this someday, and you—and your people who survived it—will have learned too many lessons." She waved her hands in frustration, but nobody tried to interrupt. All were captivated by her passion and insight. "So let's sit down and scratch out your damn 'armistice.'" She continued bitterly. "We're all too tired and bloody to go at it anymore, right now. Maybe we'll wise up before the shooting starts again, someday, but if *our* history's any guide, I wouldn't bet on it."

She shut her mouth and crossed her arms over her breasts, unwilling to speak further.

"I take your point. About our people, I mean," Gherzi told her gently. "Perhaps the Triumvirate can be persuaded. I'll try." He looked at Matt. "But that'll be much easier for me if you can secure the 'pig' I mentioned."

Keje blinked, and Matt shook his head, uncomprehending.

"See?" Silva groused. "It ain't even *in* the poke."

"Whaat are you taalking about?" Keje asked.

"*Leopardo* took no part in last night's action and Victor Gravois isn't dead. He won't respond to our transmissions, however, so I may *assume* he is, for the purposes of our negotiations. I'm also fairly certain I can convince the Triumvirate that he was entirely responsible for the disaster that befell our forces in this hemisphere." He paused and regarded Silva's hulking, bloody form. "But he is rather 'slimy and squirmy,' with a remarkable talent for avoiding consequences. I think we'd all be better off if you managed to catch him."

"Where is he?" Gunny Horn asked harshly. Like Matt, he held Gravois most responsible for his, Sandra's—and Diania's, of course—brutal internment by Kurokawa, not to mention Adar's death and the slaughter of the wounded on a hospital ship. Gravois had been the hidden architect of *so many* of their woes in this war, all across the world.

"We intercepted a transmission from *Leopardo* to *Canet*—another destroyer—directing it to proceed south in company toward Puerto del Cielo. *Canet* ignored us as well, after Gravois commanded her to do so." Gherzi hesitated, as if reluctant to put other countrymen at risk, but decided he must. "They were expecting to meet *Ramb V*—an armed auxiliary I'm sure you're aware of—and an oil tanker, but they were dispatched to carry Don Hernan upriver to New Granada and he never released them to return." Gherzi smirked. "We couldn't reach those more distant ships either. Perhaps Don Hernan controls them now, or our wireless equipment simply wasn't sufficient. It's not in best repair," he added ironically, "but Gravois's messages directed at them struck me as . . . perplexed."

"So if he wants enough fuel to run, he has to go up the 'River of Heaven' to 'Lago de Vida,'" Matt said, "right where Shinya's hammering New Granada. We'll have him bottled up." He paused and looked searchingly at Gherzi. "Any other ways out of there? Other rivers or anything?"

"Not that I'm aware of," Gherzi answered truthfully. "But the Dominion never provided maps of their interior. We were to consider ourselves 'fortunate' they gave us charts of their waters," he added bleakly.

Matt nodded. "Very well, Admiral Gherzi, you'll have your armistice. High Admiral Jenks and Sir Sean Bates, if we can pry him loose, will negotiate for the Empire. Admirals Sessions and Semmes'll probably want in, from the NUS, and Doocy Meek, and whoever's in charge of Courtney's fleet, can represent the Republic. Commodore Tassanna"—he paused, glancing at Keje before he subtly shook his head—"and Lady Sandra will speak for the United Homes and the American Navy Clan."

Sandra's eyes went wide before they narrowed in fury. "Matthew . . ."

"*No*, Sandra!" Matt stated forcefully. "Not this time. I *need* you here to speak for me—who knows my mind better?—and there's way too many wounded who need you even more. Going with me this time would only be pointless and selfish, and . . ." For an instant they all saw the desperation on his face before he forced it away, but a hint of pleading remained in his voice. "Look, all that's true, but there's another reason I couldn't even use last night—but last night's going to *make* me use it now. We're going down a hole after a cornered rat and I don't know *what* we'll find. More importantly"—his eyes strayed to the line of dead—"*after* last night, I don't know if I can still fight my ship like I may have to with you aboard. It's more than I . . ." He shook his head and cleared his throat. "I'm asking you please, this one time, to do what I say."

Sandra's fury vanished like a puff of smoke and tears sheened her eyes when she realized Matt was right, about it all. He did need her here, and so did the wounded. Worse, she *had* been selfish, and caused him needless stress and anguish, when that was the last thing in the world she wanted to do. "Yes, my love," she said. "I will."

Matt jerked his head in an abrupt nod. "Admiral Gherzi, please accompany High Admiral Jenks aboard USS *Madraas* when she arrives. The least we can do is improve on the manners we showed when you came aboard here."

"What about *New Dublin*?" Jenks asked.

"Admiral Lelaa will follow us down to Puerto del Cielo, escorted by *Gray*, and stand ready to supply air cover as necessary." Matt paused, considering the damage reports he'd skimmed. "*Mahan* and *Ellie* will join *Walker* in escorting *Sular* up the river. *Sineaa* and *Daanis* will stay with you, but you'll have the Repub fleet to protect you, and help with ongoing damage control."

"*Sular*?" Jenks asked.

"We brought her and Chack's troops to reinforce Shinya," Matt reminded. "This way, they don't have to march through the forest to get there." He glanced at Gherzi. "*Tourville*'s hard aground?"

"She is, in fact, rather sunk, I'm afraid," Sartre replied. "I doubt she could ever be pulled off the reef. She'd certainly sink entirely if she was."

Matt looked back at Jenks. "Try to find sheltered water for everything else, a cove or bay. At least until you're ready to start towing ships to Martinique."

"When will you leave?"

Matt took a long breath. "As soon as I can. As soon as rescue operations are complete and *Sular* has some of her dories back. In the meantime, the DDs that are going need to take on fuel and replenish ammunition." His eyes were roving around the ship as he spoke, as if inventorying what they could fix or do without in the time they had. The Repub ships were getting closer and the sun was coming out, still low behind them, burning through the cloud cover. It would start getting hot. Then the line of mattress covers caught his attention and he called to Spanky. "Mr. McFarlane, we'll be having funeral services almost at once. As soon as that's finished, gather all the seriously wounded on the fo'c'sle for transfer to the oiler when we take on fuel."

"Aye, aye, sir," Spanky said, looking out at USS *Steele*'s mangled hulk. "They're never gonna save *that* poor girl, an' her 'Cats are killin' themselves trying. Let me pass the word to scuttle her. We can sure use her people aboard here. *Mahan* had a lot of casualties too."

"What's the word on *Tassat*?"

"Tight as a drum from her engine rooms forward. She'll float, but that's all she can do. She needs a whole new stern."

Matt was wondering how the hell they'd ever get all these ships, and those at Martinique, back to shipyards that could do the work they needed. Even if the Nussies got some of the spoils, they didn't have the know-how or facilities. The closest—marginal—place was back through the Pass of Fire at the Enchanted Isles. Or maybe they could go all out and finish the base the Impies had ceded to the Navy Clan near where San Diego ought to be? There was little more than an outpost there, though they'd started work on a large dry dock. No matter what they did, however, it would be a monumental undertaking.

"Very well," he said tiredly, "I'll talk to *Steele*'s captain myself, but we need to break this up. We have a lot to do." Looking around at his friends, his wife, his enemies still standing, watching him, he raised his eyebrows at the boarding party. "Give their swords back, Chief Gilbert."

Gilbert hesitated. "What if they try to poke somebody?"

"They'll each have a hundred holes in 'em before they hit the deck," Gunny Horn promised.

Matt turned to get busy and didn't hear Gherzi when he spoke to his wife in a courtly tone. "You were right about the people, Lady Sandra. They truly are our most precious asset. But good leadership is necessary to get the most from them. Perhaps someday we'll find it, as your people have."

CHAPTER 51

TF-CENTIPEDE STOMP

////// The Caribbean
August 6-7, 1945

The little task force turning toward the Dominion bastion at the mouth of the River of Heaven on the evening of the sixth was steaming under an unusual name, more like one might expect for an operation. But the task force *was* the operation and its purpose was simple: kill Gravois and reinforce Shinya's assault on New Granada. No one expected those things to be easy, but just getting there might be the hardest part. At some point during the day, as the battered, fire-blackened, leaking, and rusty *Walker*, *Mahan*, and *Fitzhugh Gray* raced to provision, replace torpedoes, and complete what repairs they could, and Tikker and Jumbo scrambled to balance the air wing on Lelaa's *New Dublin*, somebody (probably Silva, as usual) coined the moniker "TF-Centipede Stomp" and it gradually stuck. Centipedes on this world grew very large and their sting was deadly but they were fairly rare, probably because they got too big to hide from things that would eat them. Everyone knew what they were, however, and didn't like them a bit.

After the rather impressive Repub fleet arrived with its prize, and Courtney Bradford politely but firmly separated himself from the Kaiser's service and relieved Tribune Nir-Shaang from his, he boisterously boarded USS *Walker*. His appearance coincided with the departure of *Walker*'s wounded—and Matt's wife—and the homecoming he'd looked so forward to was nearly blocked by Captain Reddy himself. But Courtney insisted he simply *must* go since "diplomacy might be required," and Matt was clearly in no "humor" to engage in any of that. Matt's mood had grown increasingly dark, in fact, as the running totals of the casualties they'd suffered the night before continued to rise. Just the "dead and missing" had surpassed two thousand by the time *Walker, Mahan*, and *James Ellis* steamed south into the gathering twilight, and Matt had worked himself into a smoldering rage at Gravois and Don Hernan, equally responsible in his mind.

He was still thinking clearly, however, perhaps more so than he had in a while, since he could sharpen his focus so narrowly. Finally, he was relieved of concerns for a global strategy against disparate foes with wildly different capabilities, in improbable places. Their land forces here, even the Nussies, had an edge in technology and quality, if not quantity, but that was nothing new. And that would be Shinya, Chack, and General Cox's problem in any case. *Leopardo, Ramb V*, and *Canet* were Matt's personal prey. They'd outgun his three weary ships, but he was used to that too. Especially after last night. But the odds were closer to even than they'd been since he came to this world, and he was ready for a final, stand-up fight.

Planes were sent to scout Puerto del Cielo during the day and they'd spotted *Leopardo* and *Canet* entering the mouth of the river, but Matt decided his destroyers should test the city's reception alone. *Sular* would follow with *New Dublin* at first, protected by *Gray* and two Repub battlecruisers. Matt had toyed with the idea of taking some of the little needlelike Repub torpedo boats upriver, but he expected a gunfight and they weren't heavily armed that way. Besides, burning coal, they made too much smoke. In the narrow confines of an unfamiliar river, coal smoke might give the enemy too much warning of their approach.

"I'd forgotten how cramped *Walker*'s pilothouse is," Courtney said cheerfully, beaming at Matt, Spanky, and Keje in turn, "but it's so *very* good to be back with you all again!" 'Cats blinked appreciatively, and Bernie nodded, smiling. He and a couple of strikers were tinkering with the port torpedo director.

"We're not all here anymore, Mr. Bradford," Matt reminded, but then did his best to stow his dark mood. It was obvious Courtney was trying to lighten it and it did his friends and crew no good. Juan Marcos helped, covering Matt's comment with an equally cheerful appearance, clomping up behind them bearing a tray of coffee cups. Matt always wondered how the little peg-legged Filipino never dropped anything. Two bandaged stewards, the only survivors of the destruction of the galley, carried a coffeepot and a large plate of sandwiches. Juan nodded at them. "That's all we'll have for a while, with the galley and refrigerator wrecked. At least they're not soaked with sweat. . . ." His eyes went wide, and apparently to his own amazement, began filling with tears. Dashing them away, he went on, barely skipping a beat. "We'll keep a steady supply available as long as the bread and coffee last." He smiled at Courtney. "The Nussies have even better coffee than you found on Madagascar, and the bread you brought over from the Repubs is very good as well."

"I'm glad you like it," Courtney said, reaching for a sandwich. "Is that rhino-pig I smell? It's been too bloody long!"

Matt noted Juan's reaction to his reference to Earl Lanier. The two had never been friends, and yet . . . Matt would miss Earl too. Looking at Courtney, he couldn't help but smile. He'd heard the Australian had changed a great deal during his time with the Repub army, and now navy, but he seemed pretty much the same. A little older and thinner, perhaps. Then it dawned on him. Courtney no longer displayed the slightest sign of awkwardness or self-consciousness on *Walker*'s bridge. As much as he'd professed to have missed it, he'd never been entirely comfortable there before. Matt snorted to himself. *He was called "general" in Africa and briefly commanded a scratched-together corps. Then he was the "admiral" of the Repub fleet all across the Atlantic. He may be the same guy in all the ways that matter, but he's* not *the same in others. None of us are.*

Matt looked out at the pitch-black night, lit only by the spray of stars and phosphorescent spume peeling back from *Walker*'s misshapen bow. The holes in her side had been patched with quickly welded plates, as had the jagged gash in the fo'c'sle deck, after the erupted steel was hammered down with mauls. There'd only been the slightest sliver of moon the night before and there'd be none at all tonight. He wondered if he could trust his Lemurian lookouts to navigate an unfamiliar river by starlight alone. He shook his head and rubbed his eyes.

"When waas the laast time you slept?" Keje asked, blinking concern.

Matt smiled. "I honestly don't remember."

"Then sleep now," Keje ordered. "I *aassure* you there are sufficient people aboard, myself included, to keep your ship off the rocks for a few hours. We'll be off Puerto del Cielo about four hours before daawn and I understaand you waant to be on the bridge when we are, but you'll be of little use by then without some rest."

"Go, Skipper," Spanky told him. "It's my watch, anyway."

Somehow, to his surprise, Matt did sleep. He didn't even dream. He was back in his chair at 0200, however. "Anything to report?" he asked Tabby, who had the watch, though Keje had never left the bridge.

"We're five miles off Puerto del Cielo, an' I steered seero, nine, seero an' slowed to one-third, as ordered. Lookout seen a mountain fish, the first one this side o' the Paass o' Fire. Some big pleezy-sores with tall, spiky fins on their baacks, like they got off Ja-paan, paced us for a while. They waas faast! Musta' wore 'em out, though, 'cause they finaally fell behind. Chief Isaak saays he's ready to relight the number one boiler, but number two's done for. Silva an' Caampeeti got the number one gun traackin' again. Two an' three never waas off, they just didn't haave crews. They do now. Number four's still only good for local control." She shook her head. "Nothin' else to report."

"Very well. I'll take the rest of your watch. You've got two hours' sack time before morning GQ, then who knows how long you'll be at it."

"Ay, sir. Thaanks."

Matt stopped her as she started to leave the bridge. "Your snipes work harder than anyone, keeping us going. Make sure they know *I* know, and I appreciate it." He turned to a 'Cat talker by the aft bulkhead. "Inform *Mahan* and *Ellie* we'll be turning to two, seven, zero, and will continue to steam back and forth for the next couple hours."

"Ay, ay."

Keje stepped up beside him and handed him a cup of coffee. The burly Lemurian seemed just as fresh as before. "Don't you need sleep?" Matt asked.

Keje grinned. "Yes, and I'll get some now. Not being in commaand is a very liberating experience. You should try it sometime."

"I will, someday. Maybe pretty soon," Matt added cryptically.

Corporal Neely blew general quarters on his bugle to herald the morning watch at 0400. Dawn was still an hour away, but they needed to be ready if Gravois—or Don Hernan—left any surprises for them, and 'Cats were scrambling to their stations, though "stumbling" might be a better word. Everyone was wrung out. Minnie was putting her headset on, already making reports. "Lookout reports *Graay* an' *Sulaar* approaching, five thousaand yaards, bearing tree, tree, seero, rel-aative. No comm." The fleet of wrecks and their helpers around St. Vincent were jabbering away (though the radios of all the League ships were under guard), but TF-Centipede Stomp was silent again. Gravois must know they were coming, but there was no point broadcasting it.

Gray and *Sular* had joined them by dawn, though *New Dublin* and the Repub battlecruisers stayed over the horizon. Admiral Lelaa had promised to launch fighters and keep her bombers ready in case they were needed. Daylight revealed a shocking sight, however. The whitewashed stone fortress surrounding Puerto del Cielo was as they'd expected from reports made by Fred and Kari and others, but the city itself lay under a heavy pall of smoke.

"What the hell?" Spanky grumbled.

"I'm rather new here," Courtney declared, "but I wasn't expecting that."

"Nobody was," Matt told him. "It wasn't burning when our scouts looked it over yesterday, and only five miles offshore, we should've seen the flames before dawn."

"So . . ." Courtney mused, "you're proposing that what's happening there is happening *now*? What do you suppose it is?"

"I don't 'suppose' anything," Matt said. "All we know is Gravois went upriver. Maybe he wasn't invited and shot it out with the Doms. It took this long for the fires to run wild."

Courtney scratched his chin under the white whiskers covering it. "Or perhaps the population got wind of his defeat. I'm new *here*, as I said, but not to the bloody Doms. I remember Don Hernan and the twisted Dominion mentality better than I'd like. I've also read reports of the various actions against them in the Americas, and tales of what befell towns and villages on the cusp of being overrun by the enemy. Us."

Matt blinked surprise in the Lemurian way. "You think their army and Blood Priests are wiping the people out, figuring they've *lost the war*?"

"I can imagine no other alternative," Courtney said grimly. "Though in a city that size, there's bound to be . . . opposition to such a measure. We could be witnessing civil war."

"Grikbirds, Grikbirds—an' draagons too! Sout'-sout'west!" The crow's nest lookout's voice reached them without aid.

"All ships make smoke! Stand by for air action starboard!" Matt ordered, raising his binoculars. Twenty or thirty of the Grik-like flyers were winging in at about a thousand feet. None seemed to be carrying anything and he wondered what they hoped to accomplish—other than saturating their defenses while the twenty-odd dragons behind them, all bearing bombs and riders, attacked. He was about to order the destroyers and *Gray* to close around *Sular* so they could augment her air defenses when he heard a rising roar. A small cloud of Bull-Bat fighters barreled overhead on a course to intercept the enemy creatures.

"That's the style!" came Silva's distinctive, gleeful bellow down on the fo'c'sle. "Tear those flappy bastards up!"

The Bull-Bats did. Smoky tracers drew arcing lines through the sky and Grikbirds exploded busy puffs of feathers as their bodies shattered and tumbled to the sea. To those watching down below, it was stunning how quickly and decisively the Grikbird attack dissolved. Most of the survivors veered radically away from the merciless assault, but except for their initial fire, the Bull-Bats ignored them, going for the dragons. Dragons were smarter than their smaller cousins and wanted no part of the fighters. Most dropped their bombs harmlessly in the sea and dove, flapping furiously back toward land. Matt was watching one that didn't flee through his binoculars and *saw* it snatch the rider off its back with wicked jaws and hurl the man away. That didn't save it. The Bull-Bats converged and quickly shot the half dozen more persistent dragons out of the sky.

"I'll be damned," Spanky hooted, grumbling no more, "I bet that was the fastest dogfight there ever was." He looked at the burning city. "Even the dragons an' Grikbirds know they're licked."

"We'll see," Matt temporized. "I think it's time to go upriver."

"*Ellie* should lead," Keje instantly suggested. "She's fresher, and Cap-i-taan Brister haas just as much experience in a river." He grinned, showing his long canines. "Besides, he's still unhaappy thaat he missed the great aaction off St. Vincent!"

Matt sighed, exasperated. "Very well. We'll follow, then *Sular. Mahan*'ll bring up the rear."

Courtney gazed sourly at Puerto del Cielo while orders flew, signal flags whipped up the halyards, and TF-Centipede Stomp steamed toward the mouth of the River of Heaven at ten knots. Matt suspected the Australian was contemplating the horrors taking place within those high, bright walls. "Don't you think we might land some of Chack's troops to . . . I don't know . . ." Courtney finally said.

"No way," Matt replied. "We don't know *what* the hell's going on over there. Even if it's a civil war, *especially* then, how would our people know who the good guys are?" He shook his head. "Shinya and Cox need Chack, and I won't drop him in a situation where he doesn't even know who to shoot at." He walked out on the starboard bridgewing and stared at the Dom city himself. Courtney, Spanky, and Keje joined him, edging the 'Cats at the torpedo director aside. It was obvious now that the city was convulsed by battle, though *why* remained impossible to tell. White smoke, possibly from cannon, blossomed out of the streets, and men were even seen firing muskets at one another on top of the walls. A ridiculously ornate bireme galley, drawn halfway up on shore, was burning fiercely. By the scars in their masonry, it looked like the forts on each side of the river mouth had been firing at each other. That presented another mystery since they definitely would've seen the flashes of big shore batteries like that in the dark. Maybe this fight started right after *Leopardo* passed the previous day and only got out of hand that morning?

A thought struck him. "Hoist the battle flag so they'll know we're not the damned League," he called aft to the signal bridge. "I don't know if that'll help," he said aside to Keje, "but I guess it can't hurt." He raised his voice so Spanky and Courtney could hear. "Whatever's happening over there, the Doms'll have to sort it out themselves, but if they don't shoot at us when we steam past those forts, we won't shoot at them." Turning his attention to the broad river ahead, he imagined the roughly two hundred miles they must navigate to their objective and lowered his voice. "We have bigger business."

CHAPTER

52

HOLY HELL

////// West of Nuevo Granada City
Holy Dominion
August 8, 1945

General Shinya is a devil, General Mayta decided almost calmly. This realization came as he watched the entire center of the Army of God collapse under fiery forge-hammer blows delivered by suddenly, *impossibly* massed artillery. A silent, foggy dawn had been shattered by the roar of hundreds of guns (now including many captured pieces, no doubt), and seemingly *thousands* of exploding shells smote the breastworks protecting the middle of the "final" defensive line west of Nuevo Granada within minutes of one another. The result was as awe-inspiring as it was cataclysmic. Earth, stone, and heavy timbers were hurled into the sky, joined by parts of bodies and splintered gun carriages. Mayta had never seen anything like it, even at El Corazon, and he and his mounted staff watched with a kind of fascinated horror less than three hundred yards to the rear. A few shells exploded nearby and some lancers detailed to protect them went down with their squealing horses, but considering the sheer weight of ordnance expended and their proximity to its target, they remained amazingly unscathed. The professionalism of the enemy artillery had cost them dearly throughout the campaign, but this required a precision they'd never imagined possible.

The near-surgical bombardment was immediately followed by a surging tide of white smoke, pulsing with stabbing muzzle flashes. Demonically squalling men and animals in mottled green and brown, and troops in grimy gray-blue uniforms erupted from the smoke, vaulting over the broken, steaming breastworks and collapsed trench line. What remained of the defense, actually relatively thin in the "secure" center to begin with, simply dissolved. Men in grungy, bloody, yellow and white uniforms fled before the onslaught, not even pausing to fire. Many couldn't, since they'd discarded weapons and anything else that might slow their flight.

"General Mayta," came the calming voice of Colonel Hereda, intruding on the incapacitating nightmare maelstrom of dread crowding Mayta's mind. "We must pull back and save what we can."

Mayta laughed and the shrillness of the sound surprised him enough to crack the numbing shell of shock hardening around him. "Save what?" he demanded. "The Army of God is destroyed, *erased*, and nothing remains to even slow the enemy before they reach the walls of the Holy City!" The statement was a hysterical exaggeration, but also more than likely true from a practical standpoint. There were still large forces on the flanks, but now Shinya could roll them up from the center and the survivors would scatter to the north and south. Few would be able to fight their way back even if they took the initiative to try, and Mayta knew initiative wasn't usually rewarded in the armies of the Holy Dominion. Perhaps a few thousand would make it to El Lago de Vida and be carried back to the city in boats. It was the best he could hope for.

"Then we must save *you*, My General," Hereda insisted, "for no one else can save the city. Certainly not Capitan General Maduro!"

"I can't save anything, Colonel," Mayta replied disgustedly, but he did at least turn his horse and urge it to a canter, pursued by the thunder of disaster. His staff, increasingly nervous, was happy to follow. "I marched out of Nuevo Granada City at the head of a *hundred and sixty thousand* men," Mayta seethed at Hereda, "assured by the Patriarca that I, *by name*, bore the divine guidance and protection of His Supreme Holiness Himself, a *living God*."

That had been a . . . disturbing experience in certain ways, particularly coming from the Patriarca of the Blood Priests of Nuevo Granada, but a singular honor nevertheless. And it was a glorious time: blessed by *El Papa*, and riding at the head of the mightiest host ever assembled by the Holy Dominion. The shadow of his defeat at El Corazon was behind him and he had the opportunity to crush its author once and for all. Victory and glory were assured—or so he thought.

He'd been admonished by the Patriarca not to engage the enemy too close to the city lest the inhabitants glimpse them as individuals, even something like people, instead of the demons and Los Diablos they were. That was fine. Mayta believed he understood Shinya and expected him to defend the high ground around the Footstool of God. He'd anticipated a spirited, skillful defense, but the Army of God was irresistible. Particularly since Shinya didn't have any of the dreadfully destructive flying machines at his disposal. Distance and events in the Caribbean had seen to that.

Mayta had no lesser dragons, what the enemy called "Grikbirds," and only a handful of greater dragons. The war had sadly diminished the Dominion's "airpower," and most of its remnants were kept in places vulnerable to enemy planes. But the Patriarca of Nuevo Granada (there was no *alcalde* in the Holy City) had six greater dragons dedicated to carrying messages. Mayta was allowed two at a time for reconnaissance purposes, and to toss the occasional bomb at the enemy when the Patriarca was in the mood. Not understanding how easily amateur aerial observers could be misdirected, especially over land, Mayta thought he knew exactly what Shinya was up to, and that he'd played right into his hands, waiting behind impressive trenches and breastworks festooned with heavy cannon.

Mayta's first assault went in, suffering heavy losses, but it seemed only a matter of time before Shinya's position broke. Mayta sent more men into the meat grinder and positioned a third line to press the attack. That's when hundreds of mounted troops flooded out of the ravines to the north and slammed into his right flank. His screening lancers—that had *just* explored those ravines—were decimated by point-blank fire. Even as Mayta sent orders for his fourth line to sweep right and destroy the enemy horsemen, a furious cannonade targeted his left, and thousands of troops pounded into *that* flank out of the forest! Chaos reigned, the assault on the breastworks wavered, and Mayta had no choice but to pull back and reconsolidate his lines.

And so it went, day after day. He'd witnessed the amazing agility of the enemy artillery, limbering up and galloping across the battlefield to mass at decisive points, and been envious to see how swiftly regiments, even entire divisions, could pull out of one point in the line and add their weight to another. But as far as he could tell, he still only faced about fifty thousand troops and couldn't imagine how Shinya moved them and their guns so rapidly, quietly, in the dead of night—*every night*—only to fall on him from utterly unexpected directions. And each time it happened, Mayta had to give more ground.

Prisoners were taken, even some of the dreaded "Rangers." Most confirmed under torture what he'd seen and suspected—that the enemy had been making very detailed maps—but none ever had any idea what Shinya would do next. Some babbled that they had more troops than Mayta thought, but that was only to be expected and his aerial observers would've seen them if it was true. It was infuriating, and as his reverses accelerated, he caught himself prohibiting the mistreatment of prisoners (after their initial interviews of course), and found himself making up rationalizations to placate representatives of the Patriarca.

He also got into the habit of reacting to what he thought Shinya would do instead of planning his own attacks, and started moving exhausted troops to his flanks at night so they'd be ready when the fight resumed at dawn. Shinya surprised him again by *striking* at night, on both flanks at once, and even in the rear with mounted troops. That caught the Army of God in the middle of repositioning, in disarray, and almost wrecked it entirely. Thousands were lost, nearly half the army's guns were overrun, and the raiders behind them burned hundreds of supply wagons. Another retreat was necessary.

Mayta thought the Blanco River would stop Shinya and give him and his army a chance to catch their breath, so despite threats from the Patriarca, he moved back across the river, destroyed the bridges, and fortified the fords. This time his lancers got wind that the enemy was using other fords, farther to the south than he'd have expected, and he shifted troops to counter the movement—only to have *another* force attack from the north, a force that *had* to have crossed days before to lie in wait for him! The most maddening thing about that had been, if he hadn't destroyed the bridges, he might've attacked *back* across the river and shattered the modest force Shinya left in the center. He had to pull back instead, rushing to reach the final, best defensive line remaining—in clear view of Nuevo Granada once more.

Only then, when the two armies stood opposite each other on the nearly open plain in sight of God and everyone in the city, did Mayta finally discover that Shinya *had* been reinforced at some point. None of the dragon flyers ever noticed, too intent on reporting movements they expected to see, but the forests on either flank of Mayta's army—and particularly at the Blanco River crossing, he suspected darkly—had teemed with enemies all along. That the lancers only reported what the enemy wanted them to, and the few "locals" they encountered still outside the city reported nothing at all, became more significant in General Mayta's mind.

And there the armies waited, probably equally exhausted and roughly even in numbers now, for three entire days. Constant messengers came from the Temple urging him to attack, to destroy the heretics and their demon friends, but nobody told him *how.* He was even presented with a bright red feather edged in gold and told it symbolized the desire of His Supreme Holiness Himself that he press an attack at once.

In the morning shadows of dark, fatty smoke rising from sacrificial fires all over the city, in earshot of the keening chants and sudden roars of triumph when severed heads tumbled down the rough, bloody steps of the temples, Mayta did as he was told. How could he not? With fluttering flags, thundering drums, blaring horns, and all the pageantry he'd been instructed to display for the benefit of his vast audience, the Army of God lurched forward into the teeth of a solid wall of sheeting rifle fire and a devastating bombardment by artillery that gathered in, unlimbered in massed batteries, and sprayed his men with screaming canister. No matter how fervent the soul, flesh can only endure so much. Again, in front of God—and everyone else this time—the assault was bloodily repulsed. And it was *seen* that only the forbearance of the enemy allowed thousands of men to stream back to their initial position.

A kind of collective ongoing moan reached General Mayta from the city, like a tide of despair washing at the sand of his faith, and he finally knew God *couldn't* be appeased, even by the sacrifice of His entire army, because He wasn't on their side at all. But Mayta was a soldier and he made every preparation he could imagine in the night. The forest was now too distant for Shinya to use to his advantage, so Mayta reinforced and extended his flanks beyond Shinya's ability to envelop them without fatally weakening his center.

What Mayta didn't know, and had in fact been conditioned to disregard, was the possibility Shinya would do the exact opposite.

When the long night ended, the sky began to gray, and the first lizardbirds took flight with their raucous cries, X Corps, XI Corps, XV Corps, and the entire NUS Army smashed directly into the weakened center of the Army of God and it exploded like a collection of dry, brittle bones under an avalanche of granite.

"I can't save *anything*," Mayta repeated heatedly, gesturing at the abandoned estates, clumps of ornamental trees, and ripening crops all around, even as panicked soldiers sprinted past, outpacing his cantering horse. Ahead lay a final line of tall mast trees and then the homes and stables of the affluent tradesmen directly backed by the wall of the city. "I'm leaving almost the entire Army of God out here, not to mention more than two hundred field pieces and countless draft animals." He paused and shrugged. "I can't even save myself. As soon as I enter the Great Western Gate, I won't live out the day."

"We'll see," Hereda replied, ducking slightly in his saddle as rifle bullets cracked past. They leaped the low stone fence between the mast trees and galloped up the avenue leading to the Great Gate, hooves thunderous on flat, white stones. They found their way blocked by hundreds of terrified troops, some armed, most not, flooding in from all directions—and the ironclad gate shut fast in their faces. With a hasty look at the twelve-foot walls to remind him there were no cannon emplaced on the landward side of the city—why should there be?—Mayta raised his voice at the faces peering down.

"Open the gate at once!"

"The heretics will get in!" came a frightened response.

"Yes, if we don't get as many soldiers in as we can. Who'll protect you if we don't?"

"The Blood Drinkers!" came a hopeful call. "Your rabble has already proved *it* can't."

"And *you* can?" Mayta snapped. "Open the gate!"

The firing was getting closer, even as more troops gathered, adding their pleas to Mayta's command. Somewhat to Mayta's surprise, the gate finally did open a crack, and men started squirting through. Soon the doors were wrenched wide and the trickle became a flood. Hanging back, Mayta dismounted and glared at some NUS soldiers stopping behind the low rock wall. Taking cover, they started killing his men with more careful aim and deliberation. A bullet whizzed by his face and a man fell in front of him, clawing his neck as blood spurted on the ground.

"My General, please!" Colonel Hereda urged. "Step inside! The enemy will soon rush the gate." Mayta turned and saw the mob clambering to get in the city had already thinned considerably. His horse screamed and collapsed, rolling on its side and kicking. Somehow, that affected him as much as everything else and he reluctantly drew the ornate, brass-barreled pistol from the sash around his waist.

"My General!" Hereda insisted.

Mayta cocked the pistol and shot the horse in the head. Turning abruptly, he paced into the city, oblivious to bullets striking the stone arches around him. With a heavy, creaking moan, the gate slammed shut.

Almost immediately, Mayta was confronted by Capitan General Maduro in his gaudy, red-faced Blood Drinker uniform, who positioned his broad form in front of him. "You're becoming quite good at losing battles, General Mayta." His normally deep voice was pitched higher with strain, or something else. "I never understood what His Holiness Don Hernan saw in you."

Mayta waved at the gate. "By all means, Capitan General, feel free to step outside and win it for us now. No? In that case, forgive me for a moment. Get up on the wall!" he bellowed at frightened troops. "I don't care if you're armed or not, just show yourselves ready to defend the city! We *must* hold them back from the gate until reinforcements arrive!"

A few wide-eyed men hesitated, but most hurried up the steps and began spreading out. The pop of musketry started to build. Mayta looked back at Maduro. "There. Now you may arrest me."

"In good time," Maduro snapped. "First, you must tell me."

Mayta was taken aback. "Tell you what?"

"How did they do it? How did they destroy the army entrusted to you?" He gestured at the city around him. "We performed all the sacrifices, called upon God to save you. To save *us*. How did you squander that power?" Even through his mounting fear, he sounded genuinely puzzled. "Are you in league with them somehow? Have they *possessed* you?"

Mayta sighed, all the exhaustion of the previous days washing over him. "Don't be ridiculous, Capitan General. They beat us because they're better, they deserved to, and God is probably on *their* side."

CHAPTER 53

////// **Ramb V**
Lago de Vida
Holy Dominion

"Are you entirely mad?" Victor Gravois roared at Don Hernan DeDivino Dicha, stalking into *Ramb V*'s wardroom. Capitano Ciano and a half dozen of *Leopardo*'s sailors—armed with rifles—were close behind. Ciano brought the guards because *Ramb V* still didn't respond to signals, there was clearly a major battle underway on shore, and even after *Leopardo* and *Canet* came alongside the big auxiliary, the sailors that helped secure them were unrecognizable by their defeated, subdued manner. Now Gravois barely recognized Don Hernan. The Blood Cardinal was attired as garishly as always, but his robes sagged and he seemed to have lost twenty pounds. His angular face was now quite gaunt, making the benign smile he attempted look like a grinning skull with gray whiskers around desiccated lips.

Gravois missed a step and paused, aware he didn't recognize *Ramb V*'s wardroom either. Don Hernan had clearly moved in, and drugged, naked children lounged all around on plush red cushions arranged on the deck. All bulkheads, the deck, even the overhead, were covered with deep red cloth embroidered with the gold lightning-bolt crosses of the Holy Dominion, identical to the sails on its warships. The cloth might've even been sails. It was also the same as the flags they flew—like the one now fluttering from *Ramb V*'s stern.

Gravois glared at the ship's captain, standing in his best uniform near Don Hernan's throne-like chair. "And you! You *allowed* this . . . this"—he gestured helplessly around—"after I *ordered* you to return to Puerto del Cielo with the oiler as soon as you delivered Don Hernan here! We *needed* the fuel in that oiler, damn you!" *Ramb V*'s captain said nothing; he didn't even move. That's when Gravois finally *did* recognize the same vacant stare he'd seen on Oriani's face. Despair clutched his heart and he looked at Don Hernan. "You *are* insane. You've *pirated* a warship of the League of Tripoli!"

"I wasn't finished with it," Don Hernan countered reasonably. "And you arrived safely enough, after all. As was my intent." An unpleasant thought seemed to occur to him. "After the defeat of your 'invincible' fleet, you wouldn't have abandoned me, would you? We have so much more to do. Together." He beamed.

Gravois erupted in fury. "How? My fleet's destroyed, as you apparently know." He gestured vaguely toward Nuevo Granada, under fire by field artillery from the west. "Your capital city's in peril, and the enemy will come up the river behind me! I had a *perfect* plan to salvage the situation . . . and rescue you," he added carefully, "but now you've *trapped* me here!"

Don Hernan shook his head, gesturing at his reduced form. "I've given this great consideration, fasting in prayer, and unless your plan was simple—likely brief—survival, it couldn't have worked without me. Nor will you and I be 'trapped,'" he added cryptically, waving his hand and assuming a pained expression. "The City of God may well fall, but we'll build another together. Stronger and better fortified against His enemies. How do you imagine your mighty fleet was lost? The answer isn't complicated: God wasn't with it! He must *always* be with your next fleet, as He will directly rule His next city!"

Gravois was growing impatient and started to ask how Nuevo Granada could fall if it was, indeed, God's city, but realized Don Hernan had left himself an out with the word "directly." He didn't have time to debate the man's twisted religion in any case. "So what do we do, and how are we not trapped?"

"Trust me," Don Hernan said gently, "the River of Heaven isn't El Lago de Vida's only access to the sea." He frowned. "But we can't leave His Supreme Holiness. His realm is vast, much larger and more important to your League than you know." Unnervingly as always, his frown turned to a smile as abruptly as if someone flipped a switch. "It's also quite suddenly in need of direct secular, as well as spiritual protection, and I believe your League prefers 'protectorates' to 'alliances' in any event?" He laughed at Gravois's expression. "Did you think Nuevo Granada was on a *frontier*? The Holy Dominion will one day rule the world," he recited dogmatically, "but even now it encompasses this entire continent. The heretics defile only the west coast, and have tendrils reaching here, but there's still the east! Imagine how grateful the Triumvirate will be when you deliver them *possession* of His Supreme Holiness, and through him, a direct claim to this continent!"

The frown returned. *Snap!* "But we can *only* control the people and priests, and ultimately the land, through His Supreme Holiness—the properly consecrated, direct messenger of God. If heretics lay their filthy hands on him, God will turn His face from the world and the people will know! They'll lose their *fear* of God and become unmanageable, turning to the False God of the heretics. It's happened before," he added darkly. "This time, with no bastion of the True Faith remaining, all will be lost." He narrowed his eyes at Gravois. "I know you don't believe, but from your perspective, your League—and you—will have achieved nothing here but the loss of thousands of men and a great deal of precious equipment. You'll find that difficult to justify without my help. With it"—*snap!* he beamed again—"you will still triumph!"

Gravois looked at Ciano, who blurted, "So, you need to fetch your master? Then we can go?" He appeared somewhat horrified and entirely at a loss, having had limited personal contact with the Blood Cardinal when he spoke this way.

"In a manner of speaking," Don Hernan replied evasively, "but with a battle raging around the city and all the soldiers of God engaged, I'll require an escort."

"An 'escort.' You mean us?"

"Some of you. Not many," Don Hernan assured. "I couldn't do it without *you*, my dear Gravois, and perhaps a dozen of your sailors? Your ships must be able to fight while we're gone, after all."

"Me," Gravois murmured flatly. "Go ashore here. I thought . . ."

"You'll have to be cleansed, of course," said Don Hernan as if it were a triviality hardly worth mentioning. Gravois's face turned to slate as he calmly unsnapped the flap on the holster securing his pistol to his belt. Don Hernan must've realized he'd finally pushed Gravois too far because his eyes went wide and he forced a companionable laugh. "You've grown so dreadfully *serious*! I was teasing about *that*, merely trying to lighten the gloom the heretics have laid upon us. I possess the authority to grant certain . . . indulgences from time to time, under extraordinary circumstances, of course." He became somber. "And this is such a time. If you believe nothing else, my dear Gravois, you must believe this: If we're to save anything from this disaster"—he glanced speculatively at Ciano—"and particularly our great *mu-*

tual purpose, I need your mind, and we must work together in perfect concert."

Gravois hesitated, hand still near his pistol. He was *so* tempted just to shoot Don Hernan, *Ramb V*'s captain, perhaps even himself. Or he might surrender and take his chances with Captain Reddy. Despite his assurances to Ciano, he doubted the Triumvirate would ever see things his way . . . unless Don Hernan was right. If he brought the League *outright ownership* of eastern South America, the loss of Gherzi's fleet might be overlooked, even presented as part of his strategy to manipulate Don Hernan into this concession. . . .

"Very well," he told the Blood Cardinal, "I'll take you ashore to collect your high priest as soon as our ships refuel from the oiler and a suitable landing force is assembled. But before we go, I must insist you describe *in detail* how we'll escape this place. I assume you mean there's another river outlet?"

"Lago de Vida is filled and drained by *many* rivers," Don Hernan pleasantly confirmed.

"Show Ciano," Gravois commanded, then pointed at *Ramb V*'s insensate captain. "And there'll be no more . . . subversion of my people or I *will* shoot you myself." He looked at Ciano. "Replace that . . . unfortunate creature, and develop a plan to use *Leopardo*, *Canet*, and . . ." He pondered what use *Ramb V*'s shattered crew might still be. "And this ship to defend the lake against Captain Reddy and his Allies, at least long enough for us to complete our errand ashore." He smiled mirthlessly. "I imagine Reddy himself will lead *this* pursuit, so you'll finally have your chance to destroy him. But fight only to delay, and block the channel if you can. Our only objective now is escape, is that understood?"

Ciano arched an eyebrow and nodded.

USS *Walker*
River of Heaven

Halfway through their second day on the river, tensions were rising on *Walker*'s bridge as they neared Lago de Vida, and whatever awaited there. The steaming chocolate river around them was oddly similar to the Zambezi in terms of color, massive crocodiles, and the dense bordering forest, but quite different in other ways. It stank, of course, like all rivers do, of dead fish and wet decay, but unlike the Zambezi, it didn't reek of Grik feces and larger rotting animals. And the density and variety of shrieking lizardbirds swooping overhead, crapping all over the decks, snatching morsels from the ships' wakes, and occasional painful nips from exposed 'Cats at their stations were unprecedented in their experience. So were the snakes in the water, enormous ones, half as long as *Walker*. Little more of the fauna exposed itself to an enraptured Courtney Bradford, who, for the time at least, with nothing else to do, had reverted to a devoted observer of nature. Matt was actually glad to see him scurry from bridgewing to bridgewing, binoculars ready, whenever a lookout reported "something screwy" moving in the trees, disturbing more lizardbirds off their roosts.

More often than not, Courtney exclaimed in exasperation that he always seemed to be on the wrong side of the ship. Matt suspected the 'Cats were doing it to him on purpose, to keep their own spirits up, since—despite the tumult of nature—the biggest difference between the Zambezi and the River of Heaven had been how eerily, almost dreadfully *quiet* their passage had been.

Steaming upriver as fast as they dared to arrive as close on Gravois's heels as they could, they passed a large number of forts, well-placed at narrows, or where the unusually straight river made a slight turn. None opened fire and by all indications they were abandoned. Matt suspected their garrisons had been pulled back to defend New Granada from Shinya, but they passed no boats and saw no people and that was almost more unnerving than the long, brutal slog up the Zambezi had been.

A tired Nancy clattered by, low overhead, heading north, and Ed Palmer brought Fred and Kari's radio observations to the bridge. "They spotted *Leopardo*, *Ramb V*, and the oiler. *Canet* wasn't seen, but she's got to be there. Kari also said Shinya's beating pretty hard on New Granada's front door, but the whole Dom army looks to be on their western wall." He smiled. "The wall behind the eastern docks is practically undefended."

Matt heaved a sigh of relief. "Good. If *Sular* gets our troops ashore, the whole Dom egg might crack."

"*This* is why you didn't laand Chack's Brigade and Second Corps at El Paalo as soon as we came through the Paass of Fire!" Keje exclaimed. "You plaanned this all along."

Matt shook his head. "'Planned' might be too big a word. Let's just say an opportunity like this is what Chack and I *hoped* for. What else did Fred and Kari say?" he asked Ed. "How are the enemy ships oriented?"

Ed frowned. "Broadside on, just offshore of the city, several miles from where the river opens into the lake." He nodded forward. "*Ellie*'s almost there now, an' could start taking fire as soon as she rounds the final bend."

Spanky's brows furrowed. "Any word what the shoreline's like around there?"

Ed shook his head. "Kari didn't say. They're low on gas, and since we can't stop to fill them up, they've got a long way to go." He hesitated. "Kari *did* say the Doms probably know we're coming, though. They saw a couple dragons with riders flying from our direction down low, like bats outa hell. Might've seen us while we were . . . stuck this morning." They'd slowed their mad dash to a crawl at night, but *Mahan* grounded on a sandbar just before dawn. Even their Lemurian lookouts might've missed the dragons while they were preoccupied watching *Sular* pull the old destroyer off. "But now they've pinpointed the Leaguers for her, Admiral Lelaa will send *New Dublin*'s fighters and bombers, won't she?" Ed prompted.

"That's the idea," Matt agreed, considering, "but they won't be here for an hour or more. Plenty of time for the Doms to shift troops to the docks when those dragons rat us out. They'll *damn* sure do it as soon as our planes come in and stir things up over the lake. That'll make things harder for Chack." He took a deep breath. "We have to go in *now*, to shield *Sular* to the docks and keep the League gunners busy while Chack goes ashore." With a final nod of his head, as if assuring himself, he called aft to the 'Cats waiting by the flag bags on the signal bridge. "Signal all ships: Stand by for action. Sound general quarters," he told Corporal Neely.

Courtney watched him owlishly while *Walker* readied herself for battle and Juan Marcos clumped up from below, as he had so many times, bearing his captain's sword and pistol belt. A 'Cat steward brought helmets, including extras for Keje and Courtney. "Are you quite sure you're not waiting for Admiral Lelaa's planes because you want Victor Gravois for yourself?" Courtney asked. "I wouldn't blame you, of course, but I might question your . . . detachment."

Matt regarded his friend, noting Courtney wasn't the only one watching him. "I'm *not* objective when it comes to Gravois, and that's just as much my fault as his," he confessed angrily. "You may remember we *had* the bastard once, and I let him go. If we'd hung him then and sunk *Leopardo* when we had the chance . . ."

"We would've started a war with the League *long* before we were ready," Courtney reminded, "and we wouldn't be here today."

"Maybe," Matt conceded, "but either way, we're doing this for Chack and his troops, and Shinya's and Cox's too. The quicker *Sular* gets Chack in the fight, the fewer losses our troops'll take, and the quicker this'll be over." He shrugged and raised his voice. "And if, incidentally, *Walker*, *Ellie*, and *Mahan* get a crack at *Leopardo*—and the man who's been directly or indirectly behind so much of the pain and loss we've suffered . . . well, I think that's only fair."

Two hundred yards ahead, USS *James Ellis* accelerated to twenty knots and steered slightly left, just short of a little bend in the channel. *Walker* matched her speed, and Bernie called for her torpedo tubes to be rigged out, thirty degrees on either side. *Sular* could usually only make sixteen knots, but the old Grik dreadnaught's massive engines labored to spin her twin screws faster than they'd ever gone. *Mahan* urged her on.

"Anything else, Mr. Palmer?" Matt asked as the signals officer turned to retreat down the stairs to his radio room right under the deck he stood on. Ed paused, thoughtful. "Nothing specifically for us. Mostly war news on the wrap-up north of Sofesshk, and the search for flood survivors. Nothing on General Alden, yet," he added soberly. "But I've also been getting a lot of repeated traffic about some huge blast yesterday, on that Jap island west of the Shogunate of Yokohama. Not many people there, so everything's via the Filpin Lands. They figure some big volcano must've cooked off."

CHAPTER 54

////// USS James Ellis
Lago de Vida
Holy Dominion

Lago de Vida was deep and blue and large enough that the curvature of the earth easily hid the forest-fringed southern end. The afternoon sky was clear, and purple, flat-topped mountains loomed beyond the distant, hazy sprawl of the Dom capital of New Granada. It was actually quite beautiful, but Commander Perry Brister caught only a glimpse as USS *James Ellis* sprinted out of the River of Heaven. An instant later, his bridge talker urgently echoed Paul Stites's shout of "surface target!" directly overhead on the fire control platform. "*Two* surfaace taargets," emphasized the talker, "bearing one, eight, seero, speed . . . seero. They must be at aanchor! Range nine t'ousaands!"

"All ahead full, left standard rudder, make smoke!" Perry shouted, his rough voice tight with tension. "Inform Captain Reddy on the TBS." The enemy would hear, but they could *see* them now, and shells were already splashing nearby. They could make all the noise they wanted.

"Rudder amidships," Perry told the 'Cat at the wheel. "Surface action starboard. Commence firing at will, and stand by starboard torpedoes."

"On taarget!" came the cry from above, and the salvo alarm rattled against the aft bulkhead. *Ellie*'s three 4″-50s that would bear boomed together, their bright tracers converging as they arced toward the larger, distant target. A pair of flashes lit the superstructure aft of the enemy bridge and Perry heard Stites yell triumphantly, "No change, no change, rapid fire!" *That must be* Ramb V, he thought, uncomfortably. *Word is, she's just an auxiliary, but heavily armed. Kinda like going up against the old* Santy Cat. *But we're already hitting her, and what's she doing just* sitting *there?*

Ronson Rodriguez, standing by the auxiliary conn, aft, while the number four gun spat another shell to join those from guns one and three, was wondering much the same when a 'Cat suddenly screamed, "Torpedoes! Port quaarter!" Ronson spun and saw them: four bright, creamy wakes arrowing in from aft. He saw where they came from too. *Canet*, the Alsedo Class destroyer that suddenly went missing had been snugged close to shore, camouflaged by overhanging trees. She was getting underway, now, already exchanging point-blank fire with *Walker* as the second Allied DD steamed into the lake. "Four torpedoes in the water, two, four, zero relative!" he shouted in the voice tube to the bridge. "That little bastard Alsedo bushwhacked us! Get this gun on him," he yelled at the crew of number four. 'Cats were rapidly cranking it around and *Ellie* was finally, *glacially*, starting to turn to starboard, when a torpedo hit her forward of the amidships gun platform, heaving her over under an avalanche of water and falling debris. Even as she hung there, a second fish struck just under the bridge. That almost rolled her over and Ronson went sliding off the aft deckhouse, tumbling onto the starboard 25mm, breaking his fall on the 'Cats who crewed it. He was afraid he might've killed one, who lay unnaturally in a spreading pool of blood. The ship shook again, even as it righted itself, and a tower of fire rushed into the sky. Everything forward of the amidships gun platform was a wall of flame, and Ronson knew Captain Brister, Paul Stites—all his friends up there—were dead.

"Get those hoses going!" thundered a blackened, smoldering form, physically picking 'Cats off the deck and hurling them toward firefighting gear. It took a moment for Ronson to recognize Chief Bosun Carl Bashear. His beard was burned off. "We still got power, so we still got water. Get some on those fires, damn you!" His watery red eyes caught Ronson. "I guess you know you're in charge," he snapped bitterly, not angry at Ronson, just coping with the loss of friends as well. "I doubt we can save the ship. I can't even get forward to *look* at the damage, but we better stop the engines before they drive us under."

"Do what you can," Ronson gulped, his first pathetic words of command. "I'll stop the engines and see if I can get ahold of anybody forward." His voice was firming as he spoke. "There *must* be somebody." He turned to climb back on the aft deckhouse and the number four gun barked, shooting at *Canet*, he guessed. "Get the torpedoes off the ship!" he shouted at Bashear. "Point 'em at the enemy if you can, but get 'em off!"

Back at his station, he quickly spoke to Johnny Parks in the forward engine room—at least *he* was still alive—and told him to secure the engines and send whoever he could to join the damage control parties. Looking forward at the roaring flames and destruction, and feeling the way the deck tilted forward, he suspected it was hopeless, but they had to try.

A high-pitched Lemurian cheer from the number four gun's crew drew his attention and he looked aft—just as USS *Walker* roared past, jettisoning her own life rafts in case *Ellie*'s people needed them. USS *Sular* wasn't far behind, recklessly dropping a half dozen dories down her launching rails. *Reckless, hell!* Ronson thought. *Those dories have* 'Cats *in 'em!* All were bounced and jostled radically by the big ship's wake, but some miracle preserved the brave 'Cats manning them. A wet, thundering *bong* reminded him of *Canet*, and he turned to see her doom. *Walker* had obviously savaged her badly as she raced by. *Of course she had,* Ronson thought proudly. Walker*'s got the best gun's crews on this whole screwed-up world! Sular* had four 4″-50s of her own, at the peak of her casemate, and doubtless raked the Leaguer as well. *Mahan* finished her, slamming a salvo right in her fireroom at less than two hundred yards. The sound Ronson heard was boilers bursting and shattering a sinking hulk. Looking forward, he knew *Walker, Sular,* and *Mahan* were still fighting *Ramb V* and *Leopardo*, but he couldn't see anything through the smoke. Nor could his number four gun bear on anything useful anymore. "Okay, people!" he shouted. "*Ellie*'s down, but she's not out. Let's get busy!"

USS Walker

"My God," Courtney murmured as *Walker* swept past *James Ellis.* The whole forward half of the ship had been smashed off, and flaming fuel spewed wide across the water. *Ramb V*, still inexplicably at anchor, was firing somewhat wildly, her guns uncoordinated. *Ellie* must've knocked out her fire control, and *Walker*'s and *Sular*'s salvos were tearing her apart. *Leopardo* had apparently retreated beyond the smoke of her burning consort and couldn't be seen.

"My fault," Matt said, as *Walker*'s guns boomed. "Perry . . ."

"I think the term is 'bullshit,' my brother," Keje told him. "For whaatever reason your heart sought this baattle when it did, your mind gave us a better one. And we caan never predict whaat we caan't possibly know. The enemy surprised us, thaat's all." His gravelly voice turned to stone. "And he paid for it. Now we'll make them pay more dearly."

Matt was silent only a moment before turning to Bernie. "Range, Mr. Sandison?"

"Seven thousand, three hundred. Easy shot on a stationary target, especially with the new fish. I have a solution for the port tubes."

"Give him all four, and they better all hit."

"Aye, aye, sir!" Bernie spoke into his headset while the 'Cat on the director kept it on the target. "Port mount, stand by to fire all tubes on my mark." He glanced at the director again. "Fire two, fire four, fire six, fire eight!" The ship lurched with each command and the bright afternoon sun briefly glinted off the gold-colored weapons as impulse charges flung them over the side in a swirling cloud of smoke and steam.

"Send to all ships: 'Follow me, and make for the docks,'" Matt said. "Helm, make your course two, three, zero."

"Making my course two, three, zero, aye," Paddy Rosen barked in reply.

"Cap-i-taan, Commaander Tiaa-Baari on *Mahaan* requests permission to pursue *Leopaardo*," Minnie said.

Matt spared a quick, fond glance at *Mahan*. Tiaa was taking her slightly out of line to the left, possibly anticipating his approval. And he *did* approve, on a visceral level, since he knew Tiaa was just as anxious as he was to avenge Perry Brister. Not only was *Mahan Walker*'s only real—if somewhat truncated—sister from their old world, she'd been Perry's first ship as well. "Request denied. We'll both go hunting as soon as *Sular*'s at the dock and we suppress any shore batteries that open up on Chack's troops as they disembark. All guns will keep firing at the big one, but if Mr. Campeti spots *Leopardo* as our aspects change—"

"Haammer her," Minnie finished for him. Matt managed a small grin. "Damn straight."

For a moment then, through the racket of the guns and the occasional shell splash from *Ramb V*, those on the bridge were able to view New Granada in better detail. Walls surrounded the city and numerous stepped pyramids rose behind them. One near the center of the city was much taller than the others. "What do you wanna bet that's where they keep their big cheese?" Spanky asked.

"I won't be betting," Courtney said flatly. Few Doms captured by the NUS over the years had even been to Nuevo Granada. Those who had all agreed—they believed—"His Supreme Holiness" resided in the larger structure. Only one, a certain Blood Cardinal named Don Emmanuel, acting as an early ambassador to the League at the time, was taken prisoner by their own Fred and Kari. He'd once been granted an audience (of sorts) with the Dom Pope himself, and finally, never imagining they'd actually see it, somewhat proudly revealed the meeting occurred in the "tallest structure in the City of God." There was only one possible candidate.

"Instruct Colonel Chack"—Matt paused, smiling slightly—"to make for what looks like the biggest cowflop around, only this one has steps. What is it about pyramids on this dopey world?" he asked the pilothouse at large.

"Nothing particular," Courtney replied. "They're the simplest of all complex structures. I know that sounds contradictory, but it's true, and they're found all over our old world as well, attributable to innumerable civilizations." He blinked. "Some of which *do* seem to have touched this world as well . . ."

"Sorry you asked?" Spanky quipped.

"*We* would never make something so crude," Keje—the Lemurian descendant of tree dwellers—said loftily, then chuckled at his own joke.

Not all the defenders of the Holy City were preoccupied in the west, and several large cannon opened on *Sular* as she steered for the docks. One massive shot deflected off the old ironclad and smashed the top off *Walker*'s number three funnel, scything fragments down on the crew of the port torpedo tubes. Even in their pain they had the satisfaction of watching all four of their fish disembowel *Ramb V.* Tall geysers erupted the length of the 384-foot ship, and black smoke gushed from her funnel like the cough of a volcano. Fuel washed across her, ignited, and she became a settling inferno in seconds.

"Take out those shore batteries!" Matt hollered up to Campeti, bypassing Minnie, and *Walker*'s guns started blasting masonry from around the closest embrasures. *Sular*'s 4"-50s and all her machine guns pummeled them too as she slowed. But *Sular* kept going, practically crashing ashore, splintering the docks all the way to the base of the wall that crumbled down against her. Grinding to a stop, she still kept shooting even as troops poured out and over the rubbled breach.

Matt touched the battered academy sword at his side, actually *yearning* to go with Chack and help finish this himself. But he belonged on *Walker*, and there was still *Leopardo*. . . . On the other hand, there *was* one thing he could do. "All ahead one-third. Bring us alongside *Sular*," he told Paddy Rosen. "Chief Silva!" he shouted down through the open pilothouse windows, still broken after the action off St. Vincent.

"Sir?"

"You've stormed a cowflop or two in your time. They say three's a charm. You want to go ashore with Chack, or stay with *Walker*? I *owe* you the choice."

Silva hesitated, torn. "I want to stay with you, Skipper," he finally replied.

"On your number one gun, doing what you've taught a dozen 'Cats to do." Matt pointed at the looming pyramid barely a mile away. Dried blood—and not all dried—coated the hundred steps to the top. "You can do more there."

Silva looked out over the water where *Ramb V* was turning turtle, her red-black belly rolling into the sunlight. Somewhere beyond was *Leopardo*. He turned back to look at his captain. "You *orderin'* me, Skipper? I got a score to settle with Gravois my own self, you know."

Matt considered. *Some choice, after all,* he thought. "Yes, that's an order. Gravois's as likely to be ashore as on *Leopardo*, anyway. We have to cover both bases. All astern one-third," he told the 'Cat on the EOT. "You've got one minute to arm yourself and get across," he called back down to Silva. "Go."

All hesitation gone, Silva tossed a salute and bolted for the hatch. "All stop. Ease her in," Matt told Rosen, as *Walker* leaned to kiss the side of the ex-Grik battleship. Self-consciously, he glanced at Courtney. "I know. Silly."

"Not at all. You do 'owe' him. We all do. And it was clear he wanted to go, despite his protestations. I would too, if I was twenty years younger." He chuckled. "And you're right. Chack may need him, and he *does* have a talent for it."

"Not me," Keje declared. "I'll fight my baattles on a wooden deck." He grinned at Matt, blinking ruefully. "At least the strakes in the pilothouse are wood."

Silva must've snatched Petey, as well as a BAR (Browning Automatic Rifle) and his belt festooned with weapons, because they both reappeared moments later and jumped across to *Sular*. In seconds he was lost among the 'Cats, humans, and Khonashi surging ashore. "He didn't take his big gun," Courtney suddenly exclaimed.

"He broke it," said Spanky, "and never replaced it this time."

Courtney frowned. "I hope he doesn't need it."

Spanky laughed. "He never *needed* it, except for the occasional super lizard. He just liked wagging the damn thing around."

"All back, two-thirds," Matt ordered. "Right standard rudder." A moment later, a big roundshot slammed into *Walker*'s fo'c'sle and splashed alongside, leaving a hell of a dent. Her guns pounded more cannon firing uselessly at *Sular*, but less so at her troops. "*Mahan*'ll have to stay here," Matt sighed. "Tell Tiaa to move out of range and keep covering our people. We'll go for *Leopardo* ourselves. Rudder amidships. All ahead full."

CHAPTER 55

THE BATTLE OF NEW GRANADA

////// August 8, 1945
Blas

Giles Meder, a colonel now, had wheeled his massed batteries right up into musket range of the western wall of New Granada. His gun's crews took fearful losses at first, while mercilessly battering the wall around the main West Gate, but they quickly reduced a section about ninety yards long to a crumbling mass of rubble and mangled defenders. Contrary to expectations, return fire from elsewhere along the wall was slackening, not growing, as Shinya and Cox struggled to form their tired troops behind the guns for a hasty, overwhelming assault.

"What the hell?" murmured Colonel Blas-Ma-Ar aside to Sister Audrey and Captain Bustos as Arano Garcia and Captain Ixtli ranted at their hopelessly intermixed 2nd Marines and Vengadores. And the problem wasn't theirs alone. Dao Iverson was yelling at Impie Marines, and Nussie officers and NCOs were working just as hard to bring order out of chaos.

"There's a battle on the lake," came General Tomatsu Shinya's voice behind them, speaking matter-of-factly. "A shame we can't see it from here." Blas turned to see the Army's overall commander, escorted by Lieutenant Anaar as he often was of late. More surprising was the sight of Captain Anson and a number of his Rangers. All were dismounted and armed with Allin-Silva rifles.

"Is a lake baattle still a sea baattle?" First Sergeant Spook brazenly asked, and Blas blinked scathingly at him.

"I suppose, in a manner of speaking," Anson replied loudly over the thundering cannon, while carefully checking his pair of large revolvers, "but that's irrelevant." He smiled. "What *is* quite pertinent is that wireless communications have virtually exploded from nothing, to more traffic than can easily be absorbed. Your Captain Reddy has *routed* the League fleet"—he grinned at Spook—"in what assuredly *was* a 'sea battle,' and chased its meager remnant here. He's going after that wicked *Leopardo* as we speak, and Colonel Chack has assaulted the docks with a division of your Second Corps and his own illustrious brigade." He waved at the walls before them. "That explains the sudden paucity of defenders here, and why we're in such a rush to take advantage!"

"That's wonderful news!" enthused Sister Audrey, while looking suspiciously at Shinya and Anson in turn. "But why are you here?"

"I'm with *him*," Anson answered merrily, nodding at Shinya.

"And I've come to pay my debt to Colonel Blas," Shinya said simply. "And you, Sister Audrey. To all the Marines, Ocelomeh, and Vengadores I've sacrificed so ruthlessly for so long. It's time I fought *beside* you, if you'll have me." He grimaced. "If you think I've earned the honor. General Cox has my full confidence and has agreed to obey General Blair if something happens to me."

"And my Rangers and I will prevent that 'something,' if possible," Anson said, still cheerful.

Blas opened her mouth to object, tail whipping, but finally blinked acceptance. "It would be *our* honor, Gener-aal Shinya."

"Do you have the time, Captain Anson?" Shinya asked. "In the excitement, my orderly neglected to wind my watch this morning, and I didn't think to." He looked straight at Blas. "I've grown *far* too reliant on other people to do important things for me."

"Certainly." The Ranger fished a large gold disc from a pocket in his dingy blue vest by the chain. "I have ten minutes after three."

"Your officers have five minutes to complete their preparations," Shinya told Blas. "Not much time, but the enemy's even more disordered than we are. And they're afraid," he added with satisfaction.

"What's Colonel Chack's objective?" Sister Audrey asked.

"The toughest, of course. His brigade will drive directly for the most prominent enemy temple, while Second Corps secures his advance. We—the Sister's Own—will do the same, while the rest of our forces spread out in the city."

"Another reason I and my fellows are here," Anson agreed with an engaging smile. "To represent the NUS when we seize that wretched temple."

Bugles sounded and Anson frowned at his watch. "A little early, I think, or the spring in my timepiece is losing its temper." The cannon fire ceased after a few final shots, their dense gunsmoke mingling with rubble dust. More bugles blared, then whistles and drums, even the usual, awful bagpipes.

"Shall we?" Shinya asked. "The army will follow *this* division." Tears poured down Sister Audrey's face as she quickly touched as many around her as she could, as if she never would again, then jerked a brittle nod at Blas. "This is why we came, why I'm here. God bless you all."

"Sister's Own!" Blas roared, echoed by Garcia, Ixtli, Bustos, and dozens of other officers and NCOs. "At the quickstep . . . *maarch*!" Thousands of closely spaced men and 'Cats stepped forward, moving like a relentless wave into the hazy breach.

Mayta

General Anselmo Mayta had no idea what happened to his frantically collected defense on the West Wall. The enemy cannonade was furious, certainly, even more focused and overwhelming than that morning, but its very focus made it less threatening to men spaced away from it, firing muskets at the gunners, or even those gathered in quickly assembled redoubts behind the gate. Yet Mayta *sensed* his numbers dwindling even before he saw men scamper from the walls and hastily constructed barricades. When he did, he could only stare in shock because they actually seemed purposeful, not panicked. He sent Colonel Hereda to discover the cause, even as his strength continued to flow away. The man returned, now bloodied and powdered with stone dust.

"Report!" Mayta demanded.

"The gate is down, My General! The whole wall around it has been smashed!"

Mayta expected that. "But what of the redoubt? That's what *it's* for!"

Hereda took a gulp from his water bottle and gasped, "Captain General Maduro sends them away! He says the enemy has broken through the *east* wall!"

Blinking to clear his eyes, Mayta looked toward Lago de Vida for the first time since reentering the city. He couldn't see much, but white smoke was rising from shore batteries, and dark, fat plumes towered over the lake.

"How . . ." he began, but shook his head. "It doesn't matter. *This* wall will fall without the protection bleeding away. Stay here, Colonel. I'll get to the bottom of this!" Striding away from his brave, loyal Colonel Hereda, he had no way of knowing he'd never see him again.

The devastation near the gate was complete and Mayta had to pick his way through the ruins of men and the broken wall, crouching when roundshot blasted him with whistling shards of stone. Through the haze and sleeting gravel, he saw Captain General Maduro berating a man on a horse that twitched and jerked with each booming report—until the cannon fire abruptly stopped. Knowing what that had to mean, Mayta stumbled forward as fast as he could. He reached Maduro as the horseman galloped away down the debris-strewn cobbles. Maduro turned to him, eyes wide and wild, clutching spastically at the never-used sword at his side.

"What have you done?" Mayta coughed.

"The heretics are landing on the docks!" Maduro gobbled, voice high and fast. "I've been sending men to guard the Temple. His Supreme Holiness must *not* be disturbed!"

Mayta couldn't believe his ears, and gestured at the racing horseman vanishing in a rush of smoke. There was fire in the city now. "Why was I not informed of the threat from the lake? Disgraced in your eyes or not, *I* command, not you!" he roared. "And the only way to guard the Temple is to *hold the walls*, you fool!" Bugles, drums, and other indistinct instruments sounded beyond the gaping, pulverized gap, and hoarse voices rose in a surf-like roar as the enemy advanced. Most of Mayta's remaining men, knowing they couldn't live if they resisted, flung their weapons down and fled. Even some of Maduro's Blood Drinkers joined the panic, and Mayta could hardly blame them. "You've destroyed us all," he grated lowly, pulling the brass-barreled pistol from his sash, "and His Supreme Holiness as well." Reaching to cock the pistol, he noted the steel still tilted forward from his previous shot and remembered the weapon was empty. "A dead horse just saved your miserable life, Captain General," he snarled. Bullets were whizzing around them now, and men who were slow to leave before now stampeded from the redoubt. Maduro clearly wanted to flee as well, but was transfixed by Mayta's gaze as the man calmly returned the pistol to his sash and said, "We'll join the men at the Temple, if any actually went." A bullet snatched a hunk of red fabric from Maduro's coat and he recoiled violently. "It seems I won't be executed after all," Mayta told him, "and we'll both have the pleasure of dying for His Supreme Holiness today."

Silva

"Hold up, Chackie!" Silva snapped, snatching his Lemurian friend (and superior officer) back behind cover as a fusillade of musket balls *vrooped* through the place he'd been. It hadn't taken long for Silva to find Chack, Lawrence—and Pam, of course, damn her—as well as Sir Sean Bates. They'd all been together, surrounded by Enrico Galay, Abel Cook, and Hamish Alexander—all top members of Chack's Brigade—dispatching companies of various regiments of 2nd Div, II Corps in different directions. Only Pam hadn't seemed glad to see him, muttering something like, "Can't go *anywhere* without that asshole tagging along."

Together they'd blasted their way half a mile into the city behind rifle fire and grenades against initially stiff resistance, primarily by the civilian populace. They'd been afraid of that, even though—unlike Shinya—they'd never had to deal with it before. And the civilians, whipped up by Blood Priests, resisted even more fanatically than the soldiers when they saw the invaders included Lemurians and Grik-like Khonashi—*obviously* demons, in their eyes. Chack's Brigade was forced to shoot men and women fighting as maniacally as any Grik, who remorselessly slaughtered any who hesitated with everything from muskets and bayonets retrieved from Dom soldiers, to meat cleavers and hayforks. It had been a brutal, bloody, sickening grind.

Civilian opposition began to fold, however, after Allied troops started targeting the Blood Priests. Watching them get shredded under a hail of bullets tended to take the stuffing out of their flock, possibly instilling greater fear of the enemy than the Blood Priests for the very first time. Chack's Brigade, dwindling due to casualties and the necessary establishment of numerous strong blocking forces, had it easy for a while as it closed the distance to its objective, but got stopped cold by a large number of Dom regulars and Blood Drinkers behind a barricade they'd erected in the plaza around the Holy Temple.

"Get on the horn!" Chack called back to a signal-'Cat packing one of the newer, but still very heavy field radios. "See if we caan get some air support! There's a big concentration of Doms in the open at the base of the temple." With only *Leopardo* presumably left on the water, Matt had ordered *New Dublin*'s SBD-2s to turn around and exchange their torpedoes for bombs. That would delay them, of course, but *New Dublin*'s Bull-Bats had flushed as soon as her flight deck was clear and they'd be here any time. As for *Leopardo*, if *Walker* couldn't handle her, there was still *Mahan*. And

USS *Gray* would soon arrive. With *New Dublin* protected by Repub BCs, Captain Miyata had started upriver the night before, without orders. *'Ol Miyata'll prob'ly catch hell for that,* Silva thought, then grinned. *But hey!*

"Bull-Baats're ten minutes out," the signal-'Cat replied, "but *Mahaan* says she'll put fire on 'em for us!" *Mahan* had been doing a lot of that, hammering targets for elements of II Corps as they called them in and gave her corrections. The 'Cat paused. "No, she caan't. We got friendlies on the *west* side o' the temple. Some o' Shinya's troops're in close contaact there."

Silva peeked around the wall and saw Doms firing furiously in that direction. At the sight of him, others shot his way and he pulled back as plaster-covered brick exploded where his head had been.

Pam started to rush toward him but caught herself when she saw he was fine. "Idiot," she hissed.

"Idiot!" Petey loudly agreed, shaking off powdered plaster before tearing at the bandage on his gliding membrane again. "*Goddamn* idiot!"

"Shut up, you," Silva told the little reptile, thumping him on the head. "An' quit pickin' at your stitches! What now?" he asked Chack.

"I don't 'ant to get shot again," Lawrence said.

Chack opened the loading gate of the "new" Krag rifle he'd been given, to replace the one destroyed in the Battle of Sofesshk, to ensure the magazine was full. Then he looked at the "command group" around him, noting how seriously it had been whittled down. Sir Sean had a bloody bandage around his head, but the sword in his single hand was steady. He looked eager. So did Abel Cook and his squad of Grik-like Khonashi. Lawrence didn't, but his rifle was ready and his large eyes gleamed with determination. The same was largely true of the thirty-odd 'Cats and Impies still with them. But the force ahead numbered in the hundreds. "I wish we haad some Repubs an' their breechloading caannon," he lamented. "Even some caannon of our own. I wonder whaat Shinya and the Nussies brought?"

The answer came quicker than the signal-'Cat could try to find out, and it was entirely unexpected. A chorus of low-frequency, gurgling roars thundered down the avenue and Silva peeked around the corner of the building again. "You believe this shit?" he growled. "Goddamn super lizards! An' me without my Doom Stomper!"

Nearly everyone crowded forward to see, since the Doms were suddenly quite distracted. Three of the huge beasts, mottled tan, black, and brown, and perhaps sixty feet from nose to tail, had stalked out of the labyrinth of buildings southwest of the temple and into the clear. Basically giant, walking mouths, the things had huge jaws, powerful hindquarters, but no forelegs or "arms" at all. Thick, whiplike tails stood straight out behind them, balancing their massive heads and torsos. Powerful as Silva's Doom Stomper had been, it wouldn't have been much use, since these monsters were twice as large as any he'd ever seen, or shot at. That didn't matter to the Doms, who were suddenly pouring musket fire at the closer, more horrifying threat.

Regardless of the futility, Silva was taking a bead with his BAR as well, when Chack—amber eyes glowing—told him to hold his fire.

"What for?"

"Where do you think those things came from?" Chack asked, excitement rising in his voice. "Shinya reported the Doms used 'em like taanks to break his defense at Fort Defiaance laast year, an' the same thing happened to Cox at El Paalo! They're *trained* to attaack people shootin' at 'em, becaause they get to *eat* 'em!"

"Eat?" Petey asked hopefully, if a little doubtfully. He'd learned that food was rarely available at times like this.

Chack ignored him. "Scuttlebutt waas they came to the enemy as 'gifts' from their daamn pope, from *here*, where he keeps 'em like pets! Prob'ly feeds 'em folks he doesn't like."

"Priority message on all frequencies!" the signal-'Cat blurted. "Generaal Shinya says do *not* fire on the super lizaards! His forces overraan their pens an' turned 'em loose when Col-nol Gaarcia squeezed a local into spillin' thaat the *temple's* the only place they ever get to go in the city. To feed 'em slaves an' such on special occasions, an' 'aamuse' the civvies! Soon as they were loose, they just headed this way! Oh! He also saays to waatch out for the armaabueys they use to herd 'em around. They aaccidentally got loose too, but they're only daangerous if they smush you."

"I'm so relieved," Pam murmured, looking at the alleyways around, as if expecting to see giant, armadillo-like creatures already thundering toward them.

"Ha! See?" Chack practically chortled.

The Doms around the temple apparently hadn't had time to gather any artillery, and that was all that might've saved them. Musket balls only reinforced the conditioned behavior of the gigantic predators and they quickened their pace toward the hasty breastworks around the Holy Temple. There was a stiff flurry of fire but the super lizards only shrugged it off and charged with hungry, anticipatory moans, crashing through the meager obstacles and scooping struggling, screaming men into their jaws. The defense quivered like an over-hard sword that takes a heavy blow—just before it snaps. The super lizards waded among the Doms, snatching them up at their leisure, methodically tilting great jaws up and simply gulping them down. Distant, frantic commands could be heard, but most of the panicked enemy broke and ran. The pursuit instinct kicked in immediately, and with a titanic roar, all three monsters swerved north around the temple with ground-eating strides, chasing the majority of the men who fled in that direction.

A cluster of Dom regulars and Blood Drinkers, a couple hundred, had heeded their officers' cries and clustered around an arched entrance with garish symbols engraved in stone. They started falling as rifle fire slammed into them, then a great gulp of smoke from what Silva knew must be a mountain howitzer by the sound spewed a double dose of canister among them. Men fell squalling on the blood-soaked pavement, and with more than the simple reluctance of defeat, it seemed, some of the Doms finally ducked inside the temple.

Men and 'Cats were charging from the west-southwest, and Silva was amazed to see the Stars and Stripes, and Sister Audrey's weird flag, flowing over the surge of attackers.

"Let's go!" Chack roared, and his little force, barely a company, rounded the corner, rifles firing, and joined the assault.

Blas

"Waatch your fire to the east!" Blas roared. "That's Chack . . . an' *Silvaa* over there!"

"Indeed it is!" Sister Audrey gasped, running beside her. "I never expected to see either again, especially not Mr. Silva. My word!" 'Cats and men were falling around them, Dom muskets growing more effective as they closed. And the sad, simple fact had always been that 'Cats in particular always grew more reckless when their objective was in sight. Not that they were alone in that today. The Vengadores were just as heedless of their losses as they sprinted toward the hated temple. Chack and Silva's little force actually reached the distracted enemy first, slamming into them with a stutter of shots and ringing steel. Blas thus caught them distracted as well, and waded into the desperate free-for-all with her bayonet. Even as she fought, however, she was aware of the singular, stunningly lethal machine of death that Chack, Silva, and Lawrence became as soon as they smashed their way to the center of the Doms.

Each had his own technique; Silva was raw power, complimented by the unerring aim of his BAR that blasted men down with two rounds apiece. Empty, it became a brutal club, smashing men's skulls or hands on their weapons, leaving them helpless against another quick stroke or for someone else to finish. Chack wielded his Krag with art and finesse, shooting men or bayonetting them almost casually, with profound economy of motion. Blas doubted even Pete Alden—the master of the bayonet on this world—could stand against Chack anymore. Then there was Lawrence, fighting much like Chack with his Allin-Silva rifle and bayonet, but he seemed most concerned with guarding Silva's blind side so the big man could wreak his havoc. They'd obviously fought Grik—individually deadlier opponents—like this many times, and Blas wondered if they were even aware of how cooperative, even interdependent, their style had become.

The fight was as brief as it was bitter, and not without cost. Glory and triumph walk hand in hand with tragedy and less than half who charged the temple entrance lived. Most who did were wounded to some degree. In addition to many 'Cats and men, virtually all the Khonashi died, their terrifying appearance drawing disproportionate fire. Abel Cook, leading from the front, went down with a musket ball in his thigh and his two surviving Khonashi covered the wounded youngster with their bodies. First Sergeant Spook and Lieutenant Anaar were shot dead in the melee, as was Captain Ixtli, dying in the very entrance to the temple. General Tomatsu Shinya fought with berserk abandon, cleaving heads with the katana Bernie Sandison made him from a 1917 cutlass so long ago. He'd just joined Blas, who'd almost linked up with Chack, when he took a vicious bayonet thrust in his lower back. The wound was avenged by Arano Garcia, but Shinya was gushing blood. He finally collapsed when the last Dom defenders died or ran. Pam, Sister Audrey, and Captain Anson, as well as Captain Bustos and two of Anson's surviving men, frantically worked to staunch Shinya's bleeding while the signal-'Cat, running up with his heavy burden, called desperately for assistance.

A single, solitary Dom remained, only because he'd ostentatiously held his empty pistol up by the muzzle throughout the fight—and Colonel Blas-Ma-Ar recognized him. "You want me to blast him?" a blood-spattered Silva shouted, pointing his reloaded BAR at the man's face while Lawrence roughly held him. Silva's hearing was still blown by the shooting.

"Not yet," said Blas, stepping to face General Anselmo Mayta.

The man actually smiled. "We meet again, Major Blas. I always knew you were extraordinary."

"*Col-nol* Blas," she corrected bitterly.

"A well-deserved promotion, I'm sure. You have my congratulations." He cocked his head, listening to the fighting raging through the city. Now that the shooting here had stopped, the intensity of the battle around them was breathtaking. "For that, and your achievement here." He hesitated before adding, "You haven't won, of course, and never will as long as his Supreme Holiness represents God . . . to these people . . . on this world."

"We can fix *that* quick enough," Silva sneered.

"Fix!" Petey cawed emphatically, earning an astonished look from Mayta.

"How you not in there, de'ending he?" Lawrence hissed in his ear.

"*Reptile demons* that speak as well? How marvelous," Mayta remarked in genuine amazement. Lawrence hissed at Petey, annoyed even an enemy would equate them. Mayta looked back at Blas. "Only Blood Drinkers and their Priests—including Don Hernan, of course—may enter the Holy Temple and live. At least that's what I always believed," he added distractedly. "Nothing in there is meant to be seen by mere men."

"Such as?" Sir Sean demanded.

Mayta laughed. "*I* don't know! I'm just a soldier." His face darkened. "Ask General Maduro, if you dare go inside. I'd be personally obliged if you kill him, in fact, before . . . whatever might happen to you occurs. His cowardice is why you broke through in the west so easily."

"Then maybe we'll give him a medal before we hang him," Silva quipped. "If we had medals."

Sister Audrey had left Shinya, wiping his blood on her smock. Now she moved in front of Mayta to peer at him closely.

"You must be the heretic priestess I've heard so much about," Mayta exclaimed, then nodded at the man she left. "And that's General Shinya?" His expression turned to one of genuine regret. "Such a shame he should die like this, and I never able to congratulate him on his brilliant campaign."

"General Shinya will not die," Sister Audrey stated emphatically, then turned to Silva and blessed him with one of her angelic smiles. "Don't harm this man," she said. "Unlike Blood Drinkers I've examined, he has the slightest spark of God's light in his eyes. His soul may yet be saved."

"Sure, Sister," Silva replied awkwardly. "Salvage away, when we got time. Then we'll hang *his* ass too." He'd always thought Audrey was a little nutty, especially when she informed him that he was an instrument of God! But like Captain Reddy, she always expected more from him than he thought he had, and got it too. Along with his genuine affection and respect. He stuffed a wad of yellowish leaves in his cheek and motioned at the temple entrance with the muzzle of his weapon. "Right now, we got a chore to finish."

"He's right," Shinya grated, as men and 'Cats carried him and Abel Cook up behind a hasty perimeter on the temple steps, largely composed of dead Doms. "There may be another exit, and you must finish this." Unfortunately, like Chack's, most of Shinya's force had been detached to hold the lane clear for their push to the temple. Many who reached it alive were wounded and they had to leave a guard on their prisoner, the entrance, and the injured until help arrived. It was finally decided that Chack, Blas, Sister Audrey and Arano Garcia, Captain Bustos, Sir Sean, and Captain Anson, as well as Silva and Lawrence, of course, had to be the ones to enter the Temple of God. Blas and Sister Audrey yearned to catch up with friends they'd missed so long, but now wasn't the time. They contented themselves with swiftly embracing Silva, Chack, Sir Sean, even Lawrence.

Captain Anson, already astonished by Lawrence, confronted Silva with an outstretched hand. "We have close mutual friends, and I've heard a *great* deal about you."

Silva blinked his good eye and mashed Anson's hand in his. "Swell. I don't know shit about you. Hope you can fight." He looked at Chack. "We're mighty brass-heavy, 'specially with 'Sir Sean' along." He grinned at the one-armed Impie, who'd just returned from speaking very earnestly with Abel Cook, but looked back at Chack. "By my lights, you're senior. You want I should lead the way?"

Chack looked around, blinking bewilderment. Planes had arrived, strafing positions in the distance. The city was burning, battle raged all around . . . and they were about to go down a hole. "I might *be* senior," he said, "but Col-nols Blas, Gaarcia, and Aaudrey know this enemy better. Besides, I doubt anyone's 'in chaarge' of things at this point, Dennis, so by all means, lead on."

"Be *careful*, Dennis, you big jerk!" Pam called out, eyes revealing how desperately worried she was. She'd moved away from Shinya—hopefully a good sign—to work on Abel Cook's leg. "*Everybody* be careful," she quickly added.

"Sure, doll, we will," Silva told her, then added sarcastically, "Love you too."

"Really?" Blas whispered up at him, and the big man shrugged.

"Who knows?"

The small group started to move into the entrance, but Silva stopped them with a gap-toothed grin, fishing in a bulging pouch at his side. Producing a pair of grenades, held tight in his big hand, he pulled the pins. "Only polite to knock first. Always heard it weren't gen-teel to show up at a party without a gift, neither. Stand clear!" he called, and threw the grenades down the long, dark corridor.

CHAPTER 56

////// Leopardo

Capitano Ciano had thought things couldn't get worse, but he was wrong. He'd ordered the oiler to hide on the south end of the lake and made the best plan he could to defend Lago de Vida, placing *Canet* in ambush and trying to concentrate *Leopardo*'s and *Ramb V*'s fire. But then he'd seen the enemy scout plane and had to assume there'd be more soon, at the same time he realized *Ramb V* was useless, her people somehow broken. He was sure they'd surrender if they weren't under *his* guns. She tried anyway, but the duel began at sufficient distance that the enemy couldn't see the big auxiliary haul down her flag, and after the first incoming shells smashed her communications and fire control, *Ramb V* had to fight.

She did it poorly, as Ciano had expected. Moving to conceal his ship behind her, he'd watched the Allies—*Walker*!—race to cut him off from the city. If *Walker* had been alone, Ciano would've gladly fought her, but she brought *another* destroyer, and that monstrous ship with just as many guns. There'd be no retrieving Gravois now, so Ciano and *Leopardo* fled.

Racing straight away from the action and the city, Ciano ordered his lookouts to find the mouth of the river Don Hernan described. They thought they had, and *Leopardo* steered into it—only to discover nothing but a little bay that quickly turned to swamp. Don Hernan had fooled them. There *was* no river, and *Leopardo* was truly trapped. That's when her lookouts saw *Walker* again, obviously hunting them, and she was all alone. "Battle stations!" Ciano shouted, eyes narrowing with hatred, as well as a . . . sense that this meeting had somehow been preordained. *Very well,* he told himself, *I'll oblige the fates. And if I smash* Walker *quickly enough, I might still escape down the River of Heaven and make a low-speed run to the Azores.* This intention he announced to his XO and the bridge watch. He didn't tell them if that didn't work, he'd settle for killing *Walker.*

Walker

Leopardo was harder to find than Matt expected. *Ramb V* had gone down, clearing much of her smoke, but when Matt steered *Walker* to avoid her debris—and a surprising number of survivors in the water—there'd been no sign of the heavy Italian destroyer. *Walker* immediately hove to and plucked thirty men, not already in *Ramb V*'s half-filled boats, from the oil slick on the lake before things—not flashies, but maybe a freshwater version—started tearing the swimmers apart. Shrieking men thrashed toward the cargo net hanging over *Walker*'s side, but their panicked flailing drew even more fearsome predators. Some were worse than flashies, resembling nothing they'd seen, like huge, armored, shark-mouth rays. *Walker* quickly saved a few more and even Courtney tried to help, but he was equally torn between horror and fascination. In less than five minutes there were no more men in the water.

Those who came aboard were packed in around the galley wreckage and made as comfortable as possible, watched by a portion of *Walker*'s small Marine contingent (most crewed her 25mm guns) and tended by the fine medical division Sandra had created. The boats were instructed to wait for rescue, and *Walker* resumed her hunt for *Leopardo.*

"What's that ahead?" Courtney asked, staring through his Repub binoculars as the calm, sun-sparkled water creamed away from the old destroyer's bow. There was something like a bed of dusky, red-topped reeds in the middle of the lake.

Keje squinted his better Lemurian eyes. "Floating birds, I think."

A report to that effect almost immediately arrived from the crow's nest lookout and Matt observed the creatures with his own binoculars. "Look something like big geese," he said. "Tan bodies with red and black heads." He chuckled. "Every one of 'em's looking at us, their skinny necks all stretched out."

"You mustn't just bash through," Courtney scolded. "They may be mating!"

'Cat chuckles joined Matt's and he obligingly ordered a slight course correction. Moments later, the lake between the ship and the creatures, right where *Walker* would've been, convulsed with eight towering geysers from a tightly spaced salvo of 4.7″ shells. Hundreds of large birds—they *did* look like geese—exploded as well, taking to the air in all directions amid a great, splashing, flapping frenzy.

"All ahead flank!" Matt ordered, then bellowed at Campeti above. "Where the *hell* did those come from?"

"There's a bay up ahead. One of my strikers thought she saw flashes, but there's no target."

"Commence firing! Maybe you'll screw up their aim until we get one. Come left to three, three, zero and shake her tail, Mr. Rosen. Extra lookouts to starboard!"

Even as three of USS *Walker*'s 4″-50s barked in reply to the sudden assault, a gust of steam escaped her funnels, her stern crouched down, and her screws sped up. Another salvo smashed the water short, blasting slower, fatter birds from the swooping cloud that formed. The natural phenomenon had drawn their attention for a critical, almost fatal moment, but was now disrupting the enemy's aim.

"Definite surfaace taarget, confirmed *Leopaardo*, bearing two, seven, seero, range, six t'ousaands!" Minnie reported triumphantly. "She's puttin' on steam, comin' out!"

"Make ready all starboard tubes, Mr. Sandison," Matt ordered as Bernie rushed to the director on the starboard bridgewing.

"Aye, aye, sir. Just gimme a minute!"

"That may be all you have," Spanky snapped.

"Well, I gotta get a *speed* on her, don't I?" a harried Bernie complained. "No sense throwing all our fish where she *was*. I gotta put 'em where she'll be when they get there!"

"Get aft, Spanky," Matt gently told his friend. "I know the auxiliary conn's out, but we've got too many eggs in one basket here. And you can still relay orders down to the steering engine room if you have to. Go."

Obviously reluctant, Spanky nodded and dashed away.

A salvo churned the water directly abeam, tracking *Walker* uncannily well, though still short. Ronson Rodriguez's faith was well-founded, however. Lots of practice truly had made *Walker*'s gun's crews the best in the world. Campeti's excited shouts of "No change, no change! Rapid salvo fire! Let the bitch have it!" followed flashes between *Leopardo*'s distant funnels and a roll of orange flame. Matt's eyes settled on Courtney. "Get below, Mr. Bradford. To the wardroom."

Courtney smeared sweat on his balding pate with a sleeve before plopping his helmet back on and replying with determination. "Thank you for your concern, Captain Reddy, but I don't believe I will. I'm not just a civilian to be ordered about anymore, you know." He straightened. "I'm a praetor—admiral—in the Republic Fleet!"

Matt's face turned stony, even as he blinked compassionate understanding in the Lemurian way. "Retired, I thought, but it doesn't matter. Aboard *my* ship—" He was interrupted by more towers of spume and a pair of deafening, numbing crashes. *Walker*'s gun's crews might be better, but they could only bring three of their four 4″-50s to bear—at most—at any given time. *Leopardo* could fire eight bigger guns, from almost any orientation. One 4.7″ shell struck right under the bridgewing where Bernie and his "'Catfish" stood. It mowed them and much of the bridge crew down with a spray of lethal fragments from their own ship before the shell punched through Matt's quarters below and exploded in the radio room. Lieutenant Ed Palmer and his assistants, including Corporal Neely who'd joined him there, never knew what hit them.

That wasn't the case in the aft fireroom, pierced by another shell. Aged and cranky as some valves and lines might be, even *Walker*'s original boilers were better than when she came to this world. Isak was known to push them to almost 300 psi. All the 'Cats and Impie gals in that space had agonizing, nightmarish seconds to endure being cooked alive by rushing steam—before erupting fuel oil stifled their screams.

USS *Walker*, blind and lamed, veered hard to port with no hand on her wheel, marked by a pall of roiling black smoke that momentarily shielded her from view. *Leopardo*, like the predator she was named for, maddened by her own painful wounds, dashed forward to finish her prey.

Leopardo

"Take us closer, damn you!" Capitano Ciano ranted at his helmsman. The poor man looked back, almost quivering with dread, but turned the wheel to obey.

"She's still dangerous," cautioned Ciano's XO, very carefully. He'd never seen his captain like this before. "And we've taken damage ourselves," he reminded. "Our torpedo tubes won't traverse, and only the forward guns are still linked to fire control."

"And we're leaking fuel from a ricochet that struck aft," Ciano snapped. "I know. We underestimated the enemy from the start, and this entire preposterous campaign has lurched from disaster to disaster because Victor Gravois"—he spat the name with seething venom—"*wildly* underestimated *Walker*'s commander."

"Then . . . if it's still your aim to escape into the Atlantic, perhaps we should go around her. More damage will severely . . . limit our options."

Ciano laughed. "Do you really think we can still crawl out of the pit Gravois left us in? *More* enemy ships will be in the river by now, if not already nearly here." The rumble of airplane engines punctuated his prediction. *Leopardo* was poorly protected against air attack. "We'll never get past them," Ciano emphasized.

"But the League . . ." his XO protested.

"You think the *League* will save us? After *half* its military wealth has already been squandered on this adventure? All that's left for us is surrender." He nodded at the smoke ahead and his expression twisted into a bitter snarl. "But first, one way or another, I *will* sink that ship."

Silva

"*Second*-damnedest thing I ever seen," Silva practically whispered, though the grenade blasts preceding the mixed assault force made stealth rather pointless. He was referring to the long, dank corridor they were in. Though carved from the same stones quarried to shape the massive, geometrically impressive structure, the passageway was deliberately shaped to resemble the inside of a natural cave.

"But consistent with their twisted belief that God and his heaven are in an 'underworld' of some sort," Sister Audrey agreed.

"I don't care 'hat they think," Lawrence murmured. "Us just get this o'er."

"I'm with Laawrence," Chack admitted. All 'Cats were a little claustrophobic, but so soon after he, Lawrence, and Silva had fought their way through the mazelike Palace of Vanished Gods in Sofesshk, Chack was openly uncomfortable about entering yet another constricted battle space. "Whaat's down here?" he asked Colonel Garcia.

"The 'Holy Sanctum,' whatever that is," Garcia replied, stepping over the corpses of Blood Drinkers, probably killed by Silva's grenades. "I know no more than our prisoner. Probably much less."

"Movement ahead!" Blas cried, as shapes came rushing from the gloom. They opened fire, the roar of Allin-Silvas, Blitzerbugs, and Silva's BAR painfully thunderous. Agonized, inhuman screeches accompanied toppling bodies and they waded forward, through them. One small form, unnaturally brilliant in the muzzle flashes, vaulted over the pile of dead and tried to impale Sister Audrey with a spear. Garcia fired and the attacker toppled to join the others at their feet.

"The hell with this," Silva grumped, tossing another grenade in the darkness ahead. A flash lit the passageway and they heard more animalistic screams.

"My God," Sister Audrey moaned, "I must have light!"

Silva fished out his Zippo, flipped it into flame, and handed it over. That's when they all saw the nature of the "defenders" they'd killed. All were children, and most were girls, their hairless, naked bodies entirely covered with golden paint of some kind. Blood now too.

"Oh my God," Audrey mourned, gently caressing the perfect young face of the last attacker. Eyes sightless, mouth wide, it was hideously obvious the girl's tongue had been cut out, probably in infancy. And burn scars inside the ears suggested she'd been deafened as well. Lying across her bloody golden body was a wooden spear, tipped with a foot-long, finely knapped, green obsidian point. "And we once thought the *Grik* were monstrous," Audrey seethed.

"C'mon, Sister," Silva said gently. "Can't save 'em. Prob'ly can't save any of 'em, in *here*. Let's get this done for the ones outside."

More red-gold bodies were heaped around a fringe of rich, now grenade-tattered, drapes. Chack parted them with the bayonet on his Krag, and they beheld the "Holy Sanctum" for the first time. The chamber beyond, clearly under the temple above, wasn't all that big, probably about forty yards wide and sixty deep, but nearly everything was red and gold, luridly lit by braziers lining garishly columned walls. "Shit!" Silva barked, his BAR thundering at human forms stationed between the columns. Three exploded before he realized they were gold-masked stone statues, each holding a painted, jewel-encrusted skull in its chiseled left hand.

"Hold your fire, Chief Silva," Chack snapped, blinking at the far end of the chamber. A great translucent curtain was drawn across it, yet backlit silhouettes moved like shadow puppets on the other side. Many were obviously more children, and three men were clustered near the center, one crowned by a large headdress of some sort. The outlines that gave Chack pause, however, were those of perhaps forty Doms, probably Blood Drinkers, and five or six other men armed with modern rifles.

"Yes indeed, do hold your fire," came Don Hernan's distinctive, benevolent voice, "and witness a wonder never seen by heretic eyes! The drapery, if you will, my dear Gravois!"

"Do it!" came an incredulous, impatient, higher-pitched voice Silva remembered as well. The curtain collapsed in a rush on what might elsewhere resemble a stone stage. A score of gold-painted children, these blind as well as deaf, fluttered nervously when they felt the displaced air wash around them. Silva almost fired then, but there were too many muskets and rifles pointed at the eight of them. He'd need another distraction, so he waited and watched.

Victor Gravois looked like he always had, natty and annoyed, though perhaps more disheveled than usual. Don Hernan was also easy to recognize. Even in the nude. His chiseled goatee had gone nearly white and he looked almost frail without his bulky robes, but there was no doubting who he was. A smaller, younger man beside him wore only an open, flowing robe, and a bizarre feathered headdress. And though his eyes hadn't been burned out like the children's, his milky orbs could serve him no better. His expression was perplexed, confused. "But Don Hernan, whatever are you doing?" he asked plaintively. "I heard another man's voice, not my Patriarca's . . . and did you say *heretics*? What's the meaning of this?"

"Rejoice, Your Supreme Holiness! Your Time has come at last," Don Hernan said gently, "and there will be some . . . subtle changes after you leave this place." The "Emperor of the World" seemed to have heard nothing after the opening statement and his face exploded with joy. "I *knew* you were a worthy successor!" he exclaimed. "The other voice, then, he is The One?" he asked anxiously.

Don Hernan motioned Gravois over with a curt nod and handed him an obsidian knife. Gravois blinked at it, surprised.

"Yes, Holiness. He's here to liberate you from this world. Your Patriarca already awaits you in the next, so you need not even endure all the tiresome rituals preceding the blessed event."

"Oh my!" The man in the headdress beamed.

"What?" Gravois asked in English as the Dom Messiah bared his throat with a happy smile, and Don Hernan knelt naked before him. "Cut his throat, you fool!" Don Hernan hissed, also in English.

"You said . . . I thought we were here to *save* him!"

"Don't be absurd. You'll save *me* after I take his place, washed in his blood!"

"What is all this strange talk, Don Hernan?" asked His Supreme Holiness, lowering his chin a trifle.

"Nothing, Holiness. An ancient exchange between Successors and The One, predating those we knew, and recently rediscovered in the west."

"But you spoke the word 'heretic' earlier," His Supreme Holiness now said, doubt creeping into his voice, "and the west is *full* of heretics!"

"Heretics?" Sister Audrey suddenly roared in the tongue of the Dominion, pacing forward and slightly to the right. "Your entire, twisted, murderous faith is *founded* on the most perverted and loathsome heresy imaginable!"

"Santa Madre!" Garcia objected, starting forward, but Blas yanked him back, hissing, "She knows whaat she's doing. Be ready!"

"You defile the word 'God' every time you utter it," Sister Audrey pronounced, her young clear voice booming in the chamber. "You soil the fabric of faith with the vomitous words you spew on it, and waste God's gift of life with your abominable, unfeeling cruelty!"

"A woman!" shrieked His Supreme Holiness, backing away in horror. "You brought a *woman capable of speech* into the Holy Sanctum? What insanity is this, Don Hernan?"

"You wouldn't *b'leve* what all he brung, on top o' losin' your war an' your city!" Silva bellowed. "Why there's women, Catmonkeys, Lizards, Nussies, Imperials, even a sneaky Frenchman! All *sorts* o' weird critters. You wanna eat, Petey?"

"Eat! Goddamn!" Petey squawked.

Silva pointed at a Blood Drinker officer, maybe even the one Mayta told them about. "*He's* got food, stuffed up his nose!"

Petey erupted off Silva's shoulder and flitted toward the man, who screamed and tried to flee.

"Kill them!" Don Hernan thundered, moving to catch the master he had to murder.

"No! No! Stop this at once, this is not right. . . ." squalled the scrawny little Messiah, tumbling backward into the sailors, losing his headdress and throwing the men into disarray. A musket roared, then another.

"Let 'em haave it!" Chack bellowed, shooting Petey's manically flailing victim with his Krag, launching the indignantly screeching reptile again. Everyone started shooting then, and the Holy Sanctum became an underground battlefield.

Snatching Lawrence behind a statue, Silva sprayed the cluster of Italian sailors with his BAR. Most went down, kicking and screaming, but the bolt locked back. Dumping the empty magazine, he inserted another while Lawrence shot at Doms, blowing one down with every shot. The only cover on the "stage" was the panicking golden children, who couldn't possibly know what was happening. Gravois had grabbed one around the neck, holding the struggling form in front of him while shooting his pistol at Captain Anson. Anson was dragging Sir Sean, who must've been wounded in the first shots, and bullets threw sparks off the stone floor around them. Arano Garcia was down on his face and Captain Bustos dropped with a shout of pain. Blas was firing her .45 while shoving Sister Audrey behind the meager cover of a jagged, cross-shaped column.

Most of the children, in utter confusion, had finally clustered together near the back of the "stage" and Silva emptied another magazine at the Blood Drinkers, sending several sprawling. He figured there must be fifteen or twenty left when the spattered lead and powdered stone of a near miss drove him back. "Anybody see where Don Hernan went?" he yelled.

"Towaard the baack, somewhere," came Chack's voice, but Silva didn't know where he was. Maybe he'd ducked back into the passageway. "I think he took thaat screaming maan who lost his haat, and Graavois followed."

"So either they're holed up, or sneaked out," Silva guessed. "Stands to reason there'd be a bolt-hole. We gotta get after 'em!"

"Whaat do you suggest? Your saack of grenades will kill us too, in here."

Silva had no time to reply because that's when the remaining Blood Drinkers charged toward Blas, Sister Audrey, Captain Anson, and Sir Sean on the other side of the chamber. Dropping his empty BAR with a curse, Silva leaped to his feet and countercharged with his Colt and cutlass in hand. Lawrence went too, as did Chack, howling a bloodcurdling cry.

Captain Anson, still trying to move Sir Sean, was hurled to the floor by a musket ball slamming into his left shoulder blade and blasting out his chest in a spray of blood. Rising painfully, grimacing, he turned to meet the enemy. They came with bayonets fixed and Anson's big revolvers thundered, rapidly blowing Doms down, but others finally nailed him to one of the jagged crosses with their blades. Sir Sean, blood spurting from a terrible neck wound and roaring defiance, stabbed two men in the legs with his sword before they bayonetted him as well.

Silva, Chack, and Lawrence slammed into the right flank of the rush, almost ignored, and killed men easily—since it quickly became clear *Sister Audrey* was their primary focus. Whether simply because she was a "woman capable of speech" in the Holy Sanctum, or for the scathing heresy she'd flung at them, the Blood Drinkers wanted *her* blood—as she'd known they would—and all she had left to defend her was Blas.

Colonel Blas-Ma-Ar was practically in Sister Audrey's lap, coldly firing her copy of a 1911 Colt right in the faces of men coming to kill them. She saw her friends coming too, stabbing, slashing, shooting . . . Chack was so brave! She'd always secretly loved him. And Lawrence, so strange, but so unreservedly loyal. And Silva, mighty Silva, who she'd never thanked for her life. They were close, now, but when the slide locked back on Blas's empty pistol, she knew they'd be too late. Snarling her fury, she flung herself at the enemy, hoping to distract them from Sister Audrey however long she could—biting, scratching, bashing them with her empty pistol. A bayonet lunged and she tried to twist away but it was coming too fast and hard and there was . . . *Pop! Pop! Pop! Pop!*

The bayonet deflected low and the man collapsed at her feet. Blas had only an instant to see Sister Audrey, sitting up, her own never-used pistol smoking in her hand. The instant stretched into a still image that would stay just behind Blas's eyelids for the rest of her life. Sister Audrey, the Santa Madre, smiling at her as if to say, "For you, dear Blossom, for you—but never for myself," just before two Doms drove their bayonets into her chest.

Blas screeched with agony and rage, shockingly loud enough to freeze the Dom in front of her while she drew her cutlass. But Silva saw Sister Audrey die as well, and went absolutely amok. More than half a dozen Doms remained, but he killed them all while Chack, Lawrence, even Blas, could do little more than back out of his way. They'd all seen him fight like this before—sort of—but accompanying his brutal skill there was always a lot of noise: cussing, bellowing, even taunts, because Silva dearly loved a battle. Most unnerving now, however, throughout the end of this "fight," though his face was streaked with running tears, Dennis Silva never made a sound. The same couldn't be said for the Blood Drinkers, and even after Silva hacked the last Dom down, the screaming wasn't through because that's when he started on the wounded.

"Belaay thaat, sailor!" Chack shouted in his loudest, harshest voice, and Silva checked another downward swing of his bloody cutlass. He didn't relax, he merely stood there like the blood-washed statue of some vengeful god of war, animated only by his heavy breathing. "Thaat's it, Chief Silvaa, staand down," Chack told him more gently, then spoke aside to Lawrence. "Go tell Paam to come get our friend. And make sure Gener-aal Maayta isn't there when she takes him out."

"Don Hernaan an' Graavois," Blas spat.

"I need no reminder," Chack told her bitterly, then called after Lawrence, who'd already turned to go. "Bring reinforcements, if there are more outside by now. But even if there aren't, we'll pursue those evil men as soon as you return."

"Ay, sur."

"Whaat about him?" Blas asked, blinking sadly at Silva. The big man had dropped his cutlass as if afraid he'd keep using it as long as it was in his hand, and racked by gut-wrenching sobs, was now single-mindedly flinging Blood Drinker bodies off Sister Audrey. He finally lifted her gently, effortlessly off the floor.

"His baattle *here* is done, but he maay haave a bigger one ahead. I've been where he is now," Chack told her quietly. "So haave you. Somehow I never expected to see *him* there, and don't know if thaat means he'll heal faaster or slower. But with his strength and the Maker's help, he'll find himself again. As did you and I."

Pam rushed into the chamber, followed by Lawrence and Enrico Galay, along with twenty Imperial Marines and more Khonashi. Several corps-'Cats dispersed to check the wounded and Chack was surprised to see one help Arano Garcia sit up, and another start bandaging Captain Bustos. He'd thought both Vengadores were dead. Pam gasped at the carnage, then ran to Silva's side. She didn't even complain when a blood-spattered Petey swooped over and lit on her shoulder. "C'mon, you big lug," she ordered gently, "let's take Sister Audrey out o' this lousy place."

When they were gone, Galay shook his head. "Silva's a blowtorch. Bound to break sooner or later."

Chack rounded on him, blinking fury, remembering how in spite of everything, Silva obeyed him at the end. "He may haave craacked, but he didn't break. *Praay* you're thaat strong when the time comes. Now let's get aafter Gravois and Don Hernaan."

Galay straightened. "Aye, aye, Colonel."

USS Walker

Matt came to, struggling against Keje, who was literally tying him to his chair.

"Oh!" Keje cried. "You're still alive, my brother! I'm so relieved. I feared you might not be, and knew you wouldn't waant to finish this fight lying on the deck."

"I *told* you!" rasped a furious Juan Marcos. The Filipino was tugging hard on a tourniquet around Matt's right leg. Groggy, Matt looked around. The pilothouse was an abattoir, with blood splashed everywhere. The starboard bridgewing was simply gone and light filtered through twisted conduits from jagged holes in the overhead. Pieces of 'Cats—and Bernie Sandison—lay scattered on shattered deck strakes. Rosen was down and unmoving, as was just about everyone who'd been around him a few . . . seconds? Minutes? Before. Minnie moved against the aft bulkhead, trying to rise from a pool of blood, though it was impossible to tell if it was hers. She was mumbling into the microphone suspended from her headset, but the wire lay severed on the deck. 'Cats came rumbling up the stairs aft, carrying stretchers. Some scrambled up the warped ladder to the fire control platform above. Matt finally realized there was no one at the EOT, and Courtney Bradford had the wheel. "Damage report," he croaked.

The Australian's helmet was gone and his thin white hair was plastered to his head by blood. More blood soaked the shirt, blown half off, but he didn't seem to notice. His face was a study in grim concentration as he tried to keep the smoke trailing *Walker* between her and the enemy. Glancing to the side, he caught Matt's eye and exclaimed, "Thank God! I feared I was all alone up here"—he tilted his bloody head at Keje—"with the exception of our furry friend, of course. Then Juan popped in, which cheered me amazingly, but I still felt rather overwhelmed. I may've been an admiral, but my experience in single-ship actions is somewhat limited!"

Commander Toos, following the corps-'Cats now tending Minnie and Rosen, had heard Matt's request for a report. "It's not good, sur. Aaft fireroom's out. Nobody aanswers inside. Chief Isaak an' Lieuten-aant Tabby shut the main line on deck so we got steam from number one, but we're takin' waater. Probaably in the fireroom. Chief Isaak's ventin' it so we caan get in and see how baad it is." Matt was struck by the irony that the only boiler they had left was the new one they'd done without so long. He tried to turn in his chair and look at the roaring flames he heard, but searing agony near his right hip stopped him. Toos understood. "Fire's baad, but not spreadin'. DC paarties got it under control. Haad to abaandon the midships guns an' deckhouse, though. Number two gun's crew got wiped out by the blaast, an' I ordered ever-body else off." He blinked. "Mosta the prisoners 'round the gaalley got burned up."

"Poor bastards," Matt swore. "What's going on ashore? Where's our air cover? Where's *Leopardo*?"

"I caan't aanswer the first two questions. The raadio room's smaashed and ever-body's dead. But *Leopaardo*'s coming up behind us. Crow's nest lookout sees her, barely a thousaand yaards off."

"Fire control?"

Toos looked up at the perforated overhead, then shook his head, blinking. "Mr. Caampeti waas found on the quaarterdeck. I fear all who were up there are dead or baadly injured."

Matt took a deep breath, wondering how many more old friends would die for the decisions he'd made. Worse, he wasn't even sure they were *right*. And he *couldn't* know now, without a radio. Poor Ed . . . Only one thing remained for him to do. Like Sandra always told him, "When in doubt, fight your ship."

"Are the starboard torpedoes okay?" he demanded.

"The mount crew joined the daamage control paarties, and the fish got scorched."

"But the tubes're still rigged out?"

"Ay, sur."

"Very well. Where's Spanky?"

"Fighting the fire. He never made it to the aaft deckhouse."

"Take over from him, and tell him to put torpedomen back on that mount. Then let me know as soon as you get the number three crew back on their gun."

"Ay, ay, sur."

When Toos was gone, Courtney looked at Matt. "Will you relieve me too?"

Matt was feeling faint, but smiled. "No. You're doing fine. Keje, will you take the EOT?" He shook his head to clear it. "You know, somehow it seems appropriate that we should all be here, like this."

"I agree entirely," Courtney pronounced. "But what shall we do?"

"We're going to fight the ship."

"Well, of course. But how?"

Matt looked at Juan, still standing by, a worried frown on his face.

"As soon as we get the word from Toos, we'll turn to starboard and hammer *Leopardo* with everything we have left—guns, machine guns, torpedoes . . . even foul language, if it'll help. If that doesn't knock her out, we'll ram the son of a bitch."

Gravois

Just inside the escape passage at the back of the Holy Sanctum, while the battle still raged inside, Don Hernan slammed the struggling, screaming Emperor of the World against the wall and slashed his throat with surprising strength. Blood fountained on the naked man, and after a moment he let the body drop, swiftly smearing the blood all over, on his face, in his hair. Gravois was sickly amazed and frankly suspected only *normal* behavior by Don Hernan might surprise him anymore. He was also anxious to get moving. Even if the Blood Drinkers overwhelmed the first invaders in the temple, there'd be more. Don Hernan was obviously thinking along the same lines because he quickly selected one of the dead man's robes from an alcove, swept it over his shoulders, and tied it closed around his waist before snatching a torch from the wall. "Come!" he said angrily, the first words he'd spoken since the "ceremony" disintegrated into chaos. Gravois followed.

The stone passageway began to resemble the entrance, only this was a *real* cave, carved from the ground by eons and sculpted by nature. Soon Gravois was huffing, trying to keep up. He didn't dare fall behind since it quickly became apparent that the path they were on was only one of countless passageways and corridors leading into perfect, dripping blackness. He soon grew less concerned about rapid pursuit, but more so about their destination, and whether Don Hernan himself knew the way. "Does this lead to the lake?" he gasped. "Somewhere near the docks where Ciano can retrieve us?"

Don Hernan stopped abruptly. Turning, he regarded Gravois strangely; the same friendly, open expression he'd always donned like a mask was covered by sticky, blackening blood. "I was angry with you, my dear Gravois," he confessed as if revealing a great failing, "for neglecting your duties as The One. . . . But I didn't prepare you and you couldn't have known. I *still* consider you The One, since you were present, and you survived!"

"I don't understand."

"The One is he who transfers the lifeblood of one, ah, 'pope' to another—which you *did* with all the assistance you've rendered to this point! Sadly, The One rarely survives the experience since the new Supreme Holiness"—he bowed slightly—"will equally rarely allow human eyes to rest on him." He shook his head. "If The One is permitted to live, he becomes His Supreme Holiness's closest advisor, since he alone may see him. My rule must be different, however, and all must see me for who I am. Slaying you would only deprive me of the excellent advisor I need."

Gravois decided to try his original question again. "But . . . this cave, this passage, it leads to the lake, correct?"

Don Hernan laughed. "Of course not! My dragon flyers reported great power coming up the River of Heaven, and even more gathering to do so. There can be no escape that way and the world we would make will die with us. I fear your ships *must* have been destroyed already, and I join you in grieving their loss."

"So you lied about 'rescuing' your master. And the channel you described? The other river?"

"It exists, only it is somewhat smaller than Ciano perhaps believed, and in a slightly different place. And there are rapids. Nothing the size of *Leopardo* could possibly negotiate them."

With that, he turned and strode briskly on and Gravois had to follow, hoping Don Hernan was as confident of escape as he seemed.

USS Walker

A pair of shell splashes straddled *Walker*'s fo'c'sle. The smoke was still helping, but only by blurring the enemy's range finders, and they'd resumed shooting at each other when they only had the vaguest targets. Till now, however, it had been *Leopardo*'s pair of forward guns against *Walker*'s lone 4"-50 on the aft deckhouse. With the enemy now within a thousand yards and scoring hits, the time had come to turn on her and slug it out. "Right full rudder, make your course zero, three, zero, Mr. Bradford. Spin it!"

"Aye, Captain!" Courtney cried in response, grinning through the blood running down his face.

"All ahead flank, Keje. Let's see what the old girl has left!" USS *Walker* groaned and rumbled as she accelerated, veering sharply out from behind her smoke and training every remaining weapon on *Leopardo*. That's when they saw for the first time that she was already under attack by Bull-Bat fighters, swooping and strafing her mercilessly with their machine guns. None of the fighters had bombs, however, or if they'd brought them, they'd already used them in the city. Their machine guns could slaughter *Leopardo*'s people, but couldn't much hurt the ship. *Walker*'s three 4"-50s that would bear, and two remaining rapid-fire 25mms certainly could. They all opened up at once, joined by three .50- and two .30-caliber machine guns. Even in local control, it was practically impossible for her well-oiled gun's crews to miss at seven, six, then five hundred yards. *Leopardo* staggered under the onslaught of converging tracers, and blast after blast rattled her frame and sent debris flying from blossoms of flame. She got off only two shots in return before her forward gun mount was blasted apart, but they flayed *Walker* badly, smashing through the aft fireroom and forward engine room. The ship started to buck as the engine tore itself apart and the port propeller shaft vibrated wildly before slamming to a stop.

Belching smoke and steam, *Leopardo* struggled to turn and bring more guns to bear, even as *Walker*'s speed fell off. Juan had taken Minnie's place as bridge talker and reported casualties and flooding in the engine room, and confirmed the engine was wrecked.

"Very well," called Matt. "Can you still get Spanky on the torpedo mount?"

"Aye, sir."

"Then tell him to fire at will."

The 'Cats seated on top of the starboard torpedo mount had begun tracking the target as soon as *Walker* turned, spinning the wheel that physically aimed the tubes. There'd be nothing fancy about this shot, just point the fish and turn them loose, so as soon as Spanky got the word, he ordered the 'Cats to fire. Nothing happened. "Stay on target!" he shouted. Unholstering his .45, he scrambled back behind the torpedo mount and used it as a hammer, whacking the emergency impulse charge detonators on the back of each tube as he passed it. *Boom-thwooosh-Splash! Boom-thwoosh-Splash!* Just as Spanky sent the fourth fish on its way, a shell smashed the mount and flipped it crashing into the aft funnel, tearing it away and toppling it across the shattered, steam-spewing engine room skylights. Spanky joined a cloud of clattering shell fragments that blew him over against the empty torpedo mount on the other side of the ship.

Walker and *Leopardo* were dying fast under the mutual avalanche of fire they spat at each other, and the Bull-Bat pilots orbiting above (including Tikker, now) could only watch in sick frustration. The great battle for New Granada was sputtering to an end, as General Mayta was taken hurriedly from place to place to arrange the surrender of isolated clusters of his beaten army. There'd probably be holdouts in the city for days, but they couldn't coordinate and no one but Blood Priests were left to lead them. And now that a tipping point had been reached, more and more Blood Priests were being found dead.

Every enemy warship on the lake—except *Leopardo*—had been sunk, and its lonely oiler had surrendered to the first plane that flew over it. Those below might not know any of those things, but while it was clear Captain Reddy had been trying to evade *Leopardo* and save his damaged ship, *Leopardo*'s skipper clearly had only one purpose in mind. Tikker banked his plane to see *Mahan* racing to the aid of her sister, and even *Fitzhugh Gray* was on the lake now, rushing past the smoldering *James Ellis*—but neither could get there in time. *Walker* and *Leopardo* would kill each other before anyone could intervene.

A blast of heavy machine-gun fire raked *Walker*'s bridge, bullets clattering all around Matt in a storm of shattered glass. He felt something like a punch in the side but there wasn't any pain. Then again, he already felt so woozy. . . . Juan was shouting something in his ear, but it didn't make any sense. Courtney was down, kneeling by the wheel, and Keje was trying to help him up. Juan physically grabbed Matt's face and forced his head to the side so he could see *Leopardo*, less than four hundred yards away—just as a tall column of spray rocketed up alongside her, directly amidships. "I told you it was going to hit! I *told* you!" Juan practically screeched with glee. Matt heard that. He was glad too. *Maybe now all this racket will end,* he thought. Somehow, quiet had become important. He knew he was dying, just as *Walker* was. While he drained, she was flooding, and they'd end together. He wanted quiet for that. After all the hell she'd been through, *Walker*'s death should be dignified.

In spite of everything, he maintained enough interest to watch what happened to *Leopardo*. Only one torpedo hit her, but especially after the punishment she'd already taken, one was quite enough. Flames roared to the sky as she settled in the middle, back broken, bow and stern both rising from the boiling water of the lake. Courtney was by him now, held up by Keje. "Good riddance, I say," Courtney hissed through pain-clenched teeth. "I apologize for leaving my post, but we're no longer underway, and I wanted to watch this with you."

Matt had known *Walker* was dead in the water. He could feel it. Feel the water rushing in. "That's fine," he said, smiling wanly. "Glad I saw it with you all." Then, as *Leopardo* broke in half and plunged to the bottom of the lake, Matt slid out of his chair and fell to the splintered deck strakes. He couldn't see, but he heard voices, especially cries of alarm when somebody found the wound in his side. He felt himself handled roughly, urgently, then thought he was floating. The operating light rigged over the wardroom table glared bright in his eyes as 'Cats rushed around. He wanted to yell at them to get off the ship before they all went down, but he couldn't seem to speak. Then he heard Tabby talking fast about *Mahan*, and rigging pumps, and thought he heard Spanky's pained reply from somewhere nearby. He closed his eyes again.

Gravois

Bats and lizardbirds exploded into the evening sky as Gravois and Don Hernan finally crept up out of the jagged mouth of the cave. Gravois looked around, but all he could see was trees. There was no sign of New Granada, or even the great lake. There was a small pack lying on the ground, however, and Don Hernan immediately removed the bloody cloak of his new office and carefully folded it before donning the simple peasant's garb he pulled from the pack. "You must do the same," Don Hernan said. "We have a great distance to travel, and anyone we meet might betray us now, until we reach the Godly haven of Brazil."

"Brazil?" Gravois gasped, suddenly realizing why Don Hernan had lost so much weight. He'd been *preparing* for this! "I've never been in *any* wilderness on this world. I haven't even stood on dry land for half a year! And how many *thousands of kilometers* is Brazil, across this dreadful land of monsters?" he demanded almost hysterically.

"Don't be so dramatic!" Don Hernan replied dismissively. "It's only a few hundred of your 'kilometers' to the east coast, where we can take a boat the rest of the way."

"But even so . . ." Gravois quavered, terror like he'd never known rising within him as the dense, vicious forest seemed to close around him. He probably only had three or four cartridges left in his pistol—as if its tiny bullets could save him from the monsters here!

Don Hernan handed him some filthy rags and a battered straw hat. "Never fear," he told him gently. "God loves me. The *land* loves me. It can do me no harm. And heretic or not, you're The One and I'll try to protect you because I still need your help to join our countries. That remains my fondest dream." He smiled encouragingly. "I give you at least one chance in five of surviving the trek, and if you do, you'll be transformed! The *land it-*

self will cleanse you, my dear Gravois! What greater glory or challenging *grace* could you ever aspire to achieve?"

A thunderous roar rumbled in the forest not so far away, and Gravois almost echoed it with a scream as he remembered. *That madman Dennis Silva—I saw him in the temple—once threatened to rip my spine out and use it to beat me to death.* As he stumbled after Don Hernan in a near catatonic state, he knew his backbone was already gone because all he could feel was jelly. Soon the blows would begin.

CHAPTER 57

////// American Navy Clan Base
Martinique
September 2, 1945

Bright sunlight pried Matt's eyes open, and suddenly he was standing on *Walker*'s dark blue, rust-streaked deck. Disoriented, he gazed around and saw the rest of the ship was back in her old, prewar, light gray paint. She still looked old and hard-used, but there was no battle damage anywhere. That was all very clear, almost painfully perfect, but he was all alone and couldn't tell where the ship rode at anchor. The distant city might've been Cavite, on the world he and this ship left behind, but could just as easily be Aryaal or El Corazon, even Nuevo Granada. For a whirlwind moment, he wondered if this *was* Cavite and everything he'd been through over the last few years was a dengue fever dream.

"She didn't sink, y'know. And you didn't die." The gruff voice jolted him with another kind of pain and he turned to see Chief Bosun Fitzhugh Gray regarding him steadily from under the visor of his battered chief's hat. Matt managed a smile. "It's been a while, Boats." There'd been a time, shortly after Gray's death at Grik City, that Matt dreamed about him a lot.

The old Chief Bosun sucked on a cigarette, then flipped the butt over the rail. "You haven't needed me for a while."

"That's a laugh."

"No, it ain't. Sure, you've goofed some. Like I never did? But you made it through, did what you set out to, an' I'm damn proud of you."

"So many didn't make it. You didn't."

Gray shrugged. "That's the breaks. You nearly didn't either, a time or two. But think how many you saved from the Grik, the Doms, hell, even the League! And you saved your ship. That's more important than you realize."

"Why?"

"Because of what you built, the world you made. They'll *always* need *Walker* to keep 'em together." He shook his head as if mystified himself, while kicking ironically at some rust underfoot. "It's the damnedest thing, but she's gotten to be like the Statue o' Liberty, or somethin', to 'em. If the country you an' Mr. Letts built survives, if the Alliance endures, *Walker*'ll still be here a hundred years from now." He shrugged. "And you know? Even if you'd ever sunk her proper an' they couldn't raise her, they'd have snagged some junk up off her wreck, built a whole new ship around it, and it would *still* be *Walker*."

Matt pondered that, and supposed Gray was probably right. "So . . . I guess I finally have to ask you the Big One. What the *hell* has it all been about?"

Gray laughed, and shook out another cigarette. "The only thing anything's about, son. Life."

Matt was confused and surprised. Chief Bosun Gray had never called him "son" before. "But you're dead."

"So? I died livin', didn't I?" He stomped the deck. "And everybody who came here on this old tub was dead before they got here. No *way* we would've got away from the Japs, and comin' here—however it happened—gave us all a second chance."

Matt frowned. "A second chance to die?"

Gray shrugged and lit his smoke with a Zippo. "Maybe. Call it a chance to die *for* somethin', instead of just gettin' heroically but uselessly rubbed out and forgotten like the rest of the Asiatic Fleet. And everybody you lost since then died for the best reason there is: *protecting* life. Whether that was 'Cats, Impies, Repubs, or Nussies . . . none o' that even matters. They, *you*, squared off against the killers and stopped 'em."

"We *killed* them," Matt pointed out. "Doesn't that make us killers too?"

"No." Gray grinned. "Just . . . killer killers." He seemed to grow impatient. "What the hell *else* were you s'posed to do, read 'em love poems? It really is all black-and-white, in the end. You gotta kill the killers. Don't go pokin' at 'em, but when they come for you, they don't *get* to live anymore, see? That gets bloody, an' it's scary—as you know—but hopefully, if you kill enough of 'em, the rest'll stop and so can you. It's that simple."

Matt looked at the distant city, still not sure where he was supposed to be. "What's it like to stop?" he asked wistfully. "Just enjoy life for a while with my wife and son?"

Gray snorted. "Hell if I know. I wrecked my chance at that between the wars back home, but maybe you'll find out for both of us." He smiled fondly around at the old destroyer. "For all of us."

"Matthew?" came another voice, definitely not Gray's, and real sunlight came into Matt's eyes. He smiled up at Sandra, leaning low over him, her pretty face washed with care.

"Sorry. Still dopey, I guess. Too much seep. I must've dozed off." He was semi-reclined on a chair with a footrest on the quarterdeck of USS *Fitzhugh Gray* as the CL rode at anchor in the captured harbor of Martinique. The carriers were at sea and *Savoie* was too crowded with workers just trying to save her, so *Gray* was packed with a lot of the ambulatory wounded off the battleship, or brought back from El Lago de Vida. There were so many injured clogging the CL amidships, in fact, that some wag had taken to calling it "dead lead row." For once, Matt doubted it was Silva, who hadn't said much at all since the battle in the temple, and Matt was worried about him. Pam (and Petey) were with him all the time but he seemed very low, even stiff to Lawrence and Chack. The only time he spoke to Matt was to apologize for letting Gravois and Don Hernan get away.

"Not your fault," Matt had told him.

"Sure feels like it," was all he'd said.

"I was just about to wake him myself," Courtney Bradford now proclaimed. "The man's snoring sounds like an artillery barrage, sufficient to stir stressful memories!"

Matt laughed. Ever since their last ordeal, Courtney and Spanky, both wounded as well, had never been out of earshot. The same was true for Keje and Juan, who'd miraculously survived without a scratch. Few others had been so lucky, and Matt had been forced to add the name of Gilbert Yeager, killed in the forward engine room, to Campeti's, Palmer's, Fairchild's, Neely's, Lanier's, Jeek's, Rosen's . . . and those were just the "originals," or those with very long service. Thirty-eight more 'Cats and Impies had died in *Walker* as well.

Still, most of the news they were getting was good. The war in Grik Africa was decisively over and recovery operations in the wake of the terrible flood were progressing well. The Celestial Mother was now hailed as the "*Saver* of Life" along with her other titles. Bekiaa-Sab-At was recovering well from losing her arm and she and Rolak reported continued good relations and cooperation with Halik and Jash. Perhaps the most exciting news that day was that RRPS *Servius* had been found in the shattered forest just north of Lake Nalak, having somehow survived inundation while being swept along almost a hundred miles. Searchers had frankly been looking for debris, maybe some bodies, but an off-course Nancy discovered the whole ship, partially buried in broken trees. Word that General Pete Alden was alive had slightly dulled the ache everyone felt over all their other losses.

There was still sniping by fanatics in New Granada, but Generals Cox and Blair were in firm control while General Shinya recovered. He'd very nearly died. It was he, however, who ordered the Sister's Own out of the city, along with Chack's Brigade, to establish an Allied presence on Martinique. They all needed a rest and change of scenery, of course, but after what happened to Sister Audrey, it *was* probably best to get them entirely out of Dominion territory. Captain Bustos and Colonel Garcia were allowed to remain, to begin preaching a different, gentler faith.

Other than that, they'd heard of *another* great blast in Japaan, similar to the first. The cause remained a mystery, but the Shogunate of Yokohama had dispatched a ship to investigate. Courtney had taken a sudden interest and greedily followed reports.

Matt looked at Spanky when the bandage-swaddled man rose experimentally. "Just testin' my legs," he assured Selass-Fris-Ar, Keje's daughter, who'd come over from *Savoie* to tend the latest wounded to arrive—and be with her father. Diania wasn't just attending Sandra on her rounds either, she was keeping her wounded fiancé, Gunny Horn, company.

"Me too," Matt told his wife. She frowned, but knew he'd try to stand whether she helped him or not. Nodding, she made sure he had a firm grip on her arm, then the cane she handed him. Together with Spanky, Keje, Courtney, and Juan, they carefully moved to the starboard side of the ship and gazed out at the harbor.

Most of the half-sunk ships at Martinique were only fit for scrap, but *Hessen* was in good condition and *Impero* would be raised. *U-112* was in *Tarakan Island*'s repair bay with USS *Gerald McDonald*, and the Nussie fleet—with USS *Donaghey* proudly anchored nearby—protectively surrounded the SPD. USS *Savoie* was a floating wreck, but though she was shot to pieces and still listing to port, she *was* afloat, and increasingly able to defend herself. The other survivors of St. Vincent that could make it themselves or be towed

(Allied ships and their prizes) were already here, and *Mahan* was due this afternoon with *Walker* in tow. The lightly damaged *Francesco Caracciolo* was surrounded by the Repub battlecruisers that took her surrender and they'd made it clear they intended to keep her. The Nussies wanted *Impero*, for that matter, in exchange for "letting" the American Navy Clan keep the base at Martinique. Matt knew they wouldn't push it, since they couldn't fix *Impero* themselves, and everyone recognized the Navy Clan was there for all of them. Besides, Martinique was on its way to becoming the biggest Allied cemetery on this side of the world, with new graves joining that of Orrin Reddy every day. It still bothered Matt how quickly they'd all started squabbling.

Regardless, it had been a full, busy port that received the single League troopship under a flag of truce two days before, loaded with people whose release was required before the seven thousand League prisoners who wanted to leave were allowed to embark. The Allied aircraft carriers were discreetly and ominously out of sight, but the rest of the Allied warships and all the prizes and wreckage of the League's vaunted fleet had to be grim reminders that, though there wasn't exactly peace, the Grand Alliance wasn't to be trifled with, and the League's overwhelming naval might had been whittled painfully back.

Now the troopship was leaving, and Matt recalled his last conversation with Ammiraglio Gherzi that morning when he came to say farewell.

"I trust you're feeling better, and all proceedings have gone according to the . . . guidelines you prescribed?" Gherzi had said.

"I am, and they did. A few of the Germans were angry when their families didn't show, but the percentage was low enough for us to write it off as cold feet on the part of the transportees."

"And I'm sure the Triumvirate will growl when they learn *two thousand* 'loyal' League subjects chose to remain behind," Gherzi said wryly. Matt's face had hardened. "I won't *force* anyone to go back." He paused. "I don't think *you* should go."

Gherzi waved his concern away. "Don't worry about me. The Triumvirate needs me too much now. As you pointed out, the League still feels secure in its domestic might, yet understands it needs people"—he smiled—"with recent experience confronting a military peer. Still . . . I *do* wish you'd managed to account for Gravois. His reappearance might prove awkward. For us all."

"I don't think we need to worry much about him. Natives from a village forty miles east of New Granada reported what sounded like a greasy old witch doctor claiming to be 'His Supreme Holiness,' tugging another tall man along on a leash. They demanded food and were chased away. The fall of New Granada has finally broken the perverted Dom faith, in northern South America, at least." Matt was only now learning that the Dom Empire had sparsely extended down the east coast of South America as well.

Gherzi had nodded, then his tone had turned brusque. "Now, I'm ordered to inform you that, though we have an armistice, incursions in what the League considers its territorial waters won't be tolerated. Allied ships encountered in the eastern Atlantic, from the Cape Verde Islands north to the Azores and beyond, will be fired upon. Any incursion into the Mediterranean whatsoever, by so much as a fishing boat, will be considered an act of war and full hostilities will resume."

Matt had smiled. "And as I told you, the same is true if we meet League ships *anywhere* else."

Gherzi had nodded understanding if not acceptance, then said, "It's a great shame we can't settle our differences like civilized"—he'd glanced at Keje and some Lemurian representatives of the Republic—"beings. I've come to respect you all a great deal and have no personal quarrel with you." He'd paused. "I hope . . . I *do* hope we never meet again."

Matt had smiled sadly back. "Me too. But I doubt we'll get what we want."

Now he pondered that exchange when the League troopship seemed to pause in the mouth of the bay as two shapes met her on an opposite course. Matt borrowed binoculars from Toryu Miyata, who'd just come down from the bridge, and eagerly focused them. *Mahan* led, of course. She'd taken some damage at St. Vincent, but nothing serious at New Granada. And with the help of *James Ellis*'s crew, distributed between her and *Walker* after *Ellie* finally went down, she'd had a few weeks to lick her more superficial wounds. On the whole, however, she'd suffered worse than *Walker* on this world, once practically blown out of existence. Matt was glad to see she'd come through this so well.

In contrast, coming up behind, USS *Walker* still looked terrible: scorched and blackened by fires and reddened with rust. Two of her stacks had been knocked down, and her deck from the bridge to the aft deckhouse was virtually bare of anything but what might be salvageable scrap. Still partially flooded amidships, she rode a little low in the water, but Tabby and Isak—battling as much to save the ship as to divert their grief over Gilbert—had performed a miracle just keeping her on the surface. Then Matt's heart almost burst with pride when he realized *Walker* wasn't under tow. Tabby, with Ronson's assistance, no doubt, was *steaming* her in on one engine and one boiler. *Mahan* emphasized their arrival with a blast of her horn and the big battle flags of both old destroyers broke and streamed behind their foremasts; the Stars and Stripes of another world representing the best of what it always had, but more now as well. To Matt's amazement, the League transport acknowledged the horn, and when he looked at her with the binoculars, he couldn't believe his eyes. All her crew, dressed in whites, had lined the rails, and a lot of the prisoners they'd released stood behind them. Matt was sure Gherzi ordered the honor—and it *was* an honor—but his mixed feelings surprised him. He'd *liked* the earnest little Italian admiral, whose only failing was absolute loyalty to a government that didn't deserve him—to the point he'd followed Gravois's orders to his destruction. Matt doubted they'd be where they were today if Gherzi had been in charge.

"My God," Sandra said, seeing what he had. "If we can learn to respect one another, maybe we *can* stop fighting."

"Maybe," Matt agreed aloud. *Or maybe Gherzi—or someone like him—will rise up in the League. Would that be good—or worse?* he asked himself.

Walker crept into the harbor while *Mahan* practically bustled around her wounded sister. When their anchors finally splashed in the bright, clear water, horns and cheering voices erupted all over the bay.

"Execute salute!" shouted Toryu Miyata, and only then did Matt realize all the people in the bay, of every race in the Alliance, had dressed the sides of the other ships as well. A popping sound caught his attention above, and he watched the signal flags break out on *Gray*'s halyards, repeated by every ship in view: Tare Victor George.

Sandra put her arm around him and Matt hardly trusted himself to speak.

"'Well Done,' by God, an' that's a fact!" grated Spanky, voice breaking.

"Indeed, indeed!" Courtney agreed, beaming at Matt.

All sorts of mental images would revisit Matt from that day. *Walker*'s dingy, battered shape, of course. She'd made it all possible, in a way. Gunny Horn and Diania enthusiastically (and surely scandalously, in Diania's mind) kissing in front of everyone, Fred and Kari, fingers intertwined, raised triumphantly above their heads. Keje suffused with joy, Miyata's respectful gaze, Chack and Blas, somehow looking vaguely sad and bewildered. Abel Cook, seated nearby, staring west—with Sir Sean Bates's sword resting on his lap. And the crackling little flags: Tare Victor George.

The most precious image of all, however, was Sandra's happy, hopeful face as she kissed Matt heartily and said, "Well done, sailor!"

"Quit mopin' around, damn it, it ain't like you," Pam groused at Silva. They'd been watching everything from up on *Gray*'s amidships deckhouse, and the happier everyone else seemed, the glummer Silva got. "I know you liked Sister Audrey. So did I. But she'll be a *real* saint someday, an' that's kinda funny since you know it would just piss her off."

"Yeah," Silva agreed listlessly, avoiding Pam's gaze. "I'm . . . I guess I ain't as tore up about *that*, no more. Don't know what come over me. But Sister Audrey saved Blas. Prob'ly saved us all, distractin' the bastards. I'm . . . proud of her. Proud I knew her, an' proud she thought well o' me. You may not believe it, but not many do." He shook his head. "It's this whole 'no war' thing I'm worried about." He looked searchingly at her. "You never knew me when there wasn't a war on."

Lawrence suddenly joined them, surprising everybody by feeding Petey a biscuit. "He's such a jerk, he thinks he'll lose you," he told Pam, "and he doesn't know 'hat he'll do 'ith hi'sel'."

Silva nodded slowly. "That last part's true, sure enough. I *don't* know what I'll do with myself. I know I don't wanna go back to what I was before the war. *I* didn't even like me, then."

"Well cheer up, dumb-ass," Pam snapped sarcastically, "'cause this war *ain't* over, it's just takin' a breather. It'll light off again someday."

"You really think so?" Silva asked, allowing himself to hope.

"Sure. But Captain Reddy won't want you just sittin' around, waitin', not with so much stuff to do. There's a whole, wide world out there waitin' to be explored, an' it's *packed* with scary 'boogers' for you to kill! We'll all go, even Petey. You in, Larry?"

Lawrence hesitated only an instant. "Sure. I ha' nothing else to do."

Pam grinned. "Swell! It's settled." Her eyes lit up. "Hey! If we're gonna go explorin', we might as well get somebody else to spring for it, right? Somebody who's been *dyin'* to go poke at bugs an' lizards ever since we got here!"

Silva's beatific grin, too long absent, suddenly erupted and he took a huge, triumphant chaw of real Nussie tobacco that Gunny Horn had given him. "Courtney!" he barked, spewing fragments of dark leaves. "Ha! A whole new 'Corps o' Discovery,' only this time we can go where we want. Might even be funner than fightin'!"

"Funner than fightin'!" Petey loudly agreed, then looked a little nervously at Lawrence. "Eat?" he probed gently. In the spirit of celebration and renewed purpose, Lawrence gave Petey another biscuit.

AUTHOR'S NOTE

Surprised you, didn't I? Everyone I've ever spoken to simply assumed as gospel that USS *Walker* would eventually be irretrievably lost, but I just couldn't let that happen. Not only because she's such an important unifying symbol to all the people she protected on that other Earth, but because she and *Mahan* and every single one of their *271* sisters on this world are gone. Those that weren't sunk in action were immediately scrapped after World War II, despite the various critical roles they filled throughout that conflict. Some thanks. So it makes me smile to think one or two might still exist in a parallel universe, where they're lovingly maintained and admired for their gallant service.

In any event, here's where there's usually been a long cast of characters and an exhaustive list of equipment specifications so readers could keep track of who was where, what they were doing, and what manner of tools they had at their disposal. With the exception of a few new characters, force dispositions, and technical developments (which should be fresh in your mind), all that stuff can be found in previous books, on my website, or on the thorough Destroyermen Wiki that's evolved with the tale and become a particularly helpful resource for audio listeners. I'm humbled by all the dedicated work so many people have put in there, as well as by the astonishing (to me) scope and vitality of the "Destroyermen Fan Association" Facebook page that sprang into being a few years ago.

So instead of another long list of characters, ships, weapons, and task forces, I wanted to use this space to sincerely thank all the wonderful people who joined me in the Destroyermen universe and, like the many characters I've come to love and think of as "real," stuck with me until the end. And that's what this is: the final chapter in an old-fashioned yarn about honor versus evil, love against hate, courage conquering terror, and how true friendship and understanding will always erode the foundations of bigotry. This is the end of the story of a battered old four-stacker and the destroyermen who steamed her to another world, fought a little skirmish against some Grik, and ultimately led their friends to victory in a global war. Sounds far-fetched, in retrospect, but stranger things have happened. Every battle *Walker* and her people fought has a historical inspiration of some sort, and in many of those instances, the odds were even longer.

I hope you enjoyed the tale at least half as much as I relished writing it, yet I understand many of you, no matter how much you liked it, will be relieved to see the series end. Far too many never do, and loyal readers are left hanging. That's not right, and I promised I wouldn't do it. On the other hand, I know there are at least as many people who will be disappointed that it won't go on forever. I sympathize with you as well and frankly doubt I will be able to stay *out* of the Destroyermen universe. As Pam admonished Silva, "There's a whole, wide world out there waitin' to be explored," and the possibilities for prequels, sequels, and spin-offs are endless. I have a few ideas already. But those will be *different* stories, not just further installments tacked onto this one, even if certain characters you already know might reappear. . . .

For now I only want to say thanks for your support, through *fifteen* volumes of *one* story. Who'd have ever thunk it?